PENGUIN BOOKS

WHITETHORN

Bryce Courtenay is the bestselling author of *The Power of One*, *Tandia*, *April Fool's Day*, *The Potato Factory*, *Tommo & Hawk*, *Jessica*, *Solomon's Song*, *A Recipe for Dreaming*, *The Family Frying Pan*, *The Night Country*, *Smoky Joe's Cafe*, *Four Fires*, *Matthew Flinders' Cat*, *Brother Fish*, *Whitethorn* and *Sylvia*.

The Power of One is also available in an edition for younger readers, and *Jessica* has been made into an award-winning television miniseries.

Bryce Courtenay lives in the Hunter Valley, New South Wales.

Further information about the
author can be found at
www.brycecourtenay.com

Bryce Courtenay

WHITE THORN

PENGUIN BOOKS

To Celia Jarvis

PENGUIN BOOKS

Published by the Penguin Group
Penguin Group (Australia)
250 Camberwell Road, Camberwell, Victoria 3124, Australia
(a division of Pearson Australia Group Pty Ltd)
Penguin Group (USA) Inc.
375 Hudson Street, New York, New York 10014, USA
Penguin Group (Canada)
90 Eglinton Avenue East, Suite 700, Toronto ON M4P 2Y3, Canada
(a division of Pearson Penguin Canada Inc.)
Penguin Books Ltd
80 Strand, London WC2R 0RL, England
Penguin Ireland
25 St Stephen's Green, Dublin 2, Ireland
(a division of Penguin Books Ltd)
Penguin Books India Pvt Ltd
11 Community Centre, Panchsheel Park, New Delhi – 110 017, India
Penguin Group (NZ)
67 Apollo Drive, Mairangi Bay, Auckland 1310, New Zealand
(a division of Pearson New Zealand Ltd)
Penguin Books (South Africa) (Pty) Ltd
24 Sturdee Avenue, Rosebank, Johannesburg 2196, South Africa

Penguin Books Ltd, Registered Offices: 80 Strand, London WC2R 0RL, England

First published by Penguin Group Australia, 2005
This edition published by Penguin Group (Australia), 2007

1 3 5 7 9 10 8 6 4 2

Cover design by Debra Billson © Penguin Group (Australia)
Text design by Tony Palmer © Penguin Group (Australia)
Cover photographs: bottom – Sean Ellis/Getty Images; top – George F Mobley
Typeset in Goudy Oldstyle by Post Pre-press Group, Brisbane, Queensland
Printed and bound in Australia by McPherson's Printing Group, Maryborough, Victoria

National Library of Australia
Cataloguing-in-Publication data:

Courtenay, Bryce, 1933– .
Whitethorn.
ISBN-13: 978 0 14 300484 4 (pbk.).
ISBN-10: 0 14 300484 0 (pbk.).
I. Title.

A823.3

www.penguin.com.au

BOOK
ONE

BOOK
ONE

CHAPTER ONE

Love in a Wet Sack

───────────

TRUE LOVE CAME TO me one crisp late autumn morning when the sky had lost the faded blue of the long hot summer and taken on the deeper colour of winter yet to come. I discovered it in a hessian sack floating down the bit of a creek that ran around the back of the orphanage. I waded into the shallow stream, the water reaching to just below the hem of my khaki shorts, the current pulling at my skinny legs. The stream, already icy from the high mountains, was extra cold from the frosty morning, so that I inched and ouched my way towards the floating sack, grabbed hold of it and drew it back against the current to finally rest it on the bank of wet black pebbles.

I untied the bag, no easy task I can tell you, the twine binding was knotted and slippery wet and my fingers near frozen. I peeped into the dark interior and, unable to see what it contained, up-ended it. To my surprise out plopped six dead puppies. Flippity-flop! Oh my Gawd!

With six dead dogs on my hands I knew I was in big trouble. What if someone came upon me and there were these dead puppies lying at my feet? I hastily dropped each one back into the sack, ready to return it to the stream. But as I grabbed the last one, the smallest of them all, it seemed to quiver and its mouth opened and gave a sort of gasp, so I gave it a bit of a squeeze and it vomited a jet of water. I squeezed it again

and more water came out. One back leg started to jerk, I squeezed a third
time and it must have been empty because nothing happened, except
that it started to breathe.

Well, you can't just put a nearly dead puppy back in the sack and
hope for the best, can you? So I took him beyond the shade of the
overhanging mimosa and laid him down in a patch of sunlight. Then
I quickly retied the bag and dragged it back to the stream and watched
as the current caught it and it floated away around a rocky corner and
was soon out of sight. I must say I was glad to see the last of it, five dead
puppies lying at your feet is no way to start a morning. But then it struck
me that a live puppy was going to be a lot more trouble than a dead one.
How was a little kid in an orphanage where you were not allowed to
have anything of your own going to look after a puppy?

Suddenly my life had become very complicated. I sat in the warm sun
beside the puppy, stroking its pink tummy, which by now was pumping
up and down thirteen to the dozen as it came truly alive and started to
get warm again. I was accustomed to getting into trouble, mostly because
of my surname, Fitzsaxby. I was English, well, that's what my name said
I was anyway, and I was in the Deep North, high mountain country,
Boer territory where the English were hated because of what they'd done
in the Boer War. They'd started the world's first concentration camps
and filled them with Boer women and children from the farms; many
came from these mountains. That wasn't the bad part. The reason they
hated the British was because 27000 of them died of dysentery and
blackwater fever and other terrible and unsanitary things. In a way, it
was understandable that they hated me for being English, you don't
forget things like what happened to your own *ouma* so easily, do you?

I picked up the still wet puppy and clasped him to my chest and he
began to suck on my thumb and whimper. There was no doubt he was
properly alive again and I had acquired a problem too big for a six-year-
old boy's brain. All of a sudden it struck me, my friend Mattress, the pig
boy, would know what to do.

Mattress was my friend even if he was a grown-up. If you're black you get called 'boy' even if you're an old man, you can be a garden boy, kitchen boy, farm boy, house boy or a pig boy like Mattress, because he looked after the orphanage pigs and also worked with the cows in the dairy. I can tell you, having a friend like him was good because having friends in that place wasn't easy when you had an English name. Nobody wanted to be the friend of the *rooinek*, which is what *they* called you if you were English. It means redneck. One thing was for sure, the concentration camp business never went away but was always pointing a finger at you. *Rooinek, you are evil! God is going to punish you and you are going to hell, you hear!*

This is what happened to the Boere. I know it's true because on Sundays when we had to attend church the preacher stood up in his long black robes with a little white starched bib under his chin, it must have been there to catch the spit when he got angry with the English. Which is what he did every Sunday morning without fail. He got all worked up and thumped the pulpit and started going on and on. Soon he'd be red in the face and spit came flying out of his mouth and sprayed onto his beard that almost covered the entire bib, so after all that trouble to wear it, the bib wasn't any good for catching spit. At first I would get really frightened, me being the only Englishman in the congregation and him saying I was the devil's children. Not me personally, he didn't point to me, but I guess it amounted to the same thing. All the other kids would turn and look at me and the guys on either side of me would give me a sharp dig in the ribs and whisper *verdomde rooinek*, damned redneck.

But then I worked out a scenario that went like this. The preacher, who in Afrikaans is called a *Dominee*, had this big round head with jet-black hair that was parted down the centre and was plastered down on his head with grease so that it looked just like a shiny beetle's back. He also had ears that stuck out like small saucers on either side of his head. With the light coming from a window at the back of the pulpit they'd glow. As he got more and more worked up over the English and the concentration camps, his ears looked like red lights glowing on the sides of the beetle's back. He had beady little obsidian eyes that disappeared into bushy eyebrows while the rest of his face was covered with that large black beard that came way down to the centre of his chest. So, after we'd sung a few hymns and Dominee De Jager arrived at the pulpit carrying a big Bible under his arm with pieces of white paper sticking out to mark his places, I'd be ready. I'd sort of narrow my eyes and concentrate really hard on the top part of his head so that it became the big black beetle with large red ears and tiny hard shiny black eyes. The beetle would be busy chomping on a lush crop of black beard. Suddenly he was no longer a huge frightening preacher man condemning my kind to hell, but instead became 'The Great Scarlet-eared Beard-chomping Black Beetle'. After that I wasn't frightened of him any more.

The Boer War happened in the 1890s when the English fought the Afrikaners because they wanted the gold that people all of a sudden were finding all over the place. The Boere said no way and the war went on for ages, the Boere on horseback in commandos and the British in regiments on foot. The Boere would attack and could shoot the eye out of a potato at a thousand yards with their German Mauser rifles while the British with their Lee-Enfield rifles couldn't fire accurately at that distance and besides they were mostly lousy shots because they weren't born on the veld. Then the Boere would gallop away, and at night every once in a while they'd sneak back to their farms to get food and stuff so they could fight the enemy on the run for the next week or so. It was *biltong* mostly, which is dried meat cured in the sun and you can live on it all week with a bit of flour or *mielie* meal thrown in. What the Boere did is called guerilla warfare and the British didn't like it one bit. It was like chasing galloping shadows. Even though the English outnumbered the Boer soldiers fourteen to one, they weren't winning the way they expected to, them being the British Empire and all that. So they came up with an evil plan called 'a scorched earth policy'. They burnt down all the farms and put all the Boer women and children in concentration camps where they died like flies.

Anyway, that's what the *Dominee* said happened and that's why it was impossible for any of the Afrikaner kids to be my friend. But Mattress didn't seem to mind and said that black people were accustomed to being hated by the Boere and that I could be his friend if I wanted. He said both his grandfathers had fought the British and the Boere and if they hadn't had guns the Zulu warriors would have beaten the pants off them and nearly did anyway. So he didn't give a shit because they were both bastards (present company excluded) and the Zulu Impi were, man for man, the best of the lot and would march over a cliff and fall to their certain death to show how brave they were. 'Ahee, Kleinbaas, when they attacked, the earth trembled and it was like thunder in the mountains.' I didn't tell him I thought that marching over a cliff was a bit stupid, but it certainly showed they were brave.

Now I don't want you to think all Boere are bad because they are not, they can be very good and kind people, it's just that they have a right to hate the English and I just happened to be one. I don't know how it happened because I was an orphan, but there you go, it was an accident of birth and nobody could do anything about it.

In an orphanage there's a lot of unkindness going about even for the Afrikaner kids, it's called discipline. It was just that I got a bit extra from the kids as well for having a name like Fitzsaxby that couldn't be made to sound Afrikaans, no matter how you said it. They didn't like to say my surname so they called me Voetsek, which is an Afrikaans word that you yell at a strange dog if it comes up to you. You give it a kick and you say 'Voetsek!' and every dog knows the word and runs away. It means 'bugger off' in dog language, only a bit worse. It's not a very nice thing to happen to a person's name but it was another thing I couldn't do anything about.

You'll probably think Mattress is a funny name for a person, but when you look at it through his eyes there isn't a lot of difference between Matthew and Mattress. He liked the sound of Mattress better. When I told him a mattress is something people sleep on he shook his head, 'Ahee, Kleinbaas, I am not sleep on this thing, I am Zulu and must have a grass mat.' Besides, Mattress sounds much better than Matthew because it doesn't have the 'phew!' sound in it. Anyway, that's what I thought and, besides, it was a whole lot better than Voetsek.

Mattress sat on the low stone wall of the pigsty with his elbows on his knees and his chin cupped in his hands and listened intently while I explained my problem to him in Zulu.

'*Ahee*, *Kleinbaas*, we have a big, big problem here.' He dropped one hand to rest on his thigh and rubbed his chin. 'That dog is too small.'

I explained to him that there were bigger ones but they were dead.

'No, it is too small to feed on its own. Look, its eyes are not yet open, it must have milk from the bitch and where is she, eh?'

I shrugged and pointed to a higher part of the mountains. 'Up there, he came downriver.'

'The bitch, she must be on a farm upstream somewhere.'

'Can we find this bitch?' I asked hopefully. 'You could go and take a look?'

He thought for a moment. 'You found this dog in a sack?'

I nodded.

'And the sack was tied with string?'

I nodded again.

'Intentional murder.' He pointed to the puppy cradled in my arms. 'If we find the bitch the Boer will murder the dog all over again. He didn't want those dogs.'

'That's all very well but what are we going to do?' I said, shifting the responsibility onto Mattress, the way white people are allowed to do with black people any time they like.

He didn't reply for a long time and you could hear him thinking, *Ahee*! What are we going to do? What are we going to do? What are we going to do? I could almost hear it going round and round in his head like things sometimes go in mine when I'm in the deep shit. '*Voetsek*, you in the deep shit, man,' one of the boys would say when something went wrong in the dormitory and I was going to be the one they were going to blame and I didn't know why I was guilty. Deep shit . . . deep shit . . . deep shit, the words would go round and round. I preferred just getting the *sjambok* rather than having all that deep shit running around in my head.

All of a sudden Mattress's eyes lit up and he clapped his hands and laughed. 'The sow! We'll put him with the big black sow, she won't know the difference.'

'Are you sure?' I asked, uncertain. The big black sow wasn't completely black but black and white just like my new dog and she weighed about 300 pounds. What if she rolled over all of a sudden and my little dog, which probably weighed less than a pound, was in the way? He couldn't even see to jump out of the way.

The sow had twelve piglets that were two weeks old who never let up fighting over the ten available teats, the two left out would squeal like billyo, snuffling and pushing and carrying on a treat until they pushed someone out of the way and got a go. They had fat round bums and curly tails and already they were three times the size of my new dog. I can tell you it was everyone for themselves in that pigsty, just like it was in the orphanage and I didn't like his chances. Frankly, I didn't think much of the solution, how does a puppy that can't even see compete with twelve piglets fighting over ten teats?

'Are you sure?' I asked again, holding up the puppy who was now whimpering and no doubt very hungry. 'Wouldn't he be squashed?'

Mattress thought for a moment. 'We'll give the dog a free go,' he said at last.

'How do you mean?'

'We'll take some of the piglets away from the sow, give her a chance on her own to get a good feed until she's old enough to fight back.'

'She?'

He clapped his hands and took a step closer and took my puppy by the tail and lifted its bum and hind legs. 'See, no snake, we got ourselves a bitch, *Kleinbaas*.'

I took a look for myself and Mattress was right, he was a she all right. All of a sudden everything was going wrong. Even at six I knew female dogs have babies and mongrel puppies in an orphanage wasn't possible. I'd just seen an example of what happened in the bottom of that sack. Even having a dog of my own wasn't going to be possible, but a bitch was totally out of the question.

'What will we call her?' he asked.

'Can't, she's a bitch, she'll have babies,' I said sadly.

He nodded. 'Ahee, woman, always trouble,' he agreed. He paused as if thinking. 'Shall I wring her neck?' He brought his big black fists together, turned them in opposite directions and made a sort of cluck that sounded like a bone breaking.

'No!' I yelled. My vehemence was so strong that my whole body trembled and my knees began to shake.

Mattress laughingly placed his large hand on my shoulder to comfort me.

'I'm going to keep her,' I said fiercely, my voice close to a sob. 'She's mine forever!'

He didn't tell me that was impossible, which it was, he just said, 'In that case you'll have to give her a name.'

'Tinker,' I said, not knowing why or where the name came from, it was something deep down from an unknown past, but plain as anything, sounding in my head like a stone shot from a catty striking a tin can.

'Ah, Ten-Kaa!' Mattress said approvingly, splitting her name in half and softening it, because you can't say hard sharp words in the Zulu language.

With her name out of the way I became all business, names give an identity and now Tinker was definitely here to stay.

'Will she drink pig's milk?' I asked.

'Soon see, Kleinbaas.' He swung his legs over the pigsty wall where a whole heap of grunting and sucking and squealing was going on. Pigs are not exactly silent types.

'Hey, look, Kleinbaas,' he laughed and pointed to Tinker. 'Same like her.' He said it in Zulu and what he meant was that the sow and piglets were black and white and so was Tinker. 'The sow won't know the difference.'

She'd have to be pretty dumb, I thought to myself. Tinker was about a sixth of the size of the greedy piglets. It was obvious she stood no chance if she was going to have to compete for the sow's milk.

The enormous sow lay on her side in the muddy pigsty, her great belly heaving, flies buzzing around her eyes, flicking her ear to chase them away. Every few moments she'd give a deep grunt, but you couldn't tell if it was because she was happy or was simply putting up with the squabbling going on down below. Looking at it from her point of view you had to wonder. Twelve piglets pushing each other aside to have a go, their snouts concertinaed right up into their foreheads. Each sucked like there was no tomorrow in an attempt to get as much scoff as they could before being bumped aside. It can't have been all that comfortable for her. Pigs don't muck about when it comes to food, that's for sure. I suppose it was the same at the orphanage, if you didn't cradle your plate within your arms and scoff it as fast as possible, the food on it soon disappeared into someone else's mouth.

I keep calling it 'the orphanage' and that sounds pathetic, as if it was in the olden times or something, whereas the time was 1939 with everyone saying there was going to be a war with the Germans. The English against the Germans and you can guess who wanted to fight for the Germans. More about that later. The real name for the place was 'The Boys Farm'.

It was in the country, about four miles out of a small town known as Willemskrans, which means the Williams Cliffs. This was because it was in the Lebombo Mountains and the town snuggled against a mountainside and was slap-bang up against these tall, rocky cliffs that rose nearly a thousand feet upwards. People said that the climate and the flora and fauna at the top were different to those at the bottom. I wondered how this could be. Mattress said that the people who lived up there were a different tribe. One big cliff and all of a sudden everything changes, the trees, flowers, climate and the people. Maybe Tinker came from up top and she'd come down the Letaba River. This was improbable because she'd have to have fallen down some mighty waterfalls. To do this and to be still alive would be some sort of a miracle, so I guess she came from some place not too high up, where the creek started.

Anyway, The Boys Farm was on twenty acres with its own vegetable garden, chickens, pigs, ten milking cows and a small dairy for making butter, there were also two donkeys to pull the small hand plough used for tilling. There was talk of a second-hand tractor but it never came to anything. Lots of things never came to anything in that place. We all worked in the vegetable garden and the older boys chopped wood and milked the cows.

What we did was usually considered *kaffir* work. But *they* decided that we'd all grow up to work on farms or as motor mechanics, timber cutters, lorry drivers or maybe get an apprenticeship to be a carpenter or boilermaker in the mines. We had to learn early to do things around the place with our hands, as brains were not considered a high-up commodity. It's funny when you don't belong to anyone that the people responsible for looking after you just assume you're nobody. You are the Government's children and they can do as they wish with you. So they train you to be the lowest common denominator, except, of course, for the blacks. You definitely can't be allowed to be as low as a black *kaffir*. So pigs are definitely not a white man's work, they're stinking creatures that live in mud and their own shit that gets squished up together to make a fearful greeny-black mud paste that stinks so much that you have to hold your nose as you approach. Even an orphan boy couldn't be expected to work in the pigsty, which is why we had a pig boy. Although I must say, I got used to the pigs' smell and didn't mind it. Mattress said that if humans lay around in their own shit they'd smell just as bad as the sow.

Mattress moved over to the sow, the greenish black stink-mud squelching between his toes. He had very large feet because he was a very big man and they were almost worn out. If they'd been shoes they would have needed to be thrown away long ago. The soles of his feet were about an inch thick and were splayed out with deep cracks running down the sides. It was as if he walked on an old pair of really thick leather soles about an inch and a half wider than the top part of his foot. This callused platform of hard, rough skin looked like it was glued to the underpart of his feet. He'd once explained this had happened from his having been a herd boy in the mountains when he was about my age.

'*Kleinbaas*, I was a herd boy in the mountains of Zululand and the small boys looked after the village goats. Goats like to be on the high slopes and on the rocks and they've got you jumping from rock to rock and running and slipping and sliding down the razor-sharp shale. Soon you're bleeding and sore and when you get back limping to the *kraal* at night the old men sitting under the marula trees laugh and say, "*Umfaan*, you are not a herd boy's arsehole until the bleeding stops and the hard skin comes".' Mattress laughed at the memory. 'Slowly, slowly, the soles of your feet grow hard.' He pointed proudly to his feet. 'And then when they get like this you know you have beaten the mountains and the rocks and the wicked whitethorns and the shale that cuts like a knife.'

Mattress made me see that having feet like his could be a very big advantage in life because you didn't need boots and could go anywhere you liked.

As he walked over to the sow she looked at him with a suspicious eye and grunted a warning a bit louder than usual but otherwise didn't move. Pigs can be dangerous and a sow protecting her young is not to be trifled with. She must have known Mattress because she didn't seem to mind when he picked up four piglets by the tail, two in each hand, and walked over and dumped them over the short stone wall into a vacant pigsty next door. Boy! You should've heard the squealing going on! This left two teats vacant. He turned, walked over to me and reached over the wall and took Tinker from me. The tiny, sightless puppy seemed to disappear within his large hands. With each piglet having a teat to itself the remaining piglets were going at it hell for leather and didn't even see Mattress placing Tinker next to a vacant teat. I waited anxiously as Tinker's nose bounced against the huge teat that was bigger than her nose. At first she didn't seem to know what to do but Mattress held her against the pig's great pink teat and sort of rubbed her nose on it and a small drop of yellowish milk came out. Tinker was on it like a shot. Her tiny mouth opened and I don't know how she got that big sow's teat into her mouth but she did, and then she hung on.

'*Ahee*! The mighty one!' Mattress exclaimed, clapping. 'She is a lioness this one. She will survive!'

I can tell you I was very relieved. But then disaster struck, one of the piglets let go of his own teat and wanted Tinker's.

'Quick!' I shouted to Mattress. 'Save her!'

Mattress did no such thing and Tinker was sent rolling into the stink-mud. Mattress laughed and picked her up. 'She must learn that life is hard, *Kleinbaas*,' he explained, but then he moved the piglet away and placed it back on its former teat and reinstated Tinker. It happened again. This time Tinker was sent sprawling against the wall near where I was standing and she gave a yelp and at that very moment, lying on her back, trying to get to her feet, her eyes opened and she looked straight into mine. I was the first thing she saw in her life, and I can tell you it was love at first sight. Her and me, from now on we were in this together, Tinker and Tom, a deadly combination in the making.

Mattress picked her up again. 'Back you go, little lioness,' he said and placed her on the spare teat. This time she had a good feed, sucking for dear life, her tiny jaws working overtime, the sow's rich milk running from the corners of her mouth. After a while you could see her tummy grow as big as a tennis ball so we knew she'd had enough.

'The sow's milk is good, *Kleinbaas*,' Mattress said, handing Tinker back to me. 'She will grow strong and soon she'll be eating *inyama*,' which means meat in Zulu.

The next problem was accommodation and here Mattress wasn't to prove very helpful. 'Can Tinker live with you in your *kaya*?' I asked him.

He sat down on the pigsty wall and sighed heavily, looking down at his cracked feet, unable to meet my eyes. 'This thing, it is not possible, *Kleinbaas*, the Big *Baas* Botha will not allow it. He will say I have a *kaffir* dog and they are not allowed here. We cannot have such a dog in this place, he will wring her neck.'

I should explain the word '*kaffir*'. It was used like the word 'nigger' was used in America, which wasn't very nice, so a *kaffir* dog was something that whites thought was pretty bad. Even I was shocked at the idea of Tinker being thought of as a *kaffir* dog.

'Oh, but she is *not* a *kaffir* dog!' I protested. *Kaffir* dogs were thin and scrawny with their ribs showing, they skulked around with their tails between their legs and with sores showing through their mangy pelts. They understood *Voetsek* very well and couldn't look you in the eye. Tinker wouldn't grow up to be like one of them.

'We cannot have a dog in this place, we are black.' Mattress said it without sadness, just sort of resigned. I knew he was right, we had rules in The Boys Farm and he had rules as the pig boy and you simply couldn't go against the rules, no matter what. 'I will lose my job,' he said.

I wanted to cry but what use would that be? Crying never solved anything and, besides, I wasn't much good at the business of blubbing. It was bad enough being English but if they saw me blubbing all over the place they'd really have a go. I did what crying it was impossible to avoid at the big rock where nobody ever came except me. Then it struck me. I would keep Tinker at the rock, it had plenty of overhang and I could make her a sort of burrow underneath and every day take her to the pigsty for a feed. She'd be okay while I was at school, and when she got a bit bigger I would build a stone enclosure under the overhang where she could play when I wasn't around or had to work in the vegetable garden.

I felt pretty cheered up as I outlined this plan to Mattress, although from his expression I could see he seemed less than convinced. He nodded gravely and said maybe it was a plan that could work and that he was very sorry about not being able to help, but jobs were hard to come by and he had to send money back to his wife in Zululand.

I was amazed to think that Mattress had a wife and that I didn't even know about her, but there you go, white people didn't spend much time asking black people about their lives, so Mattress was just the pig boy and didn't exist beyond his immediate occupation. I had fallen into the same white-people-total-disinterest-in-black-people trap, and even at six years old I felt ashamed.

'Do you have children, Mattress?'

His face lit up. 'One boy same like you, already he is with the goats and his feet I think they will soon be hard and will not bleed.'

'What's his name?'

'Mkiti Malokoane, but he also has a white man's name, it's Joe Louis, same like Joe Louis the mighty fighter who is *Amabantu*.' Mkiti means 'Big Feast' and Malokoane was Mattress's surname. I confess that I'd never heard of Joe Louis the boxer and thought he must be someone from Mattress's tribe. But not long after Meneer Frikkie Botha, who was Mattress's boss and who looked after the farm but was also the boxing coach, was answering a question from one of the boys, Fonnie du Preez, who was the best boxer at The Boys Farm. The question was, 'Why are American *kaffirs* like Joe Louis such good boxers?'

There was the name again, so I listened to the answer. 'Ag, that Joe Louis is good, but he was knocked out by a white man, a German, Max Schmeling. With those American *kaffir* boxers they all one-punch Johnnies, you hear. Then they come across a white man with brains who can *really* box and it's, "Good night, lights out, hear the dicky bird singing, *kaffir*!" Mostly those black guys they got glass jaws, man!'

I thought that I'd better not tell Mattress that Joe Louis had a jaw that was made of glass and what happened to him, because I didn't want him to be disappointed and maybe think he should have called his son Max.

Much later on I heard that it must have just been a lucky punch from Max Schmeling that knocked Joe Louis out, because the next time they boxed Joe knocked out Max in the first round. Meneer Botha didn't tell us that bit or that Joe Louis stayed Heavyweight Champion of the World for ages afterwards. So Mattress had every right to be proud and name his son after the great boxer. All this had happened already and Meneer Botha *must* have known it at the time. But he didn't tell us, did he? He just made us think that Schmeling was the white hero that beat the black bastard. Which goes to show you have to find out about a person yourself and not listen to all the badmouthing going on all over the place. In life you can't just take the part of a story that suits the way you think and leave the other stuff out.

'I will help you find some rocks to make a home for the little lioness,'

Mattress offered kindly. But I knew he shouldn't because if Meneer Botha caught Mattress helping me beyond his pigsty and dairy territory it could mean big trouble for him. Meneer Botha wasn't kind to black people and always referred to them as black *kaffirs* and even sometimes as baboons.

'It's okay, I can do it myself,' I said and I could see Mattress was relieved.

'Maybe if you need some big rocks moved I can do it, *Kleinbaas*.'

'She is only a very small dog,' I replied. 'There are lots of small rocks around.'

So I dug a sort of burrow under the big rock and found some old *mielie* sacks to keep her warm and this became Tinker's home and at night I'd close it using an old cut-in-half four-gallon paraffin tin so nothing could get at her.

For a while all went well and the weeks passed and I'd take Tinker for a feed in the morning before going to school and then again when we returned to the farm. Soon she was a fat, happy puppy jumping up and down and being very playful. She was still on the sow's teat but now she was the boss. Even though she was a lot smaller than the piglets they soon learned to stay away from her because she'd grab them by the tail or an ear and hang on for dear life. The piglet would try to shake her off to no avail and squeal blue murder. Mattress said that Tinker the lioness was learning to survive in the jungle. I began saving crusts for her from our breakfast bread and Mattress cut a jam tin in half and he'd bring her milk from the dairy when she was old enough not to need the sow's teat.

When things go well you tend to grow careless and I was taking Tinker for walks well away from the big rock when one day we turned a corner and there stood Pissy Vermaak with his knobbly knees and snotty nose and sort of caved-in chest.

'Whose dog is that, *Voetsek?*' he sniffed, pointing at Tinker.

'It's a dog. I found it just now,' I lied.

'Look, man, he's fat, he must be someone's,' Pissy observed.

'I dunno, I suppose,' I said.

'You jus' found him?' Pissy said suspiciously. 'He jus' came walking along all of a sudden, hey?'

I nodded. I was still learning to lie and wasn't very good at it yet. All this lying was getting me deeper and deeper into the shit. Pissy wasn't someone I needed to be afraid of, as he couldn't fight or anything, even though he was ten years old. He'd got his name when he was smaller and used to wet his bed. He was dangerous though because he had a reputation for reporting things to Mevrou, the matron. He had this bad chest and had to go to her every night to get medicine and that's when he'd tittle-tattle. He'd tell her about the things that went on in the dormitory and other places so that before you knew it Mevrou called you in and you got six of the best with the *sjambok*. Nobody liked Pissy for that reason and also, he always smelled of piss, his skin when you got near smelled like piss when it has been standing in the chamber-pot all night. People said that he could have fits 'out of the blue' if he got a fright or was beaten or something like that, although it had never happened while I'd been there. Maybe his smelling of piss had something to do with him having out-of-the-blue fits. He had ginger hair and lots of big brown freckles and his skin where he wasn't sunburnt was pale pink, all of which was unusual for an Afrikaner.

'He's yours, isn't he, *Voetsek*?' Pissy bent down and picked up Tinker who was too small to know she was in enemy hands. 'I think I'll have him, take him for me.'

'No!' I screamed. 'She's mine, she's my dog.'

Pissy Vermaak laughed. '*Ja*, man, I thought so all the time. I'm going to tell on you, *Voetsek*. Wait till Mevrou hears what you been doing, hey.'

'Please, Pissy, don't tell her!' I begged.

'Only if you give him to me.'

'She's a her, not a him.'

He mustn't have heard when I first called Tinker a she and now his expression changed to one of alarm. '*Sis*, man! A bitch dog! She'll have babies all over the place!'

He started to squeeze Tinker around the neck as if to strangle her. Tinker gave a desperate yelp and bit him on the thumb. Pissy yelled '*Eina!*' and dropped Tinker, who fell to the ground yelping and afraid. Pissy hopped up and down and wrung his hand in the air and then he brought his thumb up to his mouth to suck the hurt.

I didn't even realise I'd done it until after Pissy had doubled up and began to cough, holding his stomach and coughing like mad and staggering all over the place. I'd driven my fist straight into his stomach, hard as anything. I can tell you I didn't hang around to admire the result, but grabbed Tinker and ran back to the big rock and put her safely in her burrow.

I knew that wasn't the end of the matter. Far from it, a person doesn't get away with that sort of thing with Pissy Vermaak around. He'd be reporting to Mevrou and she'd tell Meneer Botha, that was for sure. *This time you in the deep shit, man!* I was about to lose the one thing I loved the most in the whole world. Without Tinker I was on my own again and my happy days were all over, finish and *klaar*. So I just sat there under the rock and I blubbed a bit and tried to think what I might do. But my brain was scrambled and no ideas would come and I was becoming desperate and the bell would soon go for us to wash our hands before going in to supper. I'd cleaned out Tinker's burrow so it was a bit deeper in case someone came looking for her, and we had to clean our nails for inspection before we went in to supper. Mine were bad from the burrowing and I would have to take my place at the end of the queue in the shower room for my turn to use the scrubbing brush and if I didn't get a go before the supper bell went I'd get the *sjambok*. Not that it mattered, dirty nails got three cuts and you'd only be sore sitting for about an hour before it wore off. Right now dirty nails were the least of my problems.

If Tinker and me ran away there wasn't any place for us to go. I was deep inside enemy territory and a war was coming and Meneer Botha said he'd joined both the *Broederbond* and *Die Ossewabrandwag*, both sort of secret societies made up of Boere on Hitler's side. He said the whole district felt the same and they were not going to fight for the *blêrrie* English, no matter what General Jan Christiaan Smuts said in all the newspapers and on the radio. Meneer Botha said that Jannie Smuts was a known traitor, a Boer War General who had gone over to the English in the First World War and became a hero to the British. So he was a definite traitor to the *Boerevolk*, to his very own *herrenvolk*.

'Never you mind, we know about him, Jan Smuts now has the same blood on his hands as the British for the women and children who died in the concentration camps.' That's what Meneer Botha said. So you can see, running away with Tinker, especially with me being English, was a hopeless proposition. People wouldn't lift a finger to help an English boy and his little bitch dog that was one day going to have babies that would need to be drowned in a sack.

At supper that night, which was the usual boiled potatoes and cabbage and stew that was gravy with only a very little bit of meat and lots of carrots and bits of tomato skin, I hardly managed to finish what was on my plate and I didn't mind when someone took two of my potatoes and I didn't even clean the plate with a piece of bread. I just didn't have an appetite for life at that moment. I'd looked for Pissy but his table was at the other end of the dining room and I was too small to see him over all the heads that were in the way.

After we'd eaten, as usual the superintendent of the orphanage, Meneer Prinsloo, who was big and fat and wore braces and waved his hands about a lot, read from the Bible and said prayers and then told us stuff we needed to know which were called 'daily instructions', only they were meant for the next day. Then the other staff would say things if they needed to and last of all Mevrou, the matron, would stand up and read out who had to come and see her. This was usually the small kids who needed to be punished or boys who had to get medicine. She was only allowed to give the *sjambok* to the small kids under ten. After that you would get a proper whipping from Meneer Botha who, for the most part, was the punishment master. Sometimes, because he was once a district champion boxer, he'd make a boy put on the gloves and then he'd beat the shit out of him. 'Fair and square,' he'd always say. 'If you can hit me you can get a bit of your own back.' But even the biggest boys, who were sixteen, couldn't get near him and they'd get in the ring with him and he'd really do some damage, black eyes and bloody noses and everything. Except for Fonnie du Preez who was fifteen, nearly sixteen, and schools' lightweight champion as far as Louis Trichardt, Duiwelskrans, Tzaneen, Lydenburg and Pilgrims Rest. He was the one kid who could have easily landed a good few telling punches on anyone he liked including Meneer Botha. But it never happened, because Fonnie du Preez was Meneer Botha's favourite. He'd taught him to box and the two of them were thick as thieves. People said they were like father and son. Meneer Botha said Fonnie was a natural who moved like lightning and had a knockout punch in both hands and would go far, maybe even to the schools' boxing championships in Pretoria.

The funny thing was that Pissy Vermaak was protected by Fonnie du Preez. They were said to be related, they were second cousins or something like that. Although how this was possible was hard to see, they were a complete mismatch; one big and dark and built like a blue gum tree trunk and the other a real weed. They'd often be seen together, Pissy doing things for Fonnie like he was his servant.

Going into the ring with Meneer Botha was supposed to make a man out of you. But if there was a choice of the boxing ring or the *sjambok* you took the *sjambok* every time. This was because Meneer Botha was only allowed to give you six of the best and, while nobody said how hard he could hit you, it was still better than his invitation to meet him in the boxing ring. It wasn't just about being knocked all over the place, it was that everyone was made to watch you being humiliated. Boere are a proud people and can't stand to be humiliated. It's not in their blood. With cuts from the cane you could always cover your arse with your trousers. An hour later everyone would forget about your beating, but with a hiding in the ring you'd walk around for days with a black eye, split lip and puffed-up and torn ears, maybe that's what people thought kids like us who belonged to the Government ought to look like.

While I'm on the subject of punishment, Meneer Prinsloo, the superintendent, would also do punishment, but only if it was a really big crime called masturbation or for stealing or taking God's name in vain. The other staff could pinch you, give you a clout on the back of the head, kick your arse or whack you over the knuckles with a steel-edged ruler, but they weren't allowed to give you formal punishment where you had to remove your trousers and bend over and get six of the best.

So I waited for Mevrou to call my name. It wasn't the *sjambok* I was afraid of. We all got beaten so often that you sort of got used to it and it wasn't too bad. A sore bum is a sore bum and everyone in the showers had the welts of the cuts from the *sjambok* crisscrossing their bums like Chinese writing. It was Mevrou discovering about Tinker that worried me sick. She'd tell Meneer Botha who was in charge of things outside the hostel and that would be the end of my little dog. Like Mattress said, he'd call her a *kaffir* dog and wring her neck.

To my surprise my name wasn't called out and nor was Pissy's. This was strange because you always went for medicine after supper and Pissy would always have to go to get his cough mixture. But there you go, miracles will never cease, maybe he hadn't said anything. Which was a big surprise because he could have blabbed easily enough because he had nothing to fear. There was no touching Pissy for fear of Fonnie du Preez. What's more, Mevrou never gave him the *sjambok* because he was 'too delicate of health' and it was suggested that physical violence might bring on one of his out-of-the-blue fits. His coughing condition was bad enough as it was, so you see he had nothing to lose by being a telltale. You could hear him coughing at night in the little kids' dormitory and people would shout at him to *shurrup*, but he couldn't. He was the only person in the showers to have no marks on his pink bum. And the guys would say, 'Pissy's got a girl's bum . . . Pissy's got a girl's bum.' Maybe it wasn't easy for him being sick and having out-of-the-blue fits and not being allowed to get the *sjambok* like everyone else.

And then all of a sudden I remembered about him getting a fit from physical violence, and I had punched him in the stomach. He'd staggered around coughing and I'd run away before seeing what happened. Maybe he'd had an out-of-the-blue fit. It was the first time I'd ever been brave and I might have given Pissy a fit or even killed him. I'd clean forgotten about him getting fits and, besides, I'd barely been aware of hitting him. I'd even quietly congratulated myself over the punch, which was the only good thing in the whole disaster and I intended bragging a bit to Mattress how I'd also got a strong heart like he said Tinker possessed.

Tinker, like I said before, wouldn't put up with any nonsense from the piglets that were miles bigger than she was. She was the smallest by far but she wasn't afraid and Mattress said it was because she was a lioness and had a strong heart.

'Sometimes, *Kleinbaas*, you've just got to stand up for yourself even if you are the smallest,' Mattress said. 'The lioness doesn't have to be told she's brave, she just knows and so do all the other animals, even the big male lion who is supposed to be the boss of the jungle, they all know who is the *real* boss and who does the hunting. People can be the same, *Kleinbaas*. A strong heart isn't about size.'

That night Pissy's bed in the dormitory was empty. Nobody said anything about this because it wasn't unusual for him to spend the night in the sick room when his chest was bad. All the other kids were pretty pleased by his absence because it meant we'd have a quiet night for a change. I was worried and didn't think I'd be able to sleep but I was also very tired from the long day with all the worries I had accumulated and did fall asleep soon enough. Your eyes don't always listen to your brain worrying. Mattress said that when things went wrong they'd seem better after a good night's sleep. 'In the morning the memory is washed clean,' he said, that's the closest I could get from the Zulu, which was, 'In the morning the river has washed over the worry stones and the water is clean.'

The wake-up bell went at six o'clock and we had to hurry up and wash our faces, get dressed, make our beds and our towels had to be folded over the end bedrail. By six-thirty we would be standing at attention at the end of our bed for what was known by us boys as 'half-jack inspection'. This was the daily dormitory inspection conducted by Mevrou who came round with her *sjambok* at the ready to inspect our beds and our folded towels and to punish the slightest untidiness. Even a button undone on your shirt could earn you a good whack.

I should explain about the word *sjambok*. A real *sjambok* is made of a single strip of rhino hide and is usually about four feet long and about an inch thick at the handle and gradually tapers down to about an eighth of an inch or less at the tip. While it is supple it isn't like a whip and it only really bends on contact with the flesh. It is used by prison warders and the South African Police Force and by farmers to beat *kaffirs*. In the right hands it can kill, but it always delivers a severe blow and causes great welts and, if it's correctly shaped and prepared, it will cut like a knife into flesh and even expose bone. It is much feared by the black people.

Now, Mevrou didn't have one of those, a *proper sjambok*. What she had was a thick piece of leather about the length and thickness of a razor strop nailed onto a wooden handle. We called it a *sjambok* because that's what we called anything that the staff beat you with. Her particular *sjambok* couldn't kill you or anything, but it left a pretty broad mark on your bum, and it hurt like hell. Meneer Prinsloo and Meneer Botha used a long bamboo cane as their *sjambok* and you could tell who was who by the cuts on a person's bum. All the little kids had broad marks from Mevrou's *sjambok* and the older kids had these red and blue cuts that were the marks from the cane. When a kid got to be eleven he'd show his first cane cuts and brag how he'd taken six of the best and hadn't even blubbed. It was a tradition to take your punishment like a man and not even let out an 'Ooh!' or a single '*Eina!*' which is an Afrikaans 'ouch', although I have to admit I wasn't always very good at this particular tradition.

When Mevrou entered the dormitory we'd all shout out the mandatory '*Goeie môre, Mevrou!* Good morning, Missus!'

'*Goeie môre, kinders,*' she'd reply on a good day.

On a good morning she'd wear a green, starched uniform and her hair would be pulled back in a tight bun at the back of her head, with a net holding the bun. Sometimes she'd appear first thing in the morning in her nightdress and slippers with her grey hair looking like scouring wire and falling all over the place. Her teeth would be missing so her lips sort of caved in with little slanted vertical lines pulling inwards around her lips like the drawstring on a pipe tobacco bag. On these occasions the whites of her eyes would be blood-red and the front of her nightdress would be unbuttoned and through the white thin cotton nightgown you'd see the shape of her great breasts. You could also see the teats, blackish and bigger than the sow's, at the end of her titties. The top part of her breasts pushed out of the unbuttoned part of her nightdress, great white lumps like bread dough with a black fly sitting on one of the rounded pieces of dough, only it was a hairy mole. Half-jack inspection was always a dangerous time but on those occasions when she appeared in her nightdress, you'd better watch out, man, this was no time for jokes.

Also, on nightdress mornings we'd shout, '*Goeie môre, Mevrou!*' as usual and all that would come in reply would be '*Hurrump!*' It was a snort exactly like the sow's. That's when you knew it was going to be a bad, bad day for everyone concerned because she'd been to bed with Doctor Half-Jack. Half a bottle of Tolley's five-star brandy in those days came in a flat bottle known as a half-jack. One Sunday when Mevrou had her day off to visit her brother and sister-in-law, which she did after church, she had an accident. She always carried her handbag and also one of those big brown paper shopping bags with string handles and if you got a glimpse inside you'd see all these little parcels of the same size wrapped in newspaper. Nobody knew what these could possibly be because they were too small to be loaves of bread and you wouldn't wrap a cake in newspaper like that and anyway, why would you have all those cakes? What's more, when Mevrou returned just before supper on Sunday night she still carried the paper bag, and if you got near enough to take a peek the little parcels in newspaper were still there exactly the same as in the morning when she'd left. It was a very strange business we couldn't get to the bottom of, until her accident.

On this particular morning when church was over and the beetle had chomped the beard and I'd received my mandatory punches in the ribs, we were all lined up beside the road, ready to be marched back to The Boys Farm. Sunday everywhere else may have been a day of rest, the Lord's Day, but on the farm we had to work in the vegetable garden or chop the week's wood for the kitchen and for the laundry hot-water system. It was the only day we didn't have school or sport so it became the main working day. On Saturday night after supper we'd get our weekly change of clothes, a clean pair of khaki shorts and shirt so we could wear them to church in the morning. But after church we had to get back into our last week's dirty clothes because the rest of Sunday was a working-in-the-vegetable-garden day. Then we'd shower again on Sunday night so we'd be clean and put on our going-to-church nice clean clothes again on Monday for school. You didn't get boots until you were thirteen. All us little kids had to bother about was trying to keep both items clean for a week. If you spilt gravy on a shirt or got your pants dirty so that they looked worse than anyone else's you got the *sjambok*. I was almost certain to get the *sjambok* every Wednesday because it didn't matter how hard I tried, my shirt and shorts were always the worst in our dormitory. Keeping clean was a very tiresome business and I wouldn't get the hang of it until I was much older.

Mevrou stood waiting with her fat sister-in-law beside us outside the church on the side of the road while her brother went to bring his lorry around to pick the two of them up and take Mevrou to the main family farm. She had six brothers and they all had farms next door to each other in a valley somewhere in the high mountains. She'd once told us that her father had found this valley in 1898 after the Boer War because he never wanted to see anyone that was English. He'd built his house and he never left the farm again, not even to come to *nagmaal*. The six brothers only went to school to learn to count and read a bit and then went back to the farm. In the district they were known to be very tough and you wouldn't want to pick a fight with a Van Schalkwyk if you wanted to stay alive for long.

Two of Mevrou's brothers played rugby for Northern Transvaal and Boetie, the one who had gone to fetch the lorry, was once the amateur heavyweight boxing champion of the Transvaal with twenty fights and seventeen knockouts. He was banned from amateur boxing because in a championship fight he was boxing against an English-speaking heavyweight from Johannesburg. It turned out to be a very even fight and Boetie Van Schalkwyk managed to knock the *rooinek* out but it happened right on the bell in the final round, or just *after* the bell, the three judges said. So the boxer from Jo'burg was given the decision. When the referee held up the other boxer's hand, Boetie lost his temper and turned around and smashed the other boxer in the jaw and knocked him out a second time for good measure. People said the Van Schalkwyks were wild men who talked first with their fists and were best left alone. I just thought you'd like to know this stuff about Mevrou's family.

Anyway, we're standing at the side of the road outside the church when this town kid on a bicycle comes riding towards us showing off big time, riding with his hands in his pockets. This kid knew none of us could ever own a bicycle and he was free to do what he liked and had the whole day to do anything he cared to do. He made the mistake of coming too close to Flippy Marais who was standing next to me so I saw the whole thing happen. Flippy quickly stuck his foot out, planted it against the frame of the bike and gave it a great push. With no grip on the handlebars the kid lost control. Next moment it veered straight into Mevrou who landed on her enormous fat bum and her legs stuck up in the air showing her pink *crepe de Chine* bloomers that came down to just above her knees where the elastic bands cut into the flesh. The brown paper bag went flying and landed with a crash of glass, and there were these empty half-jack brandy bottles sticking out of pieces of newspaper scattered all over the road. The town kid jumped to his feet, retrieved his bicycle, mounted it and was gone like a rat up a drainpipe. On Monday morning at school he probably expected to get the shit knocked out of him by Fonnie du Preez or one of the other tough kids from The Boys Farm, but instead we all went up and congratulated him. That's how we discovered that Mevrou went to bed with Doctor Half-Jack.

The morning following Pissy's absence was a nightdress morning and Mevrou snorted her 'Hurrump!' and walked straight to his bed and brought her *sjambok* up and smashed it down on his pillow several times until she was panting, then she said, '*Genoeg!*' which means 'enough'. As in, 'Look, man . . . I've had enough, you hear! *Genoeg!*' Then she slammed the *sjambok* down once more across the pillow as hard as she could so that the whack resounded through the dormitory, making us all jump. If your bum had been that pillow I can guarantee you'd have trouble sitting for days. This time some feathers flew out of the side of the pillow and up into the air. I watched as one was caught by a draught of air and sailed right up past my nose and turned and floated out of the window behind my bed four rows away from Pissy's pillow.

'Kobus Vermaak has had an epileptic fit and somebody here is to blame! I want to know who it is! If you don't tell who hit him then you all going to get in trouble, you hear?' She looked around, her bloodshot eyes taking in each of us. The fly resting on her tits was moving up and down with her heavy breathing. 'I don't want you playing all innocent, hey! Somebody here knows, and if you don't tell me who it is you all going to get the *sjambok!*' She waited but only silence followed. 'I'm going to ask each one of you, "Did you hit Kobus Vermaak?" and you going to look me in the face and if you done it, I'll know. It's no use, you can't fool me, you hear?'

I don't think any of us would have known what an epileptic fit was. Certainly I'd never heard Pissy's fits given a name like that. In fact, I was a bit surprised that fits had names other than 'out of the blue'. How would we know one was different to the other? But an epileptic one was obviously bad and if it came about because you hit a person then I was to blame, one hundred per cent. But I had one thing going for me; nobody in the dormitory had seen me do it and I didn't have to own up, although

I wasn't much good at duplicity. I'd have to try my hardest not to give anything away. But that's the trouble, in my experience, when you try to conceal you often reveal. I could feel the fear rising up from my stomach, and filling my throat and my knees started to shake and my whole body trembled so that I was a dead giveaway.

Mevrou started at the top bed and I knew I'd have to try to pull myself together before she got to me, but fear is something that's hard to control, the harder you try the worse it gets.

'Dannie van Niekerk, did you hit Kobus?' she asked. Dannie was the oldest boy in the dormitory, nearly twelve, and almost ready to be transferred to the senior boys' dormitory.

'*Nee*, Mevrou!' Dannie shouted out his emphatic denial.

'Willem Oosthuizen, did you hit Kobus?'

'*Nee*, Mevrou!' came the equally vehement response.

She continued down the beds. For once nobody was guilty so they could shout out their denial quick smart and with conviction. Then she came to my bed where I was shaking like a leaf, guilty as sin. I couldn't even get the words out to confess and I could feel my eyes blurring with tears. I was truly shitting myself and wouldn't have been surprised if I'd done a job right there in my pants. It's not every day you are responsible for an epileptic fit that nearly kills a person. Mevrou looked at me and said with a tone of contempt, 'Ag, you couldn't do it, you too small to swat a fly!'

She moved to the next bed. 'Bokkie Swartz, did you do it, did you hit Kobus?'

'*Nee*, Mevrou!' Bokkie answered.

She reached the last boy's bed, only to be met with the same resounding denial. She stood there panting and was very red in the face.

'Off!' she commanded, whereupon we all undid our belts and our khaki shorts dropped to our ankles, exposing our waterworks that we were quick to cup with our hands.

'*Hou vas!*' came the next command and we all turned and gripped the bedpost from which the towel hung, one hand on either side of it.

'Buk!' We all went into *sjambok* position, bending at the waist to present our bare arses for the leather strap. I could hear the whacks approaching, three to each boy. I'd stopped shaking, counting myself dead lucky, three cuts was a small price for not being found out. I gripped the end of the iron bed harder in anticipation of my turn but Mevrou just continued past me and gave Piet Grobler at the next bed three of the best. *Whack! Whack! Whack!*

She arrived back at the top bed, her nightdress clinging to her large frame due to the sweat from the exertion of giving twenty-five boys three of the best. I must say it wasn't a very nice look. Afterwards all the guys said they'd seen her great black bush through her nightdress. But I must have forgotten to look or something, not knowing about black bushes on grown-up people.

'Don't think you heard the end of this, you hear?' she screamed. 'Kobus Vermaak had a very bad epileptic fit and he could have died,' she said. 'Just lucky the pig boy found him lying in the dirt and called us. If it wasn't for the *kaffir* boy he could have swallowed his tongue and choked to death. We going to find out who done it, don't you worry about that. Kobus says someone threw him with a stone in the stomach but he didn't see who done it. But the *kaffir* saw it and he will know who is the guilty person. When we catch this wicked boy he will go to Meneer Prinsloo for punishment and spend a day in the tank!'

The tank was an empty, rusted corrugated iron 500-gallon water tank outside the laundry building that was just tall enough to hold a boy standing up and sufficiently wide to accommodate one sitting with his legs crossed. You had to climb in from a hole in the top and when they put the lid back on it was pitch dark with only tiny holes in the sides so a bit of air could get in. You could only be sentenced to the tank in the winter as it was too hot in the summer, and you could die from the hot air and the perspiration it caused. They said all the sweat would leak out of you and you'd just shrivel up and die, you'd become a piece of *biltong*.

It was my lucky day alright. I knew Mattress would never tell on me even if he had seen it happen, which he can't have, because he wasn't there. I'd punched Pissy so there was no stone throwing. It was funny. I usually got punished for stuff I *didn't* do and here I was getting away with a terrible epileptic fit crime I *did* do. But, there you go, the rule was that you took everything you could get away with because it didn't happen too often.

But the big question remained: why hadn't Pissy Vermaak dobbed me in? It just wasn't like him at all. All I could think was that perhaps he was unwilling to admit that the smallest and weakest boy in The Boys Farm had given him a hiding. That seemed to make sense, nobody, not even a sissy like Pissy, would be able to live with the shame when it was known that *Voetsek* the *rooinek* had got the better of him.

All I could think was that Tinker was safe and nobody except Mattress and me knew where her hiding place was in the burrow under the big rock. I decided I'd go and visit Mattress after school and he'd tell me his part of the story. For the first time in my life I felt as if I was in control of the information that guided my immediate future. Mattress and me knew more than all the others put together. Then I thought that maybe having an epileptic fit gives you such a shock that it wipes out your memory and Pissy clean forgot what happened and just made up the bit about how he'd been hit with a rock because he had to have someone to blame.

If only I'd known what lay ahead I'd have jumped over my own tongue in my haste to confess to Mevrou. I'd willingly have taken the punishment coming to me, even the prospect of six of the best from Meneer Prinsloo's terrible bamboo cane and a day spent in the dark and empty water tank.

But that's the problem with the road you travel in life, you never know what new disaster is waiting for you around the next corner.

CHAPTER TWO

The Terrible Consequence of Loving

I LOST NO TIME in going to see Mattress after school. Because Tinker was off the sow's teats, I didn't have to cart her over to the pigsty first thing after breakfast, an event that had always meant a rush as I'd have to let her get a good feed and take her back to the big rock. It would only just allow you time to get your pencil box for school and line up for the four-mile march into town.

Now that she was weaned Tinker ate breakfast bread crusts. Crusts were the only thing you were allowed not to eat in that place, so sometimes some of the boys would leave their crusts behind and I'd scoop a few of them up after breakfast, my own included. The reason we were allowed to not eat our crusts was that Meneer Prinsloo had these Black Orpington chickens and while they had plenty of *mielies* and all that to eat, he had this theory that bread crusts were good for their feathers. Don't ask me why. They were supposed to make the feathers more shiny or something, so that he'd win ribbons at the Magaliesburg Show. Gawie Grobler said his uncle in the Free State grew sunflower seeds that get crushed up for their oil and it's the oil that goes into the bread and that's what makes the chickens' feathers shine. How a person would know a thing like that I couldn't say but Gawie definitely wasn't a bullshitter, and was clever as well. I asked why Meneer Prinsloo didn't simply give his chickens sunflower seeds to eat.

Gawie thought for a moment. 'Have you ever seen a sunflower seed?'

'No, just a big sunflower, big as a dinner plate.'

'Well, the black part in the middle, that's the seeds, man . . . and they as big as my fingernail and they hard as a rock when they dried. Chickens can't eat them,' he concluded convincingly.

'Why not?' I'd seen chickens eating lots of things much bigger, grasshoppers for instance.

'Chickens got no teeth, man. They can eat them but they can't break them open to get the oil inside and they just pop them out their bums, which doesn't make their feathers shiny.'

I'm always amazed at the things you can learn from a person. I'd never thought about chickens having no teeth. Anyway, that was good, Meneer Prinsloo would have to rely on bread crusts for his prize chickens' shiny black feathers and this meant Tinker's food supply was happily intact. One thing for sure, a dog wouldn't be able to eat sunflower seeds, even though he did have teeth.

There were these blue ribbons that Meneer Prinsloo's chickens had won at country agricultural shows plastered on the wall behind the staff table that was raised on a platform in the dining room. The staff didn't get the same food as us because they were grown-ups and deserved better.

You see, even though Meneer Prinsloo, because he was the superintendent, could do anything he liked about the crust situation, you still couldn't just go around hollowing out loaves of bread and giving the chickens the crust. This was because food was scarce and . . . 'God will not tolerate waste and nor will I,' he'd say to us. But if we left a few crusts lying around after breakfast or any of the other meals, that was a different matter altogether. This was a definite thing God allowed you to do.

The bread was good on Monday and Tuesday, so crusts were always scarce on those days, but by Wednesday it was becoming a bit stale and by Friday or Saturday you could collect heaps. On Sunday it was the Lord's

Day, so no bread. There was only *mielie* meal porridge with brown sugar and milk for breakfast, for lunch cold potatoes and other vegetables like beetroot and grated carrot and cold pumpkin and cabbage chopped up, raw stuff like that. At night it was always potato soup and bread pudding made from the leftover stale bread you couldn't even cut with a knife, so they'd soak it on Saturday. If you looked through the kitchen window on a Saturday afternoon you'd see all the leftover stale bread with the crust removed for the chickens soaking in these white enamel basins, ready for Sunday night's bread pudding. With no bread on a Sunday I had to get a double ration of crusts on Saturday, otherwise Tinker would starve.

Because Tinker didn't need too many crusts I could always rely on a pocketful for her and also at supper you could maybe manage to rub your own crusts in the stew gravy left on your plate. Sorry to go on about it, but feeding a puppy you're not supposed to have wasn't an easy business and I just wanted you to know how it was done. So I would give her the crusts and the half jam tin of milk that Mattress got for her at the dairy that would be put in a certain place behind the empty milk churns for me to get after school. Sometimes the milk went bad in the heat and turned into sour milk but Tinker didn't seem to mind. She was a dog and a half, I can tell you, I never saw anything she didn't eat. I loved her so much she made me want to cry.

Have you noticed that food is the biggest preoccupation people have in life? If people don't eat fast and they talk while they're eating then you know they came from a good family. The speed people eat is a dead giveaway to their past. I have to say that the brown bread we had at The Boys Farm must have been full of good things because although Tinker wasn't fat, she wasn't thin either, not like a *kaffir* dog. Mattress said she was good and would grow up to be strong. Sometimes he even saved a bit of gristle from the meat he was given by the kitchen to cook with his *mielie* pap, and occasionally there would be a small bone for her to gnaw. What a happy little dog she was, with her tail that hadn't been chopped off always wagging and when you saw her in the morning she'd yelp and turn round and round and jump up to tell you how nice it was to see you again.

The day when Mevrou had walloped Pissy's pillow and shouted 'Genoeg!' I went down to the pigsty to see Mattress. Winter was coming and by the time we got back from school it was already sunset and getting a bit cold, but we didn't get our jersey until a month later. Mattress had a fire going at the pigsty where he was making a mash for the pigs – old vegetables, cabbage leaves and the like and some of the leftover buttermilk from the dairy and some *mielies*. He boiled it all up, stirring once in a while with a big carved wooden stick like a paddle. We stood by the nice warm fire and he told me how he'd found Pissy flopping like a *platanna* you've just caught in the creek.

A *platanna* is a kind of frog, dark green with a smooth skin on top and a yellowish stomach. Sometimes in the summer, when the creek wasn't so cold, you could take a bit of bread crust and tie it to a length of string and drop it into the stream just below the water. The *platanna* would come swimming up, grab it and wouldn't let go so then you could yank it onto the black pebbles or the grass. Boy, what a kerfuffle happened then! The frog would leap this way and that, land on its back and from that possie spring high into the air with no control of its movements, yellow belly then green top and shivering and shaking like all get-out, legs going like propellers. That's how Mattress said Pissy was when he had his fit. His eyes were rolled back in his head, which also happened to a *platanna*, and he was busy trying to swallow his tongue, which isn't a thing a *platanna* can do.

Mattress laughed. '*Kleinbaas*, I had to sit on his chest and hold his arms to the ground. I found a stick and I put it in his mouth just like you do with a goat if it has convulsions when they've eaten a certain poison fruit you find growing on a small bush in the mountains. If a goat swallows its tongue it will choke and it will not live, so I think that boy is same like the goat. *Ahee!* He is not a strong one, that boy, but when he had the "goat fit" he is strong like a buffalo. I have to hold him very tight with all my strength. After a while he finish that fit, but I left the stick in his mouth because sometimes with a goat it comes back. Then I go and fetch Big *Baas* Botha and he come with the Big Missus and a blanket.'

I was very glad to hear the story because now we were evens; I'd punched Pissy in the stomach and Mattress had saved his life. I confessed my role in the whole affair, telling Mattress what had happened, telling him how Pissy tried to take Tinker away from me. He shook his head slowly.

'You have a strong heart, *Kleinbaas*, that boy he is a bigger one than you, but a man, he must protect what is weaker than him always.'

I must say I was rather pleased with the compliment, as there weren't that many compliments flying about in my life.

That night Pissy was in the dining-room queue again and seemed to have completely recovered. Later in the wash house, when we were washing our faces and hands and feet so that when we went to bed we didn't dirty our bottom sheet, he came up to me and whispered, 'I'm still going to get you, you hear, *Voetsek*? Just you wait, man!' Those words with no further explanation. He had a sort of a half smile on his freckled face and I caught a whiff of his piss smell as he moved away. Now I knew an epileptic fit doesn't make you lose your memory. It made me worry a lot as we went into the dormitory to go to sleep.

You must be thinking that I didn't say we cleaned our teeth before we went to bed. Well, we didn't because the Government couldn't afford toothbrushes, let alone toothpaste. Twice a year the dentist would come in a van with a special dentist chair and a nurse and pull out your teeth if they were bad. If you couldn't wait, Doctor Dyke, who was a vet who owned the farm next door, would come in an emergency when aspirin and oil of cloves didn't help any more and you could see the swelling from the outside of a person's cheek. Mevrou would leave a white dishcloth hanging from the gate of The Boys Farm, and Doctor Dyke on his way to or from where he worked in town would see it and drive his Dodge truck in if he had the time. She could have called him on the party line but she didn't want everyone knowing our business: 'Ag, man, Boys Farm business is private, you hear? The Government doesn't like it if people go telling its business all over the place.' This was intended as a general warning to us kids not to talk about The Boys Farm to anyone at school. Later I realised she didn't want to call Doctor Dyke on the party line in case someone listening in heard that the vet was taking out our teeth.

They'd strap your arms to the back of this big dining chair Mevrou had for the express purpose and strap your ankles to its legs. The front legs of this chair were placed on two wooden boxes so that it tilted backwards. Mevrou would stand behind the chair and clasp both her big hands over your forehead and pull your head hard against the back of the chair, holding it steady with her body. Doctor Dyke would tell you to open your mouth wide and he'd tap your teeth with his callipers and when your eyes got big and frightened he knew he had the right tooth. If he was doing an emergency on the way back from town you could smell the beer on his breath, a sort of sour smell that wasn't very nice. He'd take his horse pliers and just pull that tooth out, without chloroform or an injection. He'd hold up the tooth in the pliers and smile. 'What pains no longer remains,' he'd announce happily. Except sometimes he'd say, 'Oops, wrong tooth, let's start again.' Maybe they were proper dentist teeth extractors but we called them his horse pliers because they were definitely not the same as those used by the Government dentist.

Once when Doctor Dyke took out one of my teeth he did his 'Oops, wrong tooth' routine and I started to cry.

'Never mind,' Mevrou said. 'Everybody can make a mistake and the doctor is only doing his best and does this for nothing out of the goodness of his heart, so crying is not a very grateful thing to do, you hear?'

I tried to stop blubbing but the extraction hurt like hell and I was swallowing a lot of blood and feeling sick and I was going to have to go through it all over again. Mevrou soon grew impatient with my sniffing. 'Ag, we all got to learn to take a bit of pain in our life, Thomas. Just think of the Lord Jesus hanging from the cross. He's got six-inch nails through his hands and a sword from a Roman soldier stuck in his side and he has to suck a sponge full of vinegar. That's what you call pain, man! Compared to that, what we got here is just a little bit of hurt from a tooth.' It was okay for her, she didn't have any teeth, so how would she know?

When you were sixteen and could leave the place and be in the outside world, you could always tell an orphan from The Boys Farm because the only teeth he still had were the ones growing in the back of the jaw where Doctor Dyke couldn't get at them. It is very hard to look intelligent when you've only got empty gums in your mouth. So, if you could stand the pain, you'd hang on until the Government dentist arrived, because if things were really bad he'd give you an injection so it only hurt after, when the needle wore off, and besides, it was about a quarter of the pain or even less than a Doctor Dyke leather-chair-horse-pliers-extraction.

The morning after the night before when Pissy Vermaak had warned me in the wash house that he hadn't forgotten me hitting him passed without incident. It was only when we got back from school that the trouble started. As I always did on my return I put my pencil case safely away. If you lost it the Government got very angry because it was 'Government Goods Department of Education', that is what our teacher told us it said on the back of the box. I waited until no one was looking and ran to the big rock that was a long way from the hostel building and quite deep in some bush. There were quite a lot of thorn bushes around so nobody ever went there except me because I knew a path through the thorns. I'd found it when I was quite little and had decided to run away. I had just walked and walked and when I got to this big rock I decided to take a rest and the rest made me change my mind because the situation was hopeless. But I knew I'd found a place I could come when I was miserable, which was quite a lot of the time. Now it was Tinker's home and no longer a place to come when you were sad.

Whenever I got close I'd call her name and put two fingers between my lips and whistle. She'd bark with excitement when she heard me coming. This time I called and whistled but nothing. 'Tinker! Tinker!' I called again and let go another piercing whistle. Still nothing happened. My heart started to thump in my chest and I scratched my arm quite badly on a whitethorn bush in my haste to get to the big rock, but I didn't even feel it until after. I rushed around the big rock and there stood Fonnie du Preez and Pissy Vermaak. Fonnie cradled Tinker in his arms and I could see there was a rope around her neck, and he held it in his fist and was pulling slightly at the rope so that Tinker's head was forced upwards. Tinker was whimpering and shivering with fright and she tried to struggle free when she saw me, but Fonnie was too strong.

'This your dog, *Voetsek*?'

I nodded, too overwhelmed for words.

Fonnie laughed. 'Not any more, man, we going to kill it stone dead, you hear?'

Pissy grinned. 'I told you I'd get my own back,' he said triumphantly.

I felt the tears well up but I knew that crying wasn't going to help. I knuckled them back, still unable to speak.

'Please, Sir . . .' came out in a whisper because my throat and chest were filled up with a hurt so terrible I thought I was going to split wide open.

'Watch,' Fonnie said. He released his arms around Tinker and held onto the rope so that she dangled from his arm, the rope pulling tight like a noose, her back legs kicking and her eyes filled with fear as she yelped frantically.

'No!' I screamed and flung myself at Fonnie's feet and grabbed his ankles. 'Please! Please don't kill her, Fonnie!' I pleaded, holding tightly onto his legs.

'What will you give me if I don't?' he said, ignoring my tears. I could hear Tinker choking and whimpering above my head. I had nothing to give him, even my pencil box belonged to 'Government Goods Department of Education'.

'Please, I'll do anything you want,' I sobbed, looking up at him through my tears.

He put Tinker back into his arms, releasing the tension on the rope. 'First you going to have to say you sorry for throwing Pissy with a stone so he got a fit and nearly died. It could have been murder, man!' He looked at me sternly. 'Then they'd put you in gaol and when you old enough hang you by the neck until you stone dead.' He released his arms, Tinker fell and once again started to strangle in the noose.

'Sorry, Pissy! Please don't, Fonnie!' I cried, reaching out to grab Tinker. Fonnie pulled away and Tinker swung away from my grasp and let out a terrible cry.

Fonnie grabbed her with his free hand and brought her back to his chest. 'Throwing a stone at a person is a coward's way, *Voetsek*.' He paused. 'But then you a *rooinek*, so what can you expect, you all cowards that murdered Boer women and children.'

'I didn't throw him with a stone, I hit him,' I sobbed, then turned to Pissy. 'Sorry I hit you in your stomach and you had a fit.'

Fonnie du Preez gave Pissy an incredulous look. '*He* hit *you*? The *rooinek* hit you?'

'No, Fonnie, he's lying, man,' Pissy said hastily. 'Honest to God, he threw me with a stone, a big one.' Pissy indicated his stomach. 'It hit me right here so I got a fit.'

'Show me the mark, a big stone will leave a mark,' Fonnie said.

Pissy didn't pull his shirt up. 'It's gone already, Fonnie. Mevrou put some *muti* on it.'

'You the one who's lying now, you hear!' Fonnie took a step towards Pissy who brought his hands up defensively to ward off the expected blow. Fonnie still held Tinker but he feinted with his left hand and Pissy reeled back. Fonnie took a second step and smacked Pissy with the flat of his hand, hard against the side of Pissy's head.

'Watch out!' I yelled. 'You'll give him a fit!' I expected Pissy to begin to shake and wobble on the spot right there in front of our eyes. Mind you, if he did, then Fonnie would have to sit on his chest and put a stick in his mouth and then he'd have to let go of Tinker. But I only thought of that later.

No such thing happened. Pissy just sniffed a big yellow glob of snot back in his nose and didn't even cough, he just looked down at his feet. Tinker was still held captive. Fonnie ignored the petulant Pissy and addressed me. 'You get points for hitting him and not throwing a stone.' He paused and seemed to be thinking, then he said, 'Sorry, but you not sorry enough.'

'I am,' I pleaded. 'I'm *really* and *truly* sorry, Fonnie . . . Pissy!'

'Really and truly, your father's a coolie,' Fonnie retorted, reciting the common rhyme and thinking himself very clever. 'No, *Voetsek*, you have to *show* him, you have to show Pissy you sorry, man.'

I looked at him, not understanding. 'What must I do?' I asked tearfully.

'Pissy, take off your pants!' Fonnie demanded.

Pissy didn't hesitate, immediately undoing the buckle of his belt and letting his khaki shorts drop down to his ankles. He had a grin on his face and he didn't bother to cup his *piel* that looked just like a fat worm with a snout, something a chicken could gobble up.

'Bend over!' Fonnie commanded. Pissy turned and bent at the waist, his bare bum pointing directly at me. It was this pale pink colour and it was the only part of him that didn't have freckles and, of course, no Chinese writing. Fonnie looked at me. 'Kiss his arse, *Voetsek*!'

I looked up at him in dismay. 'No,' I said in a small voice. 'It's not nice.'

'Ag, man, it's not nice to nearly kill a person with a fit! You got to pay, man.'

'I don't want to,' I said, not looking at Fonnie du Preez.

Fonnie's voice changed. 'It's just like a girl's arse. You'd kiss a girl's arse, wouldn't you?'

'No, I wouldn't!' I retorted, shocked at the very idea.

'Nice and pink and no marks.' Fonnie's voice had gone sort of gravelly. I hesitated, waiting, hoping for a reprieve. He suddenly barked, 'You kiss Pissy's arse or your dog dies!' He let go of Tinker who fell dangling, yelping and kicking, the noose about her neck tightening as Fonnie jerked her upwards and held her aloft. 'Kiss, *Voetsek*!' he shouted. 'Kiss, then lick his arse!'

All I could hear was Tinker yelping and I fell to my knees and kissed Pissy's arse.

'Kiss again, *rooinek*, inside!' came the command from above. With Tinker yelping and about to die from throttlelisation I licked the side of

Pissy's bum. '*In sy gat!* In his hole, kiss it for me!' They both laughed and Pissy's hands came around and parted his bum so I could see his arsehole. 'Now kiss or the dog dies!' Fonnie threatened. Tinker's yelp had become a weak whimper as her throat constricted from the effects of the noose. I kissed into Pissy's bum, inside the crack but my lips didn't touch the place that wasn't pink but sort of purple and nasty. It smelled of shit. I made a sort of smacking sound with my lips. 'Now do it again, *rooinek* arse-licker, and say you sorry again!' Fonnie demanded.

I kissed Pissy's bum hole but I didn't lick it. 'Sorry, Pissy,' I wept.

'Stay like that on your knees, don't turn around,' Fonnie's voice demanded. Pissy stood up and moved away from me and I remained on my knees with my back to Fonnie. Tinker was either dead or back in his arms because she'd stopped whimpering. 'Your dog is orright, you hear. Now turn around.' I was trying not to blub as I started to get up but the tears and the sobs just came out by themselves. 'No! Stay on your knees. Then turn around, *Voetsek*.'

'Please don't kill her,' I choked, turning to face Fonnie. That's the moment I got the biggest shock of my life. Fonnie du Preez had removed his shorts and staring at me was his enormous cock, fully erect.

'You like my snake, hey, *Voetsek*? Suck me.'

'No!' I cried.

'You licked Pissy's arse, that's far worse, man!' Fonnie exclaimed.

'I don't want to, Fonnie,' I said tearfully.

'I got no more patience! Suck me, or this time your dog dies, for sure!' He held Tinker by the rope and she was again yelping for her life, the whites of her eyes were showing and her legs were kicking. My little dog couldn't take much more and her legs were going slower, unable to kick because she was choking to death. I heard Pissy cackle, 'It tastes *lekker, Voetsek* . . . jus' like *boerewors*.' (It tastes nice, *Voetsek* . . . just like farmer's sausage.)

Blubbing my heart out, I took Fonnie du Preez's huge cock between my lips.

All of a sudden I heard this roar of anger, '*Mina bulala wena!*' Fonnie turned suddenly and his cock jumped out of my mouth and, at the same time, Tinker dropped at my feet. I saw a pair of black arms lift Fonnie off the ground and hurl him so that he seemed to take off into the sky above me. Fonnie's body arched, arms flailing, one coming down to try to break the fall as he crashed into the side of the big rock. I turned around in time to see him slide down the face of the rock, with blood streaming from his nose and head. He hit the ground like a rag doll, rolled over onto his stomach and then lay quite still. I thought he must surely be dead. I grabbed hold of Tinker and held her to my chest, crying and sobbing and shaking like billyo, kissing her soft little neck with the piece of rope still tied around it. She shivered and shook in my arms and started to lick the place where the whitethorn had ripped open the skin on my arm. I don't know how long we remained like that, Tinker and me. I was too frightened to look at Fonnie du Preez's dead body with blood all over his head and in his hair.

Then Mattress bent over me. 'Come, *Kleinbaas,*' he said in Zulu. He was panting and I could hear the air being pulled into his nostrils and out like an angry animal. He lifted us both up and carried us away, leaving Fonnie du Preez just lying there with his bare arse facing us in the late afternoon sunlight. Flies were already buzzing around his head like the big sow when she was feeding her piglets. Pissy Vermaak was nowhere to be seen. I rested my head against Mattress's broad chest and just blubbed and blubbed like a little kid.

I can't remember all the detail of what happened after. Mattress took me and Tinker to Meneer Botha and told him what he'd seen. He hadn't seen the arse-licking part so he could only tell the part he'd seen. I must have still been in a state of shock and words couldn't come out. But I need not have worried because the first thing Meneer Botha said was, 'You don't say anything, you hear!' He put his hand on my shoulder. 'Look at me, Tom!' he demanded. I looked up into his eyes which were fierce and frightening and he squeezed my shoulder so it hurt. '*Stom!* If I hear you told somebody, you in big trouble, you hear?'

What? Was he mad or something? Did he think I was going to walk around and tell everyone that I had Fonnie du Preez's cock in my mouth or that I'd kissed Pissy Vermaak's arsehole? *Sis*, man, imagine that! I may have been only six, nearly seven, but I wasn't a complete nincompoop. It was bad enough being a *rooinek*, but if I told, everyone around the place would know, even a *rooinek* couldn't survive that sort of shame! I nodded. '*Ja*, I promise, Meneer,' I said.

'I better go quickly and see where is Fonnie du Preez,' Meneer Botha announced. He turned to Mattress. 'You also, you don't say anything. You were not there, you hear? If you tell then you get the sack, you understand, *kaffir*!'

'*Ja, Baas*, I am not be to that place,' Mattress readily agreed.

Meneer Botha looked at both of us threateningly. 'If I hear either of you have said anything . . .' he turned to me and for the first time seemed to notice Tinker, who was still cradled in my arms. 'What you got there?'

'It's a dog, Meneer.'

'*Ja*, I can see it's a dog. You can't have a dog, it's not allowed.'

I didn't know what to say except, 'Yes, Meneer Botha.'

He seemed to change his mind and went down on his haunches and sort of smiled, then looked me in the eye. 'You can keep him, but only if you promise you will never talk about what happened. You weren't even there at the rock, you understand, Tom? If I hear you told someone, *here*, man!' He paused, looked at Tinker and drew his finger across his throat. '*Wragtig*, he's a dead dog, I swear it, or my name is not Frikkie Botha. Do you promise?'

'I promise,' I said with alacrity. It was going to be the easiest promise to keep I had ever made. But talk about a cat having nine lives, my dog was beginning to match any cat, so far everyone who had found out about Tinker had threatened to take her life almost from the moment she'd plopped out of that wet sack. Even Mattress had suggested wringing her neck, though I think it was a joke and he didn't *really* mean it.

Meneer Botha pointed to Tinker. 'He can stay in the dairy in the room at the back with the *mielies*. He's a fox terrier. They make very

good ratters. He can earn his keep, but only if you don't tell, you hear?'
he said for the third time. I didn't tell him Tinker was a she and so could
have babies all over the place. Sometimes in life it's best just to leave
some things out when you talking to a person. It's not lying, it's just that
they don't always have to know everything about a person's business.

'Where is du Preez?' Frikkie Botha asked.

'I show you this place,' Mattress said.

'*Ag*, no man, didn't you hear what I just told you, hey? You and the
boy supposed to know nothing about this. Nothing! Bugger all! Is he at
the big rock?'

'*Ja, Baas*, sorry, *Baas*, yes the rock, *Baas*,' Mattress said, looking down
at his big feet.

Here's the story as it came out. Fonnie du Preez had a broken arm,
a broken nose and sixteen stitches in his head and they had to take him
in the lorry into town to see Doctor Van Heerden. As the story went,
Fonnie and Pissy Vermaak had gone for a walk in the bush to shoot some
birds with their cattys. Fonnie had climbed to the top of the big rock
to see what was going on in the bush and there were bush doves calling
that were hard to see in the tall trees that grew next to the creek. That's
why he climbed the rock. Anyway, he started to come back down and
some loose shale came off the big rock and he lost his balance and fell.
Then Pissy ran to the dairy, the nearest place after the pigsty, and told
Meneer Botha, who promptly came to the rescue. There was no mention
at all of Mattress or me.

Whoever made it up, probably Meneer Botha, did a good job because
everyone believed that's what happened and said it was a tragedy as the
district schools' boxing championship was coming up and Fonnie du
Preez would miss out on winning the middleweight division. Meneer
Botha said it was a travesty of justice that the boxer from Lydenburg
High, Henrick Van Jaarsveldt, would probably win the championship
when everyone knew Fonnie du Preez could take him any time with one
hand tied behind his back.

What I couldn't understand was that the secret of the big rock was safe. Nobody was going to believe a *kaffir* and a *rooinek* even if we kept telling the truth til the cows came home. What really happened was safely buried for all time. Even so, I could see that Meneer Botha was very worried that the truth might come out. Fonnie would never tell. Pissy wouldn't either, no way, man. I wouldn't be stupid enough to put Tinker's life at risk or ruin whatever was left of my reputation. Nobody would even listen to Mattress because he was a *kaffir* and would only tell a whole lot of lies.

But nobody had reckoned on Mevrou and her influence over Pissy Vermaak. Mevrou liked to be the first to know everything and Pissy was her conduit to what happened on The Boys Farm. Here was something really dramatic happening, like a broken arm and nose and stitches in Fonnie du Preez's head and Pissy was an eyewitness and hadn't come to her first but had run to Frikkie Botha instead. Broken arms and other things were her department and she was supposed to call the doctor and take charge. Meneer Botha had taken over and driven Fonnie du Preez to the hospital without telling her or taking her along, and all of a sudden everyone was saying Frikkie Botha was a hero. He had got all the credit and the story was even in the newspaper, the *Zoutpansberg Nuus*, where they had a picture of Frikkie Botha and one of Fonnie in his boxing uniform, posing with the gloves on when he won the schools' district title.

PROMISING YOUNG BOXER
IN ROCK-CLIMBING ACCIDENT,
RESCUED BY BOXING COACH

Sometimes Meneer Prinsloo got his picture in the newspaper but nobody else from The Boys Farm had ever done it. Mevrou was furious because it should have been her in the paper.

Now, Mevrou was not the sort of person to let a thing like that pass so easily. Although Meneer Prinsloo was the boss of the inside of The Boys Farm and Meneer Botha was boss of the outside, Mevrou was really the boss of the inside, because she looked after the boys in the little dormitory and also the sick room. She'd been a nurse in the town hospital once, so was the medically qualified one to do broken noses and arms and dressings and such things. I can tell you there was no love lost between her and Frikkie Botha, because if a boy got hurt in the boxing ring he would always want to fix him up and take her job away from her. What he'd done by taking Fonnie to the hospital without her also in the lorry was a terrible slight she wasn't going to let pass without him knowing he was in a fight and a half because of the insult to her professional standing.

This is how the most terrible thing happened. At first Pissy swore on the Holy Bible that the story of him and Fonnie going to look for bush doves and Fonnie climbing the big rock and falling was true. But Mevrou could see from his eyes or something that it wasn't true, that there was more to the story. Every kid in that place was a good liar, because you had to be, even me, in the end I eventually learned to lie just as well as anyone else. Mevrou was an expert lie detector. To get away with a lie in front of her you had to have a special talent for lying. Besides, she knew how to work Pissy over big-time. She went to work on him.

You're going to ask how I know what I'm going to tell you now because otherwise you're going to think I made it up or something. The sick room that Mevrou called 'the clinic' was two rooms at the end of a long veranda that jutted out at right angles from the rest of the building. Maybe they'd been added on later after the hostel was built because they didn't look the same as the other part. The back of the sick room faced out to a small garden with lots of hydrangea bushes that grew right up to a window that looked into one of the two rooms, the room that was Mevrou's personal office. The other room was where you stayed if you were too sick for the dormitory or were put in quarantine for the measles and stuff that was maybe catching. If you had to go to the sick room for something and the door was closed, what you did was go into the garden and creep through the hydrangea bushes and take a look to see if Mevrou was alone and at her desk, because sometimes she'd be lying snoring on the leather examination couch she sometimes used to examine people on. You see, you weren't supposed to go to the sick room until after supper, only in an extreme emergency. If you disturbed her it was big trouble, I can tell you.

You remember the scratch on my arm from the whitethorn bush? Well, it festered badly and I hadn't gone to the sick room to have Mevrou take a look at it because then she'd ask me how it happened. I wasn't so good at lying and remember, Meneer Botha said I wasn't at the big rock when it happened. So I thought maybe she'd ask and I'd have to lie and she'd find out and next thing Tinker is 'a dead dog or my name isn't Frikkie Botha'. But Mevrou Prinsloo, the superintendent's wife, stopped me to tell me to do up my trouser fly buttons that I must have forgotten. When I did she saw my arm and how it had gone all red and there was pus coming out and she told me to go and see Mevrou at once. So that's why I was creeping through the bushes to see if it was all clear to go in and knock on the door. And that's when I overheard what I'm going to tell you. There was Mevrou and Pissy Vermaak and the window was open a little bit so I heard everything, hiding in the hydrangea bushes.

'What were the two of you doing in that part of the farm where nobody goes?' I heard her ask.

Pissy repeated the story of going to shoot bush doves with their cattys. Every kid on The Boys Farm had a catty. You made one by cutting two thin strips of rubber about a quarter of an inch wide and twelve inches long from an old car inner tube. Then you'd cut a forked stick from a branch, find an old piece of leather for the pouch and bind them all together using even thinner strips of inner tube. When you were finished you had your own deadly weapon to shoot birds with. The bigger boys were able to make really powerful ones that could take a stone high up into the branches of a stand of tall blue gum trees. There was a small forest of about twenty huge trees beside the stream, not far from where I'd found Tinker. This was a favourite place for bush doves, they'd roost high up in the very top branches and nowhere else. In the late afternoon you could hear them *cookarooing*. If the bigger boys shot three or four they'd make a fire and roast them, as they were fat and plump and delicious from eating some farmer's *mielies*. Not that I'd eaten one. I was too small to use a strong enough catty and I didn't possess the skill to bring a bush dove down from the high-up branches. I also wasn't allowed to chop any wood or light a fire. Sometimes a bigger boy would shoot six or seven doves and he'd give them to Mevrou in exchange for three C to C cigarettes. She loved to put the bush doves into a pie. She said they were her favourite food from when she was a girl on her father's farm. Anyone who wanted to get in her good books knew how to do it. So, you see, she knew all about bush doves and where they came from.

'Bush doves? You were looking for bush doves, hey?' she asked Pissy.

'Yes, Mevrou, and Fonnie climbed the big rock to take a look where they were,' Pissy replied, once again confirming the story going around.

'This big rock, is it the big rock where the whitethorn grows on the other side of the pigsty?'

'Yes, Mevrou,' Pissy answered.

'So tell me, man, this rock is 400 yards away from the stream where the big blue gums grow. How can a person climb that rock to see bush doves that are high up in the trees that you sometimes can't even see when you standing right under the tree? How come, now suddenly Fonnie du Preez is supposed to see them and gone 400 yards away in the opposite direction?'

Pissy was taken by surprise. 'I dunno, Mevrou, he's a boxer so he's got very good eyes and you can see them better at the top of the trees from a distance.'

'*Ja*, and you a very bad liar, Kobus Vermaak.'

'No, Mevrou, it's true, honest to God,' Pissy protested. 'We was looking for bush doves, I swear it on the Holy Bible!'

'You better watch out, man! After this you going to wash your mouth out with soap? God is going to strike you dead. Using God's Holy Bible like that is blasphemy, you going to go to hell and burn in an everlasting fire for all eternity, you hear!' Mevrou picked up her *sjambok*. 'You know I've never hit you before, Kobus?'

Pissy nodded.

'But now is different, all of a sudden you lying to me after all I done for you. It makes me very sad and you ought to be ashamed of yourself. All this time I've trusted you and now you go and tell me lies. You breaking my heart, man. I've treated you like your own mother and look what you done, you gone and lied to somebody who has always shown you love, who nurses you when you sick. *And* you're a blasphemer.' The tone of Mevrou's voice suddenly changed. 'Now you going to get six of the best, you hear! Take down your trousers.'

Pissy looked *really* frightened. 'But I could get a fit, Mevrou,' he said desperately.

'That's all rubbish and you know it, Kobus. We just tell people that because it's true you delicate of health, but you don't get a fit from the *sjambok*, it doesn't happen like that. Epileptic fits, we don't know what makes them happen, only that it's a brain seizure that makes you go unconscious and have convulsions. People don't die from them unless they swallow their tongue. Lucky for you that *kaffir*, the pig boy, came along and put a stick in your mouth to bite on. *Wragtig*! How a *kaffir* would know to do a thing like that, I just don't know, you can only thank God. After you've had one fit, you don't usually get another for a long time.'

I remembered how Fonnie had clouted Pissy on the side of the head and nothing had happened, when I'd thought he'd go into a fit for sure. I was in for a bit of good news. Being hit didn't bring on Pissy's epileptic fit. It hadn't been my fault after all and he'd never nearly died because of it.

Up till now I'd only been listening but I stuck my head up through the bushes so I could see what was going on. Pissy undid his belt buckle and his shorts fell to the ankles of his knobbly-kneed freckled stick legs. He stepped out of them and stood cupping his cock with his hands. 'Bend,' Mevrou instructed. I instinctively prepared to flinch as I saw her arm go up but it stopped mid-air and dropped to her side. 'Bend more, touch your toes,' came the command. Mevrou put the *sjambok* down, walked right up to Pissy's bum and carefully parted his cheeks, using both hands to expose his arsehole. 'It's bruised!' she said, then stepped back. 'What's going on, hey?'

Pissy, still holding his ankles, looked back. 'Nothing, Mevrou,' he cried. His face had gone very red and I could see he was about to cry. Mevrou had seen the same purple marks I'd seen when Tinker was being nearly murdered. I'd never looked into a person's arsehole before Fonnie made me do it and as far as I knew, everybody's arsehole could have been purple like that.

'It's bruised and there's signs of bleeding. What's going on, Kobus?' Mevrou demanded, looking the fiercest I'd ever seen her, and that's *really* saying something. 'Stand up and put on your pants,' she instructed.

She made Pissy sit down on the leather examination couch and drew up her chair. Pissy looked very frightened. His bony shoulders were hunched over his narrow chest and his hands gripped the side of the leather couch, his skinny legs dangled and his knees bumped together so that the bottom part of his legs sort of splayed out. He had three front teeth missing because of Doctor Dyke's horse pliers and his pale blue eyes were rimmed with red below his close-cropped bright ginger hair. The usual yellow glob of snot hung halfway out from his nose. I can tell you he was not a pretty sight.

About this time my heart was beginning to beat faster. Mevrou was famous for getting the truth out of a person and she'd been known to bring undone even some of the best liars in The Boys Farm. Pissy wasn't a bad liar but he wasn't good enough to compete with some of the older kids who, easy as pie, could convince you black was white and then the other way around again. Pissy was between a rock and a hard place and was about to be interrogated by the best lie detector in the business. What if Mevrou made him tell the truth? I would be in the deep shit and be known as an arselicker and cocksucker for the rest of my life, but much worse than this, they were sure to kill Tinker.

'Kobus, *genoeg*! Now you tell me the truth or we go to Meneer Prinsloo and he's going to recommend they send you to the reformatory in Pretoria. With you delicacy of health you will die in that terrible place.' She paused. 'They going to send you for sure because I'm going to sign the recommendation myself, you understand?'

How clever is that! She didn't beat around the bush, just came out with the single biggest threat known to man, the reformatory in Pretoria for boys who are bad. The stories from that place were bad and it was true a boy could even die in there, easy as anything.

'Tell me what were you doing at that rock? If you lie I'm not going to waste my time, we go straight to Meneer Prinsloo,' she repeated. 'I'm also going to tell him about the bruises around your anus.'

Pissy looked up, you could see he was scared stiff, but you really had to admire what he did next. 'If I tell you, Mevrou, will you promise not to take me to Meneer Prinsloo?' She had him over a barrel and he had the cheek to try to bargain with her.

'I can't promise because I don't know what you going to tell me,' Mevrou answered. 'But I promise I won't sign the recommendation for the reformatory if you tell me everything that happened and leave nothing out.' Mevrou was miles too good for him.

'He likes to piss on me,' Pissy declared suddenly, his voice barely above a whisper.

Mevrou was clearly surprised, not sure she'd heard correctly. 'Say again?'

'Fonnie du Preez likes to piss on me,' Pissy repeated, a little louder.

'Piss on you! How?'

I confess it's not what I expected him to say either. I thought he was about to spill the beans, tell about me and Tinker and everything. Although I don't know how you explain how somebody pisses on you, they just do it, don't they?

But Mevrou didn't wait for an answer. 'How long has this been going on?'

'He just did it that one time at that rock.'

Even I could tell it was a big fat lie, but it explained a lot of things, the way he always smelled for one thing. If the clothes you wear for a week are drenched with piss that's how you're going to smell all the time. I'd never remembered smelling him on a Sunday when we took a shower with soap and got our new change of clothes before going to church, so everyone in the congregation would think how nice and clean the boys from The Boys Farm always were.

Mevrou let the lie pass, her voice became clipped and businesslike. 'At the rock? The day du Preez had the accident, that's when he pissed on you?'

'Yes, Mevrou.'

'Explain to me what happened.'

Pissy looked down at his knobbly knees and even from where I was in the hydrangea bush I could see he was shaking. 'I don't like to, Mevrou,' he said, his voice trembling.

Mevrou sighed this big sigh. 'Don't make me angry, Kobus. Tell me at once!'

'He wanted to stand on the rock and piss down on me, like it was a nice joke.'

In my mind's eye I saw Fonnie with his big cock and a stream of golden piss cascading over the edge of the big rock on Pissy's ginger head. Splash! Trickle. Of course, that's not what happened and couldn't have happened before I got there because I would have seen if Pissy's head and his shirt were wet and I'd have smelled the extra fresh piss on him. So far Pissy was winning in the lying game and, I must say, was doing bloody well under interrogation.

Mevrou drew back in her chair. 'A nice joke? You let someone piss on you and it's called a nice joke? You an Afrikaner from a proud people and you let a person piss on you for a joke!'

'Not to *me*, Mevrou, to *him* it was a joke,' Pissy mumbled.

She'd got that bit wrong. An orphan can't be a proud anything even if he is an Afrikaner, which is better perhaps than being English, but if you just belong to the Government it's not much to be proud of because there's nobody who gives a shit about you. Also, the part where Mevrou said she'd treated Pissy like his own mother. He didn't have a mother so how could she know about that, hey?

'You didn't think it was a joke but you let him do it to you? You could have run away,' Mevrou said.

Pissy shook his head sadly. 'You can't, Mevrou, he'll jus' get you later.'

It was a good point and she let him have it. There was no hiding place in The Boys Farm. They always got you in the end. It was best to take what was coming to you, even if it was unfair, otherwise it only got worse and worse.

Mevrou sighed again. 'So far all we've got is the pissing joke. Did he masturbate in front of you?'

We all knew the word, although I wasn't completely sure how it worked, you rubbed your cock and white stuff came out, but only if you were bigger. All I knew was that it was the worst thing you could possibly do on The Boys Farm. It got you sent to Meneer Prinsloo who would give you six of the best with his vicious, specially long bamboo *sjambok*. They said he'd stand way back and run at you, and each cut was like ten ordinary ones. God definitely didn't like masturbation and Meneer Prinsloo said, 'God forbids it and so do I.' They put you in the tank afterwards, or if it was summer, in a small cupboard that was pitch dark. You could hardly breathe in there and you stayed for the whole day without food, just some water. Afterwards you had to kneel down and put your hand on the Bible and promise God you'd never do it again. I gasped at the very thought of Mevrou suggesting such a thing had occurred. But it was me who was in for a big surprise.

'He sometimes did it,' Pissy said.

'In front of you?'

'Yes.'

'Did he make you do anything?'

'Like what, Mevrou?'

'Like suck his *piel*?'

'No, nothing like that, Mevrou,' Pissy said, almost in a whisper.

What a dirty lie! I knew it was a lie because of what Fonnie made me do and Pissy saying it tasted like *boerewors*. You could just tell he did it the way he said it was *lekker* and all. I just knew that Fonnie made him do it and Pissy didn't even mind one bit.

Surprisingly Mevrou didn't make a fuss when I felt for sure Pissy was on the way to Meneer Prinsloo. She suddenly changed the subject. 'What about the accident to Fonnie du Preez on the rock? Tell me.'

Pissy was ready for her. 'After he'd finished he was doing up his fly and laughing a lot and he stepped back without looking and this piece of rock came loose and he slipped and fell down.'

'Backwards? He fell backwards?'

It was a trick question. All Fonnie's injuries were on the front, his face and head, and he'd broken his arm by frantically trying to cushion his fall. What's more, the skin inside both his arms was scraped raw from the surface of the big rock. Pissy twisted the top part of his body around. 'No, Mevrou, he sort of twisted, then suddenly lost his balance and he fell down on his face and head and broke his nose and his arm and was unconscious.' He looked up and for dramatic effect added, 'I even heard it snap, like when you step on a twig in the bush.'

My admiration for Pissy was growing by the minute. I mean, for his slyness and his ability to lie like a dog. He was proving far and away the best liar among the ten-year-old boys. I was observing a world champion liar in the making. If I hadn't been there at the big rock myself I would have been convinced that every word he said was God's honest truth.

But Mevrou wasn't finished by a long shot. 'Now, listen carefully before you answer and just understand that I will protect you, Kobus,' she said in a soft and kind voice I had never before heard from her. It was a voice you'd like to hear before you go to sleep at night. 'How many times did he piss on you? How often, Kobus? Once? Twice? Ten times, more than ten times?' It was clear she wasn't going to accept the 'just the one time' story.

Pissy swung his right leg up and down in agitation and looked in his lap for what seemed a long time. 'More than ten times,' he finally replied.

Mevrou's voice rang out like a shot. 'Then after, did he get an erection?'

Pissy jumped. 'Ja, Mevrou!'

'Did he bugger you, Kobus? Did he stick it in you, in your bottom?'

Pissy remained silent.

'Did he penetrate you, Kobus? Answer me, damn you!'

Pissy started to howl, I mean really blub, so that Mevrou was forced to wait, but she didn't get up and comfort him or anything like that. She just waited while his shoulders quaked and quaked, and the snot ran out his nose. He didn't even wipe it away with the back of his hand, he just let it run down his top lip and some went in his mouth and some over his chin together with the tears that were falling, splashing down nineteen to the dozen. He sobbed and sobbed and began to cough violently, but she still waited and didn't even slap his back.

'Speak, child!' Mevrou said at last and stood up suddenly and pointed her finger at Pissy. 'Fonnie du Preez buggered you! He fucked you, didn't he? Frikkie Botha's favourite little boxer fucked you up the arse! You were his dirty little whore!' she was screaming and her breasts were wobbling like mad.

I was shocked but also ready to applaud. In this place it was every boy for himself and the survival of the fittest was the only rule, and I can tell you for certain Fonnie du Preez was headed for Pretoria. Pissy only had to say yes and he'd made himself a victim. Although I personally doubted his innocence, he really enjoyed being under Fonnie du Preez's patronage and I hadn't forgotten 'Tastes *lekker, Voetsek* . . . jus' like *boerewors*.' Pissy, if he was a victim, was a willing one. That was easy enough for anyone to see, which, when all is said and done, was very clever of him, if you ask me. Though, if he'd escaped the reformatory, what they'd do with him I couldn't say. If Fonnie went to Pretoria then Pissy wouldn't survive for long here. Fonnie was a boxing hero and Pissy was the worst kind of a nobody, even if he was a Boer. There was another Boys Home in Pietersburg, they'd probably send him up there.

With Mevrou standing there screaming at him my whole world exploded into smithereens.

'No! No, it wasn't him, I swear it!' Pissy cried out. 'It wasn't Fonnie du Preez who done it to me. It was the *kaffir*. The pig boy!'

'The pig boy? The *kaffir*? The *kaffir* did it?' she said incredulously. 'When, for God's sake! Tell me, man.'

'When I had my epileptic fit he saved my life, and then after I came out the sick room I went to see him at his hut by the pigsty to thank him for putting the stick in my mouth, like you said I should.'

'*Here*, man! He did it to you then?' she asked. 'In his dirty *kaffir* hut where you went to say thank you?'

'*Ja*, he threw me on his bed and did it to me!' Pissy howled and looked up despairingly at Mevrou. 'It hurt a lot.'

Mevrou was nearly beside herself. 'In his stinking bed! In his dirty blankets?'

Pissy nodded and sniffed some snot and looked miserable.

'*Sis*, man . . . Why didn't you report it, child?'

'I couldn't, Mevrou, I . . . I was too ashamed. I only told Fonnie du Preez.'

'You told him what the *kaffir* did to you, everything?'

'*Ja*, Mevrou, I told him and Fonnie said he would kill the fucking *kaffir*, that's why we were – Fonnie didn't piss on me that time.'

'Say again, it wasn't about Fonnie du Preez pissing on you?'

'No, Mevrou, I jus' made that up,' Pissy said, looking sort of half ashamed. 'He was going to *donder* the pig boy, that's why we were there.'

Mevrou drew back. 'Made it up?' She looked at him sternly. 'What else are you making up, Kobus?'

'No, it's God's truth, Mevrou,' he sniffed.

'Stoppit!' Mevrou yelled. 'Calm down, no more crying, you hear? *Genoeg!* Now you going to tell everything that happened, from the beginning.'

Pissy sniffed and sobbed down to quite a quick calmness. Mevrou leaned forward and said, 'The big rock. Now I want the truth, you hear? What were you *really* doing there – first it's bush doves, then it's pissing all over a person's head, now it's . . . what?'

'Fonnie sent me to tell the pig boy one of the cows was caught in a whitethorn bush at the big rock and he must come there. The pig boy came and when he got there Fonnie hit him and knocked him down. It was a good punch,' Pissy elaborated. 'The *kaffir* got angry and he jumped up on his feet and Fonnie hit him again, a left and a right, but it was no use, the pig boy jus' kept coming at him and lifted Fonnie in the air and threw him against the big rock. I ran to tell Meneer Botha.'

I had to admit Pissy's lying was a genuine world championship performance and he'd even got Fonnie du Preez off the hook. Pissing on somebody wasn't a very nice thing to do to a person, but it could be seen as just boys' pranks, and while masturbation was a definite sin, it wasn't Pretoria material. Fonnie would get the long cane, six or maybe even ten of Meneer Prinsloo's special running-at-you cuts and then the tank. When he came out he'd be a hero, because he had the guts to take on and pick a fight with the stinking *kaffir* who, what can you expect, fought dirty and not like a white man. He'd also gone to avenge Pissy. Even if they were related, it was a most honourable thing to do. The *kaffir* was much bigger and stronger but Fonnie didn't care, he took him on all the same. That's how it would go. What's more, when it was over Pissy Vermaak's reputation wouldn't be much worse, because, like me, he was a complete nobody already and what's more, he might even get people to be sorry for him because of what the *kaffir* went and did to him.

Don't think I worked all this out on the spot because I didn't. It took a lot of thinking about it later and, at the time I was listening from in the bushes, my heart was pounding like billyo for Mattress who was in the deepest of deep shit.

Amazingly, Mevrou seemed to believe this third version of events which was still not the truth. 'It accounts for his injuries,' she exclaimed. 'I always knew he couldn't get them just falling down a rock like Frikkie Botha and you said it happened. A nurse like me doesn't get easily fooled, you understand. We trained so we know what's going on,' she said smugly.

Pissy did his masterstroke. He all of a sudden started to shake all over and to weep uncontrollably, you've never seen such a performance, it pissed on the one before with the snot and tears running over his chin.

'What am I going to do now everybody knows?' he wailed. He wailed even louder and choked and sobbed and sobbed and wailed again and threw himself down on the leather examination couch and beat his fists against it, as if he was suddenly heartbroken. I saw the surprise, then the sympathy on Mevrou's face and she went over to him and took him in her arms.

'Be still, Kobus, don't cry,' she said, brushing her hand through his cropped hair and drawing his snotty face into her large bosom. '*Shhhsh, skattebol . . .* that *kaffir* is already dead, you hear.'

CHAPTER THREE

Until Death We Do Part

I DON'T KNOW HOW long I sat there under the hydrangea bushes shaking from the shock of what I had just heard. Like a bolt of electricity through my body I suddenly realised that I had no time to waste. The days were closing in and the mountains were starting to get in the way of the sun. It would shortly become dark and the washing-hands bell would be going and then it was supper. Because it was late autumn you couldn't guess the time like you could in summer, but nevertheless I had to take a chance and get to Mattress to warn him. I crawled out from under the bushes and ran like hell down to the pigsty, hoping to find him there.

As I arrived he was pouring swill into the pig trough and at first I was unable to talk. I stooped down with my hands on my knees, trying to catch my breath. I hadn't even given myself time to compose a correct sequence of the events that had taken place between Mevrou and Pissy Vermaak. As I stood panting I tried to collect my thoughts, then translate them into Zulu as Mattress couldn't speak Afrikaans very well and might miss the meaning of what I was trying to tell him. I was six years old and a lot of the words I had to use I hadn't come across in Zulu.

I know I said I was six but, in fact, I had just turned seven by a few days. I only knew this because when I got to school one morning my class teacher, Miss Bronkhorst, told me it was my birthday.

'Can I learn to read now, *Juffrou?*' I pleaded.

'No, Tom, you have to wait until next year. You're halfway between the sixes and sevens and can't be a special case because I am much too busy to go back to the beginning again.'

I'd asked if I could sit in with the other seven-year-olds and try to catch up. But she said it was May already and that I was being a show-off if I thought I could catch up with five months of reading lessons already gone. 'Besides,' she'd said, 'Afrikaans isn't your first language and you're going to find it difficult.'

You can't argue with a teacher but I couldn't understand why this would be so. I had been in the orphanage since I was four and the first language I spoke was Zulu, and as far as I knew I'd never spoken English. It was just my name, Tom Fitzsaxby, that got me into all the trouble I've already told you about. Maybe, I thought, a person is born with a certain language in their head and so it's difficult to learn to read in a language that God hadn't put into your brain already before you were born.

Anyway, it was going to be much easier for me to talk to Mattress in Zulu. I just had to hope I could explain those things Fonnie du Preez had done to Pissy and the other things that Mevrou asked him about. I could do the pissing bit dead easy, that's *umchamo*, but things like arse-kissing, penetration, buggered, masturbation – how was I ever going to get those across to him when I didn't really know what the last three were or how they happened? I didn't even know if black people did those things the same as us, or whether any of those words I couldn't translate would mean anything to him. Maybe Pissy was accusing him of doing something to him he didn't even know how to do.

'*Sawubona, Kleinbaas,*' Mattress called cheerily to me. 'It is late for you to come and see me, but you are running very fast. I think, for sure, a lioness she is chasing you. With your strong heart, you have left her panting in the dust.' He laughed at his joke, then put down the milk churn and stepped over the pigsty wall, his big platform feet with the deep cracks in the sides making little puffs as they landed in the soft dust on the far side.

'Mattress, it is terrible news!' I gasped.

'Ten-Kaa?' He looked concerned. 'But she was at the dairy just now, she is having some milk.'

'No, not Tinker, *you*!'

Mattress looked puzzled. '*Mena?* Today I have worked very, very hard, *Kleinbaas*. There is no trouble.'

'There *is* trouble,' I said urgently. '*Makhulu* trouble, big trouble.'

Mattress took a step towards me and rested on his haunches so that we could be the same size. Next door the big sow was grunting and grumbling, waiting for the rest of the swill. Mattress placed his hand on my shoulder.

'What are you hearing? Is the Big *Baas* angry?' He looked genuinely puzzled. 'Why it is so? All the time I am work very, very hard. That one cow, that black one, it is sick all night from the bloat, she is eating too much the wet clover. I stay by that one and run her around so she farts out the sickness, but it doesn't work so I put a knife in her stomach to let the air out, now she is coming better. Big *Baas* Botha . . . why he is not happy with me, *Kleinbaas*? If I don't put in the knife to that black cow she is going to die.'

'Not him, it's Mevrou! She says you already a dead *kaffir*.' I hadn't meant to tell it exactly like that, it just came out in a rush and I started to cry.

Mattress squeezed my shoulder. 'This is not the time to cry, *Kleinbaas*. You must tell me what happened in this news you have for me. I must hear it in your way.'

The trouble was where to start. I decided to go right back to me having to kiss Pissy's arse. Mattress shook his head. '*Ahee*, that is before I am coming to you, that Fonnie he is very bad man.'

I told him about the conversation that went on in the sick room. While I had some trouble with those words I spoke about, Mattress seemed to understand and supplied the Zulu words I needed. When I got to the last part where Pissy had accused Mattress of doing it to him, Mattress slapped his knee with the palm of his hand. '*Ahee*, that one of the goat fit is very, very bad also. That one is a coward and a liar and a *skelm*.'

'You must run away at once, Mattress, go into the mountains, they will never find you there.' I pointed to his feet. 'You can go over the sharp rocks, they will not be able to follow.' In my mind I could see him scrambling like a goat much too quick for anyone to follow.

'*Ahee, Kleinbaas*, they will catch me, they have the dogs, they will follow my scent.'

I'd seen the three big Alsatian dogs the police sergeant kept when he came around to visit Meneer Prinsloo, but I had simply thought he kept them as pets. I had to admit it would be pretty hard to outrun a dog, even in the mountains.

'But what will you do?' I asked in a panic.

Mattress thought for a moment and seemed to be weighing up his options. 'I am *AmaZulu*, I am not running away. If I run away they will think I have done this bad thing. This Boer boy he is lying and he is bad.'

'Yes, I know, but it's your word against his,' I protested.

Even if we, the boys in the orphanage, belonged to the Government and so were a nobody, we were a better class of nobody than the blacks. The word of a white boy would almost always be taken more seriously than that of a black man who was a pig boy. Even at seven I knew this to be true. What's more, Pissy Vermaak had proved he was a consummate liar and if he could convince Mevrou, who was a world champion lie detector, then he could do the same with the police sergeant.

Sergeant Jan van Niekerk was famous in this part of the world, and was known to be a '*regte* Boer' who had the reputation for treating *kaffirs* harshly and carried a *sjambok*, a proper rhino-hide one, wherever he went. We'd sometimes see him on the way back from school. Black people would step off the pavement if they saw him coming, even if there remained lots of room for him and for what I had thought, until moments ago, were his three pet Alsatian dogs. The black people would step into the road and stand with their eyes averted, not daring to look at him. They could get a severe slash from his *sjambok* if they looked directly at him, because then he thought you were 'a cheeky *blêrrie kaffir*'.

Mattress looked at me. 'I am a Zulu, the grandson of a great warrior of the Paramount Chief, Dingaan, I will not run away like a village dog. *Baas* Botha, he must tell me I have done this bad thing and I will tell him this boy who had the goat fit is lying. I am not lying before to *Baas* Botha and he will believe me, he will know the truth in his heart.' Mattress said it with such conviction that I almost believed him.

Meneer Botha knew the truth, alright, but he'd warned us never to tell it so why would he come clean all of a sudden? But worse still, we were dealing with Mevrou, who was a different kettle of fish. On the other hand, Mattress was a grown-up and I was just a small kid and he had rescued Pissy when he'd had his epileptic fit. It was certainly something they'd have to take into account. Him putting the stick in his mouth and all that. '*Wragtig*! How a *kaffir* would know to do a thing like that, I just don't know, you can only thank God,' was what Mevrou had said.

I suddenly realised I had to run back because the washing-hands bell would have rung by now as only a deep orange glow showed behind the dark silhouette of the high mountains. If I was late for supper then I'd go without, and also get three of the best or six if my hands were dirty as well.

'*Sala kahle*, stay well,' I said to Mattress. 'I hope it will be all right.'

Mattress looked sad but did not reply as we shook hands in the proper African way, first like white people do and then switching by grasping hold of each other's thumb, two movements instead of one.

'*Hamba kahle*, go well,' he replied. My parting memory was of his large dark hand and my small white one, and how the black hand completely swallowed the white one.

I got back just in time to join the end of the supper queue. I didn't have time to wash my hands before the cook, Mevrou Pienaar, who always wore this greasy apron that she wiped her hands on, rang the bell for us to enter. Fonnie du Preez was with the big boys at the front of the queue, he had a plaster of Paris arm and people had written their names on it for luck. Obviously Mevrou hadn't taken any action as yet. There was no sign of Pissy Vermaak, which wasn't a good sign, although not entirely unexplainable, he'd been in a pretty overwrought state and she'd probably kept him in the sick room. We didn't have a hands inspection because Mevrou didn't appear, which was lucky.

When we'd all sat down my heart *really* sank. Meneer Prinsloo and Mevrou were not at the staff table. When supper was over there was still no Meneer Prinsloo and Mevrou. Meneer Botha took over the job of reading from the Bible and saying prayers thanking God for our food and for looking after us. In both cases I wasn't at all sure God was doing a good job and, in my opinion, was getting a bit too much praise. No Mevrou announcements followed, which meant there'd be no *sjambok* for the little kids that night. Instead, old Mevrou Pienaar said that if anyone needed to go to the clinic and it couldn't wait until the morning, they should see her afterwards on the *stoep* and she'd do the best she could. As we went to the hall where we had to do our homework, through the big window at the end, I saw the lights of a car pull up. It was Doctor Van Heerden's new Chev with a dicky-seat at the back. The outside light went on and Meneer Prinsloo and Mevrou came out to greet him and took him inside. You didn't need to think too hard to know what that was all about. Doctor Van Heerden was here to examine the bruises on Pissy's arse.

As I lay in bed that night my mind started to work things out. Not that a seven-year-old is much good at solving complex problems, as he can't really understand possible outcomes. But what I knew made me very worried. Firstly, I already knew that Fonnie and Pissy had conspired with Meneer Botha to concoct the story of Fonnie falling down the big rock. But all that had changed and there was the new Pissy confession to Mevrou version of what happened. This was all lies but she believed him and when she believed something, watch out, man! In this second version I still wasn't there, but Mattress was. Secondly, Mattress was now supposed to have penetrated Pissy in his hut before the rock incident took place and of course this was also a pack of lies.

I started blubbing because I knew if I went and told Meneer Prinsloo the real truth then Tinker would be dead. You couldn't go around accusing someone like Meneer Frikkie Botha of lying and concocting stories and expect him not to get his own back. I was also certain that the superintendent wouldn't believe me, wouldn't take my word against two important grown-ups like Frikkie Botha and Mevrou. Besides, he knew already that everyone in The Boys Farm lied to the staff all the time, so how would he know I was telling God's honest truth? So if I talked I was going to lose the two people I loved the most in the world, Mattress and Tinker. It was the saddest moment in my life because I didn't know what to do to save them. I've told you before how it was survival of the fittest in that place and now look what was going to happen, even if they didn't believe me. Tinker would be dead and Mattress would be taken away by the police and sent to Pretoria where they would hang him by his neck until he was stone dead.

It hit me all of a sudden, if I said nothing, stayed *stom*, Tinker would stay alive and only Mattress would be killed. There was nothing I could do to save Mattress. Or, if there was, I wasn't capable of thinking what it might be. The forces ranged against us were just too powerful. But I knew that somehow, whatever happened, it was my fault and that's why I was blubbing. Then someone shouted, 'Shurrup, *Voetsek*, and go to sleep!' Until then I hadn't realised I'd been crying so loud.

What I'm about to tell you is what happened next. But, of course, I wasn't present for most of the grown-ups' conversations. I only found these out some years later and in a rather sad way when I met up with Fonnie du Preez and Pissy Vermaak again. But I'll tell you about that later. So there has to be some speculation involved. Pissy and Fonnie were present for a lot of what took place and Pissy, like all good liars, had an excellent memory and seemed to recall the conversations just the way they happened.

Mevrou said, 'Doctor, I'm not an expert in such things you understand, but when I saw it I also definitely knew.'

Pissy Vermaak was hauled in front of Doctor Van Heerden who examined him in the sick room in the presence of Mevrou, while Meneer Prinsloo waited in the other room. He put Vaseline on his finger and made Pissy lie on his knees and elbows and he stuck his finger up Pissy's bum. Then when he pulled it out he said, 'Ja. Most definitely, this boy has been sexually molested. See here, contusions around the anus and severe bruising, this boy has been through a difficult experience.'

'Ag, you're not telling me anything I don't already know, Doctor,' Mevrou said. 'It's a terrible thing to happen to a child.'

Doctor Van Heerden said to Mevrou, 'Is there a camera here?'

Mevrou said she didn't know but she'd go and ask. She left the room and Pissy heard her ask Meneer Prinsloo if he had a camera and he replied that he'd go and fetch it.

Pissy had to wait, lying on his stomach, until the superintendent returned and Meneer Prinsloo came back with his wife's box brownie.

'I'm not so sure we can get the close-ups we require,' Doctor Van Heerden said.

'Ag, I think it will be orright, doctor, we use it for our snaps when we go on holiday and it always gives good pictures,' Meneer Prinsloo assured him.

'Perhaps if we light the area with a torch?' Doctor Van Heerden suggested.

Mevrou went and got a torch and Pissy had to go back on his knees and elbows and the doctor separated his buttocks and Mevrou held the torch and Meneer Prinsloo took three snaps. As it turned out later, you couldn't see anything, just some smudges and Sergeant Van Niekerk said they were hopeless and jus' looked like shots taken of the moon that he'd seen in a magazine, Die Huisgenoot, only last week. He said the magistrate would throw them out of his court but that the good doctor's evidence was all they needed. Doctor Van Heerden said he would write a report for the police and then he left.

After that they gave Pissy some dinner.

Well, that was only the beginning. What happened next was a big surprise. The next day, after Meneer Prinsloo said he'd prayed to God for guidance, he called everybody together except, of course, Mattress.

First, Mevrou told her version of what happened, how Mattress had done the penetration to Pissy in his hut. Then about the fight and how Fonnie had come off second best. All the lies Pissy had told her that she'd swallowed hook, line and sinker. As she finished, Frikkie Botha smacked his forehead with the palm of his hand.

'*Wragtig*! Now, at last I understand,' he said. 'I always thought the story wasn't the truth.' He turned to Fonnie and Pissy. 'Why did you lie to me, hey?'

They didn't say anything, just looked down at their toes so that Meneer Prinsloo demanded, 'Speak up, man!'

Fonnie pointed to Pissy and said, 'He was ashamed and couldn't tell anyone except me.' Fonnie said softly, 'I told him I would fight the *kaffir* for him.'

'And teach him a lesson he'd never forget!' Pissy added, enjoying the attention.

So you can see, they were both expert liars.

Frikkie Botha was pleased with the reply because now he was off the hook and could go along with the Mevrou version. 'He's not in your weight class, man. You now a junior middleweight and that *kaffir* is a heavy,' he said, a hint of admiration in his voice.

'You should have reported it to me at once, you hear!' Meneer Prinsloo said angrily. 'We can't have crimes like this happening around the place. I am going to have to call the police. This is a very serious crime.'

They were all silent for a moment, then Frikkie Botha said, 'I only want you to do me one favour before you call Sergeant Jan van Niekerk, who is a good friend of mine.'

'What? What favour?'

'Let me have a go at him in the boxing ring. What Fonnie did was an honourable thing, even if he should have reported the incident to you. Now what I want to do is finish the business, let that *kaffir* come in the ring with somebody his own size for a change, hey?' Which just goes to show how far people will go to cover up things. Frikkie Botha knew the truth but he must have been thinking, if it ever came out, him boxing Mattress would prove to people that he didn't know it. That the boxing was a *regte* Boer's righteous anger and his own personal revenge for what Mattress had done to one of his boys. After all, like I said before, it would only be the word of a *kaffir* and a *rooinek* against his and who was going to believe them anyway?

Meneer Prinsloo shook his head slowly. 'I dunno, man, I think we should just have him arrested right away. "Revenge is mine, sayeth the Lord."'

'*Ja*, but when he's arrested the story is going to get out, you can't hide a thing like this even if you try your hardest. People are going to hear about it, it's best brought out in the open. If they think we just called the police,' he looked at Pissy, 'and just let one of our children suffer, they'd think we don't care about our kids on The Boys Farm.'

Meneer Prinsloo frowned and still looked doubtful.

'I think it is a good idea, Meneer Prinsloo. Kobus has suffered terribly and for the rest of his life he's got a scar,' Mevrou said.

'You know, I still got one problem,' Meneer Prinsloo said. 'A *kaffir* is a *kaffir* and when a *kaffir* does something like this he will run away.'

'He is a Zulu,' Frikkie Botha said hastily, as if this explained everything. 'If he was a Shangaan he would run, but a Zulu . . .' He didn't finish the sentence.

'You know they do it all the time, even to their women,' Mevrou interrupted.

'Do what?' Meneer Prinsloo asked.

'They use the back instead of the front so the woman doesn't get pregnant,' Mevrou explained.

'*Sis*, man, that's a *kaffir* for you!' Frikkie said, happy for the confirmation.

'Also, in the mines in Johannesburg there's no women in the single men's compound so they do it to each other,' Mevrou said. Then, by way of explanation, she added, 'My cousin works in the mines, and he says they don't think it's shameful only because there are no women around. They don't think like us.' She suddenly remembered the presence of Pissy and Fonnie. 'You two not allowed to hear this, you hear?' she instructed.

'You think this *kaffir* was first in the mines?' Meneer Prinsloo asked.

'Maybe, but he won't tell you if you ask. They don't like you to know because some of them break their contract and run away and then they wanted by the police,' Frikkie said. He seemed to be thinking for a moment, then suddenly exclaimed, '*Magtig*! Why didn't I think about it before! He's a Zulu, this isn't Zulu country, it's too far north, this is Shangaan country. A Zulu who is here is hiding for sure. These are not his people, he doesn't speak their language. I think when we take a good look at his pass we in for a big surprise, man.' He looked up at the superintendent, appealing to him. 'Just let me have one go at him, Meneer?' he begged. 'Just three rounds in the boxing ring, fair and square, with him also wearing gloves so that the *kaffirboeties* in Pretoria can't accuse us of not playing fair.'

Kaffirboetie means a nigger's brother and is a white person who sticks up for a black person's rights. You can be sure there were no such people in this part of the world. Nevertheless you could see the superintendent was taking this into consideration. He felt much better now that he knew Mattress was a fugitive from justice, an escaped mine boy, but he still wasn't sure.

'*Kaffirs* can't just go around hitting white men and even if white men can hit *kaffirs* they *can't* go around fighting them in a boxing ring. *Here*, man, what would people say if all of a sudden white men and black men are fighting each other in the boxing ring and *kaffirs* are allowed to win?'

Frikkie thought for a moment. 'It's happened before, the great German boxer Max Schmeling knocked out the American *kaffir* Joe Louis.'

'Yes, in America, but this is South Africa, here we a more civilised people.'

'*Ja*, that's true, but we also *Boere* and we believe in justice. The *kaffir* boy is a heavyweight and when he picked on Fonnie he was fighting a middleweight. That is a no contest. I am a heavyweight. Let the black bastard come up against someone his own size for a change.' As his final shot he added, 'You don't want everybody to think a Boer can't take care of his own children and the boys here on the farm, they under your care, they just the same as your children.'

'*Ja*, well, I know I am a true father to them. But still I don't know . . . *kaffirs* boxing white men. I'll have to think about it some more,' Meneer Prinsloo said.

'We also got our own pride to consider, Meneer,' Mevrou said, drawing her head back and pulling her lips into a thin line. 'We also work here and Frikkie is right, a father doesn't just stand there and watch his children being thrown into a rock by a *kaffir* boy.' She pointed to Fonnie du Preez. 'What we got here is a broken arm and a broken nose and his head is full of stitches. But God willing, he will get better from that.'

She turned to Pissy. 'But Kobus Vermaak is only ten years old, and you heard what the doctor said; he has been physically molested.' She looked directly at the superintendent. 'Do you know what that means? It means he's got scars on his brainwaves for the rest of his life. The pictures we got on the camera, that's nothing, what about the pictures he's got on his brain camera? Pictures of a *kaffir* that done unspeakable things to him.' She placed her hand on Pissy's shoulder. 'If Kobus can see we care about what happened to him, if this *kaffir* is punished by us and not only by Sergeant Jan van Niekerk but by you, who the Government says has to be a father to this boy, then maybe he can get better because he will know he is loved.'

Meneer Prinsloo was momentarily overcome by Mevrou's words. 'It is true I love all the boys here on the farm,' he said, his eyes growing misty. 'God has charged me to look after them, and while it is sometimes a terrible burden I accept my duty with humility. A shepherd must always take care of his flock no matter what, and I must be a loving father to these boys.' He looked gratefully at Mevrou. 'You are right, the gospel says, "Whosoever harms a sparrow, harmeth me, sayeth the Lord".' He turned to Frikkie Botha, suddenly all business, and said, 'What are you going to say to the pig boy?'

'What do you mean, Sir?'

'Well, you can't just put him in the boxing ring and give him a good hiding when he doesn't know why you doing it.' He pointed to Fonnie. 'You can't tell him it's because he threw du Preez against the rock, he'll get suspicious and next thing you know he's vamoosed.'

'*Ja*, you right.' Frikkie Botha scratched his head and thought for a moment. He suddenly brightened. 'The night before last there was a sick cow that ate something, probably some deadly nightshade which grows down by the creek. The pig boy knows he mustn't take the cows down there except at one place by the drift where they go to drink. I'm going to say to him, "*Kaffir*, because I don't know for sure what happened, but that cow could still have died because you didn't listen to me, so I'm going to give you a second chance in the boxing ring with both of us wearing twelve-ounce gloves."' Frikkie Botha looked up at the superintendent. 'He can try and hit me as much as he likes, so what can be fairer than that, hey?' he concluded, pleased by this clever ruse.

'All right, the cow is good,' Meneer Prinsloo agreed. 'Only three rounds, you hear? We can't let Sergeant Van Niekerk think we taking the law into our own hands. If he asks, we can tell him it was nothing to do with with du Preez at that rock. The sick cow is good,' he repeated, satisfied that he'd met the requirements of fatherhood in a dignified and fair manner. Then he had a second thought. 'Frikkie, this *kaffir* is a proper heavyweight, you say?'

'Ja, 220 pounds, maybe a bit more, bigger than a cruiser weight for sure,' Frikkie Botha replied.

Meneer Prinsloo looked at Frikkie Botha who was even bigger than that, maybe 240 or even fifty, but most of the extra weight was stacked around his middle. 'You sure you can take him, Frikkie?'

Frikkie Botha was insulted. 'Any day of the week. Let him come, man, any time, any place. I guarantee it won't take three rounds.'

The following evening after supper there was the Thursday night Bible reading as usual. I haven't explained, we had a Sunday night reading and a Thursday night one, because Meneer Prinsloo said seven days was too long without a message from God in our lives. This reading was all about the Good Samaritan, how he found Jesus exhausted at the side of the road carrying this big wooden cross. It must have happened on the way to where they were going to put the six-inch nails in his hands and feet and push a sword in his side and give him vinegar to drink because he said he was thirsty. So the Good Samaritan picked up the cross, even though he didn't know Jesus from a bar of soap, and he carried it up the hill for him. Meneer Prinsloo said it was a lesson on how we shouldn't just always think only about ourselves but help others less fortunate, even perfect strangers and people who were different to us because the Good Samaritan wasn't a Jew. He said prayers and then Frikkie Botha stood up and announced there would be a heavyweight boxing match at ten o'clock sharp on Saturday morning.

Naturally we were all pretty excited but also a bit confused. There were only three sixteen-year-olds big enough to be called a heavyweight and the rugby season had just started and they were all in the school team because they were the front row forwards. But on Saturday the school rugby team was going to play Tzaneen High, which was in a town about fifty miles away, so how could they be in a heavyweight boxing contest? Besides, they weren't very good boxers and only one of them,

Jannie Marais, had managed to get to the second round of the district schools' championship and Frikkie Botha said it was a disgrace, but on the other hand all three of the referees were from other schools, so what could you expect. So who was going to fight whom on Saturday was what everyone wanted to know.

Fortunately Pissy came back to the dormitory that night and told us everything that he said happened. He lied through his teeth, of course, because what he told us wasn't at all what happened. He didn't tell us anything about Doctor Van Heerden and the box brownie snaps. Nor did he say that the boxing match had nothing to do with what was going to happen to Mattress afterwards. I only learned about that some years later. He made it sound like *only* the fight between Frikkie Botha and Mattress was happening and the rest was all forgotten.

What he made up was this. He was in the sick room and Frikkie Botha came in because he had cut his arm from fixing a barbwire fence and wanted some sticking plaster. Meneer Prinsloo came in to talk to Mevrou about something or other and the conversation about how the pig boy had let the black cow eat the deadly nightshade took place. Pissy said Frikkie Botha asked Meneer Prinsloo if he could put on the fight because if he just beat Mattress with a *sjambok* he wasn't *absolutely* certain that he was to blame for what happened to the cow and he wanted to be just and fair. He wanted to give the *kaffir* a chance to hit back. Meneer Prinsloo said all right because it wasn't taking justice into your own hands. Pissy told us how it goes to show that Frikkie Botha is a salt-of-the-earth type and a *regte* Boer. Everybody knows a good lie must contain a fair element of the truth and Pissy already knew that and had it down pat, so for a change he was a hero in the small kids' dormitory.

You have to remember that only him and me and Fonnie du Preez knew the new Mevrou version of the story of what was supposed to have happened at the big rock. Even though I wasn't supposed to know, having only overheard it by mistake. Mevrou's latest version, you will remember, was still a whole pack of lies. All the other kids still believed in the original pack of lies, that the accident happened when Fonnie was supposed to have tripped and fallen when some rock gave way.

Talk about confused, I didn't know if I was coming or going and I had to keep reminding myself that the licking and sucking and Mattress rescuing me and throwing Fonnie against the rock was the real God's honest truth. As I lay in bed I asked myself what could it all possibly mean? One moment they were going to take Mattress to Pretoria and hang him till he's stone dead and the next he's fighting Frikkie Botha in a boxing match because of a cow.

I alone knew that Doctor Van Heerden had been to see Pissy's bum. Although you couldn't be one hundred per cent certain that's why he came, you had to ask yourself why else would he come at night in his new Chevrolet with the dicky-seat when Pissy was the only one in the sick room? Even a person who was seven could work that one out. But I'd been dead wrong about everything else. When Mevrou said that Mattress was already a dead *kaffir*, what I thought would surely follow was a big blow-up, with the police coming and Sergeant Van Niekerk bringing his three big Alsatian dogs in case Mattress tried to run away up the mountains. So I'd run down to the pigsty to warn Mattress. Suddenly, everything had changed. The only bad thing was that Mattress was going to get a good hiding from Frikkie Botha for letting a cow feed on a deadly bush. I told myself this was a lot better than Mattress being 'a dead *kaffir*'.

I was still pretty worried for Mattress but I didn't cry. You got used to what was unfair about that place and if you waited around for fair to come along you'd eventually turn into a pillar of salt. What was going to happen to Mattress in the boxing ring was unfair alright. He'd stayed up all night and nursed that sick cow and saved its life. I knew also if the cow ate the deadly nightshade it wouldn't have been Mattress's fault. To a Zulu a cow is a very important person and he would never let it happen on purpose. It was just an accident that could happen to any cow. I went to sleep feeling very sorry for Mattress but also feeling a lot better about the situation than I had the night before.

The following morning before school I took my crusts down to Tinker and stopped to visit Mattress.

'Do you know how to box?' I asked him.

Mattress laughed. 'For boxing I am not good, *Kleinbaas*. I am Zulu and I can throw a spear.' He picked up a smallish stone and aimed it at the swill churn, which was about twenty yards away, and let fly. The stone crashed with a clang into the side of the churn. 'For boxing it is Big *Baas* Botha who can show you this. *Ahee*, he is very, very good that one.'

'But how will you fight him then?' I asked.

Mattress looked genuinely astonished. 'Why I am fighting Big *Baas* Botha?'

'Because he says you let the cow eat the deadly bush by the creek.' I didn't know the name in Zulu for deadly nightshade.

Mattress looked puzzled and then a little indignant. 'That one black cow she is sick from the bloat, I am telling you before, *Baas* Botha also knows, she is eating too much the green clover, she is not eating that bush by the river.'

'That's not what Big *Baas* Botha says. He says because he can't prove that you let the cow do it, that's why you have to fight him, so fair's fair.'

Mattress didn't reply but shook his head slowly. I got the impression that his silence was over my peculiar and decidedly difficult-to-believe news. If I had been a Zulu he might simply have scoffed at me and told me I was talking rubbish. You couldn't blame him, two days before I'd come huffing and puffing to tell him he was in mortal danger and to flee into the hills. Now I was telling him he had to fight Frikkie Botha in the boxing ring because of the cow whose life he'd saved. Finally, I think to be polite, he looked at me and explained, '*Kleinbaas*, I cannot do this boxing, Big *Baas* Botha, he can beat me if he wants with his *sjambok*, but a white *baas* and a black man they cannot do the boxing together, it is not allowed.'

'I know!' I said urgently. 'Only this time they going to allow it!' I added, 'I swear it's true, on my word of honour.' It was getting late and I had to go to school and I hadn't fed Tinker the scraps of bread in my pocket. I whistled and called her name. Moments later she came dashing down from the dairy at a thousand miles an hour, and a great deal of leaping and tumbling and running around in circles and yapping with pleasure took place before her final leap into my arms and the licking of my face occurred.

I stood holding Tinker and I said, 'Mattress, I just want you to know that I will be on your side.' I put Tinker down and produced the bread crusts and a great gobbling and happiness of eating took place at my feet.

Mattress smiled. 'We are friends,' he said. I shook his hand in the traditional way. '*Hamba kahle*, go carefully,' he said.

'*Sala kahle*, stay well,' I replied. It was good to know I had two things in my life that I loved.

That was Friday and the fight was to take place the following morning and when I returned to play with Tinker in the afternoon after school Frikkie Botha had informed Mattress about the fight. I found him sitting on the pigsty wall with the swill churn next to him. Even from a distance I could see he wasn't happy.

'*Sawubona!*' I called as I approached, but for once he didn't even raise his head and smile but simply remained looking forlorn. As I drew close he looked up. 'It is true, *Kleinbaas*. Big *Baas* Botha he want to fight me with the boxing tomorrow.'

I wasn't as tall as Mattress was, even though he was sitting on the wall, but I stood on my toes and put my arm around his shoulder. 'I am on your side, Mattress,' I said. 'You are a Zulu warrior and the grandson of a great warrior who fought with Dingaan against the Boere.' I added, 'It is not possible for you to be afraid.'

Mattress turned and looked at me in astonishment. 'I am not afraid, *Kleinbaas*! But what we are doing, this boxing, Big *Baas* Botha and me, it is not right.'

'Yes, but you *must* hit him back when he hits you! This time it's officially allowed, man! It's the rules in the boxing ring.' I didn't tell him that Frikkie Botha was once a district amateur champion heavyweight and had narrowly lost on a points decision in the finals of the Northern Transvaal Championships in 1933. He would be hard to hit if you didn't know how to box him back, which was likely to be the case with Mattress.

'I am a Zulu,' Mattress said.

I have to admit in my heart of hearts I didn't think that would be enough to stop him getting murdered by Frikkie Botha.

It was Saturday and it was a day everyone thought would never come, such was the anticipation. It's not every day that you see a white and a black man fighting it out – may the best man win. We'd all seen blacks getting a hiding, but that wasn't the same, they just stood there and had to take the *sjambok* without being allowed to retaliate. It's funny, there seemed to be some deep sense of satisfaction going through the place that now it wouldn't be like that, that this time the *kaffir* could fight back if he wanted. Naturally, he would be severely beaten in the process, everyone knew a black man couldn't beat a white man in a thousand years. In America maybe, but in South Africa the white man would always be better if they weighed the same.

This was the perfect match-up, two heavyweights slogging it out. Well, hopefully slogging it out. The fear was that the *kaffir* wouldn't put up much of a fight and while that would still be good, because of what it proved, it wouldn't be as much fun. Everyone hoped the fight would go the three rounds, but expected it would result in a first-round knockout. 'What does a black *kaffir* know about boxing, hey?' 'And remember he's coming up against an ex-districts champion.' That's how everyone was talking.

What I'm trying to show is what was going on in the hostel in the minds of the boys. Nobody thought Mattress had a hope and, I'm afraid, that included me. But, in my case, not because he was black, but because he lacked the skill as a boxer. Or maybe I'm telling a lie. Perhaps I did think like all the others, that it was because Mattress was a black man. In an *assegai*-throwing competition he'd have eaten Frikkie Botha for breakfast, but boxing was altogether another thing.

The saddest people in The Boys Farm were the three guys who had to get up early and go into town and catch the bus that was taking the rugby team to Tzaneen. They even talked about going sick all of a sudden, but you couldn't just go and replace a whole front row. They were very good too. In later years they would pack down as the front row for the Springboks when the New Zealand All Blacks came to play us in 1949, the first tour after the war ended.

Breakfast was finished at seven o'clock and people all over the place were jumping out of their skins with impatience waiting for ten o'clock to come along. After breakfast I ran down to feed Tinker his crusts and to see Mattress. He was cleaning the dairy floor, washing it on his hands and knees. It was red cement and it also had to be shined after with polish. I'd seen him do it before and he'd be covered with sweat when he finished. It didn't seem like much of a preparation for a boxing match.

There wasn't much conversation going on between us because we both, for once in our lives, didn't know what to say. I looked at his nice face with his white teeth and wondered how it would look after Frikkie Botha was finished with him. Frikkie had false teeth that he took out when he was in the ring and it made his face, with his flat nose that I supposed was broken, look sort-of collapsed with his chin and mouth all bunched up together under his nose. His hair stood up like the bristles of a brush in what would one day be called a GI because American soldiers did it like that. Frikkie Botha, everyone said, was 'a hard man'.

I left Mattress polishing the floor. He wore only some cut-off-below-the-knees old khaki pants with lots of holes and he had really big muscles in his arms and back that shone when he polished that dairy floor. If he wasn't as heavy as Frikkie Botha he was just as tall, about six feet and four inches, and he had a flat stomach that had ripples. If he knew something about boxing he could have been good you'd think, just looking at him. But then again I don't know, everyone said Frikkie

Botha 'was as strong as a bull'. I said goodbye and wished Mattress luck and we shook hands. 'Remember you allowed to *shaya* him back, to hit him back,' I said hopefully.

'I am a Zulu,' he replied and went back to polishing the floor. Usually when he did it he'd be singing with a deep voice and mostly what the song was about was cattle and the mountains and rivers and finding good grazing after the spring rains in Zululand. Sometimes it was about a young man hunting a lion so that he could become a man. But today he was silent. Just every now and again he gave a grunt that sounded a bit like the big sow. In two hours he would be standing in the ring and Frikkie Botha was going to beat the living daylights out of him. My heart started to beat faster.

Ten o'clock came and everyone was there, even old Mevrou Pienaar, the cook, and Mevrou herself and also, a big surprise, the superintendent's wife, Mevrou Prinsloo. The three women sat in chairs ringside and everyone else stood, including the rest of the staff. The six kitchen boys were also there because Meneer Prinsloo said it was only fair that somebody was on the pig boy's side. Although, you never know, they were Shangaan and they weren't supposed to like the Zulus, but you'd expect, just this time, they'd put the tribal thing aside and be on the side of another black man. Anyway, they wouldn't be allowed to cheer for Mattress because then they'd be cheeky *kaffirs* and get into trouble. Maybe in their hearts they'd be on his side.

In the meantime Frikkie Botha was walking around outside the ring, blowing out air in big sudden puffs every few seconds and smashing his twelve-ounces together while looking fierce with his teeth out. Mattress stood with the kitchen boys, his arms at his side and looking down at his big cracked platform feet. He still wore the dirty cut-off-below-the-knees khaki pants with holes, because he only had one other pair, a good pair that he used for going home once a year to see his wife and Joe Louis, his son. I tried to catch his eye but he just kept looking down.

Meneer Prinsloo with his fat stomach and braces holding up his trousers that only went down to the top of his polished brown boots had to be helped into the ring and was already puffing and red in the face when he got in to make the announcement. Not that he said a lot. For a start he didn't say why the fight was on. But, of course, everybody knew it was about the cow and how a *kaffir* has to be taught a lesson when he is careless. That Frikkie Botha was going to teach him a lesson he'd never forget . . . anyway, you know all that.

Meneer Prinsloo, breathing heavily, said, 'In the eyes of God all men are equal, even *kaffirs*.' He then said that there was a special place in God's heaven for *kaffirs* to go. This was because God was a merciful and compassionate God and if a *kaffir* decided to be a Christian he was saved from everlasting damnation and wasn't a heathen any more so he wouldn't go to hell. '"In my Father's house are many mansions and I go to prepare a place for you" the Bible says. So you see, *kaffirs* can have houses in heaven as well. That is, as long as it isn't with white people, but you must understand, what they've got is also very nice.'

I was busy wondering what all this had to do with Frikkie Botha fighting Mattress when he very cleverly came around to the subject. 'There are only two places where a *kaffir* and a white man can be equal,' he claimed. 'Those two places are in heaven and in the boxing ring. You see, in a boxing ring there are two separate places for the opponents, one corner for the white man and another for the black man. In the middle they come together and God is the referee to see everything is fair.' He stood back and paused expectantly and everyone knew they must suddenly clap. He smiled an acknowledgement for this clever speech. 'What we going to now have is a fair fight where the *kaffir* boy is allowed to fight back and may the best man win.' You could see everybody was very impressed. 'Now, I must ask the two opponents to step into the ring,' the superintendent said. 'I will personally see as a Christian that this is a fair fight,' he concluded. You could see he was well satisfied with his introductory speech and we all clapped again.

Frikkie Botha climbed through the ropes, walked around the ring and held his gloves above his head. Everyone cheered like mad. He went to his corner and stood leaning back against the corner post with the top boxing ring rope under both his outstretched arms. Mattress slowly approached, parted the ropes and climbed in. Nobody said anything, it was just mumbles all around. The kitchen boys stayed silent. I don't know whether it was because they were Shangaan or just afraid. I admit I was afraid to do anything, to be seen to be on the side of Mattress. He stood in the centre of the ring holding his gloved hands clasped across one of his wrists and in front of him like he was protecting his balls.

Meneer Prinsloo pointed to the opposite corner of the ring and indicated Mattress should stand there. He didn't call them together like you're supposed to in a boxing match so that they could hear the rules. He just stood in the centre of the ring and everyone said *shhhush!* When it was quiet the superintendent said to both boxers, 'Hit clean, you hear? No dirty tactics, hey? Below the waist is not allowed.' He took a whistle out of his pocket and this big gold watch that had a chain that draped across his fat stomach. 'Three-minute rounds, I will blow the whistle at the end of every round and then you must stop fighting.' I was not sure Mattress understood any of this. He just stood there looking at his platform feet.

Meneer Prinsloo blew the whistle and Frikkie Botha came charging out of his corner while Mattress just stood. Mattress hadn't ever seen a boxing match and he hadn't been to the bioscope where sometimes they showed a big world championship in the newsreel, so he didn't know what to do. But he could see Frikkie Botha coming at him and before you could say 'Watch out!', which I did without thinking, Frikkie had landed a big swinging right to the side of Mattress's head. Mattress hadn't even stepped out of his corner and already he was in big trouble. He brought his gloves up to protect his head, and next came a left hook under the jaw. Mattress's head went back and he sank to the canvas on his knees.

Meneer Prinsloo seemed to have been taken by surprise but after a few seconds he started to count. 'One . . . two . . . three!'

Frikkie Botha shouted at Meneer Prinsloo, 'The *kaffir* is bluffing, don't count some more!'

The superintendent was taken aback. You have to remember he wasn't an experienced referee, he didn't do the boxing for The Boys Farm; that was under Frikkie Botha's control. So he did what he was told and stopped counting.

Mattress rose slowly and you could see he wasn't at all sure where he was. Frikkie Botha said to the superintendent, 'Make him fight.'

'C'mon, *kaffir*, you got to fight,' Meneer Prinsloo ordered.

By this time maybe you could have counted to thirty and I could see Mattress was again steady on his feet.

'C'mon, *kaffir*, fight!' Frikkie Botha called. 'Come out and fight, you black bastard!' He was beckoning with his right glove for Mattress to come forward. He pretended to spit on the canvas and said in Zulu, 'You are *igwal*! You are a coward!'

Mattress let out a roar and ran at Frikkie Botha, his arm raised to strike him down. Frikkie sidestepped and smashed Mattress in the jaw. Mattress took three steps backwards, lost his balance and landed on his back with his legs in the air. But this time he got up right away, before even the superintendent could start to count. Frikkie waited for him and popped Mattress with a hard right hand in the eye and then drove a left into his stomach. The whistle blew and it was the end of the round. Mattress hadn't landed a single blow and already his eye was closing up big-time. All the guys were screaming and yelling and I saw the old black man who was the head cook when old Mevrou Pienaar was sick with her asthma shake his head and walk away. He didn't want to see the humiliation of the pig boy.

There was no water and no seconds so the two boxers just stood there in what was turning out to be a very hot autumn morning. The whistle went and this time Mattress left his corner. Frikkie Botha started to stalk him and Mattress tried to stay away. But a boxing ring is only a small space and there's no place to hide. Soon he had Mattress in a corner protecting his head with the gloves and Frikkie was landing dozens of blows to his stomach, hard as he could. Mattress managed to get out of the corner and Frikkie came for him in the centre of the ring, rushing at him, throwing all caution to the wind, hands open, determined to finish the *kaffir* off. Mattress threw a haymaker and it landed right under Frikkie Botha's jaw and practically lifted the big Boer off the ground. Frikkie sank to his knees and lay still.

There was silence from the crowd. Then Meneer Prinsloo said, 'We gave the *kaffir* a long count, now Frikkie has one.' I don't know exactly how long they waited but eventually Frikkie Botha got to his feet and for the rest of the round he sort of shadow-boxed around Mattress until the whistle blew.

The last round came and Frikkie Botha came out hard, he realised that Mattress had landed a lucky blow and all he had to do was box him and the time would come to knock him out. But Frikkie Botha was running out of puff, he'd thrown too many punches and his oversized stomach was heaving as he started to blow like a whale. With Frikkie slowed down to a crawl Mattress was learning fast and back-pedalling and moving around the ring, staying out of the way. You could see Frikkie's frustration as he tried to nail Mattress with the one big punch. He was throwing punches that didn't land, and at one stage had to stop and bend over, resting his boxing gloves on his knees. Mattress was a bloody mess, with both eyes closed and scarlet blood dripping from his nose, over his chin and onto his dark chest. Instead of going for Frikkie Botha he too took the opportunity to recover.

Halfway through the third round, when Frikkie had knocked him down on two more occasions, and you could feel the crowd grow silent. 'Lie down, you black bastard,' Frikkie called out, but the black man refused and kept getting up. Frikkie Botha was totally spent and he dropped his gloves to his side, trying to summon up enough strength to hit the defenceless *kaffir* with one big punch, one last time. But Mattress was trying to do the same thing while he could still see his opponent through the slits that had become his eyes. The Mattress punch came first. It was an uppercut and it hit Frikkie on the chin with a force like a runaway steam engine crashing into a solid wall and again Frikkie's feet lifted off the canvas.

He tried to regain his balance as he frantically back-pedalled, hitting the ropes and then spinning sideways before crashing to the canvas where he lay on his back with both arms stretched out. Mattress had landed only two punches in the whole fight. But when you have to polish a dairy floor your arms are strong. Frikkie Botha lay completely still and it was apparent to everyone that he'd be a long time getting up. Meneer Prinsloo stooped over him and evidently didn't like what he saw because he turned and called out for Mevrou to come and help without first counting Frikkie out. Everyone had gone very quiet. There was some blood running out of Frikkie Botha's nose. Mattress just stood there, not knowing what to do next.

'Go back! Go back to a neutral corner, you hear, *kaffir*,' Meneer Prinsloo cried out in a panic-stricken voice, his arms waving. Once again he stooped over Frikkie Botha, but obviously didn't know what to do about anything.

Mattress walked towards the nearest corner but then changed his mind and walked back to Frikkie Botha's prostrate form and said, 'I am very, very sorry for what I am doing in the boxing, *Baas* Botha.'

I don't suppose Frikkie Botha heard him because he'd really and truly had the daylights knocked out of him and he hadn't moved.

'Go away, *kaffir*! Can't you see he's hurt?' Mevrou shouted, arriving in the ring, immediately taking control. She stooped over Frikkie and you could see her huge bosoms, one with the dead fly, rising and falling as she bent over. 'Take him to the sick room,' she yelled at nobody, then turned and pointed to several of the bigger boys crowding around the edge of the ring. 'Fetch the stretcher, you hear!' They nodded and went running off.

Frikkie Botha started to stir. I reckon by this time four minutes had passed. With help from Mevrou he sat up and locked his arms about his knees and dropped his head between them. Blood dripped from his nose onto the canvas while Mevrou massaged the back of his neck.

Mattress stood for a moment at the far end of the ring with his back turned to Frikkie Botha. In the mid-morning sun his sweat-burnished black skin shone, showing all the muscles. Turned away like that you couldn't see the damage to his face and, for a moment, he stood tall and proud, a great and awesome warrior. He stepped down from the ring, then onto the grass and began walking away with his boxing gloves still tied at his wrists, the white tape stained red from trying to wipe the blood from his nose. The gloves, the same colour as his skin, looked as if they were a natural extension of his long powerful arms. No one shouted at him to take off his gloves.

Nobody knew what to do because this wasn't what was supposed to happen. I ran after Mattress and caught up with him as he passed the punishment water tank where the other servants, the Shangaan kitchen boys, were standing. Their eyes were shining with pride, but they didn't say anything, instead they reached out and touched him as he passed. In their heads they must have said something because their lips moved silently.

'You are a Zulu warrior!' I cried out.

At the sound of my voice Mattress stopped and turned around slowly. I observed that both eyes now seemed completely closed. Blood covered his chin and chest. His left ear was twice its normal size and his bottom lip was badly swollen and split, one side hanging down in a fold of raw pink flesh and ragged black skin, exposing bloody gums and several bottom teeth.

'You didn't forget to hit back,' I said.

'I am Zulu,' he replied.

'And a son of Dingaan.'

Mattress tried to laugh but he couldn't. He must have swallowed some blood or something because he suddenly bent over and spat out a tooth. He straightened up and, resting a boxing glove on my shoulder, said, 'You were right, *Kleinbaas*, now I am already a dead *kaffir*.' He turned and continued walking towards the pigsty, his big platform feet raising the usual puffs of powder dust on the surface of the footpath. I watched as Mattress, proud Zulu and the father of Joe Louis, slowly walked away from me. In the background I could hear some bush doves *cookarooing* high up in the giant blue gum trees by the creek. Four dead ones were worth three cigarettes.

Two nights later, at approximately three o'clock in the morning when the whole town was fast asleep, the body of an unidentified Bantu man was dumped outside the Duiwelskrans police station. His facial features had been removed completely and the skin and flesh from the front of his chest and stomach was largely missing. His hands were tied together at the wrists with a piece of rope that had cut so deeply that the hands were almost parted from the wrists. The rope extended for several feet where it had been cut.

CHAPTER FOUR

The Love That is Beyond Understanding

———

YOU PROBABLY THINK BY now that being cruel to black people was so common that nobody hardly noticed when one of them was murdered, but you'd be wrong. It was on the front page of the *Zoutpansberg Nuus* and everyone at school was talking about it. You couldn't just go around the place murdering people, even if they were *kaffirs*. Murder is murder. 'Revenge is mine sayeth the Lord' is what the *Dominee* said in church over the murder. He got very angry from the pulpit and for once in his life he forgot about what the English did, and said that a lynching was a sin against God and decent God-fearing *Boerevolk* and if anyone knew who was responsible they should go to the police at once. He even said never mind if it was a brother or a father or a cousin or a friend, it was our Christian duty to report what we knew to Sergeant Jan van Niekerk who, as everyone knew, was also the brother of the school headmaster, Meneer Van Niekerk, who was a church elder and greatly respected in the community.

'We know that the black people are savages!' the *Dominee* shouted and he thumped the pulpit with his fist. 'But people who go around murdering them, taking the law into their own hands, they are also savages of the worst kind! The Children of Ham' (which is what he called the black people) 'were *innocent* savages because they hadn't met Jesus Christ yet and those people who did this terrible thing to this

savage were *guilty* savages whatever the colour of their skin. God would
see them burn in hell!'

The thing was that because the murdered *kaffir* had no face left
nobody could identify him. There he was, missing and everything, but
nobody at The Boys Farm would say perhaps Mattress was the murdered
person. Everyone pretended they didn't know where he was and claimed
that maybe after the fight he'd got afraid because he'd knocked Frikkie
out and that was something he wasn't supposed to do. A *kaffir* fighting a
white man in the boxing ring was not an everyday thing, especially if he
was only a lowly pig boy. So they said that's why he'd run away into the
mountains.

It was all bullshit, because he'd left his good trousers behind and
his *knobkierie* and a few other small personal things. Like, for instance,
an enamel mug and his three-string guitar made from a petrol can with
a hole cut in it, and a copper bracelet. They were definitely things he
would have taken with him, even if he did decide to run away. He also
had an old alarm clock that didn't work any more but that he liked a lot;
I admit he probably wouldn't have taken that. And even if he was in a
hurry, a person doesn't leave his best trousers behind and a Zulu always
carries his *knobkierie* wherever he goes. There was one other thing. He
would have said goodbye.

All the guys at The Boys Farm also knew the victim had to be the pig
boy. There were whispers all around the place that it was the *Broederbond*,
a secret underground society of Boere who were determined to get rid of
the British and get the old republic back, who were responsible. There
was also the *Ossewabrandwag*, who sided with the Germans in the war
that had been going on for a year. Others said it was certain to be them. It
was suppposed to be a big secret if you belonged to these societies, except
that in our district everybody knew the secret, but nobody was allowed
to talk about it. If a policeman asked you if someone was a member you
had to swear on a stack of Bibles that he wasn't, otherwise you'd become
a traitor. Frikkie Botha belonged, of course. But then so did Meneer
Prinsloo and Sergeant Van Niekerk and just about everyone around. So

the murderers could have been anyone, except Sergeant Van Niekerk, because a police sergeant wouldn't go about lynching *kaffirs* when they can easily as anything send them to Pretoria to be hanged by the neck. Meneer Prinsloo was also not a suspect; he was a lay preacher and a church elder, and he wouldn't be game enough to be a part of a *kaffir* lynching as he was much too holy and worked for the Government.

Besides, even in the deep north, a *kaffir* wouldn't get lynched just because of beating a white guy in the boxing ring. A Boer is much too proud to do something like that. He would have a return bout and beat the shit out of the *kaffir*, but to murder him just because he was beaten in a fight was unthinkable. A lynching took more than one guy and he'd have to convince all his friends and that was very unlikely. If Frikkie Botha was a suspect, then it was against his character. After the fight he could hardly talk because of a swollen jaw, but he stood up and said that it was a fair fight and the result showed that the best man won, even if it was a lucky punch. That was because some of the boys were saying Meneer Prinsloo hadn't officially counted him out so there was no result. But Gawie Grobler, who told me that hens don't have teeth, said he'd counted Frikkie Botha out silently and it was 200 when he finally sat up. Everyone was turning to everyone else and asking, 'If it isn't about the boxing and if the *kaffir* without the face is the pig boy, then what is the motive for the lynching?'

You must remember that among us boys only Pissy Vermaak and Fonnie du Preez knew about the Mevrou version of what happened at the big rock, where Pissy said Mattress had penetrated him. So they knew, and I knew, and Meneer Prinsloo, Frikkie Botha and Mevrou knew that there was a motive, that is, if you believed the pack of lies Pissy had told Mevrou, which Mevrou and Meneer Prinsloo did, and Frikkie Botha pretended he did. If you think it was getting complicated, you are right. I was seven years old and I kept having to remind myself that the true version was the kissing and licking and sucking version where Mattress had rescued me and Fonnie du Preez had been hurt. Only five people knew the *real* truth. Us three boys, Frikkie Botha and

Mattress. Only four really, because I was certain Mattress was already dead.

The morning after the fight I had gone down after breakfast to feed Tinker before we had to go to church and, of course, to see Mattress. What a calamity! The pigs were carrying on and the old sow was kicking up a terrible fuss, grunting and running from one side of the pigsty to the other. The piglets had long since been weaned and they were in the big sty next door doing all the squealing, and the reason was that they hadn't been fed. The cows had come up to the dairy by themselves for milking and were mooing and bellowing something terrible.

I called out for Mattress but there was no reply. Clearly, something was wrong. Mattress just wasn't the sort to let something like this happen, and besides, Frikkie Botha would have been down before breakfast to check on everything like he always did.

What I didn't know was that Frikkie Botha's jaw had been broken in the fight and he'd been taken into town to hospital and Doctor Van Heerden had wired up his jaw and kept him there for observation and to drain the sinuses in his mashed nose. I walked over to Mattress's hut and peeped through the open doorway. It was always as dark as an African mud hut, called a *kaya*, and didn't have any windows.

'Mattress, *wena lapa*? Are you there?' I heard a grunt, so I entered. It took some moments for my eyes to adjust to the semi-dark interior but when they did I got a real hundred per cent shock. Mattress was lying on his grass mat and his face was about twice the size it should be, and his eyes seemed to be completely closed. Half his bottom lip hung off the side of his mouth, even worse than before, and was hugely raw and swollen. It was all the things I'd seen yesterday but twice as bad. He still had the boxing gloves on. I could see he was trying to greet me but no words came out, just a sort-of grunt.

I realised that no one had come down to see him, not even one of the Shangaan kitchen boys. He'd been on his own and couldn't take the boxing gloves off because the tape was tied too tightly and he couldn't even use his teeth to undo it because of his terribly torn lip and loose teeth. You could see where he'd tried because there was the brown of the dried blood from yesterday staining the white tape and red from the new blood of today. The yesterday blood had also dried on his face and chest and a few flies buzzed around, frequently landing on him. Luckily, it was late in the season for flies and most of them had already gone because of the approaching winter when flies go who knows where.

Mattress sat up with a great groan and held his gloves out for me to undo. I couldn't undo the knot at first, blood had soaked in and spit and stuff, and it wouldn't budge, but then I found an old kitchen knife and sawed through the tape. Using both my hands I pulled the gloves off. Mattress grunted and rose to his feet and groaned. He was bent almost double and held his hands against both sides of his waist. Later in life I would realise it was because Frikkie Botha had hit him probably fifty times in the kidneys and Mattress had been bleeding internally all yesterday and last night. He was shuffling very slowly, rocking on his big feet like an old man, and he walked towards the door of his hut and into the morning sunlight.

In the daylight he looked even worse. He sat down on the pigsty wall and I ran and got his enamel mug and filled it with water from the cow tank. He drank it, holding the mug with both hands, and maybe because of his torn lip, he spilled most of it down his front. I did it again, and after four mugs he raised his hand to say it was enough.

Mattress must have been able to see something because otherwise how would he find the pigsty wall to sit on? But I couldn't see his eyes because they were so puffed up. I told him to wait and I ran to the back of the dairy and found some old used cheesecloth for making butter and I wet it at the cow tank and wiped down his face and chest. I had to have several goes before all the old dried blood was gone. On his face it must have hurt a lot when I wiped but he didn't say anything. I didn't touch his lip because it was too sore. I also noticed that his nice straight nose wasn't straight anymore.

The water he drank must have helped because he managed to say to me, but in a very strange sort of voice, 'The pigs must eat, the cows, I must milk them.' Then he said, 'Cabbages.' I realised that the cows have to be milked twice a day and that they'd been standing there since yesterday evening making milk inside them and now their udders couldn't hold any more and it was like a bag about to burst.

I couldn't milk a cow, but behind the pigsty was this bin where Mattress kept old vegetables that had gone to seed and some perfectly good ones we didn't need in The Boys Farm kitchen. This week it was cabbages. So I went around to the back of the pigsty to the bin and got an armful of cabbages and threw a big one to the sow and three more to the piglets. The piglets started to squeal even worse as they fought over the cabbages, so I got some more and threw another one in for the sow and the rest for the piglets and things definitely began to calm down. It's hard for a piglet to squeal with a mouthful of cabbage leaves. Chomp, chomp, chomp.

Mattress rose and pointed to the dairy and indicated that I should lead him there. So I took his big hand and we walked slowly over to the cows. Those cows all knew him and I think they must have been very glad to see him because the mooing really got going. Mattress felt the side of a cow to guide him to the udder and then squatted down, his big hands found the teats and suddenly there was milk splashing in the dust. We did that for every cow. Splash, splash, splash in the dust until it was milk mud everywhere. I knew there'd be lots of trouble because there'd be no milk for The Boys Farm but the cows didn't care because they weren't sore anymore. They turned and went back into a nearby field all on their own and started grazing and being happy again.

Mattress's lips looked really bad and you could see he needed stitches. I knew this from the cut Fonnie du Preez got in his head from when Mattress threw him into the big rock. If he needed stitches for that cut, then so did Mattress for a lip that was hanging half off his face. But it was now Sunday and Mevrou had gone to visit her family at their farm in the mountains and there was nobody to ask. I told him I would try to find Frikkie Botha and maybe he would drive Mattress to the hospital where there was a special part at the back that looked after the blacks.

Mattress couldn't talk much but he said I should take him back to his hut because now the pigs had been fed and the cows milked, he had the day off until milking tonight and he'd just like to rest and I should not go to see Big *Baas* Botha. I led him back to his hut and then fed Tinker who, I forgot to say, was with me all the time this was going on, and I'd got her cut-down jam tin and filled it with milk for her.

I left Tinker at the dairy and went back to The Boys Farm because that afternoon we were getting a visit from a missionary who played the violin and had a mission station near Bulawayo in Rhodesia. Meneer Prinsloo said at supper the night before that although this missionary lady wasn't from the Dutch Reformed Church, she was still a good Christian spreading God's work among the heathen and we all had the afternoon off from working in the vegetable gardens to go and listen to her.

I must say I didn't think the violin sounded very good doing hymns, but we also prayed for the heathens who she said were 'cast into everlasting darkness unless they saw the light and repented and accepted Jesus into their heart'. Then she asked if anybody in the audience wanted to do the same, but nobody did because our hearts were too hard and we'd been to church already once that day.

I'm only telling you this because I didn't know at the time that I would never see my friend Mattress again, because usually after we'd finished in the vegetable gardens I'd go and see him and Tinker again, but this Sunday I couldn't because of the missionary.

Back to the murder. This is what the newspaper said happened and I also heard it at school.

Some persons unknown had assaulted the murder victim and tied his wrists together with a long piece of rope. They tied the end of the rope to the back bumper of the *bakkie* and drove off so that the murder victim had to run behind the lorry. They went faster and faster so he couldn't run fast enough, so he fell and they dragged him along until he was dead, and had no face or chest or the front part of his body left after being scraped along the surface of the dirt road. They'd cut him loose outside Sergeant Jan van Niekerk's police station sometime between midnight and three o'clock in the morning. Because it was Sunday night and very late there wasn't even anyone on duty at the station, except a black policeman who was asleep in the station cell and didn't hear anything. Of course, we only heard about all this later when it came out in the newspaper.

But to go back to the time before I knew of the murder, at breakfast on Monday morning after the Saturday fight, we didn't get porridge as usual because they said there wasn't any milk. Everybody moaned and complained but there was no further explanation so we only had bread and black coffee that tasted horrible and bitter, even with sugar. I knew why there wasn't any milk because Mattress and me had poured it straight onto the ground on Sunday. The milk we used was always the day-before milk, because butter and cream were made with the fresh milk and then what was left was sent up to the kitchen later in the morning for use that night in our coffee and breakfast the next day. Frikkie Botha wasn't at breakfast so I thought he was probably down at the dairy and poor Mattress was getting a terrible scolding for pouring Sunday's milk onto the ground. Of course, I still didn't know that Frikkie Botha was in hospital for his broken jaw and his sinuses.

After breakfast and before school on that Monday I took Tinker her crusts and there were the cows mooing and waiting at the dairy to be milked and the pigs making a fuss about getting no breakfast again. My heart started to thump and I thought Mattress might be sick and couldn't get up. I ran over to his hut and turned the corner and ran straight into Sergeant Van Niekerk. And then I saw there were two black policemen and the police van. There was also Meneer Prinsloo.

'What are you doing here, boy?' Meneer Prinsloo asked.

I was suddenly in a terrible fix. I couldn't tell him about Tinker;

thank goodness I hadn't yet called her with a whistle or shouted out her name. Tinker knew she wasn't allowed to come until she was called and she'd learned to stay away from everyone accept Mattress and me. If I couldn't tell the truth about Tinker I had no other choice but to say, 'Mattress is my friend and I help him to feed the pigs, Meneer.'

'Who is this Mattress?' he demanded to know.

'The pig boy, Sir.'

'The pig boy!' He looked at Sergeant Van Niekerk and shook his head and addressed me again. 'Sunday you get your clean clothes for church and they still clean on Monday so you can go to school and show them you get good care here.' He pointed in the direction of the pigsty. 'Now you come down here and feed the pigs in your nice clean clothes?'

'Yes, Sir. I'm sorry, Sir.'

'Does Mevrou know about this?'

'No, Sir,' I said in a timorous voice, then added, 'it's allowed, Sir. Meneer Botha says I can.'

'You are the English child, aren't you?' he asked.

'*Ja*, Meneer.'

Sergeant Van Niekerk stepped forward. 'You say you knew this *Bantu*, son? What did you say his name was?'

'Mattress, Sir.'

He smiled. 'Mattress, hey? Did he lie down a lot?'

I could see he meant it as a small boy's joke. 'No, Sir, he slept on a grass mat and he worked very hard.'

He went down on his haunches. He was a big man but not as big as Mattress, and he put his hand on my shoulder just the way Mattress would sometimes do. 'Did he, this Mattress, ever touch you? What is your name?'

'Tom, Sir, but they call me *Voetsek*.'

Sergeant Van Niekerk drew back in surprise. 'I will call you Tom. Tom, did this *Bantu*, er, Mattress, ever touch you?'

'Touch, Sir?' I wasn't sure what he meant.

'In places, private places.' As far as I knew we didn't have any private places at The Boys Farm.

'No, Sir.'

'Did he touch you at all?'

'Yes, Sir.'

'Oh, how was that?'

'Like you are touching me, Sir. He sometimes put his hand on my shoulder.'

'He was your friend, hey?'

'Yes, Sir, I already told Meneer Prinsloo that, Sir.'

'Don't be cheeky, you hear!' Meneer Prinsloo snapped.

'No, he's not being cheeky,' Sergeant Van Niekerk said, quickly defending me. 'He's right, he did tell you. How old are you, Tom?'

'Seven, Sir.'

'Seven! *Magtig*, and already you a farmer helping with the cows and the pigs. Will you be a farmer when you grow up?'

'I dunno, Sir, I'm an orphan,' I told him.

'But you won't always be an orphan,' he said.

'Yes I will, you can't not be an orphan.'

'He is a clever child,' he said, looking up at Meneer Prinsloo, who didn't reply. Sergeant Van Niekerk looked back at me and said, 'Did you and Mattress talk about a lot of different things then?'

'Yes, lots of things.'

'Did you talk about your bodies?'

'Only about his feet and Joe Louis's feet.'

'Eh? His feet? What about his feet?'

'In Zululand there are high mountains, much higher than here,' I explained. 'The rocks there are *really* bad and sharp and when you an *umfaan* and are minding the goats you cut your feet a lot until they get a proper platform. Until that happens you not a goat boy's arsehole,' I said, quoting Mattress. 'Joe Louis is still getting a platform.'

'Joe Louis, the boxer?'

'No, Mattress's son, who is the same age as me.'

'So, what's this platform? Do you mean the callused soles of a *kaffir*'s foot?'

'Yes, that's what we talked about.'

'No other mentions of the body?'

I tried to think but I couldn't remember any other part of the body we'd ever discussed. 'No,' I replied.

'What else did you talk about, Tom?'

'Cows and goats and the rains. It can get very dry in Zululand, you know, and even rivers dry up,' I informed him.

'What else?'

'Well, did you know goats can have fits? That's how Mattress knew how to put the stick in Pissy, er, Kobus Vermaak's mouth.'

'Kobus Vermaak?' The sergeant turned to Meneer Prinsloo. 'Isn't he —?' He stopped. 'Never mind, later,' he said and turned back to me. 'Anything else you talked about?'

'Women.'

'Women? What did he say about women?'

'That a man can never understand them. You see, Mattress has a wife and every month he goes to the post office and sends her a postal order and when she's got enough she buys a goat and then they sell six goats and buy a cow. She always complains that the milk from six goats is better than milk from one cow and it costs too much to get a bull, ten calabashes of *kaffir* beer and ten shillings and sixpence to the chief. One day he's going to go back to Zululand to sit under a marula tree and watch his cattle and his wife working in the *mielie* field and drink *kaffir* beer all the time,' I explained.

'I see,' Sergeant Van Niekerk said. He went down on his haunches in front of me again. 'How would you like to come in my van back to the police station?'

I looked at him and was suddenly very frightened. 'I haven't done anything bad, Sir!' It was all getting too much for me. Here I was in trouble with the police and I was only seven years old and going to gaol already. Maybe to Pretoria to be hung by the neck until I was stone dead because that's what a sergeant of a police station could do any time he liked.

Sergeant Van Niekerk laughed. 'No, Tom, I am not placing you under arrest. I just want you to help the police with their enquiries.'

'What's an enquiries?' I asked. It didn't sound a very nice thing to help to do.

'Just talking together and you'll get a cool drink and an ice-cream . . . an Eskimo Pie if you like.'

I'd tasted ice-cream because we got it at Christmas, also a cool drink, but I'd never tasted an Eskimo Pie, which was this small block of ice-cream that had chocolate frozen around it and was wrapped in paper like a little parcel. You saw them when the ice-cream boy came around on his bicycle at school, a rich kid could buy one for a *tickey*.

'I don't think we could allow that, Sergeant,' Meneer Prinsloo said suddenly. 'The boy is only seven years old.'

Sergeant Van Niekerk gave my shoulder a squeeze and stood up. '*Ja*, I know it's not usual, hey. But this boy is very intelligent and nobody around here seems to know anything about this native who is missing. Frikkie Botha is in hospital with a broken jaw and bandages around his nose and face, and the doctor says he can't talk for at least two days. He's the only person who can tell us anything about this Zulu, except, of course, Tom here.'

'I don't think a seven-year-old boy's testimony would be accepted in a court of law,' Meneer Prinsloo protested.

'Who said anything about a court of law? I have a corpse with no face, a lynching on my hands and a charge of indecent assault from you involving a farm boy who's missing from your premises. I have no idea who did this lynching or even if the two crimes are connected. I also know nothing about the missing Zulu you are reporting.' He glanced down at me. 'Tom is the only one who knows anything about him. It would be most helpful if you would cooperate with the authorities on the matter, Meneer.'

I sensed that the farm boy mentioned was Mattress who was somehow involved because of what Pissy had said to Mevrou, and now Meneer Prinsloo seemed to have reported it to Sergeant Van Niekerk. But otherwise nothing he said made any sense.

'No! I forbid it! The boy is too young,' Meneer Prinsloo said, flapping his hands and sticking out his great stomach with his trousers pulled high by his braces to halfway up his chest. 'Absolutely forbid it, you hear? That's my last word, finish and *klaar*!' He turned to me. 'Go now, boy.'

Believe you me, I didn't need to be told twice, but then I remembered the pigs and the cows. 'The pigs haven't been fed, Meneer, and the cows must be milked or they'll burst,' I said.

Sergeant Van Niekerk laughed. 'He is a real farmer. Can you milk a cow, Tom?'

'No, Sir, but I can get some cabbages for the pigs.'

He turned to ask if either of the black policemen could milk a cow and they both said they could, so he sent them off to do this.

'Come, Tom, I'll help you feed the pigs.'

'This boy must go to school. Go on, off you go,' Meneer Prinsloo said, pointing towards The Boys Farm.

'Why don't I drive him to school in the police van?' Sergeant Van Niekerk turned to me. 'How would you like that, Tom?'

I didn't know what to do and looked to Meneer Prinsloo for guidance. I would have liked a ride in the police van and I liked Sergeant Van Niekerk a lot.

'Over my dead body!' Meneer Prinsloo said emphatically. 'You are not going to interrogate this child alone, he is Government property and under my care.' I could see things were a bit strained between the two men. Meneer Prinsloo turned to me. 'Go on, hurry up and go, man,' he instructed me.

'One more question,' Sergeant Van Niekerk said, looking straight at the superintendent. 'Tom, would you recognise Mattress's feet if you saw them?'

'*Ja*, Meneer, I think so.'

'You are not showing this boy a dead *kaffir*'s corpse, you hear?' Meneer Prinsloo shouted. '*Genoeg*!'

'A photograph. I will arrange for a photograph to be taken of the victim's feet,' Sergeant Van Niekerk said calmly. 'Until we have a positive identification of the victim, we don't know if we've got two cases or only one.'

'Go on, off!' Meneer Prinsloo shouted down at me. He was red in the face and snorting like a wounded buffalo.

I set off at a run and heard Sergeant Van Niekerk call, 'Thank you, Tom, you've been a big help.'

Ja, I thought, thanks for nothing. You not the one who's going to get Meneer Prinsloo's extra-long cane *sjambok* when you get back from school. Him running at me, *whack! whack! whack!* Chinese writing on my bum that won't go away for a month!

I hadn't seen the last of Sergeant Jan van Niekerk. Halfway through the morning at school the headmaster Meneer Van Niekerk came to our classroom and told our teacher he wanted to see me and to come with him to his office. Now I had a second Meneer Van Niekerk involved with me and both on the same day, that was pretty frightening stuff. When we got to his office who should be there but Sergeant Van Niekerk, who was the younger of the two brothers.

'Howzit?' he said with a smile. 'We meet again, hey, Tom.'

'Sit, Tom,' the headmaster said, indicating a straight-backed chair. I knew you weren't supposed to sit in front of a headmaster, especially in his office where you only went if there was some trouble.

'Can I stand, please, Sir?' I asked.

'No, Tom, we want you to sit, this could take a bit of time.'

I sat on the chair but my feet couldn't quite reach the floor and I wasn't comfortable at all with two Van Niekerks, a policeman and a headmaster, facing me. I knew I must be in some terrible trouble but I couldn't think what it might be. Especially as Sergeant Van Niekerk had been so nice to me only this morning at The Boys Farm.

The police sergeant reached for a big envelope that lay on the headmaster's desk and from it he withdrew a black-and-white photograph. 'I want you to look very carefully at this photograph, Tom. Tell me if you recognise anything.'

He handed it to me and there, staring me in the face, were

Mattress's big platform feet. 'It's Mattress!' I said, looking at the snap of his feet.

'Are you sure now, Tom?' the sergeant asked.

I was certain. You couldn't mistake Mattress's platform feet with the cracks in the side. 'Yes, Meneer. Does that mean he's dead? Mattress is dead?'

Sergeant Van Niekerk didn't answer at once. 'If they are his feet, then yes, son,' he said softly.

I couldn't help myself, I started to sob. Mattress was the best friend Tinker and I had and they'd gone and killed him stone dead. They let me blub for quite a while because I couldn't stop, even if I wanted. Then the headmaster handed me his handkerchief to wipe my eyes and gave me a cup of water.

When I'd calmed down a bit Sergeant Van Niekerk said to me, 'Tom, we are going to ask you a few questions, you hear? The headmaster here is my big *boetie* and he's here to see that you are not harassed and he is also a witness to our conversation. Do you agree to talk to me?'

'Yes, Sir . . . but I'll get into trouble, Sir.'

'Trouble?'

'With Meneer Prinsloo, Sir.'

Sergeant Van Niekerk looked at his brother and rolled his eyes. 'Prinsloo' is all he said.

The headmaster looked at me. 'Never you mind about that, Tom. I will be writing down everything, there will be nothing to get into trouble about.'

The headmaster obviously didn't know very much about The Boys Farm where you were always guilty and innocence wasn't something anyone believed possible anyway. If you didn't do something, then the *sjambok* was thought to be a down payment on some future crime you were certain to commit.

'This morning, Tom . . . let me think, yes, you said something about Mattress putting a stick in Kobus Vermaak's mouth when he had a fit. Can you tell me what that was all about?' The police sergeant had this paper in front of him and it had about four pages and he was reading something on the second page when he looked up and asked the question. Maybe it was all written on the pages so I couldn't tell a lie because he'd know. I decided to tell the truth, but as little of it as possible.

'He had a fit and Mattress found him and put a stick in his mouth.'

'Why did he do that?'

'So he wouldn't swallow his tongue. If you swallow your tongue you can die,' I explained.

'Why did he have a fit? Did something happen?'

'It wasn't because I punched him, Sir!' I said defensively. 'Mevrou said you can just get a fit any time you like, it just comes.'

'You punched him? Why did you punch him, Tom?'

I'd clean forgotten that nobody but Pissy knew I'd been on the scene just before he'd had his fit and the only person I'd told was Mattress. I was trapped. Now the police sergeant was going to find out about Tinker! I tried to think of a lie but I couldn't think of one fast enough that might explain why I'd punched Pissy. Then I thought, well, the sergeant has three big dogs himself, so maybe he'll understand.

'Why, Tom?' the sergeant repeated.

'He wanted to take this dog I found, Sir.'

Sergeant Van Niekerk smiled. 'Not only a farmer but a dog lover as well. I also love my dogs. They are a person's best friend. A dog will never let you down. You say you found a dog and Kobus Vermaak wanted to take it away from you. Where did you find this dog?'

'In a sack floating down the creek, Sir. The other five puppies inside were dead already.'

'And you saved its life and wanted to keep it, hey? That's nice, man. What's its name?'

'Tinker, Sir.'

'So, tell me, Tom. How did Kobus take Tinker from you? Did he grab it from you? Did he punch you? Tell me, son.'

'He found where I was hiding her.'

'And where was that?'

'At the big rock, Sir.'

Sergeant Van Niekerk started rummaging through the paper in front of him and he found what he wanted. 'The big rock?'

'Yes, Sir.'

'This big rock, was it the same big rock where Fonnie du Preez was attacked by Mattress?'

All of a sudden I couldn't help myself. 'It was the same rock, but it's a pack of lies, Sir!'

'Lies?'

'Mattress didn't do it!' I cried out and started to blub again.

I was still holding the headmaster's hanky that had got all wet in my fist, but I forgot to use it and the tears just splashed down over my chin. After a while I got a bit better.

'What makes you think he didn't do it, did he tell you?'

'No, Sir, I was there, Sir.'

The police sergeant went back to the papers. 'There is no mention of you here, Tom. Are you sure you were there?'

I had trapped myself completely and there was no getting out of it, and the only good thing was that I was able to tell about what Mattress did, even though it was now too late. In between blubbing every once in a while, I told them about being made by Fonnie du Preez to do all those things to Pissy and him. Then how Mattress came just in time to save me and lifted Fonnie and threw him against the rock and then carried me away. We'd reported it to Meneer Botha who said, 'You weren't there, you understand?' He said if I told anyone what had truly happened my little dog would be dead. Next thing I knew, they'd made up a whole new story of what happened, with some rock giving way and Fonnie hurting himself. I then told them about the Mevrou version with me listening while I hid in the hydrangea bushes outside the sick room.

After I'd told them all this, Sergeant Van Niekerk consulted his papers again while the headmaster was writing furiously. Then the sergeant said, 'Tom, you said Mattress slept on a grass mat, I saw that. Do you know if he ever had a mattress in his hut?'

'No, Sir. Once when I told him that his name meant something people sleep on he said a Zulu didn't sleep on anything like that, so it didn't matter.' It was the second time he'd brought up the subject this morning.

At the time I'd clean forgotten that Pissy had told Mevrou that Mattress had penetrated him in his hut *on a mattress*! The sergeant wrote something in the margin of one of the pages and the headmaster finished writing down stuff and looked up and said, '*Indrukwekkend*,' which means impressive. He turned to Sergeant Van Niekerk. '*Magtig*! Jan, what a terrible, terrible waste of a good *Bantu's* life.'

Sergeant Van Niekerk glanced at his brother and then nodded towards me. 'The boy's been through a helluva lot,' he said, looking at me and smiling. 'Now, Tom, the headmaster says you got an hour off school, and you and I are going to go to the café for ice-cream and a cool drink, maybe even a milkshake, hey?'

I'd never had a milkshake but I'd heard about them, you could get strawberry ones. I wasn't ever going to get another chance so I said quietly, 'You said this morning I could have an Eskimo Pie, Meneer?'

Sergeant Van Niekerk laughed. 'Ag, Tom, an Eskimo Pie is only a *tickey*. We going to take a whole shilling and buy an ice-cream in a dish,' he cupped his hands together, 'so big, with lots of other nice things and with chocolate and hundreds and thousands spread all over and a big pink biscuit that sticks out of the top.'

'You are a very brave and clever boy, Tom,' the headmaster said and put his hand on my head. It was the first time in my life a high-up person had ever given me a compliment. Except that very morning when the sergeant had said I was clever, but you could see Meneer Prinsloo didn't agree and he already knew me better.

We were walking out of the headmaster's study when I remembered his handkerchief that was still scrunched up wet in my hand. 'Sorry, Sir, I nearly forgot and took your hanky,' I said, and gave it back to him. Afterwards I remembered there must be some wet snot in it from my crying, but it was too late to take it to the tap and wash it out first.

In the café, which I'd never been in before, Sergeant Van Niekerk asked the lady, who was called Mevrou Booysens, to make a big ice-cream in a glass dish that stood on one leg. 'Put on everything,' he instructed.

'Everything?' She looked surprised. 'There are ten things that can go on ice-cream,' she declared.

'Then we got all ten things on Tom's ice-cream and also a strawberry milkshake. This young man deserves only the best, you hear?'

'Don't blame me if he gets sick,' she laughed.

But I didn't.

As I ate the ice-cream and drank the milkshake through this straw Sergeant Van Niekerk found and put in it, he said to me, 'Tom, I want you to listen to me carefully now, hey?'

'Ja, Meneer,' I answered, first licking all the ice-cream off my spoon so it was nice and clean and I put it down carefully on the table. I hoped it wouldn't take too long because some of the ice-cream was melting already.

'Tom, I think it is best if you don't say anything about what we spoke about in the headmaster's office, you hear?'

'Ja, Meneer, but if they hear where I've been they will ask me.'

'Is there anyone in your class who's also at The Boys Farm?'

'No, Sir.'

'So it's unlikely to get back. The headmaster says you have permission to say it was about you maybe getting special English lessons because you the only English-speaking boy in the school. Can you remember that? Nobody knows I was there as well, so best not to mention that, hey?'

'Ja, Meneer, but I'm only English because of my name. I can't speak English, except what we learn in class.'

'It doesn't matter, that's why the headmaster wants to make the special arrangements. Do you understand?'

I said yes, but I admit I was a bit unsure of what it all meant, but I knew what to say if Meneer Prinsloo asked, which was the main thing.

In the next week Sergeant Van Niekerk's police van was seen twice in the morning at The Boys Farm and Pissy and Fonnie didn't come with us when we marched to school. What I *can* tell you is that for the whole week Mevrou came into the small boys' dormitory for half-jack in her nightgown. Her hair was all over the place and she was sweating, with her breasts jumping up and down and sometimes if you looked hard, you could see the black where her bush was. In that week, I've got to tell you, man, nobody escaped her *sjambok* except Pissy! I got blasted twice and one time when she gave me four of the best she called me *Die klein kaffirboetie!* The little *kaffir*-lover.

Of course the boys asked Pissy what was happening.

'Nothing,' he'd say, and for once you couldn't get anything out of him, not even lies. At night, it was his turn to cry. So we had his coughing and crying going on ten to the dozen. On the Friday when we were washing our hands for supper he had another fit and had to go to the sick room and the next day we all got the *sjambok* again. I'm telling you, that was a week and a half orright! But one good thing, nobody said anything about what happened at school with the headmaster and Sergeant Van Niekerk. I don't know how he did it but he kept me out of it, and when on one occasion I passed Meneer Prinsloo he ignored me like he'd always done.

In the second week after Mattress's death, when the lynching had been in the newspaper and the kids who could read had told everyone everything it said, lots of them were asking, 'What is the motive?' On Tuesday morning two weeks and two days after Mattress's death, we were lining up ready to march to school when Sergeant Van Niekerk arrived in the van and stopped beside us. Meneer Prinsloo and Mevrou and Frikkie Botha, who still couldn't speak properly, came out and stood there as if they were expecting something to happen.

We all watched silently as Sergeant Van Niekerk got out of the van. He was on his own and he walked up to Meneer Prinsloo and said in a very loud voice, so I think he wanted us all to hear, '*Goeie môre, Meneer Prinsloo. Ek is hier om Fonnie du Preez inhegtenis te neem.*' I am here to take Fonnie du Preez into custody.

There was a gasp of amazement from all of us, and Meneer Prinsloo started to wave his arms and stick out his stomach.

'You can't do it!' he said to Sergeant Van Niekerk. 'Not in front of everyone, it is not civilised, you hear!'

Before Sergeant Van Niekerk could reply, Fonnie du Preez, who still had his arm in a sling, broke from the ranks and started to run. Sergeant Van Niekerk turned around when he heard the noise from the kids and saw what was happening. He walked normally over to the police van and opened the back. Out jumped the three big Alsatian dogs. They landed beside him and sat.

'Go and stop!' he commanded.

You should have seen those dogs go! We could see them catching up to Fonnie, who wasn't running his fastest because of his arm in the sling. The dogs skidded to a halt in a cloud of dust beside him and started to bark fiercely, jumping up and surrounding him so he couldn't move, but they didn't bite him or anything. He tried to run but the dogs bumped into him, knocking him off his feet and they stood over him, showing their fierce teeth and gums, but still not biting. They weren't barking now, just growling.

'*Staan op en kom hier, du Preez!*' Sergeant Van Niekerk shouted, ordering Fonnie to get up and come to him.

We all watched as Fonnie struggled to his feet and Sergeant Van Niekerk put his finger to his lips and whistled. The dogs allowed Fonnie to walk, though they stayed right behind him, their big pink tongues lolling out of their mouths. I'm telling you now, it wasn't funny and I'm never going to try running from the police. I could see why the blacks got so scared when Sergeant Van Niekerk walked down the street with his three dogs.

Sergeant Van Niekerk never moved as Fonnie, with his head bowed, walked up to where he was standing. He took out his police whistle, blew it twice and the dogs jumped into the police van. He turned back to Fonnie.

'I am placing you under arrest, du Preez,' he said. 'If you resist again I will be forced to handcuff you. Now, come along.'

'You can't do this, you hear, Van Niekerk!' Meneer Prinsloo shouted. 'I am in authority here and this boy is under my supervision. On what grounds are you arresting him?'

Sergeant Van Niekerk had his hand under Fonnie's elbow, ready to guide him to the passenger seat of the police van. He turned and said, 'We have already discussed the need and the reason for the arrest on the telephone this morning, Meneer Prinsloo. Or would you like me to tell the boys what it's for?'

'It's not civilised, you hear! This could have been done low-key like decent people and you come here and treat us like we've done something wrong and embarrass me and my staff. *Wragtig*! You will hear more about this, that I can assure you, Van Niekerk!'

'The title is Sergeant, Meneer Prinsloo, and may I say, when you and your staff act like civilised people then that is the way the law will treat you. Please feel free to report me.'

Meneer Prinsloo went very red in the face and waved his hands frantically. I thought his tummy was going to burst open and his braces snap right off. He turned and walked away, back into The Boys Farm.

Mevrou turned and shouted at the sergeant, 'What would you know about civilised, hey? The *kaffir's* dead, so what is the use of arresting a good Afrikaner boy, one of your own *volk*?'

Sergeant Van Niekerk turned and said, 'Mevrou Van Schalkwyk, if I were you I would be very careful what I said next.'

But Mevrou couldn't restrain herself. 'You should be ashamed, you hear?' She turned and walked away and Frikkie Botha just looked at the sergeant and shook his head and went 'tsk' and followed her.

Sergeant Van Niekerk guided Fonnie into the police van, started the engine and drove away slowly.

I caught a last glimpse of Fonnie du Preez. Good riddance to bad rubbish, I thought as we were marched off to school.

———

The next week Pissy was put on the train to Pietersburg to go to the boys home there and Mevrou said it was because his mother, who'd put him in the orphanage, lived there and wanted to be near him. I knew this was a lie but I didn't say anything.

But Pissy got me one more time! Before he left he tried to become the innocent victim and put all the blame for what had happened on Fonnie du Preez, now that he was safely out of the way. In telling the whole story he said how Fonnie had made me kiss Pissy's arse and lick his arsehole and how I had to suck Fonnie's prick. Suddenly I was an arse-licker and a cocksucker *and* a *rooinek*! *And* I was the one who was left behind.

Now that everyone knew the story they also knew how Mattress had saved me, and that he was completely innocent but still got murdered by whoever lynched him, and it looked like whoever did it had got clean away with murder.

But that's the funny thing. Not one boy at The Boys Farm or even an adult thought about Mattress and what he'd done to save me. Maybe he'd even saved Pissy's life by putting the stick in his mouth, but nobody wanted to remember that either. Mattress seemed to disappear from everyone's memory as if he was never there. One day he was milking the cows with his broken face and lip hanging off and his kidneys bleeding so the cows would be comfortable and not suffer, and the next day he was dragged face down by a *bakkie* in the dust until he was dead and couldn't be recognised. Mattress had a nice face and they went and wiped it clean off his head. It was as though if you don't have a face, you don't exist. I don't suppose his wife or Joe Louis would ever know what happened to him. The postal orders just wouldn't arrive in Zululand. I didn't even know where they buried him. I started to worry about what happened to a person who had no face when he arrived in heaven because maybe God wouldn't recognise him. Just in case, I prayed and told God to look at his platform feet and He'd be able to tell for sure it was Mattress.

———

We heard that the magistrate in Tzaneen sent Fonnie to the Boys Reformatory in Pretoria. I thought that would be the last of him in my life, but I was wrong. Pissy was another one I hoped never to see again, but I was also wrong about that.

I didn't understand things properly at the time, but as I grew older I realised how it was Pissy's malicious lies that had led to Mattress's death, and that Pissy was as much the murderer as the people who dragged Mattress behind their *bakkie*. This was another thing I had to think about in life: that everything we do has a consequence and that it is beholden on all of us to stop and think what the consequence of any action we undertake might be. That lying to save our own skin and getting away with it usually results in others being hurt or wronged.

One good thing did happen. Frikkie Botha said Tinker could be my dog anywhere and any time I liked because a month after the murder she caught her first rat in the dairy. It wasn't a very big rat, but then Tinker wasn't properly grown-up yet. Meneer Botha said it showed she had 'all the right instincts'. He said that from now on she could get food from the kitchen so she could grow up strong and be good at her new job. It was after Frikkie Botha's jaw was mended that he managed to say all this.

Everyone said he was very lucky that Mattress had broken his jaw in the boxing ring and that Doctor Van Heerden had put him in hospital, because otherwise he would be suspect-lyncher-number-one in the murder case. But because he couldn't have been one of them, whoever did it remained a dark mystery and no charges were laid, even though Sergeant Van Niekerk did his best for justice.

All I knew was that I had lost the first person in my life I had ever loved, and that the love Mattress had given me had simply disappeared into thin air as if it didn't matter to anyone. I couldn't understand why that should be. I knew that I would love Mattress for as long as I lived. To have loved somebody is not something you can just go and forget, because you just can't.

CHAPTER FIVE

Falling in Love with the Word

I HAVE TO TELL you now about how I became a thief. It all had to do with having hot showers. You see, in summer we had cold showers, but up there in the mountains it got cold as anything in the winter mornings and the pipes would freeze. Not snow, there had never been snow, probably not since the beginning of time, but in the morning the frost lay like a silver blanket on the ground and the pale, smooth bark of the blue gum trees were cold to touch. Some days on the way to school, until the sun rose, your toes would freeze to death. We got a jersey for the winter and you could pull the sleeves over your hands, that helped a bit, but on cold mornings it wasn't really enough and you were cold as billyo.

Back to hot showers, which needed extra wood for the boilers. The work in the vegetable gardens was less in the winter and instead we had to chop wood on a Saturday morning. Or rather, the big boys who weren't in a school rugby team had to chop wood and all the small ones would be sent along the creek to gather tinder – old branches that had fallen and the ones you could reach to snap off.

I'd found this big branch and started to drag it back to the woodshed, which was a long way away, and by the time I got back the bell for lunch had gone and everyone had left. Lunch on a Saturday was just bread and jam that they left out on a long table on the *stoep*, and also coffee.

I knew it was useless trying to have some, because it was a free-for-all and we little kids didn't often get very much. Even if you ran like anything to be there first and stuffed some bread and jam into your mouth as fast as you could, you never got more than one slice down before the others arrived and then you'd better get out of the way fast, man!

With me bringing in the big branch I would have been much too late to get even a single bite. Maybe some crusts, but you couldn't guarantee it and that's why I always got double crusts for Tinker on Saturday. So I just stayed behind because there wasn't rollcall or a clean-hands inspection or anything like that on a Saturday. I dragged the branch to the big wooden box where we put kindling and started breaking off branches because they all had to be nearly the same size, about twelve inches.

That was when I saw a chopper resting on a woodblock. I'd always wanted to use a chopper but that wasn't allowed until you were ten years old. My hands were tired from breaking pieces of kindling, so I said to myself, Why not the chopper? Nobody was looking, so I picked it up and was surprised at how heavy it was. It wasn't one of those big choppers they used for splitting logs from tree trunks, just a small one called an axe, but it was still pretty heavy. I put a branch on the woodblock, took the chopper in both hands and lifted it up above my head and . . . *Crash!* Instead of chopping the branch in half like it was supposed to, the branch went flying into the air and landed several feet away. I remembered how I'd watched Mattress chop kindling for his fire when he cooked his *mieliepap* in the black three-legged *kaffir* pot he had. He'd hold one end of the stick and pick up the axe with one hand and, still holding the stick resting on the chopping block, he'd chop the stick in half, easy as can be, right in the middle.

So that's what I did and it worked easy as anything until I misjudged one stick and went *whack!* with the chopper and it cut deep into the forefinger of my left hand. At first there was nothing as I hopped up and down, but then the blood started to come out and I knew I was in the deep shit. If you got a cut doing something you weren't supposed to do you tried to hide it so no one could find out. But my finger seemed to be half off, not as bad as Mattress's lip, but I knew I couldn't hide it. I went to the dairy and found some of that old cheesecloth and wrapped it around my finger. It was soon red with blood because my finger wouldn't stop bleeding, and I knew I wouldn't be able to work without someone seeing it. So Tinker and me went over to the creek, because after lunch we had a free hour, and I washed it in the water, but the blood still kept coming.

There was nothing I could do but report to Mevrou at the sick room. On Saturdays she didn't like things happening, even though it wasn't her day off. She would have a good lie down in the afternoon. We knew this because if you went past the hydrangeas outside the sick-room window you could hear her snoring. She couldn't go to her own room in the staff quarters because she was supposed to be on duty, so she lay down on the doctor's leather examination couch where Pissy had told his pack of lies. Talk about sawing wood! Her snoring, if it was a cross saw, would have done the whole week's shower boiler supply in ten minutes flat.

So I crept through the hydrangeas to check to see if she wasn't asleep and she wasn't. She was sitting in a chair doing some embroidery of red roses, a tablecloth or something like that. So I crept back out of the bushes and went in and knocked on the sick-room door. By this time the cheesecloth was soaked and my finger was going throb-throb.

'Kom!' I heard her call, so I opened the door.

'What do you want?' she said, looking up. 'You know I don't like anyone to come in the afternoon, you must wait until after supper.'

'I don't think I can, Mevrou,' I said, holding up the red-coloured cheesecloth.

'Look out, you stupid boy!' she suddenly yelled. The cheesecloth couldn't take any more blood and some drops fell on the lino floor.

'Ek is baie jammer, Mevrou, I am very sorry, Mevrou,' I stammered, looking down at the crimson drops. Then I did a stupid thing and tried to wipe them away with the sole of my foot.

'Don't!' she yelled again. 'What do you think? I've got all day to clean up blood from the floor, hey?' She put her embroidery aside and went to a cupboard and found some cottonwool and told me to come over to the sink. She took the cheesecloth off and washed my finger. 'It needs stitches,' she announced. 'What have you gone and done, you stupid child?'

'I cut it on a sharp stone when I was looking for twigs, Mevrou,' I lied.

'You are nothing but trouble, *Voetsek*. When you first came here you wet your bed and had to get the *sjambok* every morning till it stopped. You always naughty and now you got that mongrel dog. It's a good thing it catches rats or we'd wring its neck, you hear? When your mother brought you she couldn't stop crying. If she loved you so much why didn't she keep you, hey? The Afrikaners wouldn't do that, crying in public like that. The bedroom is where a woman cries, not when her husband is around so he can hear. You a real little *kaffirboetie*, *Voetsek*, always talking to the Zulu that ran away up the mountains like he was a proper white man. You got no respect, you hear?'

I forgot to tell you that Sergeant Van Niekerk had taken fingerprints of Mattress off the alarm clock and sent them to Pretoria, together with the prints they took of him when he was dead. It was him all the time. So now everyone knew that the *kaffir* with no face was the pig boy and the victim of the lynching. But Mevrou *still* said he'd run away into the mountains.

'Sorry, Mevrou,' I said softly. She was the only one of the grown-ups to call me *Voetsek* and not by my Christian name.

'The lorry is broken down,' she said. 'You'll have to walk into town. Doctor Van Heerden has Saturday afternoon surgery at his house, do you know where it is?'

'*Nee*, Mevrou.'

'Ag, everybody knows where the doctor's house is,' she said impatiently. 'Just ask someone.'

'*Ja*, Mevrou.'

She dried the finger and some new blood came, but not too bad and much better than before. Then she wrapped my finger in a big wad of cottonwool and put some sticking plaster around to hold it. She gave me a cloth, a big one you use for drying dishes. 'If it bleeds some more, wrap around this dishcloth,' she instructed.

So I set off for town and just got to the gate when I thought, Why not take Tinker? So I went to the dairy and fetched her. It was nice, not so lonely with Tinker coming with me.

Mevrou had done a good job because I only had to use the dishcloth when I was almost in town. When I got there I went to the café where Sergeant Van Niekerk had taken me for the ice-cream with everything on top and the strawberry milkshake. Dogs couldn't come inside and Tinker had never been inside anywhere, except the shed behind the dairy. I told her to wait and she did, just outside the café. I entered expecting to find Mevrou Booysens, but she wasn't there. A girl, who was about sixteen, told me how to find the doctor's house. 'It's on stilts at the front, and you have to go around the side of the house where there's a path because the surgery is at the back, you hear?' I thanked her and turned to go when she asked, 'What's wrong?', pointing to the dishcloth, but there wasn't any blood showing through where she looked.

'I cut my finger,' I replied.

'Is it bad? How'd you do it?' she said, asking two questions at once.

'It needs stitches,' I said, feeling quite brave. 'I cut it with a rock,' I lied again.

'Do you want me to go with you?' she asked.

I shook my head. 'No, thank you, Miss, I can find it myself.'

'Ma!' she called out, then turned back to me. 'Wait, little boy.'

Mevrou Booysens came out from the back wiping her hands on her apron. 'Oh, hello,' she said, and seemed to recognise me, 'the ice-cream boy, isn't it?' She turned to the girl. 'He had all ten toppings on his ice-cream and still wasn't sick, then a milkshake. He's got a stomach like a cement-mixer,' she explained. 'You're from The Boys Farm, aren't you?'

'Ja, Mevrou.'

'And you also in town alone?'

'I've got my dog,' I answered.

'He's cut his finger and has to have stitches,' the girl explained. 'Can I take him to Doctor Van Heerden, Ma?'

'*Ja*, certainly,' Mevrou Booysens said. 'There should have been someone come with you in the first place.'

'They couldn't,' I explained. 'The lorry's broken.'

She shook her head and came around from behind the counter. 'Let me take a look, hey?'

I removed the dishcloth and she could see that the cottonwool under the sticking plaster was completely soaked with blood and there was quite a lot on the dishcloth, but it hadn't soaked through yet.

'*Here!* Those people on that Boys Farm should be ashamed!' She turned to the girl. 'Marie, take him quick, you hear?' Then she turned back to me. 'What colour sucker would you like? Where is your dog?'

Two questions at once again. Suckers don't come along every day of the week and you have to choose carefully. Green is nice but red is better. 'A red one please, Mevrou,' I answered. 'She's waiting at the door.'

'The boy has nice manners,' Mevrou Booysens said. 'What's your name, son?' she asked.

'*Voetsek*,' I said, not thinking.

'*Voetsek?*' she said, drawing back in surprise. 'I don't believe you!'

'That's what they call me because I'm English,' I explained. 'My real name is Tom.'

'They should be ashamed,' she said again. 'Calling a child a name like that.' She gave me a red sucker and unwrapped the top, carefully removing the cellophane. Then she took a yellow one and put it in the pocket of my khaki shirt. 'Sometimes you have to wait a bit. Saturday all the farmers come to see the doctor. Goodbye, Tom, come and see us some more, you hear? You always welcome at the Impala Café.'

The girl called Marie left me and Tinker when we got to the doctor's house and pointed to the path round the side that led to the surgery.

'Good luck, Tom,' she said. 'Come and visit again soon, hey.' She bent down and gave me a kiss. '*Totsiens*.' It was the first kiss I could ever remember getting, and it was nice and soft on my cheek. She patted Tinker, which was the first time a girl had patted her. 'Bring your dog next time also, we'll give him a nice bone,' she promised.

'He's a she,' I said, but I don't know if she heard because she'd already turned and was walking away. With all the distractions and a sucker and then a kiss and all, I hadn't noticed that my finger was really throbbing and the blood had now come through the dishcloth.

When I got to the surgery there were a whole lot of people there. Mevrou Booysens was right, they all seemed to be farm folk. You could tell because they'd brought stuff for the doctor. Here a sack of potatoes, there a case of mangoes or avocado pears, another sack of oranges, someone had six pineapples and one fat *tante* had a whole basketful of eggs and another auntie sat with a wooden box with jars of canned fruit and jam at her feet. Farm people don't like to visit the doctor empty-handed. Doctor Van Heerden was a very high-up person and they liked to give him something from the farm to show they trusted him. Even when he came to The Boys Farm he always got stuff from the vegetable garden and eggs from Meneer Prinsloo's black shiny-feathers chickens. The *Dominee* got the same. People brought stuff for him when they came to church. I don't suppose both of them ever had to buy anything to eat except flour and sugar, maybe some salt and coffee, stuff like that.

With all the farmers already waiting and being there a long time before me, I had to wait my turn. There was also an old dog asleep and I didn't want it to come and start a fight with Tinker, but it didn't take any notice or even open its eyes. So I went and sat with Tinker under a nearby mango tree because all the benches on the surgery *stoep* were already full. It was by now quite late in the afternoon and I must say I was beginning to feel very tired and glad I didn't have to walk any more because my legs felt weak. By now the dishcloth had turned red completely.

I must have fallen asleep because suddenly there was someone shaking me and it was getting dark and Tinker was growling. 'Wake up, little *boetie*,' a large woman said to me. 'Does your dog bite? Are you here to see the doctor?' Two questions again. Then she must have seen the dishcloth. 'Oh my God!' she exclaimed, drawing back. 'Get up quick and come and see the doctor!'

I tried to get up but I couldn't and the large auntie helped me to my feet, but I could hardly stand and my knees were wobbling on their own – knock, knock, knock.

'Just look at you!' she said, and I looked down and the whole front of my shirt was covered with blood. 'How long have you been waiting?' she asked.

'There were lots of farm people, eight, I had to wait, Mevrou.' I was still holding her hand so I could keep my balance and looked at the surgery veranda and there was nobody left, all the farmers had gone home to their farms. Only the old dog remained, still asleep.

'We were just closing the surgery,' she said. 'Can you walk? You've lost a lot of blood.'

With her help we got into the surgery and Tinker followed. When we got to the old dog I told Tinker to stay and the old dog got up and followed me. He sort of dragged his hind legs but I could see he liked me, his tongue was lolling out and he was panting even though all he'd done was lie asleep all day. I heard Tinker whine softly because she didn't want the old dog to go in and she had to stay outside. I think she thought it was unfair. Doctor Van Heerden was writing and looked up as we entered.

'What's this, Nurse?' The old dog lay down with a plop on the lino floor.

'He, this boy, he's been sitting under the mango tree, he's lost a lot of blood.'

'Yes, I can see.' He looked at me sternly. 'Why didn't you come straight in? When did you arrive, son? Why are you alone? Where are you from?' He pointed to a chair in front of his desk. 'Sit here.' Four questions and an instruction all at once, so I answered them backwards, in case I forgot the first one.

'The Boys Farm, Sir.'

'Who brought you?'

'Nobody, Sir, the lorry was broken so I had to walk, but I took my dog with me.'

He shook his head and got up from his chair, saying nothing as he became busy taking off the dishcloth, and then the sticking plaster and the cottonwool while I was hoping I could remember the last two questions. The old dog must have farted because suddenly there was this poo smell everywhere in the air.

'Helmut is a very old dog,' the doctor explained, shaking his head. 'We must respect the old and the young.' I think he was really saying he knew it wasn't me who'd farted.

He turned to the nurse and said, 'Make the boy a cup of coffee and put four teaspoons of sugar in.' He pulled the cottonwool away. 'Hmm, nasty! You're going to need stitches. What's your name, son?'

'Tom Fitzsaxby, Sir.' You can't go and just give your first name to a high-up person like a doctor, that much I knew for sure.

'You're the young lad who helped Sergeant Van Niekerk with his enquiries, aren't you?'

I now knew what an enquiry was, so I said, 'He asked me about Mattress's platform feet, Sir. He had this big photo.'

'Well done, Tom, I believe you were a great help to the police.'

'Meneer Prinsloo mustn't know, Sir,' I said quickly.

'Of course he mustn't, and he'll not get any information from me. I feel very sorry for the *Bantu*, your friend . . . Mattress. A great tragedy, sometimes I am ashamed of my *volk*, my people.' I wondered how he could know all this, but then I suppose doctors know everything. 'I'll just clean this up a bit. It may hurt so I must ask you to be brave because I can only give you an injection when I put in the stitches. How did this happen, Tom?'

Suddenly I was in a lot of trouble, you can't lie to a doctor or a preacher because it's like lying to God and you'll be found out and thrown into the everlasting fires of hell. 'With a chopper, Sir.'

'You were chopping wood? At *your* age?'

'No, I'm not allowed, only to collect kindling.'

'But the chopper was there and nobody was looking so you just picked it up and used it?' he asked. 'Next thing you nearly chopped off your finger.'

It's true! Doctors *do* know everything. I was glad I hadn't told him it was a rock. 'Yes, Sir,' I said, not wishing to look him in the eye, so I looked down at the bloodstains on my shirt and it was a good thing tomorrow was Sunday and clean-clothes day because I wouldn't be able to go to school in this shirt, that's for sure.

'Didn't you get into trouble with Mevrou Van Schalkwyk?'

I kept my head down and answered in a small voice, 'I told her a lie, Sir. That I'd done it on a sharp rock.' I glanced up at him. 'You won't tell Mevrou will you, Sir?'

He was cleaning my finger and it was hurting but his questions had distracted me. 'Lots of secrets, hey, Tom? Well, never you worry, doctors are good at keeping secrets and I don't think we'll bother to mention this one, eh?'

Doctors are very high-up persons and so I was surprised that he was turning out so nice.

The nurse came back with a cup of tea. 'The *boere* drank all the coffee, Doctor,' she said. Tea wasn't something we got a lot at The Boys Farm, only sometimes. I liked it and when I took a sip it was nice and sweet.

'Did Mevrou at The Boys Farm give you the sucker sticking out of your pocket?' Doctor Van Heerden asked.

I couldn't believe it! I'd clean forgot, here was a yellow sucker, a pineapple-flavoured sucker, in my pocket and I'd forgotten to suck it. Something must have been *really* wrong! 'No, Sir, it was Mevrou Booysens at the café, they told me where to come.'

'Gallstones. Terrible. Poor woman must have really suffered, never complained.' I hadn't the faintest idea what he was talking about. 'Now, I'm going to give you an injection so your finger will go dead before I put in the stitches,' the doctor said.

I must say I didn't much like the idea of having a dead finger. 'Will it drop off?' I asked.

'Will what?' Doctor Van Heerden asked, puzzled.

'When my finger goes dead, will it fall off my hand after it gets rotten?' I asked.

He laughed. 'It will come alive again in an hour or so,' he said. 'In the meantime the worst is over, you were very brave when I cleaned your finger, Tom.' It was another compliment from a high-up and I must say I liked it because I didn't think I was ever brave about anything before. Except, of course, the *sjambok* but that didn't count because if you cried it was worse for you. That was because of what the other guys would say about you being a *rooinek* who couldn't take it like a real man, and like all the English, you were a sissy. Even if your bum burned something terrible from six of the best you forced yourself not to cry.

When Doctor Van Heerden put in the needle to make my finger dead I nearly jumped through the roof. '*Eina!*' I yelled out, even though I didn't mean to.

'*Ja*, I don't like it myself when the dentist does it to me,' he said sympathetically.

He must have had the Government dentist pull out his teeth because Doctor Dyke with his horse pliers didn't believe in injections. After about five minutes, so I could drink my tea, he tested my finger.

'Can you feel this, Tom?' he asked and squeezed my finger. You could see him press the finger really hard and near the cut, but I couldn't feel a thing.

I shook my head. 'It's dead,' I declared.

He sewed up my finger, neat as anything, and put a bandage on it. The fat nurse had gone and got her handbag and said goodnight just after she brought me the cup of tea. She had a basket with two pineapples and some mangoes and avocadoes. Then the telephone rang and Doctor Van Heerden answered and said, 'Yes, fighting, *kaffir* beer, badly cut, gut, prepare the theatre, how many?' He turned to me. 'Tom, there's been a tribal fight in the native location and six *Bantu* men have been badly stabbed. I have to go to the hospital at once. Stay here and rest, I'll have someone call The Boys Home when I get to the hospital and have them pick you up. You've lost a lot of blood, so don't try and get up until you feel better, you hear? Don't leave on your own, you're not strong enough to walk back to The Boys Farm and it's quite dark outside. See Mevrou Van Schalkwyk in the morning and have her put on a fresh dressing.'

He pointed to my shirt pocket. 'Suck that sucker, it is sugar for energy.' Then he left and I heard him get into his '39 Chevvie with the dicky-seat and drive away.

I took the sucker from my shirt pocket and had some trouble removing the cellophane wrapper because I now had a giant bandage on my forefinger. Eventually, using my teeth, I got the wrapper off. I must say yellow was delicious, nearly as good as the red one, and from what I remember, better than the green, so perhaps I'd still take red any time but if someone ever offered me two, I might think about yellow instead of green.

I waited an hour and nobody came. I remembered that there was a *tiekiedraai* competition and dance at the town hall and probably Meneer Prinsloo was there with Mevrou Prinsloo because she was supposed to be a judge of folk dance and it was the district championship final that night. We knew this because after dinner on Friday, Meneer Prinsloo said that we all had to congratulate his lady wife because she had just been made head judge of folk dancing in the district. So we all clapped. He said on Saturday night she'd decide the fate of dancers who came from as far as Messina near the Rhodesian border and Nelspruit in the Lowveld. If the lorry was broken there was only Meneer Prinsloo's Plymouth, and maybe it was at the dance so they couldn't use it to fetch me, even if they wanted. Which I didn't think they would, because you needed to be dying for them to borrow the Plymouth that we had to wash and polish every week because it was the Government's property, the same as us.

I waited a long time and patted Helmut, the old dog that kept farting. I became very tired, so I left the surgery because Tinker was giving these little whines to tell me she was lonely out there on the *stoep*. I walked outside and the old dog followed me, slowly as anything, but still wagging his tail. Here's the funny thing, he just sniffed at Tinker and then they were friends. Not playing or anything, because Helmut was too old, but I think they liked each other. It was cold already and I didn't have my jersey.

Like Marie from the café said, Doctor Van Heerden's house was built on these stilts at the front because it was on the slope of a small hill, so I crept under the house with Tinker. It was getting very cold and I was hungry because I didn't have any lunch and now no supper. It was pitch-black under there and a cold wind was blowing, but luckily the veranda light was on and some light beams shone through the floorboards and I could see a large box. I crept towards it and lay down behind it to protect myself from the wind. Helmut had come with me and lay down next to me, with Tinker on my other side. I held them against my body, making sure my stitched and bandaged finger was out of the way if Tinker moved. Almost immediately I fell asleep in the soft dust, against a nice warm old dog and a little one. If Helmut farted I didn't know it because you can't smell things when you're fast asleep, not even smoke from a fire. Gawie Grobler said there was this man his uncle knew in Pretoria who was fast asleep when his house caught on fire and they called the fire brigade, and when they got there the flames were coming through the roof already and it was too late to go inside, but they knew this man was still in there because they could hear him snoring. That definitely proves that when you're asleep you can't smell things, not even smoke. The last thing I remember was that Tinker also hadn't eaten anything except her breakfast and some milk.

When I woke, early sunbeams were coming through the cracks in the floorboards where last night the light had come through. Tinker was licking my face. Helmut was still with us and now it was his turn to snore. I didn't know dogs snored, but he was nearly as bad as Mevrou. I felt a bit stiff from lying with my back against the big wooden box, so I stood up. I only had to bend my head a little to stand up straight. The box had a lid and the handle was right there in front of me so I lifted it. There was now enough light for me to see inside. It was full of mouldy old books.

It was then that I saw it. A strip of gold in the half-light that turned out to be the pages of a book with each page edged with gold. It had a red-leather jacket that was nearly all covered in green mould, and when I reached in and picked it up it felt slightly damp to the touch. I rubbed some of the mould away and you could see the name of the book done in gold lettering on the spine. I couldn't read what it said but I sort of instinctively knew it must be important, being all leather and gold. What I did know was that it was the most beautiful object I had ever seen and was seized with a terrible desire to own it. I just knew that inside that book was stuff I had to have to make my life good. It was not something I can explain, even today, but I was possessed of a certainty that I must own this wonderful object.

And that's when the devil entered me. I took the book and stuffed it inside my bloodstained shirt. I didn't know the time, it was still early, but it couldn't have been too early because the sun was up. If I was late for breakfast or Mevrou had come into the small boys' dormitory, which sometimes she didn't on a Sunday, or if everyone had left for church already I couldn't imagine how many cuts from the *sjambok* I'd get, maybe a world record.

I couldn't really run too hard because of this big book inside my shirt that I had to hold against my stomach with one hand while also holding my newly stitched finger out so it was safe. The streets were deserted but I passed the night cart with all the full tins on the back and three *kaffirs* sitting on the front of the wagon with one of them driving the four mules. If you think Helmut was bad, how those shit boys could stand it I just don't know. They had hessian sacks cut open on one side that went over their heads and covered their backs, and from the night's collecting they'd spilled a whole lot down their backs. But they didn't seem to care and they were laughing and chatting and they greeted me as I went past holding my nose with my good hand and the book jumping up and down inside my shirt. The driver patted the seat beside him and said, 'Kom op, Kleinbasie,' inviting me to sit next to him and they all nearly fell off the wagon, they were laughing so much. It's funny how people can work on the night cart and still laugh. I was very glad the cart was full and moving very slowly and not so fast that I couldn't get ahead of it because the sewage farm was in the same direction as me and Tinker were going, and can you imagine if we'd had to run behind it all the way back to The Boys Farm. Though I've noticed that dogs seem to quite enjoy bad smells.

You can sometimes get lucky in life and on a Sunday morning we got our clean clothes before breakfast. I just got back in time to hide the book in the hydrangea bushes and send Tinker to the kitchen to get his scoff, take a shower and be at the very back of the line. What happened is this, you'd take a shower and put your dirty clothes in a big wooden box and in this room next to the showers they put your new shirt and khaki shorts with your name on the inside. Even if you couldn't read everyone knows what his own name looks like on his shirt and shorts. But anyway, mine were the last still there. I just got to breakfast in time, the last to go in. Talk about lucky!

Because it was Sunday and Mevrou was going to see her sister I didn't go to the sick room like I was supposed to, anyway my finger wasn't throbbing or anything. It was trudge, trudge, trudge back to town to church.

'You lucky hey, Voetsek,' said Gawie Grobler. 'Mevrou didn't come into the dormitory for half-jack this morning so she didn't know you weren't there all the time, man. They all went to the dance in the lorry and came back very late.' Which explained her early morning absence.

'But the lorry was broken,' I protested.

'Broken? Nah, we had to go and clean it yesterday afternoon so it would be nice to take everyone to the *tiekiedraai* competition,' Gawie said.

Then they wanted to know where I'd been for the whole night. 'Ag, I stayed at the doctor's,' I said, trying to sound casual. I could see they were impressed, me not only staying in a real house, but in the house of a high-up person. I told them about having stitches and how your finger is dead but then comes alive again. When someone asked what the doctor's house was like I was in a bit of trouble, so I said, 'They drink tea with lots of sugar in it and the doctor's got all these books and an old dog called Helmut who farts and snores a lot.' They laughed about the farting and snoring, but I wasn't important enough for them to ask any more questions so, thank goodness, it turned out all right in the end.

When we got back to The Boys Farm after church, I went and found an old paraffin tin with the top cut off and the sharp edges hammered down. There were lots of these because when they were empty you'd put a wire handle on them so that you could use them in the vegetable gardens as buckets to water the orange and avocado pear trees. Old ones that had a leak were thrown away and it was one of these tins I went and got. Tinker and I went back to the big rock where she used to stay and I placed the tin in the hole that used to be her kennel. Then I fetched the book from under the hydrangeas and put it in the tin and covered up the entrance so rain couldn't get in and people passing by wouldn't see it. Not that anyone ever came to the big rock now that Fonnie du Preez had gone to reform school in Pretoria and Pissy Vermaak had been sent to Pietersburg to be closer to his mother.

Every day Tinker and I would visit the book that I'd cleaned up and you could hardly see where the green mould had been on the nice red-leather cover. I don't know why, but I just liked to hold that book, which was sort of warm and alive and you'd turn some of the gold-edged pages and the words would dance up at you, millions of them, like gnats buzzing in the air. Sometimes I thought about taking it back and creeping under the doctor's house and putting it in that big wooden box. But then I'd think it was like burying it again and I loved it to be alive the way it was

with the words dancing like that. I knew I'd committed a sin stealing it
and sometimes sitting in church with the *Dominee* raging on about the
English and the beetle he'd have chomping away at his beard I'd feel
guilty and decide to take it back, but when I held it again, I couldn't.

Lots of weeks went by and holidays came and went. Not that the
holidays were much use to us because we had to work in the vegetable
garden and around the place so that school was better. Some of the big
boys were allowed to go and work on farms during the holidays, which
they liked a lot, but it meant us little ones had to work a bit harder
when they were gone. Christmas came and we had jelly and ice-cream
and two new shirts and pants from the Government and roast pork for
Christmas dinner with second helpings and roast potatoes. At church
on the Christmas morning the *Dominee* didn't say anything against the
English because 'It was a time of peace and goodwill towards all men and
a Saviour was born on this day to die for all of us regardless of colour or
creed. Christmas was the best time to confess our sins because we and
not Jesus were born in sin and could only be saved if we were born all
over again in His precious name. We'd be washed in the blood of the
lamb.'

With all this being-born-again stuff going on I wondered if I should
tell about the book and confess my sins, but then the *Dominee* said, 'We
will become as innocent as a little child when we give our lives to the
Lord Jesus Christ.' So me being a little child and all and, besides, I didn't
much like the idea of being washed in lambs' blood, I decided I must be
innocent. I'd had a bit too much blood in my life lately, so I thought it
best to say nothing about the book and wait until I was grown up and
had become an official sinner and then I'd tell about stealing it from
under Doctor Van Heerden's house.

Christmas was soon over and nothing much changed around the
place. But when school started I was pretty excited because I was going to

learn to read. Juffrou Marais, my teacher, said I was even further behind the class that had been seven the beginning of the previous year and now were all eight and I was still seven until May. So I had to start with the reading beginners who'd just turned seven this year, even though I was now seven and three-quarters.

'Please, Juffrou, can I try to catch up?' I begged.

'Most of them have turned eight and you're still seven until May. It's the rules, you have to start with the beginner class and you can't just jump a whole year when you don't know the first thing about reading,' she replied. 'Besides, I don't have time to give you extra lessons, you hear?'

So from being the youngest in the class I'd suddenly become the oldest at learning to read. It didn't seem fair, but then fairness wasn't something you came across much so I decided I'd learn extra hard. I didn't know if I was clever because nobody ever told us if you were, but I thought I'd just work at learning because I wanted to read my big red book more than anything in the world.

You must think I'm stupid because it was a grown-up book and little kids can't just start out reading books like that but I told myself that there would be words in there that I recognised. Maybe only the very little ones, but that didn't matter because I would grow up one day and be able to read them all. I soon became the best reader in the class and, even if I say so myself, I left all the other kids in the dust. But when, every day, I went to the big rock with Tinker and we'd sit down and I'd take my big red book out and open it, nothing happened. I'd search and search but couldn't find a single word I could recognise until one day I found 'die', which means 'the' in Afrikaans. I can tell you, that was a day and a half! I was pretty pleased with myself. At last I'd begun the long journey into the dancing words. But alas, my progress halted with this single word because I couldn't find any others I'd learned from the primers they gave us to read at school. You'd think you'd find some, but with the exception of 'die' there was nothing. I couldn't understand this, because all the words we learned were ones you could speak, but when it came to my book they'd all disappeared.

Suddenly my life changed forever. Juffrou Marais, who we all thought was just getting slowly fat because she'd got married the year before, left because she was going to have a baby. A new teacher, Juffrou Janneke Phillips, who Meneer Van Niekerk, the headmaster, said was 'only temporary' and was a practice teacher from Johannesburg, came to take our class. She was very pretty and looked quite young and had red nails and was nice to us all and we soon liked her a lot. After a week or so Juffrou Phillips said I must stay back after school to see her. I was a bit worried because if we didn't march back to The Boys Farm after school we had to have a note from our teacher to say why we had to stay back. If it was because of something bad that you'd done you got double punishment, one from the school and the other from Mevrou. I forgot to say they always checked us at line-up when we got back from school. So you can see, I was a bit anxious when all the other kids traipsed out and I was left sitting at my desk.

'Tom, why are you in this reading class? Your reading is far better than any of the other children,' my teacher said.

'I don't know, Juffrou, maybe because I'm a bigger seven than they are.'

'Did you all start learning to read at the same time?'

'Ja, Juffrou.'

'So you think you're more mature, is that it?'

'What's mature mean, Juffrou?'

'No, I don't think that's it,' she said, as if she was speaking to herself. 'I'm going to put you up with the eights, you're a lot better reader than most of them.'

'Juffrou Marais said the Government won't allow it,' I replied.

She laughed. 'In this class I am the Government,' she said, then added, 'I'm not holding a bright child back because of what the Government says.'

So I was put up with the eight-year-old readers where I seemed to go pretty okay and then Juffrou Phillips put me up a class with all my other subjects as well. But nothing helped. Now I was reading well but still no words appeared that I could find in my red book.

Up to that time I hadn't really trusted anyone who was a grown-up, except Mattress. You couldn't count Sergeant Van Niekerk because, like Doctor Van Heerden, while they'd been nice to me I didn't really know them except for two occasions over Mattress with the sergeant and only a stitched-up finger with the doctor. They were both high-ups and people like me couldn't really count them as grown-ups we knew as someone to trust. I talked to Tinker about Juffrou Phillips and asked her what she thought, should I show her the red book? I know that's stupid because a dog doesn't talk or anything, but sometimes you can just tell what they're thinking and Tinker was a very clever dog, I can assure you. You'd ask her something and she'd cock her head and look at you and often she'd give this little bark, so you knew she knew what you were saying. We decided to trust Juffrou Phillips.

During morning break when we all got a small bottle of milk and a bun, because of the rural malnutrition program the Government had, I asked if I could talk to her after school. When she said yes, I also asked if she'd give me a note to say it was all right for me to come back to The Boys Farm not in the crocodile.

After school I showed her my red book with the gold-edged pages. It was getting a bit dirty and old-looking from me always turning the pages, and I suppose my hands weren't always clean.

'What's this, Tom?' she asked.

'It's a book I found, Juffrou.'

'Yes, I can see that, but why are you showing it to me?'

'Please, Juffrou, can you teach me to read what's in it?'

She picked up the book and read the gold words on the spine that had faded a bit. 'Abolition of Slavery 1834,' she read aloud.

'None of the words are the same as you're teaching us, Juffrou,' I declared.

She laughed. 'I don't suppose so, this book is written in English!'

'Can you teach it to me, please, Juffrou?'

'Can you speak English, Tom? Your name, Fitzsaxby, is that English?'

'I think I could once before I came to The Boys Farm, but I'm not sure.' In the hope that it might influence her, I added, 'Everybody says I'm English and a *verdomde rooinek*.'

She sighed. 'Children are so cruel. You can't even speak the language and they call you a damned redneck.' She seemed to be thinking for a bit, then she sighed again. 'I'm only here for another month or two at the most, it's not enough time.'

'Please, Juffrou!' I begged. 'Just so I can find some words in my book.'

She looked at me and took both my hands in hers. I could see her red nails were quite long and shone up at me bright as anything and I thought her hands looked so beautiful they shouldn't ever be used for writing things on the blackboard.

'Tom, this isn't the kind of book you can learn to read,' she said softly. She must have seen the look of disappointment on my face because she quickly added, 'until you're a lot older.'

'How old must I be?' I asked tremulously. The idea that I might never be able to read the dancing words was unthinkable.

'Just older,' she said kindly. 'In the meantime I'll tell you what I'm going to do. I'm going to see the headmaster and ask him if I can put you on the English lessons the ten-year-olds in grade five do when it is compulsorily in the curriculum for English to be taught as a second language. I feel sure you'll manage their books quite easily.'

'Then will I be able to read my red book, Juffrou?'

'Probably not right away,' she paused and smiled. 'Now, Tom Fitzsaxby, when we talk English together you don't call me Juffrou Phillips, you call me Miss Phillips or just Miss.'

'*Ja*, Miss,' I said.

'Yes, Miss,' she corrected.

I couldn't explain it but I sensed this was an important moment. As it turned out, it was more important than I could have possibly imagined. Far beyond being a carpenter or a boilermaker or a lorry driver or a bulldozer driver on the roads or an engine driver on the railways – all the things we were told were good skilled grown-up jobs for us if we worked very hard.

Miss Phillips forgot to give me the note for Mevrou and I was so excited that I didn't remember either so I got four of the best when I got back to The Boys Farm. You see, I couldn't tell Mevrou that I'd stayed back so that I could ask to be given reading in English lessons because then I would have truly been in the deep shit.

You could hear already what she'd say. 'So Afrikaans isn't good enough for a certain person who's a *rooinek*, hey?' *Whack!* 'You think we, the true *volk*, are not good enough for you, hey?' *Whack!* 'You kill our women and children and then you think you a better type of person.' *Whack!* 'You just a *verdomde rooinek!*' *Whack!* 'Ever since you come here, *Voetsek*, you nothing but trouble, man.' *Whack!* 'And if that's not bad enough, you a *kaffirboetie* making friends with that pig boy who ran away up into the mountains!' *Whack!* 'Take six of the best!' *Whack!* 'It's seven I know, but I've given you one extra because I've had *genoeg!*' No whack.

So I told Mevrou I'd gotten into trouble and my teacher made me stay back. It was worth the four new bits of Chinese writing on my bum because soon I'd be reading my red book. You see, I couldn't believe I'd have to wait until I was grown up to understand it. Not that Miss Phillips said that exactly, but sometimes you can hear what grown-up people are thinking in their heads.

CHAPTER SIX

Not Having a Friend for Love or Money

NOW I THINK I have to spend a little time telling you about Tinker who had become the champion ratter around the place. So much so that she was allowed to go everywhere with me, and both Meneer Prinsloo and Frikkie Botha would boast about her to people who visited The Boys Farm. I'm not saying that she was more of a pride than the shiny-feathered, crust-eating Black Orpingtons because Tinker had never won a ribbon at an agricultural show or anything like that. But Meneer Prinsloo kept a tally of the rats she'd caught and he'd say to visitors, 'See that little dog, so far he's caught 120 rats.' He never did understand that Tinker was a she, because you had to be a he to have done something good like that. Frikkie Botha would tell him the tally for the day and on two occasions Tinker had appeared in the after-supper news when she'd got eight rats. Not that her name was mentioned with mine. She'd all of a sudden become The Boys Farm official ratcatcher, like that was her job and everyone owned her and both times she got the eight rats she got a dining-room clap.

Frikkie Botha would refer to Tinker as 'my little rat trap' and brag about her prowess to everyone. They all seemed to have forgotten that they wanted to wring her neck in the beginning. In their heart of hearts they knew Tinker was a one-man dog and I was that man.

Frikkie Botha did one really good thing for Tinker. This big dog from Doctor Dyke's farm, the vet who pulled out our teeth with his horse pliers, came sniffing around Tinker's bum and tried to mount her. But he was an Alsatian like Sergeant Van Niekerk's dogs and Tinker was a very small fox terrier and luckily it didn't work. Frikkie Botha saw what was happening and he called Doctor Dyke who, for once in his life, came over to The Boys Farm to do his real job and fixed Tinker up so she couldn't have puppies.

When I was eight Tinker started coming to school with me and she'd wait outside the classroom all day. At morning break when we got our bun and milk for malnutrition, the kids who brought sandwiches from home and didn't want their buns would try to give her bits to eat, but unless I said so she wouldn't touch the food they offered. The password was '*Izinyawo ezinkulu zika Mattress*' which means 'Mattress's big feet' in Zulu. I know that's a bit of a mouthful but I didn't want Tinker to ever forget Mattress because if it hadn't been for him putting her on the sow's teats she wouldn't be alive. It also constantly reminded me of Mattress whom I had loved. Unless I said this password Tinker would simply lie with her nose next to a nice piece of roast beef from a rich kid's sandwich or half a *boerewors* that I would have liked to eat myself and she'd not move an inch.

Once I must have been playing or something and someone gave her a piece of *biltong*, which would be a super special treat for any dog, and the bell went for us to go back into the classroom. After school Tinker wasn't outside waiting for me. I called out and she came running up, then she ran back a bit and waited and gave this little bark and cocked her one black ear to encourage me to follow, and did it again and again until we'd reached the piece of *biltong* and then she lay down with her front paws on either side of the *biltong*, her nose next to it, and looked up at me pleadingly until I said, '*Izinyawo ezinkulu zika Mattress.*' She was suddenly the happiest dog in the whole world as she chewed on that piece of *biltong* as if all her Christmases had come at once. She'd waited three hours beside it, the delicious smell of the dried meat going up her nostrils, driving her crazy with desire.

Tinker knew when I was sad. She'd come and sit on my lap and lick the back of my hand. She could do tricks like balance on her hind legs and dance or jump up into your arms from a standing position and, of course, fetch a ball and return it. Here's the best thing she could do. Every morning she'd lay the rats that she caught during the night neatly in a row on the dairy steps and when Frikkie Botha would come to open the dairy he'd say, 'How many today, Tinker?' If there were six Tinker would bark six times, if four, then four barks and so on and so forth.

But here's the funny thing. If Frikkie Botha put six stones in a row and asked Tinker how many, she'd simply ignore him. If *I* asked, she'd bark the number of stones. You see, she knew Frikkie Botha was in charge of the ratcatching operation so she'd oblige him because that was her official job. Tinker wasn't bred on The Boys Farm for nothing, she knew when to fall into line. For everything else she only listened to me. I have to admit she couldn't count past eight and I think that's because that was her ratcatching record for one night. Now I know I said earlier that I'd send her to the kitchen to get her scoff, but I'd always say the word before she went so she knew she could eat the food the kitchen boys put out for her and then, after a while, I got them to say '*Izinyawo ezinkulu zika Mattress*' so she knew that she could take her food at the kitchen when she heard the words from one of the kitchen staff. I even taught Tinker to say thank you when she'd finished her food. She would sit up on her hind legs and bark two woofs – 'Woof! Woof!' – and the Shangaans in the kitchen would clap their hands and laugh and they'd remember to save her a nice bone or something. Old Mevrou Pienaar the cook who had four cats loved Tinker. Even the cats liked her as much as cats can. You can see, while she remained a one-man dog, she was an all-round hit with just about everyone except Mevrou who associated Tinker with Mattress and me, so Tinker couldn't be liked by her and Tinker'd always give Mevrou a wide berth.

As I said before, there wasn't much love going on around that place. Plenty of *sjambok*, but no love. I can say this for sure, I loved Tinker so much I would sometimes burst into tears just thinking about how much she meant to me. You'd hold her in your arms and her little heart would be going boom-boom-boom and you'd feel this big lump rising in your throat and there'd be tears in your eyes and before you knew it, you'd be sobbing.

I would spend another three-and-a-bit years at The Boys Farm until I was eleven and still too small to really have an influence around that place. Thanks to Miss Phillips who went to see the headmaster I was elevated two classes to learn English and he decided to try me with the other lessons as well. I must have satisfied him because I remained two years ahead of my age group. This act of generosity by the headmaster didn't help me an awful lot at The Boys Farm, because suddenly I was in the same class as Gawie Grobler and I was supposed to be just as smart as him because I was in the same class. But I was still a *verdomde rooinek* so being smart didn't count, nobody was going to ask my opinion anyway. I'd still get the *sjambok* lots – 'You think you so clever, hey, *Voetsek!* Take four of the best!' *Whack! Whack! Whack! Whack!*

I didn't really learn much English at school. This was because it was taught to us by the Afrikaans language teachers with little enthusiasm. The Government made it compulsory so they had to do it. Their dilatory lessons were received with even less inclination from their pupils. It made no sense to an Afrikaner kid to learn the language of the enemy and they all failed at the end of each year except Gawie Grobler and me. Nobody could see the point of learning a language they were forbidden by their parents to use, the same language that had condemned 27 000 women and children to death in the British concentration camps only a little while ago so that their grandmothers could still remember what went on.

What really happened concerning me learning the English language was this. After three months Janneke Phillips completed her temporary teaching and returned to Johannesburg. When she told me she had to leave I tried very hard not to cry.

'Can't you stay just a bit longer, Miss?' I stammered.

'Tom, I'm only a temporary, and I still have six months in teachers' college,' she explained.

'But you don't need to learn more, you're the best there is already,' I protested.

She smiled and took my hand. 'Thank you, Tom, but I have to get my certificate or I can't teach. But let me say, it's been a real pleasure teaching you and I wish it could go on too. Who knows, maybe it can, we'll see, hey?'

In the time she was at Duiwelskrans she'd given me English lessons every day, but in three months you don't learn a whole language, although after every lesson she'd write down notes on my progress and was a source of constant encouragement to me. I was getting praise all over the place, and I must say I lapped it up.

Now, before I tell you the rest I don't want you to think that because her surname was Phillips that she was English, because she wasn't. Her great-great-grandfather or even earlier came from the Cape, which is right at the bottom of South Africa. You see, the English had owned the Cape of Good Hope since 1795 when they took it over from the Dutch. There must have been a Phillips who came out from England way back then. But he married a person who spoke the Dutch language and that soon put an end to where he came from. Miss Phillips' ancestors from then on had been Afrikaners. Eventually they joined the Great Trek when the Boere left the Cape because of the laws the English were making that they didn't agree with. They crossed the Fish River in their ox wagons and kept going into unknown territory to eventually establish their own republics in the Orange Free State and the Transvaal. There must have been lots of sons in Miss Phillips' family because the surname persisted.

Although she was proudly Afrikaner, Miss Phillips spoke English fluently because she came from Johannesburg, where mostly English was spoken. It's important that you know all this, because I don't want you to think that this English teacher suddenly arrived in the town and rescued the little should-have-been-an-English boy who couldn't speak his own language. Nothing of the sort happened. What really happened was that I got called to the headmaster's office one morning.

I knocked on the open door.

'Come in, Tom,' Meneer Van Niekerk said in English, which was the first big surprise.

'*Dankie*, Meneer,' I said, thanking him in Afrikaans. '*Jy het my geroep, Meneer?* You called for me, Sir?'

'Yes, Tom, come and sit down,' he said in English again, which was very puzzling coming from a high-up Afrikaner like him.

I walked in and stood in front of his desk.

'No, sit down, Tom, I have a nice surprise.' He looked up and smiled. 'From now in this office we will always speak English. Outside my office, it's Afrikaans. Inside here, English. Do you understand me?'

I still didn't much like sitting down in front of him but you have to do what a headmaster says, so I sat on the chair in front of his desk. '*Ja*, Meneer,' I stammered.

'No, Tom, what did I just say? Your reply to me is "Yes, Sir."'

'Yes, Sir,' I said tentatively. It was like any moment God would strike me with a bolt of lightning. It would come right through the roof and I'd be the same as the man in Pretoria that Gawie Grobler's uncle said was still snoring when the fire brigade came and couldn't get in, and then afterwards they found only ashes where he'd once been. But nothing happened except one thing; my feet now touched the floor when I sat on the chair.

He pointed to a big brown envelope on the desk in front of him. 'This came for you, Tom.'

'*Ek*, Meneer?' I said in surprise, clean forgetting the agreement we'd just made. I'd never received anything from anybody in my life and all of a sudden I'm receiving parcels from all over the place!

'From Miss Phillips in Johannesburg. She's written you a letter she has asked me to read to you.'

Already I was getting lost with all the English words he was using.

Some I understood, but I'd never had a letter and I hadn't seen too many either. 'I have a letter, Sir?' I asked to make sure I understood. It didn't seem possible that someone so low down as me could receive a letter with a stamp on the outside that you had to tear open to see what it said on the inside. I felt sure I must have misunderstood.

'A letter in English, Tom,' he said, not chastising me this time for replying in Afrikaans. 'Now, you probably won't understand it all but I'll repeat everything in Afrikaans afterwards.'

I didn't understand much of that last sentence, let alone the letter, only when he repeated it all in Afrikaans. The letter I have to this day, it's kept inside the pages of the red book.

My dear Tom,

I have written to Meneer Van Niekerk concerning you. I have asked him to read this letter to you. I don't expect you'll understand all of it until you're more proficient in your own language, but I'm sure he'll explain.

I have enclosed a book for you to read. It is the first in what I hope will one day be your own library. With the book is a list of questions and some writing paper. What I want you to do is to read the book and answer the questions in English and send them back to me in the self-addressed envelope, also enclosed.

You will receive a new book with questions every two weeks when I will also comment on the answers you gave to the last set of questions I received from you. It will be like a test, but one that you should enjoy doing.

I feel sure that between us we'll soon have you reading English fluently and while I don't think you'll get much opportunity to talk it as a language, writing and understanding it is the most important thing for the time being.

Just remember, Tom Fitzsaxby, I am very proud of you and I know we can do this together.

With love,
Janneke Phillips (Miss)

And so began my love for the written word and I also got my first 'With love'. I would read the books she'd send at every available moment and then again and, if the book wasn't too long, once more before I would attempt the questions she'd send along with it.

After a while she began to send me poems that she encouraged me to learn off by heart and to repeat aloud to myself. I'd sit on the big rock with Tinker and recite William Wordsworth's 'Daffodils' to her and would wonder who the daffodils were, an army or something like that who had golden shields or helmets maybe, and there were a lot of them because they appeared in a host. It was only much later that I learned they were only flowers and I must say I was disappointed, that's a lot of trouble to take over some yellow flowers.

Soon the books became longer and more exciting, and reading became a life for me where there was no *sjambok*, no Mevrou, no Boys Farm. I recall crying my heart out over Hans Christian Andersen's fairy tales, 'The Little Match Girl' in particular, with 'The Little Mermaid' and 'The Ugly Duckling' not too far behind in the crying stakes.

From there I took a leap into *Peter Pan* and *Robinson Crusoe*, then even higher to Charles Dickens and *Oliver Twist* to name but a few of the many books she sent as I grew older and more proficient. When I was nine I received a dictionary from Miss Phillips as a Christmas present. It was a big book, nearly as big as the red book, and had every word in it that was in the whole English language. Miss Phillips said I should learn a new word every day and try to write it in a sentence and send every day's sentence to her along with the questions she'd ask about the latest book she'd sent me.

I never gave up on the red book and from the very beginning read from it every day but still with almost no comprehension. With the arrival of the dictionary it started to unravel bit by bit. I'd be lying if I said it was as interesting as the books Miss Phillips sent me, because it wasn't. Later I would realise that it was dry legal writing in old-fashioned English, but it was mine and I loved it and would learn whole pages off by heart. This ability to retain the information in it word for word in large lumps would hold me in good stead later in life.

Children are never sufficiently grateful for those things that are done gratuitously for them. It may be the inability of children to return advantages that are bestowed on them that makes it seem that they take them for granted. While I was aware that Janneke Phillips was single-handedly bringing about a change in my life, I didn't know to what end or even comprehend the work and attention she so lavishly showered upon me. I simply had no tangible way to thank her for the gift of learning and, as I later perceived, the love she so willingly gave to me. I saw only the schoolteacher who was at times a hard taskmaster and I tried very hard to please her with my work. I recall I once wrote to her about Tinker and told Miss Phillips how her way of saying thank you was 'Woof–Woof' and thereafter always wrote 'Woof–Woof' on the bottom of the completed questionnaire or essay she'd set for me. I think Miss Phillips liked that because once in haste I neglected to write it at the bottom of a lesson. When the new book arrived there was a small note included that asked if I was displeased with her for some reason as my 'Woof–Woof' was missing from the bottom of the last lesson.

I would very much have liked to have bought her a gift but we were never given any money and I wasn't old enough to work on a farm during the school holidays when the boys who were would come back to The Boys Farm with ten shillings.

Then, out of the blue, something happened. One of the exercises Miss Phillips had sent down was to do with these similes. You know, 'Free as a —' and then you'd think a bit and write 'bird' in the space provided. Right after 'Free as a bird' came 'Light as a —' and, of course, I wrote 'feather'.

That's when I had my big idea. You see, I'd told myself that even if I found something that I could send Miss Phillips I wouldn't have any money to send it to her. I couldn't put it in the self-addressed envelope with my homework because you paid the Government money for stamps and if what you sent was more than you paid then there'd be lots of trouble, and they'd maybe fine her. But this idea was perfect. I decided to send her a tail feather from one of Meneer Prinsloo's shiny-feathered roosters. It would be so light it could easily go into the self-addressed envelope I used when my work was completed and returned to her.

So Tinker and I would visit the chicken house every day to see if a feather had dropped off. But God must have glued those big feathers that stick out of the backside of a rooster very, very tight because one just didn't drop off.

One day I got Tinker to bail up a rooster and I grabbed hold of his tail feathers and pulled with all my might and four feathers came out, and it was like a miracle; every one of them was perfect. They were long and curved and so shiny-black you could see other colours like purple and green in them. Another miracle was they fitted into the large envelope Miss Phillips had sent without bending them. Then they were off all the way to Johannesburg with my work, the first gift I had ever been able to send to anyone. I must say I felt very pleased with myself.

What a catastrophe! That night after dinner Meneer Prinsloo stood up and you could see immediately something was very wrong because his stomach was pushed way out with the braces straining to breaking point, and his hands were flapping ten to the dozen in the air.

'Who has destroyed Piet Retief?' he shouted. Piet Retief was a famous Afrikaner leader in the Great Trek and he'd been dead over a hundred years so we didn't know what Meneer Prinsloo was going on about. 'Next week is the agricultural show in Pietersburg! Now somebody has stolen his tail feathers!' He'd gone all red in the face and his hands had become windmills. 'Tail feathers don't just fall out of a Black Orpington rooster, you hear? Somebody here is sabotaging my chance to win the silver cup and blue ribbon, not only in Pietersburg next week but at the Rand Easter Show in Johannesburg, the biggest in the whole land, you hear?'

Thank God we were sitting at the table because I could feel my knees starting to shake. If only Meneer Prinsloo had known Piet Retief's tail feathers were on their way to Johannesburg already.

'*Wragtig*! Let me tell you one thing is certain. I will find the boy who done this act of sabotage, whoever he is! He won't get away with it! Now I only have General Botha to put in the Pietersburg show and he's not good enough for the Rand Easter Show. I want all the boys who are responsible for feeding the chickens to stay behind. I'm going to get to the bottom of this if it takes all night, you hear? To do such a thing to an innocent person's chicken is a criminal act against mankind!'

The three boys on chicken-feeding duty that week each got the *sjambok* and came back from Meneer Prinsloo very grumpy, but they didn't complain because that's how it was. You often got punished for stuff you didn't do. It was called 'getting cuts on appro'. Nobody knew what appro meant until I looked it up in my dictionary. It meant on approval. Gawie Grobler said he'd like to know who approved them because *he* certainly didn't, and trust an English word to be for something nasty you got for nothing.

You probably think I should have admitted to pulling out Piet Retief's tail feathers but that's not how things worked on The Boys Farm. Even the guys who got the *sjambok* would have thought I was mad if I'd confessed. There was this unspoken rule, outside The Boys Farm you were honest, inside it was every boy for himself and you didn't complain when something unfair happened to you.

I kept all Miss Janneke Phillips's letters except one that I learned off by heart and tore up into little pieces and watched them float down the creek to who knows where. It was this one.

My dearest Tom,

What a lovely surprise! Thank you for the four beautiful feathers and now I have a story to tell you. Up here at this time of the year we have a large agricultural show called the Rand Easter Show and we also have the Easter Show Handicap which is a big horse race held at a racecourse named Turfontein. My father always takes me to these races and every year there is a prize for the best hat – the Easter Bonnet Prize.

All the ladies go in for this competition and spend a fortune on their hats and guess who won it this year? Me! Hooray! With a hat that featured your four beautiful feathers! I received a silver cup and a cheque for ten pounds!

I am enclosing a one-pound note as your share of the bounty, so don't spend it all at once on sweets and make yourself thoroughly sick.

Your essay on A Tale of Two Cities was very good. You're coming along splendidly.

With gratitude and love,
Janneke Phillips

Now I had a 'With gratitude and love' to add to all my 'With love's and a 'My *dearest* Tom' to add to my 'Dear Tom's but I couldn't keep the letter in case it was discovered and taken to Meneer Prinsloo. I thought very hard about this, telling myself that no one in the small boys dormitory could read English, not even Mevrou. But eventually discretion seemed the best way to go so I tore it up, like I said. In life you got to think ahead. You see, we didn't have any private space like lockers or anything. We had to keep our schoolbooks or anything else we had under our beds at the very end concealed by the towel hanging down, everything neatly stacked because if it was untidy or something got dusty you got the *sjambok*.

So now there was the one-pound note, which was the most money I'd ever heard that a boy could have. The sixteen-year-olds that worked on the farms all school holidays only got ten shillings from the farmer at the end of the holiday, so I had two holiday-works' worth in one hit and for doing nothing as well. How and where was I ever to hide such a treasure? If anyone saw it, then it was gone for sure as God made little apples. One of the big guys would soon have it in his pocket. Even the ten shillings the big guys got for working on someone's farm was handed to Meneer Prinsloo by the farmer and the boy who did the work got two shillings to spend and a receipt for eight shillings that he could reclaim when he left The Boys Farm. If you worked every holiday from when you were allowed at fifteen you could leave the place with three pounds for the two years of working because there were three school holidays every year long enough for you to work through.

Now I had one pound and the terrible responsibility of hiding it where it couldn't be stolen. Worse still, I couldn't spend any of it because they'd see me eating a sucker or even an Eskimo Pie and they'd think I must have stolen some money to get it. 'Now you a terrible little thief, *Voetsek!' Whack! Whack! Whack!* 'Stealing money for suckers!' *Whack! Whack! Whack!* 'Six of the best is not good enough, you have to learn a lesson, you hear?' *Whack! Whack!* 'Take eight!' No whack. And that's only if I didn't get sent to Meneer Prinsloo for the long-cane *sjambok*. Stealing a pound would probably also get you sent to the Reformatory School in Pretoria to join Fonnie du Preez. How you would go about stealing a pound was beyond me.

Talking about stealing, I suppose, technically speaking, the Great Shiny-Feather Robbery was stealing. This meant I was a thief twice over, the red book from under Doctor Van Heerden's house and now the four shiny-black feathers from Piet Retief the rooster. But I reckoned the fact that Meneer Prinsloo got to win the silver cup at the Rand Easter Show Races cancelled out the second theft, even if he didn't know about it. Anyway, the feather theft happened inside The Boys Farm so it didn't really count. Too bad I couldn't tell Meneer Prinsloo about his rooster's big win that wasn't a blue ribbon, but was even better – an Easter bonnet! It could have made me a hero.

Where to hide the pound note was the worst crisis I'd ever had, except for punching Pissy Vermaak in the stomach for trying to take Tinker and what Fonnie du Preez and him did to me after. I kept the pound note in my trouser pocket when we were watering the young orange trees down at the orchards, but my hand went in so often to check that it was still there that I practically wore the paper out. Japie Betzer, one of the big guys, noticed my hand going in and said out loud so everyone could hear, 'Look! *Voetsek's* got a hole inside his pocket and he's jerking himself off!'

My hand came out of my trouser pocket so fast the lining came out as well and the pound note fell at my feet. In a trice I put my foot on it to hide it but it was too late, and I was suddenly surrounded. We were all standing next to the water pump waiting to fill our paraffin tin buckets and the ground around the pump was muddy from water that had spilled. My pound note was under my right foot in the mud and Japie, who'd started it all, stood over me. He was fifteen years old.

'What you got there under your foot, *Voetsek?*' he growled.

'Nothing,' I replied fearfully.

'You lying, man! I seen something.'

'It's just a piece of old paper,' I protested, thinking fast.

'Move your foot and let me see this piece of paper,' Japie demanded.

'I think it's money,' someone said. 'A ten-bob note!'

There was a gasp from everyone standing around and then Japie gave me a great push in the chest. I went arse over tit into the mud and then there were seven boys diving at the pound note sticking out of the mud. Talk about a scrum! All of a sudden there were bodies everywhere fighting and kicking and rolling over each other. Gawie Grobler managed to get the pound note but the others were onto him like a pack of mad dogs.

'Stop!' It was Meneer Frikkie Botha who'd suddenly come up. Everyone stopped and got up with their clothes covered with mud, and we all stood with our hands behind our backs the way you were supposed to in a line-up.

'What's going on, hey?' he asked.

'Nothing, Meneer!' we all chorused.

'So nothing's going on and all of a sudden you all fighting and rolling around in the mud?'

We all looked down at our feet and remained silent.

'This nothing that's going on is all of a sudden going to turn into six of the best for everyone if somebody doesn't tell me what this is all about,' Frikkie Botha growled. He turned to Japie Betzer. 'Japie, I saw you push Tom, here! Why?'

'It was nothing, Meneer. We was just playing,' Japie mumbled, not looking up.

'I see, playing in the mud for nothing, is that it?' He looked around. 'You think I'm stupid?'

'No, Meneer!' we all chorused again. He looked at me sternly. 'Tom, why did Japie push you?'

I was in the deep shit. If I told Frikkie Botha about the pound note I'd be up in front of Meneer Prinsloo in a flash. If I told Meneer Prinsloo that I'd received the pound note from Miss Phillips he'd ask to see the letter that was floating in little pieces down the Limpopo River. If he believed me, which was very unlikely, he'd write to Miss Phillips who'd tell him about the four black feathers and how she'd won the Easter Bonnet competition at the Rand Easter Show. I was suddenly between a rock and a hard place and my Great Shiny-Feather Robbery would be exposed and it was Pretoria for sure, possibly not the reformatory, but hanging by the neck until I was stone dead.

'I said the Union Jack was a nicer flag than the *vierkleur*, Meneer,' I lied. The *vierkleur* was the flag of the Transvaal Republic before the British defeated the Boere in the Boer War. In that part of the world it was a sacred ensign. People kept it in a bottom drawer for one day when the Boere would rise up and defeat the *verdomde* English and restore the sacred God-given flag to its rightful place outside every police station in the land.

Suddenly Frikkie Botha's large hand landed on the side of my head and lifted me off my feet so that I landed back in the mud. 'You said what?' he growled. 'You better take that back, you hear? Stand up, man!' he yelled. I stood up. 'Now say you sorry to God!'

'Sorry, God,' I said.

'No, man, look up to heaven and go down on your knees and bring your hands together and say sorry to God for sacrilege and dishonour to the true flag.'

Back into the mud I went with my ear stinging and my head ringing.

'Sorry, God for sacrilege and dishonour to the true flag,' I said with a small sob and a sniff.

'Now say sorry to Japie Betzer,' Frikkie Botha commanded.

I rose to my feet. 'Sorry, Japie,' I said in a small voice. Japie nodded and grunted.

'And that's not all, tonight you go and see Mevrou who is going to make you wash your mouth out with soap because what you talking is blasphemy!' Frikkie Botha turned and stormed off, you could see just from looking at his back that I was now the enemy.

After Frikkie Botha had gone Japie Betzer and the other bigger boys demanded that Gawie Grobler hand the note over. Gawie's nose was bleeding and his lip was split from the fight to get at the note in the first place.

'Someone grabbed it,' Gawie sniffed. 'I haven't got it anymore.'

'You lying, hey,' Japie said threateningly, and several of the bigger boys closed in on Gawie. 'Hand it over, man!'

'You can search me,' Gawie protested. 'It's God's truth, I'll swear it on a stack of Bibles. Someone took it out of my hand!'

'Open your mouth,' Japie said. Gawie opened his mouth and Japie put his dirty forefinger inside and rummaged around. 'Pull out your pockets' was the next command. Gawie did as he was told. Still no pound note.

'I'm telling you, man, I haven't got it,' Gawie sniffed back the blood coming from his nose. The back of his hand was red from wiping the blood away.

'Take off your shirt and shorts,' Japie said.

Gawie soon stood naked in front of all of us. 'I swear on my mother's grave,' he said, clearly upset.

'You haven't got a fucking mother,' Japie sneered as he shook Gawie's shirt and then his shorts. Still no pound note.

It must have occurred to Japie that if he found the pound note he'd have to fight the two other big boys for it, because he turned around to them. 'We going to search everyone, you hear? When we find the ten bob, we each,' he pointed to the two bigger boys, 'going to get two and sixpence and there's two and six left. So all the small guys here get sixpence, even *Voetsek* because he saved us from Frikkie's *sjambok* with his Union Jack story that he made up, but it's still blasphemy.'

My pound had turned into sixpence if it could be found, except that it might turn into a shilling because it was really a pound and not ten bob. Sixpence was more than I'd ever owned before the pound came into my life and a shilling was even twice that. You could get twelve suckers for a shilling, so maybe it hadn't turned out all that badly after all.

But then came the surprise. Everyone, even Japie Betzer, took off their clothes and we could search anyone we liked, but the pound wasn't found. People started digging around in the mud and lifting any small rock or piece of wood that was lying around, but we found nothing.

'I told you it was an old piece of paper that must have blown away,' I said triumphantly, and I added accusingly, 'but no-one would believe me.'

Japie gave me a clip behind the earhole, fortunately on the opposite side to Frikkie Botha because he was left-handed. 'Why do you only make trouble all the time, *Voetsek*, saying that about the Union Jack. You just a fucking *rooinek*, you hear?'

There I was with a couple of thick ears and my first fortune lost, disappeared into thin air.

That wasn't the end of the Great Shiny-Feather Robbery because that night when I went to have my mouth washed out with soap by Mevrou, there on her embroidery table was a copy of *Huisgenoot*. On the cover of the magazine was this big picture of Janneke Phillips smiling and wearing a beautiful hat with four Black Orpington feathers sticking out of it. The words under her picture said '*Die hoed wat die Rand Passfees Wedrenne gewen het*. The hat that won the Rand Easter Show races.'

Now I knew I was *really* and *truly* in the deep shit. The evidence of the robbery was there for all the world to see. The four feathers stolen from Piet Retief's bum were on the cover of the biggest Afrikaans-speaking women's magazine. This was long-cane Prinsloo territory and with Pretoria thrown in. I waited for the dreaded words to come.

But nothing happened except that Mevrou made me wash my mouth out with Lifebuoy soap. 'This is from Meneer Botha, *Voetsek*. He told me what you said about the beloved *vierkleur*, the true flag of our noble *volk*! *Sis*, man, you should be ashamed! Under that same flag they killed 27 000 Afrikaner women and children. So from me comes castor oil because the *sjambok* is just too good for you!' I had to drink three big spoons of castor oil and I shit myself silly for two days afterwards. At the end I could hardly stand.

As far as the magazine cover went, I'd clean forgotten that neither Mevrou nor Meneer Prinsloo had known Janneke Phillips. While the cover was proudly drawing-pinned on the school noticeboard by Meneer Van Niekerk, not a single kid from The Boys Farm made the vital connection with Piet Retief's missing bum feathers. To them, a feather was a feather, and as far as they were concerned, the world was full of black shiny feathers in hats worn by ladies.

That still wasn't the end of the matter. It was now school holidays and three days later when at last I wasn't running to the shithouse every ten minutes, Gawie Grobler approached me. '*Voetsek*, why don't I meet you maybe down by the creek where you always take your little dog?' he said, and then added, 'I'll be waiting there after lunch, you hear?' While he'd made it sound like a suggestion I had no option. He was two years older than me and you daren't disobey when you're at the bottom of the pecking order. Not that Gawie would have done anything, he wasn't the physical type and won his respect because everyone knew he was the cleverest boy at The Boys Farm. Maybe I was getting nearly as clever, but, of course, that didn't count. I forgot to say it was a Saturday and we had an hour off after lunch.

I was surprised at his knowing about the creek and a bit worried. Kids always think they do things unobserved and me going down to the creek with Tinker was one of those things. If Gawie had said the big rock I would have been *really* worried. You see, that's where I kept my growing library of Miss Phillips' books. At first they went under my bed where we were allowed to keep things, then Mevrou found out they were written in English and all of a sudden she made a new law that said we could only have our schoolbooks there and three other personal things. Things such as your catty and a pocket knife if you had one, which I didn't, and maybe a ball or a top or a tin where you kept things like marbles you'd won from the town kids or other things you'd found. There was also this rule among the boys that you couldn't steal something from your own dormitory, and even people like Pissy Vermaak didn't ever. 'It's like our home,' everyone agreed.

I had to find a new place to put my books and all the letters and her exercise corrections and marked essays Miss Phillips had sent me. It was quite a pile, I can tell you, and my library was growing week by week. So I went and collected some old paraffin tins and I put my books and papers in them and hid them under the big rock. Ever since what happened at the big rock everyone thought it was a bad-luck place and stayed away. Not that very many people went there in the first place. I had it all to myself and I gave it a new name, the library rock. If Gawie Grobler had suggested we walk to the library rock I would have been very worried.

The part of the creek Gawie chose to go to was good. This was because the swimming hole was further down a bit and was the best place to catch *platannas* as well as shoot bush doves in the big blue gum trees. It was the place where I had found Tinker floating in a sack and it was a part people almost never went to. But Gawie, who was also a quiet type and very clever, must have observed Tinker and me going for walks. The reason he would have suggested we meet at this place was that he probably didn't want the other kids to see me with him. The thing about me saying I liked the Union Jack better than the *vierkleur* had spread all around the place and I was an even bigger untouchable than before. I have to say this for Gawie Grobler, he tried to explain to everyone that I only said it to save them all from a certain *sjambokking* by Frikkie Botha. But people still said, 'Never mind that, *Voetsek* still said it, and that's because in his heart of hearts he believes it, so it's still blasphemy.' Sometimes in life you have to choose your words very carefully, even when you have to find them in a hurry.

When Tinker and me got to the creek Gawie was already there waiting. 'Howzit?' he said in English, much to my surprise.

'*Ja, goed dankie*. Yeah, good thanks,' I replied politely in Afrikaans.

'I suppose you wondering why I asked you here?' he said in Afrikaans, because I don't suppose he spoke English very well, even though we'd both passed the exams. I didn't reply. 'It's about your books,' he said.

The shock I felt was worse than the clout Frikkie Botha gave me at the water pump. The inside of my mouth had gone dry. 'My books?' I said at last, my voice close to a whisper.

'Can I read them?' he asked.

'They English,' I said.

'Yes, I know,' he replied.

'But you are an Afrikaner?' I asked, puzzled.

'*Ja*, I know I can't let anybody see. I thought I could read them with you when you go down to the big rock where you go and read by yourself.' He paused. 'We could go separately to that rock and then read together and talk about the stuff that's in them, like we do with the Afrikaans books at school.'

You could have knocked me down with one of Piet Retief's tail feathers. Gawie Grobler had been spying on me all the time! He knew I went down to the library rock to read and no doubt also knew that's where I wrote my stuff for Miss Phillips. Here I was all the time thinking I was safe. I remember sometimes Tinker would start to bark at something in the thorn bushes, but I always thought it was a bird or a lizard or something like that. There were all sorts of little creatures that lived around the library rock, sometimes the *dassies*, the rock rabbits, would come out and Tinker would get very excited. Goodness me, it was probably Gawie Grobler all the time. I didn't know what to say. If I refused, which I didn't know if I even had the right to do, I'd have him as my enemy and he was the one boy who had never given me a hard time. He'd also recently tried to defend me over the flag business.

'I'll pay you ten shillings,' he said suddenly.

'Ten shillings!' Where would someone like him get ten shillings?

He wasn't even old enough to work on a farm during the holidays. Ten shillings was an amount more than any boy from The Boys Farm could have in the world that wasn't first kept by Meneer Prinsloo until they left the place.

He held out his hand and in it was a one-pound note. 'It's yours, the one that fell out of your pocket at the water pump but since then a miracle has happened to it. Finders keepers, hey?' he said, reminding me of the rule that applied to everything on The Boys Farm.

'Where did you hide it?' I said, remembering the search and how we'd all been undressed and even dug up the muddy ground and lifted the stones and sticks lying about.

'In my bum hole!' he laughed.

'You stuck it up there?' I cried. 'Up your arse?'

'Ja!' he giggled.

'Didn't it hurt?' I said, starting to giggle myself.

'No, it was only paper, but I was really scared, man! What if, when we were all standing naked around the pump, with my *poep* hole blocked with paper, I suddenly farted – it would have come flying out!'

'And everyone would make a dive for it and it would be all covered in shit!' I yelled happily. Then we started to roll around in the grass laughing and Tinker started barking and jumping all over us. It was the best laughing I'd ever done in my whole life. Eventually we stopped and I had to ask, 'What was it like when you took it out?'

'*Magtig*! That was the miracle! The ten shillings that fell out of your pocket had all of a sudden changed into a pound!'

'And you went and washed it?' I asked somewhat stupidly.

'*Ja*, it wasn't too bad, they made of stuff that's not like ordinary paper and you can wash them and they don't disintegrate, and the shit came off easy as anything.'

There was a moment's silence between us. I admired him greatly for his ingenuity but at the same time thought that, in the end, it was originally my pound that had disappeared up Gawie's bum. But there wasn't much use pointing this out to him.

As if he read my thoughts he looked at me with a serious expression and said, 'That's why you getting your ten bob back, *Voetsek*. Because I put *your* ten bob up my bum where it miraculously turned into *my* pound.' He tried to conceal his laughter. 'So the other ten shillings that was made while it was in there belongs to me!'

You have to admit that was clever talk. 'Okay,' I said. 'Stick it up your bum again and see if two pounds come out! Then I can have my pound back and you'll have your very own pound!'

Gawie laughed. 'Okay, we quits, but I'm still keeping ten bob. Have we got a deal?'

'What? With the money or reading my books?'

'Both,' he replied.

With a person who could make me laugh like we just did I felt obliged to say, 'Yes, it's a deal.' I extended my hand. 'Shake a paw.' Gawie Grobler knew he had me over a barrel all the time anyway. He was in a position to do several things. Report the presence of the pound to Meneer Prinsloo with the consequences I've already outlined. Keep the pound for himself and I couldn't do very much about it except to tell Japie Betzer that he'd had it all the time and have Japie beat him up and take the pound from him. On the other hand, I would rather have had Gawie own my pound and give me ten shillings than the horrible Japie Betzer taking the lot. Furthermore, Gawie could reveal the whereabouts of my library that was no longer protected by the dormitory 'no-theft agreement' and so would almost certainly be destroyed as a revenge for the Union Jack incident. Even at the age of nine I knew the books were far more important to me than the money. Ten shillings was a king's ransom anyway, more money than I could possibly imagine because the pound, in the brief period I'd owned it, was beyond my comprehension and was well beyond my capacity to keep it safe. Even the ten shillings was going to present a giant problem that, right at that moment, I had no idea how to solve.

After nearly five years on The Boys Farm I had my first real friend. He still couldn't be seen with me except when we were marching to and from school, and even then he had to be careful, but we were to spend many happy hours reading and discussing books together and he started doing all the same homework Miss Phillips sent me. After a while I wrote to her and asked if Gawie could also send his work and Janneke Phillips graciously agreed, although I would later realise that this must have placed an extra strain on her own workload. The next two years were the happiest I could remember. Still plenty of *sjambok* and Mevrou, but that was nothing compared to the loneliness that didn't happen anymore.

Now I know you're thinking about that pound, because unfortunately Gawie's bum didn't *poep* it out in two separate notes. He now shared the same dilemma as I had originally stumbled onto, how to turn one pound into two ten-shilling notes without someone noticing that two kids from The Boys Farm were walking around with a fortune in their pockets. We discussed every possibility and the most appealing one was to go to Mr Patel at the Indian shop on the edge of town because Meneer Prinsloo had once said that you couldn't trust him as far as you could throw him, and he'd steal the gold out of your teeth. We reckoned that he was somebody who wouldn't tell, because Indians don't have the same God, or maybe not even a God, so they didn't care if you'd stolen the money and wouldn't ask questions. What's more, we didn't have any gold in what Doctor Dyke with his horse pliers had left of our teeth.

'But Mr Patel won't just do it for nothing,' Gawie reasoned. 'Remember, he's unscrupulous.' It was a word we'd just learned in the new book Miss Phillips had sent and I'd looked it up in my dictionary. It means having no scruples, so then we had to look up scruples. What it said was 'a regard for the morality or propriety of an action'. And we knew the 'un' in front meant it was just the opposite. So that was a perfect word to describe Mr Patel, the Indian whose shop was called Patel & Sons so his sons were probably just as bad as him. I must say Gawie looked a bit smug because he was the first to use the new word. Later in my write-a-sentence-from-a-word-found-in-the-dictionary lesson I wrote, 'Mr Patel is an Indian who owns a shop named Patel &

Sons and is unscrupulous.' Miss Phillips wrote back and said she didn't like the sentence because it insinuated that because Mr Patel was an Indian he was unscrupulous, and that this was a racial slur. She asked, 'What evidence do you have to prove your point?' So then we had to look up 'insinuated'.

'We'll just have to buy something small,' I said. 'Like a sucker each, that's only a penny.'

Gawie frowned. 'But then we wouldn't have our ten shillings each, only nine and elevenpence.'

I could see his point. That missing penny had the effect of somehow reducing the fortune in one's mind. '*Ja*, but we'd have a whole sucker each,' I said. My thoughts went back to Mevrou Booysens at the Impala Café and the kiss I'd got from Marie, and the red sucker and the pineapple one. That had been about two years ago but I hadn't done a lot of kissing in the meantime, none as a matter of fact.

'Maybe I'll buy two,' I said rather grandly. 'A red one and a pineapple, it's better than green.'

Gawie thought for a moment. 'You know how I gave you ten shillings for nothing because it came out of my bum, *Voetsek*?'

'Yeah?' I said suspiciously, not seeing his self-proclaimed miracle quite like that.

'Well, to say thank you to me, why don't you buy two suckers and give me one and I can still keep my ten-shilling note?'

'You're cheating me, Gawie!' I protested.

'*Ja*, I know, but I have to hurry up and get rich and you two years younger than me, man! You can easy catch up.'

I agreed to buy him a sucker from my ten shillings as I hadn't really thought much about becoming rich, and besides, it's not every day you can make a grand gesture and have a new friend at the same time.

So after school we ran down to Patel & Sons. The idea was to catch up with the kids from The Boys Farm afterwards, before they reached the front gate and we'd be in time for the line-up. Before we entered the shop Gawie said, 'Let me do the talking hey, *Voetsek*. I'm eleven and you only nine and still a little kid.' I must say I was quite relieved and also impressed that Gawie was the one to do the negotiation because I had no idea how to go about dealing with an Indian person. We entered the shop that was full of everything you could imagine a black person would want to buy. I don't know about Gawie, but I was pretty nervous.

'Good afternoon, boys,' Mr Patel said, smiling. 'What can I do for you?'

'Good afternoon,' we said back. We didn't say 'Good afternoon, Meneer' like you had to with a white person grown-up. This was because while an Indian wasn't a black, but was a sort of halfway-up person but still a non-white that couldn't use a white person's lavatory, but different to a black and not so low. Mr Patel's skin was shiny and soft brown and he had black hair, just like a proper person.

Gawie slapped down our pound note and said quite calmly, 'Can we have two red suckers, please?'

'My goodness gracious, we are wanting two suckers and we are having one pound!' Mr Patel said, looking surprised. 'Two suckers is two pennies and we are giving for them a one-pound note,' he repeated. He looked at us suspiciously. 'And where are two boys that are walking with bare feet getting this one pound you are giving me?'

We'd guessed wrong. Mr Patel was a person who had scruples. My first instinct was to grab the pound note from the counter and run, but then I saw that Mr Patel had picked it up.

'We didn't steal it!' Gawie protested.

'I am not knowing this,' Mr Patel said. 'One pound, that is a lot of money for one boy to have.'

'It's both of ours,' I said, as if this immediately rectified the matter.

'Together you are having this pound?' he exclaimed, now even more suspicious than before. 'I am very, very worried, boys,' he said, shaking his head. 'I am wanting your mother to come and see me. If she is telling me this pound is yours then I am giving you, on the spot, two suckers and nineteen and tenpence change.'

'We don't have a mother!' we both said at once. Almost immediately I realised that this only got us deeper into the deep shit.

'Your father, he is coming then?'

'We're from The Boys Farm,' I said despairingly.

'Then I am calling right away Meneer Prinsloo,' he declared.

'No!' we shouted.

Mr Patel shrugged. 'Who am I calling to be making confirmations about this two-red-sucker pound, boys?'

'We didn't steal it!' Gawie protested again. 'I swear it on a stack of Bibles.'

I wasn't in a position to remind him that Mr Patel didn't believe in the Bible. 'Call Sergeant Van Niekerk,' I said suddenly. It just came out without thinking.

'I am calling Sergeant Van Niekerk?' Mr Patel was obviously impressed. 'At the police station?'

Gawie gave me a look as if to say I must have all of a sudden gone crazy. If I was, then it was too late. I nodded to Mr Patel who turned and went to the telephone on the wall and rang up the exchange at the post office and asked them to put him through to the police station. He waited and seemed to be listening, and then he hung up the phone.

'Sergeant Van Niekerk is in the native location,' he explained. 'I am telling you what I am going to do. For this pound I am giving you a receipt and I am keeping it until I am seeing Sergeant Van Niekerk. If he is explaining and you are explaining how this pound is yours then we are doing business, hey boys?' he smiled. 'Now you are getting a *bansella* from me.' He put his hand in the sucker jar and took out two red suckers. '*Bansella*, boys, from Patel & Sons,' he announced rather grandly. 'I must be having now your names for putting on this receipt forthwith and so forth.'

We gave him our names. 'One Afrikaner, one English, my goodness gracious me, what have we got here?' He wrote out a receipt for our pound and gave it to Gawie. 'Keep this safe, boys. If I am dying in the night then it is proving you have one pound with Patel & Sons. Tomorrow you are coming here after school and we are sorting this out. Goodbye and I am wishing you very, very good luck, boys.'

We had to run like hell and only just caught the kids marching back from school before they turned into the front gate of The Boys Farm. We didn't even have time to suck the sucker and so we had to save it and suck it in bed when everyone was asleep and hide the stick until the next morning.

'What's a receipt?' Gawie asked when we'd got our breath back and were standing in the line-up.

'I don't know. We'll look it up in the dictionary at the library rock tomorrow, but I think it sort of means Mr Patel has our pound on appro.'

'I hope he doesn't die tonight,' Gawie said.

I must say that pound Miss Phillips sent me was causing a lot of problems. I had no idea having lots of money could be such a difficult thing.

'Sergeant Van Niekerk could arrest us,' Gawie said.

'He is my friend, I'll tell him the truth, he's a high-up and I don't think he likes Meneer Prinsloo, even if he is also a high-up,' I said to reassure him. Gawie still seemed unconvinced. 'Remember the day Sergeant Van Niekerk took Fonnie du Preez away in the police van to go to Pretoria?'

Gawie nodded.

'Well, didn't you see? Meneer Prinsloo nearly broke his braces and burst his stomach open and he stormed off with Frikkie Botha and Mevrou. Remember?'

Gawie looked horrified. 'You going to tell Sergeant Van Niekerk the truth, *Voetsek*? You *can't* tell him about the ten shillings turning into a pound up my bum!'

'No,' I said. 'I'll only tell him about the feathers.'

Gawie looked at me completely mystified. 'Huh? What feathers?'

We'd become best friends so quickly that I clean forgot that I hadn't told him the story of stealing the rooster's feathers. Standing in line next to all the other kids was certainly not the time to do so.

'Shush! We talking too loud, someone will hear. I'll tell you later,' I said out the side of my mouth.

Then someone called out, 'Hey, Gawie, is *Voetsek* all of a sudden your pal? Perhaps you also like the Union Jack better than the *vierkleur*, hey?'

'No!' Gawie shouted back. 'I am a real Boer!' He immediately distanced himself from me. It was okay because that's what we'd agreed he'd do when we were not alone. He couldn't afford to be seen to be friends with the *rooinek*.

The next day nothing happened. After school we went down to see Mr Patel but there was only an Indian lady there in a long pink dress that sort of wrapped around her with it only going over one shoulder and it wasn't the sort of dress you'd see a white lady wear in the day, and a diamond in her nose and this red spot in the middle of her forehead. She also had smooth hair.

'Can we see Meneer Patel, please?' Gawie asked.

'He is going out all afternoon and not coming back until five o'clock,' she announced. 'He is going to Tzaneen today to buy *mielie* meal.'

'With our pound, I'll bet,' Gawie said bitterly when we went outside.

I'd looked up the meaning for receipt – 'the act of receiving or being received into one's possession' – which didn't help one little bit to make us feel any better because that's exactly what Mr Patel had done. He'd received our pound into his possession, alright, and it didn't look like coming back into ours in a hurry. For once in his life Meneer Prinsloo must have been right. That *blêrrie* Indian Mr Patel couldn't be trusted as far as you could throw him. We'd been cheated right out of our pound easy as anything. What's more, there was nothing we could do about it because now he was busy buying *mielies* in Tzaneen with our money.

I'd confessed to Gawie about the Great Shiny-Feather Robbery and he'd quickly pointed out that I'd committed a major crime against a grown-up, high-up person like Meneer Prinsloo, that my calling on

Sergeant Van Niekerk for help to get our pound back was just about the most stupid thing a person could do.

'It's like locking yourself up in gaol and throwing the key out the window!' he said. 'We lost our pound but now *you* still going to gaol in Pretoria, *Voetsek!*' he said darkly.

'No, that's not true!' I protested. 'If Mr Patel stole our pound he wouldn't be going around telling people all over the place. Like the lady with a diamond in her nose said, he just went to Tzaneen and while nobody was looking he bought some bags of *mielie* meal with our pound.'

'You got a point, *Voetsek*,' Gawie said, grudgingly admitting to my logic.

While we lost our pound I felt reasonably safe after such a narrow escape from going to prison. But I have discovered that life seldom goes the way you hope it will. At morning play break Meneer Van Niekerk called me to his office and when I got there Gawie Grobler was already waiting and so was Sergeant Van Niekerk. Talk about being in the deep shit!

'Good morning, Tom,' Sergeant Van Niekerk said. 'We meet again, hey?'

'*Goeie môre*, Meneer,' I stammered, then turned to the headmaster and said good morning to him as well.

'Is it true that the two of you paid Mr Patel at the Indian shop a visit after school yesterday?' Sergeant Van Niekerk asked sternly.

'*Ja*, Meneer,' we both said, looking contrite.

'So tell me, what is all this about?'

Gawie turned and looked at me. All of a sudden it was the younger person that had to do all the talking.

'Meneer, it is all my fault, I stole the feathers from Piet Retief's bum and Miss Phillips won the Easter Bonnet prize at the Rand Easter Show and sent me a pound. Gawie Grobler did nothing wrong, Meneer!' I cried in one big burst of confession.

'Whoa! Not so fast, Tom. What's this about feathers from Piet

Retief's bum? Maybe he had a feather in his hat, but this is the first I hear that the great Boer leader had feathers coming out of his backside.'

'He's a rooster, Meneer,' I stammered.

Sergeant Van Niekerk turned to his brother, the headmaster. 'I think I'll take Tom here outside for a little chat. If I need Gawie we can always get to him later.'

The headmaster told Gawie to go back to class and Sergeant Van Niekerk took me outside and then to the front gate. Tinker was waiting outside the headmaster's office and followed us. When we got to the gate, the police van was parked right there and half on the pavement. If anyone else had done it they'd have got into a lot of trouble.

'Get in, Tom,' the sergeant instructed, then he saw Tinker. 'Bring her too.' He opened the door of the passenger side of the van. I remembered he'd done the same to Fonnie du Preez so I didn't get my hopes up too far, but at least Tinker was coming with me to gaol. I picked her up and climbed in, and this time it was *my* heart that was going boom-boom-boom against *her* little chest. She licked my hand. Sergeant Van Niekerk climbed in on the other side behind the steering wheel and I asked, 'Am I being arrested and will you send me to Pretoria, Meneer?'

He turned on the ignition and the big Ford engine went *varoom!* When a person could hear again he said, '*Ja*, something like that, Tom. Only I thought perhaps instead of Pretoria prison we might go to the Impala Café and you could have all ten toppings while you tell me the whole story, hey? What do you say?'

Mevrou Booysens welcomed me like a long-lost friend. 'Where have you been, Tom? It's about two years since you came in. How is your finger? Marie and I often talk about you. She is in Pietersburg training to be a nurse. Can you still eat ten toppings? Do you still have that nice little dog?'

I must say I was amazed. You don't expect grown-ups to have a memory like that. I showed her the scar on my finger and told her Tinker was waiting outside.

'Even the dog has good manners,' she said. 'We going to find him a nice bone, hey?'

So I told Sergeant Van Niekerk everything except about the water-pump incident and the pound disappearing up Gawie's bum. By the time I was finished I'd also finished the ice-cream that still came in a bowl that stood on one leg.

'He has a stomach like a cement-mixer,' Mevrou Booysens said, beaming down at me before taking it away. 'But the dog doesn't eat the bone, Tom. It's a nice one with meat still on.'

I'd been so concerned about myself that I'd clean forgotten. 'She won't till she gets the password, Mevrou,' I explained, then looked at Sergeant Van Niekerk for permission to go outside the shop. Mevrou Booysens followed. Tinker was lying with both her paws on this big meaty bone and her nose right up against it.

'*Izinyawo ezinkulu zika Mattress,*' I said, and in a trice Tinker grabbed the juicy bone, happy as can be.

Sergeant Van Niekerk had come out and must have heard me give Tinker the password and now he shook his head.

'Mattress's big feet,' he said softly to himself. 'You loved that *Bantu*, didn't you, Tom? I'm sorry I couldn't get a conviction. The case is still open and I promise you I'll keep trying.'

We returned to the table. 'Two suckers coming up, what colour do you want, Tom?' Mevrou Booysens asked.

'Red and yellow, please, Mevrou,' I said. I was still not too sure I was safe because my sentence hadn't yet been passed, and if I was going to go to gaol the suckers would come in handy as a bit of comfort.

Sergeant Van Niekerk said, 'Well, Tom, I haven't had an official complaint from the superintendent of The Boys Farm about Piet Retief's missing tail feathers so I have decided to close the books on the case. We will now go down to Mr Patel's shop to get your pound as I am completely satisfied it is rightfully yours.' He paused and seemed to be thinking. 'It might be a good idea to stay away from Meneer Prinsloo's roosters, though. Offenders often return to the scene of their crime and we don't want him seeing you around his chickens. What did you say the second rooster was called?'

'General Botha,' I replied.

'That's blasphemy!' he laughed. 'Meneer Prinsloo should be arrested for treason.'

When we got to Patel & Sons (it later turned out the sons were in India going to Bombay University) my pound was returned, even though Gawie still had the receipt in his trouser pocket at school.

'Thank you, Meneer Patel,' I said. 'Can I please have two ten-shilling notes instead?'

'Certainly! We are giving you two ten-shilling notes quick smart, Tom,' Mr Patel said. 'Sergeant Van Niekerk tells me you are a very, very fine boy. You want anything, you come and see me. For you it's wholesale price every time.'

I think he must have liked me calling him Meneer Patel because I don't suppose it happened very often from the white people around the place, even Sergeant Van Niekerk only called him Patel. I didn't care because you have to admit he'd turned out to be a very nice person in the end, offering me wholesale and all that. Mattress was supposed to be a dirty *kaffir* and the lowest down you could get, but he was still my best friend ever. At church once the *Dominee* read from the Bible and it told us that Jesus once said to the man next to him on the cross about people going to heaven, 'In my father's house there are many mansions, I go to prepare a place for you.' Every night I prayed to God to please give Mattress a really nice house with some cows to milk and a black-and-white sow that had lots of piglets.

Outside the shop Sergeant Van Niekerk went down on his haunches and put his hand on my shoulder, looked me in the eyes and asked, 'Tom, are you sure you want to give Gawie Grobler ten shillings? It's a lot of money. You do know the whole pound rightly belongs to you now, don't you?'

'Ja, Meneer, but he is my friend, just like Mattress was.'

'That's good,' he replied. 'A man should always have a friend he can trust.' I was too young to realise that Sergeant Van Niekerk had, once again, proved to be just such a friend, even though he was a high-up and a very important person who could have had anyone he liked as his friend.

CHAPTER SEVEN

For Love of Country

BY NOW YOU CAN see there was a fair amount of politics going on around the place so I thought maybe we should talk about the war, which to me was a very confusing time. Who's right and who's wrong, that was my problem. It wasn't too hard to decide who was right if you listened to Meneer Prinsloo, Frikkie Botha and Mevrou or, in particular, the *Dominee*. Every Sunday he was saying all sort of things from the pulpit, but mainly that maybe on the surface Hitler wasn't a God-fearing man but we must look below the surface for the truth.

'God, we must understand,' the *Dominee* said, 'works in mysterious ways and maybe Hitler is the political Messiah who will restore South Africa to the Afrikaner folk who, we must remember, invented white supremacy long before he came along.' The Almighty was definitely against the English all the way and obviously against the Jews who crucified the Lord Jesus Christ, and Hitler was the same. So this proved once and for all that anyone who fought the English and hated the Jews and knew that white people were superior to other races was a God-fearing person.

'Now, let us examine for a moment why Adolf Hitler doesn't bring God into his message to the world,' the *Dominee* said one Sunday. 'It is because of the Church of Rome.' He went on about how with all the

Roman Catholics in Germany Hitler couldn't just come out and say up-front that he was a Protestant and a Lutheran. Because after the Jews the Roman Catholics were the worst there was, worshipping idols and a man called the Pope and the Virgin Mary, who was the mother of Jesus but also just a humble common woman because God wanted it to be that way. He, the Lord God Almighty, wanted His son to be *born of man* so Mary was just the womb suitcase Jesus came in. She was *definitely not* worth worshipping, not just because she was a woman, but because God said so.

'In the meantime, they, the Roman Catholics, are forgetting all about mentioning Jesus who was the Son of God and it is all Pope and Mary this, and Mary and Pope that, and so-called holy statues everywhere. With Roman Catholics in Germany and with Italy being one hundred per cent Roman Catholic, Adolf Hitler couldn't just come out and say he was a proper Christian and didn't worship idols or Virgin Marys.'

Then the *Dominee* said that because we don't live in a perfect world, sometimes there has to be political compromise. 'But just you wait and see, after Hitler wins the war the Catholics will be the next to go up in smoke!' The *Dominee* got very worked up saying all this stuff and the beetle chewed overtime on the beard grass. He kept thumping the pulpit and the light coming from the window behind made the beetle's ears blood-red and he thumped so hard the Bible fell with a mighty thump to the floor.

One of my big problems was that when you saw a person shout a lot and thump things like the Bible, you knew that he wanted you to believe stuff that maybe you should look at a bit more carefully before you did. Meneer Prinsloo was another such person, a shouter whose hands were windmills and who pushed his stomach out so his braces had to hang on for dear life, and so you also knew you had to be careful because a lot of what he said was sheer, utter and complete bullshit.

Now I must say it came as a big surprise to learn that there were people called Jews still hanging around the place after all this time since the Bible. I mean, there were no English or Afrikaners in the

Bible because they didn't exist yet. But according to everyone the Jews were still here and they were *still* guilty of crucifying the Son of God. That is not a thing you can forgive lightly, and the ones escaping from Germany needed to be kept out of South Africa at all costs. Everybody said we already had enough Christ-killers allowed in by the British and the Smuts Government. The Jews now owned all the goldmines and diamonds and wanted to sack decent-living white miners and put *kaffirs* in to work underground because the Jews could give them less wages and make more profit.

So you see I was trying to sort all of this stuff out in my head, and in one of our many discussions on the library rock I said to Gawie Grobler, 'Okay, answer me this. If Jesus died for our sins so that we could have eternal life like the *Dominee* says, then why are we angry with the Jews for killing him? He came down from heaven and was supposed to be killed in the first place. God said to Him, "Go down there and talk to people about us, then you have to die so their sins can be forgiven and they can start all over again, washed in the blood of the lamb, which is you." When the Jews did it to him like they were supposed to, all of a sudden they can't come into South Africa? Didn't God know all the time they were supposed to do it? The *Dominee* says the Jews were God's chosen people, after the Afrikaners, so God must have chosen them to do it to Jesus!'

Gawie thought for a while, then said, 'No, *Voetsek*, you got it wrong, man. It was the Romans that were supposed to do it all the time. God said Jesus had to die but the Romans had to do it. At the last minute the Jews said they wanted to have a part in it but that was never supposed to happen because up to then the Jews were God's chosen people.' He added, 'But they not anymore, we are.'

I knew he meant the Afrikaner *volk* and not me, because the *Dominee* said that the Afrikaners could easily be one of the lost tribes of Israel, so they had every right to claim that they were now God's chosen people. The *Dominee* pointed out that they'd also done a lot of wandering in the wilderness among the heathen, as a matter of fact, for more than forty years, which beat the pants off Moses's record. What's more, there had been no backsliding by worshipping craven images, like Aaron did the moment Moses's back was turned when he climbed up the mountain to talk to God about some laws to be made called the Ten Commandments. 'The Afrikaner tribe,' the *Dominee* said, 'had kept the true faith to this very moment, and mostly the Ten Commandments and so were definitely a first-class chosen people who God could trust not to let Him down.'

So if, according to Gawie, that took care of why God didn't like the Jews any more, it still didn't answer why He hated the Romans who were only following His orders.

'But why do we hate the Romans when God said they had to kill Jesus? It's not their fault, if God says something you've *got* to do it, man,' I insisted.

'Ag, *Voetsek*, you don't understand! God doesn't hate the Romans because they killed Jesus! He hates them because after they killed Him they turned into Roman Catholics, and now they worship the Pope and the Virgin Mary and Jesus only comes in third possie. That's why we have to hate Roman Catholics as well.'

'Okay, I buy that, but why do we let the Roman Catholics into South Africa and not the Jews, hey?'

'We didn't, the English did. It's just another one of their terrible sins.' To drive the point home he said, 'You don't see any Afrikaners who are Roman Catholics, do you?'

I was forced to admit that I didn't know a single Afrikaner who was a Roman Catholic. I wasn't even sure if I'd recognise a Roman Catholic or a Jew if I saw one. There certainly weren't any in Duiwelskrans. 'How do you know if someone's a Roman Catholic or a Jew?' I asked Gawie.

'Easy, man,' he said with great authority. 'My uncle in Pretoria says you can tell a Roman Catholic because they wear a big gold cross around their neck and count beads that's supposed to be their prayers. They don't do proper prayers like us, they've got this necklace and every bead on it is a prayer that's already been said lots of times before. So if they just count them, they think it's the same as saying them, and in the meantime they're saving time. Imagine if you're God and you're waiting to hear all the prayers coming up to heaven at night and on Sunday morning all you hear is click "one", click "two", click "three" going on down below. How is He supposed to remember all the prayers they've gone and turned into numbers? *Wragtig!* It's an insult to God!'

'And Jews? How do you know if you run into one?'

Gawie paused, then said, 'My uncle in Pretoria says they've got this really big hooked nose and a black beard and long curly hair and they wear a round hat.'

'You mean they all look like Jesus?'

'No, man! Jesus had a straight nose, just like yours and mine, and he didn't wear a hat,' he said, growing impatient with my questioning.

'*Oom* Paul Kruger, the President of the Transvaal Republic during the Boer War, had a beard, a hooked nose and long hair and he wasn't a Jew!' I protested. We'd recently seen this picture of the young '*Oom* Paul' in a history lesson at school, taken before he got fat, and to me he fitted the description Gawie's uncle had given of a Jew down to a T.

Gawie sighed this long sigh. '*Voetsek, Oom* Paul had a big blobby nose and all Boere at that time had beards, and his hair was long because he was so busy fighting the British he didn't have time to get his mother to cut it.'

I thought it best to leave the discussion there. You couldn't argue about *Oom* Paul Kruger because that could take me back into blasphemy territory and I was still suffering from the flag business. While I thought I might be able to recognise a Roman Catholic by the big gold cross dangling around his neck and his beads clicking away while he's counting instead of saying prayers, I wasn't at all sure about knowing a Jew should I eventually came across one. There were plenty of Boere around with black beards and hooked noses that wore big hats. The *Dominee* was one for a start. Maybe it was the hair that would give them away. Because most people around the place had the short back and sides, so if a man suddenly had curly black hair, like a girl's, you'd know he was a Jew who shouldn't be allowed into South Africa. But, on the other hand, maybe

he was just a Boer who needed a haircut. Some of the Boere coming
down from the high mountains for *Nagmaal* had their hair long, so you
could easy make a big mistake.

I was also getting a bit worried about Gawie's uncle in Pretoria. Like
most of the kids, Gawie never had any relations visit at Christmas time.
Already I'd been in The Boys Farm since I was four years old and I don't
remember Gawie's uncle ever coming to visit and he never once went to
Pretoria on a holiday. His uncle must have done an awful lot of talking
to him about hen's teeth and snoring in fires and Jews and Catholics
counting beads before Gawie came, which was when he was only five
years old.

Now that the war was on we also were getting extra lectures after
dinner from Meneer Prinsloo who, like everyone else in the district,
supported the Nationalist Party like all decent, God-fearing Afrikaners.
They were bitterly opposed to the United Party and 'that traitor to his
own people, Prime Minister Jan Christiaan Smuts, who ought to be
locked up for treason and the key thrown away!' We weren't supposed to
talk about these lectures if a grown-up who was a stranger asked. Meneer
Prinsloo wanted us to understand that there were evil things going on
that were designed to destroy the Afrikaner people, 'who couldn't be
destroyed and would still be racially pure when the second coming of
Jesus comes!'

In one of his braces-straining sessions he said, 'This whole war is an
example of British/Jewish imperialism, and we in the Nationalist Party
must fight them tooth and nail!' I hoped he wasn't expecting too many
tooth-and-nail fighters from The Boys Farm because we didn't have too
many teeth left after the horse pliers, and most of us chewed our nails
right down to the quick.

Meneer Prinsloo also agreed with the *Dominee* that Hitler was an
okay person for all the same reasons. But he also said, in the Boer War
the Germans were on our side all the way up to their eyebrows but
couldn't fight for us because they didn't want to get into trouble with
the British, but they sold Mauser rifles and bullets to us really cheap,

and gave us bandages and medicine for nothing, and built portable field hospitals also for nothing.

'Instead of killing our women and children like the British, they saved our lives!' Meneer Prinsloo's braces were stretched to breaking point and his stomach stuck out beyond the platform where the staff table was, and his hands were moving so fast in the air around him that they were blurry.

It was a good point, even coming from Meneer Prinsloo. 'Now, boys, let me be quite fair and put the case to you. If somebody says to you that you must pick a side to fight on,' he paused and looked down at us from the platform, 'on the one side is someone who kills Afrikaner women and children in concentration camps and on the other is someone who saves their lives with bandages, medicine and whole field hospitals.' He took a breath, then said, 'As an Afrikaner, who you going to pick, hey?' Another pause to make sure we all got the point. 'So, I ask you, why are we fighting on the British side all of a sudden? Let me tell you why – because of British/Jewish imperialism! The Jews and the British own the goldmines and the diamonds and because Adolf Hitler says, "No more Jews in Germany, finish and *klaar*!" so now we got to fight against our old friends. Now is that fair? Is that what a Boer, a *regte* Boer, would do? A man of high honour and outstanding principles?'

Up to this point he had been pretty calm for someone like him, but all of a sudden his hands did somersaults in the air, and his arms practically flew off his shoulders and he roared at us, '*Never*! You hear, never! Never! Never! Never! I swear it on the graves of my dead grandmother Hester Prinsloo and great *Tante* Freda, who died of blackwater fever in the British concentration camps! God rest their souls and give them a home in heaven as far away from any British as possible!' When you think about it, he didn't have to worry – how could there be any British in heaven after what they'd done?

Then Frikkie Botha and Mevrou and even old Mevrou Pienaar the cook stood up and clapped and Frikkie Botha extended his hand in the Nazi salute. All of a sudden all the adults copied. Meneer Prinsloo stood there on the edge of the platform with his right arm raised and his stomach pulled in as much as it could for a change and the braces practically not extended. We all stood up and clapped and pushed out our arms in the Nazi salute. When I stood up the two boys on either side of me pushed me down again and held me down with a hand on either shoulder so they couldn't clap but could still salute, except one of them had to salute with the wrong arm.

Frikkie shouted, '*Heil* Hitler!' Everyone shouted back and Meneer Prinsloo's arm that had been in the salute started to wave around slowly at first, then the other one did as well, and they both started to windmill and he shouted, 'Victory to the Third Reich and freedom to the Afrikaner *volk*!' Everybody cheered like mad. I've got to tell you, it was very confusing. I decided on the spot that if ever I came across a Jewish imperialist who owned a gold or diamond mine, I was going to give him a piece of my mind. I'd also tell them to have a haircut quick smart because while a beard is okay, you can't go walking around with long, curly black hair sacking white people who've got jobs in your goldmine just so they can put a bit of food on the table for their wife and children.

Later someone told Mevrou I hadn't stood up and clapped and done the salute after Meneer Prinsloo's magnificent speech, so then I got seven of the best. 'Tonight you getting three for the British —' *Whack! Whack! Whack!* 'and three for the Jews, *Voetsek.*' *Whack! Whack! Whack! Whack!* 'That's a *bansella* from me, Mevrou Van Schalkwyk!'

So there was more Chinese writing on my bum. I'd never met a Jew and already I was being punished because of them, which just goes to show you can't be careful enough with Jewish imperialists all over the place.

The next night Meneer Prinsloo stood up and said he was very pleased with what happened the night before. He announced that he'd bought a new young Black Orpington rooster from a breeder in Acorn Hoek, which was a little *dorp* that you wouldn't ever think would have pedigree anythings, let alone roosters. He said again how Piet Retief had been sabotaged by some criminal person and all his hopes had been dashed. General Botha, his other rooster, wasn't good enough for the big-time shows, so now we could all learn a lesson of hope snatched from the jaws of disaster. '*Man het 'n plan*, a man has a plan,' he said. 'In life you've got to take the hard bumps as well as the tender kisses. Last night I had a dream, more like a vision, because the spirit of the Lord was definitely with me and I knew that the hand of God was guiding me. I am going to start from scratch with a new rooster who will be called Adolf Hitler after the great and glorious leader who has been through hard times but now is a world-champion leader.' He concluded by saying, 'If Adolf Hitler had tail feathers they would shine like the sun and scrape the very roof of the sky!'

We all clapped but Meneer Prinsloo held his hand up for silence. 'Now, one thing more,' he said. 'We don't know who the criminal mind was who sabotaged Piet Retief, but if anyone sees a certain vet when he comes to pull out your teeth and is afterwards hanging around the Black Orpingtons they must come and tell me immediately. This is an order!' He let this point sink in before explaining further. 'The Great Piet Retief, who is to become chicken soup, would have entered the Potgietersrus Agricultural Show as the preliminary to qualify for the Rand Easter Show, and everybody knows it was a foregone conclusion he would have won. But now Scarlet Pimpernel, the Rhode Island Red who is owned by a certain vet, has just won Best Rooster at Show!' He looked around darkly. 'I'm not saying any more, you hear? Except maybe this, everybody who knows a chicken knows that a certain vet's Scarlet Pimpernel wasn't a patch on Piet Retief whose tail feathers left that imposter champion's sprawling in the dust!'

Meneer Prinsloo asked us to leave lots of crusts on the table because he felt in his water that in Adolf Hitler he had a potential grand champion. '*Magtig!* Already he is only a cockerel and you can see how proud he walks!'

We all clapped again because when Meneer Prinsloo made a speech clapping was compulsory. I remembered Sergeant Van Niekerk's warning to me not to return to the scene of the Great Shiny-Feather Robbery. On the other hand, Doctor Dyke's big Alsatian had come sniffing around and tried to mount Tinker, and already there were three of my teeth missing because of the dreaded horse pliers. Maybe this year Miss Phillips could wear a handful of magnificent red feathers in her Easter bonnet from a champion Rhode Island Red, but then I remembered it would be a crime if it happened outside The Boys Farm and would count against me with God and also Sergeant Van Niekerk.

Here's a funny thing that happened. Even at Christmas we didn't get roast chicken because you had to be a proper family to get chicken at Christmas. I'd never tasted chicken and it would be some time before I did. Piet Retief was too tough to be a roast chicken, him being a rooster and all. But don't think we got to taste the soup old Mevrou Pienaar made from him because one chicken, even a champion rooster, couldn't get tasted in soup by sixty kids. The soup got served to the staff at the platform table. If you watched carefully everyone drank their soup slowly, holding their spoons just so and sipping with a great politeness. This was because they were aware that this was a dark moment in chickendom, that they were drinking the soup of somebody who could have been a grand champion at the Rand Easter Show. Meneer Prinsloo was the last to finish. He put his spoon back down on the plate slowly and precisely, then he took his serviette and wiped his eyes. Everybody was silent for a while after. Guess what happened to the chicken bones? Tinker got them in his scoff bowl that night. Tinker, who was, technically speaking, also a criminal, got to taste chicken before any kid at The Boys Farm. Crunch! Crunch! Crunch!

Maybe you've had enough of the war already, but I have to tell you about Frikkie Botha and how he went to blow up a bridge and blew himself up by mistake, which turned out to be no joke, I can tell you that for sure.

Frikkie was a member of the *Ossewabrandwag*, the Ox-Wagon Fireguard, which was known to everyone as the OB, but he was also a member of *Die Stormjaer Van Afrikanderdom*, the storm-troopers of the Afrikaner Nation. They were sort of soldiers of the OB and had lots of duties that I don't think they were supposed to have, like blowing up bridges, post offices and telegraph poles, and fighting the soldiers going to the war and who in their spare time tried to break up the political meetings that were against the Government and, of course, beating up *kaffirs* for practice. You weren't supposed to ever talk about them but it seemed to me that everyone around the place was one. Maybe not Doctor Van Heerden, Sergeant Van Niekerk or Meneer Van Niekerk the headmaster because they never said and didn't go to the meetings.

But Frikkie Botha, the storm-trooper, was now in his element. His hour of glory had come and all his free time was spent training to fight with broomsticks, clubs and flick-knives. He'd stand there and you'd think he had nothing in his hand, then all of a sudden there's this pocketknife that flicks open and the blade is staring at you, inches from your stomach. Frikkie was now my enemy, not because of him becoming an OB, but because of the flag incident when Gawie stuck the pound note up his bum. Thank goodness this didn't apply to Tinker, who was still Frikkie's little rat trap and his all-time favourite dog.

On Saturday, when we worked in the vegetable gardens and the orange grove, Frikkie Botha had taken to wearing his *Stormjaer* uniform and copying Meneer Prinsloo by giving us lectures. He listened to a radio in the staff quarters and he'd give us regular updates on what was happening in the war. Of course, he only reported the German victories. Here is a 'for example' of one of them.

'Now they, the Germans, they in Poland, man, running all over the place. The Poles they came charging on horses with swords, like it's the Boer War all over again, but there's German tanks coming at them across the border and all of a sudden there's mincemeat everywhere, pieces of horses flying up in the air, and suddenly no more Poland! Next it's going to be the British, you wait and see, man! The British, they bayonet charging, while somebody plays the bagpipes, and what do they find? Only a wall of steel. *Pow! Pow! Pow!* Finish and *klaar!* All the British lying dead in their skirts with nothing underneath.'

I could see that everyone was a bit puzzled. 'Why are the British soldiers wearing skirts, and someone is playing with a pipe in a bag?' Kaag Wolmarans asked.

'Ag, man, they just do it,' Frikkie said. But still no one was any the wiser.

Then Gawie said, 'They're from Scotland and they're Scotch. What they wear is kilts that is like a skirt that men wear and the bagpipes is a musical wind thing they play when they go to fight.'

'*Ja*, that also,' Frikkie said, pretending to know all the time and giving Gawie a nice look.

Gawie and I had recently read Sir Walter Scott's *Rob Roy* and we'd learned all about kilts and bagpipes.

'Is England next to Poland, Meneer?' Matai Marais asked.

'*Ja*, I think it's right next door, just you watch, their turn is coming any day now,' Frikkie said darkly.

'But first they got to cross the English Channel,' Gawie piped up cheekily.

'Ag, man, no problems,' Frikkie Botha replied. 'Those German tanks, they can go anywhere. Before you know it they there. A channel is nothing for a tank, they are over it and up the other side like lightning. They can dig a channel as deep as they like, for a German tank it's no problem, in and out and the next thing you know the British are all lying dead.'

Gawie didn't dare point out that the English Channel was filled with water and was thirty miles wide and nobody knows how deep. And for once in my life I wasn't stupid enough to say so either or to point out that Poland wasn't anywhere near England.

'Haven't the British got tanks?' someone asked.

Frikkie Botha thought for a moment, then smiled. '*Ja*, but it's hopeless for them. Let me tell you a story of how clever the Germans are.' Frikkie took a deep breath while trying to contain his amusement.

'In this one factory they build tanks and in another they make anti-tank weapons. Got it?' We all nodded. 'So now the general in charge of the tanks says to his factory, "Here's a piece of steel that our tanks are made from and see this, it's got a hole right through the middle. That's where a bullet went right through from the anti-tank weapon factory next door. *Magtig!* Now I want you to make a tank so the anti-tank bullet can't get through it, okay?" So that's their next big problem.' Frikkie chuckled to himself. 'But then the general in charge of the anti-tank weapons says to his factory, "Hey, man, look at this!" and he shows them this piece of steel that's only a got a small dent in it. "That's the best bullets we got, man!" he shouts. "They won't go through this steel from the tank factory next door! Shame on you! Your next big job is to make an anti-tank bullet that can go through this steel, you hear?"' Frikkie paused. '*Wragtig!* By the time those German tanks come out the other side of that channel Gawie Grobler is talking about and all of a sudden there's British tanks facing them, it's . . . *Kapow! Zing! Kapow! Boom! Boom! Boom!* Finish and *klaar!* What the British tanks are made of is only pots and pans they collected at the last moment from the British people! They up to shit, man!' Frikkie Botha spread his hands. 'For a German tank it's like shooting through a paper bag and the British bullets coming back, it's like they made of putty when they hit a German tank!'

I must say I hadn't built up a lot of sympathy for the British and it certainly looked as if Adolf Hitler was well in control. But I couldn't see things improving for me when he won the war, which could be as early as next week, if you listened to what people were saying. Already being English wasn't easy, now all of a sudden with Hitler winning the war and giving South Africa back to the Boere my future didn't look too bright. So Gawie and me had one of our discussions at the library rock.

'What's going to happen to the English in South Africa when Hitler wins the war?' I asked him.

Gawie, looking down at his hands, didn't answer right off. Finally, he said, 'Unfortunately, concentration camps.' He paused and looked up at me. 'Just like you did to us, *Voetsek.*'

'All the English here, we going to die then?'

'Not all. Those that don't die we going to send to Madagascar.'

'Madagascar! What's in Madagascar?'

'It's just a place to send people you don't want,' he replied. 'Don't worry, I'll look after Tinker for you.'

'Why can't she come with me?' I was deeply shocked.

'No dogs allowed,' Gawie said firmly. 'Those boats are too full, you can't even fit a mouse in them.'

'I could hold her on my lap,' I said defiantly.

'No food, man! You all going to come out walking skeletons, some people will just be a heap of bones and a bit of skin and hair that's left behind in the Union Castle boat that takes you there.'

'But . . . but you are my friend, Gawie. Wouldn't you help me?'

'Can't!' He looked at me sympathetically. 'Honest, *Voetsek*, I would, but it's against the law. Besides, I'll be too busy running a goldmine.'

'But you're only eleven, that's too young to own a goldmine,' I said, relieved that all this was just a big pretend and he was pulling my leg. But I'd momentarily forgotten that Afrikaners are very serious people and don't go in for a lot of leg-pulling.

'No, I won't be!' Gawie protested. 'You forget, you first going to have to go to the concentration camps where you have to starve to death for a long time like we did and maybe also die. Only what's leftover goes to Madagascar. By that time I will be old enough to have a goldmine.'

'I don't think they just going to give you a goldmine,' I said doubtfully.

'Yeah, there's plenty, man! I'll have one that a Jew used to have, but because he's dead, it will be mine.' He looked at me. 'I told you already. When I grow up I *have* to be rich.'

'But we're already rich,' I replied. 'We've still got our ten bob.'

'More, much more, a hundred pounds at least,' Gawie said.

'A hundred pounds!' I couldn't believe my ears.

'*Ag*, man, to a Jew a hundred pounds is nothing if you got a goldmine.' Gawie looked at me, smiling kindly. 'I tell you what, *Voetsek*. When you go to the concentration camp you can give me your ten shillings and I'll buy some gold for you or maybe a diamond. A diamond you can hide easily as anything, if you have to, you can stick it up your bum. That's what the Jews did when they were running away from Germany.'

'They stick diamonds up their bum?'

'Not always, sometimes it's gold in their teeth. That's another way you can spot a Jew, when he smiles it's all gold, every tooth is made of pure gold.'

This was certainly a better way of recognising a Jew than long curly black hair that could be anyone who hadn't got his hair cut, a golden smile you couldn't mistake. I'd never seen a Boer with gold for his teeth. I must say it did seem a bit impractical sticking diamonds up your bum. A diamond is a very small thing and can easily get lost. What's more, gold, I'd read somewhere, is very heavy. With a mouthful of gold maybe you couldn't even chew stuff because it's so heavy. I really was beginning to have serious doubts about Gawie's Madagascan theory.

'With the diamonds, what happens when you go for a shit?'

'Ag, you take it out first, man. Like I would if I had to with that ten-shilling note that turned into a pound.'

'And gold teeth? Gold is heavy, if you've got only gold teeth how can you chew food?'

Gawie thought for a moment, then went 'Tsk!' and shook his head from side to side. 'You know, *Voetsek*, sometimes I think you don't listen. You starving, man! Remember? There's nothing to eat so you don't need to open your mouth because you not allowed to talk.'

The flaws in this argument were too obvious for me to pursue. Gawie was my friend and I didn't want to trap him, especially if I was going to need his help in a week or so when Hitler arrived and gave the whole country back to the Afrikaners. I couldn't resist one more question.

'Who told you all this stuff?' I asked.

'My uncle in Pretoria,' he replied with his usual degree of finality.

I took a deep breath. 'I don't believe you've got an uncle in Pretoria,' I said, my heart thumping like billyo.

'I have so!' he protested. 'Oom Piet.'

'Oom Piet?' I had a surge of courage. If I was headed for a concentration camp and then, after starving to death, was being sent to Madagascar, I might as well clear up my serious doubts about Gawie's uncle in Pretoria once and for all. This was the first time he'd mentioned his uncle by name, a fact that caused me to hesitate. An actual name is different to just having an anonymous 'my uncle in Pretoria'. Stupidly I decided to press on. 'Hens got no teeth, okay, this I understand. A man burning to death while snoring away with the fire brigade watching, this too because when you a little kid you can be told things like that, maybe by an uncle in Pretoria. But, Gawie, you now eleven, man! You've been here at The Boys Farm since you were five years old and not once have you seen your uncle in Pretoria. So where is your Oom Piet?'

'He told me before I came here!' Gawie persisted, raising his voice for emphasis. 'I got a good memory, man!' I could see he'd gone all red in the face.

'Gawie, Jews were not running away all over the place with golden teeth and diamonds up their bums from Germany when you were five,' I said accusingly. 'It's only happening now that Hitler has said, "Finish and klaar, no more Jews in Germany!"' I was wrong, of course, Jews had been leaving Germany long before either of us were five, but neither of us knew this then.

'My Oom Piet writes me letters,' Gawie said, digging himself in deeper. That was the trouble with Gawie, in some things he was very, very smart, the cleverest of all of us, and in others, like, for instance, him owning a goldmine from a dead Jew, he was even more dumb than me. Even I wouldn't think something like that could happen. We also both knew nobody got letters at The Boys Farm. If one should arrive a lot of fuss was made over it and it would be handed to the boy after supper, but only after Meneer Prinsloo had read it first and told us all what was in it. The parcels from Miss Phillips were always sent to the school headmaster, Meneer Van Niekerk, who then gave them to me after looking to see that the book she'd sent was alright for me to read.

'Show me one of these letters,' I demanded.

'I can't, I have to tear them up in little pieces and throw them away because they got war secrets in them.' He gave me a nervous smile. 'It's a good thing I've got a good memory, hey?'

Sometimes things come out of your mouth that shouldn't come out of your mind. 'That's bullshit and you know it!' I said, raising my voice.

We were sitting on top of the library rock and Gawie suddenly jumped up. 'Are you calling me a liar, *Voetsek*?' Before I could answer, he shouted, 'You a fucking *rooinek*, you hear! I'm not your friend any more and I'm going to tell Meneer Prinsloo about the feathers!' He turned and ran down the side of the rock and away towards the creek.

Talk about the deep shit! This time I was a goner for sure! Why had I opened my big mouth? When are you going to learn you in enemy territory, *Voetsek*? I asked myself despairingly.

Tinker, who was there all the time, could see I was upset, and she came onto my lap and licked my hand and then the tears off my face. This time nothing helped. I'd just lost the best friend I'd ever had after Mattress. As a matter of fact, the *only* friend I'd ever had who was still a boy. Now look what was going to happen to me.

I thought that hopefully Hitler might win before Meneer Prinsloo saw to it that I joined Fonnie du Preez in the Boys Reformatory or they sent me to Pretoria Prison. Then I could go to the concentration camp and starve to death and maybe eventually get to Madagascar, which would be a lot better than hanging by the neck until you were stone dead. When you're alive you've still got a chance, even without a diamond up your bum or gold teeth. But Meneer Prinsloo didn't call me up about Piet Retief's tail feathers so that was the first piece of survival-hope, that Gawie hadn't told him.

You're probably wondering how Gawie and me knew about the English Channel and Poland as well as other war things that Frikkie left out of his updates, when there weren't any newspapers and we couldn't listen to the wireless. How we learned stuff about what was going on in the war was another example of Gawie being the cleverest of all of us.

Every week from somewhere, I think from the Government, would come this big bunch of newspapers to The Boys Farm that had to be cut up into squares for the lavatories. They were old ones nobody wanted or they'd already been read. It was one of the duties you got if you were in the small boys dormitory. Then one day at half-jack, Mevrou held up this square of newspaper that was for wiping your bum.

'See!' she exclaimed. 'Perfect! It's just perfect!' You could see she was very pleased. She held up another and put it behind the first one. 'See how it fits, hey?' Then four more, all fitted exactly with none of them sticking out at the edges. 'This is the work of a very talented boy, you hear?' We all waited to hear who it was and I knew for sure it wasn't me. My squares were all over the place, some of them were even triangles, and once I'd got four of the best for the hopeless job I'd done.

'Gawie Grobler, step out from your bed,' Mevrou said in a fond voice, which was a nice change. Gawie did as he was told. 'If only the rest of you could do it like this, maybe we could learn some good hygiene lessons,' Mevrou scolded. 'Now everyone give a big clap!' So we all clapped Gawie for his perfect square shit paper.

All of a sudden we stopped having to tear up newspapers for the lavatory as a regular duty. This was because Gawie went to Mevrou and asked if he could have the job on a permanent basis. Gawie later told me how Mevrou was very impressed with his offer. This was because nobody ever volunteered to do anything around the place and she agreed that he was just perfect for the job. He was a boy who liked to do things properly so that they were just so and always exact, and the pieces he made also fitted very nicely in a person's hand so you didn't need two pieces of paper.

I've already told you how clever Gawie was, but this was the perfect example. Now Gawie didn't have to collect wood or water the oranges and avocado trees or any of the other dirty jobs around the place, like cleaning out the chicken run. All he did was sit on his bum tearing up bits of newspaper as the official shit-paper maker. How clever is that, hey? Okay, now you know that part. Here at last comes a miracle.

I'm busy sitting on the toilet having a you-know-what and I reach out for the paper hanging on the wire hook and there right in front of my very eyes is this:

POLITIEK KOMENTEER
VAN OOM PIET
Die Jude Krisis

Political Commentary from Oom Piet. The Jewish Crisis.

Dr T.E. Donges, Minister for Finance, declared in Parliament on 4 November 1936 that 'The Jew is an insoluble element in every national life.' Well said, Doctor, I couldn't agree more. I can remember how after the First World War the Palestine question arose over a homeland for the Jews and there was a proposal put forward to give them Madagascar as their Promised Land. While this big island off the East Coast is alarmingly close to South Africa, at least it would have been some sort of a solution to the Jewish problem.

But as usual the British bowed to the demands of Jewish imperialism and American Jews who said they would only settle for Palestine and then only as a token. The Jews have no intention of moving out of the cosy countries they live in and where they have a privileged existence and control the financial markets. For example, the great Wall Street crash of 1929 was manipulated by the American Jews causing the Great Depression and as a consequence millions of non-Jewish people around the globe suffered terrible hardship.

It is to our everlasting shame that since 1933 and up until 1936, when Jewish migration was finally restricted in South Africa by a government that had at last come to its senses, we accepted a total of 3605 Jews into the Union. While this is close to being a national tragedy, there is a small funny side. Not so very funny, more like amusing. I have it on good authority that many of the Jews who came here before they left Germany first had their teeth heavily capped with gold and they are said to have concealed diamonds in a certain bodily orifice that I leave to your imagination. *Magtig*! Here, where most of the world's gold comes from, and also diamonds! And people say they are clever! It is my personal opin—

There was more, but Gawie had torn off the rest to make his perfect square and I couldn't find the rest of *Oom* Piet's commentary in the bunch of paper hanging beside me on the wall. So I would never know what his personal opinion was going to be, but I don't think it would have been very nice. Now I understood how Gawie knew everything and how he had invented his uncle in Pretoria. He'd read it all in *Die Vaderland*, which was the name of the newspaper we mostly got for shit paper. So I wiped my arse on another piece and carefully folded the one I'd just read and put it in my trouser pocket.

The next morning I confronted Gawie on the way to school and said I was sorry about saying what he'd said was a load of bullshit. At first he didn't want to know me. '*Voetsek, Voetsek*!' he said, giving me a push. I persisted and told him I knew something that as far as I was concerned made him even cleverer than I already thought. So he brightened a bit and when we'd walked a few steps further he asked, 'What?'

I showed him the newspaper square and told him how inventing his uncle in Pretoria was a stroke of genius. He laughed and we were friends again and he said, 'You didn't really think I'd tell Meneer Prinsloo about the chicken feathers, did you, *Voetsek*?'

'*Ja*,' I laughed, 'I thought I was in the deep shit, man! Already on my way to Pretoria.'

'A *regte* Boer doesn't betray his friends like the British do,' he said piously.

Gawie and me were friends again. What's more, from then on he'd keep articles about the war and other stuff going on when he was tearing up squares, and we'd read them and talk about them. That's how we knew about the English Channel and where Poland was and lots of other things. We could also carry on having our discussions at the library rock and read books of which we now had a big collection that formed the library Miss Phillips had promised I would one day own. By the way, Miss Phillips didn't win the Easter Bonnet competition again because she didn't have any proper feathers from a champion rooster. Adolf Hitler, Meneer Prinsloo's new rooster, hadn't won a single competition. Meneer Prinsloo said it was early times and he was coming along nicely and next year his tail feathers would be ready for action. Perhaps next year, which would be more than a year since I visited the scene of the crime, Miss Phillips would get a nice surprise slipped into her self-addressed envelope.

I haven't told you yet about Frikkie Botha and the great bridge explosion disaster. The local *Stormjaer*, the so-called soldiers of the *Ossewabrandwag*, were kept busy guarding Nationalist political meetings around the place from hecklers and proper soldiers. But in our district there wasn't any opposition coming to disrupt and to heckle, as the Lebombo Mountain region was an Afrikaner stronghold. It got pretty boring with no opposition at the meetings, no Jews to be seen anywhere about the place, no army camp or soldiers getting ready to go off to war that you could beat up. What's more, in our district there wasn't any point in blowing up bridges or railway lines or telegraph poles or even the post office or police station because you'd only be harming yourself. Besides, in Duiwelskrans you'd have to answer to Sergeant Van Niekerk and his three dogs and that wouldn't be at all funny.

So there was Frikkie and other *Stormjaers* strutting around the place in shiny boots with their broomsticks, lead pipes, bicycle chains, knuckledusters, clubs and knives with nothing to do. Frikkie and his platoon of six other *Stromjaers* were jumping out of their pants for want of some real honest-to-goodness violent action. I should explain that the *Stormjaers* worked in groups of seven men, like a small platoon. There could be as many platoons as you liked in the district but only seven men in each who drilled and worked together to do things like guarding and sabotage. Frikkie's platoon consisted of himself and Mevrou's six brothers, later known as the 'Van Schalkwyk Six', even though there were seven of them at the beginning, the seventh being Frikkie Botha.

So Frikkie and Mevrou's six brothers hatched this bold plan to blow up a train carrying white Rhodesian soldiers to Durban who were joining South African troops going to fight overseas. Rhodesia was a country right next door to South Africa and about one hundred and fifty miles north of where we were. It was also on the side of Britain. It seems one of the Van Schalkwyk brothers had once been a guard on the South African railways and knew the railway line from Beit Bridge, which is on the Limpopo River, the natural border between Rhodesia and South Africa, and Pietersburg. The plan was to drive to near the border and find an isolated culvert or a donga with a small bridge over it and blow it up and derail the troop train.

Frikkie Botha got some dynamite from a nearby goldmine and a miner showed him how to make a bomb, how to light a fuse and how best to blow up a small bridge. All of a sudden he was the big explosive expert around the place. I don't want you to think that the *Stormjaer* were stupid or anything, and would just let an amateur like Frikkie go ahead and blow up a bridge. They had plenty of experts around the place that could have done it properly, but the district *kommandant* didn't know it was going to happen because Frikkie's platoon wanted to be heroes and hadn't asked permission, just in case they were refused. They were sick and tired of guarding Nationalist Party meetings where nothing ever happened.

So off they drove in a lorry with false numberplates, dressed in their farm clothes, not their uniforms, and without any other identification. They eventually got near to Beit Bridge where they hid the lorry off the main road. They carried the dynamite and fuses in a hessian sack and walked three miles to where the railway track was. They walked along it until they found this donga that was a dried-up creek with a small bridge over it that was miles from anywhere so nobody would hear the explosion when it went off. The plan was that they'd blow up the little bridge and the train coming later wouldn't know about it. They'd be miles away when the engine fell into the donga. *Boom!* Easy as anything, man.

As Frikkie was the one who got the instructions on how to make the bomb and where to plant it under the bridge, he got the job to climb under and put the bomb against one of the main girders. Knowing Frikkie Botha, he would have loved the opportunity to be a hero in the eyes of Mevrou's six fierce brothers. Just to be the single outside member of a platoon with the six of them making up the remainder was a source of great pride to him. He'd once boasted to us, 'Ag, man, we probably the best in the business and all we do is guard Nationalist Party meetings. If we were in Pretoria, Kommandant General Hans van Rensburg would give us all the *really* dangerous sabotage jobs, like blowing up the Union Building in Pretoria and the main railway station in Johannesburg.'

The bomb was made of sticks of gelignite tied together with a long fuse that allowed you to light it and then get away in time to hide behind a rock or something before it went off. The little bridge was about twenty feet above the bottom of the donga. Frikkie climbed over the edge at the centre of the bridge and then worked his way underneath to the central steel girder. The rest of the bridge was made of wooden beams and it was this steel girder that had to be blown out so it would collapse. That's where Frikkie was meant to put the bomb and then drop from a rope to the bottom of the donga. It wasn't supposed to be dangerous because the fuse was long enough to allow plenty of time for Frikkie to get to where the six Van Schalkwyk brothers would be hiding from the blast.

All went well and using a pair of pliers and some wire Frikkie tied the bomb securely to the steel girder. That's when he made his first big mistake. He was supposed to let the fuse hang down from the bomb all the way to the ground and climb down the rope and light the fuse and run away to safety. But he forgot and lit the fuse while he was still under the top of the bridge. He realised what he'd done, and panicked and grabbed the rope to let himself down, at the same time he hit his head against the steel girder, and was knocked unconscious and fell to the bottom of the donga.

When he didn't get to safety the brothers took a look from where they were hiding and they must have seen Frikkie lying there, but they weren't game to get closer as they could see the fuse spluttering sparks so they knew it was already alight. Ages went by and they could have easily rescued Frikkie because the fuse would take about three minutes to burn down, but nobody volunteered to go to help him. The longer they waited the more they panicked until *Boom!* Down came the bridge on top of Frikkie.

When the smoke cleared, the Van Schalkwyk brothers ran over to the collapsed bridge and the first thing they saw was Frikkie's severed hand lying in the dirt. Coming closer they saw that his skull had been fractured so they could see his brain, and his face was wiped off. They were sure that he was dead. There were wooden beams all over his body and one across his throat, and out of the bloody mess that was once his face his tongue stuck out like a little pink gravestone.

This is what happened next. Remember, nobody knew they were there. They left Frikkie Botha, who was about to be mashed even further by a train engine falling on him. They walked the three miles through the bush back to the lorry and drove the hundred and fifty miles home to Duiwelskrans and back into the high mountains to their farm where they put the correct numberplates back on the lorry. Dead men tell no tales.

But Frikkie Botha wasn't dead. He'd just lost his face like Mattress had. I didn't know it at the time, but Mattress was the more fortunate of the two because he died.

Some blacks from the Venda tribe who lived in a village some way off heard the explosion and some *umfaans* came to see what the noise was all about. They found Frikkie and these black kids ran back to the village to tell the adults who came over and lifted up the beams. They saw Frikkie Botha was still alive so they made a makeshift stretcher of cowhide and carried him the three miles to Beit Bridge and from there he was taken to the hospital in Messina.

One of the African men who rescued Frikkie applied a tourniquet to his arm and saved him from bleeding to death. That a black person would know how to do such a thing was a source of wonderment to the Afrikaans newspapers, which didn't mention the real wonderment: that they'd carried him several miles through the bush when they could have easily left Frikkie Botha to die. The Vendas also posted men on the railway line to stop the troop train before it got to the collapsed bridge. But here's the joke. It wasn't even a troop train. It was a goods train carrying copper from Northern Rhodesia to Pretoria. The troop train was due to leave Salisbury the next morning, by which time the bridge had been temporarily repaired.

The papers were full of the news of this man lying unconscious and in a critical state in the small hospital in Messina. He had no identification on him so he became known throughout South Africa as 'The Faceless Man'. While everyone agreed it was an act of sabotage, there was nothing on him to suggest he was a *Stormjaer* who belonged to the *Ossewabrandwag*. So now Frikkie was also the 'Lone Saboteur', which suited the six Van Schalkwyk brothers down to the ground.

At first we were all none the wiser at The Boys Farm. Frikkie was on his holidays and away for two weeks. He'd told everyone he was going to the Orange Free State to visit his auntie in a little *dorp* named Jacobsdal, which was in the opposite direction and several hundred miles from where the bridge had been blown up. The two weeks went by and the Faceless Man still hadn't regained consciousness or been identified, and eventually the newspapers stopped putting him in. When Frikkie didn't get back to The Boys Farm when he was supposed to, after a few days Meneer Prinsloo called Sergeant Van Niekerk who called the police station at Kimberley because Jacobsdal was such a tiny *dorp* it didn't even have a policeman, let alone a police station. They sent a policeman to visit Frikkie's auntie, who hadn't laid eyes on him for sixteen years, ever since her sister's funeral. So Sergeant Van Niekerk got the X-ray from Duiwelskrans hospital they'd taken when Mattress had broken Frikkie's jaw and put it on the train addressed to the sergeant at the Messina police station and the mystery of the Faceless Man was solved. A picture of Frikkie when he'd been a boxer appeared in just about every newspaper in the land so that everyone knew what he'd looked like when he still had a face on him.

They waited another week before Frikkie came out of his coma so they could hear his story. But guess what happened? The small wooden beam that had landed across his throat had permanently destroyed his vocal cords so he would never speak again.

Now you're asking, how do I know about what happened before Frikkie was discovered under the bridge when nobody else did? Well, I'll tell you about that later, and it isn't a very pretty story. In the meantime, this is what happened to Mevrou's six brothers. The Van Schalkwyk Six, whom everyone in the district ended up thinking of as heroes in the Afrikaner resistance movement, went from bad to worse.

You'd think they'd learn a lesson after the bridge disaster and that they'd leave exploding things alone, but no such thing. They still got bored doing nothing around Duiwelskrans so they took a weekend to go to Potchefstroom where they'd heard there were these big electricity pylons carrying powerlines. This time they were successful and managed to blow up two but they were caught minutes later. It was this act that made them famous as the Van Schalkwyk Six because they were sentenced to life imprisonment for sabotage, the first OBs in the Northern Transvaal (if you didn't count Frikkie Botha) to became martyrs to the Afrikaner cause.

Mevrou has six brothers in prison and is very proud. It's not every day you have a genuine martyr in a family, but to have six is something you could never believe could happen and people were shaking her hand and making compliments all over the place.

The next time I did something wrong and they called out my name after supper and I had to go to the sick room for punishment she said, 'I've been waiting for you, *Voetsek*.'

'Why, Mevrou?' I asked, puzzled, because the reason I was getting the *sjambok* was that I'd forgotten to wash my hands before supper, which only meant three of the best.

'*Ja*, well, you the *rooinek* and that's nearly like being the Smuts government, you hear?'

'No, Mevrou, I don't like the Government like everybody else!' I protested.

Mevrou sighed. 'It's no use trying to get out of it, I've made up my mind, we have to remember the martyrs, so what you going to get is the Van Schalkwyk Six!'

'But it's only three for not washing your hands!' I said.

She pointed to my hands. 'And what about the blood on your hands?' she demanded.

'Blood?' I examined my hands. 'There's no blood on my hands, Mevrou.'

'Ha! What about the concentration camps? If it wasn't for the English taking our country when we didn't do anything to them there wouldn't be women and children killed in the concentration camps, and we wouldn't be fighting this war on the wrong side. So then the six martyrs wouldn't be rotting in a Pretoria prison!' There were tears in her eyes. 'Do you understand?' She didn't wait for me to reply. 'Those martyrs, they are my own flesh and blood, you hear?'

'I'm . . . I'm . . . very sorry, Mevrou,' I stammered. 'I was very sad to hear about your brothers.' A big fat lie, of course, but it was a Boys Farm lie so it didn't count against God.

'Sorry? A name like yours with blood on his hands is all of a sudden sorry? How dare you insult me! Take down your pants, touch your toes!'

I did as I was told.

Whack! 'Kobus!' *Whack!* 'Johannes!' *Whack!* 'Pietrus!' *Whack!* 'Kees!' *Whack!* 'Jakob!' *Whack!* 'Frans!' *Whack!* 'Me! Because I am from the same martyred family.'

I now had Chinese martyr writing on my bum.

CHAPTER EIGHT

The Love of Two Good Women

THE *DOMINEE* DE JAGER was at it again because all of a sudden things were not going too smoothly for Adolf Hitler, who was meeting some opposition at long last. This seemed to upset the Great beard-chomping beetle because Hitler had decided to go to Russia instead of invading Britain and was now stuck in the snow. 'I'm no general, you hear? But why is Adolf Hitler all of a sudden invading Russia? What has Russia done to us? The Afrikaner people have no quarrel with Russia!' he declared vehemently.

I could have told him it was because Hitler could get some oil for his tanks and stuff, and in England they've got no oil and in Russia they've got lots. Only his one big mistake was that he shouldn't have gone to get it in the winter. We'd read all about it in *Die Vaderland* that Gawie had saved from his shit squares only the week before. But, of course, you can't just stand up in church and explain to the congregation why Hitler had to go to Russia but should have gotten out before the winter came. One, the *Dominee* is too high up and a child can't say anything to him. Two, with me being English they would think I was a spy, knowing stuff like that. Three, nobody in the congregation had ever seen snow and ice, and they wouldn't know you could get so cold in Russia your toes and fingers fell off.

So the *Dominee* thundered on. 'The sooner there's Germans marching all over Britain the better for the Afrikaner *volk*. Let the British see what it's like to have the enemy knocking on your door for a change. You go to the door and you open it and standing right in front of you is a German officer! Maybe he just wants a cup of coffee, but maybe also he wants to come and live in your house, and then you've got to wait on him hand and foot, and if you got a daughter, watch out!' The beetle started to munch his beard overtime. 'I'm speaking from personal experience, you hear? When I was a small child it happened. One morning, knock, knock, knock, and my mother opens the door and there's an English captain who is a *ware rooinek* with red hair on the *stoep*. And what's worse, the English captain is really an Australian! Next to him is a man, an Afrikaner, who is holding a big fish!' The *Dominee* stretched out his hands so we could all see how big the fish was. I can tell you that fish was definitely a big one. But later I learned people always exaggerate about fish, even a *Dominee*. 'It's a big barbel from the Vaal River that's got whiskers ten inches long! "The captain wants you to cook it!" the Afrikaner, who is his translator, explains. My mother shakes her head. "*Nee, Meneer Kaptein*, it will taste like mud. You can't eat that fish. That fish is a barbel and feeds on the river's bottom, it is no good." The translator, who should be ashamed for working for the British, explains what my mother says about the barbel. "Cook it!" the English captain demands, going all red in the face and shaking his finger at my mother. Next thing he is living with my family, sleeping in my mother's bedroom in the bed I was born in, sleeping *lekker* under the goosefeather quilt my *ouma* made for her glory box, long before she died in the concentration camp!'

We never did hear if that Englishman ate the barbel. But afterwards we all agreed he couldn't have, because nobody, not even an Englishman, could eat such a stinking fish as the barbel. But now the *Dominee* was talking about fish he clean forgot about the Germans in Russia until it was too late, and then he made a very bad sermon message connection. After talking about the barbel-eating Englishman sleeping under his *ouma*'s goosefeather quilt, he made the point that Jesus is the 'Fisher of men'. If we are not caught hook, line and sinker by his precious gospel bait telling us to confess our sins and be saved, then we going to be condemned to eternal hellfire.

Still on the fish theme, the *Dominee* also told us how Jesus had done two miracles concerning fish. The first was when some of his disciples, who were fishermen before they met Jesus, were out fishing one day on the Sea of Galilee and they looked up and there is the Lord Jesus coming towards them and here he is walking on water! 'Follow me and I will make you fishers of men,' Jesus says to them when he gets close enough for them to hear above the roar of the waves. Now, it's not every day that you're to hellangone out to sea and there's waves splashing about everywhere and it's deep water, and all of a sudden you look up and here's somebody coming over to you walking on the water with his bare feet. Next thing, he steps into the boat and his feet and the hem of his garment are not even wet. So, of course, they decide to follow him and become his disciples. You couldn't say no, even if you wanted to, with something like that happening.

The next fish miracle is when Jesus is preaching to the multitudes on the slopes of some mountain in the desert, and everyone's walked a long way to hear him preach and they've forgotten to bring any food. Except for this one man who's got a few loaves of bread and another, maybe a woman, who's got a few dead fish in a basket. 'Bring them here,' Jesus instructs and waves his hand over the bread and suddenly there's loaves of fresh-baked bread piled up everywhere. He does the same to the fish and then there's more fish than the people can eat and it's already cooked with the bones taken out! But what I want to know is this. There's no water in the desert, right? So how come all of a sudden this woman's got fish in her basket?

Now, I suppose you're wondering what this has to do with Hitler going to Russia instead of England? Well, as far as I could work it out, it was God working in mysterious ways. The *Dominee* got himself on the subject of fish and he suddenly remembered about Russia, so he had to get back to that subject again. This was because he always liked to talk to a theme and have a 'rounded message' that always ended up where he'd begun.

This is how he got back to Russia. He claimed that everyone could make a mistake, even Adolf Hitler, and being in Russia was definitely a mistake and he should have been in Britain. Now the *Dominee* had talked about two miracles and we had to pray for two more miracles. A walking-on-water miracle and a feeding-the-multitudes-bread-and-fish miracle, but it all had to happen in Russia. The *Dominee* pointed out to the congregation that it was a well-known fact that snow, that you couldn't walk on or drive tanks in it, could easily turn into ice that you *could* walk on and drive tanks over. That's what we had to pray for, snow turning into ice in Russia.

So that was how he turned the Jesus-walking-on-water miracle back into Russia. But the feeding of the multitudes wasn't so easy. First he said aeroplanes could land on the ice to bring in flour and stuff from Germany to bake bread. Then the *Dominee* made his big mistake. 'With ice you can see where the rivers run,' he explained. 'You look through the ice and there's a river called the Volga running underneath your feet, so you drill a hole and there's lots of fish you can catch. The Eskimos do it all the time,' he explained. He leaned back from his pulpit. 'A person as clever and resourceful as a German soldier would soon be eating all the fish he could catch,' he concluded, happy that he'd finally pulled Russia, Britain, English captains with red hair, his *ouma*'s quilt, two fish miracles and back to Russia together all in the one message.

Even to me this fishing through a hole in the ice didn't sound too practical, especially as, according to *Die Vaderland*, lots of the Germans were still wearing their summer uniforms and thousands of them were freezing to death, and everyone knows ice is even colder than snow. So, by praying for an ice miracle instead of snow we were condemning even more German soldiers to death. As for German soldiers being resourceful and catching all the fish they could eat through a hole in the river, in my opinion all the fish they would catch was none! But, like I said, you couldn't argue with someone as high up as the *Dominee*. As far as I was concerned it was a bullshit sermon and he'd just done it so he could get back to Russia and have his 'rounded message'.

Later, when Gawie and me were talking about this Gawie said, 'Ag, it doesn't look as though you're going to go to Madagascar, *Voetsek*.' He added graciously, 'I'm glad, man, because now we can grow up together and always be *maats*.'

I was naturally very pleased to hear this, but a person can't just go around showing your feelings, so I said sympathetically, 'But now you won't get your gold and diamond mine from a dead Jew.'

'Ag, it doesn't matter, man, I'll get one on my own because when I grow up I have to be rich.'

'And have a hundred pounds,' I remembered.

'*Ja*, maybe even more,' he said.

That night, as I lay in bed in the dark, I hugged myself. This was because Britain was beginning to look like they were going to win the war because the Americans were coming in to help, which was very disappointing for a lot of people around the place. But for me, at least two good things would happen. I wasn't going to starve to death and then get sent to Madagascar, and I now had Gawie who I could grow up with, and who would always be my friend. Maybe if I gave him my ten shillings we could have the gold and diamond mine together.

You see I still hadn't spent my ten shillings because every time I did something with the money things would go badly wrong. So I kept it between the pages of the red book because of all the books I now owned nobody would ever look inside that one, not even Gawie. Not that I didn't trust him. By now I was able to memorise whole chapters and knew all about how, under English colonial jurisprudence, which is another name for law, magistrates had to deal with disputes between the indigenous natives and *Boer* burghers in the courts in Natal and the Cape of Good Hope in 1812. Most of it had to do with cattle, grazing rights and punishment because *Boere* could no longer have slaves, so black people, who could now only be servants and farm workers, had some rights for a change. But I don't know if they still have them here in the Transvaal. Only Sergeant Van Niekerk, or someone like him, would know for sure.

Now, I'm afraid I have to take you back to church. Because if you think of all the other things the British did that upset the *Dominee*, this thing was the worst ever. The funny thing was that it didn't even have anything to do with the Boer War or what the British did to the Afrikaners or his grandmother's goosefeather quilt or even about the war that was going on. It was all about a book. The book that got him *really, really* angry was called *The Origin of Species* by Charles Darwin. *Dominee* De Jager didn't say how he got hold of it or even if he'd ever read it, but judging by what he said about it, a preacher wouldn't be allowed by God to read a book like this. I would later find out that this particular book had been around longer than my red book. The way the *Dominee* talked in church, he made it sound like it was the latest wicked thing done by an Englishman.

'This morning we going to talk about wicked books,' he said, opening his sermon. 'Ungodly books that serve the Antichrist and are written with a pen that's been dipped in the devil's scarlet ink. Before I tell you about this particular devil-written book I want you to know that Adolf Hitler himself knows about the existence of wicked books, and has done his best to stamp them out in Germany. This is yet another sign showing that deep underneath he is a God-fearing man and a good Lutheran.' He stopped and opened the large Bible resting on the pulpit. 'Here in the Bible it is clear as daylight, God tells us about words, *good* words. "In the beginning was the word, and the word was *good*!"' he read. 'You can't get plainer than that, only *good* words can be tolerated, you hear?' He slammed the Bible closed and the sound of the covers coming together echoed through the church, then he patted the gold-embossed front cover. 'Never a truer word has been said,' he declared. 'In this book, the Good Book, are all the words we need to lead a fulfilling and God-fearing life. But Satan knows how powerful and everlasting God's word is and that he can never write the book of evil that can begin to match this book of good. Make no mistake, the devil is very clever. He has a satanic plan. If he can't write one big book of evil that's the opposite to God's good book, then he puts a little evil here, a few poisoned words there, until the world is filled with evil books. Everywhere you look it's evil books. A person has to think before they read a book and ask themself, "Is this the work of the devil or not?" Maybe you are halfway through a book and it's going along nicely when all of a sudden buried there in the middle is the devil's work. An act of fornication is suddenly planted in the pages in front of your very eyes! A blasphemy against the teachings of God appears. That's why the Führer is so clever. In Germany he got Herr Joseph Goebbels to read all the books. *Magtig!* What a clever man is this Joseph Goebbels. He can smell a degenerate book, even if it's hidden in a whole library! When he discovers the evil in them Adolf Hitler takes that book and puts it on a big pile of books and burns them in the city square, where everyone can see it happening. In one burning they burnt 20 000 books! Can you imagine that? Twenty thousand bits of evil and filth that the devil has planted in those pages, and that's only the beginning. They had to do it again a bit later because the evil books started piling up again. The books were by Jews and Bolsheviks, Anarchists and Roman Catholics – all the terrible filth cleansed by the fire of truth and the smoke of righteousness!'

But we haven't reached the end of the *Dominee*'s sermon yet because now he went back to the book *The Origin of Species* and held it up. From where we were sitting you couldn't see if it was the actual book. But if it was, then later, after he'd told us what was in it, I wouldn't have been surprised if it had burst into flames right there in front of our eyes.

'In the beginning was the word!' the *Dominee* shouted out again, this time so loud we nearly jumped out of our skins. 'But this book says in the beginning was nothing but germs that eventually, after millions of years, become people and all the creatures on earth. It's called evolution, and it's blasphemy! This is true evil. The devil's masterpiece! God tells us seven days and everything is finish and *klaar*, but Charles Darwin, the Englishman, tells us millions of years and from germs!' He looked around. 'Now who you going to believe, hey? God's masterful creation in six days and then Sunday for a good rest, or germs growing up to be people and trees and animals? It's truly laughable that somebody could have the cheek to write such rubbish and expect people to believe it!' The *Dominee* paused. 'But that's where the devil is clever, you see, because inside he has put a Christian truth, it is called "survival of the fittest". God has said the white man is superior and must dominate all the inferior dark races, and we know also that the Afrikaner is one of his chosen people because we survived among the savages in the wilderness and we are definitely the fittest. So be careful when you read a book, sometimes there are truths written in evil books, just so you can be fooled. But Hitler wasn't fooled and in Germany there are no more evil books. But in England, the whole place is full of them, you can hardly read a book that isn't. I don't suppose many of you will read books in English, but if you do, beware, the devil is very clever and lurking on pages, and before you know it, you're trapped. God tells us that to think evil is the same as doing it, so I want you all to watch out, you hear? Better still, don't read anything in English, that is my final warning!'

Well, I must say, I didn't think much of the *Dominee*'s walking-on-ice and fishing-through-a-hole-in-Russia sermon. But this one, where this Englishman says God definitely didn't create the earth in six days and it was germs all the time, was different. This was sheer blasphemy, as plain as the nose on your face. In all the books Miss Phillips sent I hadn't seen anything like this. Perhaps in the future I'd have to look a bit closer for evil lurking between the pages because the devil was so clever. The fact that the English allowed it to happen and hadn't burned any books to make everyone safe like Hitler had done was a big worry. In life there's always something you've got to watch out for, and I still wasn't sure about recognising Jews and Roman Catholics and now, all of a sudden, there were Bolsheviks and Anarchists as well.

Then, on the following Saturday after the germs-versus-creation sermon we were working in the vegetable garden when I looked up and there was smoke coming from the direction of the library rock. I dropped my paraffin tin bucket, and Tinker and I started to run. Gawie must have seen me, then the smoke, because he did the same. But we arrived too late, and all my Miss Phillips books had been taken out of the old paraffin tins and thrown on a pile that was now just leaping flames. On top was the red book, and maybe because the cover was made of leather it hadn't burnt yet. Without thinking, I stuck my hand into the flames and pulled it out. The red book was very hot and one corner was alight, but I got it out and threw some sand on it to stop the flames. My hand was burning like billyo. Gawie tried to kick some of the books clear on the edge of the flames, and some of the lighted pages separated from the covers and flew up in the draught caused by the disturbance and got into the grass and dry thornbush on the edge of the library rock, and now the grass was alight and the thornbush was crackling and exploding around us. Gawie and me tried to stamp it out but it was burning in too many places, so I picked up the red book and called to Tinker, who was barking like mad, and to Gawie and we scrambled up the side of the library rock to safety and stood on the top watching the fire spread. Soon the surrounding bush was nothing but flames leaping high as a house and dense smoke everywhere.

We could hear people shouting from the direction of the vegetable garden and orchard but there was no way they could get over to us or see us through the smoke. Through a momentary clearing of smoke I saw something too terrible for words. The fire was heading for Mattress's old hut and the pigsty and dairy. Next thing the pigs were squealing in terror and I knew we were in the all-time deepest of deep shit. It was getting hard to breathe because the fire was eating up the air around the library rock. There was a narrow unburnt corridor to the left of us that led to the creek about 300 yards away, and I decided we had to try to get through.

'Gawie, we've got to run over there!' I shouted, pointing towards the creek. He was beginning to cough so he nodded, and we climbed down the library rock and ran through the smoke towards the safety of the creek. To this day, I'll never know how we made it. The flames were closing in fast and there were even patches of grass and whitethorn alight ahead of us where sparks must have been carried in the wind that had come up with the fire. Tinker was barking like mad and trying to protect me, running ahead and showing us the way around the burning patches. We both ran straight into the creek, panting like mad, and Tinker stayed on the creek bank barking. I realised that I was holding the red book under water and the cold creek water was soothing to my fiercely stinging hand.

From where we were sitting we could now see the fire had reached the dairy and the pigs were still squealing. Later, everyone said you could smell the roast pork for miles. I looked at Gawie and his face was black, and I suppose mine was too.

'What now?' he said.

'First, wash your face,' I replied. Why I would say a stupid thing like that I don't know, but he dipped his hands in the water and splashed his face clean.

'You too, *Voetsek*,' he said.

'I can't because I'm holding this,' I said, producing the red book from under the water. My other hand was too sore to splash with.

'Ag, throw it away, man! It's all burnt and wet.'

'No, I can't,' I said, and stood up and walked to the creek bank where we both sat down on the black shiny pebbles. The fire had stopped short of the creek, but was still raging everywhere else, making a sort of roaring sound.

'We in the deep shit, man!' Gawie said.

'I know,' I answered.

'So, what are we going to do? They going to think we started the fire and it's Pretoria for sure.'

I could see Gawie was on the edge of tears. I felt the same way myself but I knew he was expecting me to do something, though what I didn't know.

'We have to escape,' I said.

'Escape?'

'Yeah.'

'Where?'

All of a sudden it was the youngest having to come up with all the answers. 'Town,' I replied.

'Town?'

It was getting annoying, him just saying one word in a question like that. 'We've got to turn ourselves in.'

'Where?'

Another one word. 'The police station. To Sergeant Van Niekerk.'

'How come we always have to go to him?'

More than one word at last. 'If we go back to The Boys Farm, that is probably burned down by now, can you imagine the trouble we in, man? We'll get a *sjambokking* from Meneer Prinsloo with the long cane, and him running flat out at us and that's even *before* we go to Pretoria.' I paused, suddenly remembering. 'Oh my God! Adolf Hitler is probably roast chicken by now!'

'You're right, man!' Gawie said, quickly realising that if we went back and Adolf Hitler was just a smouldering roast chicken carcass, then we were also as good as dead meat.

The road to town was about 400 yards from the other side of the creek, so we waded over again with Gawie carrying the red book, and me carrying Tinker. They must have made books very strong in the olden days because except for the burnt corner and it being a bit swelled up from being wet, the stitching still held together perfectly, and the gold on the edges of the pages was still there to be seen.

When we got to the road we discovered we had problems. Not at first, but starting to come down the road were *bakkies* from the surrounding farms who must have seen the smoke from the big fire and were coming to help to put it out. So we had to hide in ditches and behind trees so they wouldn't see us, and I had to tell Tinker not to bark. When we were in one ditch we could hear someone driving towards us with a siren going and we saw it was Sergeant Van Niekerk in the police van.

'What now?' Gawie asked.

I had to think fast. 'Mevrou Booysens at the Impala Café,' I said, only because I couldn't think of anybody else except Meneer Van Niekerk, the school headmaster, but it was Saturday and no school.

'Who?'

We were back to one word. 'You don't know her, but she'll be good,' I reassured him. From time to time I'd pop in after school to say hello to Mevrou Booysens. But not too often because she'd always give me a big welcome, and when I had to run to catch up with the crocodile going back to The Boys Farm, she'd give me a red sucker. I didn't want her to think I was only coming for the sucker. Which was a bit true in any case, but I *really* liked her and Marie, her daughter, who was not yet completely a nurse, but nearly, and she would sometimes be home from the hospital in Tzaneen. Marie would make a big fuss of Tinker and give me a kiss. I was collecting quite a lot of kisses, ten of them, but only from her, because she said she was now my *nooi*.

We made it safely to the Impala Café and Mevrou Booysens was there and also Marie. I told Mevrou Booysens what had happened, then I started to cry, but not because I was scared, which was also true, but because my books had been burned. My precious library that was now only the red book that I'd stolen from under Doctor Van Heerden's house. Gawie also started to cry, but I think because he was scared about what was going to happen to us.

Marie put her arm around me and Mevrou Booysens put hers around Gawie. I'd had Marie's arm around me before, but Gawie probably couldn't remember if it had ever happened to him, and now he really started to blub. After a while Mevrou Booysens said, 'I've got just the recipe to stop crying in boys and it's ice-cream with ten toppings!'

It did the job, alright. Soon Gawie was right as rain, scoffing ice-cream out of his bowl with one leg and guessing what topping he was tasting next. I was eating mine a bit slow because I held the spoon in my left hand, not wanting to show my burnt hand. Marie went and got a wet dishcloth to wipe my dirty face, which she said was as black as a *kaffir's*, and then she said, 'Now your hands,' and grabbed my right wrist and lifted it from my lap.

'*Eina!*' I cried.

'Oh my God,' she exclaimed. 'Tom, what have you done to your hand?'

'I burned it when I put it in the fire to get my red book.'

'That's silly! Now look what you've done! Why didn't you just let it burn?'

That was the first time I understood that women don't think like men. 'Because I couldn't,' I said, not knowing what else to say or how to explain.

'This is a bad burn, Tom, I'm afraid you'll have to go to Doctor Van Heerden. I don't have the right dressings, only a bandage,' she explained. She must have seen the concern on my face. 'What's the matter?' she asked.

'I can't say,' I whispered.

'Look, Tom, you can't move your fingers, that's because the skin on you hand is burned, if it gets infected you could be in all sorts of trouble.'

'We already in all sorts of trouble,' I sniffed.

Marie smiled. 'This could be a lot worse, *skattebol*.' She took the spoon and dug into my ice-cream that was hardly touched, making sure there was some topping on it. 'Open your mouth or all the ice-cream is going to melt,' she said.

How could a burnt hand that hurt a lot be as bad as the trouble we were already in? Going to Pretoria was the worst thing that could happen to a person. This was another thing perhaps a woman wouldn't understand that men would. 'Only if you don't tell him about the red book,' I said.

'What's so special about that book, Tom? Why mustn't the doctor know?'

We were outside The Boys Farm so you couldn't tell a lie. 'I stole it,' I said softly, not looking at her.

'From Doctor Van Heerden?'

'From a box under his house where Tinker and me slept the night I cut my finger.'

'They should be ashamed!' she exclaimed. I wasn't sure who she meant, but then she said, 'It's okay, you've already been punished enough, God just burned your hand for stealing that book, now it's yours for keeps.'

That sounded all right, but I knew the world didn't work like that. 'You won't tell him, will you?'

'I swear it on a stack of Bibles,' she said, raising her hand to her shoulder. 'But what are you going to say when he asks how you burnt your hand?'

'Can I tell him I tried to rescue a book but couldn't?'

Marie brought her forefinger to her lip and tilted her head so she could think properly. 'Mmm, that's only half a lie, that's good because it could have happened like that quite easily.'

I turned to speak to Mevrou Booysens. 'Can Mevrou look after the book while we gone, please?' I asked. 'It has to dry out.'

'Of course, Tom. This book looks very important, we'll put it near the stove. There's a nice warm place where we dry the dish towels.' She turned to Gawie. 'Maybe some lunch while Tom is at the doctor? How about a mixed grill?'

My mouth fell open at the exact same time as Gawie's. A mixed grill cost two and sixpence! I'd never heard of anyone who'd had one. You get everything in it – sausage, chops, liver, bacon, tomato, a fried egg, chips and all the tomato sauce you wanted. The Government gives you one pound when you leave The Boys Farm when you're sixteen and every big kid always says the same thing, 'I'm going to have a mixed grill,' and then they tell you what's in it. Gawie was going to have one and he was now only eleven and I had to go to Doctor Van Heerden. I can't say I was too happy about that, but my hand was *really* hurting now and I don't suppose I could have managed to hold the knife.

All of a sudden Mevrou Booysens clapped her hands together. '*Magtig*! I must call The Boys Farm, they'll be thinking that you're two charred-up corpses and a little dog corpse, and they'll be looking for you all over the place.'

'They probably don't even know they missing,' Marie said, going all sarcastic. 'That place just doesn't care about the children, they think they just the Government's kids.'

'We saw Sergeant Van Niekerk going out, maybe you could talk to him first, Mevrou?' I asked, pleadingly.

She seemed to understand. '*Ja*, that's the best idea, Tom. I'll ask him to come to the phone.'

Marie, Tinker (who'd had a nice piece of meat and a bone) and me set out for Doctor Van Heerden's house. It was just like last time with all the farmers and their wives sitting with boxes and baskets of this and that they'd brought. One farmer had brought a pumpkin you couldn't lift in one go and Doctor Van Heerden would have taken a year to eat it all, even if he liked pumpkin, which I didn't. The old dog Helmut was nowhere to be seen.

This time there was no waiting. Marie just barged in when someone walked out, pulling me in with her. She went straight to the same lady that had been there before. You could see the lady didn't recognise me because it was now three years and I'd grown a lot bigger, nearly four inches. 'Good afternoon, Nurse,' Marie began, 'I am a registered hospital nurse, and this boy has a badly burned hand and *must* see the doctor at once.'

Then to my surprise the lady said, 'With him it's always hands.' So I was wrong, she did remember. 'What have you done now?' she asked.

'It was a bushfire, Mevrou. What happened to the old dog?'

'*Ag*, it was his arthritis, he couldn't walk any more so the doctor gave him an injection.' I knew I couldn't do that to Tinker even if she was old. I'd just carry her everywhere. 'Let me see your hand, child?' I showed her my hand.

'*Magtig!* It's not so good.' She looked up at Marie. 'You can take him straight in.' She turned back to me. 'What's your name again?'

'Tom Fitzsaxby, Mevrou.'

'Oh yes, now I remember, blood all over you and you couldn't hardly walk, you were with the little dog.'

'She's waiting outside, Mevrou.'

She rose slowly from her desk with her hand on her hip, went to the surgery door and opened it. 'Tom Fitzsaxby, Doctor. The boy with the chopper from The Boys Farm, he's done it to his hand again.' She turned and motioned with her head that Marie and me should enter.

'Hello, Tom,' Doctor Van Heerden greeted me. 'This time you bring with you a pretty lady and not so much blood, eh?'

'This is Miss Marie Booysens, Doctor,' I said, remembering my manners.

Doctor Van Heerden chuckled. 'We are old friends, Tom. I delivered Miss Booysens. Though I don't suppose she remembers much about our first meeting. She has a fine mother.'

Marie laughed and you could see she was accustomed to doctors, her being almost a nurse and all. 'Tom has burned his hand rather badly, Doctor, and he's being very brave.'

'I'm sorry to hear about Helmut,' I said.

Doctor Van Heerden looked up in surprise and his eyes brightened. 'You are a very different kind of boy, Tom Fitzsaxby. Thank you, he was a very good friend. Now let me see your hand.'

I showed him my hand and he said, 'Mmm, nasty.' He looked up: 'How did this happen?'

'I tried to grab a book out of the fire,' I replied, telling our agreed-upon half-lie. With a person as nice as Doctor Van Heerden I knew I should have told him about stealing his book, but I just couldn't, yet.

'A book? How did it get into the fire in the first place? Wait, I'll give you an injection to stop the pain.'

I didn't have to answer his question, and he put in the injection and said we had to wait a bit. Then he said, 'The book you tried to rescue from the fire, how did it get there and why was it so important?'

So the whole story came out about my books being burnt because they were in English, and Miss Phillips and me doing lessons in English because that was what I was supposed to be.

'Who would do such a thing as burn books?' he asked, shaking his head.

I shrugged because now my hand wasn't hurting all of a sudden. 'I don't know but I think it was because of what the *Dominee* said in church last Sunday, Doctor.' I had to tell him about the book called *The Origin of Species* by Charles Darwin and how it was the most evil book that had ever been written and how the English didn't burn their evil books like Adolf Hitler did.

Doctor Van Heerden was silent for a moment, then he sighed and shook his head. 'That stupid, stupid man.' I thought he meant Charles Darwin. He reached over and put his hand on my shoulder. 'Look at me, Tom,' he said. 'Just remember this, *The Origin of Species* by Charles Darwin is one of the most important books that has ever been written!'

'As important as the Bible?' I asked, thinking that maybe the *Dominee* was wrong and that the devil *had* written his own big evil book that now matched the Bible.

Doctor Van Heerden laughed. 'Different, but in its own way, just as important. You see, the knowledge of science and the history of God don't always coincide, we must remember to keep an open mind, Tom.' Then he said something just the opposite to the *Dominee*. 'Read, always read. Read everything! In books there is every opinion on everything mankind has ever thought, but in men there are only the opinions and beliefs they have acquired or have been persuaded to adopt. Find out for yourself what you believe and what you think. Never listen to dogma.'

Well, I have to tell you, there wasn't much of *that* conversation I understood at the time. I knew I would have to look up 'dogma' for a start. Then I remembered I no longer owned a dictionary. And then

Marie went and spilled the beans! 'Doctor, Tom here has something to tell you about a book of yours,' she said, smiling.

All of a sudden I went cold inside and hot in the face. I was learning about women fast, and one thing for sure, they couldn't keep a secret, even if they promised on a stack of Bibles.

Doctor Van Heerden started to look closely at my burned hand that was now properly numb. 'Oh, tell me?' he said. 'A book of mine?'

I must admit, I was taken by complete surprise, and I stuttered and stumbled and told him how me and Tinker and Helmut had slept under the house that time he'd stitched my finger. I confessed I'd stolen the red book with the gold edging on the pages. His first words were, 'I really must do something about those people at The Boys Farm. We are a close community and our children should not suffer neglect.' He was talking mostly to Marie. He turned to me. 'Tom, my dear brother died in a motorcar accident twenty years ago, those were his student books. He was a lawyer and I am a doctor. There was nothing in the packing case that interested me. I'm glad you found a book you wanted, what was its title?'

'It was the one he rescued from the fire and burned his hand,' Marie interjected. 'It's very important to him and we drying it out for him in the kitchen at the café.'

'*Abolition of Slavery 1834*,' I answered.

'And you've read this book?' he asked, surprised.

'I can now recite 113 pages, Doctor, that's four chapters,' I said, trying to be modest because I was secretly proud of what I'd done with the red book.

'*Magtig*, you are an extraordinary child,' he said.

What he didn't know was never mind the extraordinary, I was the one who was in the deepest shit it was possible to be in. In Pretoria there would be no more books, only the *sjambok*, and only if I was lucky. Starting fires that burn down pigsties and dairies is certain to be the death sentence. They were not going to believe it wasn't me at the time. Why would I burn my own books? 'Because you've already read them and they were in English and evil!' they'd say. 'Those evil books have put the devil in you, *Voetsek*. It's just the sort of thing an English person planning sabotage would do!' Having Gawie with me wouldn't help either. They'd say it was just a clever trick by me to say he was *also* to blame and *he* was an Afrikaner, so how could it be sabotage, because an Afrikaner wouldn't burn down his own country? All of a sudden I'd be responsible for kidnapping Gawie and that's the death sentence again for sure! Two death sentences in one go. 'You think now that the British are winning the war you can get away with this, hey, *Voetsek*? Well, we'll soon see about that. Bring the rope, man!'

Doctor Van Heerden started cleaning my hand with a saline solution and iodine, and then put sulphur paste on it and bandaged it. While he was doing it he asked if I could tell him what was on the opening page to Chapter Two in the red book. This was pretty easy because I could see the words plain as anything. So I told him and he said, 'Quite remarkable,' and that I should pay attention to the punctuation, that commas and full stops were very important in a person's reading.

Then he said, 'I know Mevrou Van Schalkwyk at The Boys Farm was once a nurse and she can probably change this dressing every day, but how about you doing it, Marie?'

As it turned out, the reason Marie was home was because she had ten days off to study for her final nurse exams, so she agreed. She also had to make my hand do some exercises that were just opening and closing the fingers every day for five minutes before she did the dressing. It was agreed I could go to the Impala Café after school every day and on Sunday she'd do it after church.

The phone rang and the receptionist mevrou opened the door and said it was Sergeant Van Niekerk on the other end. The doctor picked up his phone and said, 'Hello, Sergeant!' and listened for a few moments and said, 'This is a branch-line and the whole district is probably listening in by now, can you come to the surgery?' Sergeant Van Niekerk must have said 'All right', because the doctor said 'Good' and put down the phone.

Doctor Van Heerden had to see all the other people waiting outside, so he told the receptionist mevrou to take us through to wait in the parlour. What a room this turned out to be. It had a big carpet on the floor and lots of big chairs you could sit on and a large wireless with a gramophone inside it. In one corner stood a grandfather clock that was something I'd read about but never seen. On one wall was a large painting of mountains with clouds in the sky and the bush underneath. On the other wall were two coloured photographs in round black frames of what I think was Doctor Van Heerden's mother and father, because if you sort of squinted a bit you could see bits of him in their faces. There was also a piano. I'd never been inside a proper person's house before, never mind a high-up one like Doctor Van Heerden's. Against the back of the chairs there were these little squares of white lace, so when you sat in one you had to be careful not to put your head on the square in case you dirtied it. I could hear Mevrou saying already, 'So now I heard you went and dirtied one of the good doctor's white squares of lace, *Voetsek!* Take six.' *Whack! Whack! Whack! Whack! Whack! Whack!* 'Maybe next time you've got some proper manners in high-up people's houses!'

It took ages for Sergeant Van Niekerk to arrive, by which time the doctor had nearly finished with the farmers. To my surprise Gawie was with him and we sat and chatted until the doctor could come and join us. Chatted wasn't exactly the right way to describe it. Gawie and me were shitting ourselves while Sergeant Van Niekerk did the chatting. I was very sad to hear the pigsty was now roast pork because I liked the pigs a lot, especially the old sow. She had really been Tinker's mother. I was relieved to hear that while Mattress's hut had also burnt down, the dairy was saved and the fire had finally stopped when it reached the ploughed field where the new potato crop was soon to be planted. We'd all been cutting up seed potatoes so that there was an eye in each piece. The hostel building was still there and Meneer Prinsloo's chickens were safe, which meant Adolf Hitler with his coming-along-nicely tail feathers was saved. If the fire had gotten him I'd have had the whole Chinese dictionary written across my bum.

When Doctor Van Heerden came in at last, a black maid brought us coffee and cake and she was told to give Tinker some of the stew left over from the doctor's lunch. I was surprised to know that high-up people also ate stew, which was all watery gravy and old vegetables and some potato in it. That was two meals Tinker would have in one day and I had to explain that I had to go outside to give her the eating password as, judging from the marks on her face, the maid was from the Venda tribe and wouldn't understand Zulu.

I was wrong about the stew. You should have seen Tinker's dish! In it were lots of big whole pieces of meat swimming in thick, brown gravy. She must have thought it was Christmas. I'd only had breakfast and it was now late afternoon and the piece of cake was nice, but I was *really* hungry because I hadn't had the mixed grill like Gawie. Nobody was looking, so I took two big pieces of meat out of Tinker's dish and quickly ate them. It was all right to do this because there was too much in it for one small dog. The meat was delicious and I changed my mind about high-up people eating stew because it was a whole different *lekker* thing.

So now finally we were all together in Doctor Van Heerden's parlour. Sergeant Van Niekerk cleared his throat and said, 'Now boys, I want to hear the whole story from the beginning of the fire you were supposed to have started.'

If I had been a grown-up this would have been an ideal time to escape to Mozambique, which was owned by the Portuguese. I would have to cross the Kruger National Park and take a chance on being eaten by a lion but it would be better than Pretoria. But I wasn't a grown-up and besides, I couldn't leave my best and only friend behind to face the music.

Gawie and me looked at each other because we couldn't both start talking at once. '*Voetsek* saw it first, Meneer,' Gawie ventured.

'*Voetsek?*'

I knew that Sergeant Van Niekerk knew it was my nickname, but he wanted Gawie to call me by my proper name. But Gawie only looked confused. Maybe he didn't understand or he'd forgotten I was named Tom.

'It's my nickname, Meneer,' I explained. Doctor Van Heerden shook his head slowly and went 'Tsk'.

'What we doing here is taking down evidence,' Sergeant Van Niekerk explained. 'I must have proper names.' He looked at Gawie. 'Your name is Gawie Grobler.' He pointed over to me. 'His name is Tom Fitzsaxby.'

'Ja, Meneer,' we both said together, not looking at him.

'So Tom, if you saw the fire first, are you telling me you didn't start it?'

So I told him about us watering the vegetable garden and me seeing the smoke coming from the library rock. Then I told him about Miss Phillips and my books and how it was now too late and all the books were already burning and how I managed to rescue the red book that was only burned on one corner and then the fire got out of control. I didn't tell him the bit where Gawie kicked at some burning books and the pages rose up and flew away, and the thornbush and grass around caught on fire.

'As a consequence he received a nasty burn to his hand,' Doctor Van Heerden said.

'And this book that's only burned on the corner, do you have it?'

'It's drying in the kitchen at the café,' Marie answered for me.

'Good,' Sergeant Van Niekerk said. 'If we can discover who started it and why, then I may need you both as witnesses as well as the book.'

'Why it was started is simple enough,' Dr Van Heerden said, turning to Sergeant Van Niekerk. 'Were you at church last Sunday?'

'Unfortunately not,' Sergeant Van Niekerk answered. 'Saturday night the natives play up in the Location, there's plenty of *kaffir* beer around and I always have to be at the police station on Sunday mornings to write out the charges.'

'And I am at the hospital to mend the broken heads,' the doctor grinned. 'The sermon was about burning books and the evil contained in English books.' He explained what I had said to him about the *Dominee*'s sermon.

'I'm a good Afrikaner myself, but sometimes I don't know what's wrong with that guy. Too much hate.' Sergeant Van Niekerk shook his head slowly. 'He calls himself a man of God and it's just hate, hate, hate.'

I thought maybe I should tell them that the reason for the *Dominee's* hate was all about a red-headed Englishman who brought the barbel with ten-inch whiskers and then slept under his *ouma's* goosefeather quilt that came out of her glory box, whatever that was, but then I decided not to because I'd already said too much.

'I suppose I must take you both back to The Boys Farm, hey?' Sergeant Van Niekerk turned to Marie, 'And I'll drop you off at the café, Marie.' He saw the look of consternation on our faces. 'Don't worry, I'll explain everything to Meneer Prinsloo. You won't be punished.'

I know what Gawie was thinking, because it would be the same thing as me. Even Sergeant Van Niekerk didn't know how things worked at The Boys Farm. But then Doctor Van Heerden said, 'I'll reinforce what you say, Sergeant, and give Prinsloo a ring. I want to call anyway to tell Mevrou Van Schalkwyk that we'll attend to the dressings on Tom's hand in town.'

Marie sat in the front of the police van and Gawie and me at the back with Tinker, like we were prisoners which we would soon be anyway. It was quite dark in there and Tinker must have smelled the big Alsatians because she kept sniffing and whimpering. At the Impala Café we got my red book back, which was not yet dry but much better already and only some of the pages crinkly. There was this big burned scallop out of the top left-hand corner of the leather cover but only the top of the pages were burned and only a few of the words on each page were gone forever. It could have been much worse. Mevrou Booysens gave us both a sucker and then we sat in the front of the police van with Tinker on my lap. She'd had so much to eat in one day her stomach was tight as a rugby ball, especially from that delicious high-up stew.

———————

At The Boys Farm Sergeant Van Niekerk said we must come to see Meneer Prinsloo, who was already waiting. But, at first, it turned out not as bad as we expected. Meneer Prisloo greeted Sergeant Van Niekerk and ignored us, which was a good sign, but things changed when the police sergeant said he wanted to go down to the library rock and take Meneer Prinsloo and the two of us with him. I don't think Meneer Prinsloo was too happy because he would have to walk through all the blackened bush and grass, but he reluctantly agreed. Sergeant Van Niekerk asked me to take them to the spot where the fire started. He'd not mentioned any books to Meneer Prinsloo.

When we got to the library rock Meneer Prinsloo was pretty grumpy because his always-shiny brown boots were now black from walking through the burned grass. We showed Sergeant Van Niekerk the exact spot, and you could see bits of book and charred pages all over the place.

'Tom, I want you to make a list of every book that was burned here. I will need it for my evidence,' Sergeant Van Niekerk said, looking at Meneer Prinsloo.

'What evidence?' Meneer Prinsloo asked. All of a sudden his stomach started to stick out and his arms came up into the windmill position.

'I have reason to believe that someone on The Boys Farm has deliberately destroyed some very valuable property belonging to Tom Fitzsaxby. Whoever it was must be arrested and prosecuted, Meneer Prinsloo.'

Well, you should have seen the windmill and the braces stretch begin! It was an almost all-time best performance.

'I will not have police officers snooping around private property, you hear?' Meneer Prinsloo blustered. 'I must ask you to leave at once, Sergeant!'

Sergeant Van Niekerk didn't appear to be even a bit frightened, although Gawie and me sure were. When Meneer Prinsloo got like this it was like the German tanks going into Poland, the whole place could explode! It was all very well for Sergeant Van Niekerk, he didn't have to live at The Boys Farm afterwards.

'I must remind you, Meneer Prisloo, that this is government and not private property and I, like you, am a government servant. I am only doing my duty, Meneer Prinsloo,' Sergeant Van Niekerk said calmly. 'Please do not destroy this crime site as I shall be returning tomorrow for further investigation and will bring a search warrant with me.'

'*Verdom!*' Meneer Prinsloo shouted. 'You will be reported to the highest authorities in Pretoria, you hear! You come sniffing around and accusing someone of crime! I'll tell you what is a crime! These two boys who lit that fire in the first place, that is a crime! We have witnesses, you hear!' Meneer Prinsloo was so red in the face that he could easily have matched the *Dominee*'s ears.

'I have no problems with these two boys, they are now only witnesses,' Sergeant Van Niekerk said calmly.

'No problems!' Meneer Prinsloo exclaimed. 'What are you talking about, man? It is for me to decide who has problems! I am the one who must be the father! That is my government duty!' His right hand pointed directly at me. 'This boy, Tom Fitzsaxby, he is nothing but trouble and is an *Engelsman!*' He pointed to Gawie. 'This one, I am ashamed to say, is an Afrikaner, but he is lacking in his character. We are not pleased with him, he is reading English books!'

'The books you just burned?' Sergeant Van Niekerk asked.

'Not me!' Meneer Prinsloo replied hastily, bringing his hands up in front of his chest. 'But we Afrikaner people, the *volk*, must keep the faith. Even you, Sergeant!' Meneer Prinsloo said. 'First you are an Afrikaner, then you are a policeman!'

'No, Meneer, *first* I am a policeman, *then* an Afrikaner!' It was the first time I had ever heard Sergeant Van Niekerk raise his voice.

'You ought to be ashamed!' Meneer Prinsloo shouted. 'I will report you to the *Broederbond!* A police sergeant is not such a big thing nowadays!' He snidely added, 'An ignorant person can be a policeman these days.'

It had all of a sudden become a personal thing between the two men, who seemed also to have forgotten our presence. 'In my family, only my brother could be educated, you understand? There was no money for a younger brother to go to the teachers' college. Now he is the headmaster of the school and I am the policeman. But, *wragtig*! I am still my father's son and we are proud Afrikaners, but we are not bigots!'

'Who you calling a bigot? We will soon see about that!' Meneer Prinsloo shouted, and then he turned and started to walk away.

Sergeant Van Niekerk had regained his calm. '*Ja*, sure, in the meantime I will be back tomorrow with a search warrant.' He called after the superintendent, 'I should remind you that arson is a serious crime!'

Gawie and me were standing looking down at our feet and I wished all of a sudden I could be invisible or even disappear. The row between the two grown-ups had put us even deeper into the shit and Gawie had been told he wasn't a good Afrikaner any more because he'd read my books.

'I want to know if Meneer Prinsloo gives you a thrashing, you hear? I will be back tomorrow to get to the bottom of this nasty business. You can be sure we will find out who did it,' Sergeant Van Niekerk said before departing.

Ha! That will be the day! First of all, we would never tell him if we got the *sjambok*, because that would just get us another thrashing worse than before and you had to survive in that place. Second, the whole of The Boys Farm could have seen who burned my books and they wouldn't tell. Even Joseph Goebbels, who was Hitler's expert on burning books, would not be able to get a confession out of them. At The Boys Farm, except for Pissy Vermaak who was now in Pietersburg, nobody talked to grown-ups in that place. It was like some oath you took, only you never said it in words, you just knew it was so. Outside was different. Although Sergeant Van Niekerk wouldn't know this and we couldn't go and tell him.

That night after supper I had my name called to see Mevrou. Only me and not Gawie.

'So, this afternoon I got a call from Doctor Van Heerden,' she said, closing the door to the sick room after I'd entered.

'*Ja*, Mevrou.' I stood with my hands behind my back, looking down at my feet, which were still very dirty with the black from the fire between my toes because I didn't have enough time to wash them properly before supper.

'So, I am a registered nurse who worked in the theatre in the hospital also and now I am not good enough to change your bandage, *Voetsek*!'

'*Nee*, you are a very good nurse, the doctor said so,' I lied, looking up at her for the first time.

'You lying, *Voetsek*! That Doctor Van Heerden never liked me, because I saw once he left a pair of tweezers in a *kaffir*'s stomach and I wrote it in my shift report.'

'What happened to the *kaffir*?' I asked, curious despite myself.

'*Ag*, he died. But not because of the tweezers. The stabbing he got did it and we couldn't stop the bleeding. But I still did my duty, you hear? Maybe it was *only* a *kaffir*, but medical neglect is medical neglect and a person, if she is a theatre nurse, has to make a proper report.'

I didn't know what to say to this but then she asked, 'Let me see your hand?'

I held out my bandaged hand and she examined the bandage carefully. 'Tsk! This bandage is no good. See where is the safety pin.' She pointed to the large safety pin that was in the end of the bandage in the centre of my palm. 'It will catch on things,' she explained. 'This is another example of medical incompetence.' She unclipped the safety pin and began to unwind the bandage. What could I do? I couldn't exactly say that Doctor Van Heerden had said she mustn't. She lifted the gauze dressing that smelled vaguely of sulphur.

'*Ag*, it is not so bad,' she sniffed. 'If I had my way we would put on some honey. That doctor thinks he knows everything! Sometimes *volk* medicine is better. We *Boere* have used honey for burns since the Great Trek and even before that. But what would we know, eh?'

'If it was honey a person could lick it off,' I said, attempting to smile.

'You trying to be funny, *Voetsek*? To laugh at our old ways?'

'*Nee*, Mevrou!' I said quickly, sorry I'd opened my big mouth for such a feeble joke.

Mevrou sighed and replaced the gauze and did up the bandage, this time the safety pin was positioned so that my wrist protected it from being caught on anything. I must say it was very clever.

'Now take down your pants and touch your toes,' she said suddenly.

'What for, Mevrou?' I cried. 'I didn't start the fire and I lost all my books also!'

'You lucky, man. Meneer Prinsloo should do it, but he says I must. You know you can't go into town without permission, you were out of bounds.'

'What about Gawie Grobler? He came with?' I protested, pushing my khaki shorts down to my ankles and bending to touch my toes. I know I shouldn't have said this, Gawie getting off was all right, but it was just so unfair picking on me.

'You the leader, *he* only followed you,' Mevrou explained.

'But he is two years older than me!' I protested, turning to look up at her.

'*Ag*, it doesn't matter about his age. He is not a strong person and is easily led. An Afrikaner boy who reads that English rubbish with evil in it is not a leader of men.'

For a moment I wondered if it had been Mevrou who had burned my books. She'd been in church last Sunday and heard what the *Dominee* had said about books in English. But I had to admit to myself that I'd never seen her walking anywhere near the library rock. She was too fat to walk such a long way and would never go through thornbushes and stuff. When she walked she planted one leg down – 'Boom!' – then the other – 'Boom!' – shifting her weight from one side to the other. Her fat shoulders also rolled with each step. You could see her coming for miles with her great stomach sticking out and her chin in the air.

Whack! Whack! Whack! Whack! I waited for the next two whacks, but they didn't come. Out of bounds is six of the best and they always came from Meneer Prinsloo's long cane that I was now old enough to get if the crime was bad enough. Sometimes you can get lucky in life.

CHAPTER NINE

A Woman's Selfless Love

OF COURSE, SERGEANT VAN Niekerk's enquiries came to nothing. Over four weekends he conducted interviews with every boy in the place. I could have told him all along it was a useless waste of time and energy. At The Boys Farm, in terms of volunteering information, he'd have to wait for hell to freeze over first. The thing was no boy there would have wanted to help me anyway. They thought the same as I did before Doctor Van Heerden told me I must read everything, every opinion, good or bad, then make my own mind up about things. They would believe the *Dominee* about English books being full of evil with the devil's messages lurking around every corner. Whoever burned my books would think they were doing a good thing and helping God's work. Sergeant Van Niekerk sniffing around the place would have made them even more secretive, more *stom*. The only thing that came out of it was that Gawie was now a *surrogaat Engelsman*, a surrogate Englishman. 'Surrogaat' was a big word for anyone to use and nobody would have known it normally, but Meneer Prinsloo had used it in his after-supper talk the night after the fire.

The fire, of course, was a very big subject and he really went to town. 'You all know there has been a big fire and we have lost our pigs and nearly the dairy, so for this Christmas no pork on the table. We won't be able to send a gift of a nice leg of ham that Mevrou Van Schalkwyk kindly cures for us on her farm to the Inspector of Children's Institutions in Pretoria. This is a great shame because for ten years now since I came here we have killed a pig for Christmas and Mevrou's delicious cured-with-honey-in-her-smokehouse ham has gone to the good Inspector, who is always very accommodating to The Boys Farm. It is good to have a friend in high places in Pretoria, and now he doesn't get his Christmas ham.'

Meneer Prinsloo stopped and looked around the room. 'But, of course, we also know the fire that nearly burned everything down was started by burning some *English* books, by a person or persons unknown.' His hands began to wave and his lips curled and the elastic braces began to stretch and strain at the leather fasteners that clipped onto the buttons on his trousers that ended in the middle of his stomach. 'These books in question belonged to Tom Fitzsaxby and were also read by the now *surrogaat Engelsman*, Gawie Grobler.'

You could tell from his voice that he was disgusted with us, especially Gawie who was an Afrikaner and not a hard-case Englishman who caused so much trouble around the place. 'This *surrogaat Engelsman* who we thought was so clever and also an Afrikaner now we know likes to read English books and maybe believe what no good Afrikaner can believe if he has a conscience!' Then he went on to say he wanted the boy or boys responsible for starting the fire to confess as it was a big disgrace to have a policeman snooping about the place and that the good reputation of The Boys Farm was at stake. 'But maybe we can't find this person, or persons, perhaps it will be like the criminal person who stole Piet Retief's tail feathers and is never to be found!'

Meneer Prinsloo knew as we all did that nobody was going to confess. There was not a snowball's hope in hell of such a thing happening. But at least he wasn't accusing Gawie and me of starting the fire, like he'd told Sergeant Van Niekerk he definitely had witnesses who saw us do it. With Pissy Vermaak no longer here, you couldn't just go around finding witnesses that would swear on a stack of Bibles that we'd started the fire when we didn't. Maybe the other boys had no time for me but they had even less for members of the staff, particularly Meneer Prinsloo. But by calling Gawie a surrogate Englishman, it was all finish and *klaar* with him.

Poor Gawie was in the super-deep shit and all because of me. Going to school on Monday, he didn't walk with me, nor had he talked with me in the dormitory the previous night or in the wash house when we were washing our face and hands and feet before going to bed. Just before we got to school he walked past me and said in a loud voice so everyone could hear, 'Voetsek, Voetsek!' I think it was supposed to be funny, and then he clouted me behind the head and moved on. I wasn't scared of Gawie and I reckon I could have taken him any time he liked, but now I had a bandaged hand. What was the use of doing that, anyway? Everyone laughed and someone shouted, 'You not game to take him, hey, *Voetsek?*' And then the kids started chanting, '*Surrogaat! Surrogaat! Surrogaat!*' and they all laughed some more, but this time at poor Gawie, who was only trying to show them he was a *regte Boer* all the time and that he didn't like me any more.

As for me, I was pretty sad. I'd lost Gawie and my books all at the one time. Where was I? I was nowhere, that's where! A nobody, nowhere! Now there was just Tinker and me and the burnt red book, starting all over again from scratch. I would have to write and tell Miss Phillips what had happened. What if she was very cross that I hadn't taken better care of the books she'd sent? They'd cost good money of her own, and perhaps I couldn't make a person like her, who hadn't grown up in an orphanage, understand that you weren't allowed to keep things in the dormitory. On the other hand, keeping books in old paraffin tins under a big rock sounds a pretty dumb thing to do. What if just a natural bushfire came along? Maybe she'd think I was ungrateful and that I just threw her books into old paraffin tins after I'd read them. 'You ungrateful child, after all I've done for you! Paraffin tins, and not even new ones!'

I was now ten, nearly eleven, and I wasn't sure how well I spoke English. But by now, thanks to Miss Phillips, I could read and write it pretty well. I used to speak English to Tinker who would listen and put her head to one side and even sometimes bark. I also told her she was English, being a fox terrier and all. I said, 'If you even say it in Afrikaans it's *foksterriër*, so this is definite proof that, like me, you are English. It's just that we've somehow got ourselves born in the wrong place.' I don't think she really cared if she was Afrikaner or English, because she was a one-man dog and if I had been an Eskimo she wouldn't have cared less. She loved me lots and lots and didn't ask questions about a person all the time.

But Gawie was a different matter altogether. To be a *surrogaat Engelsman* was like you don't know who you are all of a sudden. All your life you've been a proud Afrikaner, *regte Boer* with an uncle in Pretoria (even if it wasn't true). Now you are an in-between something or other, neither a *rooinek* like me, nor a proper *Boer*. I mean, if someone came up to me and handed me some beads and a big gold cross and said, 'Sorry, *Voetsek*, from now on you a Roman Catholic, man!' How would I feel? Not very happy, I can tell you! You'd have to learn all those prayers so you could go 'click' one, 'click' two, 'click' three and so on, because God would know if you didn't know them off by heart and you'd be punished for trying to take shortcuts with praying! I'd probably be all right because, if I could learn to recite the red book, I reckon I could do those bead prayers also. It still wouldn't be nice one moment to be who you *really* are and talking to God direct, and the next it's beads clicking and crosses dangling and you're somebody else altogether. Somebody you never even thought you were going to be until Meneer Prinsloo said you were it.

That week in school I was trying to get up enough courage to write to Miss Phillips. I could only have two goes. You couldn't waste paper because of the war, and if you tore a page out of the exercise book the Government gave you at school then you had to go to the middle where the staples were so two would come out. That's two pages and nobody would know you'd torn them out. But four pages would be too many and maybe they'd find out. So I had to practise the letter I was going to write in my head and then write the one I decided on, and after that make a clean copy with the page that was leftover.

So after I got it all straight in my head, I wrote:

Dear Miss Phillips,

I have some very bad news. There has been a terrible fire and all my books have been burned. It is a tragedy but not my fault, somebody else did it because of what the Dominee said in church about books in English should be burned because lurking in the pages is evil. You reading along nicely and then when you not looking a bit of evil is written. In Germany it happened, but Adolf Hitler has a man called Joseph Goebbels who finds out every time and they burn that book. You can take him into a whole library and he'll go straight to the bad book and burn it. But the English don't do that and so the Dominee said we mustn't read English books because most of them have evil lurking. Doctor Van Heerden says that's rubbish, but too late, someone already burned all my books you sent me. I don't know what to say, except that I'm very sorry because you paid good money for them and I loved them very much. You must understand about the old paraffin tins, there was nowhere else, we are not allowed to keep things like books under our beds and so I had to hide them under the big rock in a small cave I dug. I am asking for your forgiveness because I am very grateful for what you did for me. I hope you are not going to be very cross reading this. Now some good news! I rescued the red book at the last minute. Hooray! Now for the bad news! It is burned on the corner and some words are also gone missing, but not a lot. Also, I burned my hand taking it out of the fire. But it is not too bad and only has a bandage and some sulphur on it and I have to exercise it so I don't lose my fingers. Did you know that the Boere used honey on burns in the Great Trek?

Your obedient student,
Tom Fitzsaxby
Woof-Woof!

I wasn't too sure about the 'Woof–Woof!' ending because I didn't know if I was going to be in disgrace. But sometimes in life you have to hope for the best. I sent the letter off with the next exercise that luckily I'd already done before the fire. I was waiting for Gawie to finish his, but now it looked as if he wasn't going to. I didn't mention this to Miss Phillips because I didn't want her to feel sorry for me losing a friend when she had every right to be angry over the burned books. And anyway, there wasn't any room left on the page.

The day after I'd posted my letter to Miss Phillips, Meneer Van Niekerk, who I now knew went to teachers' college when his little *boetie* Sergeant Van Niekerk couldn't go because there was no money, sent for me.

'Come in, Tom,' he called in English when I knocked on his open door. He pointed to the chair in front of his desk. 'Sit down, son.' It was the same chair that was always there, but now I could sit on it and my feet were flat on the floor even if I leaned back. I still didn't like sitting in front of such a high-up person, but we did it quite a lot because Miss Phillips sent her envelopes to Meneer Van Niekerk to give to me, and he'd always have a chat with me and ask how I was going and I had to answer him in English.

'I am very sorry to hear about the fire, the burning of your books,' he began, then paused and seemed to be thinking for a long time, with the end of one of the arms of his spectacles stuck in the corner of his mouth. 'There is still a lot of ignorance and bigotry in this world and the Afrikaner *volk* are not without their share. Even a *Dominee* is not always wise in what he says, and words are sometimes put into God's mouth that are not always the absolute truth. I must tell you that I was also at that sermon and was very ashamed at what the *Dominee* told the congregation. Evil can be and is written in books from time to time, but we must read each book and decide for ourselves. Reading is a way of opening minds and burning books is about closing minds. The Bible says, "Seek the truth and it will set you free". Reading books from everywhere and about everything is seeking the truth, and it will free you from bigotry and those ignorant men who would otherwise take advantage of your ignorance. Some of the greatest books ever written are in the

English language, but also in German, French, Russian and so on, no nation owns a greater share of genius or stupidity. Do you understand?'

'*Ja*, Meneer. Yes, Sir,' I hastily corrected myself.

The headmaster was saying the same thing as Doctor Van Heerden, only in a different way. He reached out and picked up a piece of paper and I saw it was the list of books I'd given to Sergeant Van Niekerk.

'I have called the CNA in Pietersburg and ordered all these books. When they arrive we will keep them here at the school, but they will be yours, not government property. They will belong to you, Tom, you understand? You can take any one of them back to The Boys Farm whenever you like, but you will always know the others are safe.'

Talk about surprise! 'Thank you, Sir,' I said. It didn't seem enough to say but I couldn't think of anything else. So I just said it again. 'Thank you, Sir.'

'Do you have a locker where you can keep one book safe, Tom?'

'We can keep four things under our bed, Sir. They are safe there because we got an agreement that you can't steal from anyone in your own dormitory.' I was having difficulty believing I was going to get all my books back. It was the best news you could get except for one thing – I'd already sent the letter to Miss Phillips. If only I could have waited one more day she would never have known about the fire. Sometimes in life a person should wait for things to cool down a bit.

In case you don't know, the CNA is short for Central News Agency. I knew this because on the bottom right-hand corner on the inside of the back cover of some of my books there was this little piece of white paper about the size of a postage stamp, and on it was written:

CNA
Central News Agency
1217 Eloff St, Jhb.Tvl.
Books & Stationery
Suppliers Nationwide

'Under your bed, that's good. Have you got anything else there?'

'Yes, Sir, an old tennis ball I found that I throw for Tinker and she brings it back, and a broken alarm clock that doesn't work anymore.' I didn't tell him that Sergeant Van Niekerk had given me the old alarm clock in Mattress's hut after he'd taken his fingerprints off it. I liked it a lot. This was because it reminded me of Mattress as well as his son, Joe Louis. Also his wife who only wanted goats when he only wanted cows so he could sit under a nice shady tree and drink *kaffir* beer all day.

'So, if you take a book back with you, there's room for one more thing?' the headmaster asked. I nodded, and from under his desk he produced this huge book, bigger even than the red book. 'It's not new as I've had it a long time, but now it's yours, Tom.' He placed the big black leather book on the desk in front of me. On the cover it said *The Shorter Oxford English Dictionary*.

I was too dumbfounded to speak, not only because it was a wonderful gift but also because a high-up person like Meneer Van Niekerk would even think about doing such a thing for someone who was only nine, nearly ten, who was owned by the Government. One other thing is for sure, if this was the shorter Oxford Dictionary, then I'd hate to see the longer one!

Later, after I'd left his office, I opened the front cover and on the inside in neat copperplate handwriting Meneer Van Niekerk had written:

> *For Tom Fitzsaxby*
> *'The truth shall set you free.'*
> *de Wet van Niekerk*
> *Duiwelskrans 1943*

I thought you would like to know the names of the books that were burned so I've written them all down for you. I had to do it anyway because Sergeant Van Niekerk wanted them and so did the headmaster. I'm not sure why but Sergeant Van Niekerk said it was part of his police investigation and Meneer Van Niekerk, who knows? There were only fifteen English books in the school library and fifty-one in Afrikaans, and I'd read all the English ones and twenty of the Afrikaans. Anyway, here is the list I wrote out three times, the last time in case some day you may want to buy some *really* good books for your children and you're not sure which are the best.

Hans Christian Andersen's Fairy Tales
Winnie-the-Pooh by AA Milne
Christopher Robin's Storybook by AA Milne
A Child's Garden of Verses by Robert Louis Stevenson
Aesop's Fables
The Book of Nonsense by Edward Lear
Struwwelpeter by Heinrich Hoffman
Reynard the Fox by John Masefield
*A collection of poetry, limericks, ballads, riddles in rhyme
and nonsense verse*

Then, when I got a bit older, from around about eight years on, this is what Miss Phillips sent to me.

Peter Pan by JM Barrie
The Adventures of Pinocchio by Carlo Collodi
The Wonderful Wizard of Oz by L Frank Baum
The Wind in the Willows by Kenneth Grahame
The Voyages of Doctor Dolittle by Hugh Lofting
Rip Van Winkle by Washington Irving

Then from there to right up to the time the books were burned, when I was reading very fast and couldn't get enough stuff to read and even Gawie's shit squares couldn't keep up.

The Jungle Book by Rudyard Kipling
The Second Jungle Book by Rudyard Kipling

Kim by Rudyard Kipling
Stalky & Co by Rudyard Kipling
Just William by Richmal Crompton
At the Back of the North Wind by George MacDonald
Swallows and Amazons by Arthur Ransome
Robin Hood by J Walker McSpadden
The Water Babies by Charles Kingsley
Alice's Adventures in Wonderland by Lewis Carroll

These were a bit harder but I liked them a lot.

Treasure Island by Robert Louis Stevenson
Kidnapped by Robert Louis Stevenson
White Fang by Jack London
Jock of the Bushveld by Percy Fitzpatrick
Little Lord Fauntleroy by Frances Hodgson Burnett
Tom Brown's Schooldays by Thomas Hughes
The Story of an African Farm by Olive Shchreiner
Robinson Crusoe by Daniel Defoe
Gulliver's Travels by Jonathan Swift
Twenty Thousand Leagues Under the Sea by Jules Verne
King Solomon's Mines by Henry Rider Haggard
Oliver Twist by Charles Dickens
A Tale of Two Cities by Charles Dickens
Missionary Travels and Researches in Africa
by David Livingstone

I can tell you, that is a lot of reading that got burned. Thousands and thousands of words just disappeared into thin smoke. But when Miss Phillips wrote back to me she said, 'Don't think of your books as gone, they are quite safe now because they are in your head forever.' To my surprise she wasn't angry with me at all. She also said she was sorry for the boys who burned them because they had been made to believe that they were doing God's work. She said it was nothing of the sort and what they'd done was an iniquity. Others, who should know better, were to be blamed and she wished this war would jolly well hurry up and be over so that we could all start working together and forget the hatred of the past and be one nation. Then she said something strange, 'Were the paraffin tins there because they poured paraffin on the flames to get the fire started?'

So I looked up iniquity in my *Shorter Oxford English Dictionary*. It means, 1 *wickedness; unrighteousness.* 2 *gross injustice.*

Words can be very clever if they want and can sometimes save you a lot of time, so it's definitely worth knowing some.

Now, I don't want to get back to the *Dominee* because I now had two high-up warnings about him and another half of a one from Sergeant Van Niekerk, who didn't say anything about the preacher but just sighed and shook his head, and I could see he was glad he was writing up charges on a Sunday morning about *kaffirs* stabbing each other in the Location so didn't have to be in church. But this sermon was about Elijah and the burning bush. Now maybe you don't read the Bible, so you don't know the story, so I'd better tell you because it happened a long time ago. There was this prophet in the Old Testament called Elijah, and his people called the Israelites who decided he was no good. So he took them into the wilderness and said, 'See that bush?' And the people said, 'Yeah, okay?' Then Elijah showed them both hands so they could see he didn't have any matches. He said, 'Search me if you like,' because in the olden days prophets wore sort of long dresses. Then still standing a long way away from the bush he shouted, 'Abracadabra!' in the Israelite language and suddenly the bush is burning and he's not even close. 'God is in that bush! Beware, oh ye of little faith!' he shouted at the multitudes. 'From now on, have some respect!'

Well, that's what the *Dominee* said in church the very next Sunday after the fire. But he said, 'Last Saturday at The Boys Farm there was another burning bush incident that just goes to show God's gospel is alive among the *volk*. Some English books were hidden under a great rock and, all of a sudden, there was a fire that destroyed them. Now I'm not trying to say this is a miracle because it isn't. But just like Joseph Goebbels could find an evil book in a whole library, some boys, who are present in this congregation and about whom Jesus said, "Suffer little children to come unto me", found these devil books buried under a big rock and burned them. You see, even in this modern age, when we have aeroplanes that can fly around the world, the God of Elijah the prophet and the God of small children and the God of the Afrikaner *volk* is not mocked. The miracle of the burning bush is still here for all of us to learn to obey God's word!'

During all of this, the beetle had practically chewed up all the beard grass and you should have seen his ears. Talk about red! Sitting right in the front row with all the high-ups was Meneer Van Niekerk. All of a sudden he stood up and turned to the congregation. 'This is a disgrace!' he shouted. Then he turned back to the *Dominee*. 'This God you talk about is not *my* God! The fire that destroyed a young boy's precious book collection was deliberately lit by someone who is ignorant enough to have listened to your wicked propaganda sermon! I blame this crime on you, *Dominee*!' Then he turned and walked out and his wife, Mevrou Van Niekerk, got up and followed him. I wished I'd had the courage to walk out, but I didn't. When he'd almost reached the church door at the back, the *Dominee* shouted, 'I will carry this crime with pride in Jesus' precious name, Brother Van Niekerk!'

But then something even worse happened. Meneer Prinsloo stood up and turned to the congregation and said, 'As God is my witness, and as the Government-appointed supervisor of The Boys Farm for twelve years already, let me tell you, what the *Dominee* said is God's truth!' And then some of the congregation clapped. So you can see, Gawie had no chance of being a *regte Boer* ever again. He was sitting in the row in front of me and someone said in a loud whisper, '*Surrogaat*!'

It was an all-over bad time. Gawie not being my friend any more was one bad thing. But what was another almost as bad was that there were no more shit-paper reports coming my way. It turned into 1944 and I was now ten, nearly eleven, and I didn't know what was going on in the war. Except you could tell England was winning because people didn't brag how good the Germans were any more. You practically never heard Adolf Hitler's name mentioned and, at long last, Adolf Hitler, the rooster, was ready for the Rand Easter Show. I've got to admit, he was even better than Piet Retief, his tail feathers were black as coal with blue and purple and green showing through and shiny as anything, and reaching up and touching the sky, and his new name for going into the show was Winston Churchill.

And then a big thing in my life happened.

Dear Tom,

I have entered your name in the Bishop's College Scholarship. This is a private Anglican school in Johannesburg and considered the most prestigious in the Transvaal. The application says that last year 2000 candidates sat the examination for only three places. The suggestion is that this year there will be even more. It is for a boarder at St John's House with all fees paid.

Now, I don't expect you to win it this year, after all, you are only ten at the moment, and the average age for Form One is thirteen. But I would like you to study for it and to sit the examination. It will be excellent practice for next year. You know what I've always said, 'Practice makes perfect!'

Don't worry if it seems too hard. I will always be there with you. I have written to Meneer Van Niekerk to ask his permission, and he has agreed that you take the examination.

By the way, he has explained to me why Gawie is no longer doing the exercises in English. What a great pity! He is such a clever boy. I have

suggested to Meneer Van Niekerk that Gawie sit for the Jan Hofmeyer
Scholarship to Pretoria Afrikaans Boys High School and I am sending him the
necessary application forms.

With love,
Janneke Phillips (Miss)

That letter was the one-hundredth *With love* I'd received in four years
from Miss Phillips.

So now I was studying for a scholarship that I wasn't going to win.
I didn't think I could win it anyway, even if I wasn't too young. In my
opinion, high-up people don't go around giving out scholarships to posh
schools in Johannesburg to boys who are owned by the Government
and are the lowest you can get, except for *kaffirs*. I'd heard somewhere
that at schools like that you have to wear underpants and I'd never even
seen what they looked like. Gawie once said they were like bloomers
for men because once when he was tearing his shit-paper squares there
was this guy in an advertisment who was wearing some. 'Only people
who ride horses at the races wear them so their balls don't get squashed,'
he explained. 'They called Jockey shorts.' There was also another very
good reason why I wasn't going to win. That reason was Tinker. I didn't
suppose they'd let a person take his dog to a posh school like that even
if you told them she'd never come into the classroom or eat somebody's
sandwiches without first hearing the password.

But I must say I really liked the idea of doing the studying because
now with no friend I had plenty of time on my hands down at the library
rock. Studying takes a person's mind off stuff and you can't worry as
much because there's other things to worry about, like who discovered
America – it was Amerigo Vespucci, an Italian navigator, born 1454,
died 1512.

When the time came to write the examination, because it was too
far for me to go to Johannesburg to sit for them, the Bishop's College
made these special rules. They wouldn't even let Meneer Van Niekerk

get the exam papers because he might have a vested interest, Miss Phillips explained in one of her letters. Instead, the sealed envelope went to Doctor Van Heerden, because a town's doctor is not only a naturally high-up person, but can always be absolutely trusted. He agreed to open my exam papers on the mornings of the three-day examination. Then the doctor had to appoint someone who was totally trustworthy to sit outside the door of the room to see that nobody entered. I was allowed only three breaks, mid-morning, lunch and in the middle of the afternoon. This had to happen for three days until four o'clock. It seemed like a lot of fuss over someone who wasn't going to win, but rules are rules and we must obey them, Meneer Van Niekerk said.

You'd have thought he'd be angry because the Bishop's College didn't trust a high-up person like him with the exam papers, but he wasn't at all and said he was very proud of me. He was going through a hard time because lots of the parents tried to have him removed from the school because of what he'd done in church that Sunday. But lots of others secretly supported him. The Transvaal Department of Education had a hearing and they said it was not a matter for them, and as far as they were concerned Meneer de Wet van Niekerk was an exemplary headmaster and that was that. Now he had a lot of enemies, including the *Dominee*.

Guess who Doctor Van Heerden asked to sit outside the classroom? Marie Booysens, who was now a full-time certificate nurse at the local hospital. And guess what again? This is *really, really* good news, Doctor Van Heerden, whose wife died ten years ago, was going to marry Mevrou Booysens. I think it must be because she was so brave when he took out her gallbladder.

Marie arrived on the first examination day and she had this big basket with lots of things for me to eat on my compulsory breaks. Also she had a thermos with coffee, and another thermos that she'd put in this big fridge that wasn't an icebox and didn't run on electricity, in it was a strawberry milkshake. Even if I didn't win the scholarship, it was still the best examination I would ever sit for and what Marie brought in that basket was nearly as good as a mixed grill that I hadn't yet had. Marie said if I did well in the examination I could have one and she'd cook it for me herself.

Doctor Van Heerden arrived at the school and Meneer Van Niekerk met him, and we were taken to a classroom that had especially been emptied for me. He broke the seal on a large envelope and removed smaller envelopes and a letter which he read. He looked up.

'I have three envelopes, Tom, one for each day of your exams and I am going to break the seal of the first one and hand it to you. Meneer Van Niekerk tells me that paper, pen and ink have been set out for you and Marie will bring you anything else you need and tell you when to take your breaks. Remember, you can't ask her anything and the only time you will be out of her sight is if you want to go to the lavatory when you will be accompanied by another boy.'

I can't say the exams were easy, because they weren't, but then again they were not that difficult either. I didn't have to go to the lavatory. We had to wait two months for the results but I wasn't anxious because I already knew I wouldn't get it. What I did know was that the next time I sat, if there was a next time, then watch me, man! I'd be old enough and I was going to *really* try my hardest.

My sitting for the examination was not such big news at The Boys Farm because Meneer Prinsloo was the enemy of Meneer Van Niekerk. Meneer Prinsloo was already an old enemy of Sergeant Van Niekerk because of Fonnie du Preez, who was now in the reformatory in Pretoria, and, of course, the fire. So anything to do with the school wasn't mentioned except if one of The Boys Farm kids in the school rugby first team scored a try.

Gawie also sat the examination for Pretoria Afrikaans Boys High School. If he hadn't been a *surrogaat*, now turned into a proper noun that didn't need *Engelsman* attached to it, they would have made a big fuss of such a clever Afrikaner. It wasn't every day a boy from The Boys

Farm got as far as matric and there had only ever been one, and he'd been before Meneer Prinsloo's time. There had never been anyone who had won a scholarship and now the two boys that everyone hated the most might be the ones who did it.

Now, I don't want you to think I'm being a nice guy when I say this, but I *really* wanted Gawie, who still wouldn't have anything to do with me, to win his scholarship. Ever since the *surrogaat* business he had been miserable. At thirteen he wasn't in the small boys dormitory anymore so he wasn't around as much. When we walked to school or worked in the vegetable garden or watered the oranges, he was always on his own. It was okay for me, because I was accustomed to loneliness, besides, I had Tinker. Gawie wasn't used to being on his own, he had always been accepted as, okay, a bit of a drip, but a brainy person as well. The other kids would ask him things they didn't know and he did, and he liked that, to be the brains around the place. Now no-one asked the *surrogaat* anything.

I would have been his friend again in a flash, but several times when I'd approached him he turned on me and shouted, 'Voetsek!', which wasn't him calling me by my nickname. When you say it as an adjective, it's what you say to a mongrel dog before you kick it. So I didn't go near him any longer. If he won the scholarship he'd be out of The Boys Farm forever and that would be a good thing because in his heart of hearts Gawie didn't have a bad bone in his whole body. It was just that he was a stubborn Afrikaner, and when they stubborn you can forget it. You can't get blood out of a stone!

Something else definitely was big news around the place. Adolf Hitler, alias Winston Churchill, won third place at the Rand Easter Show. You have never seen such a gerfuffle! That night at supper, such was his excitement, Meneer Prinsloo made his speech *before* dinner. He was wearing the usual braces over his white, open-neck shirt but the third-place rooster ribbon was draped over his right shoulder and across his huge body like a sash worn by the leader of a marching band. As he stood there smiling, with his chest out nearly as far as his stomach, you knew already it was going to be cold soup tonight.

First, he turned to the top table and smiled his fat smile. '*Dames en Here en Jongetjies*. Ladies and Gentlemen and Boys, tonight is a truly great night in the history of The Boys Farm. We, and I include you all, because of the bread crusts you have left on the table, have won the top rooster in all of South Africa, except for a Leghorn and a Rhode Island Red. I speak, of course, of Adolf Hitler, the grand champion of roosters, except for the two other birds my informants tell me had definite connections with the judges.' He tapped his nose with his forefinger. 'Never you mind how I know this. Us Afrikaners have our ways and means and people who clean out cages, change the water and feed the chickens at these shows are not stupid, you hear. God gave them ears to listen and mouths to report the politics going on to their fellow Afrikaners who are trying to compete by playing fair and square.

'But politics are always around and a *Boer* from the Northern Transvaal who is the superintendent of a Boys Farm cannot compete with the big-time politicians of Chickendom! But we *volk* from the North who those people in Johannesburg always call *Japies* are also not stupid, hey!' He paused to let this point sink in. 'With chickens it's always Englishmen all over the place as judges. I must remind you the Rand Easter Show is situated in a place where the British and the Jews live. So, "*'n Man het 'n plan*", a man has a plan. In order to have a good chance I was regrettably forced to take that noble rooster with his tail feathers that touch the sky and give him a false identity. Now we all know this great, now nearly grand champion rooster's birth name, but for purposes of politics and disguise, we entered him as Winston Churchill.' He looked around and beamed at us all. 'What a clever joke, eh, boys? All of a sudden Adolf Hitler becomes Winston Churchill!'

Meneer Prinsloo brought his arms around his great girth, but his fingers were unable to touch by about twelve inches. He began to chuckle and then to shake with silent laughter, his belly wobbling like a plate of Christmas jelly, so we all laughed too. Then we clapped at this incredible piece of cunning designed by a master chicken strategist.

At the sound of the applause he calmed down and held up his hand, still half-laughing. 'Wait, there is more, boys!' he said, delighted with himself. 'There is also the chief judge's medal that he gives at his own discretion and not always to the grand champion, that imposter Leghorn. This chief judge of chickens, his name is Colonel Ted Emery and he has a big ginger moustache.' Meneer Prinsloo was taken up again with another sudden fit of giggling, but we kept clapping and laughing because his great jelly stomach was wobbling so much.

Finally, he managed to stop giggling long enough to say, 'When this medal is announced the chief judge says, "I award my medal to the third placegetter in the Best Rooster Under Two Years Category. A fine bird indeed, but this is not my reason for making this award. The breeder comes from the Northern Transvaal, from a small town called Duiwelskrans. You may recall the notorious Faceless Man, who attempted to blow up a troop train, came from this particular town. It is known as a veritable hotbed of political dissension openly masterminded by the *Ossewabrandwag*! To my mind, the courage this particular man has shown in naming the third placegetter after Sir Winston Churchill shows great character and loyalty to His Majesty the King and deserves the highest commendation. Ladies and gentlemen, boys and girls, I award Meneer Pietrus Prinsloo the Chief Judge's medallion!"'

Mevrou and old Mevrou Pienaar, who by now was almost totally deaf, and the two wardens who looked after the senior boys, Koos van de Merwe and Jakob Fourie, stood up on the platform table. Mevrou must have remembered the occasion when Frikkie Botha did the same to applaud the great Adolf Hitler speech when we all did the Nazi salute. The five staff started to applaud. I don't suppose you can do a Nazi salute for a rooster, so we all stood up and clapped like mad, mainly because we hoped it was about to end because by now our soup was stone cold.

'No! No!' Meneer Prinsloo shouted, his arms flailing through the air, braces stretched to capacity. 'Stop at once! Stop, you fools!' he thundered. We stopped and sat down again, a bit puzzled. Meneer Prinsloo, now very angry, shouted, 'If it were true what that *verdomde rooinek* chief judge of chickens Colonel Ted Emery said it would be a terrible disgrace on my good name! I am a loyal member of the *Ossewabrandwag*, as everyone knows very well! The *Broederbond* also! Winston Churchill is the imperialist dog that barks for the degenerate British King Georgie! Can't you *stupid* people see I was making only a nice joke against the Britisher chief judge of chickens!'

There was dead silence in the dining room. Old Mevrou Pienaar, who was always a bit confused, turned and leaned towards Mevrou. In a voice loud enough for everyone to hear, she said, 'What is all this about? Is it that stupid chicken? I only wish somebody would pull out its tail feathers again!' Nobody dared to laugh, but I'm telling you, I had to put my hand over my mouth and look down into my lap, quick smart.

My old books, now all brand-new editions, began to come in dribs and drabs from the CNA in Pietersburg. Each time a parcel arrived on the train, Meneer Van Niekerk would call me to his office and make a small presentation. As he handed me the brown-paper parcel tied with white string that had a piece of red sealing wax melted on the knot, he always said the same thing. 'For your personal use, Tom. Remember always, the truth shall set you free.' Each time I opened a parcel it was like meeting an old friend wearing a clean shirt. Books are like that, you know. When you haven't got a friend they can be your best friends and one thing is for sure, they'll never let you down or leave you in the lurch.

During the school holidays at the end of the second term, at the after-supper Meneer Prinsloo talk, the superintendent held up this envelope above his head. You could immediately see from his expression that he wasn't very happy with it.

'I have here a letter!' he announced, then paused and brought the envelope down to eye level and half squinted at it, then reached back to the platform table to get his spectacles, which he placed across his nose. You could see that he was already play-acting. 'It is addressed to

Master Tom Fitzsaxby,' Meneer Prinsloo began. '*Magtig!* Now already we a *Master*. Well, let me tell you, in here he is just a boy like you all, you hear?' He extracted the letter from the already opened envelope, then looked up and across the room taking us all in. 'Where is this fine specimen? Stand up, *Master* Tom Fitzsaxby!' he said with a sneer. There was a bit of a titter from all around the dining room.

I stood up and everyone looked at me. I knew I was in the deepest-of-deep shit again, but I couldn't think why. I'd had the usual on appro weekly *sjambokking* from Mevrou, but my bum had hardly any Chinese writing on it nowadays. The punishment ever since the fire was simply ignored. Nobody had anything to do with me, I had just disappeared from the face of the earth. Besides, there must have clearly been some mistake. I'd never received a letter at The Boys Farm. This was because all the Miss Phillips letters went 'c/o' Meneer Van Niekerk at the school. I'd once told her that letters sent to boys at The Boys Farm were opened and often read to everyone after supper. So it couldn't be from her as she deliberately never wrote to me in the school holidays. Instead, she sent all the work I had to do for the holidays in advance so that it arrived at school before the end of each term. If it wasn't from her, well, I didn't know a single other person in the whole world who would possibly write to me.

'Now I want you all to listen very carefully, you hear?' Meneer Prinsloo said. 'You remember the *Dominee*'s sermon when he told us about evil hidden in books? The German ones that were burned and the English that we mustn't read because they haven't got a Joseph Goebbels to find the devil's work in them.' He raised the letter above his head again and waved it. 'In this letter there are also secret codes that a good Afrikaner must learn to interpret. You are all young boys who have innocent hearts, so now I must give you a lesson in the interpretation of evil. It is for your own good and we cannot start early enough spotting evil lurking around the place.' He adjusted his spectacles and began to read.

Dear Master Tom Fitzsaxby,

I have the honour on behalf of the Bursary Committee to inform you that your name is among the three winners of the Bishop's College Scholarship for the coming year 1945. Congratulations.

I must, however, inform you that your name must now be submitted to the Board of Governors, as the school does not, as a general rule, accept scholars into Form One under the age of thirteen years old.

Should the Board of Governors decide against making an exception for a scholarship boy, I am pleased to inform you that the Bursary Committee has agreed to defer your scholarship until the first term of 1947.

For your interest, here are the placings and the names of the three winners.

Nathan Feinstein, overall mark 98 per cent

Tom Fitzsaxby, overall mark 95 per cent

Julian Solomon, overall mark 94 per cent

Two thousand and seven hundred candidates from all over South Africa and Rhodesia sat for the examination so that you are entitled to be very proud of your effort. We look forward to welcoming you to the Bishop's College.

I will inform your sponsor Miss Janneke Phillips, your examination supervisor Dr A M van Heerden and your headmaster Mr de Wet van Niekerk by separate mail.

I remain,
Yours faithfully,
Rev. John Robertson, MA Oxon., Headmaster.

When the superintendent read out the overall mark I'd got, there was a gasp around the place and then a general murmuring. No boy at The Boys Farm, not even Gawie Grobler, had ever got an average mark for all subjects near as high as that. Nor, of course, had I. If I hadn't been standing there in the middle of a room where everybody was expected to hate me and where I was about to be humiliated, I too would have reacted with astonishment. As it was, I clasped my hands behind my back and looked down at the floor, summoning up the courage for what was to come.

Meneer Prinsloo looked up from the letter. 'Now, at first, when you read a letter like this, you see nothing,' he began. 'It is just a letter about a boy that won some scholarship, but now you must take it carefully apart. For instance, I ask now, who has bishops?' He looked down at us before saying, 'Roman Catholics. They the one that got bishops! So you see, the first thing you know is that this is an Antichrist school where they worship the Virgin Mary. Hanging on the walls are false idols and there is a Pope who, to them, is next to God Himself. Now you see, Jesus Christ who is His only begotten son only comes in fourth place after the Pope and that Mary woman they had the cheek to make a saint! So now you all know where this boy *Master* Tom Fitzsaxby is going. Roman Catholicism is where! He should be ashamed!'

I glanced up and saw that the superintendent's stomach had grown so large that if he'd been lying in the water on his back and all of a sudden there was this jet coming from his bellybutton you would have to think he was a sperm whale. His hands were going round and round so fast the letter was making a sort of whirring sound. Surely he'd have to get new braces soon because these ones must be just about worn-out from going beyond the stretch limit set for braces. You see, I had to think funny things like this because, if I didn't, I would have started to cry on the spot. It's a trick you learn so as to distract your mind from what is *really* going on. You try to think about something funny, then it doesn't hurt so much. I learned this when I was little, and I'd do it with Mevrou all the time. Then after a while, what's the use, you going to get the *sjambok* anyway. But now with Meneer Prinsloo, if I didn't do it, who knows what would happen? Maybe I'd even shit my pants.

'Now, don't you worry! That is not all the wickedness to be found in this letter,' he continued. 'Look who also wins scholarships? Two Jews! Two thousand and seven hundred children sit down to do this so-called examination and how does it end up? A Jewish sandwich! One

Jew, Nathan Feinstein, is the top slice, in the middle Tom Fitzsaxby is the *Engelsman* meat and the bottom slice is Julian Solomon, another Jew.' He glared down at me. 'Shame! Shame! Shame!' He stopped and took a deep breath. 'And another thing! I am like a father to you all. The Government picked me and my good wife, Mevrou Prinsloo, to be parents of all you boys. Wouldn't you think a bit of courtesy is due to someone who is a genuine government-selected mother and father? They, this Bishop's College, don't think so. They are now going to send a letter to Meneer Van Niekerk who *only* stands up in church and blasphemes! Then also another one to Doctor Van Heerden, who never even comes to church because he's sewing up the stomachs of black *bobbejane*! Black baboons! As for this lady.' He glanced down at the letter again. 'This Miss Janneke Phillips who is a corrupting influence and deliberately sends an innocent boy to a Roman Catholic school that's full of Jews, she *also* gets a letter!' He paused to let this iniquity set in. 'But not the hostel father! Not the official person the Government makes responsible for the welfare of this certain *Master* Tom Fitzsaxby. There's no letter for him, is there? No letter for the good Afrikaner who wins ribbons at Easter shows!'

By this time my knees were knocking together like billyo, so when Meneer Prinsloo had folded the letter and put it back in the envelope and said for me to come and fetch the letter from the platform table, I was hardly able to walk. When I approached him, he dropped the letter at his feet and I had to bend down and pick it up next to his shiny brown boots you could see your face in. My knees were still knocking for everyone to see, but at least I didn't cry in front of them all, just a bit of a sniff that I don't think anyone could see, snot pulling back, because it happened all of a sudden when I was bending down. It was very hard walking back to my place with my wobbly legs.

At breakfast four days later, it was a Saturday and we were just beginning to eat our porridge when we could see through the big window in the dining room the police van pulling up in front of the hostel. Sergeant Van Niekerk got out and went straight to the staff quarters to see, I suppose, Meneer Prinsloo, who didn't have breakfast with us boys, only supper. Then, just as I'd finished porridge someone came and told me to go to Meneer Prinsloo's office.

Sergeant Van Niekerk was waiting when I arrived and Meneer Prinsloo said, 'The sergeant wants to take you into town for further enquiries about the fire.' He sighed, 'This *verdomde* fire, will it never go away!' I don't know who he said it to because I don't think Sergeant Van Niekerk was listening, he was now looking out of the window. He then turned around to face Meneer Prinsloo. 'I must warn you, we may be away for most of the day, Superintendent.'

'Ag, man, you can take him as long as you like. As far as I'm concerned, it's good riddance of bad rubbish!'

I saw Sergeant Van Niekerk stiffen and his eyes suddenly grew hard. 'You know something, Pietrus Prinsloo? If I could arrest anyone for that fire, it would be you! We can't go on living in the past, man! What is done is done. It is not the railway workers, lorry drivers and timber cutters you turn out in this place that matter, it is clever boys like Tom Fitzsaxby and Gawie Grobler who are the future of our land. We must forget the past and get on with life.'

Meneer Prinsloo stuck out his stomach. 'I am an Afrikaner, Sergeant, first and foremost. I will die an Afrikaner with the *vierkleur*, the glorious flag of the republic, draped over my coffin. You do not know what you are talking about, Jan van Niekerk. My own mother had to sleep with an Australian sergeant who is worse even than an Englishman so we could put a little food on the table. A God-fearing woman who had never sinned in her life, now she is drinking brandy and sleeping with a drunken Australian soldier in my *ouma*'s bed and staying out all night until the early morning. You think I can forget this? Never! My mother, who was as pure as the snow. A good woman who never missed going to church every Sunday before that Australian came, now they calling her a whore. *Wragtig!* These people, they are devils who corrupt the soul, man! You think I can trust their offspring? Never, you hear? Rubbish is always rubbish!'

Sergeant Van Niekerk shook his head slowly. 'C'mon, Tom, we got to go, man,' he said.

I would have liked to ask Meneer Prinsloo if there was a goosefeather quilt from his grandmother's glory box involved in the affair with the Britisher who was an Australian. Or was it only the *Dominee* it happened to? Maybe they didn't have goosefeather quilts in England or even in Australia and this was a nice opportunity for Britishers to sleep under one. Although, judging from what Meneer Prinsloo had said, his mother and the Australian hadn't spent a lot of time sleeping under it. We only got one blanket in winter at The Boys Farm and when it got cold I can tell you something for nothing, I myself would have liked to sleep under such a cosy-sounding quilt, even with someone else, if it was big enough for two people of course.

When we were out of Meneer Prinsloo's office Sergeant Van Niekerk said, 'Better go and fetch your dog, Tom. I'll wait for you at the front gate.'

I knew Tinker would be waiting at the back door of the hostel and I brought my fingers to my lips and did a loud whistle. In only a few moments here comes Tinker around the corner of the hostel, running flat out, her little legs sending puffs of dry winter dust rising up behind.

'She is a good little dog,' Sergeant Van Niekerk said, as Tinker did her leap into my arms and started to lick my face. 'A dog can love a man better than anyone else.'

'*Ja*, she is what is called "A one-man dog",' I explained happily.

'And the best ratter in the Northern Transvaal I hear, hey?'

It was a nice compliment, but it just goes to show, a police sergeant knows everything that's going on around the place.

'Eight is the record,' I said, patting Tinker. 'That's the most she can count.' I thought momentarily of Frikkie Botha who was lying in a hospital somewhere with no face. He always hoped for nine rats. 'One day we going to get nine, just you wait and see, that little ratter will do it I guarantee.'

On our way into town we turned left into a farm road that headed towards the high mountains. It wasn't my place to ask and I thought Sergeant Van Niekerk may be visiting a farm or something before we went to the police station to do further enquiries on the fire. A subject that, I must say, I too was a bit tired of hearing about.

'Aren't you wondering where we going?' he asked after a while.

'*Ja*, I thought maybe somebody's farm you had to go and see,' I replied.

We were beginning to climb, going round narrow curves on a dirt road with Sergeant Van Niekerk constantly changing gears. Sometimes the road was so narrow the tyres sent small rocks down the steep slope at the one side of the road.

'Have you ever been on a picnic, Tom?'

'*Ja*, Meneer, once with the church to the sports field, we all had to help with the work. Nearly the whole town was there.'

'No, a proper picnic by a waterfall in the high mountains?'

I couldn't believe what I was hearing. 'No, Meneer, does it have *boerewors*?' I had heard all proper picnics had *boerewors* and a *braaivleis*.

'*Ja*, for sure. All you can eat and maybe even fish, there is a pool and sometimes you can catch bass.'

I'd never tasted fish, but it didn't matter, because if I didn't like it, I could just taste a little bit just to be polite. Then eat *boerewors* as much as I could eat. Which was a lot, because I only had porridge this morning, not even a cup of coffee.

We climbed for more than an hour and passed only one farm that had four houses on it. 'Van Schalkwyk,' Sergeant Van Niekerk said, then did this sort of spit out the window.

So this is where Mevrou lived when she grew up, I thought to myself. The four houses must be for the six brothers and the mother and father. Even with all the houses it looked a lonely place. There was also a big shed and a *kraal* but no cattle because they were probably grazing in the mountains. Outside the biggest house there was a Dutch oven and a smokehouse and a bit further on a big piggery.

'They breed also pigs. I must say their ham is the best you ever tasted, they can do it with honey so you think it's Christmas every day,' Sergeant Van Niekerk remarked.

We travelled even higher and not changing gears because only the low gear was needed. You could see further than I had ever looked. The country all around had huge rocky outcrops and the bush *veld* stretched down into green valleys, and thousands of flat-topped fever trees and aloes dotted the countryside. It was the most beautiful country I had ever seen. I became aware of something else, although I couldn't quite put my finger on what it was.

'High mountain country,' Sergeant Van Niekerk said, as if he was reading my thoughts. 'This is where the rainforest begins.'

It was true, the surrounding *kloofs* were deep green with tall trees and monkey ropes and even above the whine of the engine you could hear that the bird calls were different. At last, we turned into a roadway that you could hardly see and Sergeant Van Niekerk stopped and went to the back of the van and produced a sharp post with a small paper flag on it and pushed it into the ground at the entrance of the turn-off. We proceeded down this hardly-a-road-at-all and sometimes I had to jump out and pull a dead branch out of the way. There was very little sunlight and it felt sort of damp and cool and dark. Once a lourie called out and then a bird I'd never heard. 'Cape parrot,' the sergeant said. We kept putting down these little flags for about a mile in the bush road, when suddenly you couldn't believe your eyes. There was first this thundering sound, then we turned into a sunlit clearing and I saw we'd come right up against a high *krans* from which a waterfall tumbled, a ribbon of whitewater that must have been 300 feet high. It seemed to fall in slow motion into a deep mountain pool and all about us were tree ferns and gigantic trees that rose up to the sky. Monkey ropes twisted and turned about them as well as other vines with huge green leaves big as dustbin lids that I'd never seen before. High up in lichen-and-moss-covered tree forks wild orchards grew.

'*Magtig!*' was all I could say. 'I didn't know there was such a beautiful place in the whole world!'

'Nice, eh, Tom?' Sergeant Van Niekerk said, switching off the idling engine.

'Is this where we going to have our picnic?' I asked somewhat foolishly.

'*Ja*, don't you like it? Would you rather go somewhere else then?' he teased. 'We've got to collect some dry wood and get the fire going before the others come. For a good *braai* we need only embers or the meat will burn on the outside and be raw in the middle.'

'Others? There are going to be others?'

He grinned. '*Ja*, your friends, just you wait and see, man. Now let's get some wood. It's not so easy, hey, this is true rainforest where it rains every day, finding dry wood can be difficult.'

I didn't know I had any friends, so it was all rather confusing.

Tinker and me went looking for wood and it wasn't too hard and soon we had a big pile. When Sergeant Van Niekerk came and looked at it he laughed. 'Ag, man, Tom, this wood is all rotten, it will burn up in five minutes, look for some that has some weight.'

How could I make such a mistake? Me, above all people, who had been collecting wood every Saturday for the boiler room at The Boys Farm and now that I was past ten years old had been chopping it for ages. Sergeant Van Niekerk must have seen the shameful look on my face because he laughed.

'It's different country up here, Tom. Everything is different, wood rots before it dries, you can see the trees and plants are different and at three o'clock in the afternoon it rains every day, you can set your watch by it.'

This was the country Mattress had described to me so very long ago. I had a sudden stab of pain in my heart. Was he in heaven? Heaven was a high-up place, maybe it looked like this, waterfalls and big trees and sunlit glades. If I had been old enough when he died I would have pinned a note on his body with his name on it so God would know who he was now that he didn't have a face. But there were always his platform feet, even God, who is a very busy person, couldn't mistake them, and they hadn't been scraped off by the road.

This time it was less easy to find wood, but we got some and when it was enough we started the *braaivleis* fire. Sergeant Van Niekerk said, 'We better get in a swim, hey? Because later there will be ladies here.'

So we took off all of our clothes and he said, 'I dare you to dive in first.' So I did and when I came up I thought I must have just dived into a pool of ice. Sergeant Van Niekerk was laughing. 'It's cold, hey, Tom!' Then he dived in and came up snorting like a walrus. '*Here*, man, it's cold!' he yelled above the sound of the waterfall.

Tinker was the only smart one who didn't jump in, she just barked at the edge, maybe dogs know these things. We couldn't stay in for long because it was too cold. When we got out we lay on this big sunny rock and got warm again and our skin dried.

'Better get dressed, the others will be here soon,' said Sergeant Van Niekerk. By now the fire was burnt down and only a wisp of smoke was rising. 'A bit more wood and the embers will be perfect,' he said.

It hadn't even started properly and already this was the happiest day of my life. You'll never believe what happened. Because the waterfall drowned out the sound, I didn't hear the car coming and I suddenly looked up and there, like a ghost car, was Doctor Van Heerden's '39 Chevvie with the dicky-seat, and there in the dicky-seat is Marie. In the front was the Doctor and Mevrou Booysens. I couldn't believe my eyes! Who was going to look after the Impala Café and the farmers coming to see Doctor Van Heerden? They had come all this way on their busiest day of the week, just to see me.

I'd hardly recovered from this shock when turning into the clearing is Meneer Van Niekerk's old Plymouth and in it is his wife Anna, who once gave me an end-of-the-year prize at school for history. The back door of the car opened and it was Miss Phillips! Can you imagine? Miss Phillips from Johannesburg!

Marie came and gave me a big kiss, and then Mevrou Booysens and then Miss Phillips who hugged me and said, 'Oh, oh, you precious child!' and I thought she was going to cry because her voice went all of a sudden wobbly. She told me how she'd come down in the train and Meneer

Van Niekerk had picked her up in Tzaneen. Then Mevrou Van Niekerk kissed me. Four kisses all at once, a brand-new world record!

Well! What a day-and-a-half it turned out to be! We didn't catch any fish, but I think I ate about a yard of *boerewors,* and cakes and pudding and *koeksisters* and a big roast potato and all the cool drinks I wanted in proper bottles. They even had some *biltong* and I could take some home with me. Other nice things you couldn't take, because they'd be confiscated, but nobody would know you had *biltong* in your pocket.

Then after lunch Meneer Van Niekerk made a speech and he said how proud they were of me winning the scholarship an' all.

'It is one of the proudest moments in the history of the school,' he said. Then he added, if Gawie also won his scholarship it would make them all doubly proud, but they didn't know his results yet. 'This day is in your honour, Tom, we are very proud of you, but we not only honour you, we also honour the selfless love of a woman, Miss Phillips. Without this very special person, who knows what might have happened to these two brilliant boys. A headmaster can only do so much and they would probably have been lost in the wilderness.'

I'm glad he also mentioned Gawie because it was true about him. Miss Phillips had gone all red in the face and said she'd only done her duty as a teacher, and that it brought her great pleasure watching two fine young minds grow. We all knew it was lots and lots more than that. I loved Marie, but I also loved Miss Phillips a lot, but in a different sort of way.

After all the speeches were over, Doctor Van Heerden said how lucky it was that he'd left that old box of his dear brother's books under the house and other nice things. 'If half chopping off your finger brings young men like you into an old doctor's life, Tom, then chop away,' he said, and everyone laughed.

Then Mevrou Van Niekerk asked if they knew about the scholarship at The Boys Farm.

'They got a letter,' I replied.

'They? You mean *you* got one?' Miss Phillips exclaimed.

'Yes.'

'Did you tell them about your scholarship?' Mevrou Van Niekerk asked.

'They knew already, Mevrou. We are not allowed to get letters that haven't been opened and read first by Meneer Prinsloo,' I explained.

'Was there a little celebration, maybe?' Mevrou Booysens asked, offering me a brown-paper packet. 'Have some dried peaches, they come from the Cape.'

I didn't know what to say. I couldn't tell them what had happened and I couldn't lie because we were not at The Boys Farm and they were all high-up people I loved and respected. I took a dried peach to cover up.

'Perhaps I can explain,' Meneer Van Niekerk suddenly interjected. 'Jan and I have an old aunt, Mevrou Pienaar, who is the cook at The Boys Farm. She told me what happened.' He went through the whole story and everyone was very quiet until the end when Doctor Van Heerden said, 'I am ashamed that man calls himself a proud Afrikaner.' Everyone shook their heads and Miss Phillips said, 'What an iniquity!' Marie came over and kissed me and gave me a big hug.

Which just goes to show, a person shouldn't go around in life criticising people who go, 'Eh? What did you say?' all the time when you speak to them. It was obvious from how the headmaster told the story that Mevrou Pienaar had heard every word that went on that night. Now I also knew how Sergeant Van Niekerk knew so much about everything going on around the place and how Tinker was a famous ratter.

But then, all of a sudden, I knew something else. I now knew that they all knew the story of the letter before they came here. By deliberately telling it again in front of me it was Meneer Van Niekerk's way of telling me, 'Remember, Tom, the truth shall set you free.' Badness doesn't always win and good people *must* fight bad people and not let them get away with stuff. That was why they had all given up their valuable time to give me such a lovely picnic.

At two o'clock, because of the high *krans* the waterfall tumbled over, the sun was already gone and the glade grew quite chilly. Sergeant Van

Niekerk said we would need to go because at three o'clock sharp the rain would come down and the road out would be slippery and dangerous. Then another nice thing happened. Doctor Van Heerden said, 'Why not drive home with us and sit in the dicky-seat with Marie and enjoy the open air.' I looked at Sergeant Van Niekerk to see if it was all right.

'I dunno, man,' he said, shaking his head. 'That's a very pretty *nooi* you got there, Tom.' He turned to the others. 'Do you think they can be trusted?'

They all laughed and I dunno why, but I got all red in the face. This was because Gawie and me had seen this word *geslagdrang* in one of his shit squares. After a lot of puzzling we'd finally worked out from reading the rest that it's what happens sometimes when you get close to a girl. In English it is 'sex urge'.

'Can Tinker come? She's a very good watchdog,' I replied. 'Then there's two women and only one boy.'

'*Hy is 'n slimmetjie!*' Mevrou Booysens exclaimed, clapping her hands. 'Naughty too!' I don't know why they thought I was clever, because it was only something Gawie and me had talked about once. One thing was for sure, if I had to put my snake into Marie, in a dicky-seat it couldn't be done! Even if I knew how to do it, which I didn't, and if I did, I wouldn't. You can't go doing something like that to somebody you love.

It was pretty squashed in the dicky-seat which stuck out of the back of the little '39 Chevvie where in other cars you'd have a boot, but it was also wonderful with the wind in your face and the countryside flashing by. Not really flashing because it was quite slow with all the bends and twists in the road, and sometimes looking over the side it was a bit scary with rocks tumbling down over the edge of the road when the tyres hit them.

Marie said she *really* liked Miss Phillips and she wished she was her older sister because she was an only child. 'You are a very lucky boy to have Miss Phillips in your life, Tom,' she said.

'I know,' I replied, 'she got me the scholarship I can't have yet.

I could never have had it otherwise. I don't know how to say thank you properly.' Then the big idea hit me! It was so simple I couldn't believe it. 'Marie, you a girl, hey?'

She laughed. 'However did you guess, Tom?'

But I was so taken with my new thought that I hardly smiled. 'If I gave you ten shillings, could you buy something for Miss Phillips?' I forgot to tell you that when I rescued the red book, it wasn't only that it was *really* important to me above all my other books, but also because that's where my ten shillings was hidden. You'll be glad to hear, my ten-shilling note was still as good as new, and so were my burned fingers.

'Ten shillings! That's a fortune, Tom. Where did you get ten shillings?'

I was discovering in life that women always need details that are not important and sidetrack a person. Before you know where you are, you telling them stuff you don't want to even tell yourself. Now I had to tell her about the Easter bonnet and Piet Retief's shiny feathers. So another person would know the crime. First Sergeant Van Niekerk, then Gawie and now Marie. 'If I tell, will you promise on your word of honour this time not to tell anyone?'

'What do you mean, *this time*,' she said suspiciously.

'Well, last time you swore on a stack of Bibles that you wouldn't tell Doctor Van Heerden about me stealing the red book from under his house.' I didn't say this unkindly or in an accusing voice, I just wanted her to know that the truth would set her free.

'Look what extra good came from me telling him?' she exclaimed. 'Now you not a thief any more. Don't you think me blabbing was worth it?'

I couldn't argue with her because I was also learning . . . no, that's wrong. I'd known all along from dealing with Mevrou that you couldn't win an argument with a woman because they've got a special logic that defeats you every time. So now I had to tell her about my second big crime, the plucking of the great Piet Retief's tail feathers.

'I'll only tell you if you don't think I'm a criminal again,' I said carefully.

'You don't mean to say you stole it! I don't believe it! *You* stole ten shillings!' she exclaimed in amazement.

'No, of course not!' I shouted. We'd come to a straight section of the road when the '39 Chevvie had speeded up, and I had to shout because the wind was whipping our voices away from us.

When we slowed down again, she said, 'You'd better tell me, Tom. I hope I am not going to be disappointed in you.'

The way she said it made me quite scared. I simply couldn't afford to lose another friend, even if she was older. So I had to tell her everything and take the risk that the truth would set me free. When I'd finished the story, she was laughing and clapping. 'But Miss Phillips sent you a pound and now you've only got ten shillings. What did you spend the other ten shillings on?'

See how it works? With a woman you start with just a simple fact. Next thing you know you're telling her about the ten shillings that turned into a pound up Gawie's bum and then back into ten shillings again. Which was the same ten shillings I now had. I thought Marie was going to die laughing, and Tinker got quite excited and barked like mad.

Then we were down the high mountains and back into the hills on the road to The Boys Farm when Marie had her brilliant idea. It was so brilliant that I thought, maybe Marie is a mind-reader? But she couldn't be, because the idea she came up with hadn't been a subject on my mind when she'd been present. In fact, the last time I'd thought about it was in Meneer Prinsloo's office that morning when he was talking about the drunken Australian sergeant and his mother who turned from pure as snow into a whore.

'Tom, I have a good idea. Maybe you'll like it, hey? I'm very good at needlework and sewing. I do it in the hospital ward when I'm on night duty. I've made several of these quilts and I've just finished one for my mum's wedding present. With your ten shillings I can buy the cottons, tapes, backing material and the stuffing, and I have this big rag bag full of material scraps I've collected since I was a little girl. All the colours in the whole world, as well as lots of different patterns. Why don't I make Miss Phillips a nice quilt? I don't want to boast, you hear, but I'm good and have won several sewing prizes around the place.'

'A quilt!' I couldn't believe my ears. 'Does it have goosefeathers?'

'Ja, Tom, all good quilts have goosefeathers. You're not getting rubbish, you know!'

Sometimes in life you can get *really* lucky. That ten shillings had had a difficult journey. First, causing a big fight at the water pump, and it completely disappearing and me getting into trouble with Frikkie Botha saying the Union Jack was a nicer flag than the *vierkleur*. Then, all of a sudden reappearing as a pound up Gawie's bum. Then turning into my ten shillings and back into a pound that was nearly used to buy *mieliemeel* in Tzaneen by Meneer Patel of Patel & Sons. Then, at the last moment getting rescued by Sergeant Van Niekerk. Then getting buried in the red book and having a very lucky escape from a bushfire! At long last, it was going to turn into the biggest surprise a person like Miss Phillips could ever have after her big win with the Easter bonnet that started everything. In life you never know what's going to happen around every corner.

CHAPTER TEN

Unrequited Love

WELL, I'M TELLING YOU, that Bishop's College met their match when they took on Miss Janneke Phillips! When she heard they wouldn't take me because I was too young, she went to see the headmaster. It was some years later that she told me what had taken place, recalling the conversation almost word for word.

'My dear Miss Phillips,' the headmaster began. 'While pastoral care is one of the features of this school, in our experience an almost twelve-year-old boy, especially one as precocious as young Fitzsaxby, would not yet be mentally and physically mature for the boarding-school environment. It would be much better in the long run if he remained where he is for another two years.'

Miss Phillips said that the whole of Johannesburg must have heard her laughing her head off. 'Headmaster, do you not know this boy's background?' she asked the Reverend John Robertson.

'Essentially no, but the boy is very bright, very bright indeed, which suggests intellectual parents and a carefully nurtured home environment, which doesn't always suit a boy for the rough and tumble of a boys' boarding school.'

'But you addressed a letter to him at The Boys Farm?'

'Well, yes, the name of his parents' farm? Now I think of it, perhaps a little strange, but names can be like that. When I was a boy in Sussex, I recall a farm near my village was named "Doomsday Farm". As a further example, whoever would have thought of calling the town from which I believe young Fitzsaxby comes, the Devil's Canyon. Rather ante-mortem and dark, don't you think?'

Janneke Phillips laughed. 'For this town, I can assure you, it is a very appropriate name. Most of its inhabitants have a Great Trek mentality and the Boer War is refought every day!'

'And this curiously named Boys Farm is what?'

'It is an orphanage started for some of the child survivors of the British concentration camps and has simply continued to exist. Past wounds are still very much felt in this society and The Boys Farm, along with the local Dutch Reform Church, is a seedbed of bigotry and Afrikaner resentment against the British. Tom's surname, Fitzsaxby, has been translated into the Afrikaans expletive, *Voetsek*, by which he is known, even by some of the adults at the institution.'

'Good heavens!' the Reverend Robertson exclaimed. 'We had no idea.'

'Tom Fitzsaxby has been at The Boys Farm since the age of four which makes his results even more remarkable, don't you think? A successful graduate from The Boys Farm might, at best, be expected to become a lorry driver, railway worker or timber cutter. Many of them end up in trouble with the law. What's more, as I've just indicated, with his English surname, Tom has been constantly and systematically persecuted, not only by the Afrikaner children, but also by the staff. Paradoxically, when I met him at the age of seven, he had entirely forgotten his native tongue and spoke only Afrikaans and Zulu. His English essay in your scholarship examination, for which your markers were kind enough to award him 95 per cent, was written by a boy who has almost no opportunity to practise the spoken language. Sir, this young boy has been beaten almost every day of his life and has suffered some sexual abuse. His only friend, a Zulu farm worker, was murdered by an unknown group of white men. Yet he has survived with his personality remarkably intact. Do you honestly think your boarding-school environment is going to have a negative effect on his character? If you don't take him at the Bishop's College next year he is condemned to spending a further two years in that vile institution,' Miss Phillips said, laying it on a bit thick.

'Well, yes, of course, my dear Miss Phillips, I can see your point, most unfortunate circumstances.' He appeared to be thinking. 'Is he a big child . . . big for his age?'

'No, he's slightly below average for an English-speaking boy. Certainly small among his Afrikaner peers.' Miss Phillips saw a look of uncertainty cross the headmaster's face. 'Don't worry, he'll hold his own, and won't be asking for any favours. I'm told he is a promising young scrum-half,' she said, as if to confirm that I was tough enough.

This last bit was stretching things a bit. We started rugby at the age of nine, mostly just the little kids fooling about with a senior kid handling the ref's whistle. It would be one pick-up team against another. I always got scrum-half, simply because I was the smallest. Scrum-half is a position where you get bashed a lot by the forwards if you don't get the ball away to the back line quick smart. So I got quite okay at playing it, mainly because I was scared stiff. Miss Phillips had based her laudatory remark on a conversation at the picnic, when Sergeant Van Niekerk had asked, 'What rugby possie do you play, Tom?' I had replied, 'Scrum-half, Meneer,' to which he had said, 'Ja, that's good, I think you will be a good scrum-half.'

'Scrum-half, eh?' The headmaster was suddenly interested. 'That says something for the lad. Nippy, agile, feisty, courageous, that's the scrum-half for you. In my rugby football experience he is usually the boy who gives the team its character.'

Miss Phillips seized on the word. 'Character! Let me assure you, Headmaster, Tom Fitzsaxby has heaps and then some to spare.'

The Reverend John Robertson smiled, no doubt accustomed to importunate parents and their like. 'Very well, Miss Phillips, I can't promise, but I'll put it to the school council. I will point out to them the unique circumstances and ask that Master Tom Fitzsaxby gain entrance to the Bishop's College at the tender age of eleven. I understand he will turn twelve at the beginning of the second term of 1945.'

Now, you're probably thinking that I'd be happy as anything when the Bishop's College decided it was okay for me to start in the first term of 1945, but I wasn't. I couldn't tell anyone this because I knew they'd be disappointed in me and think I was letting them down. But you see I thought maybe I was going from the frying pan into the fire, and the devil you know is better than the one you don't. I had read *Tom Brown's Schooldays* before it was lost in that fire. Now maybe you haven't personally read this book, so if you haven't read it let me tell you something for nothing, it was almost a dead swap over for The Boys Farm. Talk about cruel and hard! That Tom Brown could have been me all over again, except it happened long before I was born, so it's probably the other way around. I was him all over again. What's more, it was even worse because there were no Afrikaners involved and the English didn't put their own people in concentration camps to die. So why so cruel at this rugby school? I said to myself, if that's how it was at an English boarding school, and they did cruelty for nothing, I was now going to the Bishop's College which was an English boarding school, so what was the point? The point for me was that I couldn't take Tinker. So now all of a sudden I'm going to Johannesburg without my little dog, just so I can have a hard time somewhere else.

The thought of being parted from Tinker was unbearable. She was my every day, my first thought in the morning and my last at night. She wasn't just my dog, she was my everything. Now, I know I shouldn't also say that, because there were lots of kind and loving people in my life – Miss Phillips, Meneer Van Niekerk, Sergeant Van Niekerk, Doctor Van Heerden and Mevrou Booysens and, of course, the wonderful goosefeather-quilt-making Marie. While I don't suppose kids can really comprehend something like death, although when Mattress was murdered I think I understood it well enough, I'm sure I would have been willing to lose my life to save Tinker. So you can see that I wasn't very happy, but if any of these people were around I had to look as if I was.

Doctor Van Heerden married Mevrou Booysens and they invited me to the wedding and what a to-do that turned out to be.

'They only having a quiet wedding, you hear,' Marie told me. 'That's because it's second time around for them both. He's a widower and my mum's a widow, so no fuss please. Only a few guests and you're going to be one, Tom.'

It was hard to believe that they'd all be high-ups and then there'd be me.

'Is it on a Sunday?' I asked anxiously.

'No, Saturday, why do you ask?'

'I was only asking,' I said lamely.

'No you weren't, you never only ask,' Marie said sharply. 'What is it, Tom?'

'I can't come if it's on a Saturday.'

'Why not, man? There's no school.'

I was trapped. 'I still can't come,' I said.

'For goodness sake, Tom, why ever not? You're being silly and that's not a bit like you, you hear?'

'It's my clothes,' I said at last. 'On a Saturday they're always very dirty because I've worn them all week.'

Marie laughed. 'Ag, Tom, that's nothing, you hear? The doctor will get Meneer Prinsloo to allow you to get your clean clothes. When do you always get them?'

'Saturday night.'

'Well, on this Saturday afternoon, they'll already be there waiting for you, you just going to be wearing them a few hours early.'

But she didn't know The Boys Farm. 'We not allowed to wear them until Sunday morning for church, so everybody will think we always nice and clean. It's our good reputation at stake,' I explained.

'Another rule made by that hypocrite Pietrus Prinsloo!' She put her arm around me and kissed me. 'Just say you'll come and we'll sort out the clothes situation.'

'Can I bring Tinker? She's never been to a wedding.' I'd stopped counting Marie's kisses because she did it all the time.

'*Ja*, of course, but not in the church, hey.'

'The *Dominee* says dogs haven't got souls, they not even allowed in a church.'

Which was a pretty worrying point also. If, according to the *Dominee*, animals didn't have souls and didn't go to heaven, how was I going to have Tinker in heaven with me and Mattress? I'd done some praying on this matter, although in my experience God doesn't give you answers on stuff like that. He only answers you if you pray and ask, 'Can I please pass my exams?' Then when you do, you know He answered your prayers. What I said to God was, 'Okay, I know about what the *Dominee* said about dogs not having souls, but could you make perhaps a special case? Because Tinker definitely has one, I can absolutely guarantee it.' I couldn't explain all of this to God, because you are not allowed to argue with Him. When God says something, there's no ifs or buts. The last person who tried arguing with Him was Jonah and, all of a sudden, the next day he is swallowed up by a whale. But, frankly, if Tinker couldn't come with me, I'd rather not go to heaven by myself. Not only because Tinker wouldn't be coming, which was a big thing on its own, but also because all the people I'd ever met who said they were definitely going to heaven, because God had saved their soul, weren't very nice to know. For instance, Meneer Prinsloo, Mevrou, the *Dominee*, to mention the main three.

Can you imagine it? You arrive in heaven and there's Mevrou in her white half-jack nightdress wearing wings sticking out the back. She's holding a bunch of Gawie's shit squares in one hand and a *sjambok* in the other. 'So, we meet again, *Voetsek*. Drop your pants, touch your toes, we got Chinese angel's writing for boys' bums up here! Welcome to heaven, man!' If heaven was full of such people I'd be better off just turning into rotten meat. But then I thought of Mattress being there, already waiting for me. Can you see how complicated things get in life?

Anyway, here's some good news. Gawie got his scholarship! And here's the even better news. His name was put on the front page of the *Zoutpansberg Nuus*.

BOYS FARM BOY
WINS IMPORTANT
SCHOLARSHIP!

It was truly big news and even the *Dominee* brought it up in church. He said how it goes to show what a brainy people the Afrikaners are. 'Look, this good Afrikaner boy has no help from a mother or a father or even brothers or sisters and *still* he is a young genius, which shows what high intelligence lurks in the blood of the *volk*.' He said it was a true credit to Superintendent Pietrus Prinsloo from The Boys Farm, who must be like a true father to this boy, Gawie Grobler.

Well, you should have seen Meneer Prinsloo after church! For once in his life his chest was almost sticking out as far as his stomach, and people were coming up and shaking his hand, and he was saying, 'Ag, man, it is nothing, a man does his best to be a good father to them all.' Then he called Gawie over to come and stand next to him so the people could come and also shake his hand. I could see Gawie was very happy because now they couldn't call him a *surrogaat* any more, and he was back to being a *ware Boer*. Sometimes in life things that go wrong can come right again for a person, and we must never give up hope.

That night, being Sunday, was supposed to be the Bible reading, but Meneer Prinsloo said we were going to give it a miss because he wanted to talk about brains for a change.

'Now, some of us have brains and some of us haven't,' he began. 'That's because, unfortunately, God doesn't pack the same amount of brains in every skull he makes.' Then he told us this stupid story called an analogy. How there is this big bucket of brains and heads going past ten to the dozen on a conveyer belt in heaven, and God is there scooping up brains with this special brain shovel made of solid gold with diamonds set in the handle. 'And, you know when you shovelling dirt sometimes, more comes on the spade and sometimes less,' Meneer Prinsloo explained. 'So if the head passing is a more, you got brains, if a less, you stupid.' He pointed to Gawie. 'Now, Gawie Grobler here, he got a shovel that was piled so high there are even some bits dropping off the side of the spade. You see, there is much more there than he's going to need in life. Praise the Lord such a boy is gifted, and when he grows up he can be anything he likes, even the President of the Republic when one day we get it back again. He will also be rich and famous,' the superintendent concluded. I hadn't realised that Meneer Prinsloo knew about Gawie one day owning a gold and diamond mine.

'Stand up, Gawie,' Meneer Prinsloo ordered. 'Let everyone see what a good brain looks like.' Gawie stood up. 'No, on the bench, man. Stand on the bench.' Gawie stepped up on the bench. 'See how he stands tall with his head above everyone else? *Wragtig, daar staan 'n mens met 'n hoer verstand*! Truly, there stands a man with a higher understanding.'

Then Gawie did something *really* brave. 'Can I ask a question, Meneer?' he said.

'*Ja*, of course, ask away,' Meneer Prinsloo said, beaming. 'When a genius speaks we all got to listen, hey.'

'Does this now mean I am no longer a *surrogaat Engelsman*, Meneer?' Gawie asked.

'*Surrogaat Engelsman*? Who said this?' Meneer Prinsloo looked puzzled, then puffed his cheeks out and wagged his forefinger at all of us. 'You show me the person who called you that and he'll have to deal with me personally, you hear? You are a *ware Boer* with a superior Afrikaner brain. Nothing but the best!' He turned to look over all the tables. 'So now we going to show our appreciation.' Then he walked to the wall behind the platform table and carefully removed the Adolf Hitler alias Winston Churchill Rand Easter Show third-place rooster ribbon. With the ribbon draped over both hands and his arms held out in front of him, about two feet apart, he walked over to where Gawie was standing. Even with Gawie standing on the bench Meneer Prinsloo was still taller. He lifted the ribbon over Gawie's head so it draped over both his shoulders, like one of those long scarves Tom Brown wore after he invented rugby. On the ribbon it read, 'Third, Class 20A, Two-year-old Rooster'. But now some of the words were at the back and some on the front. On his right shoulder, it read 'Third Class' and on the left it read 'Rooster'. At long last he was no longer a *surrogaat* but a Third Class Rooster.

You could see some people were starting to giggle. Meneer Prinsloo puffed out his chest and announced, 'Ladies and Gentlemen, as the chief judge and government-appointed father of all the boys at The Boys Farm, those who have some brains and also those who are stupid.' He stopped to take a deep breath. 'It gives me great pleasure to announce Gawie Grobler the Best Brain at the Show!' He turned around, beaming. 'Clap and cheer, everybody!' he shouted. So we clapped and cheered and some of the boys even whistled, and Gawie went very red in the face and stepped off the bench again. I'm telling you, man, in that place Gawie was all of a sudden a hero and a half! His *surrogaat* slate wiped completely clean.

Now, I don't want to be nasty or anything, but kids don't like a person to be too clever around the place. From then on sometimes, like when we were watering the oranges and Gawie would be walking towards a group of us boys filling up our paraffin-tin buckets at the water pump, you'd hear someone say, 'Look, man, here comes that fucking third-class rooster again!' And when he got close they'd all go 'Cock-a-doodle-do!' For a good brain he was having a hard time all over again. Sometimes in life it's best to leave things alone.

———

Now I have to tell you about the wedding. Remember Marie said a small private affair at the church first and then a reception at the Impala Café, where she also said on the big day a person could have all the ice-cream they want.

First, the business of the clean clothes. Doctor Van Heerden phoned Meneer Prinsloo and asked if I could attend the wedding and also get my clean clothes early. Meneer Prinsloo told him yes, but that was not the end of the affair by a long shot.

After supper that night he stood up to give us the usual messages and read out the punishment names. He said, 'In this place are sixty boys, fifty-nine Afrikaners and one *Engelsman*.' He paused to let this point sink in and I felt the old jolt in my stomach because I knew I was about to be up to my eyebrows in the deep shit, but didn't know what for.

'In this town there is only one doctor and one café, and now the doctor is going to marry the café,' he announced. 'Now, I'm not against this, you hear? If a wife dies then a man can marry again and that's nobody's business because it isn't a divorce. Both parties in this wedding are Afrikaner and well known around the place as you all know. So you'd think they'd show some respect and invite the important people in the *dorp* to come and celebrate the big event, wouldn't you? It's not every day a widower marries a widow, and one is nearly fifty-five years old and the other is forty-five. Understand this is no spring-chicken affair, believe you me! So why are children involved, hey? Tell me that, please?' Meneer Prinsloo's lips curled into a sneer. 'But now the good doctor calls me on the telephone and he says, "Pietrus, we only having a small wedding, just a few close friends at the reception." So I say, "Thank you, Doctor, I am honoured. Mevrou Prinsloo will be very excited." Then he says, "No, no, you get me wrong, man, not *you*, I want to invite Tom Fitzsaxby!" "Say again?" I say, because maybe I didn't wash out my ears this morning. "You want to invite the *Engelsman?*" "*Ja*, he is our personal friend," the doctor says.'

Meneer Prinsloo stopped talking and looked around. 'So now *Master* Tom Fitzsaxby is going tippy-toes and sneaking off behind our back, and making friends with a person who spends Sunday stitching up black *bobbejane* and never comes to church, and also a café owner who sells sweets, cool drinks, cigarettes and pipe tobacco on a Sunday. They invite a snotnose *Engelsman* who is turning soon into a Roman Catholic! *Here*, man, is it strange times? Has the sun fallen into the sea? Has the weather changed outside? What was hot is now freezing cold? Maybe Armageddon is coming soon? Or are we all going mad or something?'

The superintendent, now all red in the face, and arms and hands whirling, paused to catch his breath. 'Also, the doctor asks me, "Can this boy get his clean clothes early in time for the wedding?" I tell him, "Excuse me! I'm not the dirty clothes man around the place, you know. You can telephone Mevrou Van Schalkwyk if you like, but we not savages you know, *Doctor*."'

At this remark Mevrou, seated with her arms crossed over her huge breasts, jerked her head backwards and sniffed, and I knew instantly that the clean-clothes business was far from over.

Meneer Prinsloo went on. 'Now, as you can see, I am not a small man, but in this 450-pound body is not hidden one single jealous bone.' He held up his fist with the small finger extended. 'Not even one the size of my pinkie.' Which, when you think about it, on him would have been quite a big bone. His hands started to whirl around again. 'But what we talking about is respect. Respect for other people who have to represent other people in this *dorp*. Government-appointed fathers and mothers that are churchgoers and have a good standing place in this town. But now you see what happens? Respect is thrown out the window like piss in a chamber-pot! Tom Fitzsaxby is going to this so-called wedding and the people who, out of common respect, *should* be invited have to stay home and feed the chickens and read about it in next week's *Zoutpansberg Nuus*!'

Saturday, the wedding morning came, and still Mevrou hadn't called me. After breakfast I summoned up the courage and went to the sick room and knocked at the door.

'*Ja*, come!' she called.

I turned the big brass door handle we sometimes had to shine and went in. Mevrou was sitting at her table doing her embroidery and she looked up. 'What do you want, *Voetsek?*'

'I came about getting my clothes early, Mevrou. Can I have them please and also have a hot shower with some soap?'

'Oh, so now we going all hoity-toity, hey. It's a good thing all your hair is cut off or next thing you'll be asking me for some Vaseline Hair Tonic and a comb.' She smiled, but it was her crocodile smile. 'Now we the wedding boy?' Her lips turned down. 'I don't think so, we can't go around making special clean-clothes rules just because someone has been going tippy-toes around our backs!'

'I didn't go tippy-toes, Mevrou. I just got asked all of a sudden. It was a big surprise.'

'We can't have you making friendships all over the place without permission, next thing you speaking to *kaffirs* again, like the last time,' she said, referring to Mattress.

'They not *kaffirs*, Mevrou,' I said quietly. I'd never realised that you were supposed to ask permission to make a friend.

'Of course not, I didn't say they were, but we are responsible to the Government. What do you think that high-up inspector who doesn't get his leg of ham this year is going to think when he knows one of our boys is making friends with people who are non-churchgoers, like a certain doctor and a certain police sergeant? Or even people who open their café and sell tobacco on the Lord's Day?'

'That's because people like to go to the café to have a mixed grill after church, *die boere*, that come in from the farms, it's their Sunday treat,' I replied. Marie had told me that Sunday lunch was the big day for mixed grills with the farmers after church, many booking their places and having permanent chairs they always sat in.

'You trying to be cheeky, hey?' Mevrou shouted, unable to think of a reply. I was beginning to do this a bit lately, use stuff called logic, but you had to be careful, like now with Mevrou, people don't like it when you've got them stumped for words.

'No, Mevrou. It's just that if *boeremense* think it's okay to go into the Impala Café after church then they must have asked God, and He would have said it was okay. These are very religious people, you know? The best churchgoers there are, the *Dominee* is always saying that.'

Mevrou sniffed. 'The mixed grill is the devil's temptation. You can smell it when you passing by that café, and next thing Satan is pulling your arm into that place for ice-cream also. But the coffee, you can't drink it! You'd think a good Afrikaner woman could make a decent cup of coffee for a change.'

I thought getting Mevrou onto other subjects would soften her up a bit. I was wrong, she went back to the clean-clothes business.

'Meneer Prinsloo has to say yes to a high-up like Doctor Van Heerden, so that's the reason why you got his permission to go to this old people's wedding, *Voetsek*,' she explained.

'*Dankie*, Mevrou,' I said, thanking her. 'Can I go get —'

'Hey, not so fast, man! You can go but you go dirty, you understand?' She laughed. 'A dirty little *Engelsman*!' She suddenly turned grim-faced. 'You think I'm frightened of that doctor? *Ek is 'n Van Schalkwyk*! We Van Schalkwyks are frightened of no-one! Ha! Let him see he can't go around giving me orders. I'm not in his theatre where he's cutting up black baboons any more, he can stick his scalpel up his bum!'

In my head I said, Ouch! 'Please, Mevrou!' I pleaded. 'Just this once?'

'Since when did I start changing my mind, *Voetsek*? With me, no is no, finish and *klaar*!'

I was too old now to try the trick of crying, anyway with her it didn't work.

'If you've got any pride you won't go, you hear?' she said. 'A person, even an *Engelsman*, can't go turning up at weddings all dirty and smelly in front of all the nice clean guests.' She stared at me for what seemed a long time. Then she sniffed, then sniffed again. 'All of a sudden there is a bad smell around here. You can go now, *Voetsek*.' I turned to go with my eyes downcast and there, under her chair hidden behind her sewing basket, was the half-jack of Tolley's five-star brandy.

I must say I didn't usually take much notice of the state of my shirt and shorts. Dirt is dirt and boys get it. By Saturday we were all the same and you don't take any notice. But, because I knew there was the possibility of a refusal to let me get clean clothes, I'd done my best to stay clean all week. But life doesn't work like that. Only that morning when Tinker and I had been taking a walk by the creek, we had been playing, me throwing a stick for her to fetch, and I slipped in the mud and now I'm also dried mud all over the back of my arse and shirt.

So there was now a big predicament. What to do? The answer, of course, was nothing. Without saying you can't go to the wedding, Mevrou and Meneer Prinsloo had found a way to make it impossible for me to attend. But I couldn't just not arrive, that would be the worst bad manners. I had to let Marie know I couldn't come. The arrangement was that I would meet her at the Impala Café at one o'clock and we'd go on to the doctor's house where she was doing Mevrou Booysens' make-up, whatever that was, something to do with weddings, I suppose. So I decided I would walk the four miles into town immediately to tell her I couldn't come, so they would know well before one o'clock and not have to wait around wondering what had happened to me. I whistled for Tinker and we set off.

It must have been around ten o'clock when we arrived at the café, and Marie was in a real tizz. The little daughter of the woman who was doing the icing on the wedding cake had taken sick suddenly the night before and was vomiting all over the place. So, not only was the cake not ready, but also Doctor Van Heerden had been called. But that wasn't the problem because he fixed up the little girl with some *muti* and put her in hospital. Now the woman was shaken and upset and couldn't do all the squiggly bits and the writing on the cake. Marie had to do this, as well as sew some artificial flowers on her mum's to-be-worn-at-the-wedding hat. And suddenly Tinker and me turn up on the doorstep.

'Tom, you're three hours too early!' she cried, bringing her hands up to cover her mouth. You could see from looking into her eyes that things were not going too well. Then she explained about the cake and the little girl and the hat and she hadn't even ironed her own dress and the toe of one of her high heels she suddenly noticed was scuffed. Boy! When things start going wrong, they go wrong all over the place!

I explained that I couldn't come to the wedding. 'Now, Tom, things are bad enough already,' she exclaimed. 'What's this now?'

'I slipped in the mud and anyway I'm already too dirty, Mevrou wouldn't let me have clean clothes.'

'Why, that stupid bitch! She's a typical Van Schalkwyk! They wouldn't tell you thank you even if you saved their life.'

I was beginning to realise, except for their legs of honeyed ham, Mevrou's family was not generally liked around the district.

Marie turned to me and said, 'Off!'

'Off?' I asked. 'Must I go now?'

'Your clothes, man! Hurry up, Tom, I haven't got all day.'

I hesitated. You don't just take off your clothes in a girl's mother's kitchen when you're nearly twelve years old. 'My clothes? Take them off?' I asked stupidly.

'Ag, man, I am a certified nurse, I have to wash grown men every day when they got nothing on, not even pyjama pants. Now hurry up, I got lots to do and we only got four hours before the wedding.'

I removed my shirt and shorts and cupped my hand over my cock. Marie had disappeared into a bedroom. I forgot to say the house was directly behind the café. She reappeared moments later with a pink kind of woolly-looking dressing-gown. 'Here, wear this, Tom,' she instructed.

Talk about all business suddenly. Before you knew it there's hot water and bubbles in the sink, and my shirt and shorts are in them and out again, and rinsed and hanging on the washing line in the bright mid-morning sunshine. Even though she was so busy she couldn't scratch her bum, I think she was quite pleased with what happened, she came in from the washing line with this sort of half smile on her pretty face.

'We'll show that bitch!' she sniffed.

'What colour are your shoes?' I asked.

'Black.'

'Got any black polish?'

'*Ja*, I think so, look under the sink.'

I found some that was a bit dried up and cracked in the tin. I managed to soften it, and after half an hour or so working on her black high-heel shoes, if I say so myself, no scuff to be seen, even if you looked through a microscope. They were also so bright they would have left Meneer Prinsloo's shiny brown boots in the dust.

The bush *veld* sun dried my clothes in no time flat, and then I had to take a shower and wash my hair and between my toes. By the time I came out of the bathroom there were my clothes already ironed. That Marie was a woman and a half, I can tell you. The cake was iced with all the squiggly bits and the writing in pale blue icing, and little statues of a man in a black suit and a woman in a long white dress all made out of icing sugar standing at the top of the cake. But Marie didn't make them, they came from Patel & Sons who'd sent for it from Pietersburg. Even the artificial flowers were sewn onto a white straw hat so it looked brand-new. Marie's dress was ironed, and it was now one o'clock on the dot. I was surprised to see Sergeant Van Niekerk arrive in the police van and blow the horn.

'Tell him five minutes, Tom!' Marie shouted from her bedroom.

The police van was all shiny bright, and had white ribbon tied on the mascot on the front and stretched back and tied to the mirrors on either side of the van, but it wasn't the bridal carriage, Marie said, because they were both married before and it wasn't a white wedding, the Doctor and Mevrou Booysens were arriving together in his car. Mevrou Booysens had gone to his house just before I arrived and she was going to get her hat when Marie came to do her make-up.

'Marie will be here in five minutes,' I said to Sergeant Van Niekerk.

'Typical woman, hey, Tom, always late,' he replied with a grin.

This didn't seem fair knowing what Marie had just been through. 'There's been disasters everywhere,' I said in Marie's defence.

'Ja, man, put a woman and a wedding together and you got a disaster on your hands every time!' he laughed.

I was beginning to understand that men seldom see life through a woman's eyes.

Marie came out to the van and, I must say, she looked really pretty with a pink dress and a little white straw hat and white gloves also. She wore lipstick that was very red and she looked like a film star. Sergeant Van Niekerk did a whistle of admiration and Marie smiled. So it was Marie and the sergeant in the front, and me and Tinker in the back of the van that had been scrubbed and cleaned so Tinker didn't even smell the Alsatians, and she just sat quietly on my lap panting happily.

Make-up, it turned out, was putting lipstick and powder on Mevrou Booysens' face with something called 'rouge for a bit of colour'. The hat looked nice and you'd never have known it was an old one.

To my surprise, Doctor Van Heerden said, 'You and Tinker are in the dicky-seat, Tom.' So there I was with Tinker at my side arriving at the church with the bride and groom, and Marie and Sergeant Van Niekerk following in the police van. Oh, I forgot to say, the '39 Chevvie also had this white ribbon on the front and a big bow and a kewpie doll tied on the radiator. Marie said she'd also got it from Pietersburg and it was 'a nice finishing touch'.

Remember I said it was only going to be a small affair. That's not what the Boerevolk thought. All the farm folk in the district and lots and lots of the people in the town had come to the wedding service, because you don't have to be invited to go into God's house any time you like. So, instead of a handful of invited guests, the church is full and there's people standing up at the back. Because, you see, Doctor Van Heerden is their doctor and they love him a whole lot because he brought some of their children into the world, and took out their tonsils, and so on and so forth. Afrikaners don't forget a good deed in a hurry.

The *Dominee* doesn't say, 'How come someone who never comes to church because he's stitching up *kaffirs*' stomachs and other wounds, gets such a big crowd?' He says, 'As a man of God I take my hat off to our dear brother in Christ, Alex van Heerden who even if he is a man of science, it is God's hand that guides the knife and helps to stitch up the wounds.' He indicated the audience with a sweep of his hand. 'All these good Afrikaner *volk* have come to pay tribute to him and his lovely wife-to-be.' After this he didn't do a whole well-rounded sermon, nor did he bring up the subject of that other man of science, Charles Darwin. This is because he had to do a thing called 'nuptials', which is stuff they ask the bride and groom at weddings.

And so the wedding begins. Meneer Van Niekerk is the best man and Sergeant Van Niekerk, it turns out, is the bride's father pretending, because Mevrou Booysens' father is long dead. The joke is that the sergeant is ten years younger than the bride! Marie is the bridesmaid and I'm sitting in the front row of the church with all the high-ups. Talk about posh! I was scared to even sniff, but I was quite good with the singing because it was two hymns we did at school.

So now you thinking, that's over? Now for the quiet reception. *Magtig!* Those *volk* who'd come from far and near hadn't come empty-handed. They'd come to a wedding, invited or not, and brought food and meat and drink, and because *Boerevolk* are very musical they've also brought fiddles and banjos and concertinas and even two musical saws and a harp. They've come to dance and *tiekiedraai* because there's no better time to do this than at a wedding. Everybody was turning to each other and saying, 'No point in going home to the farm and back again in the morning for church when a good party can be had for the making.'

To cut a long story short, Sergeant Van Niekerk closes off the street in front of the Impala Café at both ends for about a hundred yards and the biggest party at a wedding you've ever seen breaks out. Inside the café are the invited guests and outside the uninvited, but soon it's all mixed up and a good time is had by all until deep into the night. It was a full moon and so bright outside you could read a newspaper without glasses. A better night for an outside party would be impossible to get.

At five o'clock in the afternoon, when I was supposed to walk back to The Boys Farm, Marie got the good doctor to call Meneer Prinsloo to ask if I could stay out for the night, that I'd be staying with Marie in Mevrou Booysens' house. When he came back from the phone he was laughing and told Marie what happened, and then later she told me.

Meneer Prinsloo picks up the phone and Doctor Van Heerden says, 'Can you hear all the noise going on, Pietrus?'

'*Ja*, what's going on, man?'

'Well, the supposed-to-be-quiet little wedding turned into a big crowd all of a sudden, so why don't you and your wife come and join us? The whole district is here, man.'

'Ag, I've got better things to do with my time,' the superintendent answered petulantly.

'Sure, whatever you say, Pietrus. By the way, young Tom Fitzsaxby will be staying with us overnight. You don't mind, do you?'

'Listen here, man, I am the Government-appointed parent and —'

Doctor Van Heerden cut him short. 'He's got several nasty bumps on his ventriculi cardio-cular appendage and I'd like to keep him under observation overnight.'

'What's a ventriculi cardio-cular appendage?' I asked Marie.

'It's just made-up nonsense words, but you better not get it,' she warned. 'Because it can be serious and has definitely well-known complications. Medical science is very worried and completely puzzled by these mysterious bumps!' She grinned. 'But not as puzzled as Meneer Prinsloo!' We laughed and laughed our heads off.

Only one bad thing happened at the wedding. Well, not *really* bad, I suppose, because it couldn't happen to a better person. About ten o'clock on the wedding night, when the party in the street was still going full swing, I couldn't stay awake any longer. So I went over to Mevrou Booysens' house to find a place I could lie down. Earlier Marie had said I could take the spare bed in the sewing room where she was making the goosefeather quilt. It was right next door to the bathroom.

So I said good night to Tinker and showed her where to sleep on a sack outside the kitchen door and then walked through the darkened house. I had to pass the open parlour door. It was full moon and light was coming through a window into the parlour and there on the settee was Marie and Sergeant Van Niekerk, and they were holding each other and kissing, and they didn't have anything on! Marie drew back slightly from Sergeant Van Niekerk and sighed with closed eyes. I felt this sudden stab in my heart, like a dagger had gone right through it. I'd never seen a lady with nothing on, and you could see all of Marie's top half, and her golden hair streaming down her back, and I knew what I saw was beautiful, but I didn't know why. So I cried a bit in that spare bed, but very softly. I don't think they would have heard because there was some sort of grunting sounds going on. Then I must have fallen asleep. It just goes to show in life you can love somebody with every bone in your body, but you can't always have them only for yourself.

I went straight to church from Mevrou Booysens' the next morning and then went in the crocodile back to The Boys Farm. It was Mevrou's day off when she carried her paper bag with the empty you-know-what's-in-it to visit her family so I didn't see her until my name was called out after supper on Monday.

I don't know if the news of my clean clothes at the wedding had reached her. If it had this would be the reason for sure for the *sjambokking* I expected to receive. 'A person can't go turning dirty clothes into clean ones without permission, you hear! This is government-supplied property, only the high-up inspector in Pretoria and me also can decide when they allowed to be washed. Next thing they all worn out from too much washing, and even a *kaffir* is ashamed to wear them! You getting six of the best and no questions asked. Take down your pants, touch your toes.' I was the only one on punishment rollcall that night, which was also pretty unusual. I knocked on the sick room door.

'Come!' she shouted.

I entered the sick room to be confronted by Mevrou with her arms folded across her big boobs. On the table beside her, neatly folded, was a khaki shirt and shorts. 'You clean clothes are here,' she said, pointing at them. 'So now it's bumps? What is this bumps business, *Voetsek?*'

'Ventriculi cardio-cular appendage, Mevrou,' I answered.

'So where are they, show me where are these bumps?'

It wasn't a question I'd prepared myself for. Anywhere I indicated on my body she'd want to see the clear evidence. I panicked. 'On the eyes, Mevrou.'

'On the eyes? You got bumps on your eyes? I never heard of such a thing before,' Mevrou said suspiciously.

'*Ja*, medical science is very worried and completely puzzled by these mysterious bumps!' I said, trying to sound convincing.

'Let me take a look.'

'Too late,' I said. 'They all gone. This morning when I woke up, not a bump to be seen. Then later Doctor Van Heerden gave the all clear.'

Mevrou still looked suspicious. 'I'm a medical person myself, you hear? I never heard of bumps on a person's eyes,' she repeated.

'*Ja*, Mevrou, little bumps, all red and itchy, like mosquito bites on your eyes,' I lied.

'Itchy eyes, now you making sense, itchy eyes, I know.'

'Like there's chillies been rubbed in.'

'Chillies? When a person has chillies rubbed in their eyes they can't see.'

I had to decide quickly whether I could see or not and decided being blinded by chillies meant I couldn't.

'No, seeing was out of the question.'

'If you couldn't see, how did you know they were red and looked like mosquito bites, hey?'

'I saw them just before I couldn't see. There was this mirror,' I added hastily, 'in the bathroom. I was looking, and these red mosquito bites are popping onto my eyeballs and all of a sudden it went all dark and then the itch like from chillies came.'

'*Jy praat kak, Voetsek!* You speak shit, *Voetsek!*'

I was getting in deeper than I cared to be. 'No, honest, Mevrou, the itching came after I went blind, that's how Doctor Van Heerden knew it was ventriculi cardio-cular appendage. That's the certain sign, first, red mosquito bites that are these little bumps all over your eyes on the white part, then everything goes black and then the itching starts. That's another one of the mysterious medical mysteries. You can ask him if you want.'

'But then you woke up this morning and you can see again?'

'*Ja*, perfectly, as if nothing had happened. A miracle.'

'Then another miracle happened, hey?'

I looked at her, not quite knowing what she meant. 'No, just that I could see good as new.'

'And what you saw was that your dirty clothes that left here to go to the wedding are now all of a sudden clean?' she pointed to my shirt. 'Turn around.' I turned so that my back faced her. 'There was mud on the back of your shirt and on your backside too, now it's gone. Turn back.' I turned to face her again and she looked at me accusingly. 'So be so kind as to tell me how the miracle of the disappearing mud came about?' She pointed at my chest. 'This shirt is clean and so are the shorts.'

I had done all that tap-dancing for nothing. We were back on the business of the forbidden clean clothes. Lying to Mevrou was compulsory, but with her one-track mind you had to be very careful because she'd always come back to the first point.

'Germs!' I said. 'You get them from mud. They had to wash my clothes because they might be holding germs that gave me ventriculi cardio-cular appendage.'

'So now we got germs in the eyes that make red lumps like mosquito bites that itch like chillies been rubbed in but only after when a person goes blind, and all of this is caused from mud?'

I must admit, even to me, it didn't sound very plausible. The germs theory was the straw that broke the camel's back. The idea of linking my dirty clothes to a medically mysterious disease wasn't going to work. Mevrou wasn't going to buy the mud theory.

'I'm a farmer's daughter, you hear? Also a highly trained three-certificate nurse, I could even have been a sister, and I'm telling you straight, *Voetsek*, the only thing that comes from mud is wet dirt!' She jabbed a fat finger at me. 'Take off that germ-free shirt and shorts!' she barked.

I removed my Marie-washed shirt and stepped out of my shorts, and stood naked in front of this large, terrifying woman.

'Ventricle means a sort of hole or cavity in an organ and cardio means your heart.' She pointed at my little dangling dick and sniffed in obvious disdain. 'Appendage means something sticking out, but what's there isn't big enough to be one,' she said. 'It all has nothing to do with bumps on your eyes, man! You think I was born only yesterday? I wasn't a theatre nurse for five years for nothing, you know. I've seen plenty of eyes in my time but never even one with bumps on it. You going to have to wake up very early in the morning before you can fool a three-certificater like me!' She paused, then asked, 'Who washed you dirty clothes? Was it that one-certificate nurse that you went tippy-toes around our backs to befriend without getting first our permission?'

There wasn't any point in lying any longer. '*Ja*, Mevrou.'

'Well, you can tell this so-called "mixed grill" nurse, who works in a mother's café and knows from nothing things that are medical, that

if Meneer Prinsloo and Mevrou Van Schalkwyk decide to send a dirty
person to a wedding we don't expect a clean one to come back. We
won't be insulted like we just pieces of dirt!'

'It was my fault, Mevrou, I didn't tell her I had strict instructions to
stay dirty.'

'*Ja*, I can see you also to blame and that's why now you getting
six of the best, *Voetsek*. Bend! Now touch your toes.' *Whack! Whack!
Whack! Whack! Whack! Whack!* 'And now two *bansella* to remove the
bumps on your eyeballs.' *Whack! Whack!* 'And put some bumps on your
arse.'

The months passed quickly, and it was soon coming up to the time to
leave for the Bishop's College. The closer the time came the more I
worried about Tinker. I simply couldn't imagine being without her at my
side, or even how she'd cope without me. Doctor Van Heerden asked if
he could look after her while I was away, saying he missed Helmut a lot
and it would be a great honour to have Tinker around.

'I know she's a one-man dog, Tom, but I could sort of be her uncle.
There's plenty of rats around the place and they take the newly hatched
chicks, she would be doing me a great favour.'

I could see he *really* wanted her and that was one small good thing,
that she didn't have to stay at The Boys Farm. Even though old Mevrou
Pienaar loved her a lot, but with Mevrou and Meneer Prinsloo you could
never tell what might happen.

Tinker and me, we'd have these long talks when she'd sit on my
lap under a tree by the creek or down at the library rock, and I'd try to
explain to her what was going to happen and assure her that she'd be
all right. I'd tell her about how I had to get an education and this was
an opportunity not to be missed, and that I'd come down every school
holiday to be with her. She'd prick up her sharp little ears and then
sometimes lick my face, but if you looked into her eyes you could see

that she was just as concerned as I was. Leaving somebody you love that much is a very hard thing for anyone to do.

You begin to realise that in life nothing stays still, just when you not looking, everything changes and not always for the better. Not that I can say this next change that happened was bad because it wasn't. But I'd be lying if I didn't say that I had in my mind decided when I grew up to marry Marie. I knew she was older than I was, but eleven years was the same as Mevrou Booysens and the doctor. So, if they could do it, why not us? But, of course, all my hopes were smashed to smithereens by the scene that had taken place in the moonlit parlour. I couldn't get the picture of the soft light on her shoulder and the gold of her hair, like a halo, out of my mind. Marie had drawn back from Sergeant Van Niekerk at the same moment I passed the parlour door and the moonlight also showed the curve of her breasts. I don't know what it was, but I knew it was very beautiful. Also, that something inside me had changed forever.

Now that Mevrou Booysens wasn't herself any more and had turned into Mevrou Van Heerden, the Impala Café was up for sale. To everybody's surprise, it was bought by Mr Patel, of Patel & Sons, for one of his sons who was coming back from Bombay with a brand-new wife. They were going to change the place into an Indian restaurant. Mr Patel said they were going to call it the Impala Curry House. 'We are keeping old tradition and having new one as well, mixed grills we are having any time you want, but also very, very jolly good curry,' he'd announced. This didn't go down too well with the town and here are some of the things the *volk* were saying all over the place. 'What does an Indian know about mixed grills? Next thing you know you getting curry chops, man! Nobody is going to eat that Charra food. It is a well-known fact that Indians are always looking for ways to cheat a person. Take, for instance, old meat that's not so fresh, put a bit of curry on it and you can't taste that it should be given to the dogs. Curry is little pieces of meat that burns your mouth so much that drinking water doesn't help. That's step one. Step two is that you have to drink lots of beer and eat lots of rice so they make a bigger profit all-round. Can't you see how clever that is? But if Patel's son thinks he can trick a *boer* then he and his new wife, who doesn't even speak Afrikaans, have another think coming, we not stupid, you hear? The *boere* won't go to eat there after church on Sunday because it's a heathen place, and it's the Lord's day also, so they go back to their farms drunk from all the beer and with their mouths still burning all over the place.'

Those were the things people were saying. I must say I was a bit surprised at Mr Patel doing a stupid thing like this, even if it was for his son. One thing was certain, he was not a stupid man. If cheating was his main business, as everyone said, answer me this. He was not the only shop in town that white people and blacks could go into to buy stuff. The other shops were all owned by good Afrikaners, so why was Mr Patel the only person in Duiwelskrans that drove a brand-new Buick straight eight? People don't go twice into a shop where cheating is going on unless they are the stupid ones.

When I asked Sergeant Van Niekerk about this, he said, 'Ag, Tom, it's simple, Patel gives credit. You can put it in the book and pay at the end of the month.'

'Don't the other shops give credit?'

'*Ja*, but only to white people.'

'Why don't they also give credit to *kaffirs*?'

'Because they think *kaffirs* won't pay at the end of the month,' he laughed. 'That's where Patel's clever. Black people *always* pay. It's the whites who sometimes don't. I'm always going around and knocking on white doors and saying, "Pay up, or else".'

See what I mean? But you learn in life that the same people can be very clever in some things and very stupid in others. Clever giving credit to *kaffirs* and stupid opening up an Indian restaurant in a town like Duiwelskrans.

So Marie said, 'I'm going to cook you your last mixed grill before the Impala closes and becomes an Indian restaurant that my mum told them isn't going to work, but they don't want to listen, what can you do, hey? At least we had the decency to warn them that this isn't a curry-type town.'

I don't know where that 'your *last* mixed grill' came from, because Gawie had had a mixed grill the time I burned my hand, but I hadn't had one yet. But I didn't say anything. A mixed grill doesn't come along every day and having the last one that was really only the first, but wasn't ever going to be cooked again was a big honour, I can tell you. Now, I suppose you're wondering how come I'm suddenly eating the last mixed grill at the Impala Café after church on Sunday and not eating stale bread sandwiches at The Boys Farm. How did I get permission to do this?

Well, you've got to give credit where credit is due. It was Meneer Prinsloo's one and only brilliant idea called Government Permission Monthly Outing. He got the *Dominee* to say it in church. Anyone who wanted to invite a boy to lunch on Sunday could, and the boy only had to be back at The Boys Farm by five o'clock in the afternoon. A boy was allowed to go only once a month because, remember, we had to work in the vegetable gardens and water the fruit trees on a Sunday. So that was why I could go to the Impala Café and have the last mixed grill in history.

Let me tell you, it turned out to be a mixed grill and a half! Here's what was in it: sausages two, piece of liver, bacon rashers two, chops two, piece of steak (not small), fried egg one, chips (lots), tomato sauce. You could have cold slaw also, but I didn't. You could get cold slaw at The Boys Farm when the cabbages were in the vegetable garden and they had too many, so why eat it now. I couldn't finish it all because I had to leave room for a one-legged bowl of ice-cream. Tinker got her football stomach with what was left over, and we could hardly walk back to The Boys Farm we were so full. At one stage on the way home, Tinker did this little vomit and it was tomato sauce. I don't think dogs like it.

After the mixed grill Marie said, 'Come into the house, Tom, I want to talk to you.' She'd gone and brushed her hair and put on the same bright-red lipstick she'd had on at the wedding, and she'd taken off her apron. So we went into the parlour and sat on the same settee where you-know-what happened in the moonlight. 'Tom, you know I love you, so I want you to be the first to hear the good news, after my mum, of course.'

I tried to smile because I was pretty sure I knew what the good news was going to be. But my mouth, all of a sudden, went sort of all squiffy. 'Is it Sergeant Van Niekerk?' I stammered.

'Clever boy!' she exclaimed, clapping her hands. '*Magtig*, there are no flies on you, Tom Fitzsaxby. How did you guess?' Her eyes were shining and I could see she was very happy.

'I'm good at guessing things,' I said.

'We're going to be married before you go to that posh boarding school in Johannesburg, just so you can be there. You're going to be best boy, you hear? It's something you can have in weddings.'

'I don't think I'm allowed, Marie,' I said, thinking it best to warn her right off. 'Mevrou is very against weddings. I have to get permission from Meneer Prinsloo, otherwise it's called "tippy-toeing around people's backs". You also have to wear your dirty clothes unless you've got the high-up inspector from Pretoria's permission because Mevrou won't give it.' It all came out at one time, like speaking vomit. This was because I didn't know what to say and I was angry that she was going to marry before I could grow up and be the lucky husband. Not that I didn't think Sergeant Van Niekerk wasn't a very good choice. He was the best there was, you couldn't get better. It was just that everything a person loved was now changing.

'Don't you worry about the clothes, you hear? And guess what? You're *also* getting a wedding present from Doctor Van Heerden and my mum.'

'But I'm not getting married!' I said, surprised. 'You the one who gets the presents.'

'*Ja*, that's true, but you're like our little *boetie* now. You'll see, you'll like it.' Then she took me in her arms and gave me a long kiss on the mouth. 'Oh, I do love you, Tom,' she said. She smelled of roses, and the lipstick had this sort of greasy taste. She drew back and looked directly into my eyes, her hands gripping my shoulders. 'There's also a big, big secret, but you've got to swear on a stack of Bibles you won't tell, hey?'

I didn't think it would be polite to remind Marie that I wasn't the one to swear on stacks of Bibles and then go and tell people all over the place. 'I promise on my word of honour,' I said solemnly.

'Tom, the sergeant and me, we also going to have a little baby!'

CHAPTER ELEVEN

The Love That Can't Wait for Weddings

———————

NOW KEEPING A SECRET is one thing, but growing fat in the front is quite another. Either Marie was eating too much and putting on weight in only one place or the secret was well and truly out for all to see. People were giggling behind their hands and saying, 'Shotgun wedding, hey!' I wasn't quite sure why it's called that, and I couldn't find out because my main-asking people were all involved. I mean, I knew it was because Marie had got the baby in her stomach before the wedding, which is, it seemed, a sort of a sin, but one that happens quite a lot in our part of the country. But why shotgun?

Anyway, when the *Dominee* said in church, 'If anyone should know any just cause or reason why this man and this woman should not be joined in holy matrimony, let them declare it now or forever hold their peace,' you could hear the start of a giggle or two around the place. He has to do this for three Sundays, and on the last one when there were a few too many giggles coming from the congregation, the *Dominee* glared down at us and thumped the pulpit with his fist. 'Marriage is a serious business, you hear? Let me tell you something, this kind of marriage has a long tradition among the *volk*. In the olden days when the Great Trek was not long over, people were scattered far and wide and could only come into a *dorp* for *Nagmaal* once a year. That was the time for the young people to take a look and see what was available for a nice wife or a good husband. You think only church and communion takes place at *Nagmaal*, hey? You are quite wrong. These, you must understand, are *regte Boere* with red blood in their bones, and the young men and women have got natural urges!' He chuckled suddenly. 'I can assure you many a young girl must get married long before the next Easter comes around, and some after the offspring have sprung off!' He paused as this got a good laugh from the congregation. 'God is a practical man who likes to take shortcuts. For example, six days only to create everything, and then a nice day of rest. The Lord does not see this example of natural urges as a deep sin, but only as a God-given opportunity to defeat the tyranny of distance. So, I will not tolerate this sniggering in my church when an essential God-sanctioned tradition is taking place. Can you even imagine a better combination than a policeman and a nurse? To keep the law and to heal the sick and then, together, to bring forth the fruit of the womb. Hallelujah!'

That stopped the giggling quick smart.

As for Marie, she said to me, 'Ag, Tom, who cares what people say. I love Jan van Niekerk and I want more than anything in the world to have this baby, and anyway he asked me to marry him long before I didn't have my time of month.'

'What time is that?' I asked.

Marie laughed. 'I keep forgetting you still little and don't know these things, it's called my menstrual cycle and it happens to a woman.'

If that was supposed to inform me, let me tell you something for nothing, it didn't. But when later I got out from under the bed my Meneer Van Niekerk's *Shorter Oxford English Dictionary* I was in for an even deeper mystery. I looked up *menstrual cycle*. This is what it said: 'The process of ovulation and menstruation in female primates.' So I looked up menstruation and what a shock I got: 'The process of discharging blood from the uterus.' That definitely couldn't be it, if a person was discharging blood all over the place there would have to be something seriously wrong with them, and Marie was a very healthy person. So I looked up ovulation.

Ovulate to produce ova or ovules, to discharge them from the ovary.

So now I've got to find what is an ovary and ovules discharging? Back to the dictionary, but now there's two explanations, the first one is:

Ovary (1) each of the female reproductive organs in which ova are produced.

We are definitely going around in circles now. There's that ova again, but I still don't know what is a reproductive organ. Then I see the second explanation.

Ovary (2) the hollow base of the carpel of a flower containing one or more ovules.

Gottit! Remember how I told you when Marie kissed me on the lips that she smelled of roses? Ovulation was when a woman smelled of roses. So Sergeant Van Niekerk must have asked her to marry him before she started smelling of roses, which just goes to show how much he loved her. He didn't even wait until she smelled nice. Although, I must say, in my opinion, she always smelled nice, sort of clean, with a bit of a nurse's smell of methylated spirits added. Mevrou, for instance, always smelled of brandy and peppermints and sweat.

Later, of course, I learned that ovulation was called 'my monthly' and also 'menstruation' or 'my period' and when you didn't get it you got a baby. That's why Doctor Dyke had to give Tinker her operation to stop it happening otherwise his big dogs would come sniffing around.

Mevrou called me in several days before the big day because, thank God, Meneer Prinsloo hadn't made a big fuss in front of everyone at supper about this particular wedding. While Sergeant Van Niekerk was a high-up, he was about the same height in community standing as Meneer Prinsloo, so it was no insult not to be invited. Besides, the two men obviously didn't like each other, mostly because of Mattress's death and the book fire. So when Doctor Van Heerden called Meneer Prinsloo to ask if I could attend the wedding, Meneer Prinsloo must have said okay right off and didn't bring it up. But, of course, Mevrou knew I was going, so the usual clothes issue came up.

'So now we going to the one-certificater's wedding with the stomach already big out front. *Sis*, man! You'd think a policeman would be more careful when he shoots his revolver,' she cackled. 'But, what can you expect? People like that just don't know how to be God-fearing. Take, for instance, selling a café to an Indian. That is disrespectful to this town and the *Boerevolk*. It's dirty money, you hear? It comes from cheating people.' She sighed, her voice slowing down. 'But always greed comes first in this world. Even someone who is now a doctor's wife can be totally corrupted when it comes to money. A person should be ashamed selling a café to a curry-muncher over other people's heads. There's plenty of good Afrikaners who would like a café like that. People whose husbands are away in Pretoria, and who must try to make an honest living. But because they haven't got cash, but want to pay it off from the profits, this greedy person won't do it. Six good women who could sell also honeyed ham that's the best in the land from such a café. But no, it must go to that dirty crook, Patel, who pays the rich doctor's wife blood money from robbing people blind!'

It was the first time I realised that the wives of the six Van Schalkwyk brothers now in prison in Pretoria for blowing up the power line in Potchefstroom were interested in getting hold of the Impala Café.

'I'm sorry to hear this,' I say to Mevrou. Of course, it was a lie and I wasn't really sorry at all. Can you imagine what it would be like with lots of junior Mevrous running about town? It was bad enough having them up there in the mountains making honeyed ham. At church, since their six husbands went to prison, they'd all come down in the one big lorry, the two old people *ouma* and *oupa* in the front and the rest of the wives in the back, sitting on a mattress, with about fifteen children. They'd all sit in one row in church with their arms folded over their big bosoms and wouldn't sing hymns or anything. The kids don't come into the church but play outside. There are no babies because of the husbands being you-know-where. They're all big fat women with their teeth missing.

When church is over, they only talk to the *Ossewabrandwag* members, and scowl at the rest of the congregation. Now on a Sunday, Mevrou goes back to her farm on the back of the lorry. I can tell you it's a tight fit all round. They've got this little ladder they climb up to get to the mattress in the back, and if you look you can see their bloomers and hairy legs.

About the six Van Schalkwyk wives and their missing teeth. Now I know you thinking missing teeth means only one or two gaps here and there, like a picket fence with some planks missing, but you wrong. In these farming parts, having no teeth is your twenty-first birthday present from the family. All your teeth are taken out, except the big molars at the back. This way you don't get toothache when you on a faraway farm and suddenly there's no dentist. It also saves future costs. The molars stay in the back of your mouth for chewing meat. If you've got to spend money at the dentist it has to be on the molars and not on the pretty teeth. Then one day, when you get rich enough, you can get false teeth to wear to church. But the six Van Schalkwyk wives didn't worry about getting them. What's the use? It's a lot of money for only one day a week, and by the time you get home from church your mouth is sore, the gums rubbed raw as anything. Mevrou had them, but sometimes after a bad night she'd come in half-jack in the morning, and she'd forgotten to put them in, and she's all gums mashing as she shouts at us, with her chin nearly touching the tip of her big nose.

'So now it's wanting clean clothes for the shotgun wedding again, I suppose?' Mevrou asked.

'Ja, Mevrou,' I answered meekly.

She did this long sigh. 'Ja, well, I'm not a spiteful person, you understand? This is not an important wedding, where not to be invited is not an insult to a person like Meneer Prinsloo, so the answer is yes. You can get your clean clothes early. But you got to understand, Voetsek, going to this wedding means you can't have your Government Permission Monthly Outing for three months, because a wedding is like a feast, so one wedding is worth three invitations to Sunday lunch.'

The three months, I realised, included Christmas. I'd been invited to spend Christmas Day with Doctor and Mevrou Van Heerden, Sergeant Van Niekerk and Marie, and Meneer Van Niekerk and his wife. Lunch was to be held at the doctor's house. It was going to be the first Christmas I had ever spent away from the orphanage.

'Does that mean Christmas also?' I asked anxiously.

Mevrou seemed taken by surprise, obviously she hadn't thought about Christmas when she said what she'd just said. Then her lips drew a thin line across her flat face, and her big nose did a sniff as she made up her mind. 'Ja, we can't go making exceptions, you understand? An outing is an outing. The Government can't go giving permissions all over the place. In life, you always got to make choices, Voetsek. So, now you got to choose again. It's the one-certificater's wedding that is nearly going to turn into a christening or Christmas with all your tippy-toes-behind-a-person's-back friends? So make up your mind.'

I'd already been to a wedding, but I'd never been to a Christmas. So, all of a sudden I was faced with a big problem of what to do. I knew I'd rather choose Christmas, because all the same people I loved would be at the wedding and at Christmas lunch. But I knew I wasn't allowed to choose because if I didn't go to Marie and Sergeant Van Niekerk's wedding they might think I was jealous and angry that he'd married her, and she hadn't waited for me to grow up.

I admit, I was jealous and unhappy. It's not every day you love someone enough to want to marry them, but in life you can't show these feelings, and when you can't change something happening, being unhappy is a waste of time. Also, I knew I was too young to give Marie a baby, which is what she said she wanted 'more than anything in this world'. A policeman's baby, if a boy, would be a good thing to have because nobody would bully him at school. But a half-English baby, you couldn't guarantee. And like I said before, you couldn't fault Sergeant Van Niekerk for being a first-class father-to-be in every department.

'I'll take the wedding, Mevrou,' I decided. At least, I thought, I'll be getting my Christmas present early and the food at a wedding would be much the same as on Christmas Day. We got quite nice food anyway at The Boys Farm for Christmas. Not chicken, but other stuff; plum pudding and custard, meat pies, stuff you didn't normally get.

'That's a very stupid decision, *Voetsek*, but if you want to go to a social-disgrace wedding, then I can't stop you. Remember, at a wedding you don't get presents.'

I didn't tell her about my early Christmas present. So what was the difference? At The Boys Farm you didn't get presents either, but saying this would be cheeky, ungrateful and disrespectful of the Government, and would lead to a certain *sjambokking*.

But then, all of a sudden I thought, Wait on! Mevrou is only the clean-clothes person. Meneer Prinsloo is the permissions person. How come she's banning me from going to Christmas lunch? So I said, 'Excuse me, Mevrou, are we talking clean clothes here or am I allowed to go to only one thing, the wedding or Christmas lunch?'

'What are you talking about, *Voetsek*?' she answered, raising her voice. 'Didn't I make myself perfectly clear the first time?'

'*Ja*, Mevrou, but I was just thinking, doesn't Meneer Prinsloo give the going-out permissions, and you give the clean-clothes ones?'

She glared at me threateningly. 'What are you trying to say, *Voetsek*? That I haven't got the authority?'

'No, Mevrou. I was just asking, does Doctor Van Heerden call you now, or is it still Meneer Prinsloo?' I realised it was a direct question and I'd probably get into trouble for asking it, but I was eleven years old and in two-and-a-half months when I went to the Bishop's College I would be free of Mevrou forever. All she could do now was give me six of the best for being cheeky. She'd been doing Chinese writing on my bum since I was six years old and one more *sjambokking* on top of the hundreds I'd received from her wasn't such a big ordeal.

To my surprise, instead of exploding and reaching for her *sjambok*, she seemed to be seriously considering my question. Then she began talking, almost as if she was thinking aloud.

'In a funny way, I owe you something. You know when your books got burned, and the fire got out of control, and the pigs died?'

I knew she didn't expect me to answer, so I remained silent and merely nodded as she continued.

'All Meneer Prinsloo's power around this place comes from that high-up inspector of orphanages in Pretoria. Without the honeyed leg of ham every Christmas he has got no power whatsoever. Now that the pigs are all gone up in smoke, he is a desperate man.' She glanced at me. 'I am a Van Schalkwyk and not stupid, you hear? A donation of a special blue-ribbon honeyed leg of ham sent as usual to the Government inspector in Pretoria this Christmas from your humble servant Superintendent Pietrus Prinsloo is a problem easily solved. But in return, maybe I can also decide a few things around the place, hey?' She paused, looking at me steadily. 'From now on it is yours truly who decides that you can only go to one thing, the shotgun wedding or the tippy-toe Christmas. Do you understand me now, or must I explain it to you all over again, *Voetsek*?'

'*Ja*, I understand, Mevrou,' I said, totally defeated.

'You tell Doctor Van Heerden to call me, the theatre nurse who saw him leave those tweezers in that *kaffir's* stomach. I know it's only a dead *kaffir*, but murder is murder and the law is the law. And he's the one who's taken the Hypocrite oath!' She stabbed her forefinger at my chest. '*Wragtig*! As God is my witness, if he gives me any trouble I will swear it was murder in front of any judge you want to bring to me!'

The last time she told me the story of the *kaffir* who had died, it was not because of the tweezers, but from the stab wounds in his stomach. Mevrou claimed she'd put it all in her report afterwards. Now she was claiming it was murder, and she was willing to swear it in front of a judge. It's funny how people can take something that means one thing at one time, and then turn it around to mean something else that suits them better at another. Mattress once told me that people's eyes see different truths at different times. 'It is like looking at the big rock, *Kleinbaas*. In the morning it is a wet rock from the dew, at midday the rock is bright and shimmers in the hot sun, in the late afternoon it is in dark shadow, and at night it has disappeared and you can swear there is no rock there at all. People always decide what time of the day or night it is when they tell the truth.' Not only was I totally defeated, but also, if Doctor Van Heerden tried to get permission for me to go to Christmas lunch at his house, I might be responsible for getting him charged with a murder. But, of course I knew this couldn't happen, and that Mevrou was bullshitting. But a woman like her – if she wanted revenge she could still cause a lot of trouble.

Now we've already done one wedding, don't worry, I'm not going to do another one. It all went off without any hitches, even if Marie's stomach in her white wedding gown was by now sticking out all over the place. It was late October and the baby was due at the end of January. You could see it kicking already and Marie had let me put my hand on her stomach, and I think it must be a boy because already it's got a truly powerful kick. Sergeant Van Niekerk said, 'Tom, with a kick like that maybe we got us another Benny Osler here, hey?' In case you don't know, Benny Osler was a famous Springbok rugby fly-half.

No more about Marie's wedding, except you'll never guess what my early Christmas present was. We'll start with boots. Marie and Sergeant Van Niekerk gave me a pair of brown boots. I don't know how she found the time, with babies kicking and cafés being sold and wedding arrangements having to be done and goosefeather quilts being sewn, but Marie knitted me three pairs of grey socks to go with the boots. How they got my foot size was dead simple, next to the kitchen steps was some damp sand, and I must have left some footprints behind. Sergeant Van Niekerk, who had also once done a detective course in Pietersburg, knew just how to measure my footprint and take the information to the bootmaker. Next thing you know, there's a perfect-fitting pair of boots that never once gave a single blister.

A boy's first pair of boots is very important. At The Boys Farm, you got them from the Government along with two pairs of socks when you were thirteen, and what that meant is that now you beginning to be a grown-up man. The boys who had them would spit-and-polish them until they shone better than Meneer Prinsloo's. Then they'd tie the laces together and wear the boots around their necks and resting on their chests until they got to church when they'd put them on and then after church put the boots around their necks again, so the Government didn't have to worry about the boots ever wearing out. But sometimes if the boy's feet would grow and the boots would get too small, the boys could apply for a new pair. When you got these from the Government you had to give the old pair, that sometimes had hardly been used and still had hundreds of miles of walking left in them, back to Meneer Prinsloo. He sold them in town and said he used the money for something called general expenses, which everyone said was just another name for his own wallet.

Then the next part of my early Christmas present was five white shirts made from some of Marie and Mevrou Booysens' single bed sheets, because now nobody could use the single sheets because both women were married and now slept in double beds with their husbands. Which is another thing I didn't know about being married, you are forced to sleep in one bed. Marie made the shirts on her Singer sewing machine. Boy, was she ever a sewer and a half! All the shirts were a bit big, but it didn't matter because they allowed me to grow into them, which was beginning to happen at long last, and you could always turn up the sleeves at the cuffs.

To top everything off, from Doctor Van Heerden came three pairs of grey flannel shorts and a navy blue blazer and a navy tie with silver stripes. On the blazer pocket was the school badge, which is a bishop's hat and a crossed mitre, and under these the words in Latin, *In deo speramus*. Doctor Van Heerden said it means 'In God we trust'. Miss Phillips had bought the blazer and tie and the grey flannel material, and sent them up from Johannesburg to Doctor Van Heerden who paid her for them. Marie also made the shorts. A leather belt and six white handkerchiefs were from Meneer Van Niekerk and his wife, Anna, who also knitted me two pairs of grey socks and a navy blue jersey with the school colours on the 'V' around the neck.

Being the best boy, my job is to stand next to the best man in church, Meneer Van Niekerk. Instead of being in my clean khaki shorts and shirt and bare feet, I am about the best-dressed person in the congregation, wearing boots and a blazer and tie and, of course, one of Marie's lovely new white shirts with the cuffs of the sleeves rolled up a bit. Talk about posh all of a sudden.

We're talking a lot about me and I apologise but it's just that I want you to get the picture of all this kindness that's coming my way. But Gawie is also in the same boat, with school uniforms and stuff he needs.

So the *Dominee* announces there's going to be a *braaivleis*, a fair and a *tiekiedraai* put on by the church, that's going to go all day Saturday and it's all in aid of the new Afrikaner genius, Gawie Grobler.

The *Dominee* is in a good mood for once, and the beetle isn't munching angry-beard grass. At the end of his usual well-rounded sermon, that was about Jesus in the Garden of Gethsemane when Judas Iscariot turns out to be a traitor and the cock crows thrice, he says, 'Now we just had a sermon about loyalty and betrayal. To be loyal is to support your own kind and this is what I am asking you to do now. We need to help a boy, who has no mother and no father, but is still a genius. We are not a big community, but we are a generous one. So bring your canned fruits and vegetables and your jams and your sewing and embroidery, and sell it for charity next Saturday. We'll have a *braai* and a *tiekiedraai* and we must have enough money at the end to pay for Gawie Grobler's uniforms and a suitcase and some pocket money. Also, he needs socks, grey, if we have some knitters in the congregation. Now listen, this is God's work also, a boy like this from a small town who has brains can change the world of Afrikanerdom. Who knows, maybe he is also a Moses who can lead us out of the wilderness? So we calling Saturday "Meet the Genius". I don't want to hear you couldn't come, you hear? Because, if we don't all support the next generation, then it is the same as the cock crowing thrice in the Garden of Gethsemane. It's finish and *klaar* for all of us. Our salvation and true revenge must come from the next generation.' He paused and looked around. 'And God in His infinite mercy may have chosen an orphan to bring us justice.'

So the next Saturday the big event took place in the church grounds. As far as the business of Gawie the Afrikaner Boy Genius was concerned, two chairs were placed on a special platform, one for him and the other for Meneer Prinsloo, who was there as the official Government Father. And behind the chairs is a banner that says:

Meet the Genius 6d!

It's sixpence to shake their hand and congratulate them. A member of the congregation was standing there to take the money and encourage the crowd. He has an old-fashioned megaphone that helps his voice to be louder. 'Roll up! Roll up! Meet the genius! Only sixpence a head, the body is free!' he yells. People like this joke and soon there's a long queue waiting to shake hands and say a kind word.

There's a tin bucket on the platform that you throw your sixpence into and it's going 'ting, ting, ting' every minute or so and they're raking in the money. It doesn't take the Third Class Rooster long to get into the swing of things, and the announcer is saying, 'Ask the genius anything you like, he'll know the answer. If he doesn't, then it's a stupid question below his dignity to answer.' Most people are too shy to ask, but some say things like, 'What's 124 plus 209 minus sixty-three divided by nine?' And Gawie would think for a moment and say, '*Dertig, Meneer, baie dankie.*' Him giving them the answer straight off and then saying, 'Thirty, thank you, Sir,' really impresses them. You'd hear people moving away from the platform saying things like, 'Not only a genius, but also respectful. He will make a very good president.'

Then Doctor Dyke comes to the edge of the platform with this half smile on his face. 'So tell me, genius, what is the theory of Pythagoras?' he asks. You could see Gawie was caught out, but luckily it's something I know. I'm standing near so I walk quickly to the back of Gawie's chair and whisper, 'Say after me, Gawie, the square of the hypotenuse.' So Gawie says, 'The square of the hippopotamus.' I'm trying not to laugh, '. . . of a right-angled triangle,' Gawie gets this part right '. . . is equal to the sum of the squares on the other two sides.' Gawie completes this correctly, shouting it out loud to Doctor Dyke, who is standing far enough away for him not to hear me whispering behind the chair.

'Not only correct, but also funny!' Doctor Dyke laughs. 'Hippopotamus, eh? Very amusing. The boy has wit as well as brains. An Afrikaner genius is worth more than a sixpence, here, take two shillings, son.' Big ting.

In the chair next to Gawie, Meneer Prinsloo clears his throat and sticks his nose in the air. He still thinks it was Doctor Dyke who cut off Piet Retief's tail feathers so his own miserable Rhode Island Red rooster could win Best Rooster at the Pietersburg Agricultural Show. Then when Doctor Dyke had gone Meneer Prinsloo said, 'He's just showing off, throwing two bob in the bucket.'

Anyway, the whole event is a big success and they going to do it every year for Gawie, so the town can take care of its own genius so he doesn't have to ask for handouts. After supper that night Meneer Prinsloo is smiling and still puffed up with pride from the whole day because more than a hundred people came up to him and congratulated him for producing a Government-owned genius. Sitting in the big leather chair on the 'Meet the Genius' platform he had smiled modestly and said to these people, 'On The Boys Farm they are all like my own sons, you hear?' Then he'd turn to face Gawie. 'But right from the beginning I knew *this* boy was a *big* brain. It wasn't always easy because we on a strict budget and I don't believe in mollycoddling, you understand? But it was worth the sacrifice to bring him up with a few extra learning privileges. After all, a genius is a genius and God only makes a very few.' He'd shrug his shoulders, 'What can I say? We can't all be geniuses. I only did my job to encourage him like any decent human being would do that is also a good Afrikaner.'

So now Gawie Grobler has gone from *surrogaat* to Third Class Rooster to Afrikaner Genius, and I think he was very happy for a change. It's not every day you get called a genius. After we'd come out of the dining room he came up to me. 'I still can't be your friend any more, *Voetsek*,' he said, 'but now, what I'm going to do is let you have shit squares again. I'll put them under your mattress, you hear?' Then he asked, 'That word you said that sounded like hippopotamus, what was it again?'

'Hypotenuse,' I replied. 'It's the side opposite the right angle in a triangle.'

'*Ja*, that's right, I just forgot for a moment. Hypotenoose.'

'Hypote*nuse*, it's like *news*, not *noose*.' He didn't say anything and just walked away. I don't suppose geniuses like to have ordinary people correcting them.

I was really pleased at getting the shit squares again. Keeping up with the war news was very hard work because there were six lavatories, and I'd have to secretly visit them all and go through the wad of shit squares on the wire hooks. If there was any war news on them I'd rip that square off the hook and so on. But you never got the full story in one go. Mostly you were left in mid-air with a headline that said, 'Russians liberate —', and then 'Jews burned in ga—', then 'Dresden bombed —'. How did these Jews get themselves burned? Was the 'ga' a garage, garden, gap, gang, gallery, gaol, garret? You'd look and look through the shit squares, and sometimes like a miracle you'd find the connecting piece. Mostly someone had already wiped their arse on where the Jews were burned, and it was gone forever, and you never knew what happened to them. Of course, months later you learned that the 'ga' stood for terrible inhuman things, gas ovens.

But you could tell, even from these only-bits-of-shit-square-news, that Adolf Hitler was on his last legs. There was also other ways that things were going badly for the Germans because suddenly there were no more *Ossewabrandwag* meetings, and all the guys in uniforms had disappeared from the face of the earth. The *Dominee* had also stopped telling us that underneath everything Hitler was secretly a God-fearing man. But he did say when Italy surrendered in 1943, 'What can you expect from Roman Catholics? They cowards that Hitler should have known would let him down in a crisis.'

Then one night at supper, Meneer Prinsloo said, 'If anyone asks about the *Ossewabrandwag* you say nothing, you hear? If any boy says they know someone who is one, all I can say is God help him because that boy better start fearing for his life, and they going to hear the *sjambokking* he gets from me in Pretoria.'

The weeks flew by like a flock of startled birds. The school holidays soon came, and Christmas and January went, and it was time to say goodbye. Then the last day came, and after breakfast, Tinker and me went down to the big library rock. The grass around it was long since summer brown, grown green after the fire, and now dried out in the late January heat. The lemon-stemmed whitethorn was back, cicadas shredded the vapoury air, and the sky was a don't-care blue.

We climbed to the top of the rock, and Tinker sat on my lap and I stroked her silky little ears and began to sob. There was no use saying anything, so I just let the tears come from deep down in my chest where the loneliness stones lived. Tinker licked my wet face and I could feel her little heart beating against my chest. My throat was so full of pain I couldn't even say goodbye out loud. I just kissed her and kissed her and kissed her, and sobbed some more.

Then Tinker and me had to wait at the front gate for Marie and Mevrou Van Heerden to come and pick up Tinker and me and take us to the doctor's house. I had Tinker's old sack that she'd always slept on at the dairy with me, so she'd know she had to stay at her new home. We didn't have long to wait, and Marie could hardly fit in the front of the car as she was 'any day now', with her stomach bigger than a prize pumpkin. The idea was for me to go home with them and spend the rest of the day to settle Tinker in, and then around four in the afternoon they'd drive me back to The Boys Farm to pack my suitcase and get into my school uniform.

The church planned a big send-off at seven o'clock for Gawie that was to take place at the railway station an hour before the train left. Gawie was to be taken to the station by Meneer Prinsloo in his Plymouth, and I'd be taken in the back of the lorry with some of The Boys Farm boys who sang in the church choir. I was leaving on the same train, but I wasn't included in the big farewell. I didn't mind because Marie and Sergeant Van Niekerk, and Doctor Van Heerden was going to try if he didn't have an emergency at the hospital, and Mevrou Van Heerden were coming along to see me off. Unfortunately Meneer Van Niekerk the headmaster couldn't make it because he was attending a regional headmasters' conference in Pietersburg with his wife, Mevrou Van Niekerk.

So when the '39 Chevvie stopped at the gate, Marie's mum, who was driving, stopped and then called out, 'Take a look in the dicky-seat, Tom.' I looked and there was the most beautiful quilt you have ever seen. Colours like the rainbow and rolled up and tied with two cloth straps that's joined with a cloth handle so it could be carried.

Then Marie called out, 'Do you like it, Tom?'

'Ja, it's truly beautiful, Marie.' I walked round to her door and climbed on the running board. 'Thank you, thank you, Marie! Miss Phillips will love it more than anything!'

'It's amazing what can come from a few rooster tail feathers,' she laughed.

'What's this about rooster tail feathers?' Mevrou Van Heerden asked.

'It's nothing,' Marie said hastily, 'just an old joke.' Then she turned back to me. 'Tom, take the quilt and put it with your suitcase, we'll wait for you here. But *maak gou*, because we in a bit of a hurry, hey, I've been getting contractions since midnight last night, but don't worry they not hurting yet and they still half an hour apart.'

It was nice to know that Marie hadn't told her mum about Piet Retief's tail feathers because it means perhaps women can sometimes keep a secret. Even though it's only goose feathers and bits of cloth a quilt can be quite heavy, but still it was the best thing I could imagine to buy with my ten shillings and now I had a proper thank you for Miss Phillips. 'What's contractions?' I asked.

'The baby's beginning to come, but it could be not until tomorrow, first pregnancy is always a long time.' I can tell you, I grabbed that quilt and took it to the dormitory, then I ran back to the gate and Tinker and I got into the dicky-seat quick smart.

I was really worried about Tinker adapting to her new home, even though it was a much nicer place to live than behind the dairy. I'd told her this a hundred times and, if she was a bit homesick, she still had her sack to smell. I didn't want her going back to The Boys Farm looking for me and then not knowing what to do when she couldn't find me.

When we got to the doctor's house there was a big surprise waiting for Tinker. Not only did she have a new home, but also her own house and a backyard. Doctor Van Heerden had painted Helmut's kennel with new green paint, and above the door was stencilled in white, 'Tinker'. Helmut was a big old labrador and Tinker was a tiny fox terrier so it was more like a mansion than a house for a dog like her. I put her sack inside the kennel and she went in and turned around three or four times, then lay down. This was taken by all of us as a very good sign. You never do know just what dogs understand when you talk to them. Tinker was, of course, a super-smart dog and must have understood right off that this was her new home. I only hoped she understood the next part, where I told her I was going away for a little while, but would be back for the school holidays. Around the kennel Doctor Van Heerden had built a fence of chicken wire so that Tinker had a yard of her own. He'd explained that this was so Tinker could grow accustomed to her new home for a few days after I left. 'After that I'll take it down, Tom, because, like Helmut, she'll be one of the family.'

We had a nice lunch, but early about eleven o'clock, some cold meat called polony and salad with a cold potato. This was because the maid had her afternoon off so couldn't cook. Marie said to Mevrou Van Heerden that she wasn't hungry and didn't want any lunch but she better have a bit of a lie down because of all the excitement coming later with me catching the train. Marie's mum said she had to go and fetch the midwife in Tzaneen as the lady who did it in Duiwelskrans was sick. Then, on the way back she'd see if the doctor was finished at the hospital where he was operating, taking out an appendix, tonsils and something that sounded very complicated with a name you couldn't remember. She said she'd be back around four o'clock when the midwife would be with Marie so she could drive me back to The Boys Farm.

So Tinker and me went exploring the doctor's backyard, and looking at the chickens. Tinker found a hole beside the garden-shed wall, and started sniffing like mad and whimpering, and I knew that the rats that lived in there better say their prayers. Then I heard Marie shouting my name from the house and to come quick.

What I saw you'd never believe. Marie was sitting on the kitchen floor with her back against a cupboard and her legs wide open. She was sweating like mad and groaning.

'Tom, get on the telephone in the surgery, my baby is coming,' she gasped. 'Tell the doctor the contractions are coming very close together.'

'What's a contraction?'

'For Chrissake, Tom, just do it!' she screamed. 'Ooh! Ahhhh!'

I ran to the surgery that was at the back of the house and on the opposite side to the kitchen. I'd never used a telephone in my life, but, of course, I'd seen it done lots of times. Doctor Van Heerden's phone wasn't on the branch-line and I was halfway to the surgery when I remembered I didn't know the hospital number. I rushed back.

'What's the hospital phone number?' I called from the kitchen door.

'Fifteen . . . Ahhhh!'

My hand was shaking as I pushed my forefinger into the little round holes and dialled. What seemed like ages passed before a female voice on the other end said 'Duiwelskrans Hospital.'

'Marie's having her baby, can you fetch the doctor quick!' I shouted down the phone, forgetting to say please.

'Can you bring the patient in?' the voice asked calmly.

'No, no. It's happening on the kitchen floor!' I yelled.

'The name of the patient, please?' the voice asked, still all calm and unconcerned.

'Marie Booysens, I mean Van Niekerk,' I shouted.

'Marie! Our nurse Marie?'

'Yes, quick, it's happening, her baby, it's happening!' I called in a panicked voice.

'Wait there!' the voice instructed, no longer sounding calm or disinterested.

Ages passed and you could hear Marie screaming from the kitchen. 'Ahhhhhh!' Sounds like that and also, when I ran back from the surgery after the phone call, you could hear the 'Ooh! Oohs!' as well.

Then the voice came back, but this time it was Doctor Van Heerden.

'Tom, I can't leave here for two-and-a-half hours at least, I'm in the middle of a tricky operation. Isn't my wife back from Tzaneen with the midwife?'

'No, Doctor.'

'Is Katrina the maid there?'

'No, it's her afternoon off.'

'So you're alone with Marie?'

'Yes, Doctor.'

'Don't worry, son, I'm sure the midwife will be there any time now,' he reassured me. 'Now tell me, Tom, how far apart are the contractions?'

I still didn't know precisely what a contraction was, only that they came. 'What's a contraction look like?' I asked.

'What's the time between every time Marie screams out?' he answered calmly.

'Very close, every minute, maybe less,' I said, trying to estimate the time between the 'Ahhhhhhs'.

'Damn!' I heard him say. 'The ambulance has been called out on another maternity call at an outlying farm. Now listen, Tom, you'll have to be the doctor until my wife arrives with the midwife. Labour for a first child can take anything up to twenty-four hours, sometimes more, I don't expect the baby will come until later tonight. Stay calm, babies are born every minute of the day. Next to the bathroom is a cupboard with lots of towels, take them all out and put them in the bedroom ready for Marie's birth.'

'She's on the kitchen floor!' I was still shouting down the receiver, not knowing how to use the phone properly.

'Damn!' I heard him say again, then, 'Ja, okay, that's a hard surface, that's even better because she's going to get a bad backache if she hasn't got it already. Put some towels under her bottom and the base of her spine, Tom. I'll get someone to call Sergeant Van Niekerk. If my wife and the midwife don't get there in time I want you to hold Marie's legs as wide apart as possible. She'll kick and scream but take no notice, just hang on. But don't worry, Tom, just comfort her, the first baby is unlikely to come so soon.'

Back in the kitchen Marie had jammed her back into the corner where the two kitchen cupboards meet. She was completely wet with perspiration, and her dress was soaked, and her huge pumpkin stomach was rising and falling, her dress was clinging to her skin so you could see her bellybutton through the thin cotton. She was gasping for breath, and then screaming out, 'Ahhhhhh!' and the screams were longer than before but coming more often. I put the big black cast-iron kettle filled with water on the stove, which was cream enamel and very posh and electric. I had to turn the stove to high, but I didn't know which switch was which plate and there was no time to work it out so I turned them all on to high. Then I fetched the towels and managed to get three of them under Marie's bottom, which was quite a business, I can tell you.

A person gets accustomed to everything and Marie's oohing, ahhhhhhing, and screaming out has been going on so long, and I've been wiping her sweating face with a wet towel so that it's got like there's only her and me in the world and we just have to put up with everything until something happens. It was now four hours since she called out to me the first time.

'Tom, take off, aaaahhh, my bloomers,' Marie gasps. She is pulling at her dress, making it come up above her waist. 'Pull them down!' she sobs.

I get down on my knees and grab her bloomers but she can't get her legs together and they won't come off.

'Cut, cut them!' she cries. 'Ahhhhhhhh!' Another big pain comes.

I managed to find a large pair of scissors in a kitchen drawer and cut the elastic around her legs and waist, then cut through one leg and then the other and pulled the bloomers away. Suddenly there's sort of water coming out from between her legs that soaks the towels, running across the floor. I pulled the wet towels away and put some new ones down. I was trying to mop up the water, and at the same time trying not to look because what I've seen is all red and pulsing and I think maybe Marie is going to die because there's lots of blood.

Now she really starts panting and crying out and she grabbed the handles of the kitchen cupboards with each hand, jamming her back further into the corner. Tinker is at the kitchen door barking, and knowing something is terribly wrong but she's not allowed in. I take a quick look over at Marie and I could see something coming out between Marie's legs, and she's still screaming blue murder. Then I remember I'm supposed to hold her legs apart. So I grab them and stand up and then hang on. But she's miles too strong for me. She's knocking me this way and that and ahhhhhhing and sobbing, and I'm hanging on trying to keep her legs apart and her bottom's bouncing on the towels and her back is arching and she's screaming her head off and still holding onto the cupboard door handles. Then she yells the biggest scream of all, 'Ahhhhhhhhhhhhhhhhh!' Suddenly, plop, and there's something that's covered in blood and slime that's definitely a baby lying between her legs. It's got this sort of meat rope that looks like *boerewors* going from its bellybutton back inside Marie, and I start to cry because there must be something terribly wrong with all the blood and the rope thing. Then Sergeant Van Niekerk bursts into the kitchen and kneels down beside Marie, putting her head on his lap while she sobs and sobs.

Mevrou Van Heerden arrives, and takes one look and kneels down and picks up the baby by the feet and holds it upside down and spanks its bottom, and all of a sudden there's this crying coming out of its mouth. Sergeant Van Niekerk starts to cry and laugh, and so does Mevrou Van Heerden. There's a whole first-class crying match going on with some laughing thrown in. Mevrou puts the baby on Marie's stomach and that's when Doctor Van Heerden arrives.

When it's all settled down and the baby, a girl, so now she can't be Benny Osler when she grows up, is cleaned up and turns out to be a sort of deep rosy pink colour with lots of wrinkles, like an old person. Everyone says how pretty she is, just like her mother, but she isn't. Maybe when the wrinkles go she'll look a bit better. Doctor Van Heerden cut the *boerewors* rope, which is called an umbilical cord, and he told me it was always supposed to be there. Mevrou Van Heerden explains that the Tzaneen midwife had another pregnancy to attend to and was still busy and was going to get her husband to drive her when it was over. Now, of course, it's too late.

With all this excitement going on it's suddenly nearly four o'clock and lots of things are happening. The doctor has to go back to the hospital, so he's taken the '39 Chevvie. Sergeant Van Niekerk has to go to court because the district magistrate is in town and there's court cases going on, so he has to leave Marie, who is now in bed in the spare room. She's had stitches down there, and Doctor Van Heerden has given her a pain-killing needle. She has to stay the night and can only go back to her own house in the morning. The midwife still hasn't arrived and Mevrou Van Heerden is staying, of course, to look after Marie.

So now I'm in the deep shit because it's a quarter to five and that's the curfew for The Boys Farm today. This is because we're having our supper at five o'clock as there is going to be this big farewell for the Afrikaner Genius at the railway station that begins at half past six, because the train leaves at eight o'clock. Even if I run it's going to take me half an hour to get back. I knock on the half-open bedroom door and Mevrou Van Heerden calls out, 'No need to knock, Tom. Come in.' But I'd never been in a room when a lady was in bed, and you couldn't just walk in.

'My hero!' Marie called out weakly. 'Come here, Tom, let me give you a big hug, hey.' She is so tired she can hardly talk. So I go over to her and she gives me a hug and whispers, 'I couldn't have done it without you, Tom! You were wonderful, you hear?' Then she puts three kisses all over my face. She didn't smell of roses, just sweat, so I suppose after the baby comes out, the rose smell goes. She looked a bit sad and said, 'If the baby had been a boy we were going to call him Tom.' She closed her eyes and was quiet for a moment.

'You must have a good sleep, Marie,' I said.

'Ja, it's far too much excitement for one day,' Mevrou Van Heerden exclaimed.

Marie opened her eyes and said, 'I've just thought of a name, we're going to call her Saxby. I don't know what her other name will be, but her first name will definitely be Saxby.'

'But it's English,' I said, surprised.

'Ja, and that's nice too,' she said softly. 'Goodbye, Tom, we'll see you in the holidays.'

Mevrou Van Heerden came out of the bedroom with me, and I

thanked her for everything. The first one-legged ice-cream, and the red and pineapple suckers, and Marie taking me to Doctor Van Heerden, and everything that happened to me that was kind ever since.

'Tom, we love you, you know? We want you to come and stay with us during the school holidays. This will be your home. Doctor Van Heerden has written to Pretoria to get the papers to release you from The Boys Farm.' She gave me a kiss and a big hug and she said that under the circumstances, she didn't think she could come to the train. 'Tom, I'd like to stay here with Marie, do you think you can make your own way back to The Boys Farm?'

'*Ja*, of course,' I said. 'Thank you for everything you and the doctor have done for me. I'll just go out and say goodbye to Tinker.' I wish I could have found all the words I needed to thank her, but all of a sudden I couldn't find the right ones because of the lump in my throat.

But now the hard part. I took Tinker to her chicken-wired-in yard and held her to my chest and kissed her, and I couldn't help it, I started to cry again. I put her down and closed the wire gate, and didn't look back and ran away as fast as I could down the road. I only managed to stop blubbing when I got to the gate of The Boys Farm, where I didn't get any supper and got the last *sjambokking* of my orphanage career. Six of the best and I didn't feel even one of them.

This is what happened. Gawie, being the big hero, was taken to the railway station with Meneer and Mevrou Prinsloo in the Plymouth, which was polished to within an inch of its life. Oh yes, I forgot to say Gawie had a brand-new trunk with all his clothes, also brand-new and bought in a proper shop paid for out of the Meet the Genius money. People were very happy, because it showed you could help others less fortunate and be a proud community as well. Here's the funny part, remember how the *Dominee* said if anyone in the congregation knitted, that Gawie needed grey socks? The *Dominee* forgot to say how many socks. In the next three weeks Gawie got forty pairs. Forty pairs of socks every colour grey you could find in a storm cloud! So Gawie took six pairs that matched and the rest were given to the kids at The Boys Farm. There was one pair left over at the end too small for anyone, and Mevrou called me in. 'Here, *Voetsek*, you can have these,' she said.

I didn't even try them on for size. 'Thank you, Mevrou, but I have six pairs already,' I told her. I was very happy to be able to refuse the socks, they were the wrong colour grey from my other ones anyway. To tell you the truth, what I was really thinking was, 'You can stick those grey socks up your fat bum!'

Doctor Van Heerden had given me his own leather suitcase, the one he'd used when he'd gone to the university in Stellenbosh to study medicine. On the outside lid it had 'A. van H.' embossed on the leather, the letters were once in gold but now the gold had worn off. All my stuff fitted into the suitcase nicely, I can tell you, when you saw it all packed: white shirts, and grey pants, and socks, and a new toothbrush and toothpaste, and a dish that had a lid that contained a cake of Lifebuoy soap. And, of course, my Meneer Van Niekerk *Shorter Oxford English Dictionary* and the red book, which I had completely memorised, all 783 pages. All my things together in the one place in that suitcase were something else to see.

There was one other thing I haven't told you about. Just before he was murdered and lost his face, Mattress had plaited a leather collar out of cowhide for Tinker. He'd scraped off all the hair and chewed the thin thongs until they were very supple, then he'd plaited them together. '*Ahee, Kleinbaas*, it should be made from the hide of a lioness for such a mighty dog!' he'd said, but it was still beautiful and Tinker looked very good with it on. Then just before I left for boarding school, Sergeant Van Niekerk brought this new dog collar with a brass tag on it that said 'Tinker – If lost, Tel. 00', which was the telephone number of the police station. I couldn't say that I wanted Tinker to keep the Mattress collar on, because having a tag on the collar was a very good idea. So I kept the beautiful Mattress-plaited collar. When I was packing my suitcase I tried it around my wrist. It turned out to be a bit big but it didn't fall off over my hand, and if you pushed it up your arm a bit it remained tight. Now that I was wearing long sleeves on my white shirts nobody would know it was there. Now I had a bit of Tinker with me all the time wherever I went.

As I mentioned before, the boys who sang in the church choir were also coming to the railway station in The Boys Farm lorry driven by Koos van de Merwe, with Mevrou sitting in the front next to him. There we were on the big Afrikaner Genius farewell night, me in my new uniform and them in clean khaki shirts and pants. It was only a Wednesday, so it just goes to show how much more important the occasion was than a wedding. The choirboys didn't tease me too much because of the funny badge on my blazer pocket.

'What's that funny pointy cap and the two crossed walking sticks mean, *Voetsek*?' one of them asked, and they all laughed. But they weren't really mocking me because I think they were a bit jack of all the attention the Afrikaner Genius had been getting.

One of the boys, Willem Kriegler, who was fifteen but his voice still hadn't broken so he was still in the choir, said, 'You know, *Voetsek*, if you weren't a *Rooinek* maybe you'd be even cleverer than the Third Class Rooster.'

Everyone laughed and nodded their heads. Afrikaner Genius was the name the *Dominee* gave Gawie and Meneer Prinsloo was using it all the time, so The Boys Farm kids definitely wouldn't use it. Like I said before, it's not a good idea to be seen as a super-clever person in such company. It wasn't really Gawie's fault because he wasn't boastful or anything, it was just that he was trapped between the *Dominee* and Meneer Prinsloo, and couldn't escape all the new attention he was getting all of a sudden.

When we got to the station there were a lot of people there, more even than would fit in the church on Sunday. It looked as though the whole town had come to see Gawie leave. Two big timber trucks with those long trays at the back were pulled up right on the platform next to the waiting train, and on one was a *boere musiek* band with violins, banjos, concertinas, guitars, piano accordions and even a small portable organ. On the other truck there were chairs on the end of the tray facing the train for the high-ups to sit, and behind these chairs was where the church choir stood. The trucks were decorated with crinkle paper in the four colours of the *vierkleur*. On the high-ups truck were Gawie and Meneer Prinsloo and the *Dominee* and Doctor Dyke and some of the church elders and the stationmaster and someone I hadn't ever seen before, it turned out he was the district court magistrate.

Mevrou told the choirboys to climb up and join the rest of the church choir on the back of the high-ups truck and then turned to me. 'Take your suitcase and that stupid quilt and get in the train, your compartment is number four, you hear?'

'*Ja, dankie*, Mevrou, *totsiens*,' I said, offering her my hand as I thanked her and wished her goodbye.

She didn't accept my hand, and clucked her tongue. 'Tsk! *Maak gou!* Nobody wants to see you around here, *Voetsek*.'

Koos van de Merwe, The Boys Farm lorry driver, went to pick up my suitcase and the quilt.

'Leave it!' Mevrou said. 'The *Rooinek* is big enough to do it himself!'

'There's a big crowd and it bulky, and he's only a small guy,' Koos protested.

'No, leave it! Let him carry it, you hear, the little *kaffirboetie* must learn he can't have people running around after him all the time. He thinks he can get away with everything!'

So I lugged my suitcase and Miss Phillips' quilt through the crowd on the platform. It was a pretty heavy and bulky combination and I had to keep saying, 'Excuse me, Meneer,' and 'Excuse me Mevrou,' to people who were standing on the platform, who I was bumping into because I couldn't help it. Finally I managed to get both items up the steps and onto the train, by which time I was puffing and panting, and my arms were practically pulled out of their sockets. It was a hot summer night and in my new blazer and tie I was sweating like billyo when I finally got into the compartment. From then on things were good because sitting alone in that compartment, looking through the open window, I reckon I had the best view of the grand proceedings that were about to commence. Gawie's trunk was already in the compartment, so I knew we were travelling together.

It had been a long day that had started at dawn, and with all my secret blubbing and saying goodbye to Tinker, and then Marie having her baby, and having to run all the way back to The Boys Farm, I was pretty exhausted. I was glad I was alone watching through the train window. I was a bit hungry though, missing supper and because it had only been a cold polony lunch, these thin, round, pink slices of meat you cut from this huge sausage that's got white blobs of fat in it. Polony is very nice but the thin slices were not enough with only beetroot and tomato and lettuce and a cold potato. You don't get full-up in a hurry on that kind of food. But I couldn't ask for more because Marie and her mum were talking about the baby coming, maybe in the next day or two, and what a pity I wouldn't be there, and they clean forgot to ask if I was still hungry, which I was. Anyway, the jelly and banana custard after was truly excellent.

All of a sudden the music started. Let me assure you, there's nothing better than *boere musiek*. The band played all the old tunes and people began to sing and *boeremense* know how to sing a good song, believe you me, they got voices like an angels' choir. People had bottles of Lion lager beer and half-jacks of brandy and there was true merriness all around the place. The choir sang two hymns, 'Abide with me' and 'Jerusalem', both in Afrikaans, of course.

After the hymns the *Dominee* stood up and started to talk. '*Dames en Here*, we are all gathered here on a very auspicious occasion.' He paused and looked down at the assembled crowd. 'Now, some of you may think it's only a young boy going to school in Pretoria and that this is not such a big occasion to celebrate. But you be wrong! What we are doing here is looking into the face of the future. In this boy, Gawie Grobler, we are seeing our Afrikaner destiny —'

I'm afraid that's all I can tell you about the *Dominee*'s speech, or any of the other speeches that may have followed, because I was already fast asleep. Then something must have woken me, and what it was was a disturbance in the crowd. You know how you're asleep and there's sounds you can't hear happening in the world that's awake, and then they change suddenly and you're wide awake because of these new noises going on?

I looked out of the train carriage window, and there's Doctor Van Heerden followed by Sergeant Van Niekerk climbing up the ladder onto the back of the high-ups and choir lorry. The *Dominee* is no longer speaking, and now it's Meneer Prinsloo, who's standing up with his stomach practically falling over the back of the lorry. If it plopped onto somebody's head below it would definitely kill them, good thing the braces were strong. He must have been addressing the crowd. He's probably been talking about being the Government father of Gawie and how he is a loving father to us all. How he spotted Gawie early on and single-handedly he's made him into an Afrikaner genius. But now he's silent and surprised as he looks at the two men climbing up towards him. The crowd is also silent, waiting to see what will happen next because both the doctor and the sergeant have a lot of respect in this town.

You can see the crowd thinks, with the doctor and the policeman suddenly making an appearance, something bad or serious has happened. This is confirmed when Doctor Van Heerden puts up his hands for silence, which is already there. '*Dames en Here*, Sergeant Van Niekerk and myself have come here tonight to try to make right a serious wrong.' He paused and looked down at the silent crowd. 'Let me first offer my sincere congratulations to this young man, Gawie Grobler from The Boys Farm.' He turned to Gawie. 'You have done well, son, and we are all rightly proud of you.'

Sergeant Van Niekerk is by now standing beside Doctor Van Heerden, and Meneer Prinsloo doesn't know what to do and looks at the *Dominee*, who points to his chair, showing that he must sit down. So Meneer Prinsloo sits down, but you can see he is not one bit happy.

Doctor Van Heerden doesn't even appear to see Meneer Prinsloo. 'We Afrikaners are a proud people and a stubborn people and some may even say a narrow-minded people, but they mistake this for a single-minded people, a people with a purpose.' This gets a clap from the crowd. 'But one thing you can never say about an Afrikaner is that we are an ungenerous people.' This gets a big clap. Doctor Van Heerden holds up his hand again. 'In this town, at The Boys Farm is another orphan and I want to tell you about him. Recently he sat for an examination for a scholarship to a school in Johannesburg. A very famous school, believe me. Two thousand four hundred students sat for this scholarship, it is the biggest and perhaps the most prestigious school in the land. With an astonishing average mark of 95 per cent this boy, who is only eleven years old, won one of the three scholarships available. This makes him capable of achieving anything he wants in life, simply because it makes him one of the most gifted and brilliant young men in South Africa! But because his name is Tom Fitzsaxby and not a good Afrikaner name like Van Heerden, Van Niekerk, Prinsloo, Van Schalkwyk or Grobler, this community, as well as those people responsible for running The Boys Farm, have completely ostracised him.' Doctor Van Heerden stopped and looked around at the people below, and then turned around and looked at all the high-ups sitting behind him. Then he said, 'I have served this town and this farming community for twenty years, and you have all been kind and generous to me, more so than I know I deserve. But tonight I am ashamed of us. Ashamed of my own *volk*. This bitterness towards a young orphan's name is a truly shameful thing and not worthy of the Afrikaner people.'

There is this silence that follows, and then a few claps, and then it's like sudden rain on a tin roof, all the clapping and cheering. Sergeant Van Niekerk steps forward and puts up his hand until finally there is silence except for one voice from the crowd who shouts, 'Where is this new genius?' And the clapping starts again but then finally it stops. 'Later you'll see him!' Sergeant Van Niekerk says. 'But first I must tell you something else. I have known Tom Fitzsaxby since he was six years old and I consider him a very good friend of mine. But today he did something astonishing, you hear! Simply astonishing, and there is no other word for it.'

You could see the *Dominee* and Meneer Prinsloo were not happy, and they were scowling all over the place, and there's no smiles or clapping coming from the church elders either. Doctor Dyke has got his legs crossed and is looking up in the space above his head. But the district magistrate is clapping with the rest of the crowd, and even the *Dominee* doesn't have the authority to tell the doctor or the policeman to sit down, let alone make a fuss in front of an outside high-up like the district magistrate from Pietersburg.

The crowd has now become completely silent so you can hear a pin drop. 'This afternoon my wife Marie went into labour quite suddenly,' Sergeant Van Niekerk began. 'She and Tom Fitzsaxby were alone in Doctor Van Heerden's house. Marie tried to get to the doctor's phone but could only get as far as the kitchen because the pain stopped her from crawling further. So she called out to Tom who was outside in the back garden. Tom went into the doctor's surgery and called the hospital.' The sergeant turned to indicate Doctor Van Heerden. 'But the doctor here is doing an emergency operation and he can't leave or the patient will die. The ambulance has gone out to fetch a farmer's wife, so can't be sent. I am in court with the district magistrate, Meneer du Plessis. Mevrou Van Heerden is out and can't be contacted. So the doctor tells Tom what he must do if he can't get there on time. And with nobody there, Tom Fitzsaxby delivers my baby daughter on the kitchen floor.'

Now there's the most clapping and shouting and cheering of all, and I can see some of the women are crying. Even if I wanted to I couldn't tell them the truth, which was that the baby just plopped out while I was trying to hold Marie's legs, and she was busy kicking me halfway into next week, and at the same time she's hanging onto the cupboard door handles so hard that she pulled one of them off, screws and all. I wasn't brave at all, and crying all the time because I was so frightened seeing that long sausage umbilical thing coming out of her baby's stomach.

After a long while the cheering and clapping stopped and Sergeant Van Niekerk said, 'Before you meet Tom Fitzsaxby I want to announce that my little daughter's name will be Saxby van Niekerk! If you all turn around, Tom Fitzsaxby is sitting in the middle compartment and isn't expecting any of this to happen.'

I just had time to duck below the train window because I truly wasn't expecting it. I know it sounds funny, but it was as if they were talking about somebody else. How can I put it? I knew it was me alright, but it wasn't, if you know what I mean? I wasn't used to having people pay attention to me, except Meneer Prinsloo and Mevrou and that was always bad. So people saying good things was something I'd never had in public, and it was as if it was another me out there on the platform, and the real, private listening and looking me was sitting hearing all of this in the train compartment.

'Show your face, Tom!' I heard Sergeant Van Niekerk shout out. But I wasn't game to do it. 'Please, Tom!' he said. So I put half of my face above the train window ledge and everyone laughed.

Then Doctor Van Heerden came into the compartment behind me. 'C'mon, Tom, don't be frightened, son,' he said softly. 'Now it's your turn for a bit of the glory around here.' He took my hand and we went down the corridor of the train and down the steps to the platform, and the crowd parted and I could feel hands touching me and patting me on the back and people saying, 'Congratulations,' and smiling at me. We climbed up the ladder and I stood between Doctor Van Heerden and Sergeant Van Niekerk, and my knees were shaking worse than the time when Meneer made me pick up the already opened scholarship letter on the floor next to his shiny brown boots.

People were cheering all over the place. Then the stationmaster blew his whistle and said the train must leave immediately or it would miss the connection at Louis Trichardt. The *boere musiek* band struck up and played 'The Maori Farewell', which later got called 'Now is the Hour'. It had become a popular song after the New Zealand All Blacks' last rugby tour and had been translated into Afrikaans and was now used a lot for saying goodbye when a person left on the train. It was a lovely song, and after the *volk* had sung it they cheered a lot and the stationmaster dropped the green flag and blew his whistle, and the engine tooted twice then went 'choof-a-choof' as Gawie Grobler and me began to move away from Duiwelskrans.

'Goodbye, Tinker, see you soon,' I whispered. I could hardly remember when my beautiful little dog hadn't been at my side, because, you see, that wet sack floating down the creek was truly the beginning of my proper life. I said quietly, '*Sala kahle*, Tinker,' which means in Zulu, 'Stay well, Tinker.' If Mattress had been alive he would tell you that it means much, much more than this when you truly love someone. The loneliness stones were already piling up and getting heavy in my chest.

Gawie Grobler began to cry, I was very tired and closed my eyes. The train wheels were saying, 'Clickity-clack, what's in the wet sack, clickity-clack, he's caught his tenth rat, clickity-clack, we're closing the case, clickity-clack, they've rubbed off his face.' I didn't know the wheels could speak.

After a while I opened my eyes and Gawie was still crying.

'You okay, Gawie?' I asked.

But he didn't answer at first, then he said with a sob, '*Ja*, I'm okay, Tom.' He hadn't called me *Voetsek*.

'I think it must be very hard to be a genius, hey?' I said, trying to comfort him.

He looked at me and said in this small sort of voice, '*You* the genius, Tom. I'm *only* the Afrikaner Genius.'

'No, I'm not!' I replied, surprised he would say such a stupid thing.

'Can we be friends again?' he said hoarsely.

'*Ja*, of course,' I replied.

We shook hands.

Gawie grinned, his eyes still wet. 'Maybe we both geniuses, hey?'

Then we laughed and laughed until our heads came off.

He pointed to me, '*Rooinek!*'

I pointed back and said, '*Surrogaat!*'

'*Voetsek!*'

'Third Class Rooster!'

'Genius!'

'Afrikaner Genius!'

Then, all of a sudden, at the exact same moment, we both started to blub.

CHAPTER TWELVE

Everlasting Love

NOW I SUPPOSE YOU'RE expecting a whole heap of stuff about going to a posh school. But I've decided against that because everyone has already read a book about going to boarding school, like the one I've already referred to, *Tom Brown's Schooldays*. Oh, by the way, I have to correct what I said about the Bishop's College probably being much the same as that because I was wrong. Boarding school was very good compared to Tom Brown's story and also compared to The Boys Farm. The food was much better and you hardly ever got beaten, and then only for proper things done wrong. Even though I was the youngest, once again I discovered a surprise about myself, this was that I was tough. What wasn't tough at The Boys Farm was tough here, I won't say butter wouldn't melt in my mouth, nothing like that, but when it came to defending myself I wasn't scared, and I had a mouth that could fire verbal bullets very accurately, if it had to. *Voetsek* was one person, Tom Fitzsaxby was quite another.

I'm only telling you this because maybe you'll hear me say things that I wouldn't have said before. I can't think of an example, you'll just have to wait and see. The thing was that at The Boys Farm, if a guy wanted to have a go at you he wouldn't do it alone; the kids would work in a pack. Unless it was a Fonnie du Preez. Here at the Bishop's College it was one on one, so you knew if you had the courage you had a good chance to defend yourself. You'd put on the gloves and go into the gym and settle the matter. Not that I was much of a boxer, but at The Boys Farm you had to do it, and so I wasn't scared of putting on a pair of boxing gloves.

The guys at the Bishop's College had never boxed, so even though I was smaller, on the few occasions I was required to stand my ground and fight it was only against a single opponent and I was able to give as much as I got. In life a person doesn't mind getting a hiding fair and square because afterwards you can still walk away with your self-respect intact.

While I had always been a loner, I now had to be a different kind of loner from the one I had been on The Boys Farm where my 'lonerness' was caused by being a *Rooinek* and not an Afrikaner. At a boarding school for rich English-speaking kids there were three reasons I had to hide and be a loner. The first was that I was illegitimate, a fact I hadn't previously known, thinking my mother had simply left me at the orphanage because she and my father couldn't afford to have me. But two days before I left The Boys Farm, Meneer Prinsloo had called me into his office.

'Tom, Doctor Van Heerden is writing behind my back to Pretoria about you staying with him in the school holidays. Now, Pretoria wants to know what I think because I am your *surrogaat* father. Without my permission, you coming back here every school holiday, you hear?'

'*Ja*, Meneer,' I muttered, looking down and shuffling my feet. The idea that I would be forced back to The Boys Farm at the end of every term filled me with horror.

'But I'm a generous man, and I'm going to tell Pretoria it's okay by me because you been nothing but trouble to us here.' He picked up a sheet of paper from his desk. 'This is a copy of your birth certificate and it says here "Born out of wedlock", do you know what this means?'

'*Ja*, Meneer.'

'It means you a bastard,' he said gratuitously.

If he expected me to react he had about as much chance as a snowball in hell. I was long past caring what he or Mevrou said about me, but afterwards it worried me a lot. Being an orphan with parents somewhere or even dead is different from being illegitimate, meaning that you were not only not wanted but were a mistake in the first place. You can tell a lie with a clear conscience if you're an orphan because you don't really know what has happened to your parents, but when you know they didn't want you in the first place it's a different kind of lie and one you've got to live with forever. So this was my first worry at the Bishop's College, what kind of lie to tell if I was forced to explain. The second reason was because I had no parents, I had no home. The third was that I had no money.

The problem with lying about not having parents is that you can't just say you don't have a mother or a father, and don't know who they are, because you have to have at least a mother and she must be somewhere. In my case, all I knew was that my mother delivered me to the orphanage and cried a lot, and then disappeared forever. If you say this then you're telling the truth, and that points to one direction, you back to being illegitimate. The only thing that was good about The Boys Farm was that everyone was more or less in the same boat, but even then everyone wants to have someone somewhere, that's why Gawie had to invent his uncle in Pretoria.

You can only invent one lie and the best one is that both your parents are dead and that makes you an orphan. But how did they die is always the next question. Then you've got to invent a whole new lie. The trick here is to invent a very simple lie, like, for instance, they died in a motorcar crash when you were still a baby and you couldn't even remember them. That's a safe lie and you can keep telling it, but it's not much of a story. There you are, a baby in a basket in the back seat, and bang-smash-tinkle, it's all over, and now all of a sudden you're an orphan. There are no memories or past, just this black hole called coming from nowhere and being a no-one. It may sometimes work, but even nowhere has a history, and a no-one was once a someone. So people want to know who these dead people were. Where did they come from? Why no relatives? Where were they going at the time of the crash? What did your father do before he died? Where did they live? If you can't answer these questions they'll think you're lying, and you just want to cover up that you're illegitimate. So back to the drawing board you go. This time you decide to design a new and improved lie, and that's where the trouble begins.

So here is my new-and-improved lie. Remember the waterfall Sergeant Van Niekerk took me to on the day of the grand picnic? Where when you stood in a certain position and called out, your voice kept echoing? It was the most beautiful spot I'd ever seen, and if someone had to die that was about as nice a place to die as you could think of. A great sheet of white water tumbling down into a tropical rainforest, strange and beautiful birds calling out, diamond sunlight and every day rain when the world would begin all over again. So I put this beautiful woman and handsome man at the very top of the falls. They'd left their baby in the shade of a giant tree at the bottom of the waterfall. Then they'd climbed up the cliff and undressed and stood on a rock, and kissed and then, holding hands, they'd jumped down into the waterfall and disappeared, never to be found again. A young herd boy looking after his father's goats in the high mountains heard the echo of a baby crying, and followed the great echo to find the child lying swaddled in a blanket under the tree. His name was Mokiti Malokoane, but he also had a white man's name, Joe Louis, and was the son of a mighty chief named Mattress Malokoane who sat under a marula tree all day and drank *kaffir* beer, and was terribly wise and greatly respected for his platform feet. The question of my name was easily enough solved because my parents had written a message across my chest and stomach in beautiful copperplate handwriting:

Tom Fitzsaxby,
the legitimate son of
Rosemarie and John Fitzsaxby

The woman's name came from Marie smelling of roses and the man's name was the English version of Jan, which was Sergeant Van Niekerk's Christian name. I decided to always end the story by saying, 'Now the truly amazing thing is that you can search every phone book in every town and city in South Africa and you won't find a single Fitzsaxby.' Whether this was true or not I was unable to prove, but Miss Phillips had once said that because it was such an unusual surname she'd looked through the Johannesburg phone directory and found no Fitzsaxby, so I reckoned I was pretty safe.

In reviewing my new-and-improved lie I discovered one rather sad fact. I was unable to refer to my erstwhile parents as young or beautiful and handsome or even that they'd kissed and held hands as they jumped. If they were destined to disappear forever and nobody had seen them arrive at the great waterfall, how would I have known they loved each other and were young, beautiful and handsome? The key to the new-and-improved lie was that I told it very sparingly, and only after a great deal of prompting. This was to give the impression that I was myself reluctant to believe it. If having heard the story someone was to say, 'Is that *really* true, Tom?' I could shrug my shoulders and answer, 'How can I possibly know? But all I can say is that I've been taken to the spot where it was supposed to have happened and it is exactly the way it was described to me. The echo is there, the big tree is there, the waterfall is there and the big rock they're supposed to have jumped from is there.'

Now my third problem was money. Everyone had pocket money and I had none. Not a single penny. I'm sure if there hadn't been the excitement of the birth and the event at the railway station that Doctor Van Heerden or Sergeant Van Niekerk would have given me maybe five shillings, but in all the gerfuffle they didn't remember. The guys would go to the tuckshop and buy a cream bun or a Cornish pastie and a Pepsi-Cola, and if you were in a group you couldn't do the same. They were all rich kids, and often one would offer to buy me a bun or a Pepsi, but, of course, you couldn't accept because you couldn't reciprocate. So you'd always just say, 'No, thanks, I'm not hungry,' or something dumb like that. Of course, everybody knows you don't have those nice-tasting things because you're hungry. So you could never hang around with a bunch of guys after school because all roads led to the tuckshop.

Maybe all of this sounds like a little thing, but being illegitimate isn't, and a nobody with no money in a school made up of kids with rich parents who knew exactly who they were and had the money to prove it was a difficult situation. If I was going to be forced into being a loner then I had to decide what kind of loner I wanted to be. In my experience there are only two places to hide if you're a 'nobody' and a forced-to-be loner, either at the back of or at the front of life. At the back is to be a nothing person, someone who is present but seldom noticed, whose opinion is never sought or given, and who is the last to be picked for anything. Until Miss Phillips came into my life and, of course, with the exception of Mattress, this was what I had been at The Boys Farm. Hiding at the back of life wasn't a very successful method of living, and contained a fair amount of unhappiness, but it had nevertheless allowed me to survive reasonably intact in an institution from which most kids emerged damaged.

Now an entirely different set of circumstances again required me to be different. I lacked the means or the background to be the same as everyone else, so I had to decide whether I would revert to the nobody-at-the-back version, or to hide at the front where I would simply attempt to be better at everything than anyone else. Doing this up-front way would never cause anyone to think to ask about my past, my successful present would be sufficient evidence of a normal background, and the lack of detail about my past would hopefully be seen as a sign of modesty.

So this is the path I chose at the Bishop's College. I had a head start by winning the scholarship and by being the youngest boy in the school. This translated into me being thought of as brilliant. The two other scholarship winners, Nathan Feinstein and Julian Solomon, matched me in intellect, and often enough surpassed me, but it was always pointed out that I was two years younger than them. I was also in for another big shock. Jewish noses were exactly the same as everyone else's and they wore their hair short, and both Nathan and Julian said their fathers didn't have curly black hair and beards; one was bald and the other one was sort of mousey brown. When I asked them how many solid-gold teeth their fathers had, they both looked at me in a bemused way, and replied, 'None.' Of course, I couldn't ask them about diamonds. I mean, after you'd already asked about the solid-gold teeth you couldn't just come out and say, 'Oh yeah, and how many diamonds does your father have stuck up his bum?' But I realised that was probably also untrue, and there'd never been any such thing happen to Jewish mouths or bums.

Throughout the school, the Jewish pupils in general and the scholarship guys in particular tended to be the very brightest academically. I became the token gentile brain. This gave me a special status among the mainly gentile boys at the school. It also meant that I had almost earned the right to be a loner, as someone thought to have a superior mind doesn't have to make excuses for himself or even behave the same as everyone else. I'd also become fairly quick with a quip, which was another way of keeping people at arm's length. So having brains and a sharp tongue that usually brought laughter proved an excellent means of camouflage, a way of hiding myself in front where nobody could see who I really was.

As time went by I joined the debating society and chess club and represented Transvaal schools in both. While I was small, I proved to be wiry and agile and I was toughened by my previous life at The Boys Farm. I became a successful, if not exceptional, rugby scrum-half and cricket wicket-keeper/batsman. Eventually I made it into the first team for both sports, and in my final year became a prefect, earning my school colours in rugby and chess, a combination that once again confirmed my loner status and largely did the speaking for me. I'm not telling you all this stuff in order to brag, but simply to get the information about the formal part of my schooling at the Bishop's College out of the way. There was another aspect of my life when I was growing into adulthood in the big city that you could be more interested in hearing about.

So now back to the beginning. Gawie and me arrived in Pretoria early the next morning and I helped him drag his shiny new trunk off the train. We'd slept pretty well in the top bunks on either side of the compartment we'd gotten into when we changed trains at Louis Trichardt. Two old men had been in the compartment when we joined the train, and they both wanted the bottom bunks so we got lucky and got the top ones. The conductor rattled on the compartment door at five o'clock the next morning and shouted, 'Pretoria one hour! Dining car open for breakfast!'

The two old men, Meneer Uys and Meneer Viljoen, asked us if we were going to breakfast and Gawie said yes he was and showed them a railway breakfast voucher. We'd already discussed this the night before and Gawie said he'd bring me back a slice of bread if it was allowed, or if nobody was looking. I can tell you one thing for sure, I was starving hungry.

Meneer Viljoen said, 'A boy is always hungry in the morning, come along, son.'

'I don't have a voucher, Meneer,' I replied.

'Who said you need one, hey? Isn't my money good enough to buy a hungry boy some breakfast?'

I don't know how he knew how hungry I was, but that was a breakfast and a half. One of the best you could hope for – bacon and eggs and as much toast as you liked and a whole big silver pot of coffee on the table and you could take as much sugar as you liked. We all sat together and it turned out that Meneer Viljoen was a stock inspector looking for foot-and-mouth disease in cattle, and Meneer Uys trained people how to do morse code on railway stations. They both got off at Pretoria, and both shook my hand, wishing me and Gawie luck at our new schools.

'A good education is a precious thing, Tom, you don't want to grow up to be a stock inspector,' Meneer Viljoen laughed.

'Thank you for breakfast, Meneer, I will try to do my best.'

'*Ja*,' he said. 'After the war, we going to need clever young people like you and your friend to build South Africa.'

'And maybe get a Nationalist government for the *volk* and get rid of that imposter Jan Smuts,' Meneer Uys called out.

The train pulled out of Pretoria and soon enough the land outside the compartment window was flat and not very interesting with here a tree and there another, and when you passed a farm it had a windmill and grew only *mielies*. Then we passed huge expanses of tin shanties, single-room houses made of this and that; bits of corrugated iron, hessian sacking, box wood, canvas and old paraffin tins beaten flat that had gone rusty. Dirt roads with oily puddles wandered through these makeshift shelters and black people, especially little kids, were everywhere you looked. It was the biggest *kaffir* location you could possibly imagine. But then these huge hills of white sand called mine dumps started coming up and I knew from my discussions with Gawie this must be the region of Witwatersrand and that Johannesburg would soon be next.

When it did, I couldn't believe my own eyes! You'd never seen building like this in your whole life. They just went up and up and up forever, and how a person would be expected to climb to the top I couldn't say because they'd be exhausted long before they got there, and what about old people? Of course, up to that time, I'd never seen or heard about an electric lift that was a little room that went up and down tall buildings, and even had its own driver in a smart uniform and cap.

The train pulled into Johannesburg Central Station. People, hundreds of people, milling around and shouting, happy, welcoming faces everywhere, arms waving, whistles blowing and black porters expertly navigating trolleys on the crowded platform. I couldn't imagine how I could possibly find Miss Phillips, what if she got the wrong day, what would I do? I suddenly panicked, nobody had told me how big the station was, and the whole city was a place where I didn't know a single person, except for her.

I waited until everyone had left the carriage because with my Doctor Van Heerden suitcase in one hand and the quilt in the other, I filled up the whole corridor. When I got onto the platform the crowds were already starting to thin out, people's backs walking away with porters carrying suitcases. Still no Miss Phillips. If she'd got the wrong day could a person sleep on a railway station? How lucky that I'd had eggs and bacon and four pieces of toast for breakfast because I could now definitely last until tomorrow. If I ever met Meneer Viljoen again, I'd tell him how he'd saved my life. I sat on my suitcase thinking about the pickle I was in when Miss Phillips' voice said quite casually, 'Oh, there you are, Tom.' She'd come from behind, and the next thing she said was, 'And the first thing we're going to do is to let you grow your hair!' Then she ran her gloved hand over my shaved head and gave me a truly super big hug. She smelled of roses.

Boy, was she pleased with the quilt! You've never seen anybody so happy about something. I explained to her about the ten shillings and how it had escaped the big fire, but I didn't tell her about Gawie's bum hiding hole when it was still a pound and its other adventures on the way to turning into a quilt. She started to cry and said it was the best present she'd ever received and she gave me another big hug and I wasn't wrong, she definitely smelled of roses and, as far as I knew, she was still a Miss Phillips, maybe there was another shotgun wedding coming up?

'It's still early, Tom, and we have to go to John Orr's to get you some underpants, then I'll take you to the art gallery, and after that we'll have lunch. We'll store your suitcase in a locker here at the station and get it this afternoon, you have to be at the School House at three o'clock.'

'Underpants?' The last time underpants had come up for discussion was with Gawie, who said he'd seen them advertised on a shit square, and they were called Jockeys and were only worn by men who rode racing horses. 'Are we supposed to ride horses at school, Miss?'

'Horses? Why, of course not, Tom. What on earth gave you such a strange idea?'

'Gawie says they're called Jockeys and so must only be worn by people who ride racing horses.'

Miss Phillips laughed and explained that this was only the name of a brand of underpants. I didn't want to ask any further questions because I didn't understand why I had to wear them in the first place. It would be like boys wearing bloomers, and why would you do a thing like that? Thank goodness no-one at The Boys Farm would see me. 'There goes *Voetsek* the *Rooinek* who wears girls bloomers!' Talk about shame. 'Is it compulsory?' I asked.

'You need them when you go to high school because, you see, that's when young boys reach puberty and your body will start to change,' Miss Phillips explained. But it wasn't much of an explanation and I made a note to check puberty in my dictionary when I got my suitcase back. There had already been some talk of body changes at The Boys Farm when Meneer Prinsloo did his lecture about masturbation. Mevrou and old Mevrou Pienaar had to leave the dining room, and then about twice a year we'd get the body-changing talk that led to masturbation, which was known as 'slogging'. With Miss Phillips talking about body changes I thought it must have something to do with slogging because, according to Meneer Prinsloo, that happened when a boy was about thirteen. It was also forbidden, and if you got caught you got six of the best from Meneer Prinsloo with the long cane. It was supposed to be against God's will and if you did it too much you would go blind, but everyone said that was bullshit because lots of the older kids did it a lot and they hadn't gone blind and nobody knew of anyone who ever had. Before Gawie became a *surrogaat* and couldn't afford to be my friend and after one of Meneer Prinsloo's 'boys only' lectures we'd once discussed masturbation.

'You're nearly thirteen, has it happened to you yet?' I'd asked him.

'*Ja*, I'm trying it on,' he giggled.

'But it's supposed to be a sin against God?'

'That's only if you do it a lot, man.'

'How much is a lot?'

'Hundreds of times! Every now and again is okay.'

I don't know how all of a sudden Gawie became such an expert on God's opinion on masturbation, but he did point out that the *Dominee* had never brought it up in church and we only had Meneer Prinsloo's word for it.

'It's going on all over the place, and if God was angry the *Dominee* would have said so,' he assured me.

So I tried it when Gawie showed me how it was done, but I couldn't make it happen yet because I was only eleven.

I wondered if I should tell Miss Phillips that it was still too early for underpants and she mustn't waste her money, but then again, she might ask me why, then how would I answer her question? I couldn't say, 'Because I can't masturbate yet, Miss.' But answer me this, if it sent you blind or was a sin against God, were underpants some sort of protection against blindness or becoming a sinner?

So we got these six pairs of underpants and Miss Phillips said I should wear one pair, and after a while you got used to them and they were quite comfortable. There was this hole in them like a fly in your pants but without buttons, and you didn't have to take them off like a girl's bloomers when you had to take a piss, quite convenient really.

Then it was on to the art gallery that was in a big park with ponds and ducks and trees, with benches for people to sit on, but only if you were a white person, and lots of lawn and flowers, and black nannies sitting together on the grass laughing and talking, and one taking charge of looking after lots of little white kids running around.

Now, of course, I'd seen pictures before but I don't think they were paintings. Some were on the classroom walls at school, and at Doctor Van Heerden's house I think two were real paintings because if you looked closely you could see brush marks. There was also a picture of a wagon being pulled by oxen over a mountain in the Great Trek in the dining room at The Boys Farm, but it didn't have brush marks, and then, of course, there were pictures in books, but nothing like the art gallery. Here was picture after picture, and proper paintings called oils, some were almost as big as a whole wall of a room. Miss Phillips said some of the paintings were worth thousands of pounds, and you could easily see why, they had frames painted gold and were very elaborate. Never mind the paintings, if you just owned the frames you'd have to be very rich. But after a while you couldn't look any more because there were so many, but you could see people painted just about everything that happens in life, and even something called still life, which is mostly bunches of flowers or pieces of fruit. There were even painting of ladies with no clothes on that you were allowed to look at, and see parts you'd never seen before with just a piece of wispy-looking cloth covering their you-know-what, but nothing to cover the top. Miss Phillips must have seen me go red in the face and back away when all of a sudden we came around a corner and there's this big painting of a lady lying on a bed. She's got no clothes on and everything's showing, and the wispy covering you could almost see through and it took no imagination. But you had to wonder how a whole baby could come out of there. Miss Phillips said, 'It's proper art, Tom, you're *supposed* to look at it, the human form is a feast for the eyes.' All I can say is that she was very lucky the *Dominee* wasn't there. But also, if this was proper art then there had to be something that wasn't proper, and I wondered what it might be.

So after the art gallery we had to have lunch. 'What would you like to have for lunch, Tom?' Miss Phillips asked.

First underpants, and now a question I'd never been asked before in my whole life, we'd only been in Johannesburg a few hours and already life was getting very complicated. I only knew two things you could eat at a place where you had to pay and that was a mixed grill and ice-cream on one leg. In Duiwelskrans a mixed grill was a very expensive treat to have, and a person couldn't just come out and say you'd like something like that for a lunch out of the blue when you'd been shopping for underpants.

Miss Phillips must have seen my hesitation because she said, 'How about roast chicken? They do a nice roast chicken with chips at a restaurant near here or perhaps you'd like a curry?'

Remember how I was supposed to go to Doctor Van Heerden's for Christmas and Mevrou said I couldn't because Marie's wedding took up three months' worth of Government Permission Monthly Outings? Well, that was the time I was supposed to taste roast chicken because Marie said the *boere* always gave the good doctor several nice roasting chickens for Christmas lunch. She said that was why he had all the chickens in his backyard, because he got so many he couldn't eat them all and kept the rest for laying eggs. So now, at long last, I was going to taste my first roast chicken. As for having a curry instead, that's a funny thing I forgot to tell you, the Impala Café was still doing mixed grills under the direction of Mr Patel's son and daughter-in-law, but the Sunday lunch *boere* were taking to curry like nobody's business. But I had to choose the chicken because I hadn't waited all my life to taste curry.

All I can say is that it was simply delicious, just as good as people said it was, and it wasn't even Christmas time. Did you know that a chicken has two sorts of meat, brown and white, and the brown is definitely the best tasting?

But at lunch Miss Phillips dropped her bombshell and, of course, it was about her smelling of roses.

'Tom, I have some news,' she began. 'I'm getting engaged to be married.'

'Are you going to have a baby?' I asked.

'Good heavens, no!' she exclaimed, adding in a softer voice, 'Well, not right away.'

Ha! She didn't even know herself. I had learned somewhere that what you said at a time like this was 'Congratulations, and who is the lucky man?' Although I don't know where I would have learned this saying, because with both weddings I'd attended I already knew who the lucky man was. But I didn't with Miss Phillips, so that's what I said to her.

'Thank you, Tom, he's a colonel in the army and on the General Staff, but before the war he was in the Foreign Service. If we win the war, he'll be returning to his old job and I expect we'll have to live in Pretoria and if he gets a posting overseas, who knows.' She reached out and touched my hand. 'Tom, wherever I am or we are, you'll always be in my life.' Then she smiled and brought her other hand across the table so both her hands rested on mine. 'I make you this promise, I will never ever part with my beautiful quilt and it will be on my wedding bed and will remain there until the day I die.' Her nails were painted bright red and were longer than they'd been before, and a person sort of knew she was saying goodbye even if, like her shotgun wedding to come, she didn't know it herself. My life was becoming full of goodbyes and I felt truly sad that I would lose Miss Phillips once the war was over. I don't know how you can tell a person that not only are you grateful for what they've done, but you also love them. It was something I'd never had the opportunity to practise, and so I hoped that when the time finally came to say a real goodbye to her I'd be able to find the right words.

That was my first day away from The Boys Farm, except for one small further thing. Where we had our roast chicken wasn't very far away from Johannesburg Central Station where we had to get my suitcase, and then we were going to the Bishop's College. So we walked and as we were going into the station, on the pavement was a white beggar sitting on a box, and next to him was a little dog, a fox terrier, and my heart gave this terrible jolt. The dog wasn't like Tinker because it had a brown spot on its chest, but it had a face almost the same as Tinker's, and suddenly the loneliness stones began piling up in my chest and I had to fight very hard not to cry. In front of the dog was an old felt hat lying upside down and inside it were a few coins, sixpences and shillings, and the little dog looked up at me as if to say, 'How about a sixpence, Sir?' And if I'd had a sixpence I would have put it in the hat for sure, a person couldn't turn a dog like that down flat. Then I looked closely at the beggar, not that there was much to see, but what you could see wasn't very nice. He wore a dirty black hood over his head with a hole cut out for one eye and another hole for one ear, so this hood only had an eye and an ear sticking out, but his right hand was just a pink stump with no fingers, and it was on the top edge of a neatly painted wooden board hanging around his neck and resting in his lap. The sign read:

Are you game? See my BOMBED FACE! Pay a shilling.
Children *only* sixpence.

The beggar started making grunting and snorting noises, and furiously pointing at us with his stump, getting very excited with the painted board wobbling up and down on his lap as he jerked his head to get our attention.

'Come, Tom,' Miss Phillips said, grabbing me by the elbow. 'The poor man is harmless but not quite right in his head.' I wish I could have asked her for sixpence. Not to look at his face, but to give to his little dog guarding the money.

We got my suitcase and put the underpants inside and left the quilt in the locker, and Miss Phillips said she'd get it on her way back from the school. To my surprise we took a taxi and that was another first thing I'd ever done. Underpants, art gallery, roast chicken and a taxi, all first things on the same day. The taxi had a meter with a handle that looked like a little flag sticking out of the top. When we started out the driver pulled the little flag down and it began to tick and show an amount of money on a black-and-white enamel dial that kept changing by a penny. I kept looking at it because it was getting to be quite a lot by the time we got to the Bishop's College – two shillings and sixpence – because the school was way out in a suburb next to the highway to Pretoria. Miss Phillips must have seen the worried look on my face when she paid and she said, 'I know it's expensive, but it's such a business lugging a heavy suitcase on a bus and from the bus stop through the grounds to the School House.' She was right about that, once we went through the school gates, we travelled past several rugby grounds and a cricket pitch, and along an avenue that was lined with huge old English oak trees, until we eventually got to the boarding house known as School House.

We hopped out of the taxi, which then drove off, and Miss Phillips said she'd catch the bus back to town and she gave me a hug, but not a kiss because there were some boys standing around. She started to walk away, and then stopped and turned. 'Oh, Tom,' she called out. 'I nearly forgot!' She opened her bag. 'It's a book of stamps. I think you should write to Marie and Doctor Van Heerden, and perhaps you can find time to drop me a line every once in a while? I won't see you until the end of term and I'd love to know how you're getting along.' I thanked her and she said, 'The school knows how to contact me if I'm needed.'

I didn't know how to thank Miss Phillips for everything she'd done for me, which was only to change my whole life. How can a person find words to tell someone that? So I took a deep breath and put my arms around her neck and kissed her on the cheek. 'Thank you for everything, Miss Phillips,' I said. I'd received a number of kisses from Marie and Mrs Van Heerden, and even six from Miss Phillips, but this was the first kiss I'd ever given out all by myself. A boy from The Boys Farm can't go giving kisses to people without permission, that's because we are owned by the Government, and other people who get kisses all the time are privately owned with a proper family who kiss because you're allowed to do it as much as you like. But I don't suppose Miss Phillips knew that it was the first kiss I'd ever had the courage to give on my own. I mean, when you got the kisses (I'd already had thirty-two) the lips that touched your skin were soft and wonderful like something coming into you, but when you did the kissing, the feel of your lips on the soft skin of a lady's face was even more wonderful because something that was inside you was going out into Miss Phillips. Something you couldn't say with words.

'Oh, you are such a darling, Tom,' she whispered, and then turned quickly and walked away, and I watched as she got smaller and smaller, in her nice blue and pink floral dress with the sun catching her blonde hair as she walked down the long avenue of English oaks. I remembered I hadn't even asked the name of her going-to-be colonel husband or what a Foreign Service was. When I'd kissed her she still smelled of roses, and I wondered if I'd be invited to the wedding, and whether I should have told her about the baby in her stomach that was a shotgun for sure.

Let me tell you, those stamps were a godsend because without them I wouldn't have been able to write letters. As it was, I had plenty of paper from exercise books but no envelopes. That was easily solved because all you did was find an old envelope and take it apart and then get some scissors and make one with a bit of glue and a page from your exercise book. The post office doesn't say an envelope can't have these blue lines across it. Guys would see me doing this and offer to give me one of their envelopes, but you shouldn't take something if you can't pay it back – that was my new rule for being a loner in front.

Marie wrote to me and told me about Saxby, her new baby, and about how the new owners of the Impala Café had asked if she could come back on Sundays to cook mixed grills because the *boere* were complaining that they were not as good as before.

Dear Tom,

How are you in that posh school? I hope you are well. The sergeant and me miss you a lot and so does Mum and the doctor. Look after yourself. Ag, man, Tom, how can you go wrong with a mixed grill? It's just meat and an egg and some chips, but they can't get it right. I think it's the gravy and I'm not telling them the secret, you add a little speck, but those Indians, they won't use pork, and what's a mixed grill without bacon or a bit of pig fat added to the gravy just before you take the pan off the stove? So on a Sunday, after church when the boere come in for lunch, it looks like I got a job for as long as I want. That's nice because a policeman's salary isn't so much and we can use the extra. Doctor Van Heerden is always stitching up kaffirs on Sundays and the sergeant is writing out charges, so my mother can look after Saxby and I can work at the Impala Café.

My husband now sends up one of the native policemen to get him a curry lunch. Can you believe it? He also wants chapati! But I must say I never thought it possible, but curry is quite nice and has all sorts of different tastes. They also building a Tandoor oven, which is for cooking chicken, but I don't know who can afford chicken for a Sunday lunch. The Patels can't ever say I didn't warn them. Patel says he's going to build a chicken farm at the back of his shop with all these chickens, hundreds and hundreds in a big shed, every one in a little wire cage without a floor, just standing and getting fed crushed mielies. When they fat enough they go straight into the Tandoor oven. In the meantime, the eggs can go to Pietersburg on the train to be sold in the market, maybe even to Pretoria. Eggs on a train and all the trucks shunting when they get to Louis Trichardt to join the proper train. The Charras don't think like us, no commonsense. Chickens in little cages! Everyone knows a chicken has to walk around the place and scratch and bath in the dirt and they won't lay eggs where you want, but only in places they choose themselves. You can make five nice nests all in a row and they'll only choose one and all of them will lay their eggs only in the one nest. Four empty nests and one full of eggs, some even breaking from their chicken feet, that's a chicken for you. A chicken is a very stupid thing, and only a turkey is more stupid. The Dominee had a heart attack, not so serious, and Doctor Van Heerden says next time it's maybe finish and klaar, and he mustn't eat so much meat with fat, and butter on his bread, and he must lose some weight. But the Dominee says he's not the worst in the congregation by far, and eating meat with fat on it and a bit of butter on his bread, how can that harm? He explained that it's what the Boerevolk have been doing for 200 years because they were in the land of Canaan since they left the British in the Cape and went on the Great Trek. As a reward for wandering in the wilderness for longer even than Moses, God gave the Boerevolk the land of milk and honey, and it's God's will they can now eat well because butter is made from milk. And Doctor Van Heerden says, 'That's the trouble around this place, nobody listens to scientific advice.' And the Dominee says, 'Since when is God suddenly a scientist? Why should I believe someone who thinks Charles Darwin is right?' I don't know who is this Charles Darwin, but the doctor says how can you help people who think the world was created in seven days? Wasn't it, Tom? You the clever one. So you can see, nothing has changed around the place, except that the boere are all becoming curry-munchers and buying lots of Lion lager to stop the burning in their mouth. Who would have ever thought such a thing could happen, hey? Miracles will never cease, but still, I guarantee chickens will never lay eggs in wire cages, the straw will just fall out the bottom. Saxby takes up a lot of my time, and that's her crying now so I better end now.

With lots of love from the sergeant, the doctor and my mum. Write soon, we dying to hear from you, you hear? We thinking of you a lot. Remember, don't become all stuck-up at that posh school.

Marie and Saxby van Niekerk xxxx and Tinker, Woof!

Marie wrote every week and I wrote back, and always with the urgent plea to tell me how Tinker was getting on in her new home. But the only mention was always at the very end of her letters with a 'woof' added. Marie loved Tinker and so did Doctor Van Heerden, Mevrou Van Heerden and Sergeant Van Niekerk, and so it was strange that no other mention of her was ever made. Maybe they thought if they spoke about her I'd become homesick, but a person couldn't get homesick for The Boys Farm, although I admit I was terribly homesick for Tinker. Sometimes I'd dream she was sitting on my lap down by the big library rock, and I'd wake up in the middle of the night sobbing. When you are a loner who is busy hiding at the front, to have someone like Tinker in your life, even at long distance and for the school holidays, is what keeps you going. Not getting news about her in Marie's letters was terribly distressing, so I wrote a letter to Doctor Van Heerden begging for news of my little dog.

Then came his reply.

Dear Tom,

It is with some regret that I find myself penning this letter. In my profession we come across a great deal that is a painful part of the human condition, and we must learn to cope, but sometimes we are confronted with circumstances beyond our control, and even a doctor must bow to the will of the Almighty.

I had only read this opening paragraph and all of a sudden my heart was pounding, and the loneliness rocks were tumbling into a cavity in my chest. Tinker! Something was wrong. I didn't want to read on because I knew Doctor Van Heerden was going to tell me something really bad had happened to her. I don't know how I knew he was writing to me about Tinker, I just did and I needed the time to prepare myself. It was almost as if I stopped reading so that what was to come would go away. Of course, that's stupid, but I had to find a place where nobody could see me, like the big rock. I folded up the letter and went outside and climbed up into one of the English oaks, high up into the top branches where I was completely concealed by a thick canopy of leaves.

As you know, the plan was for Tinker to spend a few days in the small containment I erected around her kennel and then, when she'd become accustomed to her new surroundings, we'd give her the run of the place, just like old Helmut. I know she's always been an outside dog, but my dearest wish was that she'd come into the surgery and lie down at my feet. Things never felt quite right after Helmut was gone from under my desk.

Everything went to plan, and Tinker took her food after the password and seemed to be enjoying the love she was receiving from Mevrou Van Heerden and Marie as well as yours truly. Tinker is such a loving little dog. Then, after four days in the enclosure we let her out and within minutes she was gone. We looked everywhere and I finally phoned Sergeant Van Niekerk who immediately said, 'She'll be at the school looking for Tom.' He offered to go and look, and sure enough, Tinker was waiting under a tree at the school gate, so he brought her home. But the next day it was the same, and this time Meneer Van Niekerk brought her home.

Tinker is a clever little dog, and after the third day she would go to school and when school came out and you weren't there she'd come back here. She was eating her food, but I noticed each day she'd eat a little less. Then she stopped altogether, drinking only water, but she still managed to go to school every day until last week, when she was too weak to walk.

Of course I examined her, and have been doing so ever since she started to lose her appetite. I know something about animals, and dogs in particular, and I don't trust Doctor Dyke's judgement. Maybe he's good with cows and chickens, who knows? But Tinker is a different kettle of fish. I took her into the hospital for X-rays but could find nothing, and her little heart seems sound enough. Then I put her on a drip in the surgery where she has been for three days.

Tom, this is a very difficult letter to write, but if Tinker doesn't respond she cannot last more than a week, or a little more at the very most. We had thought to wait before writing, but your letter sounded so distressed I decided it

was unfair to keep you in the dark. I am supposed to heal people, but I simply
don't know what else I can do other than try to keep her alive in the event
that she makes the decision to live. This is the first time I have ever witnessed
an animal that is dying of a broken heart, and it is not a prognosis I fully
understand.

You can be quite sure I will do everything possible to keep her brave
little heart beating. Last night we all went down on our knees, Mevrou Van
Heerden, Marie, Sergeant Van Niekerk and myself, and prayed to God to
save the life of this little creature we know you love so much. This is a gesture
very uncharacteristic of a person like me and I also imagine Jan van Niekerk,
but I want you to know that we did so with the utmost sincerity.

I remain your friend,

Alex van Heerden

It was not a long letter but it took me almost an hour to read because I
just couldn't stop blubbing. When I had recovered sufficiently, I looked
at the envelope to see how long it had taken to get to me and it had been
three days. If Tinker could stay alive for another four or five days then
I could somehow get to her. When she saw me her broken heart would
start to mend, and she would recover. It had been terribly wrong to leave
her, and for what? To become a loner hiding in the front? You can't go
around breaking hearts just because you want to get a nice education
and get away from The Boys Farm. I loved Tinker more than anything
on earth, she was my sun and my moon and all the stars in the sky, and
I had woefully deserted her. I started to cry again, knowing I was a piece
of shit.

The afternoon was drawing to a close and we were all due indoors.
Several guys noticed I'd been crying and said, 'What's the matter, Boots?',
which was what they called me because I was the only kid in school who
wore boots and not shoes. Which was another thing, my boots were my
pride and joy in Duiwelskrans but not at the Bishop's College, here they
all wore shoes. So I had to invent a dose of weak ankles to cover up

my boots. I didn't tell the guys why I'd been crying because a plan was beginning to hatch in my brain, and it was the kind of plan that is best not shared with anyone.

The school was near the highway to Pretoria. In fact, it ran right past the cricket ground and if I walked for an hour or so I could be more or less on the open road. The habit of getting up early had followed me to the Bishop's College and I'd often wandered across the cricket ground to the school fence at five o'clock in the morning to watch the traffic. In a boarding school you don't get out of the grounds and I liked to see the world going by. Especially all the cars and trucks, you've never seen so many makes and, of course, cars and trucks were a bit of a hobby of mine. I'd be back at the School House before the wake-up bell went and we had to take our shower. I don't suppose it was allowed, leaving the dormitory early, but Big Porridge, the night-watchman who spoke Xhosa, a language very close to Zulu, liked me a lot and he wouldn't say anything. Besides, as he explained to me, his job was to prevent anyone coming in and not to prevent anyone going out, and also because a native boy can't tell a *Kleinbaas* where he can and can't go early in the morning.

That night at supper I managed to put four slices of bread in my pocket, and just before evening prep I went through to the house library with a pencil and piece of paper and looked up the map of the Transvaal in the atlas. I reckoned Duiwelskrans was approximately 300 miles from Johannesburg. I wrote down the names of the places you would pass heading back to Duiwelskrans: Pretoria, about 40 miles away, then all the bigger towns: Nylstroom, Potgieterus, Pietersburg, and then off the main highway onto the road to Tzaneen about 70 miles away, and finally Duiwelskrans. If I got lucky and got some long lifts, I could do it in two days, maybe even less. Two slices of bread was enough each day to keep me going. The trick was to get to Pretoria early enough before the big trucks left for the north. I was quite familiar with hitchhiking, though only for very short distances, as sometimes walking back to The Boys Farm from town you'd hitch a ride from a timber truck or a farmer. But I told myself it was still the same thing, whether it was a short or long ride.

When everyone was asleep, I got out of my bed and knelt down beside it. Usually, if I wanted to say a prayer I just did it lying down in bed. I meant no disrespect to God, but kneeling down to say your prayers wasn't what you did. We had evening prayers after prep, always the same prayer and read by the duty master pretty quick so as to get it over with as fast as possible. For a God's-place school they weren't very fussy, and Meneer Prinsloo would have left them in the dust for so-called godliness. The guys probably thought that was enough so you didn't go on your knees later and say your prayers for everyone to see, you just did it lying down, hoping God didn't mind. But now I asked God to keep Tinker's heart from breaking into pieces before I got there to rescue her. I also asked Him to look after me tomorrow. 'I know it's asking two things, which is quite a lot at one time, God, but you must understand this is an emergency and I'll make it up to you later in good deeds.' If it was possible to feel a bit better after speaking to Him, then I did.

I woke up with a start, and could see it was pitch-black outside, even more so than usual, so I knew it was earlier than five o'clock. Then shortly afterwards the clock on the school tower struck four. I got dressed very quietly, leaving my blazer and tie behind because they would be a way of identifying me, and crept downstairs and left the School House. Big Porridge was fast asleep at the front gate as I tippy-toed past him, not using the gravel path but walking on the lawn beside it. I crossed the cricket ground that was wet with dew and it wasn't long before I found myself on the main road to Pretoria. The idea was to walk far enough to leave the suburban houses behind and find myself on the open road, how far this would be I really couldn't say.

I'd been walking for about twenty minutes, not bothering to glance back at the traffic or to use my thumb as I was still in a suburban area. Suddenly there was a screech of tyres and a military jeep stopped right beside me. Two soldiers sat in the front seat of the jeep, and the one on the passenger side called out, 'Are you all right, son?' I nodded, and he said, 'Where are you off to?'

'Pretoria,' I answered.

'Bit early to be on the road, hey?'

'*Ja*, Sir, I was hoping to get a big truck, they always leave early in the morning.'

'Is Pretoria where you live?'

'No, Sir, I live in Duiwelskrans in the Northern Transvaal.'

'That's near Tzaneen,' the driver called. 'I myself come from Pietersburg.'

'You're a long way from home, man,' the first soldier said.

'Three hundred miles,' the driver added. They had these white bands on their caps and on the arm of the one nearest me was a red armband and sewn on it were the words 'Military Police'.

'*Ja*, but I have to go home, it's an emergency, Sir.' I was suddenly very scared. I'd only been gone for about half an hour, and here I am caught by the police.

The soldier must have seen me staring at his armband. 'We're military, don't worry, we can't arrest civilians.' He jerked his head to indicate the back of the jeep. 'Hop in the back, son, we'll get you onto the open road.'

I thanked him and jumped into a khaki canvas seat, and we moved away from the kerb. But at the very next cross street they turned left and drove about a hundred yards and stopped outside a house. The street was quiet and everyone was still asleep in the houses. A dog came to a gate and barked, then stopped.

The soldier in the passenger seat turned around, resting his arm on the back of his canvas seat. 'So what's going on, hey? You running away from home or something?'

'No, Sir, I'm . . . I'm only trying to get back to my home, it's an emergency,' I stammered.

'School? You're running away from school?'

'*Ja*, but only for a bit, I have to go back.'

'This emergency,' the driver asked, 'can you maybe tell us what it is about? Perhaps we can help?'

'A dog,' I answered.

'Your dog?'

'Yes.'

'What about your dog?' the soldier in the passenger seat asked.

'She's dying, Sir . . . of a broken heart. I have to go home to mend it.' A smile appeared on both men's faces and I began to despair. Grown-ups, especially men, wouldn't see a dog's broken heart as important. Animals are just supposed to live and die, and because they've not got souls and can't go to heaven they're not important enough for a boy to run away from school to the rescue. I felt sure they were deciding to take me back to school. Then I had a sudden inspiration, and took Doctor Van Heerden's letter from my shirt pocket and handed it to the passenger soldier.

'What's this?' he asked, taking the envelope.

'Will you read it, please, Sir?'

He turned away from me and began to read, and when he had finished reading he handed it silently to the driver of the jeep, who did the same. The driver turned and handed it back to me, and looked at the other soldier and said, 'We're only going to Pretoria, but you're welcome to come along.' He turned back to me and stretched out his hand. 'My name is Gert,' he flicked his head in the direction of the passenger soldier. 'This is David. Best not give any surnames, hey? And your name is?'

'Tom Fit—'

'No name, no pack drill, Tom!' the passenger soldier cried, cutting me off mid-word.

The driver, Gert, handed me back the letter. 'Welcome aboard, it's a pleasure to be able to help in such a worthy cause.' With this he started the engine and did a U-turn, and in moments we were back on the Pretoria road heading north.

As we approached Pretoria, David unfolded a map and spread it out on his lap, the wind snapping at its edges because the jeep didn't have its top on. Then he folded it and spoke to Gert, who nodded and turned to me, shouting above the wind and noise of the engine. 'We're taking you on the ring-road so you'll miss Pretoria and get on the road to Nylstroom and be on your way.'

On the north highway on the other side of Pretoria we passed a military truck, a ten-tonner with a canvas top. 'This could be your lucky day, Tom,' Gert shouted and put his foot on the accelerator, tooting as we passed the truck. When we'd gone about a quarter of a mile, Gert pulled over to the side of the road, and David jumped out and I saw he was holding a torch, only it had a red light. As the truck approached David waved the torch, and with his free hand he signalled the truck driver to pull over.

'Stay where you are, Tom,' Gert said, jumping out of the jeep. I watched as they both approached the truck driver's door and started talking to him. I couldn't hear what they said. There was another soldier in the front of the truck. Then David walked over to the jeep. 'It's certainly your lucky day, Tom, they're two army transport guys, Cape Coloureds. You'll never guess, man! They're going through to Pietersburg!' My mouth must have fallen open, because David laughed. 'Come, you better get going.'

Talk about prayers being answered! God sure must get up early to go to work. I thanked Gert and David as profusely as I could manage.

'Ag, it's nothing, man, glad to help,' Gert said. He glanced at his watch. 'Here, we better be on our way.'

David shook my hand. 'We told the two transport guys no names, no pack drill, just first names. Don't worry, they won't talk. Good luck, Tom. If anyone can mend a dog's broken heart I reckon you the man.'

'Totsiens, ou maat,' Gert called as I climbed into the front of the big truck and sat beside the other passenger. We waited until the jeep did a U-turn and sped off in the direction of Pretoria.

'Fok, man! I thought for sure I'm going to have a heart attack on the fokken spot. Already the police have found us and we only gone a fokken hour,' the driver exclaimed, switching on the ignition.

The other man laughed, his laughter lost in the sudden roar of the engine. Then as it quietened he offered me his hand. 'Stoffie.'

'Tom,' I replied, shaking his hand.

'This is Dippie,' Stoffie said, jerking his head towards the driver.

'Hello, man!' Dippie said, turning the truck back into the road. 'Those cops. *Fok*, I shit my trousers so much, if they wasn't open at the bottom they would have filled up.'

'They're nice guys,' I volunteered. His trousers were not open at the bottom and were held by gaiters around the top of his boots, but it was still a nice picture in my head.

'You still young, man. When a cop is a nice guy, then Stoffie here is a *fokken* angel with *fokken* wings like a butterfly,' Dippie laughed.

Stoffie turned to me to explain. 'You see this truck? It's supposed to be in the depot getting a service, it needs an oil change and new brake linings, the drivers they ride the clutch all the time, no disrespect for Dippie here, who is an army driver. Me, I'm a mechanic and these guys who call themselves drivers are always riding the clutch. On a jeep the handbrake doesn't last ten minutes, they forget to take it off. Downhill you use the gears to slow down, these guys use the brake.'

'*Fokken* mechanics, always *fokken* complaining,' Dippie laughed. 'It takes lots of energy to change gears in these big *fokken* trucks, the foot is stronger than the arm!'

'We're *boeties* from Cape Town, District Six,' Stoffie explained, 'but we stationed in Pretoria where we also got an auntie. Our auntie has a husband who is a drunk, you understand, which for a Cape Coloured is not a hard thing to be, but now she's sick and tired of being beaten black-and-blue, and she says, *genoeg*, finish and *klaar*! She's got a sister who lives in Pietersburg and has a laundry for washing clothes, mostly sheets and towels from the hospital, and she needs some help, so my auntie calls me on the telephone at the mechanic shop in the camp.' Stoffie held his hand up to his ear with his thumb and little finger extended to indicate a telephone receiver, and his voice went up high and shrieky. '"Stoffie, that you and you brother Dippie?"

'"No, *only* me, Auntie. Dippie, I don't know where he is at the moment."'

"'*Ja*, well you'll be glad to hear I'm leaving that good-for-nothing you can't even call a husband, because how can you call a piece of shit a husband, hey?'"

"'It's about time, Auntie,' I say, because she's always, for the last twenty years, going to leave him.

'She says to me, "No, it's true, this time it's for keeps, you hear! No more black-and-blue from you-know-who." I wait, because I know this is not why she's calling me. "Stoffie, I must have some help to take my furniture to my sister in Pietersburg."

'I tell her, "Auntie, we can't! Dippie and me, we in the army now, military service, we'd like to help, but you understand, we can't just do it."

'Of course Auntie answers back, "*Ag, jong*, never mind military service, what I want now is some auntie service! Stoffie, now you listen to me! I'm not asking, I'm telling. When you were a little baby and your mother got sick with I-can't-tell-you-what because it's not a nice thing for a woman to get from a sailor, who do you think gave you my own milk from my own breasts? I got your cousin Bokkie, who is now in gaol in Port Elizabeth and always never complained when I asked him to do something, on the left one and you I got on the right one, both pulling and sucking like you think maybe this is a big tug-o-war for babies! No wonder I now got razor strops!"'"

Stoffie turned to me and grinned. 'So we take this ten-ton Fargo I'm servicing, and Dippie here gets us a forged vehicle destination pick-up consignment from a coloured guy, who's a second cousin twice removed like everyone else in District Six. Us coloured guys we got to stick together because we very far from home. We put some jerry cans of petrol in the back, and from another second cousin twice removed who works in the colonel's office we get a forged forty-eight-hour leave pass. Only this morning, when it's still dark, we leave the camp and go and get my auntie's furniture. Her husband, who a person has to refuse to call uncle, is fast asleep and snoring, just lying there on the planks of the front *stoep*, with the moon shining on his bald head. He's so drunk he can't get his key in the lock so the keys are lying where he threw them away on the front path. My auntie opens the door and says, "Don't step on him because you'll get a mess on your boots that smells to the high heavens and you got to wash it off later under the tap!" Then we only half an hour out of Pretoria and we stopped by the military police! Can you see now how it's no problem for a man to fill up his trousers with the creamy brown already digested, Tom?'

'*Fok!* You can say that again, brother!' Dippie cried from behind the steering wheel.

During the course of the day I was to learn that Dippie did the swearing and Stoffie did all the explaining, although in the process taking great care not to use a single expletive.

We stopped for breakfast just outside Nylstroom, pulling into a side road. 'We got a primus in the back and we'll make some coffee and have some breakfast, but first we got another surprise.' Stoffie indicated that I should follow him to the back of the truck, and when he let down the tailgate there was the surprise. Sitting in this big old lounge chair was a very small lady. 'Auntie, we stopping for some breakfast,' Stoffie announced, adding, 'This is Tom, he's coming with us.'

'*Here, jong,* just in time, I'm telling you! All this jogging and bouncing, and for the last hour I need to go to the lavatory! Hello, Tom. Quick, Stoffie, or we going to have a terrible accident in our bloomers, you hear.' By this time Auntie had left the chair and was standing on the tailgate, and Stoffie picked her up and put her on the ground. 'Some paper! Give me some paper!' the tiny, dark-skinned woman yelled.

Stoffie's hands started to tap all over his khaki tunic, and then his back pockets, then back to the top pocket of his tunic and he came up with nothing. At that moment Dippie came around to the back of the truck. 'Paper! Auntie has to do number two!' Stoffie yelled.

Dippie did the same with his hands, but almost immediately came up with a piece of paper that was snatched from his hands by the desperate auntie. 'More! This is not big enough, Dippie!' she cried. Dippie found another piece of paper and handed it to her, and she went scuttling off like a small rodent into the nearby bushes.

Then Dippie started frantically patting his pockets again. '*Fok!*' he yelled.

This particular '*fok*' had a definitely desperate sound.

'What now, man?' Stoffie asked.

'Auntie's wiping her arse on the forty-eight-hour leave passes and the vehicle destination pick-up consignment!'

I couldn't help myself and I started to giggle, then it was on for one and all, talk about laugh! Stoffie was thumping the side of the truck, and Dippie was bent over double and we're all howling with laughter when Auntie comes out of the bushes and asks, 'What's the *lekker* joke, boys?'

So we try to stop laughing and Stoffie, who is the serious brother, says, 'Auntie, come show me where you did your business, we got to get back the paper!' And now Dippie fell on the ground holding his stomach, rolling around, and I've got tears running down my face and my tummy is hurting from laughing. Stoffie had his forehead pressed against the side of the truck again, and his back was shaking, and he was beating the side of it with his flat hand – bang, bang, bang. 'Oh, ahh, oow, ha, ha, ha, ha, haw, haw, haw! Oh, shit! Ha, ha, ha, haw, haw, haw!' It was the only time he said a swear word all day.

After Stoffie and Auntie came back, Stoffie explained it wasn't too bad. They'd found a small stream and the 'you know what' was all gone, but the ink with their names and forged signatures on the official forms were washed away as well. But the papers would dry on the dashboard on the way to Pietersburg, and if you looked carefully you could maybe see where the writing originally was. When the paper dried it could be better. I was beginning to wonder what it was in my life that made shit paper play such a big part in it.

Then Auntie lit the primus stove and she brought out a big basket and we had eggs and sausage and bread and butter and she made coffee with Nestlé condensed milk in it and the whole thing was simply delicious, the best there could be.

We stopped again for lunch. This time it was cold meat and bread and hard-boiled eggs and cold roast potato and milk tart and *koeksisters* and more coffee with condensed milk, all stuff from Auntie's big basket.

After lunch we were riding along, and so far Stoffie and Dippie hadn't asked me any questions about why I was going home. I mean, it's not every day you see an eleven, almost twelve-year-old boy hitchhiking all over the place, yet they'd kept their curiosity to themselves. I decided that while I would have liked to keep the reason to myself, they had shared everything about themselves and it was only fair that they also knew something about me.

'Stoffie, you and Dippie haven't asked why I'm going home all the way from Johannesburg?'

Stoffie seemed to be thinking for a moment. '*Ja*, in life everybody has a story but they don't always want to tell it. It's you business, Tom, you don't have to tell it.'

I reached into my shirt pocket and fished out Doctor Van Heerden's letter and held it out to Stoffie. 'The reason is in there,' I announced.

'What's this?' Stoffie asked, drawing back slightly, but not taking the envelope I held out to him.

'A letter, it says why I'm going home, will you read it?'

Stoffie hesitated. 'Letters are very private things, Tom.'

'*Ja*, but I'd like you to read it,' I insisted.

'*Fok*, we can't read, man,' Dippie suddenly said. 'Until the army, we both *fokken* juvenile delinquents!'

'We can only write our names,' Stoffie said quietly. 'In the Boys Reformatory we learned our trade, him driving trucks, me a mechanic. We did it so we could steal cars better, but we didn't do much book learning.'

I was taken aback, and in an attempt to recover, asked, 'Can I read it to you?'

'*Ja*, man, we'd like that. I admit we a bit curious to know.' Stoffie grinned, trying to put me at ease. 'You see, Dippie and me, we experts at running away, man.'

I read out Doctor Van Heerden's letter and when I'd finished it, I looked up to see that Stoffie was crying and Dippie suddenly pulled the truck to a halt at the side of the road. 'Fok!' he said, his head was turned away from me and he was looking out of the side window.

After about four hours on the road and half an hour after leaving Potgietersrus we hit a police roadblock. Dippie saw it first. 'Police!' he cried out.

'Quick man, Tom, get under the dashboard,' Stoffie commanded. There was plenty of room in that big Fargo and all I had to do was to sit hugging my knees. I was suddenly very frightened. I heard Stoffie say, 'There's four cars and a lorry stopped, and they searching the cars!'

'Fok!' Dippie cried.

But then a miracle happened. As we began to slow down, we suddenly picked up speed. 'Hey, man, he's waving us through!' Stoffie shouted happily.

There must be a definite difference when you take the trouble to be a bed-kneeling boy when you pray to God, because His hand was definitely guiding me. First Gert and David in the jeep, then finding Dippie, Stoffie and Auntie in the army truck, now this narrow escape from the police. In church the Dominee would sometimes say, 'If you got faith in God, then He's going to have faith in you. With God, you understand, it's not only a one-way street.' Although, in this case, I was hoping for it to be a one-way road, with me being the one to get to the end safely.

Ten minutes or so after leaving the roadblock, Stoffie told Dippie to pull over. 'We don't know if that's the last roadblock, Tom, so I think you better get in the back with Auntie. If we is stopped, then hide behind some furniture or get in the wardrobe at the back and let Auntie do the talking. She was on the game when she was young and beautiful, and knows more about talking to the police than anyone in South Africa, you hear. Take it from me, when she's finished talking their ears will want to go on a holiday from listening.'

I couldn't help wondering what sort of a game Auntie played when she was young and beautiful. It must have been a pretty rough sort of sport, like wrestling or boxing, because she was not very pretty any more. But, of course, I knew women can't wrestle or box, so it was a mystery. Perhaps, I decided, when I got in the back with her she might tell me. There were two of these big lounge chairs, and Stoffie and Dippie arranged them side by side in the back of the truck. Auntie seemed pleased. 'It's nice to have some company, Tom. Sitting here alone, I'm nearly breaking a world record for *stom* and I'm not a person that doesn't like to talk.'

Lucky I was a good listener because she started up and never let off. Talk about talking the hind leg off a donkey! She told me her whole life story in District Six in Cape Town where her people had lived for 300 years. 'Maybe, who knows, even the same street,' she said. 'In the Cape it's not like up here, you understand? Down there a coloured person is not a black and not also a white man. But everyone knows some hanky-panky has been going on a long time now, so we in the middle, not the one and not the other, also in the olden times some Malay thrown in, so in the Cape we got some respect, you hear. Up here in Pretoria they ignorant *boeremense*, and they show no respect for a person. When you on the game you soon learn it's the *boere* who always wanting it. They think because we brown and not black and we don't have peppercorn hair that it's not such a big sin to play with a coloured woman.'

Try as I might I couldn't guess what sort of game involved policemen as referees and was obviously played by coloured women mostly against the *boere*. How could a game be a sin? The *Dominee* said gambling was a sin, maybe it was some sort of gambling? If I could have got a word in sideways, I would have asked her to explain the rules of this mysterious game. But then she got onto the topic of Frankie Bezuidenhout, who turned out to be the person lying on the front *stoep* with the moon shining on his bald head. He was the subject that took us all the way to Pietersburg, and not once did Auntie have a good thing to say about him. 'Ag, Tom, my sister Elsie says that washing the sheets and towels from the hospital is not always nice work. "Ha!" I said to her. "Never you mind that, Sissie! With Frankie you don't need a hospital! You can't tell me about dirty towels and sheets and the mess that comes from inside a drunk! This time it's not my own blood, you hear? No more black-and-blue!'" She turned to me and placed her forefinger on her nose and pushed, and it practically disappeared into the soft flesh of her face. 'Once it was straight and I was beautiful, now it's mashed potato!'

I must admit that while I think I'm a good listener, there was a point, like the paintings in the art gallery, when you can't take in any more. I knew we were getting closer and closer to Tinker, and my mind became totally occupied with getting to her before her little heart finally broke. So I didn't hear some of the stuff about Frankie Bezuidenhout, which was more than you could find in a book about one person. One thing was for sure, I wouldn't have liked to be married to him, but on the other hand, maybe he did some of his black-and-blues just to shut Auntie up. Talk about a talking machine!

It was getting late in the afternoon when we reached the outskirts of Pietersburg and Dippie pulled over to the edge of the road. Stoffie came to the back of the truck. 'Tom, we safe now, man, come sit in the front again, we wondering where you living in Pietersburg so you will show us, hey?'

'Stoffie, can you drop me at the turn-off to Tzaneen?' I asked.

'Tzaneen? You don't live in Pietersburg?'

'No, in Duiwelskrans.'

'How far is that?'

'About sixty miles.'

Stoffie was somewhat taken aback.

'Don't worry, I can get a lift,' I assured him. 'There's plenty of trucks on that road, farmers who come here to shop,' I half lied, anxious to impress him.

'Let me talk to Dippie a moment, Tom,' he said, and walked back to the driver's side of the truck. He returned in a few moments. 'We'll take

Auntie to Auntie Elsie's house, unload the furniture and then take you home, Tom.'

'No, no! Please, Stoffie,' I begged. 'I can get a lift, I promise. You've already done enough.'

'Ag, *jong*, it's only sixty miles, about two hours, that's not far, man,' he said.

'And two hours back to Pietersburg, and then back to Pretoria.'

'No, man, don't worry, we'll take a mattress and put it in the back of the truck and sleep at Auntie Elsie's house and go back tomorrow.'

'Are you sure?' I asked again.

'*Ja*, no trouble, man.' He paused, then said, 'Tom, can you do running writing?'

'*Ja*, of course.'

'Dippie and me, we need a favour?'

'What is it?' I said, hoping it might be something I could do to repay their kindness.

'Have you got a fountain pen?'

My heart sank. 'No.'

In the distance, as there seemed always to be on the outskirts of any town, there was an Indian shop. I pointed towards it. 'There's an Indian shop, we can borrow a pen from there. What must I write for you?'

Stoffie pointed to the forty-eight-hour leave pass and the vehicle destination pick-up consignment that were now dry, the papers glued to the dashboard from the water drying. 'The ink has washed away, can you write it all out again for us, also make up some signatures, we'll give you the names.'

'Give me the papers, I'll take them into the shop.' But it soon became apparent that the papers were stuck to the dashboard and wouldn't separate without tearing.

'It's okay, man, as long as we got them in the truck. Can you write on them stuck down, Tom?'

'*Ja*, I think so.'

———

The Indian turned out to be an Indian wife who looked doubtful when we asked if we could borrow a fountain pen for a few minutes.

'Why do you want it?' she asked suspiciously.

I'd already learned that the red dot on her forehead meant she was married. 'We have some documents in the lorry, army documents, we have to fill in please, Mevrou,' I explained, smiling at her.

She gave this little smile, and I knew she was smelling a rat. 'I am thinking also you are too young to be in the army.'

'No, not me, it's for the two soldiers outside.'

She'd heard enough and went into a back room that was separated by strings of beads hanging down to keep flies and other insects out. I wasn't sure what to do. If I'd been a grown-up and white she wouldn't have dared to leave me standing like that, but she could see I was still a young boy and it didn't matter. Then the hanging beads parted with a rattle and a male Indian appeared. 'We are wanting now a fountain pen. I have a very, very nice fountain pen, Waterman, solid-gold nib, you are wanting to buy? I give you a very, very good pre-war price.'

'No, Meneer,' I pointed to the fountain pen clipped to his shirt pocket, 'I just want to borrow yours for a few minutes to sign some important army papers for the two soldiers outside.'

'Papers? What papers? Important papers you are signing for the army? Bring in so we can see them.'

'I can't, the papers can't leave the truck,' I explained.

'You are wanting my fountain pen for confidential documents? My goodness gracious me, we don't want trouble, you hear?' He turned to his wife and shrugged. 'How can I lend my Parker 51 gold nib and gold-cap fountain pen for the signing of secret war documents? I am telling you, definitely no.'

'Go away! Go, please!' his wife said with a sweep of her arm. 'We are not wanting trouble.'

At that moment Stoffie walked into the shop. 'Here, man, what's going on? We can hear the gentleman shouting from outside.'

I'd never heard an Indian called a gentleman before, but from the way Stoffie said the word I'm not sure it was the same meaning as usual. 'He won't lend his fountain pen to us.'

A nice smile appeared on Stoffie's face. 'I see,' was all he said, and then took a step closer to the Indian, looking him directly in the eye. The Indian immediately clasped his hands over his pocket to conceal the fountain pen. Stoffie wasn't a big man, only slightly taller than the shopkeeper. Now he simply stuck out his hand, waiting for the pen to be placed in it. 'Please,' Stoffie said politely, the smile still on his face and his eyes still locked on the Indian man's face. Slowly the Indian man's hand lifted from his shirt pocket, then the other followed, then he plucked the pen from his pocket and placed it on Stoffie's outstretched palm. 'Thank you,' Stoffie said. 'If you send your wife outside in five minutes she can get it back when we finished using it, you hear?'

We both turned to return to the truck, and as we were going out of the shop the Indian shouted, 'India also is fighting the war on our side! We are not being the traitor and we are also liking Winston Churchill very, very much!'

I was rather proud of my handwriting. I'll say this for Duiwelskrans school, we all had to do running writing in copperplate and they were very strict, so my handwriting didn't look like it was written by only a nearly twelve-year-old kid.

I returned the fountain pen to the shopkeeper and thanked him.

'My goodness gracious me, what is happening now?' he said accepting the pen.

'Honesty is the best policy, Meneer,' I replied haughtily, and giving him a cheeky smile asked, 'How about a *bansella*?'

'*Bansella*! Who is giving a Parker 51 fountain pen, you or me?'

'*Ja*, you right, *you* gave it, but I *gave* it back!'

The shopkeeper shook his head and sighed, then reached into a glass jar and gave me a green sucker. I didn't have the courage to ask him to exchange it for a red one.

We got going again, the two documents were still stuck to the dashboard but now neatly signed with the two pretend signatures of Captain Rigby and Lieutenant Crosby. I asked Stoffie what he would have done if the Indian had refused to give him the pen.

'Ag, *jong*, easy man, I would have sent Auntie in to get it,' he replied, and both brothers laughed.

We spent the next hour unloading Auntie's furniture. Her sister Elsie lived on the outskirts of the whites section of Pietersburg and just before you came to the native location. The house was in a dusty street full of scrawny chickens and stray, mangy-looking dogs that had long tails that never rose above the curve of their hind legs. The chickens squawked, and the dogs snapped and growled a lot amongst themselves. The house was small, and I wondered how all of Auntie's furniture would fit in. Elsie's house was in what was known as the coloured section. She had this old rusty *bakkie* parked in the front garden with a sign painted on one of its doors in faded letters: 'TANTE ELSIE'S LAUNDRY'. The front fence was half broken down with some palings standing and others lying flat in the tall grass. Inside the house it was very clean and smelled of wax polish, and outside at the back the lavatory smelled of Jeyes Fluid, but she had a nice vegetable garden. She also had shit squares nearly as good as the ones Gawie made. One read, 'Allies cross the Rhine'.

It was nearly six o'clock in the evening before we left, and Auntie came out to say a second goodbye because we'd already done it in the house. She gave me a kiss, and even for me she had to stand on tiptoe. 'When you grow up, take my advice, don't marry pretty, marry clever. Pretty gets ugly, clever stays clever.' She stood back and looked at me carefully, then smiled approvingly. '*Ja*, Tom, I can see you not the black-and-blue type.'

It was almost eight o'clock when we finally arrived at Doctor Van Heerden's house. It was just getting dark, and the fireflies were out dancing under the deep shadows cast by the mango trees, green phosphorescent pricks of light in the approaching darkness. I asked Dippie and Stoffie to come in, assuring them that they'd be welcome, but you could see that they'd already sniffed the nature of the town.

'No thanks, Tom, this is no place for an army truck, you hear? We got to get going, man.'

'Some coffee, maybe?' I asked.

'No, man, really, we got to kick the dust,' Stoffie insisted.

'*Fok!*' Dippie suddenly exclaimed. 'Look over there!' Our eyes followed to where he was pointing at Sergeant Van Niekerk's police van parked at the side of the house.

'Oh, it's nothing,' I laughed. 'It's only Sergeant Van Niekerk. He is my friend.'

'A policeman is never a nothing,' Stoffie said quietly. 'We got to go, Tom.'

I shook their hands and thanked them, and then they were gone. I watched until the rear lights disappeared in the distance before walking around the house to the back so that I could enter through the kitchen, like I always did. The maid was washing the supper dishes as I walked in and greeted her. She looked shocked to see me, as if she'd suddenly seen a ghost, and she brought her hands up to her mouth and you could see the white soapsuds popping on the back of her dark hands. '*Baas* Tom!' she exclaimed. 'It is you!'

'Katrina, can you please tell the missus I'm here?' I asked.

Katrina grabbed a dishcloth and hurriedly dried her hands, and then went running into the rest of the house. '*Missus! Missus! Kom gou!*', which means 'Madam! Madam! Come quickly!' Moments later the kitchen filled with all the people I loved. Marie came first, took one look at me and burst into tears, grabbed me and pulled me to her bosom.

'Thank God! Oh, thank God!' she bawled.

Then Mevrou Van Heerden started to cry, and Doctor Van Heerden,

Sergeant Van Niekerk and Meneer Van Niekerk all surrounded me. I disengaged myself gently from Marie, and still sobbing Mevrou Van Heerden kissed me and the three men shook my hand, everyone was talking at the same time and saying things you couldn't hear all at once.

Then Sergeant Van Niekerk put his hand on my shoulder and said, 'Tom Fitzsaxby, you under arrest.' Everyone laughed and he turned to his brother. 'You owe me five bob, I told you it would take more than a few police roadblocks to stop Tom getting here.' He squeezed my shoulder. 'This boy never gives up.' It was a nice compliment and I would have to tell him later how easy it had been so he didn't think nice things about me that I didn't deserve.

'You're the first boy from Duiwelskrans school to become a general alert on the wireless all over the Transvaal,' Meneer Van Niekerk said.

'Tom, we know why you've come,' Doctor Van Heerden said.

'Tinker?' I asked anxiously.

He nodded. 'She's still alive.'

'I've come to mend her broken heart,' I said, trying to hold back my tears.

Doctor Van Heerden touched me lightly. 'Tom, Tinker is a very sick little dog, you mustn't —'

'I can make her better!' I sobbed. 'When she sees me her heart won't break any more.'

There was silence and I couldn't see anyone because of my tears.

'Come, Tom, she's in the surgery.' I felt Doctor Van Heerden take my hand and lead me out of the kitchen. I stopped at the door, and wiping my eyes with the back of my hand turned and said, 'Sorry.' I saw that Marie and Mevrou Van Heerden and Katrina were all weeping silently.

Tinker lay on a big cushion covered with a towel, and next to her was a stand that held a rubber bag and a rubber tube that went from the bag into her little pink tummy. She was so thin her hipbones stuck out, and her tiny rib cage showed through her fur. I dropped to my knees sobbing and started to stroke her and she gave this tiny little whimper so I knew she knew it was me, that I'd come back. 'I'm sorry, I'm so sorry, please forgive me,' I sobbed. 'If you get better I promise I'll never leave you again.' I just couldn't stop crying and crying, and then I felt her tongue licking my hand.

'You stay with her, Tom. You may put her on your lap. Here, let me help you,' Doctor Van Heerden said gently. He sat me on the floor, making sure my back was against the wall, and put the cushion with Tinker on it and the drip still in her onto my lap. 'I'll call by later,' he said.

So I sat there and talked to Tinker. I told her how I'd found her floating in the stream in the wet sack, the smallest but still alive because she was the bravest from the very beginning. I said how I'd squeezed the water out of her and dried her in the sun. Then we talked about Mattress and the big black-and-white sow and Mattress's platform feet. How he always said she was a lioness, and how she'd lived in a paraffin tin under the big rock and had grown up to be the world champion ratter. I told her about all the other times we'd talked at the big rock, and what had happened to her with Fonnie du Preez and Pissy that time they tried to choke her. Then about the big fire, and even the time she got to taste chicken, the carcass and bones of Piet Retief, even before anyone at The Boys Farm themselves knew how chicken tasted. I reminded her of the story of the Easter bonnet feathers she'd helped me to get for Miss Phillips, and the pound up Gawie's bum and the great day of our visit to the waterfall in the high mountains. And then, because it had been a long day and I hadn't meant to do it on purpose, I must have fallen asleep. When I woke up it was dawn and a rooster was crowing in the backyard, and both my hands were resting on Tinker, and she was dead. Her heart had been too badly broken to be able to mend.

BOOK
TWO

CHAPTER THIRTEEN

Love Thine Enemy

IT SEEMS TO ME that a child's past can be one of two things: a generally pleasant experience roughly summed up as childhood; or a graveyard of past happenings, the fatal emotional accidents that occur in the process of growing up without love. Too many emotional tombstones existed for me in Duiwelskrans, and the road to this cemetery of the psyche was paved with loneliness stones. Not only the murder of Mattress and the death of Tinker, but also the days, months and years of accumulated unhappiness. Mevrou's acerbic voice constantly undermining my fragile confidence. Waking up to a thousand mornings of half-jack misery, and with it the greedy presence of the air-scything *sjambok*. Meneer Prinsloo's windmilling arms grinding out self-righteousness, hypocrisy, hurtfulness and constant God-bothering. The incident at the big rock where Fonnie du Preez and Pissy Vermaak were involved. The prevailing presence of the *Dominee's* vitriolic hatred of my kind that seemed contained in the air I breathed. The book-burning inspired by his fist-thumping-pulpit and right-wing dogma. Doctor Dyke's disregard for our pain and the sense of worthlessness his horse pliers provoked in us as he mutilated our laughter. The endless humiliations of *Rooinek* and *Voetsek* and the constant need to lie in order to survive. Once my soul had escaped this umbrageous mountain town it couldn't ever return.

Anyway, enough of that. I'd been a general alert on the wireless and now all the papers wanted the story of the boy and his dog. It was even printed in *Die Vaderland*, so maybe one of the kids at The Boys Farm would be about to wipe his bum and there we'd be, Tinker and me, being famous on a shit square.

Sergeant Van Niekerk took me up the high mountains to the waterfall, where we buried Tinker under the giant tree. The picnic had only been one day in her life but it was the best one. At first I thought about burying her under the big rock, but that held too many sad memories. If Tinker couldn't go to heaven then she shouldn't be buried among the whitethorn with the sad memories, or near people that were not always nice. The waterfall, white and clean and eternal, was as good a place as heaven could possibly be. If she wanted to bark, then the *kloofs* and *kranses*, the deep valleys, canyons and high buttresses, would carry the echo for miles and miles, and the herd boys would swear among themselves that it was the roar of the lioness Mattress always claimed her to be.

Anyway, when it all came out in the papers, Miss Phillips, who had a bit of Auntie in her when it came to persuading people, went to see the headmaster. He ummed and ahhhed a bit, but with a letter added from Meneer Van Niekerk, he eventually agreed I could come back. So that's how I got my first bit of education.

The war came to an end in early May and Miss Phillips married her colonel and became Mrs Hammond. He was once again a nobody, but quite a high-up nobody because he was in the diplomatic service. He was an official in a consulate and they sent him to Australia, to the capital Canberra, a city designed by a man called Burley Griffin that goes around in circles. So I couldn't see her any more, and it was back to writing letters to a person I would always truly love.

Before I leave school and go to university, there's something I have to tell you about. It's the school holidays. Because I had no money and things wear out, like shirts and shoes and other bits and pieces, such as, believe it or not, underpants, or when I had to get into long trousers or save up for a new blazer, the school holidays were the time I had to find a job to pay for them.

Now just after the war it wasn't easy to get a job with all the soldiers returning and needing work. When you're only thirteen years old it was even harder to get temporary employment. When the first school holiday came along, Doctor Van Heerden applied successfully to the Government for me to stay with them rather than to return to The Boys Farm and he sent me my rail fare to return to Duiwelskrans. I have to say they couldn't have been nicer to me, and Marie and Sergeant Van Niekerk and his headmaster brother Meneer Van Niekerk as well. They were the salt of the earth and the pillars of my limited wisdom and I will always love them. I returned three times during my twelfth year because that was when I had no real necessities. So, apart from having no money I was able to survive the first year at the Bishop's College.

I knew these good people would look after me, but I just couldn't go back to Duiwelskrans. Each of the holidays spent in that high mountain town alienated me further and, besides, I had always depended on others, and it was time I took care of myself. Sergeant Van Niekerk and Marie, Doctor and Mevrou Van Heerden and the headmaster and his wife would remain my friends for life and I wrote to them regularly thereafter, but I was almost thirteen and practically grown up. If I was going to make it on my own in life then the sooner I found work and a place to stay during the school holidays, the better.

I found my first job in the 'situations vacant' column of *The Rand Daily Mail*. It was for the Born-again Christian Missionary Society situated upstairs in a smelly and untidy arcade off Pritchard Street, Johannesburg. It was a place where unsmiling European migrants with thick accents and a babble of various languages began their precarious and fearful middle-aged lives all over again. A small, crooked concrete burrow jammed between the smooth-walled skyscrapers where optimism had long since been abandoned and hope was a dirty word.

The office of the Born-again Christian Missionary Society was, by the standards of its neighbours, a shining example of business virtue, an oasis of light in a disconsolate semi-dark desert of forsaken dreams. It was contained in three offices on the first floor, each lit with two central strips of neon that extended the width of the ceiling to produce an incandescent light almost blinding to the eye. The centre room, leading from the rickety balcony and stairs, contained a Christian bookshop with the injunction above the door, 'Come in and browse for Christ' and directly below it in smaller letters, 'Prop. Pastor Jellicoe Smellie'.

From either side of the interior of the bookshop a door led into two small offices. The office on the left, untidy and impossibly cluttered, contained two desks, each serviced by a stiff bentwood kitchen chair. The second office was the home of a small offset printing press set amid an equally untidy landscape of paper stacked on the floor and shelves filled with printing clutter. When the printing press was in operation it emitted a mixture of clanking, humming, hissing and slapping sounds. To anyone passing through the arcade below, it was as if this cacophony was responsible for manufacturing the sharp blue neon light pumping into the general gloom below.

The tiny advertisement in the 'situations vacant' column read: 'Energetic b.a. Christian required, must have excellent handwriting, apply personally, 9 a.m to 6 p.m., no age limit.' This was followed by the address in the city. With my Boys Farm and *Dominee* background, my passing for a born-again Christian was a cinch. While I expected the 'no age limit' meant they might accept an elderly person, I convinced myself that this also extended to the young, providing that I could prove myself a sufficiently worthy candidate.

Moreover, I knew myself to have a terrific hand, as this was one of the very few qualities about me that was constantly admired. The education dished out at the Duiwelskrans school was a fairly hit-or-miss affair, but the highest standards of handwriting were rigidly inculcated. I guess the reasoning behind this was that a *domkop* with seriously immaculate handwriting would not as easily give away his innate stupidity. In the handwriting department I'd have to be an outstanding candidate for the job, and besides, I had boundless energy.

Fake the born-again Christian, demonstrate the handwriting and evidence the energy, and all I possibly had against me was my age. I arrived at the Born-again Christian Missionary Society believing I was in with half a chance

Pastor Jellicoe Smellie appeared to be quite old, perhaps sixty. He was tall, bald and dried out. His skin was the colour of parchment, with the exception being his nose – it was sharp and heavily veined. His pale grey eyes were slightly rheumy, pink-edged like those of a white rabbit, and he wore rimless spectacles, two squares of heavy glass on either side of his purple nose. He had Albert Einstein hair and was dressed in a once-white linen suit that was badly ink-stained, and it hung untidily from his six-foot-something frame. This general sense of untidiness was refuted by his highly polished black boots, with the toe-cap of the right boot removed. He wore brown cotton socks from which the toe of his right foot protruded at a right angle from the sock to point directly at the shiny left boot. This was because either it had broken through the restraints of the cotton, or a deliberate hole had been created for it to emerge. This misplaced big toe had the peculiar effect of throwing him slightly off-balance so that he leaned permanently to the right, a bit like the Tower of Pisa.

'Yes, what do you want, boy?' he asked, and because of the angle of his body, the one pale grey eye looking down at me through the square prisms looked larger and more pink-rimmed than the other.

'I've come about the situation vacant, Sir. The one in *The Rand Daily Mail*,' I said, holding out the postage-stamp-sized piece of newsprint I'd cut from the paper.

'Oh no, definitely not, far too young, far too young, definitely not, definitely not!'

'Can I show you my handwriting, Sir?'

'No, no, definitely not, definitely not! Simply atrocious, your generation, atrocious, atrocious!'

I had prepared a page from an exercise book with a carefully crafted copy of Alfred Lord Tennyson's poem 'The Charge of the Light Brigade'. If I say so myself, it looked very good, every swirl identical, all the i's and the t's carefully dotted and crossed, and the angle of the copperplate script leaning at about the same angle as Jellicoe Smellie was. I reached into my shirt pocket and handed the folded page to him. 'Can you take a look please, Sir?' I persisted.

He snatched the folded paper from my grasp just as a customer walked in, and Pastor Jellicoe Smellie left me and walked over to the customer with a decided limp. I had no idea a toe taking a left-hand turn could so affect a person's walk. 'Praise the Lord, can I help you, my sister in Christ?' he asked the customer.

The customer, a woman about the age of Miss Phillips, took one look at the tall, leaning man with the fly-away steel-grey hair, pink eyes and purple nose, and turned and fled without a word, her footsteps echoing down the rickety stairs to the level of the arcade.

'Hmmph! Definitely not, definitely not a born-again Christian. Hallelujah, praise His precious name,' Jellicoe Smellie said, as if talking to himself. He turned to pass through to the little office leading from the book room. 'What are you doing here, boy?' he said, surprised to see me still there.

I pointed to the folded piece of paper in his hand. 'You have my piece of paper, Sir. You haven't looked at it.'

He looked down as if surprised to find he was still holding the folded page. 'Umph! Definitely not, definitely not,' he said, opening it, and then he looked surprised, his rheumy pink-rimmed eyes widening. 'Can you do fifty an hour?'

'Fifty . . . an hour?' I asked, bewildered.

'Are you deaf, boy? I said fifty an hour – envelopes, addresses – no, I don't think so, definitely not, definitely not!' he said, still staring at the poem in his hand.

I had no idea whether I could address fifty envelopes in an hour but I needed the job badly. 'I think so, Sir.'

'A born-again Christian? Taken Christ into your life, into your life?'

'Yes, Sir, definitely, definitely!' His speech mannerism was beginning to affect me.

'Washed in the blood of the lamb?'

I was on solid ground here. The *Dominee* had said we needed to be washed in the blood of the lamb, although I'm not so sure he'd intended to include me together with the *volk*. 'Oh yes, Sir!'

'Praise the Lord, praise His precious name! Boys' wages, one pound ten a week, not a penny more, don't argue, I can't be persuaded, definitely not, definitely not!' He glared down at me as if he expected me to object. 'Own fountain pen?'

'No, Sir.'

'One pound and eight shillings a week, two shillings a week to hire my fountain pen, fountain pen!'

I did a quick calculation. I needed one shilling and sixpence to eat once a day. Should I find weekly lodgings, say a bed and breakfast for ten shillings, that left seven and sixpence a week I could save. I'd set my target for the month of the school holidays at two pounds saved, and what Jellicoe Smellie was offering me was ten shillings short.

'Sir, I could work during my lunch hour if you don't charge me for the fountain pen?' I offered hopefully.

His pale, papery-looking hand came up and slapped hard against his breast pocket concealing his fountain pen. For a moment the impact of his hand on his chest looked as if it might make him teeter out of control and crash to the floor. 'Definitely not, definitely not! Can't, can't! What lunch hour?' he exclaimed.

I had nowhere to stay that night and while I'd scoffed-up during the last meal at school and would be okay until the morning, I knew I'd soon be hungry. I'd naively convinced myself I'd get the job and get down to work immediately, and at the end of each day I'd be paid and be able to eat at night. Now this first opportunity to be solvent was about to slip through my fingers. I knew this sanctimonious old bastard was cheating me and there was nothing I could do about it. The loneliness stones began to build up within my breast. It was The Boys Farm all over again. 'To thine own self be true, Tom', the words Meneer Van Niekerk had written in the inside cover of the *Shorter Oxford English Dictionary* sprang as if from nowhere into my head.

'Then I can't take the job, Sir,' I heard myself saying, and turned to walk to the door just a few steps away, my heart beating like billyo. I knew I must escape quickly as I could feel tears begin to well. I was about to make a fool of myself. The last time I'd wept was for several days when I'd been truly heartbroken and I'd promised myself that the next time I did so it would be for something or someone as important to me as Tinker.

I had reached the top of the rickety stairs when I heard him shout, 'Wait, boy! Wait, wait!' I turned and waited as Jellicoe Smellie, leaning diagonally across the doorframe of the bookshop, ordered, 'Come back at once, boy! At once, at once!' I sensed a hint of panic in his voice.

'It's not boy, Sir! It's Tom, Tom Fitzsaxby!' I said somewhat petulantly. It was the first time in my life that I'd contradicted an adult and I could feel my face burning.

'Fitz? Fitz-Saxby, royal bastard,' he said. 'Most curious, most curious.'

I was astonished that he knew I was a bastard, as for the royal I had no idea what he was on about, but I told myself that if he'd already found my weak spot there wasn't much point in hanging around. So I ran down the stairs, which visibly shook and trembled with each step I took.

'Come back! Come back, come back, can you write tracts? An extra ten shillings a week if you can *and* a free fountain pen, free fountain pen!' he shouted down to me from the edge of the balcony.

I looked up and saw that his large papery-coloured hands now gripped the edge of the wrought-iron balcony but failed to pull him into an upright position. The railing began to sway under his weight, and he appeared as if he was about to hurl himself to his death below. His right-angled big toe, protruding from under the bottom rail, pointed directly at me, wriggling accusingly as if it was telling me his death would be my fault.

'What's a tract?' I called up to him.

'Definitely can, definitely can! Come up, come!' He gestured with his right hand.

It was by now quite clear that Jellicoe Smellie was completely bonkers. But then, he was no worse than Meneer Prinsloo with his chickens and windmilling arms or Mevrou in praise of shit squares and her lopsided logic or the *Dominee* with his well-rounded sermons and preposterous dogma. So I returned up the shaky stairs. I thought, however, that I should establish my identity once and for all, though this time avoiding my surname. 'My name is Tom, Sir,' I announced as I entered.

'Jellicoe Smellie,' he said, bowing sideways as if we were starting from scratch.

I followed him into the small office just as a customer walked in, this time a man. 'You have a customer, Sir,' I said to Jellicoe Smellie's back.

'Definitely not, definitely not! Can't, can't!' He turned around, almost losing his balance, but upon seeing the customer he suddenly cried out, 'Praise the Lord, can I help you, my dear brother in Christ?'

'Amen, praise His precious name, Pastor!' the thickset man called back in a heavy Afrikaans accent, respectfully removing his battered felt hat in the presence of the preacher.

Confronted by a born-again Christian who appeared deferential, Jellicoe Smellie relaxed and smiled for the first time, and I saw that he had large yellow teeth. Pink eyes, purple nose and yellow teeth in what was otherwise a bloodless paper-coloured face. 'Give and thou shalt receive,' he called out to the *boer*. 'Praise the Lord, I am at your service, my precious brother in Christ.'

'*Ja*, thank you, Brother . . . ?'

'Jellicoe.'

'Brother Jelly,' the Afrikaner repeated. Smelly Jelly! The name just leapt into my head and seemed perfect, although I wasn't conscious of any particular smell, it was just that some sort of smell must emanate from so strange a creature. Musty came to mind.

'Now listen, man,' the *boer* said, abandoning the religious cant, 'we got a big problem, hey! This tract is a very nice one.' He dug into his coat pocket and produced a rectangular piece of paper about eight inches long and two inches wide, and held it up. 'Unfortunately it is in English and we from the Apostolic Faith Mission and where we come from English is not a big-time language, you hear?' He pointed to the bottom of what I now knew was a tract. 'It says here, printed by the Born-again Christian Missionary Society and —'

'Praise the Lord, praise His precious name!' Jellicoe Smellie interjected.

But the *boer* wasn't to be put off. '*Ja*, okay, us too, but what we want to know is can you translate this tract into Afrikaans? We'll take 1000, you see, we got a tent revival coming up in Bronkhorstspruit already next month.'

Jellicoe Smellie drew back in horror. 'Definitely not, definitely not! Can't, can't!' he exclaimed.

'*Ja, nee, met plesier, Meneer. Ons doen dit vir u met graagte.* Certainly, Sir, it's our pleasure to do it for you,' I called out in Afrikaans.

The *boer* looked at Jellicoe Smellie and then back to me, obviously confused. '*Here,* man, what's going on here, hey?' he asked.

Speaking to him in Afrikaans I reassured him that while we were very busy with orders from all over the Christian world, I would personally see to it that his tracts would be translated and done in time for the revival.

Observing that I was only a boy and judging from my perfect Afrikaans accent, he took me for one of his own and decided it was no longer necessary to be polite to me. 'How much?' he demanded.

'You'll have to ask the *Dominee*,' I replied, pointing to Jellicoe Smellie.

'*You* ask him!' he said in a peremptory manner, again in Afrikaans.

'The gentleman wants to know how much?' I asked Jellicoe Smellie.

'It's for the Apostolic Faith Mission, we all born-again, you hear?' the *boer* said in English, addressing Jellicoe Smellie directly. He hesitated, clearing his throat. 'We always get a discount for God's work.'

'We already rushing your job through, it's costing us money, Meneer,' I replied sharply. 'This is also God's work!' The new Tom Fitzsaxby with the quick mouth was emerging in front of my very eyes.

Jellicoe Smellie looked anxiously from me to the *boer* and back again, obviously not understanding Afrikaans. He grabbed a small pad and began working out a price. 'Fifteen shillings,' he announced after a few moments, 'and we'll include the run-ons.'

'Plus two and sixpence for the translation and 10 per cent tithe, that's another one and sixpence. It goes to the missionaries in the Congo,' I explained. The *Dominee* always said that members of the congregation should give 10 per cent of their income back for God's work, and that it was a definite instruction from the Bible or else you'd go to hell.

Jellicoe Smellie looked at me in amazement, but only took a moment to recover. 'That comes to nineteen shillings,' he announced in an almost-happy voice.

'*Here*, man, it's a lot of money, *Dominee*,' the *boer* said in English, clucking his tongue and shaking his head in dismay.

However, old Jellicoe knew an extra bob earned when he saw one and he jumped feet-first into action. 'Hallelujah! Praise His precious name! Nineteen shillings is not much to pay to save a damned soul! To bring just one sinner to Jesus! To give just one poor wretch life everlasting! A thousand tracts may save a host of sinners. A revival tent overflowing with sinners down on their knees demanding to repent!' He turned to me. 'Tom, here, is the Poet of Salvation! The Poet of Salvation translated into Afrikaans! How can you count the cost of this blessed harvest of sinners for the Lord in sixpences and shillings?'

There was not a single twinned word in the entire diatribe and the *boer*, now totally bewildered, knew he was beaten. He turned to me and said truculently, 'Okay, nineteen shillings, it's a lot but we'll pay it. But I don't want the tithe to go to the *kaffirs* in the Congo, you hear?' He was speaking in Afrikaans to prevent the Englishman from hearing.

'I'll see what I can do,' I said rather high-handedly. 'What about the starving children in India?'

'No *Charras*!' he shot back, alarmed. 'Definitely not, man! They heathen and they come here to get rich and go back to India to worship their gods, not one God like decent people, they got lots of them, some with ten arms and two heads and worshipping monkeys, they can't be born-again, it's a waste of money. When must I come back?'

'Day after tomorrow, after four o'clock,' I said, hoping this could be done. 'How about Cape Coloureds?'

'*Ja*, okay, as long as they born-again Christians, you hear? Lots of Cape Coloureds they just hopeless drunks.'

I thought at once of Auntie and her good-for-nothing black-and-blue husband lying on the front *stoep*, while Dippie and Stoffie stepped over him as they moved her furniture into the army truck. 'Isn't that the sort of person who needs to be born-again?' I asked, a trifle sarcastically.

'*Ja*, it's all God's work, you hear? But we leave them, the Cape Coloureds, to the Assembly of God, they not so fussy who they save,' he explained.

Jellicoe Smellie could barely contain his delight as he ushered the *boer* to the door, spouting a further half-dozen God-bothering imprecations. The *boer* shook his hand and after the sound of the last of his footsteps on the wonky stairs had faded, Smellie turned back to me. 'Excellent! Excellent! Praise the Lord! Praise His precious name! The Lord has rewarded me with your second coming, Tom.'

I took my second coming to mean my return up the rickety stairs. In the meantime, he seemed to have completely forgotten all his previous 'Definitely nots' and 'Can't, can'ts', and now extended his hand and shook mine vigorously. 'Welcome to the "Come in and browse for Christ" bookshop, the Born-again Christian Missionary Society, the Evangelical Mechanical Printing Press, and my accounting arm, Heavenly Prophets. We will proceed henceforth to gain riches for the Lord while keeping a small portion for ourselves.' I was to learn that the only time Jellicoe Smellie twinned words was when he was nervous or agitated.

'Does that mean I have a job, Sir?' I asked.

'A job? Why, Tom, we are to form an entirely new arm of the business, you are to become the Poet of Salvation in Translation!' he said gleefully, yellow teeth now dominating his purple nose and pink eyes. 'Two pounds a week and free penning, that's the very best I can do,' he said, his pink eyes narrowing in case I should argue.

My time spent at The Boys Farm had taught me very little to use in life but one of the more important lessons I learned was to press home any advantage I might momentarily hold. 'That ten extra shillings was for writing tracts, Sir. I am now the Poet of Salvation in Translation?' I said, my eyes downcast so as not to sound too opportunistic. I must admit my new title had a certain ring to it, but on the other hand you couldn't go around the place saying 'Guess what? I am the Poet of Salvation in Translation in the Born-again Christian Missionary Society.' So, practically speaking, it wasn't going to do much for my ego or my future salary.

'Ah, yes! But I am *the* Poet of Salvation! That is the senior position!' Jellicoe Smellie said pointedly. 'May I remind you it is I who write the tracts and you who *merely* translate them into that abominable gutter language.'

This was true enough, and I told myself I needed this job which now satisfied my saving requirements with even a little over. But I also knew that he who hesitates is lost, another sound lesson learned from Mevrou's *sjambok*. For instance, Gawie's exclusive job sitting on his arse, tearing up shit squares had come from grabbing a single rare opportunity and turning it into easy work, while the rest of us laboured in the vegetable garden, chopped wood and worked in the orchards.

'How many tracts have you written, Sir?'

'Oh, dozens and dozens, hundred and hundreds, some very, very good ones too.' The twinning of words was back.

'And how many have you sold?'

'Ah, grains of sand on the seashore, thousands and thousands, grains of sand, grains of sand.'

'At fifteen shillings a thousand?'

Jellicoe Smellie hesitated, then said, 'Well, no, I cannot tell a lie, the normal charge is twelve and sixpence, but, after all, that dreadful man *was* the enemy and so I was forced to add a small surcharge.'

I ignored this racist remark. 'Do people get tired of tracts, you know, want new ones?'

'Ah, my dear fellow, I regret to say, fashion prevails in the business of Jesus Christ like any other.' He was beginning to relax.

'So you're always having to write new ones?'

'A burden I willingly bear for the Lord,' he said sanctimoniously.

'And you said you've written hundreds?'

'Scattered far and wide.'

'If I translate them and we charge fifteen shillings a thousand, you can use all the old ones you've written, can't you?'

'I say, what a grand idea!' he exclaimed.

I wasn't fool enough to think this thought hadn't already occurred to him. 'You make your original profit all over again plus one and sixpence, then the translation fee and tithe, that's another four shillings!'

'Splendid!' he declared, clapping his hands.

'You make your original profit and keep the one and six for the enemy factor *and* the 10 per cent tithe, and I keep the two and sixpence for each translation into Afrikaans.'

'And you *don't* get the extra ten shillings for writing tracts, writing tracts,' he said, as quick as can be. He was twinning again, which was a sign that he was nervous.

'Fair enough,' I replied, 'but only when my Afrikaans translation income becomes greater than the ten shillings extra in my weekly wages.' I smiled ingenuously and shrugged my shoulders. 'We taking a chance on each other, Sir, ' I said cheekily.

He pointed a bony finger at me. 'Not correct! I am the one *taking* the chance.' A flash of yellow, purple and pink occurred and he extended his hand. 'Welcome to the Born-again Christian Missionary Society, you seem to have an admirable grasp of the Heavenly Prophets aspect of the business, Tom,' Jellicoe Smellie said, welcoming me for the second time.

I needed to clear up one final detail. 'Sir, what did you mean about, you know, Fitz and er . . . royal bastard?' I asked.

'Astonished you don't know, Tom,' Jellicoe Smellie exclaimed. 'Fitz? All Fitz's are royal bastards! Fitzgibbon, Fitzpatrick, Fitzgerald, Fitzsimmons, your name, all derive from an illicit liaison occurring at some time in the past with a commoner and royalty. A promiscuous lot, your English royalty. Not at all born-again!'

So, that's how the Government-owned and now right-royal bastard Tom Fitzsaxby came to be employed during his school holidays.

I'd like to say that once it got going and we'd printed samples of my translated tracts and sent them in envelopes, addressed in my copperplate handwriting, to all the Pentecostal and other faiths that preached in Afrikaans that business boomed. But it didn't. I was receiving the extra ten shillings without being able to justify it. Instead of the avalanche we'd anticipated, orders for my translated tracts were merely trickling in and I could only think it must be me. I was a lousy translator and I expected to be fired at any moment.

But after the second holiday spent in Jellicoe Smellie's employ, I came to realise that the Mechanical Evangelical Printing Press lay idle for most of the time. Dare I presume that Smelly Jelly's tracts were simply not good enough? I'd had my original suspicions, many of the words he used in his tracts were composed of three syllables and, besides, when he could find a fancy word or turn a simple sentence into a convoluted one, he never hesitated to do so. Finding equally complicated words in Afrikaans proved difficult, and probably made my translations even more obscure. The need to confess one's sins and become a born-again Christian required a reader of Jellicoe's tracts to be highly literate, and my pedantic translations would have been well beyond the comprehension of your average Afrikaner sinner seeking redemption.

Then one day while he was out, I was searching for a pencil sharpener in the drawer in his desk and I came across a bunch of tracts tied together with an elastic band. They seemed well used and somehow different from our own and so I began to read them. After a few minutes I paused to see where they came from. They were all American, from various charismatic faiths, though the majority came from the Assembly of God. It became obvious that Smelly Jelly had helped himself liberally to the themes and ideas contained within them, but that he wished to stamp his work with his own imprimatur. In the process he had lost the simplicity and directness and the dire warning and consequences of remaining unrepentant that was the hallmark of the American tracts. He may have been bonkers, but as it transpired, he had an educated and complicated mind and he simply couldn't think at the level of the repent-or-burn-in-hell vernacular of the American hot gospel tracts.

It was then that I had my big idea. I had practically teethed on the Dominee's well-rounded sermons and dire imprecations. I'd listened to hundreds of Sunday sermons while the beetle munched the beard grass. So I wrote my first tract, always bearing in mind my own people, the good citizens of Duiwelskrans and the boere in the surrounding mountains. I would think about how I might go about bringing Mevrou's six brothers, the Van Schalkwyk Six, now languishing in prison in Pretoria, to Jesus.

The result was almost impossible to believe. Orders started flowing in from all over the country and every new tract was snapped up. That is how I eventually became the Poet of Salvation in both English and Afrikaans. Most of the successful tracts translated back to English sold as well as their Afrikaans counterparts. The Mechanical Evangelical Printing Press was working overtime, and in two years it had been replaced with a bigger and better one made by Goose & Pratten, a UK engineering firm, which Smelly Jelly aptly named the 'Gospel-gobbling Goose'.

I would pen a tract while at school and, because of my success, I now demanded and got a pound for every tract I wrote. I had gone from having no money to practically swimming in the stuff. But every extra penny earned had to be gouged from Smelly Jelly's Heavenly Prophets department. Beneath the leaning bony body, ink-stained linen frame, nervous word-twinning, sanctimonious prattle and sudden panic was an educated mind as cunning as a shithouse rat. Nevertheless, I couldn't complain, on that first day he'd seen in me an opportunity and I had, in turn, successfully exploited his greed.

However, on that first day of my employment I had an immediate problem. Another lesson learned at The Boys Farm was to never compromise your position, to appear to be vulnerable and to show yourself to be less than your opponent had assumed you to be. Humans crave status above most things, and dominance is the bully's way of obtaining it. I had no place to sleep that night and no money, but I couldn't bring myself to ask Jellicoe Smellie for the means to eat or sleep and by so doing diminish the equality of status that in my mind I believed we'd established.

I had all afternoon in which to find a safe place to sleep, and I already had a half-formed idea in my mind. Remember when I first came to Johannesburg when the train pulled into Central Station, and how I'd been overwhelmed by the size of the crowd and the hubbub and general business? When Miss Phillips failed at first to arrive and I thought for a moment that I'd been abandoned I'd wondered at the time whether a person could sleep in a place like this? So that's where I was headed, to seek out some nook or cranny in that giant building that might conceal me safely for the night. I carried a brown-paper shopping bag, one of those with two string handles. It contained a spare shirt and pair of grey shorts and a couple of pairs of underpants and spare socks, my toothbrush and a bar of soap I'd nicked from the school.

As I approached the station I noticed the same faceless hooded man I'd first seen when I was with Miss Phillips, seated on his box outside. More correctly, I saw his little dog first, so very like Tinker but with a brown patch on his chest. I had such a sudden and overwhelming desire to hold the little dog that my eyes filled with tears. I waited a few moments and knuckled the wet from my eyes. I felt that if I could just pat the little terrier once or twice, I'd be okay again.

The hooded man had his chin slumped on his chest, and may have been dozing. Anyway, he didn't stir and I knelt beside the little dog who welcomed my pat and was immediately friendly, placing his front paws on my knee, his tiny pink tongue lolling. I felt he really liked me and he nuzzled his nose into the palm of my hand as I fingered his collar. It was then that I got the shock of my life. On the tiny leather collar hung a metal disc, and I turned it face-up to read the dog's name. For a moment I thought I was hallucinating, because the inscription on the disc read 'Tinker'. I started to weep silently, nuzzling the little dog's head into my thigh, the tears rolling down my face. I became aware of a series of frantic grunts and guttural sounds to my right, and looking up I saw the hooded man holding out a piece of paper and acting in a very agitated way. I didn't know whether I should depart in haste or accept the note he was proffering in his left hand and with increasing vehemence gesticulating with the stump of his right.

I accepted the small single sheet of paper and, brushing away my tears for the second time in several minutes, glanced at it. The handwriting was elegant and the note read: *I am Frikkie Botha and you are* Voetsek. *I can't speak.*

It was written in Afrikaans, of course, as Frikkie couldn't speak English, the elegant hand came from Duiwelskrans school where he too had been educated, mostly with a steel-edged ruler across his knuckles, until the slant and formation of the letters were perfect. I was dumbstruck and it took me several moments to recover from this second shock.

'Can you hear me, Frikkie?' I asked at last.

He nodded his head. I was suddenly lost for words. Where was I to begin? How could I ask him questions that simply required a nod in reply? So much water under the bridge. The Frikkie of the dairy, cows, vegetable patch and orange orchard. The Frikkie who'd allowed Tinker to live on the condition that I stayed *stom* over Fonnie du Preez and Pissy Vermaak. The Frikkie who'd beaten Mattress to a pulp in the boxing ring and, in turn, received a broken jaw. The Frikkie who referred to Tinker as 'my little rat trap', and would brag about her prowess to everyone. The Frikkie who'd knocked me into the ground because I'd tried to cover up the fight over Miss Phillips' pound residing in Gawie's bum and confessed that the reason we were scrapping was that I'd stupidly said the Union Jack was prettier than the *vierkleur*, the hallowed flag of the Transvaal Republic. The Frikkie in his *Stormjaer* uniform, giving us ill-informed lectures on the latest German triumph while we watered the orchards or worked in the veggie garden. The Frikkie of the disastrously bungled railway bridge explosion and the cowardly Van Schalkwyk brothers. Then the Frikkie that followed the explosion as the notorious Faceless Man whose identity the newspapers had speculated over for three weeks. And now, finally, Frikkie the broken, the hooded beggar. The Frikkie who now sat before me, one hand reduced to a stump, and his little dog, who pathetically derived his name from my own beloved Tinker.

'Howzit going, Frikkie?' I asked. 'Fancy meeting you here. What a surprise, man.' I spoke in Afrikaans, of course, trying to sound cheerful.

Frikkie nodded his head.

'You have a little dog and you've called him Tinker?'

Another stiff nod. I wasn't getting very far and an awkward silence ensued. Frikkie had a spiral notepad resting in his lap and now he started to write. He was a left-hander and it was the only means of communication left to him. He now wrote: *I saw you with a lady a long time ago.*

'I'm sorry, man. If I'd known it was you I would have stopped to talk,' I said.

He wrote again, tearing off the page: *What are you doing here?*

'I'm going to school. I won a scholarship,' I replied.

It's nice to see you, Tom.

'Ja, you too, Frikkie.'

We go back a long way.

'Ja, since I was just a small brat.'

A series of glottal stops followed from Frikkie, these I took for laughter or, more likely, a chuckle.

Where you staying?

There seemed no point in lying to him. 'Ag, as a matter of fact, right now, I don't know. It's the school holidays and, well, you see I'm broke. I thought that maybe I could find a place to sleep in the station here.'

He shook his head furiously, scribbled rapidly and ripped the page from the notepad. *No, man, the railway police, they arrest you.*

'Maybe you know a place I can go, Frikkie? I've got a job, starting tomorrow. Perhaps somewhere that will let me pay them back in a week, a boarding house or something?'

He scribbled again. Not that it was *really* a scribble, like I said, he had a beautiful hand. *Come and stay with us, it costs nothing.*

I had no idea who the 'us' was meant to be. Himself and the surrogate Tinker still at my side nuzzling me, or were there other people involved?

'*Ja*, I'd be most grateful, thank you,' I said, accepting his generous offer.

He wrote again and handed me the note. *Tom, come back at half past five. I have to wait here for the rush hour. Today is payday and it's worth at least a quid to me.* I forgot to say that his spelling in Afrikaans wasn't all that good, but I've translated it here correctly into English.

I was a bit hungry, but it wasn't too bad, though I knew for certain that tomorrow I'd have to lower my dignity and ask Smelly Jelly for an advance or I was going to starve to death. I'd not had the opportunity to explore Johannesburg other than the time Miss Phillips took me to John Orr to get underpants and then the art gallery and the lunch where I tasted roast chicken. So I had a good time exploring around this big skyscraper place. All in all, it had been a wonderful day, I'd got myself a job and now I had somewhere to sleep, as for the food department, well, I wasn't that hungry, yet. But that's the problem with life, just when you not looking something bad happens, something you never going to forget in your whole life.

I haven't explained to you that for a few months now I'd been thinking a lot about girls and waking up in the morning and not being able to go to the showers until it went down, which sometimes took ages. I was trying not to do 'you know what' too much just in case Meneer Prinsloo was right about going blind from overuse, which I doubted, but a person shouldn't get too cocky. So part of my exploring the city was to keep my eye out for pretty girls.

So, now it's rush hour and I'm making my way back to Frikkie Botha and walking along Rissik Street, which is packed with people going towards the railway station, when I see this beautiful girl. She's grown up already, but even I know how beautiful she is. Long, blonde hair and a nice body and she is swinging her hips in her summer dress. I really had to worry about what was going on in the front of my grey flannel shorts, and had to put one hand in my trouser pocket to keep things looking normal. I worked my way through the crowd until I was right behind her. We stopped at this robot and waited for the light to turn green. Then, just as the light changed, she stepped off the pavement and, all of a sudden, her bloomers fell down around her ankles. Only they were not like Mevrou's bloomers, but a little light thing that's black and has red roses embroidered on it. So she steps out of them with her high heels and keeps walking. I am so shocked that I don't think and I bend down and snatch up the bloomers and go running after her. 'Miss! Miss! Stop! You've dropped your bloomers!' I shout. There's lots of people who hear, and the girl just keeps walking, and everyone is laughing, and I panic and catch up with her and tap her on the shoulder.

'Go away!' she hisses.

So I'm standing holding the bloomers. I don't know what to do. So I put them in my trouser pocket and start to run in the opposite direction bumping into people. Now my perfect day has become far from perfect because the Poet of Salvation in Translation is just a stupid young boy idiot!

When I eventually regain my composure and double-back to reach Central Station, Frikkie is waiting. He's stowed the box and the display board with the coloured man in the magazine kiosk. Now we're walking along with Tinky on a lead, which is what I've decided to call his little dog, because I can't say Tinker without wanting to cry. It's pretty slow going because Frikkie is bent almost double, and isn't exactly the prancing boxer of the past. He walks with a stick, and his arm with the missing hand almost scrapes the pavement. He is still wearing his hood and I haven't yet seen what he looks like underneath. The eyehole keeps slipping away from his one eye, so I don't know how he can see. But then I realise that Tinky has worked this out long ago and he's taking his master home. Only not directly, as the little dog leads him into a small Indian curry place. Not so much a restaurant, but a sort of a hole in the wall with two tables and a curry smell coming from it.

'We are very, very happy to see you, Meneer Botha. You are looking very, very well and absolutely blooming also. Mrs Naidoo has made a very, very excellent curry for you,' the Indian guy, who I take to be Mr Naidoo, says, welcoming Frikkie. How he can possibly know Frikkie is looking well with the hood over his head is a mystery. Maybe Frikkie was walking a bit better. 'For Tinker we have a lovely, lovely and very nice meaty bone,' Mr Naidoo adds. 'Now you are please introducing me to your friend?' he says, smiling and extending his hand over the counter. 'Naidoo, Bombay University, B.A. failed,' he announces by way of introduction.

'Tom Fitzsaxby, how do you do?' I reply, taking his hand.

'Very excellent, top notch and jolly, jolly good,' he replies, and turning to Frikkie, says, 'The usual you are having?'

Frikkie nodded and pointed to me, raising two fingers.

'You are wanting for your friend, Mr Tom too?'

Frikkie nodded again.

I couldn't believe Frikkie was going to buy me dinner, then I immediately thought he might expect me to pay.

'I'm not hungry, Frikkie,' I said hurriedly.

'For Mrs Naidoo's curry a boy is always very, very hungry, it is something very, very delicious, Bombay chicken!' Mr Naidoo protested.

'I haven't got any money, Sir,' I whispered urgently to the Indian proprietor.

'We have rice and pappadam also, no charge tonight, we are having Hindu sacred feast, everything is free.' He looked at me and smiled. 'You are coming please?' Whereupon he turned and led us through a door at the back into what was no more than a passageway with a lone small table set for one. 'We are getting you a chair at once, Mr Tom,' he said. Frikkie sat down and Tinky collapsed at his feet with his nose on his master's boot.

Then, to my horror, Frikkie removed the dirty hood.

I'm ashamed to say my mouth fell open and I visibly pulled back in shock. Frikkie's face was as flat as a plate and the colour of beetroot with white scars running every which way, like well-grained beef. Two holes served as his nostrils, which pumped in and out, popping mucous bubbles. The hole directly under was without lips, and looked more like an anus than a mouth. His left eye was completely missing and was simply a pinkish purple dent in his head while his right eye was completely normal, though without an eyebrow. One ear was perfect and the other was sheared cleanly from the side of his head.

'Jesus!' I heard myself exclaim.

Frikkie had the notepad out and wrote hurriedly, then handed the pad to me. *You owe me a shilling! Ha! Ha!*

I'd never tasted curry before but I took to it right away. The meal was simply delicious and was washed down with a big enamel jug of orange cordial that Frikkie had to sip through a straw. Mr Naidoo came to the table as we completed the meal. 'I have some very, very nice *ganja*,' he said to Frikkie.

Frikkie nodded and produced two half-crowns from his purse, and the Indian returned shortly with a cellophane packet containing some sort of crumpled brown leaf. I looked at Frikkie curiously and he wrote on his pad, *dagga*. I had never seen marijuana before and it certainly didn't look like a whole five bob's worth of anything to me.

'Very, very good, Durban Gold,' Mr Naidoo said, then turning to me, 'For Mr Botha's pain,' he explained. Then he added, 'You are please not touching, Mr Tom, this *dagga*, it is very, very bad for boys, but also good *muti* for Mr Botha.'

We left soon after and went a few doors down to a Solly Kramer's bottle store, and Frikkie purchased a bottle of brandy. The bottle store was opposite Joubert Park, where Miss Phillips had taken me to visit the art gallery and it came as some surprise when Frikkie and Tinky crossed the road and we entered the park, heading directly for the art gallery.

When we arrived I saw that the steps and the veranda with its huge

Gothic columns was now a place where a dozen or so men were sitting smoking and taking in the mild evening air or lying, covered by grey army blankets, despite the mild weather. Most of them nursed bottles wrapped in brown paper or newspaper, and one or two of them greeted Frikkie, who pointed at me and gave the thumbs-up sign, which seemed to be all that was needed to introduce me. One very tall and exceedingly thin derelict called out in Afrikaans, 'What's your name, son?'

'Tom,' I answered, not adding my surname.

'Lofty . . . Lofty van der Merwe,' he replied. 'Welcome, Tom.'

'*Dankie*, Meneer van der Merwe,' I said, thanking him.

'*Ag*, man, we not all hoity-toity here, Tom,' he replied. 'Just call me Lofty, hey?'

Nothing lasts forever, and towards the end of my fourth year at school Smelly Jelly was working back catching up on a bit of printing on the Gospel-gobbling Goose. I must say we had become a formidable team, and for some time now had been sending tracts to America. Talk about hot gospel! Some of our efforts practically burned your fingers! Smelly Jelly would read a new tract I'd written and say, 'Congratulations, Tom, this one is positively proselytising pyrotechnics, you have lit a bonfire for Jesus!' I had become an international tract-writing success, with one of my tracts, 'When Jesus Came to Dinner', a truly big-time hit. The Gospel-gobbling Goose was burning the midnight oil, pumping blue fluorescent light into the dark arcade below.

So this was the reason Jellicoe Smellie was working back one late November night. He finally packed up and prepared to set off for home, a flat he shared with a ginger cat in Hillbrow. The cat didn't have a name and was simply referred to as 'the cat that pisses'. On this night, like many others recently, Smelly Jelly was the only one left in the arcade. Although nobody actually witnessed what happened next, the conclusion seemed obvious. Jellicoe took the one step too many in the accident waiting to happen. Under the weight of that terminal tread the stairway crashed down into the darkness below. The following morning they discovered his lifeless body buried under four cedar steps and a length of moulded banister.

While I missed working with Smelly Jelly it wasn't the financial disaster that it might at first have seemed. I'd saved twenty pounds from my tract writing and this was more than enough to get me through my final year at school, as well as pay for my clothes.

Now here's a funny thing. After the first year of working for the Born-again Christian Missionary Society and dossing down each night with Frikkie's friends on the art gallery veranda, I suppose I could have afforded some sort of cheap boarding house or even the YMCA, but I continued to stay with this brotherhood of drunkards in what was referred to as the Starlight Hotel.

In the winter we'd move over to the back of Johannesburg Central, or Park Station, as it was commonly called. We'd camp among the huge steam pipes pumping heating into the railway station. With two army blankets, even though the Johannesburg temperature often dropped to below freezing on some winter nights, we were snug enough among those big old heated steel pipes. Of course, it was pretty noisy with the trains coming and going all night and the constant shunting in the goods yard, but drunks sleep through anything, and boys quickly grow accustomed to noise.

Most of the alcoholics were ex-miners who'd worked underground and had been the victims of accidents and were on a small fortnightly pension from the mining group who'd employed them. My contribution for being allowed to stay with them unharmed was to write letters to the various mining companies, Goldfields Limited, Consolidated Mining, Anglo American and the like. I'd try to solicit extra payments for wives long-since deserted or sick and dying children whose names they often had trouble recalling. I grew quite skilled at penning these pathetic pleas for help. While they were not always successful, I managed over the years to extract several hundred pounds in *ex gratia* payments with a letter that must have, once in a while, touched the heart of someone in the head office of a giant mining company. Solly Kramer's bottle store was where the cheques were usually cashed, the payment always being returned in excellent spirits.

My tract-writing career was an ideal apprenticeship. A good tract requires a mixture of guilt, persuasion, remorse, reward and compassion, as well as a tincture of dire consequence. A soliciting letter isn't all that different in nature. After a while my facility with the pen assumed a mystical quality among the drunks who used Joubert Park and Park Station as their home.

Lofty van der Merwe had once been a mine captain underground, which was one rank up from shift boss, and, apart from the fact that he could hold his brandy better than all of them, his previously exalted station made him the undisputed leader when occasionally one was required. Alcoholics listen to a lone voice inside their heads and they're not apt to follow anyone as the demon drink is the only shift boss they know. But the company of regularly inebriated men is seldom held together without occasional violence, and Lofty understood this and earned their respect by ending many a fight with a straight left that had a fellow drunk sitting in the gravel wiping the blood from his nose.

These were men who hailed from the bottom of the social barrel, even when they'd once lived sober lives. In the landscape of a large city they were referred to in the popular vernacular as Poor Whites. Where I came from in the deep north there was nothing unusual about them, they were farm hands, timber cutters, railway workers, road gangers or worked in the saw mills, mostly gainfully employed and always drunk on a Saturday night. They beat their wives and children as a matter of course and then went to church on Sunday. I knew them intimately and understood how to act in their company. After all, The Boys Farm was a factory that set out to produce men for precisely such rural activity. Completely accepted in a backwoods community, they became social detritus in the City of Gold where their only usefulness lay 2000 feet under the towering skyscrapers as underground miners.

Lofty must have been a bit of an exception, and well beyond the sober aspirations of his peers at the Starlight Hotel. During the soft summer evenings on the high *veld* I would act as Lofty's shift boss, writing letters, running a book on the Turfontein races and even, after a while, dispensing advice and keeping an eye on the health of the brotherhood.

Drunks usually ignore even the most serious medical problems by masking the pain with drink. In the first few days of the school holidays I became a familiar sight at the Emergency Department of Johannesburg General Hospital. On the first evening out of school, Lofty would line the boys up for inspection and then, next morning, I'd bring the sick and the lame into Emergency and complete the necessary paperwork and see to it that they received treatment.

It wasn't unusual for me, first thing on a bitter winter morning, to have to go to the public phone to call an ambulance to cart one of the boys to hospital or even sometimes to the mortuary. I don't mean to say they were dying all over the place, drunks are amazingly resilient and these were men who, even in the sober periods of their lives, did it tough and lived rough. But every winter you'd say goodbye to a couple of the boys who'd ignored their conditions just one cold night too many and lost what Lofty referred to as 'the big gamble called life'. 'Ag, Tom, it's short and sweet and hard and bitter all mixed up together, it's the big gamble called life.'

I don't want you to think I was some sort of hero. These were not the kind of men who show gratitude or even respect and I expected neither. The Bishop's College was teaching me how to be a gentleman but my roots still lay deep in the red soil of the high mountains, even if I was determined never to return to them. In a strange way, the school holidays spent with Frikkie and his fellow alcoholics were an opportunity to relax and to drop the pretence of being a somebody when you knew you were a nobody. The term 'a nobody' does not necessarily derive from a sense of low self-esteem, though I confess I'd had my moments in this emotional department of life. I was already beginning to understand that I had a modicum of brains and that opportunity awaited me in the big wide world. Rather, it was the sense of having no continuity, of emerging from a dark space, a void, a place where no loving or touching existed, a perfectly blank background.

Here among the brotherhood of drunkards there was no need for explanations or antecedents, they too had divorced the past, I was accepted and regarded with, at most, a benign acceptance or, at the very least, with a complete lack of curiosity. Here I was Tom, without even a surname. It was good.

Frikkie Botha remained my friend. Although, despite his initial kindness to me, I was to discover, perhaps not surprisingly, that he'd become a very lonely and bitter man. He was also in constant pain. The *dagga* he used at night helped him cope with the pain but coupled with a nightly bottle of Tolley's brandy, he was a spent force quite soon after we'd had our dinner. Communicating with him was a painfully slow process that took weeks and months and finally even years.

Towards the very end of the school holidays when I'd first found him and Tinky outside the railway station, he'd slipped me a note. *Tom, do you want to know what happened to Mattress?*

My heart started to beat rapidly. 'Frikkie, please tell me, I *really* need to know!' I'd replied urgently.

Not now, man. It's a long story.

'Can you write it all down, please, Frikkie? I don't care how long it takes. I'll bring you paper . . . everything!'

Those bastards, we'll get them, hey, he wrote.

'Please, Frikkie, it's very important for me to know,' I begged.

But somehow Frikkie could never quite get around to writing the details down. I took to picking him up after work from outside Park Station whenever I could, although I couldn't always get away. He'd wait for me until six o'clock, milking the commuters, and then we'd usually go to Mr Naidoo or some other cheap café or eatery that had a back room where he could take off his hood in order to eat. Frikkie ate with great difficulty, jabbing the spoon into his little scarred arsehole of a mouth and spilling food everywhere, but he was a proud man and wouldn't let me feed him.

He always left a terrible mess behind and we were often requested not to return. It was only Mr Naidoo's Indian eatery that always welcomed us.

This was the only meal Frikkie ate all day, though he would consume a dozen bottles of Pepsi-Cola to get high on the caffeine. Whenever he required a Pepsi he'd tap Tinky four times on the head, and the clever little terrier would trot off to the kiosk 20 feet away and bark twice to get Stompie the proprietor's attention. How Frikkie managed to train him to do this trick was a complete mystery. Stompie would then deliver an ice-cold Pepsi with a fresh straw to Frikkie, but then I discovered he was charging him a threepenny premium for the service. I thought this unfair and remonstrated with the little Cape Coloured, who immediately went on the defensive.

'Ag, man, Tom, what we got here is a tit for tat situation,' Stompie protested.

'Tit for tat, how come?'

'When my friends come and also the family and they want to see what's under the hood, Frikkie won't do it for nothing, it's one shilling every time!' He spread his hands. 'I'm only trying to get my money back,' he explained.

'How often do your friends want to see what's under the hood?' I asked him.

'Lots of times, man. Two, three times a week, sometimes more.'

I did a quick calculation. 'You're robbing him blind, Stompie! Three times a week is three shillings. Frikkie drinks twelve Pepsis a day, so you're making a tickey every time, that's three shillings just for a day!' I quickly calculated. 'One pound one shilling per week, less three shillings, that's eighteen bob profit you're making. That's daylight robbery, man!'

'Ja, but what about transport and everything?'

'Transport! It's 20 feet!'

'Here, man, Tom, I also got to bring water for the dog,' Stompie protested, but then, suddenly in a fit of remorse, added, 'Okay, fair's fair, if he's game, I'm game.'

But Frikkie wouldn't hear of giving Stompie three free facials. He replied to my request in a long note in misspelt Afrikaans. Here is a rough translation of what it said. *He's a half-*kaffir, *man! I'm not going to show my face for nothing to a half-*kaffir! *Personally I got my dignity, you hear? I'm in showbiz and he is in selling cold drinks. I pay him so he must also pay me for my performance!*

My argument that his dignity was costing him money didn't wash with Frikkie. When a *Boer* goes stubborn on you, you might as well try to shift Table Mountain. So I was forced to go back to Stompie and tell him the bad news, but I also decided to take things into my own hands in an attempt to obtain an outcome fair to them both.

'Now, listen here, Stompie, I'm allowing a penny extra a bottle for transportation, so if you pay for three facials a week that's still 100 per cent profit. You way ahead, man, at the end of the week you've got three shillings extra in your pocket.'

Stompie shook his head vehemently. He wasn't taking Frikkie's refusal to make a deal at all well. 'That *Boer* can go *fok* himself!' he exclaimed.

'Now, come on, Stompie, fair's fair, you'll make three bob for taking a few steps and you still got the normal profit from selling twelve Pepsis a day.'

'What about the water for the dog?'

'Water is free, Stompie, it comes out of a bloody tap!' I exclaimed indignantly.

But Stompie's feelings had been hurt and he wasn't going to give up without a fight. '*Ja*, but the tap is inside the station wash room, that's another long walk. I'm a busy man, you hear.' Then he looked at me shrewdly. 'So tell me, where is the *Boer* going to get his Pepsi? I'm the only one who's got this personal service going,' he said, smiling like a crocodile.

It was time to play my trump card. I pointed to Mary, the African flower lady who sold carnations from a stall nearby. 'Mary, she'll do it for two shillings a week *and* she won't buy the Pepsis from your kiosk, she'll get them from the café over the road. She's *very* happy to do it,' I added for emphasis.

Stompie shook his head sadly. 'Now you *really* playing dirty, Tom. You giving my Pepsi business to a *fokken kaffir* woman who sells carnations that's four days old already. You can ask anyone, she always buys the old stock at the market that hasn't already been sold and is four days already in the water. I know, man, my family's in the flower-selling business. Take a look at the stems, you can see she's cut them above where the water stain on the stem is. It's a fresh cut. A good carnation will last ten days, with her you lucky if you get three before their heads already dropping like a Zulu night-watchman's!'

I refused to be distracted. 'Three shillings, 100 per cent profit each week and you continue to bring the dog his water.' I looked him directly in the eye. 'Take it or leave it, Stompie. I'm serious, it's my final offer.'

'Ja, okay, man, Tom, for you I'll do it,' Stompie agreed unhappily. 'I like the little dog.' Then he suddenly jabbed a finger at my chest. 'But you tell that *Boer* I want him to take the hood off for more than five seconds, you hear? He takes it off and then he puts it back so fast you can hardly see anything properly. You looking at the no-eye and before you can see the no-nose it's finish and *klaar*. It's not fair, all my friends are complaining, and sixpence is too much for a child, it should be only a tickey!'

I received a letter at school from a city law firm inviting me to the reading of Jellicoe Smellie's will. The housemaster gave me permission to go into the city after school, and I arrived at an old building in Market Street that had a birdcage lift. After a great deal of rattling and whining it took me to the fifth floor whereupon it stopped with a jar, a jolt and a clank.

I had been disgorged outside the chambers of Jacobs & Tremaine, Solicitors & Attorneys at Law. No secretary attended the front desk, there was only a bell and a sign that said, 'Ring for service. Please be seated.' I pressed the buzzer-type bell and heard a faint ringing somewhere in the interior of the office. Then I sat to wait in a wicker chair as instructed.

The waiting room was as old-fashioned as the building, old black-and-white photographs of mine dumps and shaft heads on the walls, and two law certificates, one for Jacobs and the other for Tremaine. The battered reception table contained ancient pre-war copies of *The Tatler* and *Punch*, two magazines I'd never seen before. I didn't understand any of the jokes in the cartoons in *Punch*.

After some time, a short, fat, balding man came out. He wore a striped grey suit that might once have fitted him but it must have been a while since he had any chance of buttoning the jacket, under which he sported a brown cardigan with the third button missing. His trousers rested under his belly and at his rear the shiny-arsed material hung in two distinct drapes, all front and no arse. He also had these small glasses perched on the end of his nose that didn't have any handles and seemed to be stuck to his nose. Later I would learn they were called *pince-nez*, but at the time I thought to myself, What a clever new invention. He looked around the reception, his actual eye level was well above the glasses.

'Mr Fitzsaxby?' he enquired, looking directly at me, yet he didn't appear to see me and was obviously looking for someone else.

'Tom Fitzsaxby, Sir,' I replied, rising and standing in his presence.

'Oh, a boy!' he said, looking me up and down suspiciously. His podgy little hands grabbed the lapels of his ill-fitting suit jacket, and they reminded me at once of a bunch of pink sausages. 'Mr Jacobs,' he announced, introducing himself without offering me his hand. 'Follow me, Boy,' he barked, turning and passing back through the doorway from which he'd recently emerged.

I wanted to ask Mr Jacobs why it was necessary for me to be present for the reading of Jellicoe Smellie's will. But his peremptory manner left me no option but to follow him into a small cluttered office. A large porcelain ashtray on his desk was overflowing with cigarette butts, each of them having been ground into the ashtray with such severity that they were bent double at the cork tip. The whole place smelled of stale cigarettes.

'Sit!' he commanded, nodding towards a leather chair. He took his place at the desk opposite me, then reaching forward, his little pink sausages began to pluck at a small pile of manila folders, each tied with red tape. Finally he plucked one from the pile, pulled the tape, opened the folder and began to read aloud, the glasses on the end of his nose coming into play for the first time.

'This is the last will and testament of Jellicoe James Wilberforce Smellie, of Parkington Mansions, Cross Street, Hillbrow.' He paused and appeared to be reading to himself, his eyes darting along the lines. 'Etc., etc., etc., blah, blah, blah,' he said at last, as if I had been privy to the reading all along. 'I leave the sum of ten thousand pounds to the Apostatical Society of Great Britain.' Mr Jacobs paused again and looked up at me over his perched spectacles. 'Do you know what an apostate is, Boy?'

'No, Sir,' I replied, not certain.

'It means non-believer.'

'How can that be, Sir? Mr Smellie was a born-again Christian.'

He looked at me disapprovingly, peering over his nose glasses. 'Stuff and nonsense, man! I am a Jew and an agnostic!'

I knew what an agnostic was. 'That's not the same thing as an apostate, Sir,' I ventured, albeit in a subdued voice.

'What? What did you say?' he barked. 'No, it isn't. Quite right, absolutely, well done! Is there a semblance of a brain in that young head after all?'

If there was Mr Jacobs didn't pause to find out, and returned to reading. 'My business, known as the Born-again Christian Missionary Society, is to be sold and the proceeds to be given to the RSPCA to be used for the euthanasia of cats, as there are far too many cats and not enough laps. It is a condition of this bequest that "the cat that pisses" is to be the first recipient.

'There is also a sum of one hundred pounds owing on the Gospel-gobbling Goose and this debt should be settled with the proceeds of the sale before the remainder of the bequest is honoured.'

Mr Jacobs looked up over his *pince-nez*. 'Pissing cats and Gospel-gobbling geese? Do you know anything about this, Boy?' he demanded, as if somehow I was responsible.

'His ginger cat and the printing press, Sir. The money is still owed by Heavenly Prophets to the firm of Goose & Pratten.' I realised at that precise moment that my career as a tract writer of international repute had come to an abrupt end. 'Sir, when did Mr Smellie make this will?' I asked.

'Make it? You mean unmake it! He's changed his will on the first day of every month, providing it wasn't a Sunday, for twenty years. At one stage I recall he left everything to a foundation to be named "The Mahatma Ghandi Foundation Dedicated To Drinking Your Own Urine". On another occasion it was to be for "The Propagation of Rabbits in Australia"!' He cleared his throat. 'Smellie's current will is his most sensible yet and made only a week before he died.' Mr Jacobs paused and looked directly at me. 'This cat that urinates, will you be able to find it?'

'It's ginger, and according to Mr Smellie is rather timid and afraid to do its business outdoors, Sir,' I replied. 'But I've never been to Mr Smellie's flat or seen his cat.'

'I see. Mr Jellicoe Smellie has been dead for ten days, either the cat has starved to death or been forced to compromise the habits of its urinary tract and found more pleasing places to piss.' He gave a small chuckle, which sounded more like an amused cough. 'I imagine it won't be too difficult for you to find a ginger cat to take its place on death row, hey, Boy?'

I now knew why I had been called to the reading of Smelly Jelly's will. I must say, I thought it bloody unfair that the responsibility of finding a cat to snuff to meet the requirements of the will had been allocated to me. I knew absolutely nothing about cats. I'd never known a cat intimately in my whole life and I had no idea where to find one willing to commit euthanasia.

I was about to protest when Mr Jacobs commenced reading again. 'To Tom Fitzsaxby I leave Flat 22, Parkington Gardens, 18 Cross Street,

Hillbrow and all the goods and chattels within it. I am aware that he has not enjoyed the best of accommodation during his school holidays over the past three years. Now that he has but one year to go before entering university he will need somewhere other than the park or the railway station steam pipes to live.'

I couldn't believe my ears. I had never told Smelly Jelly of my holiday living arrangements and could only surmise that he must, on some previous occasion, have followed me to the art gallery, and again later to the steam pipes. Now, all of a sudden, I owned somewhere named Flat 22, Parkington Gardens, 18 Cross Street, Hillbrow. I was fifteen years old, nearly sixteen, and owned a completely furnished home of my own! I wasn't sure I had heard Mr Jacobs correctly.

'Do I now *own* this flat, Sir?' I asked, somewhat incredulously.

'Do you have a guardian, Fitzsaxby?' Mr Jacobs asked, ignoring my question.

'No, Sir.'

He looked up at me over his glasses. 'I'm afraid that simply won't do! You're too young to take possession, papers to sign, deeds. Do you have a birth certificate?'

'I don't think so, Sir.'

'Well, man, how the devil do I know you are who you say you are?' he exclaimed, stabbing a single sausage in the direction of my chest.

It was a good question and one to which I had no answer. 'I just am, Sir, well, me. I'm an orphan, Sir.'

'Good Lord, Boy! Orphans don't just appear from under toadstools! They get born properly! Hospitals, records, that sort of thing!'

'Maybe they've got something at The Boys Farm, Sir,' I said.

'Boys Farm?'

'The orphanage at Duiwelskrans, Sir.'

Mr Jacobs made a note, then looked up. 'Well, I'm afraid you're going to have to bring someone in who can positively identify you. Someone who can act as your guardian until you come of age. Do you understand, Boy?'

I wondered if this meant that I wasn't going to become a property owner after all. 'What kind of somebody, Sir?'

Mr Jacobs was growing increasingly impatient and clucked his tongue. 'Someone who has known you for a period of three years, and who is prepared to sign an affidavit that you are who you say you are and agrees to hold the deeds to the property until you're old enough to take possession. Do you know someone like that?'

I thought of Reverend Robertson, the headmaster, but just as quickly dismissed the thought. Mr Jacobs would have to read the will to him and he'd find out about me sleeping rough all these years. 'Yes, Sir, Mr Lofty van der Merwe.'

'Dutchman?' he sniffed disapprovingly.

'Afrikaner, Sir.'

'Knows you well? Three years at least?'

'Yes, Sir.'

'You're to bring him in,' Mr Jacobs ordered. 'When? Can you call him on the telephone?' He jabbed a nicotine-coloured sausage in the direction of the telephone resting on his desk. 'I want to clear this matter up as soon as possible.'

'He's not available on the telephone, Sir.'

'Oh, where does he live?'

I swallowed hard. 'At the Starlight Hotel, Sir.'

'And they don't have a telephone? All hotels have telephones, Boy.'

'They won't take messages, Sir,' I lied. 'I can bring him in for you after school tomorrow.'

'Very well, and be sure to be on time, Fitzsaxby.'

'What time would that be, Sir?'

'On time is on time, Boy!' he reprimanded me sharply, half standing up and dismissing me in the direction of the door with a backhand wave of five pink sausages. 'Bring along two guineas for stamp duty!' he called after me.

So now I had a different problem. It was nearly five o'clock and Lofty van der Merwe would be well on his way to getting drunk. I had to get to the park and somehow persuade him to stay sober the following day until I picked him up after school. There was also the matter of clothes to be considered. Both cleanliness and tidiness are not usually associated with alcoholics living rough and Lofty was no exception. I'd have to persuade him to wash his shirt and his worn khaki trousers, as well as himself, first thing in the morning. His customary footwear was a pair of filthy takkies with a hole cut into each of their canvas toe-caps to allow his big toe to be exposed on the right foot and three of his smaller ones on the left. Lofty's exposed toes were not a pretty sight. I decided I'd solve this problem by buying him a new pair at the army disposal shop on the way in to see Mr Jacobs.

Lofty was at his usual place on the top step of the art gallery when I arrived, and appeared to be comparatively sober. 'Hey, what you doing here, Tom? It's not the *blêrrie* school holidays already? *Here*, man, time flies, it's only just the other day you went back again.'

I sat down next to him. 'Lofty, I need to ask you for a big favour,' I began.

'Ask away, Tom. We friends from way back.'

'*Ja*, thank you, Lofty, do you know what an affidavit is?' I asked.

'A what? No, man, I wouldn't know one from a bar of soap.'

'Well, it's like signing a document that says you know me and that I am who I am.'

'Who's asking, hey, Tom?'

'Well, this lawyer, Mr Jacobs.'

'Jacobs? I don't like the sound of that name, you hear? Take my advice, Tom. Stay away. Those Jews are very clever people, they got brains coming out all over the place, you can't beat them, you only going to end up worse-off than before.'

'No, it's not like that, Lofty.' I explained the business of Smelly Jelly's flat to him and with me being underage and having no birth certificate I needed him to positively identify me on a piece of paper called an affidavit while at the same time acting as my guardian.

'Guard? *Ja*, I can do that, Tom. Anyone who touches you has to deal with me, you hear? I'll knock his *fokken* block off,' Lofty declared fiercely.

'*Ja*, thank you, Lofty, I've seen your straight left in action before.'

Lofty looked pleased. 'Any place, any time, Tom. Just ask, man.'

'Guardian just means you agree to look after my affairs, like you're sort of, you know, my father.'

Lofty looked down at his knees, then back up at me. 'Tom, I have to tell you I wasn't a very good father.'

'No, you don't have to be one, you just have to sign a paper to say you'll do it,' I explained.

Lofty looked relieved. '*Ja*, okay, bring it here, man, I'll sign it.'

'No, it's only tomorrow, you have to come with me to the lawyer. He has to witness your signature.'

Lofty looked shocked. 'I have to come with you?' He took a quick slug of brandy and then shook his head slowly. 'Tom, I dunno, man. Lawyers, they always trouble, you hear?'

I spread my hands. 'Lofty, it's no big deal, we just go into his office and you just sign this piece of paper to say you know me and we get the deeds, finish and *klaar*.'

Lofty thought for a few moments, then nodded slowly. '*Ja*, okay, I'll do it,' he said.

'Thanks, Lofty, you're a real pal,' I said gratefully. Now, for the hard part, the bit about him having to take a shower and wear clean clothes. Lofty was a proud man and I wasn't sure how to broach the subject. But he saved me the embarrassment.

'What must I wear?' he asked, glancing down at his dirty blue shirt and torn khaki trousers. His tone of voice suggested that he had a wardrobe full of clothes and all I had to do was nominate the appropriate apparel for the visit. 'At the Salvation Army, I can get a clean shirt and some trousers,' he volunteered, then added, 'I can't promise a jacket, you hear?'

'No, no, that's fine, you don't need a jacket, and I'll buy you a pair of new takkies. Thanks a lot, Lofty.'

'For you it's a pleasure, Tom. I'll also take a shower, hey.'

Everything was falling into place but for one last thing. 'Lofty, you must promise me you won't have a drink until after the interview with Mr Jacobs.' I paused. 'That's after five o'clock tomorrow afternoon.'

Lofty took another long slug of brandy. 'Ag, Tom, you got no faith in a human being. You think I'm an alcoholic or something? You talking to Lofty van der Merwe, you know!'

'Please, Lofty,' I begged, 'just this once? Half past three tomorrow afternoon I'll be here.'

'Don't you worry, Tom. I'll be waiting, all spick-and-span, just you wait and see.'

The following afternoon I arrived to fetch Lofty. He was sitting in his usual spot on the art gallery steps, and from a distance I could see he wore a clean white shirt and a pair of dark brown trousers, but as I drew closer I saw the brandy bottle in his hand. 'Oh, Jesus, no!' I exclaimed. Drawing closer still, I saw that Lofty was completely legless. 'Lofty, you promised me!' I shouted angrily.

Lofty tried to focus on my face. 'Ag, Tom, ish my nerves fir that affydavy,' he explained drunkenly. 'Jes one little sip fir the nerves, man!' He looked at me sadly. 'But it did . . . didn't help, so I took nutha . . . you unnerstan, fir me nerves . . . not let yer down, Tom, I jes fine . . . no prob . . . prob . . . lem . . . man!'

'Lofty, you're drunk as a skunk!' I shouted at him.

'Ja, skunk asha drunk . . . but I can . . . sign the *blêrrie* affy, davy . . . look, I'll show you,' he placed the brandy bottle down beside him and began to trace squiggles with his forefinger in the layer of dust lying on the surface of the step.

'Christ, what's the use!' I cried, thoroughly disgusted. It was my fault, I'd put pressure on him and that's one thing you can't do with an alcoholic. The scrub-up and clean clothes and the expectations of the visit to Mr Jacobs had all been a bit too much, and he'd taken just the one little drink to calm his nerves, everyone knows all it takes is that first little drink.

Lofty looked up from his fancy finger-work. 'Ag, be heppy foh a change, Tom, ish notshow bad!' he slurred.

I turned and started to walk rapidly from the scene.

'Tom! Tom!' Lofty called out.

I turned to see him standing up and then somehow managing to stumble down the art gallery steps. He stopped at the bottom, swaying unsteadily. '*Fok* you!' he shouted after me.

Desperate times call for desperate measures. Mr Jacobs was expecting me around four o'clock and I had no time to waste. I walked straight over to Park Station where Tinky was very excited to see me, yelping and leaping up so that I caught him and held him as he planted a series of welcoming kisses all over my face. Frikkie was waving his stump so I knew he'd seen me.

'Frikkie, you've got to help me!' I cried, squatting down and explaining the situation as quickly as I could. 'You've got to come and sign the affidavit, you've known me since I was four years old.'

Frikkie rose slowly from his box and reached for his walking stick, and I fixed Tinky's lead to his collar. Then I took Frikkie's advertising sign from around his neck and lifted it over the hood, taking it together with the box to Stompie to keep in the kiosk. Then we set off directly for Market Street. Such was my anxiety that it never occurred to me that Frikkie Botha, hood or hoodless, must have been a strange and bizarre sight. The beggar and the schoolboy, wearing the blazer and tie from one of the poshest schools in the country, being led by a fox terrier along the street. Yet, in truth, Frikkie came closer to being my guardian than most of the people in my life. He'd watched me growing up and I'd spent more actual time in his presence than any other adult, except perhaps for Mevrou. Had I chosen Frikkie in the first instance, I would have seen to it that he was suitably cleaned up. With me away at school he had neglected himself badly and his once white and now filthy woollen vest, old suit coat and baggy cotton trousers were in a frightful condition. His garments were splattered with grease and every other kind of food stain, besides he stank to high heaven.

We finally reached our destination and I pressed the buzzer bell and we sat down, Tinky panting at Frikkie's feet. We waited for what seemed quite a long time before the door to Mr Jacobs' office opened and he stepped out. 'Good God! What is this?' he demanded in an alarmed voice. His glasses began to wobble as his nose, twitching, searched for the nasty smell that pervaded the reception area.

I stood up and indicated the seated Frikkie. 'This is my guardian, Mr Frikkie Botha, Sir,' I announced.

'Have you gone quite mad, Boy! Who is this . . .' he seemed momentarily lost for words, then added distastefully, 'creature?'

'My guardian, Sir,' I repeated. 'He's not a creature, Sir. He's here to verify that I am who I say I am and to sign the affidavit and take possession of the deeds to the flat.'

Mr Jacobs drew further back into the doorway to his office. I could see he was about to protest or dismiss us with a sweeping sausage-like backhand when, all of a sudden, Frikkie reached up and removed his hood. I had never before heard a grown man scream. Ten pink sausages were clasped to his breast in terror, his eyes popping out of his head as he reeled backwards into the interior of his office. The door slammed behind him with such ferocity that a small portion of greyish-coloured plaster fell to the floor from the wall directly above the lintel.

Frikkie reached out and with his left hand held my arm above the elbow making the glottal sounds that passed for laughter. I reached out and replaced his hood and had a bit of a giggle myself. What now? I thought. I decided, then and there, I wasn't going to budge. Frikkie might be dirty and smelly but he had the same rights as anyone else. Who says a person's guardian has to wear clean clothes or smell nice? He'd come to sign an affidavit and get the deeds, and that's exactly what we were going to do.

I walked over to the door, knocked and opened it slightly so Mr

Jacobs could see my face. 'Don't come in or I'm calling the police,' he said in a frightened voice.

'Sir, Mr Botha is quite competent to sign the affidavit. It's just that he once had a bad accident, he can't help the condition of his face.'

'Go away, both of you!' Mr Jacobs shouted.

'No, Sir, we're going to stay here until the affidavit is signed.' I closed the door. Then an idea occurred to me and I opened the door again. 'Sir, why don't you prepare a statement and slip it under the door and Mr Botha will sign it?'

Mr Jacobs seemed relieved at this suggestion. 'Very well, but he's not to come in or I'm calling the police.'

Frikkie and I sat waiting for a further twenty minutes before a sheet of paper appeared under the office door. I read it quickly and handed it to Frikkie who appeared to be reading. It was in English so I knew he didn't have a clue. 'Do you want me to read it to you, Frikkie?' I asked in Afrikaans. He shook his head and then produced his little pad and wrote, *Show me where*. I handed him the Waterman fountain pen Smelly Jelly had given me the previous year for Christmas and showed him where and what to fill in the blanks. Frikkie signed his name, the period he'd known me at The Boys Farm and accepted the role as my guardian and custodian of the title to Smelly Jelly's flat until I came of age.

I tapped on the door of Mr Jacobs' office. 'May I come in, Sir?'

'Alone!' Mr Jacobs called out fearfully. I opened the door and the stale cigarette smoke pervading the office seemed to slap me in the face. Two half-smoked cigarettes burned in the overflowing ashtray, twin curls of pale smoke rising to the ceiling. He was obviously still not entirely in command of his senses. I placed the affidavit in front of him. He read it quickly and witnessed it.

'May I have the deeds of my flat, Sir?' I said, putting down the two guineas for stamp duty he'd instructed me to bring along.

'You must first bring me a dead ginger cat,' he said quickly.

'Bring you a dead cat? A dead cat in here?' I exclaimed.

'No, of course not! The RSPCA! We must see a certificate of euthanasia. The will requires it.'

I walked to the door and opened it slightly. 'Frikkie, will you come in please? Take off your hood,' I called in a louder-than-necessary voice.

'No, no, please!'

I turned to see that Mr Jacobs looked truly terrified. I remained, deliberately waiting at the slightly open door as if to let Frikkie in. 'You shall have the deeds, Fitzsaxby!' the lawyer called out in alarm. 'Let me affix the stamps and hand you the deeds and the keys at once!' He reached for a packet of Craven A cork-tips.

I pointed to the ashtray. 'You have two alight, Mr Jacobs.' It was the first time I hadn't referred to him as Sir.

'Quite right,' he apologised, and reached over and murdered the two half-smoked fags, squashing them deeply into the pile of brown and white butts, bending them double at the cork-tip in the familiar manner of the others, then he handed the deeds to me.

'Thank you, Mr Jacobs,' I said, extending my hand. He reached over and took it, his grip flaccid, the fat little fingers feeling as boneless as their sausage-like appearance.

It was nearly half past five when I dropped Frikkie and Tinky at Mr Naidoo's Indian eatery and caught the bus back to the northern suburbs, and then walked the short distance to the Bishop's College to arrive just in time for supper.

On the way in the bus I kept fidgeting with the two keys to Flat 22, Parkington Gardens, 18 Cross Street, Hillbrow. The deeds to the flat felt secure within my inside blazer pocket and fitted snugly against my chest and armpit. At the age of fifteen, nearly sixteen, Tom Fitzsaxby now owned his very own palace. Perhaps, I thought to myself, now that you're the owner of property, it's time to stop hiding from the front.

CHAPTER FOURTEEN

Let Music Be the Wings of Love

THE LATE JELLICOE JAMES Wilberforce Smellie's flat was a small, dark two-room affair with bathroom and toilet and a cupboard that opened up to reveal a small fridge and hotplate and a few assorted dishes, two pots, an electric kettle and a frying pan. A single overstuffed club chair in the sitting room faced a small table on which a bullnose bakelite wireless and a gramophone of the wind-up variety sat. On the floor to each side of the table were two 2-foot stacks of 78rpm records, one jazz and the other classical. The remaining floor space was covered with a tired grey carpet, much in need of cleaning, and the walls, floor to ceiling, were fitted with bookshelves crammed with books on every subject imaginable, except religion.

The bedroom was so tiny that it could be better described as a monk's cell. It contained a narrow single iron cot and a small chest of drawers. Above this a rod protruded from the wall, and from it hung half a dozen tired-looking white shirts, three ties, two black and one maroon, frayed at the edges, another of his Gospel-gobbling Goose stained linen suits and a bright-red woollen dressing-gown. On top of the chest of drawers sat a monogrammed silver brush-and-comb set, in every appearance unused, which accounted for Smelly Jelly's Einstein hair. A window, blackened with grime and from all appearances never opened, cut through the wall above the bed, its sill acting as a bookshelf containing leatherbound copies of the works of Charles Dickens and Sir Walter Scott. Between the outer covers of each book, apparently to prevent them rubbing or becoming damaged, Jellicoe had placed an unfolded tract. These makeshift book-savers were the only reference to religion I found in the entire flat.

I'd taken possession of the flat on the last day of school on 5 December 1949, a year after the Nationalists came to power. The Afrikaners were back in control under Dr Malan, the new prime minister, and the *volk* were on the long march back to the past. If the *Dominee* hadn't already died of a heart attack, the beard-munching beetle, with no more vitriol to feed on, would have been out of a job. God's chosen people were back in business. The 'Bitter Enders', the true believers, were overjoyed and the cliffs and canyons in the high mountains around Duiwelskrans would have echoed with their triumphant cheering. What a mighty well-rounded sermon the *Dominee* would have delivered on the Sunday following election day, had he lived to see the 'Lost Tribe of Africa' find their way back home. Not that I was too fussed about politics at the time, my dealings with the Apartheid Government would come much later.

In retrospect, the Hillbrow flat may have been described as small, dark and dingy, but to my mind I wouldn't have swapped it for Buckingham Palace. I counted the early December day I moved into Smelly Jelly's flat as one of the happiest of my life. The single exception was perhaps the first visit to the great waterfall with Sergeant Van Niekerk, Marie, Doctor and Mevrou Van Heerden, and Meneer Van Niekerk the headmaster and his wife.

Now, you may be thinking that the day I found Tinker would be my happiest. But, of course, it wasn't. At the time I was filled with anxiety about how to keep her and the severe punishment I would receive from Mevrou if a puppy was to be found in my possession. Mattress Malokoane had saved my bacon on that day and still, nearly ten years later, hardly a day passed when I didn't think of the big, generous-hearted Zulu with the world-champion platform feet who had been my friend when no-one else could afford to be. How inextricably linked we'd all become. Mattress's death continued to plague me, and Frikkie Botha, who claimed he knew the circumstances of the Zulu's murder, was increasingly coming to depend on me as his physical condition continued to deteriorate.

Almost my first task every school holiday was to cart him to Johannesburg General where, because of his numerous operations and terribly scarred condition, he'd become an object of medical curiosity. The senior medical staff always seemed anxious to put him on display for their interns. There was hardly a branch of the medical profession that didn't find something of interest to them in Frikkie's face or poor broken body, with the result that I could obtain the sort of expert medical attention for him that a run-of-the-mill down-and-out was unlikely to receive. I also used these connections with the various top doctors to get due attention for the brotherhood and, as a result, by comparison to some of the other small communities of alcoholics in Johannesburg, the Joubert Park lot were, medically speaking, reasonably well looked after.

Frikkie's breathing was becoming increasingly laboured and we were making frequent stops on the way to Mr Naidoo's eatery for him to catch his breath. He was complaining of chest pains as well. Shortly after I'd moved into the Hillbrow flat I took him in for a complete medical examination. A cardiac specialist took X-rays and some soundings, and diagnosed a slightly enlarged heart. Professor Mustafa, the chief medical officer who had taken it upon himself to be the doctor in charge of Frikkie's medical, took me aside. He told me that the drinking and life of a derelict was taking its toll on Frikkie and that his tests showed he was a diabetic, probably from the sugar contained in the dozen bottles of Pepsi-Cola that Frikkie consumed each day.

'Along with his heart condition, in my opinion Mr Botha will be fortunate to make it through the next winter at the steam pipes, Tom,' he advised, then added, 'How he's survived this long sleeping rough is almost a medical miracle.' Then he invited me to sit down for what he described as 'a bit of a serious chat'.

'Tom, you've been bringing these alcoholics to us for three years, tell me, why do you do it, son?' Before I could reply he said, 'You know they all trust and love you, don't you?'

I shrugged. 'Drunks don't love or trust, Professor. I understand them, that's all.'

'You mean you don't judge them? Was your father an alcoholic?'

Two questions. 'No and no, he wasn't,' I replied, not wanting to say any more. It wasn't a lie because I had no way of knowing about my father. I hated people asking personal questions. When you hiding from the front, personal questions are definitely a no-no. I wanted him to stop, but you can't just come out and say, Mind your own business, Professor.

'Tom, we regard you very highly here at the General,' Professor Mustafa said kindly. 'We've made some enquiries, you see, and . . .'

I couldn't hold myself back any longer, he was a famous doctor and therefore a very important person, someone you'd never normally dream of contradicting or even interrupting, the most high-up of high-ups. But we were entering *Voetsek* territory, and I'd been around a long time and could read the silent sentences forming in people's heads as soon as they started happening, sometimes even before they knew themselves what they were about to say. Where this conversation was heading was only going to get me into a lot of trouble.

'Sir . . . er, Professor, I'm a born-again Christian and doing God's work,' I lied. 'Hallelujah! Praise His precious name! Are you saved, washed in the blood of the lamb, Professor?' I asked, laying the Smelly Jelly vernacular on thick as peanut butter in an attempt to put him on the defensive.

Professor Mustafa was silent for a moment, and then a sort of half-smile appeared on his face. 'Well, I'm not at all sure, Tom,' he said, scratching the side of his head with his forefinger, and appearing to be thinking. 'My parents were originally from Egypt and are Muslim, personally, I don't know about being saved by the blood of the lamb.' He grinned. 'But Egyptians eat a lot of lamb, if that's any help.'

I guess he wouldn't be a professor if he hadn't been a lot smarter than a schoolboy of fifteen, almost sixteen years old. He had me in one, and I started to giggle. 'Sorry, Professor, I lied, I'm not a born-again Christian.'

Professor Mustafa threw back his head and laughed. 'And I'm not a practising Muslim and have even been known to eat bacon,' he said, attempting to put me at ease. We were silent for a moment, and then he cleared his throat. 'Hear me out, Tom, I don't want to invade your privacy. If I go too far, then stop me, is that okay?'

'Ja, okay,' I said softly, but I wasn't, and he'd already gone too far as far as I was concerned. The God-bothering vernacular hadn't worked and I had no more tricks left to avoid being exposed, and I felt myself defenceless.

'Tom, about two months ago we were at the dinner table and I was talking to Mark, my eldest son, about his school results. They weren't bad, just not as good as I thought they ought to be, he's really quite a bright boy. Maybe I was being a little heavy-handed because he took exception to something I'd said about not wasting the opportunity he'd been given. "Ja, well, we can't all be as clever as Tom Fitzsaxby, Dad!" he replied. It seems he's in the same form as you at Bishop's.'

I nodded, knowing Mark Mustafa. 'He's no slouch, Professor.'

'Thank you, but that's not my point. Fitzsaxby is not a common name and I even took the precaution of looking it up in the phonebook. There's no Fitzsaxby in it. Your name was, of course, familiar to me. You've been bringing the alcoholics to Emergency for three years and signing for them. They often enough speak about you to the medical staff, how you stay with them in the park or the steam pipes during the school holidays, but none of them seemed to know the name of your school.'

I was pleased to hear him say this because I had gone to some trouble to make sure none of the brotherhood knew the name of the school I attended. Frikkie was the only one who knew anything about me. He'd indicated that I was okay and given the initial thumbs-up and that had been sufficient. Alcoholics are a self-preoccupied and incurious bunch anyway. Moreover, being unable to speak, Frikkie couldn't volunteer anything that might give me away. Besides, I'd never told him the name of the school, and I'd been careful never to wear my school uniform during the holidays. Hiding from the front becomes an ingrained habit, almost an instinct.

'But you concluded that I was the same Fitzsaxby that went to Bishop's?' I asked the professor.

'Well, *ja*, but not quite yet. It just didn't make sense. Exclusive private school to sleeping rough in the park and the steam pipes, it just seemed improbable. I tried to imagine my son doing so and simply couldn't. I kept asking myself how such a thing might occur. Then by fortunate coincidence, I found myself at a dinner party in Houghton where Reverend Robertson was also a guest. To cut a long story short, I mentioned that my son attended his school and inevitably the conversation got around to academic results and whether today's boys took their studies seriously enough. The headmaster seemed to think nothing much had changed, but then added that occasionally a student came along to gladden a headmaster's heart. "We have a young boy in the fourth form, Tom Fitzsaxby, who is the brightest student I can ever remember attending the school, quite, quite brilliant!" he said.'

I could feel my face starting to burn and I didn't know where to look. 'Nathan Feinstein and Julian Solomon are better than me, Sir,' I stuttered, averting my eyes. So much for hiding from the front, all of a sudden I was being found out all over the place.

Professor Mustafa continued as though he hadn't heard my response. 'This, I immediately thought, was an opportunity to question the headmaster. "What is the boy's background, headmaster?" I asked.'

I froze inwardly. The moment of truth had arrived. The headmaster had spilled the beans.

'Your headmaster is a very circumspect man, Tom. As a doctor I expect people to give me their most intimate details, it goes with the profession and I suppose we take it for granted. But the Reverend Robertson simply said, "He's a scholarship boy, I'm afraid we don't divulge their backgrounds, some of them may not enjoy the wealth and privilege most of the boys who come to the Bishop's College take for granted."' The professor grinned. 'Your headmaster put me well and truly in my place, Tom, but what he'd said was enough. I knew the Fitzsaxby he was talking about could only be you.' He paused. 'Tom, what we'd like to know is whether, when you matriculate next year, you would consider accepting a scholarship to Witwatersrand University Medical School?'

'No!' I cried out, my response so immediate and vehement that I had no idea where it came from.

Professor Mustafa drew back. 'I . . . I really don't quite understand.' He was clearly astonished at my reaction. 'You've had a better offer, Tom?'

'No, Sir, it's . . . it's nothing like that. Thank you, it's a huge compliment . . . honour. It's just . . .' I was incapable of finishing the sentence.

'This is the moment, then?'

'Moment, Sir?'

'Not to interfere.'

'Yes, thank you, Professor,' I said, grateful to be let off the hook.

'If you change your mind the offer still stands,' he said generously. He extended his hand and I took it. 'You're a pretty complex young man, aren't you, Tom?'

'No, Professor, it's just . . .'

He raised his hand. 'I understand, say no more.'

Phew! When an idea grows in your mind from the age of seven, at first it doesn't even have a shape. It is more like a shadow, not even that, a change in the light, a faint possibility. Gradually it begins to grow, fragile, unlikely, seeming impossible. But then it begins to articulate, to have clearly distinguishable parts. I sensed what it was I was going to have to do one day, but no alembic shape had yet emerged. I wasn't prepared to talk to anyone about it. Though one thing I knew for sure, it was an idea that had nothing to do with becoming a medical doctor.

While I had twenty pounds saved but for the two guineas stamp duty I had to pay for the title to Smelly Jelly's flat, I still needed to get a job for the Christmas holidays. I felt quite certain that I wouldn't be able to find another job as a tract writer, despite my rapidly growing international reputation.

I had been rather shocked to discover that Smelly Jelly was an apostate. I confess to always having had the odd pang of guilt over the tracts, but I told myself the fact that Jellicoe Smellie was such an ardent and enthusiastic born-again Christian served to let me off the hook. They were, after all, *his* tracts and it was *his* gospel mission. God's work was being done and I was only his amanuensis. But now, with him declaring his true beliefs, which were absolutely none, the Born-again Christian Missionary Society proved to be a cynical and exploitative exercise and I felt truly guilty and ashamed. The born-again Christians of this world definitely deserved better than two such covert blasphemers. Even if God may be said to work his wonders in mysterious ways, and despite the many testimonials we'd received saying my tracts had helped to save the souls of unknown sinners, we'd done the wrong thing.

While I had never been born-again, the *Dominee* had instilled in all of us a fear of God and the need to repent our sins. If I never got around to doing so, salvation was not such a bad idea. After all, it often turned drunks into sober men, criminals into honest men, and wilful and selfish men and women into loving and caring people. Confession and redemption are a part of every religion and seem to be a necessary part of the emotional lives of humankind.

But I'd been surrounded by God's business all my life, even attending an Anglican school, and I thought I might like to see what the secular world had to offer, which all added up to my getting another job as far away from the born-again business as possible. I chose the music business.

MUSIC SALESMAN

Well-known music retailer requires young, enthusiastic
trainee salesman. Trial position over Christmas period.
Tel. JB 7596.

I knew almost nothing about music, but I reckoned if I listened to all Smelly Jelly's 78s – I counted 197, almost equally divided between classical and jazz – I might learn something. Until I did, which might take several school holidays, the advertisement did say trainee salesman and trial position. Of course, I don't think they intended that their new trainee should be completely tone deaf. But, anyway, at the time I didn't know I was. While quite a lot of things seemed to stay fixed in my head, tunes were not one of them. I'd have trouble singing 'Baa Baa Black Sheep' in tune.

I went to the corner telephone box and called the number, and a Mr Lew Fisher answered. He asked my age and whether I had any previous business experience. Judging from his tone of voice, he didn't sound too impressed.

'The Born-again what?' he asked.

'Christian Missionary Society, Sir,' I answered.

'What did you do there?'

'I wrote tracts.'

'Tracts? What are they?'

It was a good question and one I'd never stopped to ask myself. 'Little stories that tell you how to repent and be saved,' I answered, knowing the conversation over the telephone wasn't going all that well.

'Saved from what?' he asked.

'Your sins, Sir.' The conversation was going from bad to worse.

'Oh! I see, sins.' A moment's silence followed, and Mr Fisher then said, 'Have you ever sold anything?'

Now the logical Smelly Jelly answer here would be 'Only Jesus Christ and Salvation', but I wasn't that stupid. 'Yes, books.'

'Where was that?'

The conversation was becoming intolerable. 'The "Come in and Browse for Christ" bookshop, Sir.'

'How old are you, Mr Fitz . . . ?'

'Saxby, fifteen, nearly sixteen, Sir.'

'Hmm. I don't think you'll suit our requirements, we don't sell very much religious music here at Polliack's.'

'Please, Sir, it says trial position, I mean, the ad, it says trainee, a temporary position over Christmas.' I swallowed hard. 'You can sack me if I'm no good,' I pleaded. Silence followed. 'Just give me an interview please, Sir,' I said, filling the void.

'Okay, maybe, what's your first name?'

'Tom, Sir.'

'Okay, Tom, you've got an interview,' he said suddenly. 'Tuesday, three o'clock, Polliack's.' I heard the click at the other end as he put the phone back on the receiver. I must say the music industry didn't sound too friendly and whoever he was, Mr Fisher was no Jellicoe Smellie. I didn't much like my chances of being accepted for the job.

I knew where Polliack's was in Eloff Street, it was supposed to be the biggest music emporium in Africa, or that's what they said when they sponsored a music program on Springbok Radio. I arrived early and stood outside on the pavement waiting so I'd be exactly on time. In one of the plate-glass windows facing the street was a white Steinway Baby Grand tied with a huge red ribbon. Or that's what the sign said it was, because it certainly was oddly shaped, fat and squat, and didn't look very much like any sort of piano I'd ever seen. A beautifully lettered sign with a tartan ribbon and a sprig of pretend holly pinned on the corner read: 'The greatest pianoforte in the world! Steinway Baby Grand. One thousand guineas.'

The ground floor turned out to be a shop selling not only musical instruments but also electrical goods. It all looked very posh with thick grey carpet on the floor and glass showcases all over the place, filled with expensive-looking goods. I walked up to a tall, slim salesman dressed in a very neat-looking blue suit, blue-and-white striped shirt, starched white collar and blue polka-dotted bow tie with a hanky to match sticking out of the breast pocket of his suit. I told him I had an appointment with Mr Fisher. 'Take the lift to the fifth floor,' he instructed, then brought his forefinger up to lightly touch his bottom lip, cocked his head to one side and gave me a quizzical look. 'Hmm!' he said, slightly raising an eyebrow.

A notice stand positioned near the lifts had an arrow pointing to a set of stairs leading downwards, it said: 'The Music Basement. Recording Sound Booths Syncopation Studio.'

I had no idea what those words meant. The lift neither clanked nor whined but was completely silent, white-walled and enclosed. I pressed the button and the lift glided upwards, and moments later the automatic doors slid open and I'd arrived on the fifth floor. Talk about posh! This was a long way from the rickety killer-stairs in the arcade or even the birdcage lift that juddered and shuddered, shook, clanked and whined on the way up to Jacobs & Tremaine, Solicitors & Attorneys at Law. I wasn't sure I was quite ready for all this opulence and mercantile splendour.

The neatly dressed salesman with the raised eyebrow who had hmm'd me downstairs had left me feeling somewhat disconcerted. I was wearing a brown sportsjacket from the Salvation Army that was a bit too big for me and by no means new. My school grey flannels were a bit too short, as I'd suddenly started to grow. I also had on a plain white shirt and brown shoes (highly polished) and one of Smelly Jelly's frayed-at-the-edges maroon ties. I'd ironed the shirt and pressed my pants under a piece of brown wrapping paper to prevent them from shining, so I wasn't exactly untidy. But I sensed that I'd entered a world a long way away from the Born-again Christian Missionary Society and the squabbling assortment of babble in the arcade beneath it.

Stepping out of the lift I was confronted by a dozen neat offices running along a corridor, all of which had their doors closed. I could hear a solitary typewriter tapping away, almost emphasising the silence. Fortunately, a large black guy was washing the opaque glass-front of one of the offices. You can tell a Zulu anywhere.

'S'bona,' I said, approaching him.

'S'bona, Baas,' he said, returning my greeting.

'Can you show me the house of Baas Fisher, please?' I asked him in his own language, not knowing the word for 'office' in Zulu.

He pointed further down the corridor, and placing his cleaning rag back into a sudsy bucket, bid me to follow him.

'What is your name?' I asked.

'Union Jack,' he replied, then suddenly halting and standing to attention and saluting, he smilingly added in English, 'King Georgie, he is my king.'

'I am Tom,' I replied, just as we reached an impressive-looking office somewhat larger than the glass-and-wood panelled ones surrounding it. An unoccupied secretary's desk stood immediately outside the door. On the door was painted 'Mr Lewis Fisher. General Manager'.

'The madam, she is not here,' Union Jack said, again in English, indicating the secretary's desk.

'Ngiyabonga,' I said, thanking him for his courtesy, and he seemed surprised when I extended my hand. He took it and I shook his own in the double-grasp commonly used by the African people. Then I knocked on the door and a voice that didn't sound all that friendly called, 'Come!'

I opened the door and entered. Mr Fisher looked up from some paperwork he was doing. 'Oh, is it three o'clock, already?' He capped his gold fountain pen and placed it on the glass-topped desk. 'Tom, isn't it?'

'Yes, Sir,' I replied, somewhat nervously. 'Tom Fitzsaxby, and I have an appointment for the trial trainee music salesman,' I reminded him, just in case he'd forgotten.

'Ja, of course, please sit, Tom,' he said in quite a friendly tone, indicating the chair in front of his desk. The office was of a sufficient size to have a separate area with a leather lounge and two matching chairs, a fancy sort of oriental-looking carpet and a coffee-table on which rested a cut-glass vase of yellow roses. On the wall was a large oil painting of an African village with the Drakensberg Mountains in the background. You could tell from just looking that Mr Fisher was a pretty important person and I was surprised that he'd be interviewing such a low-down as me.

Mr Fisher leaned back in his chair. 'So, what have you got to say for yourself, young man?' he asked.

How do you answer a question like that? 'Nothing much yet, Sir,' I replied. My instinct told me not to mention my international reputation as a tract writer.

'Yet?' he seemed amused.

'Well, I'd like very much to learn how to be a trainee music salesman, Sir.'

'Well, I must warn you, it's a far cry from the religious business, Tom,' he said, recalling our previous phone conversation. Then he chuckled, though more to himself. 'There are some people who think jazz is the music of the devil. What do you think?'

I didn't know how to answer him. 'I've only heard it on Springbok Radio, Sir.' Then I added, 'It sounded okay to me. Dizzy Gillespie and all that,' I said, remembering a snatch of an announcer's conversation overheard in passing on the radio in the prep room at school.

'What do you know about music, Tom?' he asked, looking directly at me.

'Nothing, Sir.'

His eyebrows shot up in surprise, 'Nothing?'

'That's why I need to be a trial trainee music salesman, so I can learn,' I said, perhaps a little too ingenuously.

He smiled and leaned forward. 'Well, at least you're honest, I like that. What school did you attend?'

'Still attend, Sir. The Bishop's College.'

To my surprise his arms spread wide. 'Well, I never! Why didn't you say so in the first place, Mr Polliack's three boys all went to Bishop's. I myself wasn't that privileged,' he added.

'I'm a scholarship student, Sir,' I explained.

'Not from a wealthy family, eh?'

'No, Sir.' Please don't ask me any more, I thought desperately, but I need not have worried because I was about to learn the abracadabra, open sesame of the private-school system among English-speaking South Africans.

He seemed pleased. 'And you need a job for the Christmas holidays?'

I nodded. 'Yes, please, Sir.'

Mr Fisher, half-rising, reached out across his desk, his hand extended. 'Welcome to Polliack's, the largest musical emporium in all of Africa,' he said, smiling broadly. 'Now, let's have your personal details. What did you say your surname was again?'

And so ended my career as a writer of religious tracts and I began as a salesman in the ungodly business of jazz music and what was known in the firm as popular syncopation, a musical style in which Miss Patti Page, among others, featured hugely.

I'm a Lonely Little Petunia (in an Onion Patch)
***
Put Another Nickel In (Music! Music! Music!)
***
Bongo, Bongo, Bongo (I Don't Want to Leave the Congo)
***
Please No Squeeza Da Banana
***
Five Minutes More (Give Me Five Minutes More,
Only Five Minutes More)
***
It Might As Well Be Spring

I could learn a set of lyrics in ten minutes, but if my life depended on it I couldn't have hummed the tune to which they were attached. Over Christmas, after the trial was dropped, I became simply the trainee musical salesman and general factotum who appeared every school holidays. Over the following year I learned to fake a musical prowess, listening to the drumbeat in the background, and keeping time by snapping my fingers, or shaking my shoulders, or tapping my feet, and in the process becoming the complete musical phoney. The Boys Farm was paying off at last. A customer would ask me about the latest hit record, and while I found it for him or her, placed it on the turntable

and handed them a set of earphones, I'd recite the entire set of lyrics
with the result that I fooled almost everyone but myself. I was learning
to be a salesman. Smelly Jelly had taught me how to praise the Lord
using well-rounded vowels, and it worked just as well with lyrics. I could
make a set of inane lyrics in plain-speak sound like the meaning of life
to your average teenager, particularly if it was a love song. For instance,
with Perry Como's 'Some Enchanted Evening' I could often reduce a
young woman to teary-eyed euphoria and the sale was made long before
the actual record started to spin on the turntable.

Now here's a funny thing. My Salvation Army too-big brown
sportsjacket and my too-short school grey flannels, my turned-up-at-the-
collar white shirts and frayed-at-the-edges Smelly Jelly black or maroon
ties seemed to add to my musical authority. I became the teenage
eccentric, the one-off, the *wunderkind*, all the while using influence I
didn't have. Kids would wait for me to serve them, ask me earnest
questions about the artists and hang on every word I uttered as if I was
the Holy Grail of pop music. 'All you need is a pair of horn-rimmed
glasses,' Graham Truby of the first-day 'Hmm' would declare. 'A little
myopia to add to that hapless boy musical-genius look.'

The point being the sniffy Graham of the tucked-in-at-the-waist
blue suit, striped shirt, bow tie, matching handkerchief and pronounced
lisp disliked serving the kids. Bobby Black, who was the department
head, a jazz drummer in black stovepipe pants, jacket down to his knees,
black string tie, lolly-pink shirt and shoes called winklepickers so pointed
that if he kicked you up the arse you'd end up with lockjaw, stuck to
selling jazz. He had a semi-famous band called Bobby Dazzle that played
strictly purist jazz, jazz and only jazz. Louis Armstrong, Count Basie, Ella
Fitzgerald, Lena Horne, and so on.

The three of us turned out to be an ideal combination for the music
basement. The adult jazz *aficionados* were drawn to Bobby with his
gollywog hairdo, long sideburns and early teddy boy suit. Graham greatly
fancied himself as Mr Opera, Ballet and Classical music, attracting the
pretentious, the serious-minded and the older foreign-accent customers.

While the young and uninformed, the musical plethora were left to
'Fitzy', who knew the words to every popular song you could name and
left you feeling like a champion because you knew enough to have
purchased a hit song before it became one. Smelly Jelly's born-again
imprecations such as 'Praise the Lord! Praise His precious name, my
dear brother in Christ' became adapted to the music biz in statements
such as, 'Yeah, good one! You've so very prudently picked Patti Page, the
Princess of Pop!' Or to a pretty young girl customer, 'Perry Como will
touch the love chords in your deeply musical soul!' My customers ate all
this rhetoric up in spoonfuls, and I confess I enjoyed the attention. Here
was a place you didn't have to hide from the front. At the end of the day
Mr Fisher simply looked at your sales figures.

Thank goodness my sales were pretty good as we were on a salary
and commission, and by the time the July holidays came around I'd
made sufficient money to buy myself an entirely new outfit. The pair of
honey-coloured corduroy trousers I'd lusted after for a year, dark-brown
suede brothel creepers with thick crepe rubber soles, three new shirts,
two knitted ties, a Fair Isle jumper and a brand-new, properly fitting
Harris Tweed sportsjacket. Six months saving, but worth every penny. It
was the first time ever that every single thing I wore was brand-new and
in the latest fashion. Boy, was I ever pleased with myself!

I remember it was a Saturday morning, the busiest time of the week
because the shops closed at noon. I arrived in the music basement
looking like a million dollars only to be confronted by Bobby Black.

'What the fuck?' he said, staring at me. 'Graham, get here quick,
man!' he shouted across the basement.

'What's the matter?' I asked, smiling proudly, thinking he was pulling
my leg.

Graham now stood at Bobby's side, forefinger poised on lip, free
hand placed on tucked waist, head cocked. 'Oh dear! Oh dearie me!' he
exclaimed.

'What?' I asked again, hunching my shoulders and spreading my
hands.

'Home!' Bobby ordered, pointing to the stairs.

'What's wrong, Bobby?' I asked, totally bemused, looking down at my brilliant new duds.

'You've just fucked your entire image, son! Now go home and get into your usual gear and get back here, pronto, we've got a busy morning ahead of us.'

'And wash that ghastly Brylcreem out of your hair!' Graham added.

If I sound like I was killing them at Polliack's, while I was doing well enough I was still the kid around the place doing chores and messages when it wasn't busy in the basement. I seldom got a lunch hour as I'd have to mind a floor while the floor manager of, say, the electrical department – 'fridges, washing machines, toasters, radiograms, floor polishers, electric fans and the new-fangled dishwashers' – was out to lunch. I was never allocated lunch-hour duty at front of house, the grey-carpeted ground floor. This, I knew, had a lot to do with my being a callow youth in the Salvo gear that worked so well for my persona in the basement.

Often I'd be given the piano department, the poshest place of all, to mind. It was separately located on the fourth floor where the musical behemoths rested in an atmosphere of splendid, highly polished calm. The three Steinway Baby Grands resting separately from the uprights on a platform decorated with potted palms planted in cut-down beer barrels with the hoops made of highly burnished brass, one of the many chores allocated to Union Jack.

I hated the piano department because, as you'd expect, it was never busy. People don't exactly walk off the street to buy a piano, or didn't in those days anyway. Instead, they made an appointment with Mr Farquarson who, in turn, 'made a suitable appointment' and then put them through a long and often harrowing interrogation. Buying your piano from Polliack's added an extra dimension to its value and so you had to earn your piano-playing rights by establishing your credentials as the 'the right kind of people' to own one from the largest musical emporium in all of Africa.

My dislike for the piano department extended to Mr Farquarson, a fat, effete Englishman who was a terrible snob and who referred to his forebears as 'County', his pronunciation rich with such perfectly rounded vowels that he'd have left Smelly Jelly for dead. He was also a sometime– concert pianist, although nobody knew quite where his illustrious career had taken place. To his credit he could certainly tickle the ivories better than most, though of course always classical.

He wore striped grey pants without turn-ups, ending over black patent leather shoes fitted with white spats. His jacket was a black linen cutaway without lapels or buttons and slightly flared where the sleeves met the shoulders. It fell down to the back of his knees in the manner of an Oxford don. He always wore a highly starched white shirt topped by an Eton collar, and instead of a tie an exaggerated maroon bow frothed from under his several chins with the ends of the ribbon resting on his enormous stomach. If he'd worn a prep school cap he would have been a dead cert for Billy Bunter's father. He was known around the place as 'The Ship of State', or by Graham as 'That disgusting old queen upstairs!' Bobby Black had once picked up on Graham after he'd heard him expressing his sentiments concerning Mr Farquarson and said, 'Look who's talking.'

Graham got very upset. 'I'm *not* fat and I'm *not* disgusting, I'll have you know I'm a perfectly respectable and rather nice queer!' he replied indignantly.

Later he confided in me that jazz drummers are deeply into pain and habitually place their dicks on the kettledrum, which accounted for all that grimacing in jam sessions. 'No names, no pack drill, Fitz,' he'd pouted, then, indicating Bobby's cubicle with a flick of his head, 'That's the only way the prick can manage to get a free bang!'

I can tell you, I was moving further and further away from the Born-again Christian Missionary Society, even if it was a pretty feeble joke.

I tried to imagine what sort of tract I'd have to write to bring Graham or Bobby to their knees, begging for salvation, but was forced to concede that I wouldn't know where to begin. 'The drummer that banged for Jesus,' an unfortunate ambiguity. 'The faggot that lit a spiritual bonfire!' I was definitely losing my touch.

At the end of that year, 1950, I sat for my matriculation exams and then it was school holidays once again. One lazy afternoon in January, with Christmas well and truly over and empty pockets prompting 'sale' signs in almost every shop in town, my biggest break ever came seemingly out of the blue and into the piano department one lunchtime.

It appeared in the form of a large *boer* who looked decidedly awkward in his soiled moleskins, khaki open-neck shirt, scalloped under the armpits with sweat, scuffed working boots and wide-brimmed hat that had seen 10000 sunrises and defied a hundred dust storms. In the pristine, softly glowing sheen of Polliack's piano department he looked as incongruous as a gorilla in a cathedral. I don't mean he looked like a large ape, because he didn't, it was just that he seemed completely out of context standing in front of the lift holding a string-handled brown-paper shopping bag.

But first a little background explanation. The Cold War between Russia and America was beginning to hot up. Korea, North and South, tucked in between China and Japan, was beginning to look like the place where a showdown between the Communists and the Free World was likely to take place. There was a great deal of sword-rattling going on between the two superpowers and the coming conflict was being touted as a peacekeeping mission under the aegis of the brand-new United Nations. North Korea was Communist and supported by Russia, while South Korea was a so-called democracy propped up by America. Communist China, the crouching dragon puffing smoke, looked on from across the Yalu River, all potential players waiting on the sideline. The world it seemed was returning to war. Gold and copper prices soared and so did the price of wool. Sheep farmers in the Karoo, the dry, flat desert country east of Cape Town, for generations barely eking out a living with their vast flocks on an unforgiving landscape, became overnight millionaires. The wool boom was on for one and all. Korea was a land where the winter temperatures fell to 30 degrees below zero and the American army, among others, had to rug up in anticipation of the big conflict in the cold.

I'd only just arrived to spend what might be anything up to three boring hours babysitting the pianos. Mr Farquarson was about to leave for an extended lunch hour to be spent, he unnecessarily informed me, 'over lunch at the Carlton and a few glasses of excellent libation with the conductor of the Johannesburg Symphony Orchestra'. He was preparing to depart, arranging his large black felt hat at a jaunty slant, the brim on one side up and on the other down, when the *boer* walked in. The Afrikaner stood hesitantly at the entrance to the lift, holding the brown-paper shopping bag with both hands in front of him. Though the Ship of State must have seen him, he showed no reaction whatsoever. He took one finally admiring look at himself in the mirror and, turning to me, said, 'Get rid of *that*, Boy!' Then he pontificated towards the lift, passing the *boer* as if he simply wasn't there. Thankfully the lift was still stationary and opened immediately to accept his corpulent prow.

'*Goeie middag*, Meneer,' I said, bidding the *boer* good afternoon.

At first he didn't reply. A look of consternation appeared on his face as his eyes swept over the department. '*Here*, man, how is a man supposed to make a choice?' he said in Afrikaans.

I was about to ask if he had an appointment but then realised, of course, he didn't. 'Do you wish to purchase a piano?' I asked.

'*Ja*, of course,' he said, looking at me as if I was mad. 'You think I come in a place like this to get out of the sun?'

My heart began to beat faster, and I thought for a moment to ask him to wait and then try to catch up with Mr Farquarson and bring him back, but quickly realised that all I would receive in return would be a stern rebuke.

'How much is a piano?' the *boer* asked.

'Various prices, Meneer,' I answered politely, 'but first maybe a cup of coffee or a cool drink?'

He nodded, accepting the offer, and extended his large hand, the fingers blunt, nails broken, skin rough. 'Odenaal, Johannes Odenaal.'

'Tom Fitzsaxby.' My hand completely disappeared into his fist.

'*Engelsman?*'

'*Ja*, Meneer Odenaal,' I said, admitting to being English-speaking.

'*Jy praat die taal goed*, Tom. You speak the language well, Tom.'

'My *eerste taal*, Meneer. My first language, Sir.'

'*Ja*, coffee,' he said, and then added, 'should a person take his hat off in a place like this?'

I laughed. 'It's only a shop, Meneer.'

He shook his head and then indicated the pianos with a sweep of his hand. 'Tell me, how much polish do you use in the place?'

'*Ja*, I never thought about it before, but you right, quite a lot, the Zulu is always polishing around the place, he's even got an electric floor polisher.'

'You don't say? Electric floor polisher, hey? Why don't you use a *kaffir* woman like everyone else?'

'Have you ever seen an electric floor polisher, Meneer Odenaal?'

'No, man, I can't say I have, if I said so it would be a lie, you hear?'

To kill the boredom of babysitting the pianos I would often help Union Jack with the cleaning and polishing around the place, and so I was familiar with the workings of the floor polisher, in fact I had become quite an expert. 'Let me show you,' I offered. I went to the broom cupboard and removed the floor polisher, plugged it in and turned it on, demonstrating it around where we were standing for a few moments before turning it off.

'*Wragtig!* That is a contraption-and-a-half!' Meneer Odenaal exclaimed.

'You want to have a go?' I asked.

He seemed reluctant. 'It's not my line of work, Tom. Sheep I know, electric floor polishers, I'm not so sure, man.'

'Ag, it's dead easy,' I replied, pushing the polisher towards him. 'Just grab the handles and lead it around, you don't even have to push, one brush goes round left and the other right, the handles are the same.' I switched it on and the floor polisher came to life with its usual whine, its floor brushes whirring. I kicked the button that lowered the brushes to the surface of the polished wooden floor. 'Now just push it, Meneer,' I instructed above the noise of the machine.

The large man placed the brown-paper shopping bag down at his feet and began to push the floor polisher tentatively, but soon got the hang of it and before you knew it, he was doing circles and zig-zags and smiling broadly in the process, even at one stage doing a neat little circle around the shopping bag. After a while I turned it off.

'Let me tell you, it's better than ten *kaffir* women!' he said admiringly, patting the machine as if it were a favourite canine.

'Coffee, I nearly forgot,' I said suddenly. Mr Farquarson kept a Kona carafe of coffee constantly warming on a small hotplate in his office. It was usually remade by Union Jack in the afternoon, but with him going on one of his protracted lunch hours it probably hadn't been replaced. But I knew that *boer* farmers sit an enamel pot of coffee on the kitchen stove all day and prefer it to be bitter and black. The carafe was still about a third full, sufficient for two or three mugs. 'How many sugars?' I called.

'*Ja*, a lot, five!' Meneer Odenaal called back.

I handed him the mug of sweet black coffee and he took a sip. '*Ja, dit is goed*,' he said, smacking his lips, congratulating me on the coffee. I motioned him towards a small lounge setting reserved for important 'appointment only' visitors and we sat down to drink our coffee.

'A biscuit!' I cried, leaping to my feet, remembering that in the country coffee is never served without something to eat. The Ship of State kept a packet of Marie biscuits in the bottom drawer of his desk, and I'd occasionally help myself to one.

'*Ja*, that would be *lekker*, Tom. Can a person smoke in here?'

'*Ja*, of course, go ahead,' I invited, pointing to the ashtray on the coffee table.

By the time I returned with the packet of biscuits, the *boer* had lit up a large meerschaum pipe and a miasma of sweet-smelling smoke surrounded his great balding head.

'Sorry, I couldn't find a plate, the Zulu must have taken them to wash up,' I apologised. I referred to Union Jack as 'the Zulu' not so that he would appear to be inferior but because his name might have upset the *boer*. Union Jack is about the dirtiest word you can use in front of a *regte boer*. Besides, we were soon to get down to the nitty-gritty and I was becoming nervous, not wanting to put a foot wrong. If I could sell him the cheapest piano on the floor the commission alone would be at least twice what I would earn for the Christmas and January holiday period. I'd be able to go to university at the end of Febuary with money in my pocket. In the meantime, Meneer Odenaal was scoffing four Marie biscuits to every sip of coffee, his mouth too full to talk.

'Another cup?' I asked, seeing him drain the last of the mug.

'*Ja, dankie*, Tom,' he thanked me, placing the pipe, which seemed to have gone out, in the ashtray.

I drained the Kona, added sugar, stirred the bittersweet concoction and returned it to him, by which time he'd consumed almost the entire packet of biscuits. I only hoped I could replace them in time before the Ship of State returned from his claret-and-conductor luncheon.

'*Ah, lekker jong!* You make good coffee,' he said, smacking his lips. 'The coffee you get in the Transvaal, it's not like the Cape, it tastes like shit!'

'You're not from the Transvaal, then?' I asked.

'No, man, never! The Karoo.'

'I've never been to the Cape,' I replied.

'Really? You must come soon, you hear? It's a very civilised place, people greet you, not like here in Johannesburg.' He laughed suddenly. 'Over here, *jong*, if a man takes his hat off for a lady in the street they think you mad and they want to call a policeman!' He looked at me seriously. 'When you come to the Cape you must visit us, you hear? I got a nice little daughter, my little *skattebol*, only fifteen, she'll suit you down to the ground, Tom.'

I thanked him for his invitation, smiled at his generous and gratuitous matchmaking with his *skattebol*, which means 'little treasure', and tried to imagine what his fifteen-year-old daughter might look like. 'What brings you up to the Transvaal?' I asked.

The big *boer* leaned back, crossed his legs, removed his wide-brimmed hat and placed it over his knee, folded his arms across his chest and, reaching out, picked up his pipe, and relighting it, he started to tell me the story of his recent travels.

'First you got to understand, Tom, I got four daughters. Hester and me we haven't been blessed by the Good Lord with sons, only daughters. But we can't complain, the first two, they married well, Karoo sheep farmers like us, they doing well. We all doing well for a change. They only live next door, down the road from us, forty miles maybe. Already the first one, Hanka, has got twins, both boys, and the next, Gertie, she's got a little girl and is now pregnant again. But never mind what she has, we got the two boys already. But the next again, Anna, she's always the wild one, you hear? This young *kêrel* from the Transvaal, he's going to Agricultural College in Potchefstroom and he comes to stay on the farm to learn practical stuff about sheep. Next thing you know Anna is pregnant and he is the guilty one. It's a shotgun wedding, I admit, but not so bad, maybe two months, nothing's showing already and the *Dominee* doesn't make trouble.

Now they living on his parents' farm near Rustenburg in the Western Transvaal. It's a long way from home and it makes the *ouvrou* sad, a woman doesn't like to lose her daughters. Now they want one hundred sheep and a good ram for a wedding present. I'm not so sure, man. "Since when is Rustenburg good sheep country?" I ask him. But he's now gone to farm school, so he knows everything, you hear? "I've studied the conditions, *Oom* Jannie. It's not too wet, you hear?" So, what can a man do? I can put the sheep on the train, but it's ten days and you can never tell what will happen, someone will maybe forget to give them water and that's the end, finish and *klaar*. So I tell Hester to come with me and she says, no, Gertie is the most pregnant of the two daughters and expecting any day now, so she's not going with me. It's a long way on your own, but I put the sheep in the big trailer and I take the Rio up myself, it's a good old lorry, but it's still five days on the road. I've put in five extra sheep and my fourth-best ram, because with sheep some always die, they can't help themselves, a sheep is a stupid animal and they die and don't give you a reason. But I only lose one on the last day, so the dogs on my son-in-law's parents' farm have got some nice meat.'

The meerschaum had gone out again and Meneer Odenaal placed it back in the ashtray and reached forward and took the last two Marie biscuits, popped both into his mouth and, chewing, said, 'Now I'm going home and coming through Krugersdorp and there is this whine in the differential.' He swallows the last of the biscuit. 'I stop at a garage and the mechanic says he hasn't worked on a Rio, the diff is different. So he looks in the telephone book and says in Johannesburg is the Rio people, in Braamfontein.'

'That's just the other side of Park Station,' I say, getting a word in at last.

'Ja, not so far, but it's going to take all day to fix the diff so I might as well take a look, hey?'

'So you found yourself here?'

'Ja, you walk and you thinking and jumping out of the way of people and then I get an idea. I'm not a man who makes up his mind in a hurry, you understand? But this idea it just comes, like a bit of rain you not expecting. You look up and there it is, clouds coming over the *Komsberge*, and the next thing I've made up my mind.'

Just then Union Jack comes into the piano department and looks disapprovingly at the empty Marie biscuit packet and at the crumbs scattered on the coffee-table and the floor at the feet of my visitor, and then quizzically at the floor polisher standing nearby. He knows very well where the Marie biscuits come from. He also knows the pecking order around the place. While we've become good friends, he is aware that the big coarse-looking man in working clothes sitting with me isn't the usual sort of Polliack 'by appointment only' piano customer. He knows

I'm probably out of order and using influence I haven't got by sitting him down and serving him the Ship of State's coffee and Marie biscuits.

'Can you make some coffee, please?' I ask him in Zulu, careful again not to use his name.

'Yes, *Baas* Fitzy, I am also taking the floor polisher?' Union Jack asks in English, giving me a questioning look. He is very particular about the piano department and takes great pride in the gleaming pianos and the immaculate setting. To see him using a chamois to polish a piano is to observe a master at work. I nod and he moves off with the polisher, and hopefully also to make coffee.

'Man, that electric floor polisher! It's modern times, hey? You never know what they going to think of next,' the *boer* says.

'So, Meneer Odenaal, you find yourself in the middle of town and all of a sudden you've made up your mind.' Even though I was enjoying his story I was anxious to cut to the chase and get back to the subject of pianos.

'Ag, Tom, just call me *Oom* Jannie, we old friends already. *Ja*, well, you see it's different times now. A Karoo sheep farmer is naturally a poor man, we a proud people, you understand? But my *oupa* was poor, my papa was poor and Hester and me we also poor. The Karoo is a hard country to make a living, but we there six generations already, you understand? We all buried there, six generations! Thank God there is always a bit of food on the table, but sometimes it's very hard and you have to go to the bank again. Now last year and the year before the rains are good and we have the best lambing seasons I can remember since I'm a small boy. Then comes this war that's coming in Korea, and then comes the wool boom and now, all of a sudden, we rich.' He said it quite simply and not in the least ingenuously, almost as if the whole thing had come as a surprise.

'That's good, *Oom* Jannie, it's nice when that happens to good people,' I said, genuinely pleased for him.

'Thank you, Tom, but that's not why I'm telling you all this. You see, Hanka and Gertie and even Anna, they never had anything when they growing up, it was always skimp and scrape, dresses handed down, even shoes. But we were a happy family, see, very musical also, except me, all the girls got nice voices, and Gertie would play the old piano accordion and Hanka the guitar.' *Oom* Jannie smiled, remembering. 'It was nice times, Tom, but poor, and always you wanted them to have better.'

Sensing that he was growing over-sentimental, *Oom* Jannie suddenly straightened and clapped his hands. '*Genoeg!* Enough!' he said. 'Here comes the idea. The Rio is empty and we going back home tonight when that differential is fixed. For Hester, my wife, who stuck with me through thick and thin, all the hard times and now the good, I want to buy a peeano. Also for Gertie and Hanka who never complained and worked hard. Anna has the sheep and my fourth-best ram and they all going to die in that new place that's not sheep country and that's enough spent already on her.' He sat back, clasping his hands together. 'So, now you show me some peeanos please, Tom?'

I couldn't believe my ears. 'You want three pianos and you want to take them away with you tonight?' I asked, incredulous.

'*Ja*, I'll pay cash,' he added.

'*Oom* Jannie, do you know what a piano costs?' I asked.

'Ag, Tom, they waited a long time, maybe next year there's no rain or that war goes away again, a man must do the right thing by his woman.'

'Let me show you,' I stammered, my voice suddenly squeaky. Just then Union Jack arrived with a silver tray, the Kona pot filled to the brim and steaming, Wedgwood cups and saucers and side plates with four pieces of fruitcake on a small silver cake stand with a white paper doily and two white linen serviettes. He placed the tray down in front of us with a smug look on his face.

'*Umbulelo*, thanks,' I said.

'*Injabulo, Baas*. A pleasure, Boss.' I could sense his amusement, the bugger was sending me up.

'More coffee, hey?' *Oom* Jannie said, then looked about. 'Tom, where can I take a quick piss, man?'

Fortunately there was a toilet in the piano department, more at the insistence of the Ship of State, who had a dodgy bladder, than because it was in frequent use by the public or staff. I pointed out the toilet and when *Oom* Jannie had entered I called urgently to Union Jack in Zulu. 'He's going to buy three pianos!' I exclaimed. Union Jack's mouth fell open. 'For cash!' I added excitedly.

'*Ahee!*' the big Zulu exclaimed, bringing his hands up to his mouth.

'Do they all have removal covers?' I asked. He nodded. 'Can we get them down to the loading dock by five o'clock?' He nodded again, still not having found his voice. 'Quick, show me the cheapest ones and then the next cheapest, in case he wants something a bit better.'

Union Jack led me over to the cheapest uprights, and then pointed out the next up in price. He lifted the lid and showed me where the price tag for each piano was located. Even if he bought the cheapest, *Oom* Jannie was up for six hundred pounds! You could buy a brand-new small car for that sort of money.

Oom Jannie returned back from the toilet, his hat planted back on his head. 'First we look, then coffee, hey, Tom?' He stooped down and picked up a piece of fruitcake as I escorted him towards the rows of pianos.

'These are the most reasonably priced,' I said, showing him a small upright.

'*Ja*, it's nice, Tom, can you play it, please?'

I know it's stupid, even obvious, why would someone buy a piano without hearing it, it was like buying a car without first driving it, but the thought hadn't occurred to me. '*Oom* Jannie, I can't play the piano,' I confessed.

'*Here*, man, Tom, I can't take it home and tell Hester I didn't even hear a tune on it. Anything? Can't you play maybe a small tune?'

Then I remembered that Mr Farquarson, in what was a private joke, had taught Union Jack to play 'God Save the King' with a fanfare of chords at the front and the back. Union Jack was terribly proud of this accomplishment, but the Ship of State would snigger, 'Small minds. Primitives. It doesn't take much to train them, old boy. You can teach a chimpanzee as much.'

I swallowed hard, I had to take a chance. I knew Bobby Black could play the piano, but if I called him up it would become his sale, he'd take over. 'Union Jack!' I called out.

'Yes, *Baas*!' he said, standing just within earshot with a cloth, pretending to polish a nearby upright.

'Come and play for the big *Baas*,' I said to him, making it sound like an order.

The big Zulu in his blue overalls with 'Polliack's' embroidered on the back needed no second invitation. Union Jack opened the keyboard and with a flourish of the keys banged out 'God Save the King'.

'That's nice, you hear,' *Oom* Jannie said to my surprise, not reacting at all adversely to the dreaded anthem. 'Now we going to try them all.'

'It will have to be the same tune, *Oom* Jannie, it's the only way you can compare them,' I said quickly.

'*Ja*, I know, that's a nice tune.'

And so Union Jack went from one piano to the next until we had tried all sixteen uprights on the floor.

'I like the second-last one,' he said pointing at an upright, 'have you got three?'

I looked at Union Jack who shook his head. '*Nye*,' he said, raising his forefinger.

'Only the one, I'm afraid, maybe you can pick two others, *Oom* Jannie?'

He thought for a moment. 'Those ones, there's three of them, we haven't played them.' He was pointing at the three Steinway Baby Grands on the raised platform.

I had difficulty finding my voice. '*Oom* Jannie, that's a Steinway Baby Grand, the best piano made in the world.'

'Why is it such a funny shape, hey, Tom?'

I couldn't think why. 'To get perfect sound, they make it like that so the inside is bigger and the sound is better,' I invented hastily. 'It's all about acoustics, the Germans are the best at it.'

'*Ja*, that makes sense, Germans, they make these? That's also good, you hear?' He turned to Union Jack. 'Play it,' he instructed.

Union Jack's eyes grew wide, Mr Farquarson would never have allowed him to play a Baby Grand. He looked at me hesitatingly. I nodded. 'You heard the big *Baas*,' I said.

Union Jack sat down in front of the Steinway, I could see his hands were shaking. I had a sudden premonition that the Ship of State was about to enter half-pissed and ready for his afternoon nap. I glanced furtively towards the lift. Then Union Jack hit the Steinway keyboard with a flourish, knowing he might never get another opportunity, and a short while later ended the anthem with a glissando of sparkling notes.

'*Ja*, definitely, that's the one, Tom, I'll take them.'

'All three?'

'*Ja*, of course.'

'*Oom* Jannie, they're very expensive, 1000 guineas each.'

He paused, thinking. 'That's 1000 pounds and 1000 shillings, 3150. You right, Tom, it's a lot of money!'

For a moment I thought I'd blown it. 'There's always the others, I'm sure we can find you three pianos very similar to the one you liked, *Oom* Jannie,' I said, hoping he hadn't sensed the rising panic in my voice.

Oom Jannie appeared to be thinking. 'You know, Tom, forty-three years is a lot of years and a lot of loving. Hester only asked me for one thing in all that time. When we got the first big wool cheque, only last year, the one when we became all-of-a-sudden rich, she said to me, "Jannie, do you think now we can have an inside lavatory? I'm getting too old to go outside in the dark." You can't pay enough for that kind of loving, Tom. Now can we go have some coffee, hey? Then I'll count it out for you.'

To my astonishment the money, in large-denomination notes, was in the brown-paper bag. It also occurred to me that buying three Baby Grands he was probably entitled to a discount, but I had no idea what to offer him. I realised that I should be calling Mr Fisher, but I wanted to make sure that nobody could take the sale away from me. I poured coffee while *Oom* Jannie first emptied his pipe and then refilled it from a small leather tobacco pouch and stoked up before starting to count banknotes.

Finally, with the air about us thick with the fragrant tobacco smoke, he picked the pile of banknotes up from the coffee-table and, tapping them together, handed me the large bundle.

'Count it, Tom,' he instructed.

'No, they'll do it later in Accounts, but thank you, *Oom* Jannie,' I said. I thought I might excuse myself and go up to the next floor and see Mr Fisher and tell him the story and ask him about the discount. Then an idea struck me. I had never forgotten Mr Patel and the misadventures of Miss Phillips' up-Gawie's-bum pound note, how at one stage Mr Patel had offered us a *bansella*, a free gift of a penny sucker each. I was about to use influence I didn't have again.

'*Oom* Jannie, may I offer *Tante* Hester a small token of my esteem, would you accept the electric floor polisher as a gift from Polliack's?' Then I added hastily, 'I know it's not new, but we only got it last month.'

Now it was his turn to be overwhelmed. 'Tom, that's very, very generous of you, you hear. *Jy is in regte Boer*! You are a proper *Boer*. All of a sudden she's got that inside lavatory, you pull the chain and everything disappears, a grand peeano, and now also her own electric floor polisher!' He chuckled. 'Martha, the old house girl, now she's going to sit in the sun and gossip all day, hey?' He stretched out his hand and my own disappeared once again into his huge fist. 'I'm proud to know you, son,' he said. 'The Marie biscuits they nice, man, but the coffee and the fruitcake, it's the best in the Transvaal.'

CHAPTER FIFTEEN

Learning to Love with La Pirouette

AT FIRST MR FISHER looked at me as if I had suddenly gone stark staring crazy. 'You what?' he cried, springing from his chair.

'Sold the three Steinway Baby Grands, Sir.' I placed the large bundle of banknotes on his desk. 'For cash.'

'Where? How? What are you trying to tell me, Tom?' He'd taken off his glasses, tweaking the marks the spectacles made on each side of his nose, his eyes tightly closed, as if he was trying to take it all in. 'Sit down,' he said finally, pointing to the chair. He flopped back into his chair and, somewhat recovered, said, 'Tom, in the history of Polliack's, we have *never* sold three Steinways in one sale, much less for cash!'

I told him the story as quickly as possible, starting from the very beginning when Mr Farquarson had told me to get rid of the big *boer*. In the back of my mind I realised that the Ship of State was likely to kick up a huge fuss, the commission on the sale was going to be big and I needed to establish that the sale had been entirely my own. 'Sir, I thought there might be a discount involved, I mean for Mr Odenaal buying all three?'

'Certainly, and for cash as well,' he replied magnanimously.

'And I gave him the floor polisher for a bonsella.'

'Bonsella?' he asked.

'Free gift, Sir.'

'You gave him the piano department floor polisher?' Mr Fisher started to laugh. 'Tom, congratulations, you're a born salesman, son.' He stretched over and shook my hand. 'Come.' He rose and picked up the bundle of money. He patted me on the shoulder, flapping the bundle of banknotes. 'Some of this belongs to you. It may well be the biggest commission paid for a single item sale in the history of Polliack's. We took a hiding on the Steinway Grand Mr Farquarson sold to the Johannesburg Symphony Orchestra.' He chuckled gleefully. 'The old chap is going to have a blue fit!'

'Mr Fisher, I used Mr Farquarson's personal Marie biscuits with the coffee,' I confessed.

'Don't worry, we'll buy him ten packets,' he laughed.

By the time we got back to the piano department Union Jack had called the company odd-job man, who was removing the legs from one of the Baby Grands. They were going to be repacked into their original packing cases ready to be loaded onto the Rio by five o'clock that evening.

Oom Jannie was delighted to get a 10 per cent discount amounting to 360 pounds. 'Do I still get the electric floor polisher?' he asked anxiously.

'Of course, that was a personal gift to your wife from Tom,' Mr Fisher said generously.

The big boer looked over to where Union Jack and the coloured man were working.

'Hey, kaffir!' he called out suddenly. Union Jack turned and looked back, surprised. 'Ja, you, come here!' Oom Jannie ordered. Union Jack was a Zulu and a pretty proud guy and, besides, he was one of King Georgie's men, so probably had a fairly poor opinion of the Afrikaners. He might well have ignored the big boer had not Mr Fisher been present. 'Ja, kom!' Oom Jannie demanded impatiently.

Union Jack approached and it was plain to see he wasn't happy. But

Oom Jannie seemed oblivious. 'You play a good tune, you hear?' The Karoo sheep farmer peeled off a ten-pound note from his discount and handed it to Union Jack, who dropped his eyes and accepted it with both hands in the *Bantu* fashion.

'Thank you, *Baas*,' he said quietly, not losing his dignity.

Oom Jannie turned to Mr Fisher. 'You got a good *kaffir* there, man,' he said as Union Jack backed away. 'It's funny how they so musical, hey?' The big Zulu had just received four months' wages as a bonsella.

Now *Oom* Jannie, still looking at Mr Fisher, said, 'Tom here did a very good job, I'm telling you, the boy will go far. When I came in I thought maybe a nice peeano for Hester my wife, now I'm going out with those three Steinways made in Germany.' He shook his head in an exaggerated fashion. '*Magtig*, I don't know what happened, man!'

It was completely untrue, of course, I knew *Oom* Jannie was giving my career a boost in front of the general manager. He shook Mr Fisher's hand, then turned to me. 'You come visit us in the Karoo soon, you hear, Tom? My little daughter, she's just right for a young *kêrel* like you. He threw back his head and laughed. 'Hey, maybe we buy *Skattebol* a Steinway for a wedding present?' He peeled off five ten-pound notes. 'Here, for you, Tom.'

'No, no, *Oom* Jannie, I can't take it,' I said, holding up my hands in protest.

'What's wrong, Tom? You won't take a Karoo sheep farmer's money?'

'Tom will receive a commission on the sale,' Mr Fisher explained. 'He'll be well looked after.'

'*Ja*, well, I only hope it's a good one. When I came in that fat *Engelsman*, he told Tom here to get rid of me. What kind of a salesperson is that, hey?'

'I'm sure there was a misunderstanding, Sir,' Mr Fisher said in a conciliatory voice.

'Mistake? My *gat*! My arse!' Only in Afrikaans it's an even worse expression.

I was glad Mr Fisher didn't understand Afrikaans. I had enjoyed talking to the big *boer* and even if he hadn't bought a thing I was glad to have met a salt-of-the-earth type like him. 'If I ever go to the Cape I'll definitely look you up, *Oom* Jannie,' I said, smiling.

'Tom, already my family is going to like you, I guarantee it, you hear?'

After *Oom* Jannie had been shown the loading dock and how to get the Rio to it and had once again invited me to visit, he'd departed, refusing Mr Fisher's offer of a taxi. 'I got a long way to drive, I must walk first a bit.'

'That's a nice man, Tom,' Mr Fisher said to me, then clearing his throat he added, 'I'll leave a message with the ground floor to call me as soon as Mr Farquarson comes in. What do you want me to do?'

'How do you mean, Sir?'

'Well, this is your sale and you'll get the commission, that much I can promise you, but Mr Farquarson is not going to be happy when he returns. Do you want to be present? It's entirely up to you and I won't blame you if you'd rather not.'

I felt a huge urge to say I'd rather not be there when the Ship of State came sailing in from lunch. But in life you've got to take the bad with the good, and I'd certainly had my share of the good in the last three hours. 'I'm supposed to look after the piano department, Mr Fisher, so I had better still be here when he returns.' Then I suddenly thought of something. 'Can we send a dispatch boy out to get a packet of Marie biscuits? I'll pay for them tomorrow, I haven't got any money on me.' I routinely walked to work from the Hillbrow flat and I'd made a couple of peanut butter sandwiches for my lunch, which I hadn't managed to eat yet.

The young African in dispatch had only just returned with the packet of biscuits and I'd barely had time to replace it when Mr Fisher and Mr Farquarson arrived in the lift. It was just after four o'clock.

I must say this for him. The Ship of State had a reputation for being able to hold his booze. When he'd had too much claret you could only tell by his increasingly rubicund complexion, his exaggerated ebullience, the fact that his left eyelid was shut and that his vowels gradually slowed in their intensity, like a gramophone record losing speed. At this final stage, if seated, he would often fall asleep mid-sentence, waking with a grunt once in a while before returning to his afternoon nap. But this, I felt sure, wasn't going to be one of those 'fly-buzzing-against-the-outside-windowpane' somnolent afternoons.

'*Three* Steinways? He sold *three* Steinways? Codswallop!' Mr Farquarson shouted as the two men entered the department.

I braced myself for what was to come.

'A wonderful sale, don't you think, Mr Farquarson? Mr Polliack will be ever so pleased,' Mr Fisher said cheerily, cleverly bringing the founder's name into the conversation in an attempt to defuse the explosion to come.

'Bollocks! How dare that snotty-nosed young imbecile sell *my* pianos! You must fire him at once, Fisher!' He pronounced it 'Fishshaar'.

'No, I don't think we're going to do that, Mr Farquarson,' Mr Fisher said evenly. 'Come now, I think you ought to congratulate Tom.'

This served to set off the full conniption as the Ship of State suddenly observed me standing several feet away and directly in his path. 'You nasty little turd, you effluent, purgation, piss off, you pusillanimous little fart!' he shouted, glaring at me through one open eye.

Pusillanimous means lacking in courage, I thought. I'd been through (if not accompanied by so eloquent a quintet of adjectives) worse abuse certainly at the hands of Mevrou and Meneer Prinsloo, but even by those two invective dab-handers, I'd never been accused of lacking courage. Fuck you! I said to myself. I earned that sale fair and square. I'm not backing off. The new Tom Fitzsaxby with the potentially acerbic tongue raced to the fore. Stay calm, Tom, an inner voice urged.

'How was your luncheon at the Carlton Grill with the chief conductor of the Johannesburg Symphony Orchestra, Sir?' I began, then, not waiting for a reply, quickly added, 'You'll be pleased to know

Union Jack and I have been quite busy in your absence.' I was surprised at the calm tone of my voice and would dearly like to have said in addition, 'Those few glasses of excellent libation are clearly showing in the sanguineous state of your nose, Sir.' After all, one big pompous word deserved another of equal pomposity. But, of course, I said no such thing.

'Why, you scruffy little swine!' Mr Farquarson roared, pointing a blunt finger at me. 'Dismiss him, dismiss him at once!' he shouted again at Mr Fisher. Then a new thought must have entered his claret-soaked mind. 'The commission is *mine*! My department! My Steinways! My entitlement! Where's Polliack? Where is the little Jewboy? By Jesus, we'll soon fix this!'

Mr Fisher froze. 'I'll have you know I too am a Jew, Mr Farquarson. I think we'd better call a taxi to take you home,' he said, his voice ice-cold.

'Intolerable! I will not put up with this a moment longer, I shall resign! Get out of my way, boy!' the Ship of State demanded, hands flapping and coming at me full-steam ahead, attempting to use his stomach as a prow to knock me out of the way. I stepped aside and he lumbered into his small office and practically fell into his swivel chair, immediately scrabbling around for pen and paper. He found his fountain pen and had barely managed to remove the cap when he promptly fell asleep, his forehead hitting the surface of the desk as if in a skit out of a Mack Sennett comedy.

'Come, Tom, we'll sort all this out later,' Mr Fisher said, his voice still frosty. Then he added, 'Perhaps what happened since Mr Farquarson's return from lunch should go no further than the two of us?'

'Of course, Sir,' I replied, knowing full well the kind of merciless grilling I was about to receive from Bobby and Graham the moment I got back to the basement.

Union Jack must have observed the whole thing because he was standing near the lift, and when I pressed the button he said in Zulu, '*Usebenze kahle, Baas* Fitzy,' which means it is good, or well done! Mr

Fisher looked up questioningly, not understanding what the big Zulu had said to me. Then Union Jack added hurriedly, 'Baas Fisher, for now we are not having electric floor polish machine.'

Mr Fisher grinned. 'Union Jack, go down to the electrical department and tell them to give you to a new floor polisher, tell Mr Saunders to call me.' He left me at the lift. 'Tom, I'll take the stairs up, I must say I have a new respect for what they taught you at . . . what was it again?'

'The Born-again Christian Missionary Society, Sir.' If only he knew, there was a lot more Boys Farm involved than there was Smelly Jelly's influence.

It's amazing what a difference something like the Steinway incident makes. All of a sudden I was a bit of a hero around the place and Bobby and Graham decided that I could wear my new gear to work, but not the Brylcreem. I'd only been with Polliack's for a year of school holidays but after the three pianos I was told I was no longer a trainee and my salary went up a pound a week. Money! I was rolling in the stuff! The commission for the sale of the pianos was 5 per cent, so I also got 157 pounds. If I was careful it was sufficient to see me through my entire university degree.

At the Reverend Robertson's suggestion I applied for a scholarship to Witwatersrand, Wits as it is known, and also scholarships to Natal, Cape Town and Stellenbosch. The selection of Stellenbosch was of my own volition as it was an Afrikaans university, which I wouldn't have minded as it was very prestigious among the Volk and the Nationalists looked like being in power for some time to come. Their proposed 'apartheid' policy was gaining tremendous support. To ever-increasing applause from the white minority, the country was beginning to run backwards into the nineteenth century at a great rate of knots.

The end-of-year results came out in late January and I'd obtained a First Class matriculation and, to my surprise, I headed the entire country in both English and Afrikaans. The first was undoubtedly due to Miss Phillips and her early reading curriculum, the second, I suppose, because it had been my first language. In early February, the university scholarships were announced in the newspapers and I'd been granted a full scholarship at all four universities. But here's a funny thing, Gawie Grobler's name was on the Stellenbosch list. I'd written to him on three occasions when I was in First Form at school, but he'd not bothered to reply so I'd lost touch with him. You can't keep writing letters into a vacuum and stamps were too precious anyway. Seeing his name as a scholarship student at Stellenbosch decided me against going there. The distance between *Voetsek* the *Rooinek* and The Boys Farm was beginning to widen, and in life you don't go back to the past to see if it still hurts.

But in the end, that's exactly what happened, The Boys Farm came back to bite me on the bum. Frikkie Botha's physical condition was deteriorating to the extent that he could no longer live the life of a derelict and still beg effectively for a living. Despite the warning from Professor Mustafa that Frikkie wouldn't make it through another winter, he'd refused to give up his way of life and he somehow survived the steam pipes for another year. Despite my urging, Frikkie was intractable and refused to entertain the idea of the Salvation Army men's home. No amount of persuasion could make him change his mind. *If I die, I die*, he'd written.

During my last year at school he would often neglect taking his medication for diabetes whereupon his blood sugar level would became too high and he'd become tired and have trouble focusing, which in his particular vocation probably didn't matter too much, but he often ended up pissing himself, which only added to his generally disgusting appearance and smell. On my instructions to Stompie, the dozen Pepsi-Colas a day he consumed had been reduced to six, alternating with water, but without his diabetic medicine this didn't help him that much. Now that I was a law student at Wits University I had time to see that he took his medicine orally every day, but it was fast becoming apparent that Frikkie was coming to the end of his useful life as a mendicant. I finally persuaded him to come and live with me in the Hillbrow flat.

Before you start thinking how generous of me to take him in, let me put things straight. In four years of school holidays I'd never managed to get the entire story of the murder of Mattress as well as the story of the great railway culvert explosion from him. It wasn't that Frikkie was particularly evasive, but simply that he was never sufficiently sober for long enough when I was with him to write it all down. He'd either be outside Park Station begging, including the weekends, or we'd be having dinner, a tedious and laborious process I've previously described. After dinner he'd smoke a *toke* and the marijuana combined with a bottle of brandy meant he was soon comatose or, to be more precise, completely blotto. It must be remembered that Frikkie was in constant pain and so it was difficult to become impatient with him.

Over four years I had collected notes on roughly what had taken place on the night of the murder, but I needed a lot more detail, every detail if I could possibly get them. The tiniest, I told myself, might end up being the most important. Now time was running out, he'd survived the winter Professor Mustafa said he couldn't, but he most certainly wouldn't survive another one living rough. It was approaching April and the high *veld* nights were closing in, and the promise of winter to come was heralded by a chilly evening breeze that whipped across the park soon after sunset. Increasingly, I was beginning to panic, thinking that Frikkie might die before I had a complete set of notes.

If this sounds callous I don't suppose I can disagree, but the task I had set myself wasn't an easy one. Cleaning Frikkie up in the first place wasn't simple. Alcoholics who sleep rough suffer in the main from three antisocial maladies: lice, bedbugs and scabies. Again with Professor Mustafa's help I obtained a large container of Ascabiol, which he referred to as 'Benzyl Benzoate'.

'Shave his head, armpits and pubic hair, then rub this stuff all over his body, except on his head because it will damage his eyes . . . eye,' he corrected. 'Leave it on overnight, Tom, then wash it off in the morning, give him a bath if you can. Repeat for three days.'

It all sounded pretty matter-of-fact, but it wasn't easy, Frikkie Botha was still a *Boer* and therefore a proud man, and I know he suffered terrible humiliation. I confess it wasn't easy for me either. Seeing him sitting huddled in Smelly Jelly's red dressing-gown, rocking backwards and forwards with his thumb in the contorted little hole that was supposed to be his mouth was terribly distressing. His mutilated face was incapable of an expression beyond the horror permanently affixed to what were once its features, but you just knew he was thoroughly miserable and decidedly pissed off with me. Cleanliness may well be next to godliness, but for Frikkie Botha achieving it proved to be pure and utter hell.

But I must say, Frikkie, bathed and with a fresh set of clothes every day, was now the cleanest and the un-itchiest he'd been for several years. I'd bought an apron made from aeroplane cloth to catch the food he spilled, and with a three-times-a-week scrubbing in the bathtub, in the cleanliness stakes anyway things were definitely looking up. It's a curious thing, but people who go unwashed for months will do almost anything to avoid water. The smell of soap, on the first two occasions I bathed Frikkie, caused him to vomit into his bathwater. At first, the process of bathing him in Smelly Jelly's ancient bathtub would cause his good eye to weep real tears, and the pathetic glottal sounds that emerged from his useless vocal cords made me feel like the biggest bastard ever.

However, Tinky took to the new clean regime very well. A regular wash with an application of flea powder and a proper diet and his coat began to improve no end, and unlike his master I was sure he felt grateful for these changes in his personal circumstances. Doubling around with one foot in the air nipping at fleabites all day must have been a miserable existence. I have to add that I was very fond of him and he was quick to respond to affection. If you ever want a small dog you'd be hard-pressed to go beyond a fox terrier.

The sale of the three Steinway Baby Grands meant I had more than sufficient money to keep us both and I tried again without success to discourage Frikkie from working. He'd written me a pleading note: *Showbiz is my lewe, sonder dit is ek 'n dooie man.* Showbiz is my life, without it I am a dead man. Frikkie had never accepted that he was a beggar but always saw himself as a performer. I was finally forced to concede that leaving him incarcerated in the dark little flat wasn't an option and that he'd die all the sooner left alone all day. Neither he nor Tinky would be able to tolerate the confinement. Both were creatures of the street, accustomed to living their lives on a busy city pavement.

The problem was that Hillbrow was a mile-and-a-half from Park Station, and Frikkie's heart condition coupled with his diabetes made walking all that way quite impossible and the tram wouldn't allow pets on board. With the cooperation of Professor Mustafa, I managed to obtain a second-hand wheelchair from the hospital workshop for nix and sixpence (almost nothing). The workshop foreman reinforced it wherever he could, which added a fair bit of weight but made it ideal for street work rather than the polished lino hospital corridors for which it was originally constructed.

Frikkie thought it was magic, a theatrical prop that added an extra dimension to his act. It was as if an old, tired vaudeville warm-up actor found himself togged out in a new top hat, starched shirt, bow tie, dancing taps and tails. The wheelchair gave him a legitimacy and, in his eye, new respectability. It was almost as if his act, cleaned up and rewritten, had finally made it onto Broadway. But the funny thing was that the freshly laundered Frikkie in his wheelchair evoked far less pity or curiosity, and made less money than the filthy smelly version sitting on an old wooden crate under a dirty hood. I guess the public prefers its freaks to be thoroughly wretched.

Pushing him to Park Station in the morning was easy enough, the mile-and-a-half from Hillbrow was virtually all the way downhill. Taking him home at night was a different matter and improved my fitness no end, but the real problem became getting him up to the third floor. I solved this by paying the janitor, a solidly built African named Six-gun, five shillings a week to piggyback Frikkie up the stairs, while I stored the wheelchair in the basement. Six-gun reversed the process each morning. It was good pay for Six-gun, but worth every penny. Frankly, I don't know what I would have done without him and towards the end the big African claimed his back was giving him trouble, and demanded and got seven and sixpence. It was daylight robbery, only slightly less than his weekly salary as janitor, but I had no choice.

I'd moved Frikkie into the little bedroom and bought a second-hand divan for the sitting room that served as the lounge with a blue chenille cover in the daytime and as my bed at night. I also got one of those enamel bedpans and another spouted one for pissing into from the hospital because Frikkie, in a semi-comatose state, wasn't capable of getting out of bed at night and finding the bathroom. You don't think of these things when a person lives in the open. There was a public toilet next to the art gallery the brotherhood would use at night and at the steam pipes the guys just moved slightly away from the sleeping men and pissed on the pipes. The hot piss turning to steam as it hit the pipes created an unpleasant effluvium, but on a freezing night the cold bit so hard into your nostrils that it neutralised most of the stink.

What I hadn't reckoned on was Tinky, who like Tinker had never lived indoors, and had no idea of toilet-training and, at first, got very upset being restrained and unable to be outdoors at night. But that's the thing with a fox terrier, they never stop learning. After a few weeks with newspaper spread everywhere he might think to do his business, he finally got the idea and learned to go out last thing at night and first thing in the morning. He now had his own basket with an old blanket, and eventually seemed happy enough, though sometimes on a cold winter's night he'd wake me up whimpering with a paw resting on my arm and I'd haul him into bed with me for a bit of a snuggle.

I wish I could say the same thing about Frikkie, who proved impossible to bed-train. He was an alcoholic and wasn't about to attend Alcoholics Anonymous. He still needed his *dagga* and brandy at night, and he'd often mess his bed in his sleep or his casual aim into the spout of the urine jug would, more often than not, miss the mark. I had a rubber mat under his sheets to protect the mattress and kept three sets of sheets for him, one always at the local Spotless laundrette, with his blankets making the same journey every Saturday morning. I'd pay Hettie, the coloured woman at the laundry, a shilling extra for a scrubbing brush and the loan of a bar of Blue Velvet soap. This allowed me to use her large washtub to remove the crud off Frikkie's blankets before she'd let me consign them to one of the semi-industrial washing machines. I can tell you there were times when a person felt pretty desperate, but what kept me going was that slowly but surely I was getting the information I wanted.

I wouldn't allow Frikkie his smoke and brandy until we'd completed half an hour of what I suppose can only be termed interrogation. I know he grew to hate it because I'd constantly cross-reference the stuff he wrote to make sure he wasn't inventing any of the facts. I was aware that alcoholics often develop delusional disorders and become paranoid, so I had to be careful. I guess I was pretty remorseless, and in retrospect it must have seemed cruel, but it worked. Despite the alcohol and the marijuana his recall was amazing, facts he'd written months and even a couple of years previously would be repeated unchanged on paper. From the very beginning I dated the spiral-pad notes and kept them together with my own. Frikkie may have been uneducated but he was a country boy and he'd learned early in life how to listen and to acutely observe his surroundings. Besides, righteous hate and the desire for revenge becomes the best way to stimulate and to keep the memory sharp. Invariably his last written sentence would be, *Those bastards we'll get them hey.* Frikkie had no idea of punctuation or exclamation marks and often even saved himself the trouble of a full stop. Curiously he didn't mind photographs being taken of his face, in fact if a tourist wanted to do so he charged an extra shilling. I borrowed a camera from Bobby Black and took a series of pictures of Frikkie from every possible angle, although I wasn't quite sure why I wanted them. Certainly not for vicarious reasons, the living, breathing Frikkie was a constant reminder of the tragedy of his broken body and his pathetic life. I simply filed them with the rest of the notes.

Mixed into all of this was life as a first-year student, which I found absorbing, and I loved the study of law. For the first time I realised that the big red book I'd stolen from under Doctor Van Heerden's house, and which I'd long since completely memorised, had served to train my mind. The learning of torts and the more detailed aspects of law came easily to me, whereas they seemed to be anathema to the other students. This ability to commit stuff to memory was probably a good thing. I was kept very busy caring for Frikkie, working at Polliack's during the varsity vacations and on Saturday mornings, and checking every Saturday afternoon after work on the brotherhood to see who among them needed emergency treatment. So I had very little time to study and my assignments were almost always late. My law professor called me in. 'Tom, you have the ability to win the university medal when you graduate in law if you apply yourself,' he said. Then, giving me a meaningful look, he added, 'May I suggest a little more application and a little less play, eh, young man?'

Then the 'winter of one too many' finally arrived, and on the evening of 10 May 1952 Frikkie died in the bathtub while I was soaping his back with a flannel. He simply jerked once and his body slumped forward so that I reached out and grabbed his arm. 'Wees kalm, ou maat. Be calm, old mate.' I called. But his head lolled awkwardly and his body became a sudden dead weight, and I then realised his breathing had stopped and moments later he evacuated in the bathwater. The farmer, boxer, resistance fighter, accident victim, showbiz personality, park and steam-pipe derelict was finally dead, his suffering over. Only moments later Tinky started scratching frantically at the closed bathroom door and commenced to howl his dear little heart out.

I'd be lying if I said I missed Frikkie Botha. But I was grateful to him for three things: a complete set of notes on how Mattress was murdered; another of the incident where he lost his face at the railway culvert; and finally, the custody of the nicest little dog after Tinker that you could possibly imagine.

The year 1952 proved to be a very good year for me. I was seventeen years old but my life to this point hadn't exactly been a load of fun. I'd learned a fair bit about the process of staying alive in a hostile world, but it had been all work and very little play, and I suspect Tom was in danger of becoming a very dull boy. Even though I was known at Polliack's for my enthusiasm and easy laughter, you can fake life and happiness for just so long before the process starts getting too difficult. I'd never been drunk or smoked a cigarette and, most of all, never kissed a girl, much less fondled, as almost every other young male my age claimed to have done, a set of firm and luscious breasts with nipples pointing to the moon.

The university campus was full of young female students, many of them gorgeous enough to render one trembling at the knees, while the basement at Polliack's was a veritable Mecca for pretty girls. More than once I'd received the 'big eyes', especially when it was followed by an elaborate compliment about my musical knowledge. I'd know in my pounding heart that this was a thinly disguised invitation to take the next step and to ask them out. Furthermore, the news of the Steinway triumph had swept through the company and several of the young women who worked in the accounts departments paid a visit to the basement. They always lingered much longer than was necessary to enquire about a pop song currently climbing up the charts on Springbok radio.

Bobby Black would tease me and say things like, 'Tom, you've got more young crumpet walking into your life than Frank Sinatra has bobby-soxers at his concerts!' And Graham would raise one eyebrow, prop, pout and make remarks such as, 'My dear, if you wished to do so, you could get laid more often than the centre table at the Carlton Grill.' They were teasing me, of course. In those days before the pill, getting a nice girl to part with her knickers was a very difficult process, even for the Casanovas of this world. While my imagination ran to lurid detail, in reality my wildest hope extended to a chaste kiss on the lips (never mind tongues becoming involved), and a bit of a fumble at the front of a straining sweater.

Alas, I had no idea how to behave in front of a girl or how to go about achieving this inept ambition. I knew that my easy confidence, chatty demeanour and lyric patter would disappear in a puff of smoke the moment I stepped out of the Polliack's basement. The instant I hit the pavement I felt certain I would turn into a mumbling, clumsy oaf. While my fantasy life appeared in panoramic Technicolor, my sexual reality was a black-and-white, faded, cracked-and-curled-up-at-the-corners box-brownie snapshot. The memory of a cheek once briefly kissed, its softness never quite forgotten.

Then all of a sudden, out of a clear and wholly translucent blue sky, La Pirouette came into my life. Metaphorically speaking, one moment I'd been trundling along in a squeaky pedal car and the next I was behind the wheel of a Formula One Jaguar racing at Le Mans.

It all happened when old Mr Polliack had his annual garden party at his mansion in one of the very posh outlying suburbs. It was a very important affair on the musical calendar of Johannesburg and involved a marquee and French champagne by the silver bucket-load dispensed by an army of waiters in white uniforms and cotton gloves to match. The food was catered for by the one and only terribly famous Carlton Grill with practically every delicacy known to man laid out on a table in the marquee the length of a cricket pitch. An outdoor stage and dance floor featured bands representing almost every aspect of music, except *boere musiek*, as well as the top musicians and singers in the country. Termed 'Polliack's Annual Musicians' Garden Party' on the invitations, it was intended to take place during a Saturday afternoon but was habitually known to continue until the early hours of the following morning.

While no expense was spared, this wasn't a stuffed-shirt affair with the usual compulsory high-ups such as the mayor in attendance, but was instead strictly a party for musicians. Even so, it was considered a most prestigious event and an invitation to attend was regarded as a badge of honour and a sign that you were considered to be among the *cognoscenti* in your profession. A fact, according to Bobby Black, that in no way prevented a great many of the participants from behaving very badly, which, he pointed out, was considered almost compulsory.

The other aspect for which the garden party was evidently famous was the calibre of the females who attended with their invited male partners, or the glamorous singers who were there in their own right. 'Let me assure you, Tom, this is a party-and-a-half, man!' Bobby would say to me. 'When it starts to get dark you begin to hear the moaning taking place in the bushes. If you walk into the maze on the third lawn, ooh-la-la! You better be wearing dark glasses, man! Behind the hedges and the swimming pool cabana, you wouldn't believe what's going on.' He'd say all this in a conspiratorial voice, almost reduced to a whisper. And, of course, I lapped it all up, my febrile imagination recreating this modern-day Sodom and Gomorrah taking place in Mr Polliack's manicured garden. I tried to isolate the goings-on behind the neatly clipped hedges, in the cabana and within the dark recesses of the exotic maze on the number three lawn, creating for each location a new and increasingly erotic fantasy.

'Bobby, do you . . . you know, also . . .' I'd once attempted to ask him.

Bobby's hands shot up in protest. 'Tom, it's not a question you can ask a person. I'm supposed to be there as the company's representative, you know, strictly kosher. Also the Bobby Dazzlers, they one of the official bands. It's the three monkeys, you understand? No see, no hear, no speak.' He hunched his shoulders, rolled his eyes and wiggled his hands. 'But I'm a jazz musician, man! What else can I say, does a bird fly, does a camel fart in the desert?'

I must say, with such a famous wicked event going on and the Nationalists now in power I wondered why the Government allowed something like this to happen in front of their very eyes. The South African police force was not exactly known for its unconventional viewpoint, such goings-on would, in their opinion, have the potential to undermine the whole society. Boy, oh boy! If the *Dominee* was still alive and he happened to get a hold of the details! *Magtig*! What a well-rounded sermon Polliack's Annual Musicians' Garden Party would make, with old Mr Polliack starring as the solid-gold-toothed, dark-haired, black-bearded, diamonds-concealed 'you know where', Christ-killing, devil-incarnate Jew!

For days after this company-sponsored musicians' afternoon champagne gargle and subsequent drunken sexual soiree, Bobby would hold his head in his hands as if his hangover still persisted, and recount yet another lurid tale involving the opposite sex. I listened wide-eyed and open-mouthed, while at the same time I tucked away in my memory the conclusion that French champagne and a woman was a deadly effective combination. One to be resurrected, if ever I could afford the first and was fortunate enough to find myself in the company of the second. I also knew that even should I know the lyrics to every pop song in the world, with me unable to sing a note I was unlikely to ever receive an invitation to this simultaneously famous and infamous garden party.

So you can imagine my surprise when Mr Fisher called me into his office and told me that Mr Polliack had personally suggested that I be invited. 'Tom, I'm not at all sure it's a good idea, but the old man was fairly adamant.' Mr Fisher grinned and his voice changed. '"Let me tell you something for nussing, Lew. Any vun vat can sell already three Steinways for cash, this is a mensch! A boy who is goink right to the top, I guarantee it. Invite away, believe me, for such a boychick, it can't harm."' But you could see he mimicked the founder in the gentlest possible way, drawing me into a mutual conspiracy of laughter.

Now I have to mention something else. With Frikkie dead I had the responsibility for Tinky who, like his late master, was not accustomed to being left on his own in a dark little flat. Like the great Tinker, he wanted to be in on all the action. But this meant I couldn't use public transport to get to university. So I bought a second-hand bicycle with a carrier stand at the back to which I wired a butter crate lined with a piece from one of Frikkie's oft-scrubbed and constantly laundered blankets. Tinky took to it like a duck to water, viewing the world whizzing by with imperious disdain and giving any hoi polloi dog we happened to pass on the way a piece of his exalted mind. He attended university with me, and was even allowed to come to Polliack's where I trained him to do the 'Woof! Woof!' part in Patti Page's 'How Much is That Doggie in the Window?', which almost doubled our sales of the hit record, as well as turning him into a star in his own right. Bobby even had a sign made that we put outside the lifts on the ground floor:

The Music Basement. Mr Lyrics and Tinky, the singing dog!

It was a stroke of genius and we continued to sustain big sales of the record long after it had lost the number-one spot on the charts. Although this was Bobby's idea, I seemed to get all the accolades these days. I was discovering that in life you only had to do one big thing and people would give you credit for successes not of your own making. My one big thing was, of course, the three pianos and now, all of a sudden, I was the boy genius, the super-salesman around the place. When you protested and gave the credit where it was due, they quietly added modesty to your virtues.

So when the big day of the garden party arrived, I gave Tinky a wash and a good brushing and we set out on the bicycle for the Polliack mansion situated in a new posh suburb named Emmarentia that was miles out of town. As it turned out, it was on five acres of landscaped gardens with a natural stream running through it. When we got to the elaborate iron gates, wrought with a motif of two peacocks with their tail feathers flared, facing each other, the security guard looked highly doubtful, holding his hand up in a command to us to stop. You could see he was thinking, how could a low-down like me with a dog in a box, arriving on an old bicycle, possess an invitation to such a swish affair? Fortunately, moments later, Mr Fisher and his wife arrived in a brand-new Chevrolet. Sticking his head out of the car window, he called, 'Glad you and Tinky could make it, Tom!' So the big Afrikaner in a pretend-policeman's uniform reluctantly allowed us through the massive gates and pointed to the garages where he said I must put my bicycle. If only he'd known that he'd been right, I was really and truly an imposter, a mere lyric-spouter and about as far from a musician as you could possibly get.

The garages alone were bigger than Doctor Van Heerden's house, and the house itself was nearly as big as The Boys Farm hostel. Later I would be told it was built in the Spanish colonial style, though when, on one occasion, I mentioned this to Graham Truby, he raised one eyebrow as usual and quipped, 'My dear, pure Hollywood Spanish! Straight off the Paramount set, à la Cecil B. De Mille!', whatever that was supposed to mean, other than bitchy. Let me tell you it was a house-and-a-half and I'd never seen better! Though, of course, I didn't see inside.

The gardens, for there appeared to be several, each in a different style, lived up to Bobby's description. Neatly trimmed and flowering hedges divided one garden from another. When eventually I found and entered the maze you could easily imagine how all these little secret nooks tucked away under the stars were perfect for doing 'it' on a camomile lawn as soft as a double pile carpet. As for the cabana, it was huge and filled with spare sun lounges and, believe me, you didn't have to have too much imagination to know how they would be employed soon after sunset!

As for the rest of the set-up, it was just the way Bobby said: the marquee with a long table groaning with food, lots of stuff I'd never eaten before, such as lobster and prawns flown up from the Cape that tasted like you wondered what all the fuss was about. But also lots of *really* good things to eat that you'd never get normally. Black waiters in white mandarin-collared jackets with polished brass buttons and cotton gloves served French champagne and any other kind of drink you wanted. I had a Coke and they didn't seem to mind getting it for me specially.

When I arrived, the Bobby Dazzlers were already on the bandstand and were going at it hammer and tongs with people jitterbugging on the dance floor, so I couldn't say hello to Bobby. Apart from Mr Fisher, who must have gone into the house, I didn't know anyone. I was later to discover that the older musicians attended a separate cocktail party. The posh inside-the-house classical-music people, such as hailed from the Johannesburg Symphony Orchestra and the ballet orchestra, naturally wouldn't have been too interested in what was going on in the garden, especially after dark. But I didn't mind being on my own because Tinky proved to be the number-one hit of the day. All the pretty girls – Bobby was right, they were everywhere – wanted to pet him. I'd since learned that smelling of roses didn't mean you were pregnant because if it still did, then every beautiful woman there was going to have a baby. Talk about nice smells around the place!

Tinky must have thought he was back on the pavement outside Park Station begging for alms and photo opportunities for the hooded Frikkie. He'd sit up with his paws held up with his best pleading look accompanied by a soft whimper that was designed to evoke the maximum sympathetic reaction from the punters. Beautiful creatures would come up and kneel down and pat him and say, 'What an adorable little dog! What's his name?' When this happened, a person could tell them and look them in the face. Which was something someone like me wouldn't normally do, except, of course, when they weren't looking or in the music basement, when I was hiding behind the lyrics of the latest pop song and wasn't being the real me.

I watched the dancing for a bit, but then an older lady came up to me and asked me to dance and said her husband wouldn't dance with her so would I? I felt a real fool. 'I'm sorry, madam, but I've got a badly sprained ankle,' I lied. So I had to leave, affecting a pronounced limp in case someone else who might be beautiful asked me. One day you're going to learn to dance, I told myself. Sometimes in the newspapers you'd see these ads for Arthur Murray – 'Why be the one left out of the fun? Learn to dance the Arthur Murray way. Guaranteed results in six easy and exciting lessons!' There was this photograph of a beautiful girl and above her head in quotation marks it said: 'Will you dance with me?' I had written this down on the mental list I kept, along with the deadly effect champagne had on girls, as one of the things I was definitely going to do one day.

It was a hot day and the sun hadn't set, but you could see there was a lot of spontaneous laughter going around the place and the girls seemed to be getting very friendly with the guys, grabbing their arms and sometimes putting their heads against their chests. You could feel it in the air that things were about to happen the moment the sun went down.

From all the excitement and the heat Tinky's little tongue was hanging out and he was panting, so we walked through two of the gardens and passed the maze to get to the little stream so he could have a drink. We found this lovely spot with a rock and waterlilies with a tiny fall of water turning the stream into a quietly tinkling brook. It was late afternoon and the sun was now pleasantly warm on my back, and I thought I'd probably had enough of the crowd for a little bit, so Tinky and I decided to sit there for a while. Sometimes it's nice to be just on your own in a pleasant place like that, like some good days at the big rock when you could read a Miss Phillips book or sit beside the creek coming down from the high mountains.

I must have been sitting daydreaming for a while when suddenly I heard this nice voice call, 'Hello! Would you mind if I joined you?'

I turned around, and I suppose my mouth must have fallen open. I'm not saying she was beautiful because it was more than that, perhaps she wasn't even pretty, she was startling. Jet-black hair, cut almost like a boy's, and green eyes highlighted with what I later learned was eyeliner and mascara to emphasise their vivacious beauty. She also had full lips with a very red lipstick and her face was lightly tanned. I must have looked the full dumbstruck idiot because the next thing she said was, 'Move over, handsome.' Then I saw that she was carrying two glasses of champagne. 'Here, hold these,' she instructed, holding them out. I accepted the champagne and she sat down beside me and arranged her skirt, then reached out and picked up Tinky and placed him on her lap, natural as anything. Tinky seemed to think it was perfectly normal to be seated in the lap of this astonishingly exotic creature because he simply settled in. She reached out again and took one of the glasses of champagne. 'Cheers,' she said, holding it out towards me.

What could I possibly do? Here was this startlingly beautiful person, arriving out of the blue, and now sitting so close to me that I could feel the warmth of her thigh, and my first words to her were going to be 'Er . . . Miss, I don't drink.'

'Cheers,' I replied, touching her champagne glass lightly the way I'd seen it done all afternoon. She took a tiny little sip and I followed suit. It tasted like sour lemonade and, as with the earlier lobster and prawns, I wondered briefly what all the fuss was about. Now my big problem was what to say next. 'I'm Tom Fitz-harrumph-saxby,' I said, my voice faltering in the middle of my own surname.

'Yes I know, three Steinways for cash already,' she laughed.

I guess I must have turned completely beetroot. Tinky was licking the back of her hand and I wanted to die on the spot. 'June Hayes,' she said, offering me her Tinky-licked hand. 'I'm Mr Polliack's granddaughter.'

Now instead of saying 'Pleased to meet you, June,' I took her hand and blurted out, 'But that's not a Jewish name!'

She smiled and my heart skipped a beat. 'In one of the more stupid of the many mistakes in my life, I was married to a gentile doctor named Hayes.' She laughed. 'My mother liked the doctor bit, but wasn't at all happy about the *goy*. The trouble with Jewish mothers is that they usually turn out to be correct about their daughters and affairs of the heart.'

'Goy?'

'It's a not very polite Yiddish word for a gentile,' she laughed again.

I was still a long way from 'Y' in Meneer Van Niekerk's *Shorter Oxford English Dictionary*, and my stupid brain couldn't help itself. 'Yiddish?'

'It's a *patois*, no, not really, probably a complete language that German and Polish Jews use among themselves.'

Thank God I knew what *patois* meant. 'Oh,' I replied, continuing my brilliant monosyllabic dialogue.

June Hayes laughed again, then throwing back her head she emptied her champagne glass. 'Bottoms up, Tom,' she commanded.

I wasn't caught out this time, it was an expression I'd read in some book or another and I knew what it meant. Besides, her meaning was obvious.

So I upped my glass and swallowed. Suddenly there was champagne issuing spontaneously in a fine spray from my mouth and bursting through my nostrils in an exit that landed partly in my lap and partly on the rock. 'Shit!' I cried. Another single word!

'Well, at least that's an exclamation and not a question, Tom,' June Hayes quipped, plainly amused and seemingly not at all concerned with my dreadful champagne accident. 'My turn now, Tom. Is this the first time you've had champagne?'

'Yeah, afraid so,' I said, sheepishly, finding my handkerchief and wiping my dripping, snotty nose.

'Any alcohol ever?' I shook my head. 'How old are you, Tom?'

'Seventeen, eighteen next month.' I'd made such a complete balls-up of everything that there seemed no point in lying.

'Eighteen, that's a perfect age for a young stud.'

'Stud?' Shit, here we go again!

'I tell you what, Tom, why don't we start all over again? You go get two more glasses of champagne and we'll take it from there.'

'Tinky, stay,' I commanded. At least I was in control of something around the place. I rose and made my way through the two gardens to the main party area and returned without having spilled a drop.

'*Salut!*' June Hayes said this time as we touched glasses. 'Just take it slowly, Tom, it was vulgar of me to quaff it like that.' The smile that followed was stunning, all teeth and mouth and virescent eyes.

'I'm sorry,' I apologised.

'Shush! Never say you're sorry, Tom. It's a word that's lost its true meaning. Besides, nobody will believe you. When we're *really* sorry we usually lack the courage to say so.' She paused, taking a sip from her glass. 'Now, starting all over again, my name is June Hayes, *née* Polliack, my friends call me Pirrou and when they don't like me, which is quite often, they call me La Pirouette. That's because I can be a spoilt bitch and, besides, I'm a professional ballet dancer. I'd very much like you to call me Pirrou and to try to like me.' She looked at me, tilting her head. 'Now, it's your turn, Tom.'

What was I supposed to say? 'I'm Tom Fitzsaxby, otherwise known as *Voetsek* the *Rooinek*, world-record-holder of Chinese writing on my bum, internationally successful gospel-tract writer, tone-deaf lyric-spouting phoney pop-music salesman and a member of the brotherhood of derelicts'? 'I'm a second-year law student at Wits and in my spare time I work for your grandfather,' I said lamely.

'And what do you do for fun, Tom?'

'Fun?' Oh, Jesus! Another monosyllabic answer! To my surprise, in the process of all this questioning I had emptied my glass. 'Shall I get another glass of champagne?' I asked, stupidly examining my empty glass with some bemusement as I hadn't remembered taking a single sip from it.

'You're making me quaff again, Tom!' Pirrou accused, smiling, then downed her glass instantly and handed it to me. 'After all, a girl has to protect her virtue.' She glanced at me out of the corner of her beautiful eyes, absently fondling Tinky's ears.

There it was! The deadly effect of champagne on members of the opposite sex working in front of my very eyes! After one glass of sprayed-all-about champagne and another I'd managed to drink down effortlessly, I was feeling quite good and the sour lemonade taste seemed to have completely disappeared.

'Ask them for a bottle of Bollinger, Tom,' Pirrou suggested. Only it was the kind of suggestion that suggested that she expected me definitely to return with the bottle. I wasn't at all sure that I could command sufficient authority to grant her request. But a man has his pride and so off I went through the two gardens again. It was beginning to grow quite dark, but I couldn't hear any moaning and as I passed several hedges and the maze on the third lawn with the double-pile camomile lawn, it was completely silent.

Back at the marquee I looked around for a waiter who appeared to be Zulu. Soon enough I found one. 'I need a bottle of champagne for *Miss* Polliack, the little *madam* of the *big baas*, the big *induna*, who owns this place,' I said in Zulu, pointing to the house. He glanced at the Polliack mansion and then looked back doubtfully, so I quickly added, 'I think you better come and see her yourself, she's a very angry person and could have you fired like this.' I snapped my fingers and gave him a meaningful look. I was using authority I didn't have again, and I wasn't sure whether this would be meaningful as a threat. I imagined that a waiter employed by the Carlton Grill was probably a very prestigious position in the Johannesburg waiter scene, and that a quiet word in the right place from a high-up such as a Polliack could see him on his way back to Zululand with his last pay packet in his pocket.

'I will get it, *Baas*,' he said, 'but the other people mustn't see.' He moved away to the rear of the marquee and returned with a bottle wrapped in a damask napkin.

I dipped into my pocket where I had a bit of loose change and up came a shilling. It was too much and I'd hoped for sixpence, but he'd stuck his neck out, so dipping back in again would have seemed churlish. 'I am grateful,' I said quietly.

I confess I returned to Tinky and Pirrou somewhat triumphantly. I wanted to hold the bottle aloft and say, 'Da-da-da-dah!' Instead I unwrapped the napkin to reveal the champagne, which by some miracle happened to be Bollinger.

'Nice work, Tom!' Pirrou exclaimed as if she *really* meant it. I had the feeling that I'd passed some sort of important test. But I wasn't to know that the real trap for young players lay immediately ahead. I had absolutely no idea how to open the bottle and I stared at it completely bewildered.

'Remove the gold foil covering the cork,' Pirrou instructed. I did as I was told, tearing the foil from the neck. Now I was confronted with a large cork held in place with, I couldn't believe it, wire. 'See the little wire loop, turn it anticlockwise.' Again I did as she said. Suddenly there was this loud bang! and the cork shot into the air and landed with a plop in the middle of the stream. My heart missed several beats and Tinky's ears pricked up and he let out a sharp bark. 'Well done, Tom!' Pirrou exclaimed, clapping her hands.

A small effervescence composed of white bubbles emerged from the bottle and spilled slowly over the lip and down the side of the neck, halting about three inches down.

'Done like an expert, see, you haven't wasted a drop!' She leaned over suddenly and kissed me on the cheek.

Now I'd like to tell you what happened after that. But the next thing I vaguely remember is street lamps whizzing by, strips of elongated light almost joined together, and looking up into the canopy of leafy trees hurling past me at great speed. Or so it seemed, because everything was spinning as well as rushing by. I remember my hand searching for Tinky and finding him against my side, but after that, complete oblivion. I had finally joined the brotherhood as a drunk in my own right.

I woke to the most incredible feeling of softness, or was it smoothness? Whatever it was, it was a sensation I'd never experienced before and it was happening to 'you know what' immediately below my waist. I opened my eyes slowly to see the sun streaming through a large picture window that faced out into a garden where a Jacky wagtail perched on the head of a small bronze statue of a naked cherub on a stone pedestal, its tail moving up and down. My head was perfectly clear and to my surprise the sensation continued – velvety smooth and rhythmic, absolutely exquisite. I let go an involuntary moan, the feeling from below sending sensations up through my body that completely dissolved the loneliness stones. They just melted and were gone, finish and *klaar*. I felt a sudden indescribable lightness of being. With my ecstatic moan the rhythm stopped abruptly and a female voice said quietly, 'Oh, you're awake, Tom.' I didn't answer, I *couldn't* answer. Then there seemed to be some disruption of sheets as a head of shining dark hair emerged from between my thighs and suddenly I was looking into a beautiful pair of green eyes. 'Shush!' the voice said, even though I hadn't spoken. Soft lips closed briefly over my mouth, and I felt a hand taking me and I entered a new kind of glorious tightness, then the rhythm started all over again. It continued and continued, soft and then urgent and soft again and gradually it became more and more urgent until I cried out and my body heaved and flattened and heaved and flattened again and again. The green eyes above me filled with laughter and then they too seemed to lose focus and the rhythm above me became increasingly urgent and I moaned and shouted out and clung to warm, smooth, wonderfully soft flesh. Then something inside of me burst as if I was witnessing, at some primordial time, the great cascading waterfall in the high mountains as it tumbled for the very first time into the vast canyon below. The green eyes above me became very still, it was like looking into deep, clean water, and the rhythm slowed down and, with a soft sigh, finally ceased. 'Oh, Tom, my beautiful, beautiful boy,' the voice above me whispered, then sighed deeply once more and Pirrou's lips came down to touch my own with a softness so delicate that I began to weep.

CHAPTER SIXTEEN

A Labour of Love

———————

AS I LAY IN Pirrou's bed with the morning sun streaming through the window I wept for the many things in my childhood past. Now, with this first intimacy, this first-ever touching, the loneliness stones within my breast had disappeared, the demons were cast out and I became clean. I wept that such a miraculous power to heal existed in the body of a woman. In a single act of spontaneous loving I had at last been born again and baptised in the name of five softly spoken words, 'Tom, my beautiful, beautiful boy'. In gratitude for this benediction, I also wept.

Pirrou moved to my side and reached out and silently held me so that I lay with my head against her breasts. It was the first time I could remember having been held in a woman's arms like this. My earliest memory was of standing in a corner somewhere, trembling and fearful, knowing that I must make some kind of gesture to please a huge woman towering above me and not knowing what this should be. Perhaps it happened at The Boys Farm when I first arrived and that mountain of indifference may have been Mevrou. This was because I sensed that at some earlier time, however briefly, I had been held with love and in tenderness, rocked in a woman's arms.

With the tears for a childhood past finally gone we lay together silently for some time. Then Pirrou moved me gently aside and propped on her elbow beside me, so that she could look down into my face.

'I'm sorry,' I ventured softly.

'Shush! I thought we decided yesterday not to use the "sorry" word, Tom Fitzsaxby,' she chided. 'Besides, of much greater concern, blue and green should never be seen.'

'What do you mean by that?' I sensed that she was attempting to change the mood.

'It's something my mother says about fashion. These two colours, according to the dictates of her day, were never to be used together.' She smiled. 'Our eyes, yours so startlingly blue and mine green. Mine the colour of envy and yours of serenity and trust. Do you think this is a bad omen, Tom?'

'Nature wouldn't agree, after all they are the colours of the sky and the land. Does that mean the firmament and the earth beneath it is out of fashion?' I asked, trying to add a little to her frivolous tone, but only succeeding in sounding pompous.

'Nice reply, neatly put, you'll make an excellent handbag, Tom.'

'Handbag?'

Pirrou laughed. 'We could make a deal.'

'What sort of deal?'

She rolled over onto her back, kicking one shapely dancer's leg into the air and holding it aloft, her instep arched, painted toenails pointed to the ceiling. It was my turn to prop onto my elbow and it was now, for the first time, that I observed her entire dancer's body. I couldn't believe what happened next. As we looked at each other my entire body began to tremble with desire. It wasn't a conscious thought, the moment my eyes rested on her loveliness, my mind took over and delivered a set of instructions to my inexperienced body, urging it to do something it had contemplated a thousand times before. But now that the opportunity had finally arrived, I hadn't the slightest idea of how to accomplish it.

'My goodness, I am impressed!' Pirrou exclaimed, bringing her leg back down.

'What sort of deal?' I asked again, trying to contain my desire, though

I could feel my throat constricting and my voice sounded different, even to me.

'This is part of it,' she sighed happily, her arms reaching out.

I had no idea love-making could be such hard work! Mind you, nice hard work, but a person's hips were practically worn out by the time Pirrou started to jerk and moan and arch her back to physically lift me into the air, her convulsive strength quite astonishing, and with me hanging on for dear life. This time it was tumbling arse over tit over the imaginary waterfall, such a thrashing around you've never experienced in your life before. Well, you probably have, but I hadn't and it was altogether wonderful.

We lay side by side, panting, not saying anything, then Pirrou turned and placed her head on my chest, and I put my arm around her and this touching and the stillness that followed was almost as nice as what had just happened. It was the first time I'd held a woman in my arms, and I felt such a strong sense of needing to protect this beautiful creature that I wanted to cry out. Though, if I'd done so, I have no idea what kind of primordial sound might have issued from my mouth, whether a grunt or a howl or maybe even a growl. Although, I must say, a growl didn't seem all that likely coming from me. What, in fact, I could do to protect such an assured, worldly and sophisticated ballet-dancer-type of person, I simply couldn't imagine.

So, those were things that were happening to me, but my intellect told me Pirrou was probably experiencing quite a different set of emotions. Taking the known facts into consideration, the evidence of her potential high regard for me wasn't in the least promising. She'd come across the two of us, a teenager out of his social depth and his dog, sitting alone absently throwing pebbles into a stream. With a garden party filled with talented and eligible guys roaming around I wasn't exactly the catch of the day. Whereupon, possibly for her own amusement, she'd proceeded to get me drunk on champagne and then, out of kindness perhaps, she'd carted me home and put me to bed like a naughty schoolboy.

Then I reminded myself, What about what happened this morning?, but I quickly saw through this argument as well. Taking my virginity was obviously yet another feather in her cap. Not exactly an exotic trophy, not anywhere near as shiny and bold as the tail feathers stolen from Piet Retief, Meneer Prinsloo's prize Black Orpington rooster, and finally featuring resplendent on Miss Phillips's Easter bonnet. But why, having extracted the virginal tail feather, had she allowed me to make love to her a second time? More amusement, perhaps?

Then, as suddenly, I realised that it was *Voetsek* the *Rooinek* who was thinking all this stuff. Not the born-again Tom Fitzsaxby, brand-new lover and recipient of a blessed five-word benediction, where the past had been forgiven and now everything was new.

Almost as if she'd read my thoughts Pirrou said quietly, 'Tom, I do hope you'll stay in my life, for a little while at least?'

'Why would you want that?' I asked, astonished, having just decided that what I'd been through, glorious as it turned out, was a one-night stand or, more accurately, a one-morning stand.

She pulled away from my arms, and jumping on top of me proceeded to land several kisses on my face. 'I told you! Because I need a smart new handbag!' Then she sat up, straddling my torso.

I grinned, trying not to look confused. Despite the laughing tone in her voice 'handbag' didn't sound a very propitious word, even to a recently born-again, former low-down, suddenly turned-upside-down-by-recent-events-type person like me. Besides, I hadn't yet grown accustomed to a naked woman sitting on my stomach. Too much was happening too soon! 'You said earlier we could make a deal?' I said, in an attempt to cover my confusion.

She didn't answer, remaining seated with her knees bent, legs neatly tucked on either side of me. Then she reached down, picked up a pillow and started to lambast me across the head until I laughingly brought my arms up to protect my face. 'I'm selfish,' *Bam*, 'and bitchy,' *Bam*, 'and as a prima ballerina,' *Bam*, 'overindulged,' *Bam*, 'and horribly, horribly spoilt!' She threw the pillow aside, her green eyes looking down at me. 'Besides, I like to get my own way,' she pronounced happily.

I thought for a moment, then said, 'And having your own way is having me as your handbag?'

'Tom, it won't be like that!' she said, suddenly serious. 'But we might as well face it. That's what people will say. This may be a big city but it's a small town, and full of careless gossip, especially in art circles. You'll be called my handbag and I'll be called La Pirouette, the cradle-snatcher! Seventeen doesn't go into twenty-eight.'

'Nearly eighteen!' I replied brightly. 'And anyway, it just did!'

Pirrou laughed at this half-good quip. 'Tom, my beautiful, beautiful boy, you're probably wondering what's in all this for you?'

Which I wasn't at all! What was in it for me was sitting naked on my stomach, and it was more than I could have possibly imagined happening to me in a hundred thousand years! Even if it only happened once, I mean, twice.

'Well, as a matter of fact, at a recent ballet reception with my grandfather, I met Professor Mustafa and your law professor, what's his name? I should remember, both of them are good friends of the Johannesburg Ballet.'

'Professor Rack, Shaun Rack,' I said quickly.

'That's right, and the chamber orchestra conductor, David Levi, was there as well. My grandfather recounted the incident of his junior trainee salesman and the sale of the three Steinways, telling the story to amuse David, and in passing he mentioned your name. Mustafa and Rack reacted almost simultaneously, both calling out your name and exchanging glances in some surprise. Then each told us of the Tom Fitzsaxby they knew, Mustafa laughingly saying that law had stolen you from a potentially spectacular career in medicine, and Rack saying that you were the most brilliant first-year student he could ever remember attending the law faculty. Then, Tom, to everyone's astonishment, Professor Mustafa told us about the way you attended to the needs of the alcoholics in Joubert Park. How they'd huddle for warmth among the steam pipes behind Park Station in the winter where you'd gather up the ones who were sick with pleurisy and other bronchial complaints, and bring them to his hospital's

Emergency Department. Then he added the equally astonishing facts that you were an orphan and a scholarship student at the Bishop's College and from necessity spent your school holidays living with these destitute men. He also told us about the faceless beggar and your special care of him until he passed away earlier this year.'

By this time I had turned multiple beetroot, and grabbing the pillow I covered my head in an attempt to conceal my shame. All the hiding out in front had been in vain, people all over the place, the founder old Mr Polliack, Professor Mustafa, Rack, my law professor, and now the prima ballerina from the Johannesburg Ballet all knew everything there was to know about me. 'Please stop!' I cried out.

It may have been the miracle of the loneliness stones and all the loving earlier that had put me completely off my guard. Pirrou's words had suddenly made me revisit the past and it consumed me. The air around me suddenly filled with the abuse I'd silently accepted at the hands of Mevrou and Meneer Prinsloo. I could hear the laughter and derision and saw myself knocked down, my mouth bleeding and my ears ringing, grovelling at the feet of some bigger kid, looking pleadingly up into his bully grin, apologising for being a murderer of *Boer* women and little children. I saw the light streaming from the window behind the *Dominee*, and the small child that I used to be, trembling at the back of the church as the promise of God's punishment of my kind came in words as blunt as bullets from his thundering pulpit. As Pirrou recounted her conversation with these high-ups, all of this stuff was being resurrected, sharp images roiling around in my consciousness. My careful anonymity had vanished in a puff of magician's smoke and the past had come rushing back to destroy me.

I know you may be wondering how this could be. That I was beginning to sound like some sort of a pathetic neurotic with a penchant for melodrama. But Pirrou's words filled me with a terror that these people she'd mentioned would see right through me, see who I *really* was, *Voetsek* the despised *Rooinek*, untouchable and guilty. Why couldn't I be left alone, just for a little while longer until I became a little stronger? Did they not see that my punishment forever was the harsh cruel words, the never-ceasing hurtfulness that cut deeper into my soul than any *sjambok* ever could my flesh? Did they not understand that the suppuration caused by constant hatefulness came from wounds that never heal? I was unclean, wicked and unlovable, and if they hadn't discovered this yet, they soon enough would, and then what? So much for my being born again and becoming brand-new. My lucky-day fuck had turned out to be my complete undoing. It wasn't just my body that lay naked and exposed in this strange bed with the sun streaming though a picture window – it was my very soul.

Pirrou climbed off me and I immediately turned onto my stomach like a recalcitrant child, discarding the pillow. She lay beside me and began to gently stroke my back. 'I've said something terribly wrong, haven't I, Tom?' she asked softly.

'No, it's just me,' I replied. 'It's difficult for me to accept —'

'What? Praise?'

'Yes, I suppose so.'

'But why, Tom, you have so much to be proud of. You've succeeded against all the odds.'

'*Ja*, sort of.' I couldn't think of anything further to say. How do you explain all that stuff? 'It's just that here, today, it's . . . well, it's all so unexpected, overwhelming, like a wonderful accident.'

Pirrou laughed. 'I have to tell the truth. It was no accident, darling Tom.'

'How do you mean?'

'I confess, I asked my grandfather to invite you to the garden party. You see, I wanted to meet you.'

I turned and sat bolt upright. 'But why, Pirrou? You knew all about me, all that bad stuff!' I decided it was time I attempted to go on the offensive. 'We come from entirely different worlds! We have absolutely nothing in common!' I said, deliberately raising my voice.

'I see, I'm the spoilt rich bitch and you're . . . well, never mind . . . is that what you're saying, Tom?' Pirrou shot back, putting me firmly in my place. I lacked the courage to reply, and besides, there was some truth in what she'd just suggested. Then she added, smiling, 'There you are, you've just caught a glimpse of La Pirouette, the nasty one!'

'Where's my dog?' I said, alarmed, turning and looking around. I was suddenly ashamed that I hadn't thought of Tinky once since waking up.

'In the kitchen, Tom. I gave him almost half a leg of lamb to chew on.'

'He'll be sick,' I said churlishly, then added, 'We have to go.'

'It's a long way to walk, Tom.'

'I've got my bike,' I said, not thinking.

'It's an even longer walk to my grandfather's place. We left it there, last night, remember?'

What was the use? I wasn't any good at this sort of bickering, even with guys, never mind the opposite sex. So I grinned and looked at Pirrou. 'I don't remember anything about last night, just the first bit beside the stream, and then trees and lights whizzing by. Did I make a bloody fool of myself?'

'Oh, Tom, you were delightful, you told me about that lovely sheep farmer from the Karoo and how Union Jack the Zulu played "God Save the King" sixteen times on the pianos.' She hesitated and then said, 'I'm afraid I quite fell in love with you, darling.'

That was two 'darlings' in English, a word I'd never had applied to me before. I know people use it all the time, and I was to learn that in ballet circles it was so common among the dancers that even the men used it among themselves and they weren't *all* of them Graham Trubys. 'I didn't . . . er, brag about the pianos?' I asked, feeling myself blush.

'No, of course not! You just told a lovely story about a nice man who wanted to buy his wife a gift for loving him so much. It was very touching and it's nice to think this kind of enduring love still exists.' She smiled. 'Does this mean our first lovers' tiff is over? Will Tinky really be sick?' she asked, switching tack, the two sentences following closely so as to allow the one to ameliorate the other.

'Yes and no. Tinky will be in doggie heaven. He'd be scratching at the door and yelping long before this if he wasn't gutsing himself.'

'Come here, Tom,' Pirrou said, her arms reaching out to me. My only hope was that my brain didn't send out the same set of instructions as before, because I would be totally stuffed. She hugged me, then drawing back, planted a kiss on the centre of my forehead. 'C'mon, let's have a shower and then breakfast, I've stocked up on everything a hungry man could possibly want.' She tilted her head and looked at me questioningly, to see if I realised she'd gone young-guy-grocery-shopping, anticipating my presence at the breakfast table all along. If all women in conquest were as confident and as prescient as Pirrou, a man was a goner for sure.

Thus started the true education of the brand-new, born-again Tom Fitzsaxby, by definition the shiny new handbag attached to Pirrou in good times and La Pirouette in bad ones. I must say right at the beginning of the relationship and in her defence that she was starting out with very crude clay. I guess I possessed an intelligence way above my knowledge of how to behave in the company of Johannesburg's wealthy arts patrons. These consisted of older European Jews, the rich part of the locally born Jewish community and others of the wealthy classes that lived in Houghton Ridge, Sandton and the posh suburbs beyond.

Johannesburg for the wealthy white population was a city that is essentially concerned with money, where the arts became a way of outwardly displaying one's wealth. We were besieged with invitations to cocktail and dinner parties, opera, theatre, symphony concerts, gallery openings, the races, mayoral receptions, parties and the like, and when Pirrou accepted an invitation, her handbag tagged along. She was regarded as good company not only because she was principal dancer in the ballet company, but also because she was a sparkling conversationalist, laughed easily, was witty, had a naughty sense of humour and knew how to flirt with older men. She also possessed wide cultural interests and a very good brain. Added to this, long before it was fashionable for a woman to pick up the instrument, she played the classical guitar very well, and had a clear, clean and pleasant voice. And, of course, she had been right; among the bitchy, of whom there were certainly many, she was referred to not as Pirrou the dancer or ballerina or musician, but as La Pirouette the cradle-snatcher.

Now that I was sharing Pirrou's bed, though at my own insistence, not her home, I had grown in confidence and could soon hold my own in a conversation involving the arts and a number of other topics, including finance, an essential requirement in the City of Gold. I admit, a lot of it was due to my prodigious memory, grown all those years back by learning verbatim the entire contents of the stolen red book. But I was steadily catching up with the actual experience of the arts and was less often sounding like a fake to myself. Literature, of course, had never been a problem, and in addition I was devouring Smelly Jelly's enormously eclectic library as well as reading law. I would sometimes surprise myself with what I apparently knew, or I would make an observation or offer a point of view, often in much older company, that made people seem to stop and take notice.

Pirrou was a hard taskmistress, but a good one; she had a wicked temper and she knew how to humiliate me if I messed up. She worked very hard at her profession and suffered anxiety and depression, and I learned to take a fair bit on the chin. Pirrou and La Pirouette were both very much a part of the relationship. By today's standards, she could be called a control freak. By Mevrou's standards, she was an angel. By my own standards, I was eager as a puppy to learn and to slough off the uncouth mannerisms of the past. This was not because I was a snob, as Pirrou explained. 'Tom, you're too young and too poor and not influential enough to be crude, rude and lack basic manners. People will judge you initially by what they see and while you may have sufficient intelligence for them to alter their opinion when later they get to know you, why put yourself at a primary and unnecessary disadvantage? You have instinctive good manners, but very poor physical mannerisms. Just remember, in essence, everything people react positively to in life is sound, dance and movement. How you speak, how you hold yourself and how you act.'

She taught me how to cook, to drive and how to dress, although it shamed me that she purchased my clothes. In this I had no choice, I simply lacked the means to dress the way her lifestyle and my associated handbaggery demanded. She tried not to humiliate me, though she often succeeded with her quick temper, impatience and outrageous sense of privilege. Of course, there were a great many compensations, among them perhaps her greatest gift of all – the many ways there are to make love, to always attempt to satisfy her needs and by so doing enhancing my own experience and ultimate joy of sex. She taught me that slow and patient was infinitely more rewarding than what she termed 'the snorting rhino charge' that so often exemplified the male ego in bed. She also taught me that a rampant phallus isn't the only physical appendage available to bring about coitus or even necessarily the best one available. I can tell you, this, and the various demonstrations and instructions that followed, came as some big surprise!

She would sometimes pick up the guitar and sing me a song. I suppose refrain would be a better word, more in the idiom of the old English 'Hey nonny no' folksong tradition, for it carried with it a gentle nostalgia.

In the Mood

My love is always 'in the mood',
His technique is no mystique,
A rhino charge with snorting horn
And then a good night's sleep!

How very much I've come to long
For a gentler style of loving,
For tenderness and slow, soft ways,
Not grunts 'n' groans 'n' shovin'!

If only he would sense my mood
Then we could share the fun,

And bed would be a loving place
Where both of us would come!

And so two years went by very quickly and I graduated in law with honours and was awarded the university medal and, more importantly, a Rhodes scholarship to Oxford that I was to take up in October the following year. Pirrou was anxious that I do a year with one of the many prestigious law firms that had offered me a place as a junior in the hope that I would rejoin them after I returned from England.

However, I had decided on quite a different course for the year that I would be free. I suppose this must sound strange, even contradictory. But despite all the culture and splendid occasion, the high society and the wealth I'd been integrated into, the social metamorphosis I'd undergone and Pirrou's careful tutelage to achieve all of this, I was left with an anxiety and concern that I was losing the sense of where I came from and who I intrinsically desired to be as an adult.

In effect, I was forgetting my roots. Now, you might even ask, 'Wasn't that the whole idea?' Well, yes and no, my roots were not only The Boys Farm, they were also the high mountains and the *Volk*. I had been fortunate to have the lovely rose-scented Marie, Mevrou Booysens, now Doctor Van Heerden's wife, and the indefatigable and wonderful Miss Phillips as the equalising element in my life as a child. These three generous women allowed me to understand that kindness was an emotion that, when given unselfishly by a woman to a child, became the precursor to understanding that a notion such as love does exist. That love wasn't just between a man and a woman, that it was a universal condition of the heart.

Then there was Sergeant Van Niekerk, who had defended and protected me. His older brother, the headmaster, gifted me with a way to regard myself, 'To thine own self be true', together with a compendium of words I would never conquer. Miss Phillips, who discovered and nurtured my intellect and so opened up infinite possibilities for my future life. Doctor Van Heerden, whose stolen red book and patronage had trained my memory and given me protection. Frikkie Botha and the brotherhood were also a part of who I was, they taught me that humans, despite their shortcomings, are worthwhile whatever their status in life. Although I had only known the three of them for a long day on the road, Dippie, Stoffie and Auntie, together with Mr Patel and Mr and Mrs Naidoo, had also shown me a generosity of the spirit I had never once witnessed among Johannesburg's rich and important people. Finally, there was Mattress waiting for me in heaven. He had given me comfort and the gift of Tinker's life as well as love and friendship when I lacked all three.

All the glitz and the glory of university and the pampering by the *cognoscenti*, in effect, was placing me at odds with those essential values in my past. I was living in a city that had managed the dichotomy of rich and poor, black and white so completely that people such as Pirrou could live their entire lives oblivious to the misery surrounding them. As an example, Pirrou had a housemaid called Martha, a laughing, happy woman who cooked and cleaned and with whom I would sometimes share a cup of tea in the kitchen. Martha had been in her employ for five years, yet it was me who told Pirrou that her maid rose at three in the morning, had two children going to school, and lived in a two-room shanty with one other family of four in Soweto. Before she left home she would iron the children's school clothes, leave their breakfast for them, make their school lunch and then leave in a crowded commuter train at four-thirty in the morning to arrive on time to wake Pirrou with a cup of tea at seven-thirty. She left at six to get home just before nine at night. It was not that Pirrou was uncaring and unkind, it simply never occurred to her to ask about the welfare of her maid. Martha was clean, honest, seemed happy in her presence, was a good cook and cleaner and well paid by the standards of most maids and so, in Pirrou's mind, each had admirably fulfilled their side of the employer/employee contract.

And so in my year off I decided to go to the copper mines in Northern Rhodesia where copper bonuses were being paid to young guys to work underground with high explosives. I could earn more in one year working in an isolated copper mine than I would in five years at Polliack's or as a junior in a law firm. I was conscious of what I was giving up, and even that it might ultimately prove to be to my disadvantage, but I needed time and space to reconcile who I was and what I had learned that was worth keeping.

I had discovered that the very rich are unforgiving, accustomed to getting their own way in most things and judgemental in all. To some real extent Pirrou and her coterie of wealthy and influential friends had an almost proprietorial interest in me. As inevitably happens, those with whom Pirrou commonly associated had learned my background and felt as though they should be a part of my future. A joint rehabilitation program for which they could be seen to be responsible or were able to assume the credit.

Of course to some extent they were correct, they had all helped to smooth the edges, modify my vowels, remove some of the guttural intonations, the strong Afrikaner-speaking English accent I had naturally acquired at The Boys Farm, and in various ways turned me into a sophisticated young man. I was grateful to all of them, but stopped short of feeling beholden. Handbaggery on the arm of a powerful and charismatic woman is very hard work if you refuse to capitulate and become the invisible silent partner, and instead are determined to give as much as you receive. The time had come to reaffirm those values I believed were important to me ('To thine own self be true') and to walk away from that which was not. More specifically, walk away from those things that were over, where the lessons in life had been learned, and the hardest of these was going to be the wonderful as well as potentially redoubtable Pirrou, who had given me so very much of infinite value.

One other thing occurred that had persuaded me to break away. As I was writing my final-year examinations at university, Tinky became unwell. I needed to wrap him in a bit of a blanket when I put him in his butter crate on the bike, and he no longer barked imperiously at the hoi polloi dogs on the pavement, and he slept most of the day. I took him to a vet who gave him a thorough examination. I had been worried for some time because he had become very grey around his snout and eyes, and was beginning to look and move like an old dog. He appeared to have arthritis in his left hip joint and had developed a constant though mild cough.

When he had first come to the flat he had a bad smell, despite my bathing him regularly. I'd taken him to the vet then too and the poor little blighter had almost everything a neglected fox terrier could have, with the fortunate exception of mange. He needed two teeth extracted and some work on his other teeth and as a consequence had very bad breath, his ears were waxy and infected and he had an anal gland infection that added to his malodorous condition. Finally he had a skin infection known as malassezia in between his paws and on his groin. At the time the vet wanted to put him down. 'It's too expensive trying to get an old dog like this healthy again,' he said to me.

'Old dog? I don't think so, it's just that he's had a tough life.'

'No, son, he's an old dog,' the vet replied.

'Can he get better?' I'd asked.

I remember the vet looking me up and down. 'Is he a stray you've found?' He hadn't waited for me to answer. 'No use wasting sympathy on a stray, better to let him go, only cost you money in the end.'

'No, he isn't a stray. Can you make him better?' I repeated.

'In time, I daresay, and with sufficient money.'

'It's not about money,' I said, swallowing, 'it's about not letting him down.'

He looked at me curiously. 'He's been badly neglected, whose dog is this?'

'Mine now.' I didn't wish to explain further.

'I see,' he said, but you could tell he didn't see. 'He's an old dog, son, his life is over.'

'No, it isn't, Doctor, if you can make him better, it's about to begin.'

He sighed. 'It's your money, son.'

I'd always thought that Tinky had belonged to Frikkie as a puppy and had never asked him how he'd come to own him. I'd always assumed that he remembered Tinker the world-champion ratter with great fondness and had somehow found a puppy who resembled her and had taken it from there. But this evidently hadn't been the case and, according to the vet, Tinky was around twelve years old when Frikkie got him, which meant that he was now fifteen and coming to the end of a fox terrier's life. The cough was the worrying factor and a visit to the vet confirmed this. It indicated a severe heart condition.

My darling little Tinky died in my arms a week later, like Frikkie, of a sudden heart attack. He'd simply looked up at me with a tiny whimper, and I'd picked him up and held him against my face. He licked me and then I felt a slight quiver and he was dead.

Although I was terribly distraught, this time I had kept the faith. I borrowed the Ford *bakkie* used by old Mr Polliack's head gardener, had a small pinewood box built for Tinky's body and then drove north to Duiwelskrans to arrive just as night came to the high mountains. I drank the last of a thermos of tea and ate the sandwiches I'd made, and then slept in the back of the truck on the outskirts of the town.

I was aware I would have been perfectly welcome to arrive unannounced at the homes of Doctor Van Heerden or Marie and the Sergeant, but I wanted to complete this particular mission on my own. At dawn I drove through the still sleeping little town and passed the nightsoil cart drawn by the same two patient old mules. The three Africans were laughing and chatting among themselves, wearing the hooded hessian sacks soaked with excrement over their heads. I thought how much had happened since the night I'd spent under Doctor Van Heerden's house and had stolen the red book and then fled into the rising sun back to The Boys Farm to be greeted along the way by these three denizens of the night. So much in life changes, but in the end remains the same.

I started to climb up into the high mountains, passing the Van Schalkwyk farm, and wondered if the six brothers were still incarcerated in Pretoria. With the Nationalist government in power, the nation had been delivered back to the *Volk*. The six Van Schalkwyk brothers were more likely to be regarded by the present government as the freedom fighters they themselves believed they'd been, rather than the saboteurs for which they had been convicted and incarcerated. The law, I was learning fast, was a matter of popular convention, rigid only in those things that can be based on a past example, mostly small crimes committed by small people. Sabotage is a question of opinion, a notion based on the popular sentiments of the day; that peculiar barometer that measures the febrile temperature of a nation at any given time and which politicians learn to read in order to suitably adjust their principles.

I finally arrived at the waterfall around seven o'clock. The sun had risen sufficiently to send its light into the dark *kloof* to reach the old tree where my darling Tinker lay sleeping. Tinky was laid to rest beside the little lioness, to become a great black-maned lion to partner her in their celestial life together. The circle was complete, the two of them, Tinker and Tinky, safely in the happy hunting grounds of eternity where she would teach her city partner the good, clean ways of the country, where no brutal concrete towers bruised the perfect blueness of the African sky.

It took me nearly two weeks to gain the courage to inform Pirrou of my resolve to leave Johannesburg, and therefore remove the handbag from her shoulder. My decision to leave was made all the more difficult because, while I had never loved her in the infatuated way of first love, I had most certainly loved her and would always do so. I mean this in a quite separate way to being grateful to her. In my mind, my gratitude for what she'd done for me was more than offset by her demanding nature, fiery temper and mood swings. I had paid back, in patience, calmness and loyalty, the debt I owed her for all her generous instruction. I'd learned how to calm her sudden anger, and I think I'd even gotten rid of the foot-stamping, tantrum-throwing little brat that I could clearly see would eventually cut short her career. La Pirouette was no Margot Fonteyn and, prima ballerina or not, there was only so much the directors of a ballet company would tolerate. But Pirrou was still someone who insisted on getting her own way, and the idea of me walking away from our association would not be the way she saw things happening.

She'd often laughingly said to me, 'Tom, the time will eventually come when you'll be too old for me, when you'll take me for granted as all men eventually do when they come to believe they own a woman. When that time comes I'll throw you out without the slightest compunction and find myself another young lover.'

'Sure, like in some of your songs,' I said, not believing her, then added, 'but then you'd have to train a brand-new handbag.'

She grinned. 'No woman can have too many new handbags, darling,' she'd replied, one eyebrow slightly arched.

I was to have dinner with Pirrou the Saturday night after returning from burying Tinky and so I'd purchased a bottle of Bollinger, wincing at the cost. I arrived at Pirrou's place with my heart more or less in my mouth. I'd much rather say I arrived with a firm resolve to end things as nicely as possible. But tame endings were simply not a part of her nature and I knew my farewell, or rather confrontation, would be made to La Pirouette and not to Pirrou. I'd once met her erstwhile doctor husband who'd seemed a really nice guy. He'd wished me luck with La Pirouette. 'Tom, you will one day appreciate, as I have, that you were fortunate in your youth to have experienced one of the most exciting women in this country.' He'd paused, thinking, then added, 'However, you should be aware that you are sitting on top of a barrel of dynamite watching the fuse burning. My advice is not to become fascinated with its sparkle and fizz until it becomes too late to jump.' So this was the Saturday night I proposed to jump from the barrel and, quite frankly, I was pretty scared.

Pirrou called from the bedroom as I entered the flat. 'Hello, darling, I won't be long, will you turn the oven down to 150 degrees and open a bottle of wine? Oh, turn off the wireless, the SABC keeps playing Strauss waltzes until I want to scream!' What all this meant was that I had plenty of time, as Pirrou's 'won't-be-longs' were a minimum of twenty minutes. I did as she asked, noticed that the dining-room table had been set for a formal dinner and I was relieved to find it was only for two. I found a damask napkin and a champagne bucket and emptied into it three trays of ice cubes from the freezer, set the champagne into the bucket, surrounding it with ice just as I'd been taught to do as a good little handbag. Then I settled down to read the evening paper.

Saturday nights, if she didn't have a performance or we weren't going out, were relaxed affairs, as often as not with cold chicken or a leg of ham, a salad and a couple of glasses of wine. We might listen to records or read a book, or she'd play the guitar and then, quite early, we would go to bed and make love, and I'd stay over for Sunday breakfast. Except for tonight, when I was going to do the dreaded 'farewell, my love', these were among the nicest times we shared.

She walked through the dining room and noticed the champagne. 'Oh, lovely bubbly, you've remembered, Tom! How wonderful!' she called out. She entered the kitchen, looking absolutely stunning in a little black dress, high heels and pearls. Except for her astonishing green eyes she could easily have been mistaken for Audrey Hepburn. She embraced me warmly, glanced up at the clock on the kitchen wall and said, 'It was about this time two years ago exactly when we were seated beside the stream and you brought me a bottle of Bollinger.'

My heart sank. I'd entirely forgotten. How was I possibly going to end our affair on this night of all nights? On the other hand, perhaps this was how it should be done, the anniversary of two years of loving her during which I'd grown up and she'd possessed me longer even than she'd managed to remain married. She put her arms around me, seated at the kitchen table. 'Tom, my beautiful, beautiful boy,' she said softly, 'I do love you so very much.'

'Pirrou, it's been a lovely two years, how could I have been so lucky?'

Pirrou threw back her head and laughed, her sentimental mood suddenly changed. 'Darling, luck had absolutely nothing to do with it. As I told you once, when my grandfather told me about you I became immediately interested, nearly eighteen-year-old boys don't sell three Steinways for cash. Then when your name cropped up in an entirely different context I knew that unless you had two heads and a long tail I wanted to get to know you. I watched you at the Musicians' Garden Party as you separated from the crowd and went to sit by the stream. I'd approached close enough on two separate occasions during the afternoon to discover that you were a beautiful-looking boy. My eyes have always been my glory, I knew this even as a small child, but it was *your* eyes, more than anything else, that made me fall in love with you. They were so intensely, so absurdly blue that they lacked a metaphor, and so innocent that I felt it was a meeting of two kinds of eyes. Mine so spoilt from attention, so cynical in outlook, so self-indulgent and yours so steady and . . . well, clean. Your eyes had no ego, they seemed to look out on a world that was still innocent as if they'd lived in the Garden of Eden before the serpent came along and fucked things up.'

I laughed, embarrassed as usual by her extravagant tone. 'It just goes to show eyes don't tell one very much, The Boys Farm was no Garden of Eden, I assure you,' I said, attempting to cover my underlying anxiety. 'Shall I get you a glass of champagne, darling Pirrou?'

'Lovely!' She kissed me. 'We're having roast lamb, do you know why?'

'Because it's my favourite?'

'It's in honour of Tinky. The morning we first made love he had what was left of a leg of lamb.'

My heart sank. Things were rapidly becoming more and more difficult, she'd made an anniversary dinner and dedicated it to Tinky and taken the trouble to look absolutely ravishing. I poured two glasses of champagne and handed her one, saying, 'You make a toast, darling.'

Pirrou looked at me steadily, holding my gaze, then reached forward and clinked. 'Blue and green should never be seen,' she said, smiling, taking a tiny sip of champagne. Then reaching out she took my hand and led me silently into the living room and sat me on the lounge. I opened my mouth to say something and she immediately brought a finger to her lips, 'Shush!' She placed her champagne glass on the coffee table and left the room, moments later returning carrying her guitar. She sat on the corner of the coffee table so that she looked directly up at me and began to play and sing.

Where the Green Meets the Blue

You entered my life so wondrously bright
By a stream where the green meets the blue
If you count the stars on a summer's night
Darling, those are the ways I'll miss you!

Farewell, sweet Tom, my beautiful,
beautiful boy

Clouds tumble and turn to scurry away
While as Earth I must stay still to wonder
Will my heart's love return to me some day
Or was he only a sharp clap of thunder?

Farewell, sweet Tom, my beautiful,
beautiful boy

May you reach for the sky, my beautiful boy
And may your life find love and perfection
I'll remember forever your laughter and joy
But oh, how I'll miss your erection!

Farewell, sweet Tom, my beautiful
beautiful boy.

And so Pirrou had the last laugh and the last say, and we sat down to dinner and drank champagne and she was bright and vivacious and seemingly quite relaxed. So much so that I began to feel that the 'Farewell, sweet Tom' wasn't as imminent as it had seemed, perhaps only her prescience that the time to part was approaching. Besides, I felt a familiar stirring and I moved to kiss this gorgeous woman who had so generously, humorously and lovingly sent me on my way, if not tonight, then at some time in the future. Perhaps it was the confidence the champagne gave me because I foolishly thought one last loving would be appropriate and then I would be able to take the initiative and end our affair.

Pirrou allowed the kiss, then pushed me away. 'No, Tom, if we made love that would mean you'd won and I couldn't bear that, you know how I am about having my own way. I've packed your clothes and now I want you to leave.' I could see she was on the verge of tears.

I was tempted to say that the clothes she'd packed no longer belonged to me, but to Tom the handbag. I knew that would be unnecessarily hurtful and so I entered her bedroom and lifted a medium-sized suitcase from her bed. I imagine I looked a little hangdog as I returned to the dining room. Standing in front of her, holding the suitcase I said, 'Pirrou, I owe you ever —'

'Stop, Tom!' she commanded, raising her arm. Then she rose and reached out for my hand and led me to the front door. Leaving the door open, she put her arms around my neck and kissed me tenderly. I placed the suitcase down and put my arms around her. 'Tom, my beautiful, beautiful boy,' she sighed, then she released me and I did the same to her, feeling her soft warmth for the last time. She stood on tiptoe and kissed me again, though this time lightly on the cheek. 'That was from Pirrou,' she said softly. Suddenly her right hand shot up and I felt the sting as her nails raked down the side of my face, piercing the skin. 'And this is from La Pirouette, you bastard!' Then she turned on her elegant heels, entered the flat and slammed the door damn near off the hinges.

I stood with my left hand clamped against the side of my bleeding face, looking foolishly down at the suitcase. I shall give those to the Salvation Army, I decided, then smiled quietly to myself. I wonder what the Salvos will do with the dinner suit or will they realise the clothes come in a Louis Vuitton suitcase? I began to laugh, then cried out, 'That's it, Tom Fitzsaxby! That's *exactly* it! You've learned too much stuff that's totally irrelevant to your life!' Then a curious thought occurred to me – while Pirrou had consciously acted to leave me, how the hell did La Pirouette know I intended to do the same to her?

BOOK
THREE

CHAPTER SEVENTEEN

A Place Where the Loving Arrives in a DC-4

———————

THE IDEA OF GETTING away from everything and everybody, and then from a distance trying to decide who the hell Tom Fitzsaxby really was seemed like a good idea. The mines, set deep in equatorial jungle in Central Africa, sounded just the place for such as me. It would be a purely physical environment away from Pirrou's people. I'd told myself in a quietly superior way that I'd had my fill of the powermongers, gossiping socialites, pseudo-bohemians, covert communists, prancing dancers, artfully shabby artists and writers from upper-middle-class wealthy Jewish and gentile families.

Of course, this made me just as bad as I've just painted them. Here I was making judgements about people who had helped me in a great many ways to grow up, and I knew that what I'd essentially learned from them was invaluable. This was the biggest joke of all, I'd been hiding all my life and never, ever getting away with it and now Pirrou's people had given me the best camouflage there was and I was dissatisfied with the effect it was having on me.

On paper, anyway, my credentials were pretty convincing. I had been educated at one of the country's best private schools, was considered a brilliant student and I guess people found me likeable. I had been rewarded with the gifts of intelligent and sophisticated conversation and an inevitably modified accent. With my new, carefully tutored social manners and pleasant demeanour, I appeared to be a bright, well-bred young man on his way to Oxford. I spoke Afrikaans like an Afrikaner, which was yet another asset in a country gripped in the thrall of apartheid. This almost inevitably meant I was destined to find my rightful place among the very privileged in South African life, those who exercised the real power in society. And it was with this prospect that I began to have doubts. Power, I had long since learned, cannot be trusted, it will always abuse, it cannot understand the viewpoint of those who have no say or ability to change things, and it is always self-serving. I had never seen an exception to this, a situation where power justified its actions. Power is somehow never guilty in the present tense. When it is eventually exposed or terminated, the social, financial and emotional atrocities it has created can almost never be repaired. If, in fact, I allowed myself to be seduced by those in power to join the select few who inevitably end up exploiting the many, then I was on the verge of betraying something essentially important within me. If I couldn't articulate, even to myself, what this precisely was I knew that it had something to do with natural justice. So I convinced myself that a complete withdrawal – spiritual, physical, emotional and intellectual – from everything I knew and from anyone who knew me was the way to go. Tom Fitzsaxby was taking a year off to discover his future direction.

With my bumpy-road upbringing I should have known better and asked a few more questions before buying a second-class train ticket for the nearly four-day journey into the heart of Africa. Physically I was no Charles Atlas, and while I was thin and wiry and cycled everywhere I hadn't done any really hard manual work since The Boys Farm, although I'd played rugby for the university, and so I suppose I was in reasonable shape. But underground miners are generally big men and if Lofty van der Merwe and the others in the park were any indication, then brawn seemed more important than brains and there was probably a good reason for this. It just went to show that in the difficult process of making the correct decisions in life, I still had a fair way to go. To voluntarily sign up as a miner working underground using high explosives wasn't exactly a sign of maturity.

To be absolutely fair and not quite as high-minded as I'm beginning to sound my decision, as I mentioned earlier, also had a lot to do with money. I'd never really had any in a single large amount with perhaps the exception of the commission on the three Steinways. Much of that had been spent caring for Frikkie and maintaining some small financial independence from Pirrou. I'd always had to scrimp and scrape, and I longed for a time when I might have enough to plan further than a week ahead. My scholarship to Oxford took care of my tuition and lodgings, but I would need to find the money for any add-ons. I also hoped to travel through Europe during university vacations, rather than having to work. I would be able to achieve all this if I saved most of what I made in the copper mines. The rent for my hut in the single men's quarters and the meals at the mine mess that were subsidised came to three pounds a week, so I could save virtually all that I made. It all sounded too good to be true. I, above most people, should have known that there are very few neat solutions in life and that nobody pays you more than you rightfully earn. An underground 'grizzly' man in the mines in Northern Rhodesia could, together with his copper bonuses, make up to 100 pounds a week, fifteen times more than I would earn as a salesman or a junior in a Johannesburg law firm.

I rented my Smelly Jelly flat for two pounds ten shillings a week, and appointed Mr Naidoo as landlord, paying him ten shillings a week to collect the rent. The remaining two pounds he deposited at Solly Kramer's, the bottle store near Joubert Park, as credit for Lofty van der Merwe and the boys when their disability pensions ran dry. Lofty may have been a drunk but he was once a mine captain and still carried authority among the men in the park. He was also a fair man and I knew he would distribute the brandy in an equitable manner among the derelicts.

I'm going to skip telling you about the almost four-day train journey to the Copper Belt except to say that it was hot and slow. The country in Southern Rhodesia was much like that in the northern part of South Africa, but on the afternoon of the third day we crossed the bridge across the Zambezi into Northern Rhodesia with the Victoria Falls only a few hundred yards away on our right. The Africans call it 'the smoke that thunders' because the spray from the falls rises to 1000 feet and gives the appearance of smoke, while the roar of the tumbling water may be heard fifteen miles away. The two minutes crossing the bridge spanning the gorge immediately below the falls remains among the most spectacular things I have ever seen.

Once within Northern Rhodesia we seemed to stop at every little tin-shed siding on the way to pick up half a dozen or so frightened blacks clustered together, each clutching the traditional recruiting gift: a new blanket and a brightly coloured tin suitcase. These were future mine workers garnered from the bush where drought had driven them from their villages to be trained to work in the copper mines. They were known as bush monkeys, raw recruits who, when confronted by their own face in a mirror for the first time, reeled back in terror. They had never climbed a ladder or seen a train – 'the snake that runs on iron'. They would be brought to the mines and trained to do work they'd never imagined existed, and in order to communicate with their fellow mine workers, tribesmen recruited from all over Africa who spoke a dozen different languages would learn a new language, Kiswahili, the *lingua franca* of the mines. They'd be driven onto the train by a recruiting officer, jeered at by recruits gathered earlier who were by now accustomed to the rattle and the roar of the iron monster and considered themselves old hands at this sophisticated business of travelling without using your own legs.

The Northern Rhodesia landscape was largely flat with an occasional range of low hills and appeared to be covered by largely equatorial forest, not quite the jungle of the Congo basin, but nevertheless tall trees with open woodland beneath them that took on all the autumnal shades of the Northern Hemisphere in midsummer: yellows, maroons, deep purples, rusts and reds. It was as if the seasons had gone haywire, autumnal colours under a blazing tropical sun.

The train took me as far as Ndola, a sleepy town that serviced the surrounding copper mines and served as one of the outposts of the British Colonial Service. I was destined for the Roan Antelope Mine situated adjacent to the small mining town of Luanshya, about half an hour's drive along a dusty dirt road from Ndola.

I was met on the Ndola station by a mine official who, extending his hand, introduced himself as Ian de la Rue. De La Rue is a South African name of French Huguenot derivation and so I was surprised when he spoke with a strange and distinct twang until moments later when he introduced himself as an Australian. He announced this in a manner that suggested this single fact was perhaps the most important part of the introduction. I was to learn that this wasn't too far off the mark.

There were over forty Western nations represented in the mines and a great many of the men who found themselves in Central Africa had left other parts of the world in an unseemly hurry. I was to discover that truth was a very rare commodity among the men who lived in the single quarters and that a simple rule prevailed: you never asked a man anything about his past and you accepted what he was prepared to volunteer about himself. If a man talked about his past history, this invariably proved to be an elaborate fabrication told during the course of a bout of heavy drinking. In this manner, ex–German SS officers turned into Polish Jews who had survived Hitler's concentration camps. Ian de la Rue, by telling me he was Australian, was in effect telling me I could trust him and that he had no past to hide.

He indicated to a black porter to take my suitcase and led me to a *bakkie* with the insignia 'Anglo American Mines – Roan Antelope Mine' painted on the door of the small truck. A few minutes later we left the town and were travelling along a bumpy, rutted dirt road.

'Tom, there's a couple of things you should know that the Anglo American recruiting officers in Johannesburg probably didn't tell you,' Ian de la Rue began when we were finally on our way.

'*Ja*, I'm sure you're right, Mr De La Rue, apart from a medical and testing the speed of my reactions, they really didn't tell me very much.'

'By the way, Tom, please call me Ian, Australians are not big on formality.'

'Thanks, Ian,' I replied, thinking that he seemed like a friendly sort of guy.

'Did they explain why they needed to test your reactions?' he then asked.

'Not really, I guess it seemed a sensible thing to do, after all, I was going to work underground and I imagine it's a place where you need to keep your wits about you.'

Ian de la Rue grinned. 'You can say that again, brother! You're going to be trained to be a grizzly man.'

'Yeah, that's what they said.'

'Did they explain what a grizzly man does?'

'Not really, only that it was the first job the young guys do when they go underground.'

He turned and glanced briefly at me before his eyes returned to the road. 'Do you know why that is?'

'Well, I guess most young guys don't have any previous mining experience?'

'Yeah, right, apart from the diamond drillers. But grizzlies are different, it's a job where older blokes are too careful and so the ore tally suffers.'

'Ore tally?'

'The amount of muck you move out in a shift. Young blokes will take chances, matter of pride, they won't leave the mouth of a stope blocked so they . . . well, take chances and get themselves injured or killed.'

'You mean it's a dangerous job?' It was all I could think to say; the terms muck, stope, diamond drillers and even the word bloke were new to me.

'We've got a young bloke in hospital in Ndola at the moment, two broken legs and fifteen breaks in his left shoulder and arm, as well as a broken pelvis. That's where I was before I met your train. Another young grizzly man died last month, climbed up into the mouth of the stope and while he was up there the muck started to run, poor bastard never had a hope.'

I looked at him. 'Ian, what are you trying to say?'

'Mate, I'm trying to warn you to be fucking careful. Scare you, I suppose. We've lost six young blokes on grizzlies in the past two years and dozens have been injured, some so badly they're in wheelchairs for life. This is Central Africa and the price of copper is going through the roof. A grizzly is the most efficient way to get the muck out of the stope, it's also the most dangerous but the company doesn't care, there's no miners' union and you can't even insure your life, no insurance company will take the risk on a miner working the grizzlies.' He was yakking on as he wrestled the steering wheel from one side to the other across the rutted road. 'Rainy season, road's history,' he said, suddenly jerking the wheel to miss another deep rut. 'Sixty per cent of grizzly men are injured in one way or another. You're supposed to do three months on and then three months off. But we never have enough young blokes to do the change-around. Then, if you're any good, there's pressure from the bloody diamond drillers to keep you on.' The *bakkie* hit a sudden bump and our heads nearly hit the roof of the cabin. 'Fucking road!' Ian exclaimed. 'You'll end up doing five or six months without a break, and that's mostly where the trouble starts. Your nerves are shot, and you're so bloody whacked you're not thinking straight. Six months of night shift where you're setting off a blast every few minutes is hell on your system.'

'What's your job, Mr De La Rue?' I asked, forgetting to call him Ian and not quite knowing what to say. Was he suggesting I turn back while I still could? It seemed odd that he would be talking to me in such a manner when he was the mine's official representative.

He grinned. 'Name's Ian,' he corrected. 'Can't you guess what I do?'

'I know nothing about mining, Ian. I'm afraid most of the terms you've used don't mean very much to me.'

'I'm the mine safety officer, mate.' He glanced at me again. 'You've just received lesson one, which is don't try to be a hero. You're going to be trained under Gareth Jones, a Welshman, in the underground School

of Mines. I can personally guarantee it will be three of the hardest bloody
months of your life. You'll have good reason to hate him by the time
you're ready to go onto a grizzly on your own, but remember his job is to
see you stay alive in a very dangerous environment. The Roan Antelope
Mine has the lowest grizzly injury record on the Copper Belt, and we can
thank Mr Jones for that. You'll think he's a bastard – no, correction, he
is a bastard, but his bastardry may well save your life one day.'

I instinctively liked Ian de la Rue. I'd never met an Australian, but
would later learn that he was a fairly typical representative of his corner
of the British Commonwealth and, furthermore, his refreshingly direct
vernacular didn't sound in the least crude.

Ian de la Rue drove me to my hut in the single quarters, which was
close to the recreation club and at the opposite end of town to the homes of
the married miners. 'Hut' is a correct description, my home-to-be was built
as a traditional *rondavel*, with a small enclosed veranda attached. That is to
say, a single brick room in the round with two barred windows and a steel
door leading out onto the veranda, which was a simple construction made
of wood and mosquito wire. Ian opened the screen door to the veranda,
and then handed me the keys to the hut, and I unlocked the heavy steel
door to enter the hut. The room contained a single iron-framed bed and
bare mattress on which two folded blankets lay, the remaining furniture
consisted of a wardrobe and a dresser, and from the ceiling hung a rotating
fan. The floor was red polished cement. No thought whatsoever had been
devoted to comfort, and on first appearance it seemed more like a prison
cell than what was to be my home for the next year. The only concession
to any thought of comfort was two old wicker chairs on the veranda.
Uninvited, Ian plonked himself down in one of these. I left my suitcase in
the hut and joined him in the vacant wicker chair.

'Just a couple o' things you should know before I take you to the mess,
Tom. Sort of rules of behaviour. Firstly, never leave your hut unlocked
when you go out.' He pointed to the door. 'It's not made of steel for
nothing, mate. Next, don't use the *chimboose* late at night. During the
week you'll be on night shift, so I'm talking mostly weekends.'

'*Chimboose?*'

'Lavatory, shower block, there's several known turd burglars among the German miners, they're an evil mob and bloody dangerous when they're pissed on *schnapps*. You'll hear them singing "*Deutschland über alles*" and other kraut songs, and my advice is to stay well clear of the bastards at all times.' He glanced at me and said, 'Now a bit of town and club advice. Leave the married sheilas alone.'

'Sheilas?'

'Yeah, women. Fraternising with a married woman is not on. If they come on to you a bit pissed at the club, get on yer bike, quick smart. You don't want some big South African diamond driller and his mates pissed to the gills on Cape brandy breaking down the door of your hut because he thinks you've fumbled his missus. The single sheilas are all mostly taken, well the good sorts anyway, but if you do get one, remember, if you get her up the duff it's either leave town without bothering to pack or you marry her the next day. Schoolgirls are out! Even if they are over the age of sixteen, touch one of them and you're dead meat.' I think he must have seen the rather embarrassed look on my face because he said, 'Mate, I told you, I'm the mine safety officer and this is as much a part of keeping you alive as going underground.' He grinned. 'Now, as a young healthy bloke you are probably wondering what, apart from taking yourself in hand, the alternative is? Well, it ain't any of the above and, of course, it ain't black velvet either, but as a South African you'd know that. Officially there's no colour bar but that's bullshit, the Brits are as bad as the Afrikaners when it comes to that sort of thing.' He paused and grinned again. 'The alternative is the plane from Brussels.'

'Plane from Brussels? What do you mean?'

'Every four weeks a DC-4 lands with a plane-load of sheilas from Brussels,' Ian de la Rue explained. 'Some are your genuine whores, the older European miners like them, no name, no pack drill, they know how to get drunk, get laid, get paid and get going. But most of them are young Belgian girls working for a dowry. Good sorts mostly, although they're a tad worn-out by the time they get to us. You see,' he explained further, 'there's more sheilas in Europe than there are blokes, I guess that's because of the war. To get a good bloke a girl has to have something to offer, usually a house or a flat she personally owns or money in the bank. She's also got to be respectable and from a good family. That's a big ask in the war-torn Europe of the present. So, to cut a long story short, there's an agency in Brussels that charters a Sabena DC-4 to Katanga province in the Belgian Congo which is an extension of this Copper Belt. The agency in Brussels takes a percentage based on every girl getting laid thirty times for the same fee by the French miners. If a girl happens to do a bit better than that she keeps the rest. Now, the "bit better than that" is obtained by giving a nice tip to the pilot to make a short hop over the border to our part of the Copper Belt, where they spend two days at each of the mines on this side. It's fifty quid an hour and they'll leave here with a bundle of banknotes that would choke a draught horse.'

I laughed, shaking my head. 'As safety officer is this also in your brief?'

'Christ no, officially it's not allowed. The British won't tolerate such scandalous goings-on, but the mine management turns a blind eye and so do the local cops, so we make sure we keep the private airstrip graded and in good order. There's also plenty of penicillin available at the mine hospital when one of the girls leaves a miner with a small token of her esteem.'

'You mean a dose?'

'I can see you're not slow, son,' Ian de la Rue declared. 'The girls arrive in Katanga clean, having had a medical inspection before they leave Brussels, but by the time they get here after the miners across the border have dipped their wick, they're second-hand goods. They'll get another medical when they return home to Brussels, but they've not infrequently picked up something nasty on the way because some of the miners will pay double if they can do it without using a franger . . . er, a French letter. So if it gets too hard to contain yerself, always use a condom, mate.'

I couldn't help laughing. 'Let me see, these appear to be my options. I die working as a grizzly. Or I get beaten to a pulp by a bunch of

Afrikaners for a dalliance with the inebriated wife of a diamond driller. I'm lynched for fraternising with a schoolgirl. Forced into marriage or have to leave town for getting someone pregnant. End up being ostracised by the white community for indulging in a bit of black velvet. Finally I could contract a nasty disease from a Belgian whore earning her right to a respectable future life by means of an ill-gotten dowry.'

'Too right, mate! Never better said,' he laughed. 'Take my advice, Tom, stick to wanking, that way you'll meet a better class of woman! *And* you'll be safe.'

I grinned, the mine safety officer was a character, alright. 'While you're at it, is there anything that's nice about the place?'

Ian de la Rue looked down at his shoes and appeared to be thinking. 'You can play a bit of sport, they've got it all here: tennis, squash, rugby, cricket, and the swimming pool's nice. There's an Anglican church, you can join the choir or the fellowship.' Then he looked directly at me. 'The money. It's the only reason we're all here, son.'

I extended my hand. 'Thanks, Ian, for picking me up, and for the friendly advice.'

He shrugged. 'It's my job.' He shook my hand. 'Do you play poker, Tom?'

'A bit.' I'd learned the game from one of Pirrou's dancer friends and quite fancied myself as a poker player going through the motions deadpan, and I was secretly thrilled when I won.

'Don't. The cardsharps, like the whores, move into town regularly, only they'll cost you a lot more than fifty quid an hour.' Ian de la Rue rose from his chair. 'I'll walk you over to the mess and sign you in, the tucker's not too bad and if you get tired of it you can get a half-decent steak at the club.' We turned and left the enclosed veranda when he cleared his throat. 'Ah, the hut, mate,' he said, pointing to the steel door, 'you've left it open.'

I locked the hut and we walked in the direction of the mess, Ian de la Rue talking all the way. 'I'll pick you up at seven o'clock tomorrow morning and take you to Number Seven shaft. That's where the

underground School of Mines is situated and you'll meet Gareth Jones.'
He hesitated, then added, 'Tom, Welsh miners have a different attitude to
mine protocol, while you're in the school always call him Mr Jones, even
when you meet him in the club, after that you're free to call him anything
you like and it probably won't be very complimentary. I can see you're not
stupid, which makes a nice change, but don't let Jones know you're clever,
it will put you at a distinct disadvantage.'

Ian de la Rue's advice concerning Mr Jones was certainly timely. The
underground School of Mines proved to be hell on wheels. It was pretty
difficult, even with my training at The Boys Farm, to appear to be
consistently stupid and it didn't take Mr Jones long to cotton on that
I was brighter than the rest of the trainees. He immediately thought I
was secretly laughing at him. Nothing could have been further from the
truth, I was fully committed to staying alive and coping with the manual
work. The procedure in the School of Mines was to do every job that
existed underground. That is, every job that an African did and every
one that a white miner performed. Not only do it, but do it harder and
faster and longer. Lashing was the business of loading ore from a freshly
blasted tunnel end, simply referred to as 'lashing an end'; that is, loading
solid lumps of rock blasted from the face, which is simply the surface
of the rock drilled to extend the tunnel, known as a haulage. Most of
the blasted rock proved too big to pick up with a shovel, and needed to
be manhandled. Jones was never satisfied until you collapsed with your
hands raw and bleeding. I was the smallest in a group of big Afrikaner
guys, all young and strong and, dare I say it, some of them thick as a
bull's dick, as the saying goes. Mr Jones wanted me to be the first to
collapse, proving perhaps that in this environment brains didn't triumph
over brawn. But in this one respect the years on The Boys Farm paid
off, as except for the time at the Bishop's College, I'd been teethed on
manual labour. I knew how to use a pick and shovel and how to lift

and carry, and although Jones would routinely get me on my knees and finally unable to continue, I was never the first or even the second or third of the trainee miners to collapse. It was the same drilling an end prior to blasting it. We'd have to manhandle a 60-pound jackhammer on our own, when it normally required two men to operate it, and it was backbreaking work sufficient to reduce several of us to tears.

Jones would examine us on mining theory, a question-and-answer session every morning that my fellow trainee miners grew to fear as they struggled for the answers he demanded. If a trainee failed, as they invariably did, he took enormous delight in humiliating him. By sheer coincidence the entire group were South Africans and Afrikaners to boot, and Jones seemed to take a particular delight in bringing them undone. I remained silent, not wishing to add to their sense of being thought of as stupid, whereupon he'd think of some nasty punishment for the entire class because he didn't get the reply he needed. But my playing dumb didn't last too long because he'd glare at me and say, 'Okay, Fitzsaxby, if you don't answer the next question you all do an extra hour's lashing.' Then he'd ask me a question out of the training manual on something we hadn't yet done in class or in practice. But the red book would always save me, it had trained my memory to a fairly prodigious level and a law degree had given me further training in absorbing detail. The manual was pretty simple stuff anyway, and I'd read the entire contents of the training course in the first three nights after we'd received it, and I would invariably know the answer. This would infuriate Mr Jones and we'd receive a punishment for 'having a fucking smart-arse among you'. There was no getting the better of him, and I soon began to realise that part of the training was his attempt to exasperate us to the point of breaking our spirit. Humiliation and constant and unfair punishment are both sound methods for bringing a man to his knees or having him resort to violence, whereupon he'd be instantly dismissed and given his train ticket back to South Africa. I was to learn that if Mr Jones was unable to eliminate at least three trainees from a group, he wasn't satisfied. Moreover he was invariably successful in this endeavour. 'Eliminating the no-hopers and

the weak' was, to his perverted way of thinking, all part of the training
to be a successful underground miner.

The Afrikaner temperament is not without arrogance and a sense
of superiority, and so Jones had just the right sort of material to work
with: quick-tempered, argumentative men unable to retaliate physically
as they normally do. For me, anyway, it was back to the future, this was
simply a grown-up Boys Farm. I guess I could read Gareth Jones like an
open book; he wasn't a patch on Mevrou or Meneer Prinsloo or many of
the boys who had bullied and harassed me in the past.

However, I could see it was getting to the class. I felt that Jones's
attempt to alienate me from the rest of them by making me the cause of
further punishment was something they might also be coming to resent.
Jones probably knew this, and used me as the straw that broke the camel's
back. Even though I spoke Afrikaans as well as they did, I was still the
Rooinek and they were getting punished because of me. Jones's attempt
to alienate the so-called smart-arse from the rest of the class I thought
might well be working.

I decided to apologise to my fellow trainees. We were back on the
surface after a particularly gruelling day when we'd received two extra
hours of hard work with attendant humiliation and abuse for my smart-
arse-ness. We were showered and changed and sitting in the change
room too exhausted to walk the 2 miles along the mine railway track
back to the single quarters. I spoke in Afrikaans, which I now translate
here.

'Hey, *kêrels, mag ek praat, asseblief*? Hey, guys, may I say something,
please?' They all looked up, too weary to speak, though one or two of them
nodded. 'You guys are getting a lot of extra shit because of me, and I want
to apologise. But I'd also like to tell you what I think is going on. Is that
okay by you?'

'*Ja*, tell us, man. I'm glad you know, Tom, because I'm fucked if I
do,' a trainee named Karl Joubert said. Several of the others laughed and
nodded knowingly.

'Well, this training is a bit like going into the army, the idea is to reduce us to the point where we don't think and simply obey without questioning. It's all designed, Jones thinks, to keep us alive in dangerous situations. So we take no chances, do everything according to the book and all will be well. You could call it a kind of brainwashing. Jones regards thinking as dangerous, and in some respects he may be right, a grizzly is a dangerous place with the constant use of gelignite, so always doing things by the book will reduce, somewhat, the danger factor.'

'You mean all this shit is good for us?' one of the guys asked.

'Some of it is,' I said quietly. 'Last year six grizzly men died, and according to the safety officer Ian de la Rue, all of them did something on a grizzly they shouldn't have attempted. Because the grizzly is the first job we do after we come out of the School of Mines, such a death can mean we weren't properly trained and that points the finger directly at Jones. So, in a way, he is to blame. So what does he do? He tries to overcompensate, he works us to a standstill in order to eliminate the weak among us and turn everyone else into people who never vary procedure. He expects some of us to fail our blasting licence the first time around and some of us never to get it. In this way he can continue to put the boot in and condition us for grizzly work. Only the strong must survive is his motto. When someone like me comes along, someone who seems to know all the answers, he decides he must eliminate me because I'm not good for the group.'

'What are you saying, that he wants you to quit?' someone said.

'*Ja*, and the best way to do that is to exert group pressure on me, get you guys to blame me for what's happening,' I answered.

'So that's the bastard's game, hey?' Dirkie de Wet, a huge Afrikaner, exclaimed. 'Listen, man, I'm not going to get through, I can do the hard work but the theory, man, no way, my brain goes numb when he asks me something. I know myself, one of these days I'm going to smash him.'

Several of the others nodded. Dirkie turned to the others. 'I don't know about you, but every time Tom here answers one of Mr Jones's trick questions it's worth it to see the bastard's face.'

There was a murmur of agreement among the men. 'So, Tom, we not going to let it happen,' Dirkie assured me. 'Maybe yes, but he's not going to break you, you hear?'

I thanked them all and then added, 'Look, there's no reason why we can't all pass the blasting licence test, it's all verbal anyway and Jones doesn't conduct it, the mines inspector in Ndola does. What say I devise a system that will help you to remember the questions when the time comes, a sort of *aide-mémoire?*'

'A what?' several of them chorused.

'A way of remembering things, like a game, we'll practise it every day for the next two months. Do you all like rugby?'

They all agreed they did.

'Do you know the rules of the game?'

They nodded.

Over the next few weeks we got a lot of fun out of a simple system of code words and analogies I devised, based on the game of rugby. We'd sit during the breaks and I'd be the inspector of mines in Ndola, and ask them questions, and it wasn't long before Jones was having trouble finding ways to make us look stupid. That's the funny thing about confidence, they all started absorbing stuff on their own, and we had become quite competitive. I have discovered in life that a person who thinks themselves stupid and then is allowed to gain confidence in their own ability will blossom beyond all expectations. Doctor Van Heerden had once said to me, 'Tom, no man can make you inferior unless you give him your consent.'

Then we received our application papers to obtain our blasting licences and, on the spur of the moment, during a rest break Karl Joubert said, 'Why don't we all do the International?'

The group looked at him as though he'd suddenly gone mad. 'You're crazy!' two of them echoed.

'Not a bad idea,' I heard myself saying.

'Whaddayamean?' Dirkie called, almost panic-stricken. 'I'm shitting myself anyway, the International Blasting Licence? No way, man!'

'The point is, if you get your International you can work anywhere in the world, but the Local is only for here,' I said. 'Anyway, if we miss out they hold the exams every three weeks, first the International and then a week later the Local. It also means because we've studied for the International we'll be bound to pass the Local as it will be a lot easier.'

'I dunno, man,' Dirkie said, shaking his head.

'Ag, it will give you confidence, Dirkie,' Karl assured him. 'Like Tom said, if you fail the International it's *blêrrie* good practice and you'll pass the Local easy as anything, man.'

And so we all decided to sit for the International Blasting Licence, an occurrence that had never been attempted by a trainee-mining group.

Three weeks from the end of the three-month course, after another particularly difficult shift using jackhammers to drill an end for blasting, Jones stopped me as we were about to enter the cage to take us to the surface. I was soaked to the skin, cold and dirty, my face blackened from the wet, powdered muck kicking back from the holes we were drilling, and I was looking forward to the glorious promise of a hot shower and clean, dry gear.

'Fitzsaxby, stay! We need to talk, Boyo.'

I looked at him and he must have seen my dismay, the next cage was in twenty minutes and I was tired as a dog. 'Mr Jones, can't we do it on the surface?'

'You being cheeky, Boyo?'

'No, Sir, er, Mr Jones.'

I watched as the cage left with the others in it, whereupon Jones drew me into a side haulage. 'Sit!' he commanded.

I did as he'd instructed and sat on the bottom rung of a ladder leading up into a grizzly escape tunnel.

'It's got to stop!' Jones barked, standing directly over me.

'What has, Mr Jones?' I asked, confused.

'You're fucking giving them the answers, Boyo!'

'But I'm not,' I protested.

'But I'm not, *Mr Jones*!' he shouted down at me. 'Yes, you bluddy are!'

'Honestly, Mr Jones, I'm not.'

'It's some sort of sign language, with your hands. What do you take me for, Boyo, a bluddy idjit?'

I shrugged. 'I can't help you, Mr Jones, I honestly can't,' I pleaded.

'Look, Fitzsaxby, I've been teaching young idjits like this for ten years, they don't change, this class is no more intelligent than any other, which means they're stupid to the fucking core. Of the ten trainee miners, on average three will get through the Local Blasting Licence the first time, then four weeks later, when I've drummed a little more sense into their thick heads, four more and we'll piss the other three off. But you've all applied to be judged for an International Blasting Licence and that's fucking absurd! You're the only one capable of getting one, but take my word for it, Boyo, you won't be going for it because unless you tell me how you're doing it, I'll break you before you get to take the exam.'

'But wouldn't it be to your credit if they all did get their blasting licence, Mr Jones?'

'That's bullshit, Boyo! Because they won't! You can't turn crap into chocolate pudding! We'll have lost six grizzly men, my reputation and my copper bonus and that is definitely *not* going to happen, son!'

I was caught between a rock and a hard place. Gareth Jones could do exactly that, prevent me from taking my blasting licence by coming up with some reason why I shouldn't work underground. Ian de la Rue had warned me that Jones had absolute power over the trainee miners and that he couldn't interfere unless it was a safety matter. Jones was a good miner, but that's all. He knew his stuff but not a great deal beyond it. He believed in the school of hard knocks and everything he'd ever learned had been by doing it tough. He also knew the nature of miners and the capacity of the trainees. Nothing on earth was going to convince him that all ten of us could pass the test or that even three of us could pass the difficult International Blasting Licence. He was, he believed, facing a wipe-out and with it personal disgrace. All his trainees were going to fail with the exception of myself, and he'd convinced himself this was an act of revenge on my part, my personal payback for the hard time he'd given me. As usual, I'd been too smart for my own good. Here I was once again rescuing drowning puppies and, in the process, had landed myself in the shit. The two-and-a-bit months of sheer hell I'd been through under the Welsh git's direction had all been for nothing. Without his imprimatur it was as good as over for me.

The stupid thing was that I was convinced all ten of us could pass; the guys had really enjoyed the study and had come ahead in leaps and bounds. I'd used a game they loved and understood intimately to teach them something that had been made into a daily purgatory that they had come to hate, but now enjoyed. They would test each other constantly, proud of their new-found knowledge. Besides, if one or two of them failed the International test they could still do the Local one the next week, and I knew even Dirkie de Wet could get his Local Blasting Licence in his sleep.

The whole shebang was about to come apart for me. This stupid man was capable of upsetting everything. The three months in the School of Mines barely paid for the rent on the hut and my mess bill. Until we obtained our blasting licence we couldn't share in the prosperity brought about by the copper bonus. Instead we endured, for four pounds a week, the daily misery Jones seemed to enjoy inflicting on us.

It was all put down to the reality of mining, Jones was thought to be toughening us up for the environment in which we were eventually to work. Even Ian de la Rue believed that young mining students ultimately worked better when they were faced with the so-called reality of the real world of mining. Jones worked us all to the point of exhaustion and commonsense indicates that's the point when men have accidents. Whenever one of us collapsed or hurt himself, this was put down to stupidity or a lack of hardness or physical ability. It was almost always due to exhaustion or because of some deeply resented punishment that preoccupied a trainee to the extent that he took his eye off the ball. In reality, no miner ever worked under anything like the conditions Jones put us through. We accepted that initially some of us were soft and needed hard physical work to condition us, but this was achieved in a fairly short time. After this point it simply became bloody-minded perversity by our instructor.

The salient point seemed to be overlooked that we'd all come to the mines for the singular purpose of earning more money than we could expect to earn elsewhere. Our future salaries would depend on our own efficiency. Even the dullest trainee among us was anxious to learn and absorb as much information as possible and besides, we, like almost all humans, had a personal interest in staying alive. This was the framework on which I had based the simple method of learning, using the game of rugby as the matrix. Curiously, every trainee seemed to work harder than under the acerbic tongue and constant harassment that was our instructor's method of learning how to survive underground. Gareth Jones simply couldn't conceive of a method of instruction that depended on cooperation and the practical intelligence most men with personal ambitions possess. Hard graft and punishment was how he'd learned mining in his native Wales, and what was good for the goose was also good for the goslings.

I sighed, then shrugged. 'Okay, it's an association of ideas, Mr Jones, a mental game.'

'Ha! Gotcha, Boyo! Brainwashing, eh? I knew it!' he exclaimed triumphantly.

'Hardly that, it's simply, like I said, an association of ideas, each object or move or association is intended to act as an *aide-mémoire*. We used rugby because everyone knows the rules. It's very simple really, a mental game that helps them to learn. I can show you how it works, if you like.'

Jones reeled back in horror. 'That's it! Mental telepathy! Oh no you don't! You're not getting inside *my* mind, Fitzsaxby.'

'Of course not! There's no such thing as mental telepathy, Mr Jones.'

'Don't you go denying it now, Boyo, I know what you're up to! Do you think I'm stupid? They'll all go in front of the blasting licence examiner and you'll wipe their minds clean and they'll all fail. It's your revenge, isn't it?'

I sighed, the whole thing was suddenly becoming ridiculous. 'You're becoming paranoid, Mr Jones, no such thing can happen.'

'Don't you go using them big words on me, Boyo! I know what you're up to and it won't work, you're on report and that means you're out of my school!' He paused, and then smacked his palm against his forehead. 'Christ, of course! It's hypnosis!'

If it hadn't been so serious I would have laughed. 'Please, Mr Jones, this is ridiculous, first it's hand signals, then brainwashing, mental telepathy and now hypnosis. I admit we've been coaching each other using a game everyone likes to play. But what's wrong with that? If they know the answers they'll pass and you'll get the credit!'

'But they *won't* fucking pass, in ten years one trainee in every three intakes might get their International. I don't mind telling you I had to sit three times to get it and it took me four frigging years! Now you're telling me nine bluddy Afrikaner gits are going to pass the first time they try?' He leaned back, a sneer on his face. 'Do me a favour, son!'

'But if they fail, the following week they can sit for the Local and be confident they'll pass. Honestly, Mr Jones, the guys know their stuff, even de Wet does. It wasn't my idea that they sit for the International, they want to and they know if they don't make it they can have another go at the Local Blasting Licence.'

'It's brainwashing, you're making them think they can do stuff they can't do.'

I thought of Doctor Van Heerden's advice to me. 'No, Mr Jones, most of these guys have been constantly told they're *domkops*, it's probably happened from the first day they went to school. You constantly tell us how stupid we are and for them, anyway, it's a reinforcement of what they already believe about themselves. That's a form of brainwashing. They believe you and that's the problem. No-one can make you feel inferior without your own consent. All I've managed to do, by using the rules of a game they all consider they're experts at, well, to use a rugby term, I have helped them sidestep this belief they have of themselves as stupid. You're a Welshman, you know that every Welsh kid, like every South

African one, believes he knows the game of rugby inside-out. It's like using baseball as a medium to teach an American kid or to an English one the rules of football. Probably for the first time in their lives they've become interested in learning.' I shrugged. 'That's all that's happened, Mr Jones. You've seen it for yourself in the past three weeks, very few of your questions go unanswered, the guys are even eager to participate, and the practical mining we do, you have to admit, has greatly improved.'

Jones shook his head, unable to deny that this was true. 'They won't pass the International, Fitzsaxby, even *you* may fail it. It's not your responsibility to get them through, it's fucking mine! If the whole class fails there's enough people around here and in management who'd just love to put in the boot. Two more years and I can go home a rich man. Nobody, you least of all, is going to fuck that up for me. The mine needs six grizzly men out of your intake and, by Christ, they're going to get them. But listen to me carefully, Boyo. You won't be one of them!'

'But even if they fail, they can sit for the Local Blasting Licence a week later!' I persisted.

'Listen, Boyo, don't think I don't understand you're setting me up. Nobody sits for the International the first time, let alone a whole new intake of mining trainees who combined haven't got the brains of my dog Spot!'

I had to think fast, by making the class believe they could go for the big one, the International, I'd clearly over-reached myself. Gareth Jones knew such an achievement to be impossible. It was a task well beyond his certain knowledge of the ability of his trainees. Underground miners are not generally known for their mental acuity. Only the diamond drillers possessed an International Blasting Licence and most of them, like Jones, had taken years to obtain it. He had become convinced that I'd hatched some diabolical plot to bring him undone. He seemed to truly believe that I could somehow enter the minds of my fellow trainee miners and make them believe they could succeed when they'd fail, vastly over-reaching themselves. He was about to become the laughing stock of his fellow miners and, in his own eyes, lose the respect of the mine management.

While Jones had absolute authority within the school, every trainee was free to choose which blasting licence he undertook. I had foolishly thought that the extra pride my fellow trainees would gain having an international accreditation would be worth it, and I hadn't thought how the idea of ten novice miners getting the big prize first-time round was likely to put every miner's nose out of joint. What's more, such a result didn't help the mine, they only needed young men with quick reactions to qualify for working on a grizzly, an efficient but very dangerous method of getting ore from the stope, outlawed everywhere with the exception of the Copper Belt.

It wasn't too hard to see Jones's point of view, and I felt stupid that I hadn't worked it out before this. The problem was that I'd found myself back at The Boys Farm where a single, constantly bullying authority decided what was best for me. I'd resented Jones to the point where I wasn't thinking clearly. All I'd wanted to do was prove him wrong about us all. That we weren't useless and stupid as he constantly told us. But, if I was honest with myself, what I was *really* doing was showing off, a sign of my own immaturity. I had put the idea into the heads of my fellow trainees that they could achieve the marks required for an International Blasting Licence. I had become philosophically convinced that given the right training, encouragement and confidence, almost anyone could achieve results way beyond any previous intellectual assessment they'd made of themselves. If I was wrong, I told myself, they hadn't lost much and they could sit for the lesser licence a week later. After all, I thought of myself as just such an example: Miss Phillips had believed in me and allowed me to escape the almost certain mediocrity The Boys Farm would demand from me. Mediocrity is just as much a habit learned as achieving good results. It was time to back down in the hope that I could save my own skin.

'Mr Jones, do you honestly believe if the class sits for the International that they'll all fail?'

'Nothing more certain, Boyo!'

'Well then, you're probably right.'

'Probably? Fuckin' oath I'm right!'

'And if they sit for the Local Blasting Licence, that only three will pass the first time and another three the second, that is counting me out because you'll not allow me to sit for it?'

'Yeah, that's right. I've been a miner, man and boy, for twenty years, I ought to bluddy know.'

'And, as far as you're concerned, there's no exception to this rule of thumb?'

Jones sighed. 'Look, Fitzsaxby, I don't know how you got here, but you don't belong, see. You'll never be a miner's arsehole. Clever young gits like you don't belong underground. You may get your blasting licence, but you won't last on a grizzly, you'll do something clever and kill yourself and I'll be the first to applaud when that happens. Mining is a job where men work to a procedure, you drum it into them until they can't think for themselves, it becomes an instinct to do as they've been taught and that way they mostly don't get killed.' He pointed his forefinger at my chest. 'Or, perhaps, Fitzsaxby, you're too much of a smart-arse to understand this? I don't give a fuck if you hate me. I do care that you stay alive long enough as a grizzly man to earn me, as well as the rest of the workers, a copper bonus! I need six of you working grizzlies in the next three weeks and, by Christ, I'm going to get them.'

While I knew that his logic was curious to say the least, this wasn't a time to argue that initiative and intelligence might also play a part in mining.

'Look, I'm truly sorry, I'm obviously in the wrong, Mr Jones. I'll try to get the fellows to back off and to sit for their Local Blasting Licence. But I need to go to them with something.'

'Something? What do you mean?'

'Well, if they pass the Local, can they sit for the International the following fortnight? They'll need your approval to do this.'

'You're blowing hot air the wrong way up your own arse, Boyo.'

'They'll be on grizzlies, on night shift, and the exam is during the day, so they won't be losing any mine time, and they just need your approval, Mr Jones.' Then I added, 'You'll have your usual quota of passes, and as you say they're not likely to pass anyway and you'll be proved right.'

Gareth Jones looked at me shrewdly. 'You mean *you'll* pass it, don't you?'

'Yes, I hope so, that is if you permit me to go with the others to take the Local?' There was no point in saying that I thought some of the others would pass as well.

'Rugby? You seem to know a bit about it. Do you play?'

It was such an unexpected question that I was somewhat taken aback. 'Yes.'

'Scrum-half?'

'Yes.'

'Any good?'

I shrugged, not knowing where his questions were leading. 'I played for my school and then the Old Boys Club.'

'What grade?'

'First,' I replied. While it was true, in fact I'd played for the University Club. But letting him know I'd been to university would have been the final blow to any hopes of convincing him to allow me to sit for my blasting licence.

'Fancy playing here on the Copper Belt?'

'I hadn't really thought about it.'

'Season starts in three weeks. I'm the backline coach.' He shrugged. 'We need a scrum-half.'

'The blasting licence examination takes place in three weeks.'

'I can see you understand, Fitzsaxby.'

'Sure, I'd like to try for the team, Mr Jones.'

'And you'll get the other trainees to sit for the Local licence?'

'If you'll let them go for the International two weeks later?'

Jones laughed. 'I told you, you're blowing hot air the wrong way up your arse, Boyo,' he repeated. 'But, okay.' He extended his hand. 'You'd better be a bluddy good scrum-half, Fitzsaxby,' he grinned.

Three weeks later we all sat for the Local Blasting Licence, and to the enormous credit of Gareth Jones we all passed, even Dirkie de Wet. Only four of the trainees, now all grizzly men, volunteered to go back two weeks later to sit for the International and three of us passed – Karl Joubert, Kolus Pienaar and myself. This result was put down to our being a rare and untypical intake. So Mr Jones managed not to lose face, the previous fortnight's 100 per cent success having served to cement his reputation as the best mining instructor on the Copper Belt. I also made it onto the rugby team.

That's the trouble with theory, rules and procedures, they seldom translate into real life and a grizzly proved the perfect example of this. It was simply impossible to stick to procedure and at the same time to work for a required ore tally. That is, put sufficient ore through the grizzly bars from the stope to get the required count of fully loaded ore trucks waiting to be filled on the main haulage below the grizzly. If your grizzly shift didn't empty the diamond driller's stope so that he could drill and blast the next day he wanted to know why. Moreover your copper bonus as well as his was affected. The rules we were taught that applied to working a grizzly were complete nonsense. Everybody knew that you were expected to cut corners and to take chances and that the possibility of being injured or killed from falling rock, by a badly timed blast, or falling through the grizzly bars and dropping 60 feet to be crushed to death was extremely high. Three months was thought to be the maximum time a grizzly man could safely work, and for many this proved too long. I would often set forty blasts on a single shift and end it almost too weary to climb down the 60-feet length of ladders onto the main haulage and walk to the cage. Invariably my head would be splitting from a powder headache, a throbbing pain of migraine proportions caused by working with gelignite.

Older miners wouldn't or couldn't work a grizzly because their reactions were too slow. The job was given to young guys, myself included, who thought themselves bulletproof. Besides, we were too proud not to get the required tally from our grizzly by the end of each shift, even when to do so meant placing your life in jeopardy at least a couple of times a shift. We took a certain perverse pride in being the gunslingers whom no life insurance company would cover. But slowly the stress began to tell, and by the time I'd completed my three-month tour of duty I was close to being a nervous wreck. Kobus Pienaar, the smartest of the Afrikaners among our trainee group, was dead, caught halfway up the walls of his grizzly to set a charge where a bunch of grapes (rocks seemingly jamming the mouth of a stope) sat. The jammed rocks suddenly collapsed, scraping him off the wall of the grizzly and smashing his body against the grizzly bars below. He would have died instantly. Big Dirkie de Wet had lost an arm at the elbow from a premature blast and was back on his parents' farm in the Orange Free State. The rest of us were pretty battered and bruised, physically and mentally, and jumped at any sudden sound, while some of my group had grown so morose they barely spoke.

A grizzly man coming off his three-month stint was given an easy job supervising a gang of African mine workers lashing, or working as a pipe-fitter keeping the water and air pipes in repair or building new ones. This was meant to give us the required time to recover for the next three months on grizzlies, whereupon I'd have completed my year in the copper mines. If I managed to stay alive and uninjured my worries would be over and I'd be on my way to Oxford, with sufficient money to live and travel without having to work while I was in Europe.

Ah, the best-laid plans of mice and men. A week after finishing my three-month stint the guy replacing me on my grizzly was injured, and the mine captain came down to the 1100 level where I was working as a pipe-fitter.

'Bad luck, Tom, you're back on your grizzly,' was all he said.

There was no point in arguing, each grizzly is different and you learn to know its peculiar character. An experienced grizzly man never works a grizzly he doesn't know, except when he first goes onto one straight from the School of Mines. Besides, the diamond driller was demanding me back. It seems the new guy had tried working to the book and hadn't emptied the diamond driller's stope for four nights running. The Afrikaner, a man named Koos Kruger, put in a complaint and the young grizzly man had been given a bollocking. In an attempt to improve his tally he'd left his safety chain off, and had fallen through the grizzly bars. It was extremely fortunate that the grizzly was two-thirds full so he'd only fallen 20 feet and was in hospital with a broken arm and pelvis. Of course, none of this was explained officially, he'd just had an unfortunate accident. But it meant I was back on the grizzly for three more months and I knew I was in big, big trouble.

But then the fickle hand of fate reached down and plucked me out of the grizzly, out of the mine and out of Northern Rhodesia and into Llewellyn Barracks, the territorial army base on the outskirts of Bulawayo in Southern Rhodesia. My call-up papers to do my three months' military service in the name of Queen and Country had arrived, and attendance was compulsory. What's more, the mine was required to pay my full copper bonus while I was learning to protect a country I would leave three months after I'd completed my military service. Sometimes in life a person gets lucky.

CHAPTER EIGHTEEN

Love Can Be a Lonely Stranger

I HAD INSTRUCTIONS TO report to the Ndola airport with no more than one small suitcase containing an extra shirt, underpants, civilian socks and personal toiletries. Nothing else, I was told, could be contained within my barrack-room locker except the clothes in which I arrived at the army camp.

What appeared to be a well-used World War II DC-3, with khaki paint peeling in patches on the nose and the tail of the fuselage, awaited us at the airport. A stiffly starched sergeant in tropical uniform took my name and ordered me to join a bunch of guys lined up on the tarmac. I must have been one of the last to arrive, because shortly afterwards he made us up into three rows of ten, told us to place our suitcases on the ground on our left-hand side, then brought us up into a ragged and uncoordinated attention. Sighing heavily at the result of our efforts, he commanded us to stand at ease.

'Right then, it just so happens you make up a complete platoon, and for the sake of convenience that's how you're going to stay when we get to Llewellyn Barracks. I am Sergeant Bolton, your training officer. As of this precise moment you are in the army, the Rhodesian Army, you are not privates, you are riflemen and will be so addressed at all times, everything I say to you or command you to do you will do without prevarication and instantly. Stand at ease. Any questions?'

We stood at ease and one little guy three places from me in the centre row immediately put up his hand.

'What's your name, Rifleman?' the sergeant barked.

'Vermaak, Sir,' the recruit answered in a thick Afrikaans accent.

'Not *Sir*, you blockhead. You will call me *Sergeant*,' the non-commissioned officer barked. 'You're not in a classroom and need permission to go for a wee-wee.' His tone became less strident. 'Besides, Rifleman Vermaak, take my advice, in the army you *never* put up your hand. There will be plenty of opportunities to get yourself killed without volunteering. Now come to attention and I will ask you what it is you wish to ask me. You will now do as I have just told you!'

Vermaak came to attention and said, 'What was that big word you jus' said again, Sergeant?'

'I'm losing my patience fast, Rifleman Vermaak, I haven't given you permission to talk!'

'Sorry, Sergeant,' the recruit said.

The sergeant sighed. 'Rifleman Vermaak, you still don't have permission to talk. You need my permission to say you're sorry! Now what *big* word, Rifleman Vermaak?'

'Prevari-something, Sir.'

'Sergeant, not Sir, you cretin! *Sergeant!*' Bolton roared, making me jump inwardly. 'It means instantly, at the double, and don't argue!'

I told myself that I had serious doubts that Vermaak would know the meaning of cretin.

'Yes, thank you, Sergeant.'

Sergeant Bolton shook his head despairingly. 'Don't thank me! Just say, "Yes, Sergeant!" I can promise you will never have any reason to thank me for *anything*, Rifleman Vermaak. Now stand at ease and pay attention.'

I wasn't game to push my head forward to glance at Vermaak. It was, of course, a name that brought back several earlier traumatic memories from The Boys Farm. Vermaak is a fairly common Afrikaner surname and I had no reason to suppose the guy Sergeant Bolton was taking apart was the infamous and epileptic Pissy Vermaak of my childhood. I quickly told myself that they would never allow an epileptic into the army so it simply couldn't be. But I was nevertheless aware that I was trembling slightly at the recall of the name.

'Righto, now listen carefully,' Sergeant Bolton said, raising his voice slightly. 'The DC-3 hasn't any seats, that's because you're not entitled to them, not being gentlemen. So you will sit on your arses on the deck. You will note that there is a webbing wall across the back of the plane and a door that opens up at the arse-end. You will stow your suitcases in the back and then enter,' he pointed to the hatchway in the centre of the plane, 'by the centre hatchway. The walls of the plane are also covered with webbing so you will sit against the wall, one man next to the other, holding onto the webbing if this proves necessary. You will do this on either side of the aircraft, leaving a corridor down the centre. Do I make myself understood?'

'Yes, Sergeant!' we all yelled like a bunch of schoolkids, the Vermaak lesson having been suitably absorbed.

'Right then, I will hand you a brown-paper bag when you enter the aircraft and this is to be used in case of turbulence.' He turned to Vermaak. 'That means in case you are airsick, Rifleman Vermaak. Now, if any one of you is sick on the floor of the aircraft, I will make you clean up the mess when we land using your own shirt, and you will be placed on report. Do you understand me?'

'Yes, Sergeant!' we chorused again.

'Your brown bags will be retained by all of you until we find a suitable place to dispose of them. Righto, now there are two webbing seats available, one for myself and one . . .' He looked around and then pointed to Vermaak. 'And one for Rifleman Vermaak. We will now do a final rollcall before we board the aircraft. When I call your name you reply, "Sergeant," that's all.' He then proceeded to call out our names and at the conclusion paused, looked us over slowly and shook his head. 'You're a pretty ordinary-looking lot! May Gawd help the defence of Rhodesia!' Then, in the middle of the grin this evoked from us, he suddenly barked

'Attention!' We all came to the same ragged and mistimed attention as on the previous occasion. 'At the double, load your suitcase and board the aircraft. Dismissed!' he shouted.

Seated against the starboard wall of the DC-3, a couple of guys from the front, was when my big shock occurred. There against one side of the door leading to the pilot's cockpit was Pissy Vermaak. Even after all these years there was no mistaking him. My heart began to beat faster for a second time, why, I can't say because I had never feared him. But it nevertheless did, while at the same time I found myself wondering if he still smelled of piss.

I had never been in an aeroplane before and was fortunate enough to be placed beside a window. Although taking off was a bit hairy, with the engines straining and the wings arocking and ashuddering, and a definite feeling that we weren't going to get airborne, suddenly we were in the air and I heard a thump as the undercarriage withdrew into the wheel-well. Once in the air I was able to rest on my knees in order to see out of the plane window and I must say it was a wonderful experience, like playing God and looking at the tiny world of man below. Here and there I spotted a native village, just a few huts and a *kraal* made of whitethorn bush to keep the cattle safe at night, and the usual patches of maize and vegetable gardens where the women worked. Sometimes there'd be a few cattle or goats, with a small child acting as herd boy, everywhere else to the furthermost horizon was covered in the amazing spring colours of the Northern Rhodesian woodland forest, with an occasional rise of rocky hills to break the appearance of a large randomly coloured quilt that appeared to be covering the earth.

While we met with turbulence from time to time when I was required to sit tight and when several of the guys were sick, I think I was too enchanted with the prospect of watching the landscape below to think about feeling queasy. All I wanted to do was get back on my knees to look out of the window. At one stage I glanced up to see Vermaak with his face buried in his brown-paper bag. 'Nothing trivial I hope,' I heard myself saying under my breath. I was surprised at the sharp sting to my memory that his reappearance in my life had caused. I guess your childhood is never quite over and the early hurts are the ones you're most likely to take to your grave unhealed.

Almost three hours later we flew over Bulawayo, a small city with the usual outlying African shanty town with higgledy-piggledy dirt roads and without trees, known in white-man-speak as the native location. Neat, leafy European suburbs with manicured subtropical gardens followed, and finally we flew over the centre of the city's broad tree-lined avenues with three or four blocks of square buildings five or six storeys high. A central square of palm trees and lawn contained an imposing courthouse of granite, built in the Victorian era, with the Union Jack flying imperiously from a flagpost at the front of the building.

At the airport we were told to deposit our sick bags in a bin placed on the tarmac, and after retrieving our suitcases, we were lined up into our platoon and marched off to a waiting bus to take us to the military camp.

Llewellyn Barracks, left over from World War II, was situated about 15 miles from the city and appeared somewhat weary-looking, the usual creosote-splashed rows of wooden barracks with a few new buildings added. It contained all the expected infrastructure: guardhouse, company headquarters, gymnasium, various storage sheds, obstacle course, dusty parade ground and rifle range. This parade ground was shared by the King's African Rifles, an African battalion with a separate set of barracks at the far end. My home for the next three months was altogether dreary-looking and seemed to speak clearly of a difficult time ahead for all of us. Still, whatever they dished up, it was going to be better than working a grizzly and no worse than The Boys Farm or the School of Mines. I comforted myself with the thought that I was being paid my full copper bonus while being trained to fire a rifle or a mortar, leopard-crawl under a tangle of barbed wire and scramble over wooden walls or swing from ropes across pretend crocodile-infested rivers.

I guess preparing a young man for the army is a universal procedure. If you've done any army training or read about it you'll have a fair idea of what it's all about, square-bashing, route-marching, rifle and machine-gun practice being the major component. Sergeant Minnaar, the sergeant-in-charge of our barracks, or those who drilled us or taught us how to defend ourselves, forcefully possessed exactly the same mindset and vernacular and attitude to abuse as Gareth Jones. To go over our military training in detail would be much the same as repeating the experience of the School of Mines, though this time in the sunlight or under the stars. That is, the singular purpose seemed to be to reduce the recruits to instant and unquestioning obedience with repetition and exacting standards involving spit and polish, and the immaculate condition at all times of the barracks room seeming to be the major objective. So much so that our bunks, the blanket and sheets, were made to a precise formula by using a ruler, and when pronounced perfect by Sergeant Minnaar, we used needle and cotton to carefully sew them into a permanently fixed position. At night we would lie on top of the bed so as never to disturb them. This continued for the entire three months, so that while in training we never once crawled between the sheets.

Punishment, like at the School of Mines, was usually collective, with individual punishment involving extra guard duty during the weekends known as CB, meaning that you were confined to barracks and had to report in full kit to the guardhouse every hour. Or *jankers*, which was less severe, lugging a full pack and with a rifle held above your head at the double around the parade ground for twenty minutes or so, or marching around it for two hours after the training day was over. Most of it was mindless and seemingly meaningless, and even activity such as bayonet practice seemed like acquiring a skill we were never likely to need. No group of soldiers had been required to fix bayonets and charge the enemy since the Kaffir Wars in the latter part of the nineteenth century when, even then, it had proved a senseless way to fight this type of enemy.

The lectures we attended proved more interesting as, by contrast, they clearly served a purpose. It wasn't hard to see, in theory anyway, that we were being trained to combat an African insurrection. In East Africa, in Kenya in particular, the Kikuyu tribe had risen up and several outlying farms and coffee estates had been attacked and ransacked, with the white farmers and their families murdered. What had at first appeared to be a small and localised uprising had quickly gathered momentum to escalate into a full-scale state of emergency. Britain responded to Governor Evelyn Baring's request for help by sending several battalions of troops to Kenya.

This small, cruel and often barbaric uprising became known as the Mau Mau rebellion, and involved a new kind of guerilla warfare where witchcraft and ritual murder gave the enemy its fanatical strength and determination, while cruelty and draconian measures armed the resolve of the white settlers and the British Government protecting them. The terrorists hiding within the almost impenetrable forests on the slopes of Mount Kenya and the Aberdare Mountains were a clever and resourceful enemy who would emerge, mostly at night, to launch an attack. Conventional tactics and weaponry were proving ineffective and the enemy very difficult to capture or contain.

Rhodesia was coming to realise that the same thing could happen with the Matabele, the largest and most sophisticated of the local tribes, and historically warlike by nature. Like the Kikuyu, they were possessed of many of the same deeply felt resentments against the colonial government that had caused the Kenya uprising. If they were to take note of the Mau Mau successes to the east they might similarly rise up to demand their independence.

The more interesting of these lectures were conducted by Captain Mike Finger, who had been seconded from the Kenya Regiment via the King's African Rifles and had a previous connection with Rhodesia where he had done his basic military training. Kenya, prior to the outbreak of the Mau Mau rebellion, lacked the military infrastructure to train its young men and they were sent to do their basic training at the George VI Barracks in Salisbury, the capital of Rhodesia. Mike, it seemed, had enjoyed army life and had decided to take a commission with the King's African Rifles there. Then, with the declaration of the state of emergency, he'd requested a transfer to the King's African Rifles Kenya Regiment in Tanganyika, Kenya at the time lacking their own native regiment. From here he was seconded to train mounted counter-insurgency units known as the Kenya Police Reserve (KPR) made up of resident farmers and members of the Kipsigis and Nandi tribes. Their task was to mount roadblocks, lay ambushes, guard the farms of members who were on duty and make the Mau Mau wary of entering the north-eastern area of the Aberdare mountain range.

He'd laugh. 'With the Mau Mau operating from within the forests on the slope of the Aberdares, the farmers in the North-Eastern District became pretty jittery. While we never really managed to make serious contact with the Mau Mau, who were rather too slippery for us, we at least managed to give the farmers and their wives an occasional good night's sleep.'

Mike Finger had a great, though quiet, sense of humour and told me of a time in the Molo District where he'd arranged for members of the KPR to guard several of the outlying farms because the male owners were on patrol. He'd noted that several of the men and women in the district had divorced, and then paired with other men and women in the district. By careful matching and rostering over several weeks he'd managed 'thoughtfully' to pair several of the ex-husbands to guard the homes of their ex-wives, all of them on the same night. This had become known in Molo history as 'The Night of the Wrong Wives'.

However, Mike felt that he wasn't being used to the greatest benefit commanding the Molo and North-Eastern District of the KPR. He requested a transfer to the Kenya Regiment and became a special branch officer in Nyeri Province, deep in the heart of the Kikuyu tribal lands. He spoke fluent Kikuyu and had been brought up to deeply understand their culture. I would later learn that the Kikuyu regarded him as one of their own tribesmen, and a white man who could read their secret thoughts. Among the Kikuyu tribe there was a legend that he was a great medicine man, who had turned inside-out to be white on the outside and black on the inside. He was often employed by the army and government authorities to negotiate with the Kikuyu people. Prior to doing so he would dye one half of his tongue black to confirm the legend, while being careful to never talk about it and so give the impression that he was unaware of this physical aberration. This simple visual manifestation was confirmation enough to the Kikuyu people that he could speak on their behalf to the white man, and that if the Mau Mau should attempt to kill him this would bring a great disaster to the Kikuyu people as a tribe. Mike seemed to have a high regard for the Kikuyu people and would openly admit that the Mau Mau insurrection was not entirely without just cause. He would privately talk about the issues involved.

'Tom, I guess all nations have long memories, but Africans never forget and seldom, if ever, forgive. With the Masai their wealth is measured in cattle and the land is communal, but with the Kikuyu more than any of the other forty tribes in Kenya, personal ownership of land is everything. They keep stock but are also maize growers and market gardeners, and they regard the soil as their wealth. Of all the tribes they are the most hardworking and prized among servants, but they are also an independent people and have never regarded the white *bwana* as absolute lord and master.' Mike looked up. 'Personally I like them for this lack of subservience.' He laughed. 'As you may expect, this is not a characteristic much admired by some of the settlers.'

I grinned. 'I guess you can say the same of our Zulu people under Dingaan and Shaka who gave the white man, both Afrikaners and English, hell when they tried to intrude on or take possession of their land.'

'That was, of course, in the nineteenth century,' he said. 'Things in your country have been settled, if badly, a fair while now. But in Kenya the injustice is still within the memory of most adults.'

'I'm not sure about that,' I ventured. 'History evolves and accumulates and the longer the injustice, the more deeply felt the resentment.'

'You keep surprising me, Tom, one doesn't come across too many left-wing liberals in the army or anywhere else in Africa for that matter.'

'There's an old Xhosa saying, "People are people because of other people",' I explained. 'What it means is that we all belong to each other and can't exist without the one for the other. As a small child the person I loved the most in the world was a Zulu named Mattress. I think he probably taught me that there is no human pecking order, that God didn't specifically create a bunch of white-skinned people as the Afrikaners around me insisted and tell them they would forever rule the black world. Besides, if the anthropologists are correct, Africa is the cradle of mankind, and so we all started out black anyway.'

Mike spoke often of his imminent return to Kenya, and I must confess I'd wondered how someone as useful as he must be in the state of emergency could be sent to Rhodesia on a passive training assignment. One evening, while enjoying a beer or five in a bar in Bulawayo on weekend leave, he told me that his reason for being a special instructor in Rhodesia was because he was recovering from the accumulated effects of malaria. He then added, with what I took to be a somewhat bitter laugh, 'And one or two other reasons.'

I waited until a beer or two later before asking, 'Mike, you suggested it wasn't just the malaria that brought you to Rhodesia and the camp.'

He paused, both his hands clasped around his beer glass, and seeming to look directly into it. 'It's difficult to talk about it, Tom.' He glanced at me. 'In the work I was doing I was seeing both sides of the war, and frankly I was pretty disappointed in the way our side was conducting themselves.'

'You mean the military, the British?'

'The military only do what they're told to do, they don't generally make the rules, they simply follow instructions,' he replied.

'What are you saying, the colonial administration . . . Britain tells them what to —?' He didn't allow me to finish.

'Perhaps it's different in South Africa. I know more than half of the whites there actively hate the British. But in Kenya we have always seen Britain as the home of a benign and fair-minded parent. They are supposed to be an example of how a decent nation should behave towards lesser nations. You know, the whole Rudyard Kipling thing, generally summed up by the expression "It's simply not British, old chap!" Well, eliminate the expression "old chap", and it is this prevailing sentiment that sums up the way young Kenyan kids like me were brought up to think.'

'And now in the state of emergency this isn't proving to be the case?'

'Exactly. Now all that's changed, the white Kenyans are the worst offenders, we've formed the Kenyan Regiment, that is the locals, chaps with whom I went to school. Chris Peterson is the commanding officer, once one of my best friends, now he's the main instigator of the white atrocities against the Mau Mau.' He looked at me, plainly distressed. 'We, Peterson and myself, were brought up with the Kikuyu. They were our playmates, we trusted them, they trusted us, we never thought of it as a skin thing.'

'But isn't that the case in any war? You know, throw out the moral scruples, forget the high-flown principles, play dirty and win at any cost?'

'Maybe you're right, Tom, but there was and is so much we could have done before we started to employ our present tactics. The Kikuyu, as I've told you, have legitimate reasons for rising up in revolt. The maths simply don't work, at this very moment approximately 250000 Kikuyu are restricted to 2000 square miles of land while 30000 settlers occupy 12000 square miles.' He pointed a finger at me. 'Now remember, Tom, both whites and blacks grow the same things: coffee, maize and vegetables; and both are skilled farmers, and to a Kikuyu man land is everything, without it he becomes a non-person. Now the white settlers didn't buy this land in the first instance, it was granted to them by the colonial administration. The Highlands and parts of the Rift Valley, the two most fertile areas, were simply declared vacant land and taken from the Kikuyu and, in some cases, other tribes and given to the settlers. We're not talking about some nineteenth-century bloody conquest or tribal treaty! We're talking recently, from World War II onwards. We're talking about a stroke of the colonial pen!' He was plainly angry. 'Ninety-seven thousand African Kenyans, many Kikuyu tribesmen, fought for the Allies in the war and returned to Kenya to nothing, bugger all! Their experience serving alongside white British soldiers as equals gave them a sense of entitlement. This, especially when white Kenyan returned soldiers and immigrating white men who'd fought in the war were given land grants, angered them greatly.'

I sighed. 'Mike, it's not a unique situation, the apartheid government of South Africa is creating Bantu homelands as we speak. When it's all over, 88 per cent of the land will be owned by 12 per cent of the population who are white, while 10 per cent of the land will be owned by 75 per cent of the population who are black, with the remaining 2 per cent owned by the other 13 per cent of the population who are non-European. Justice and Africa are contradictory terms.'

Mike shook his head. 'I know, but two wrongs don't make a right; here in Rhodesia things aren't all that equitable between black and white either and I guess that's why we're both here.' He grinned, and picking up his beer, drained it. 'C'mon, Tom, that's enough politics, there's a dance on at the YWCA, let's check it out.'

'But you haven't explained the other reasons why you're here,' I protested.

'Another time! If I tell you now I'll just end up drunk and morbid.' He grinned. 'Anyway, I'm your senior officer, Fitzsaxby, it would never do to be seen arriving back at the barracks legless, carried past the guardhouse by a bloody rifleman.'

'Come to think of it, that wouldn't do me a whole heap of good either,' I said. 'Fraternising with a permanent-force officer wouldn't exactly impress the guys in my hut, much less Sergeant Minnaar.'

Mike grinned. 'Minnaar, eh, one of the old school, as blinkered as a brewer's horse. Rather die than be an officer, they think as sergeants they run the army and to some extent they're right.'

As we left the bar, Mike Finger put a hand on my shoulder. 'Tom, I've been meaning to talk with you about that. Colonel Stone is anxious to have some of the brighter guys among your lot go through officer training; we made a list and your name is on it. What do you think?'

'You mean after I've done my basic training?'

'Yeah, we'd start after you'd completed the first two months, which is in a fortnight. That's all the stuff every recruit has to know. Then a further three months of officer training. It would mean an extra two months in the army.' We stopped on the pavement outside. 'What do you think?'

It wasn't a hard decision to make. It would mean two more months away from a grizzly, and only a month before I would be due to leave the mines for good. It would certainly be more intellectually stimulating. I would have to check to see if the mines would continue to grant me my copper bonus. But in life it's never a good idea to accept a proposition too eagerly, that is, unless it is plainly stupid not to do so.

'May I think about it?' I replied.

'Sure thing. I probably shouldn't have mentioned it when I'm half-pissed anyway. When it comes from the commanding officer, kindly appear surprised.'

The dance at the YWCA was the usual polite meeting of the sexes with all the girls carefully chaperoned. A stout, somewhat imperious-looking elderly matron with pouter-pigeon breasts moved among the dancers to ensure there was a degree of daylight to be seen between the chests and thighs of each dancing couple. We arrived back at the barracks just before midnight curfew – Mike and I, officer and rifleman, sitting on separate seats in the bus.

You're probably wondering by now what happened when I finally confronted Pissy Vermaak? Well, let me begin by saying every barrack hut has one: the inept and stupid guy who is the butt of everyone's jokes and the bane of every sergeant and, in particular, Sergeant Minnaar who ran our hut. It became abundantly clear in the first month of training that Pissy Vermaak was the cross we were destined to carry. Pissy spent more time on CB, reporting to the guardhouse in full kit, or on *jankers* with full pack or trudging around the parade ground, than the rest of us combined. He was always exhausted, so his kit would be in disarray, his locker untidy and his bunk a mess. Parts of his uniform, such as a single gaiter or a piece of webbing, would go mysteriously missing or he'd forget to shave or to polish his boots and, as well, he possessed two left feet. He used his hands a lot in order to communicate and possessed a high-pitched and simpering tone of voice, coupled with a somewhat effeminate manner, so that everyone was convinced he was a queer. He was also an Afrikaner, where being a sodomite is regarded as the one irredeemable sin in the eyes of God, and meant automatic consignment to hell, repentance and salvation being out of the question. In other words, the poor bastard hadn't a hope in the company of young, mostly Afrikaner guys who, often as not, found themselves on the receiving end of a group punishment brought about by some Pissy misadventure.

I shamefully confess that at first I didn't give a shit. While I don't think I took pleasure at seeing him suffer, I can't say I was over-sympathetic. But after a while it was plain to see that someone had to help the poor bugger. That is, bring some semblance of order into his life. In other words, do what the army was trying to do but was failing miserably in the attempt. In fact, the more Pissy was punished the more exhausted and disheartened he became, and therefore more of a hindrance to the progress of our hut. Carrying Pissy Vermaak was becoming an unacceptable burden.

I guess, as in the School of Mines, it didn't take too long for the guys in the hut to single me out as perhaps a bit more educated than most of them. When Pissy had finally been the cause of both our first and second weekend leave being cancelled, the first two we'd been granted since arriving at Llewellyn Barracks, I knew it was time to do something. The guys were going stir-crazy and were ready to lynch Pissy. I felt I probably had the unspoken authority, so I called a late-afternoon meeting. Pissy, as usual, was running around the parade ground with full pack as punishment for yet another misdemeanour. We all knew the drill, he'd return in an hour or so and lie on his bunk sobbing, and often enough would go without his evening meal. In my opinion he was getting close to a complete mental breakdown.

'Okay, you guys, what are we going to do about Vermaak?' I asked.

'Kill the fucker!' someone replied to all-round laughter and a general nodding of heads.

'No, seriously, it's affecting us all.'

'He needs a fuckin' nanny,' someone called out.

This was exactly what I wanted to hear. 'You're right, there's thirty of us in the hut, we've got two-and-a-bit months to go, that's two days for each of us.'

'What are you saying, man? We got to look after him, wipe his arse? He's a fuckin' queer, man!' a big *boer* named Piet Kosterman yelled out.

I ignored this remark. 'It's not a big deal, hey. Just see he cleans his boots, check his gear, see he tidies his locker, showers, shaves, his bunk is in order, rifle cleaned . . .'

'Wipe his nose, take him for a shit, wipe his arse,' Gert Boeman added. 'I wouldn't touch him with a fucking barge pole, man. The bastard smells of piss!'

'Look, I'll go first and nanny him for a week, see if it helps, if it doesn't work we'll try something else.'

Piet Kosterman shook his head. 'I dunno, man. He's a fucking homosexual, why don't we just break his arm, hey?'

At six feet seven inches Kosterman was the biggest guy in our hut and fairly thick, but he had the support of most of the Afrikaners, who comprised two-thirds of us.

'Because if he blabs to Minnaar we'll all be on a charge, Piet. Grievous bodily harm, that's six months minimum in the bloody military clink, man!'

'Bullshit, Tom!' Kosterman objected. 'He won't talk, we'll tell him if he reports us because of "the unfortunate accident falling over his own feet", we'll break his other arm and both his fucking legs.' Kosterman was pretty typical of his kind, where blatant intimidation is considered the subtle approach to solving a problem.

'*Ja*, that's definitely one way,' I agreed, 'but we'll try my way first.'

I looked around. 'Any objections?' I was using influence I wasn't sure I possessed.

The hut fell silent, the Afrikaners waiting for Piet Kosterman to react. After a few moments he said, '*Ja*, okay, Tom, as long as you go first. Two days, hey?' He turned to the other Afrikaners. 'Tom does a week, we only do two days, that's fair enough, do we say okay?'

They nodded agreement.

'Right then! It's Operation Pissy Vermaak,' I announced cheerily, and then realised that I'd referred to him by his Boys Farm nickname. It was too late, the men in the hut all laughed and that was that. Poor old Pissy was certain to be back to being called 'Pissy'.

I could have backhanded myself, to say the least, it was a stupid slip of the tongue. You see, I hoped to get some further information from Pissy about what actually happened between Frikkie Botha, Fonnie du Preez and himself when they'd concocted the story of Mattress sexually assaulting him. There was also a part of his blatantly lying confession to Mevrou and Meneer Prinsloo that I hadn't heard. While I had Frikkie's version of events written down in detail, if I could only get Pissy to corroborate Frikkie's confession of a conspiracy to murder Mattress, then I had a potential live witness on my hands.

I'd tried on three previous occasions to approach Pissy, and while he'd not rebuffed me outright he was obviously cautious, and when I'd mentioned The Boys Farm he simply didn't want to know.

'Ag, I've clean forgot about all that a long time ago, man,' he said.

Then, later, when I asked him again if he'd talk to me about the time we'd been together as kids, he'd looked me directly in the eye. 'Whatever you ask me, Tom, I've already forgotten, you hear?'

I'd tried a third time, and on the last occasion he'd grown very agitated and threatened to call me *Voetsek* in front of the others guys in the hut. When I'd laughed and told him to go ahead, he'd spitefully remarked, 'Now, even more than before, I'll forget *anything* you ask me, man!'

So my volunteering to be the first to play nursemaid to Pissy wasn't exactly going to be welcomed by him with open arms. On the other hand, it was plain that he'd reached the end of his tether, and I didn't want him to have a mental breakdown and be dismissed from the army before I could get the vital information I needed.

So you can see my little talk to the guys in our hut about helping Pissy was, in a large part, not brought about by any sense of kindness or pity, but by my fear that I was going to lose him before he'd talk. When we'd had our weekend leave cancelled for two weeks in a row because of Pissy, I was aware that it was possibly my last chance to get to him. Approaching him on my own hadn't worked, whereas he'd have to buy our collective decision to keep him out of trouble and might just decide to talk to me. It was a long shot, I knew, but one well worth trying.

Pissy arrived back at the hut well after sundown, and only half an hour before the bugle was due to sound for dinner parade. He could barely drag himself to his bunk and his fatigues were completely soaked, the camouflage pattern turned a single shade of dark by sweat. His face, coated with parade-ground dust, was a deep orange colour, with twin skin-coloured streaks down either side of his cheeks, cut through the dust by recent tears. A sticky wash of mucus ran from his nose, covered his upper lip and crossed his mouth and chin.

'Jesus Christ, look what the cat brought in!' Steven Hudson, seated on the bunk nearest the door cleaning his rifle, called out.

Arriving at his bunk, Pissy simply let his rifle free-fall to the polished cement floor with a clatter that made us all wince, removed his pack and dropped it beside his weapon, followed by his cap and webbing. He then threw himself onto his bunk without removing his dirty boots. Lying on his stomach, his head cupped in his arms, he commenced to sob into his pillow. Pissy Vermaak was completely knackered and beyond caring what we, or the army for that matter, thought of him. If Sergeant Minnaar had entered the hut at that moment, the rifle on the floor, together with the careless disposal of his hat, pack and webbing would have earned him a similar punishment to the one he'd only just completed. The never-ending vicissitudes of Pissy Vermaak were once more in progress.

'Hey, Tom, the cry-baby snot-nose queen is all yours, man,' Kosterman called gleefully from his bunk.

All eyes turned to look at me. This, I guess, was the moment of truth. We'd showered, polished our boots back to the required see-your-face-in-them shine demanded by the army, and put on clean fatigues in preparation for dinner parade. The hut was spotless but for the sobbing, pathetic human mess that lay upon, and the disarray of government equipment lying beside, Rifleman Vermaak's bunk.

I walked over to Pissy's bunk and retrieved the rifle and placed it against his bunk number in the rifle rack. Miraculously, the hard cement floor hadn't damaged the sight or marked the butt. I returned and opened his locker and removed a set of clean fatigues, hung up his webbing and pack, and pegged his hat. Then I moved to the bottom end of the bunk and removed his boots, yanking them off his feet in an unnecessary pantomime of disgust. Meanwhile Pissy remained inert and continued to sob quietly. The boots were too dusty to wipe indoors, so I took them and placed them on the back step of the hut, and returned to consider what to do next. Grabbing a towel from his locker, I placed it over my shoulder, then bent down and touched him on the shoulder.

'Get up, Vermaak,' I said quietly.

Pissy didn't move.

'C'mon, get up, I'm here to help you, man!' I said, raising my voice somewhat. Pissy remained as he was, his shoulders jerking with a sudden sob. I could sense everyone was waiting to see what would happen next. Shouting at him army-style, I sensed, wasn't going to help, he was way beyond caring. I bent over so that my lips were close to his ear. 'If you don't sit up I'm going to tell them about you at The Boys Farm,' I whispered. Then to cover myself I said in a loud, near-threatening voice, 'I won't ask you again, now sit up!'

Pissy rolled onto one elbow and then wearily moved to sit on the edge of his bunk, his khaki-stockinged feet planted on the floor, his dirty face a mess of dust, mucilage and tears, eyes puffed up and almost closed.

'You have to take a shower,' I said. 'C'mon, man, I'll help you.'

'Why you doing this, *Voetsek*?' he said, too weary to realise what he'd called me.

'I'll explain in the shower, now come on, the bugle for dinner parade is about to go.'

'I don't want any fucking dinner!' he sobbed suddenly.

'C'mon,' I urged. 'You'll feel better after a shower.' Maybe he suffered from a leaking urinary tract or he'd pissed his fatigues, but Boeman was right, Vermaak did smell – stink is a better word – of piss. The same smell he'd carried at The Boys Farm, although, in fairness, I hadn't noticed it on any of the previous occasions I'd been close to him.

Pissy stood up slowly, sniffed back a glob of snot and tried to look defiant. I put my arm around his shoulder, his shirt still sweat-damp, his body giving off the strong smell of urine. He shrugged and pulled away. 'I can walk by myself!' he protested.

I took this to be a good sign, so I grabbed his clean fatigues and a pair of underpants and socks, and handed him the towel that hung from my shoulder. '*Ja*, okay, but hurry, man, we haven't got a lot of time.'

All eyes were on us as he shambled out of the barracks to the communal ablution block that fortunately happened to be situated directly behind our hut. While Pissy showered and changed I returned and removed his snotty pillowcase and walked through to the hut laundry, and placed it with his dirty fatigues in one of the washing machines, then polished and buffed his boots. We re-entered the hut to all-round clapping and cheering. Moments later, the bugle sounded for dinner. I had passed, it seemed, the initial test involving the nannying of Rifleman Kobus Vermaak of the Rhodesian Territorial Army.

Keeping Pissy on the straight-and-narrow wasn't easy, he was a walking disaster, but by the end of the week he hadn't received a single hour of punishment. I must say, by the weekend I was exhausted. We drew straws for who was to be the next nanny and the short straw went to Angus McClymont, Rhodesian-born and the son of a magistrate in Kitwi, a decent sort of chap who would take the job of nannying Pissy seriously. My fear had been that it would be Piet Kosterman or one of the other Afrikaners who might help Pissy get organised, but with an extremely ill grace.

If I hoped that Pissy would talk to me about what happened at The Boys Farm I was mistaken. While we'd grown quite close, Pissy was as cunning as a shithouse rat and knew what it was I wanted from him. Not giving me the information I craved gave him some sense of being in control, and I guess he enjoyed having someone looking after him. I admit, I had it coming to me, but I confess that the coincidence of running into him again had seemed like a minor miracle and now it was proving nothing of the sort. I had one more ploy up my sleeve. If I could get Pissy out of the army he might agree to talk to me. One big favour granted in exchange for another. Afrikaners have a deep sense of honour and don't like to be beholden to anyone. Although I didn't expect Pissy would have inherited this characteristic. Where from? The Boys Farm, or the reformatory in Pietersburg? Hardly likely. Nevertheless it was worth a try.

So, in the process of playing nanny I'd asked him about his epilepsy. 'How come the army called you up when you're an epileptic?' I asked.

'They don't know about that,' was his reply.

'Don't know? Why didn't you tell them?'

'My job.'

'What do you mean?'

'I drive an ore train underground at Nkana Mine, if they find out I can get fits they'll fire me,' he said simply. 'But I haven't had one for five years,' he added.

'*Ja*, but you could have one at any time, couldn't you?'

'*Ja*, I suppose, but I haven't and maybe it doesn't happen, hey.'

'So letting the army know you're an epileptic is out of the question?'

'*Ja*, definitely, man.'

Even though he wasn't on *jankers* or being punished Pissy still smelled of piss, and I'd make him change his underpants several times a day. At night all four pairs of army-issue underpants went into the washing machine and dryer. 'Look, Pissy, I don't want to be personal, but you go for a leak lots. Yesterday, for instance, sixteen times.'

Pissy looked embarrassed. 'So now you counting how many times I take a piss, *Voetsek*?'

Now that he was known as Pissy by one and all he'd taken to calling me *Voetsek*. 'No, it's not that, you seem to have an insatiable thirst too, and I think there might be something wrong with you. It's not normal to piss that much.'

'You mean I'm sick, hey? What's insatiable?' he asked hopefully.

'You can't drink enough water. It could be some sort of renal failure.'

'Now it's renal all of a sudden? What's a renal, hey?'

'Your kidneys. There may be something wrong with your kidneys. I'm not a doctor, of course, but you know how when you are on *jankers* doing the parade ground and you always piss your pants, maybe it isn't your fault.'

Pissy blushed deeply. '*Ja*, I don't even know I'm doing it. What you trying to say, *Voetsek*?'

'It could get you out of the army. It's not like epilepsy, you'd keep your job in the mines.'

'Say again, man? This renal thing could get me out? I could vamoose, fuck off?'

'Like I said, I'm no doctor, but nobody deliberately pisses his pants, maybe there's something wrong. It's worth finding out, don't you think?'

Pissy sighed. 'Ag, who's going to believe me, man. I've already tried going to the medical officer so many times he won't even see me anymore. The medical clerk tells me to bugger off. Sergeant Minnaar says next time I go on sick call it's *jankers* for a whole week!'

It was true, Pissy spent what little free time he had, when he wasn't doing *jankers* or reporting to the guardhouse or undergoing some or other punishment, sitting waiting in the medical officer's surgery looking miserable.

'*Ja*, okay, I understand. Look, I'm prepared to go to Captain Mike Finger on your behalf. I'll ask him to write a report to the doctor about your possible renal problem. They'll give you a urine test.'

'A what test?'

'Test your piss.'

He looked suddenly hopeful. 'And if it is this renal business, I'm out of the army, hey?'

I sighed. 'Pissy, if you're constantly leaking or pissing yourself then there's definitely something wrong. It's just a possibility they'll send you home. Mind you, if you told them you are an epileptic that would definitely do it.'

'No, no way, man. I've got a good job, and with the copper bonus I can leave at the end of the year with enough money to do what I've always wanted, man.'

'And what's that?' I asked, more from politeness than out of curiosity.

Pissy hesitated for a moment and then, to my surprise, he answered in a shy voice, 'Ag, nothing, just to open a club in Jo'burg.'

'A club? What sort of a club?' I could hardly believe my ears. The idea of Pissy, who could barely tie his shoelaces, running any sort of a club seemed like an absurd idea.

'Just a little private club,' he answered. I could see he was at once reluctant to explain any further, then again perhaps not; sometimes we have a need to talk about things that should remain private, the human need to confess is deeply atavistic.

'What, a nightclub?' I guessed.

'Ja, sort of. Only it's for men. Drinking, meeting each other.'

I looked at him incredulously. 'You mean a club for, you know, queers?'

He grinned. 'Ja, there's a big opening in the Jo'burg market, man. For Afrikaners, they not like you English, they don't want people to know, they very private people, there's a lot of shame to it, you understand.'

What could I say? Pissy for the first time seemed to be openly confessing to being queer, although perhaps not quite; running a private club for Afrikaner homosexuals wouldn't necessarily mean he was that way inclined himself. I'd met several homosexuals with Pirrou, some dancers, some not, but all of them highly articulate, intelligent and generally amusing guys. Then there was Graham Truby from Polliack's, again quite different but essentially well-bred and articulate. Pissy Vermaak didn't fit these stereotypes at all, and I couldn't imagine him running any sort of establishment for the kind of men I'd met who were homosexuals. I could only conclude that homosexuals came in all social types, and that there must exist a morose and guilt-ridden Afrikaner version that needed to hide their guilt, but still needed somewhere to meet. Though, for the life of me, I couldn't quite get my head around Pissy as the proprietor of any such establishment. 'You may need a good lawyer from time to time, Pissy. Most of the police are Afrikaners and not likely to approve. Just remember, I'm your man,' I joked.

Pissy may have suddenly realised the implications of what he'd just confessed to me. 'You won't tell the guys in the hut, hey, *Voetsek*?'

'I don't know,' I chaffed. 'Piet Kosterman could be your first signed-up member, those big Afrikaners who go in for homo-bashing, you just never know, do you?' Then, seeing the look of concern on his face, I reassured him quickly. 'We go way back, Pissy, your secret is safe with me,' I lied.

Completely out of the blue he'd presented me with an unexpected opportunity that my training as a lawyer was quick to seize upon. If I could get Pissy out of his army training, he might consider he owed me something in return, namely the confession of the plot to accuse Mattress of sexually abusing Pissy. Although I admit I was clutching at straws, I knew neither he nor Fonnie du Preez as children could have possibly been privy to the actual decision to murder the big Zulu. But he could tell me what additional lies they'd told Mevrou and Meneer Prinsloo, and so confirm Frikkie Botha's written evidence that together they'd hatched a plot to accuse Mattress of sexually abusing Pissy which, in turn, had led to his brutal murder.

The fact that I now knew Pissy harboured an ambition to open a club for homosexuals was an additionally powerful piece of emotional leverage. This was in 1956 when the benign and universally accepted word 'gay' had yet to be coined. 'Queer' and 'queen' were the only common colloquialisms available in the popular vernacular, and they were only a slight amelioration to the then dark and deep revulsion that existed among the general population for the word 'homosexual'.

If I was forced to do so, I knew I wouldn't hesitate to use this new-found knowledge of his intention, unlikely as it seemed, to open a club for Afrikaner homosexuals to get Pissy to tell me the truth about Mattress. My hope was that it wouldn't be necessary, or that, in addition, I might threaten to tell his mine management that he was an epileptic and shouldn't be driving an ore train underground. Nannying Pissy Vermaak for a week hadn't been much fun, but it might well be turning out to be a very fruitful exercise.

At the time I didn't know Captain Mike Finger as well as I later would and, in addition, I was going over the head of Sergeant Minnaar. But I had no doubt that Pissy had some sort of medical problem and I'd convinced myself that it ought to be looked into.

One thing was for sure, one way or another, Pissy Vermaak wasn't going to last the distance. I had to take the chance or he might disappear from my life once again. My instinct told me he would be an important witness in what had been formulating in my mind for a very long time, the re-opening of an enquiry into the murder of Mattress.

Not that there had been much of an enquiry; Sergeant Van Niekerk had simply concluded that no sufficient evidence existed to prosecute anyone. He stated in the official police notes that the victim, Zulu Mattress Malokoane, had been murdered by a person or persons unknown. Mattress was simply another dead *kaffir* buried in the native location graveyard with neither headstone nor name, but the number PO 289, which stood for *Polisie Ondersoek* 289 (Police Investigation 289).

In fairness, Sergeant Van Niekerk had done all he could at the time, and while he may have had his suspicions he hadn't the means or, I now realised, the skill to mount a proper investigation. A murdered African didn't merit the time of a detective sent from Pietersburg, or even a post-mortem examination. In all probability, Doctor Van Heerden would have signed the death certificate without examining the victim.

Mike Finger listened as I explained Pissy's problem to him, unofficially, after a late-afternoon lecture. 'He's not malingering, is he? Some recruits will go to extraordinary lengths to get out of their military training.' He looked at me shrewdly. 'Tom, it isn't just that Rifleman Vermaak is creating problems for your platoon, is it?'

'No, Sir, I admit he's not popular. We've had our first two weekend passes cancelled because of him and we'd all love to see him gone, but I do believe there's something medically wrong with him. He has an insatiable thirst as well, he can't get enough water.'

'Hmm, pissing your pants systematically could be a clever ploy, I've seen stranger attempts to avoid training. I'm not your commanding officer so I can't officially interfere or send him to the medical officer, but I'll talk to Captain Crawford. Is there anything else I should know about him?'

I didn't think there was any need to tell Mike Finger about Pissy's effeminate nature or nightly sobbing sessions. 'Well, he's got two left feet, and he's an incompetent soldier and always in trouble with the sergeant, he tries to go on sick call at every opportunity, so much so that Sergeant Minnaar has forbidden him to do so.'

'But you don't think it's designed to get him out of the army, you think it's something genuine?'

'Yes, Sir, I do, Sir.' Although I was suddenly beginning to experience some doubt. I thought back to The Boys Farm, where Pissy had used his epileptic fits to gain favour with Mevrou and avoid work, particularly on Sunday afternoons when we had to work in the vegetable gardens and orchards. He had also allowed Fonnie du Preez to sodomise him in order to obtain protection from the other kids. Now that I thought of it, the bastard was certainly capable of devising a ploy such as incontinence, regularly pissing in his pants for all of us to see, in an attempt to get out of the army.

But, as it turned out, the medical officer sent a sample of Rifleman

Vermaak's urine to a lab in Salisbury, and a week later they confirmed that he was suffering from diabetes insipidus, and this diagnosis was sufficient to earn him a dismissal from his army training.

Pissy was pathetic in his sycophantic gratitude, sobbing and mucoid as he thanked me over and over again for what I'd done for him. The commanding officer called me to his office to congratulate me for caring sufficiently for a comrade in arms to raise my concern with an officer. The incident also became one of the reasons why I got to know Mike Finger a lot better, so that we eventually became really good friends. I was once again receiving credit when none was due, my motives being far from altruistic, with kindness and sympathy playing no part whatsoever in my seeming concern for a fellow recruit.

Pissy was placed in Bulawayo General Hospital for observation and further tests, and on the following weekend leave pass I called in to see him. He was obviously surprised and delighted to see me. 'Voetsek!' he shouted out as I entered the ward. This caused all the other male patients to look up, whereupon Pissy announced, 'Hey, everyone! This is my best friend who saved my life!'

I blushed. 'I did no such thing,' I protested.

'Ja, man, definitely! If it wasn't for him —'

'Shut up, Kobus,' I interrupted. 'You're a diabetic, it's not life-threatening.' This caused smiles from the other patients. 'I didn't bring you any sweets because I don't think you're allowed to have sugar,' I apologised.

'No, man, you wrong, what I got is not *sugar* diabetes. It's called "insipidus", and with this diabetes I can have chocolates and lots of things I like a lot,' he said, looking pleased with himself.

'It's a nice day, can we go out and sit in the gardens? Hospital wards give me the creeps,' I said quietly, hoping I might be able to get him on his own so that we could talk.

'Ja, I can go anywhere I like in the grounds, I know a nice place.' He rose from the bed and put on a hospital gown and slippers, and we left the ward.

'Now, Pissy, you'll be back underground soon and then it's only until the end of the year, that's six months and then you're free to open your club.' I admit it was a pretty crude attempt to cut the preliminary crap and get down to business.

Pissy grabbed me by the wrist, speaking in a low voice. 'You won't tell anyone about that, promise me, *Voetsek*?' He looked directly at me and attempted to grin. 'It was all a big joke, you hear?' he lied.

'Why? It's a bloody good idea,' I said. 'I know one or two people in Johannesburg who may be of some help to you.'

'Really?' he exclaimed, suddenly excited.

'*Ja*, but if it's only a joke . . .'

Pissy was silent, and then he said quietly, 'No, I lied, man. It's a definite plan, we opening next year.'

'We?'

'*Ja*, my partner and me. He's someone who knows how to run front of house, a very respectable old man and a good Afrikaner. We also going to have these Turkish baths. You know what that is?'

'*Ja*, I've read something about them, a steam room, isn't it?'

'*Ja*, sort of.'

'And your partner knows how to run such a place?' I asked.

'No, me, man. I worked at one as a towel and laundry boy, you see, they don't have *kaffirs* for that job. You can't have *kaffirs* walking around in a steam room. The Afrikaners don't like *kaffirs* to know their private business. It's degrading for them to be naked in front of one. It was in Pretoria when I was sixteen and when I came out of the orphanage in Pietersburg. I worked there four whole years, I done all the jobs there were. I know the steam-room business backwards, man, also front of house and the bar and kitchens.'

'There's Turkish baths in Pretoria?' I asked, surprised.

'*Ja*, in the front it's quite respectable, anyone can go in, it's a health club. At the back there is another big steam room and a big hot bath, this is the private one. If you didn't know, you wouldn't know it was there. That's where the money is. I'm telling you, *Voetsek*, there's lots of us Afrikaners who, you know, are homos, but they don't want people to know. They'll come to the steam room and afterwards have a drink in the club and maybe eat something with all the respectable people, the professors from the university and foreigners from the embassies who use the saunas and steam rooms in the front.'

'What, male homosexual partners?'

He started to cackle, his face creased with amusement. 'No, man, *not* partners. These people like to be alone, they feel safe on their own.'

'Alone? But how . . . ?'

'With all the steam everywhere you can't see what's going on and what's going on, *jong,* is nobody's business, because you can't see the nose on your own face. There's just naked bodies you can feel with your hands and it's no problem to help yourself. Everyone is there for the same thing and afterwards, hey, it's no name, no pack drill. Later, if they have a drink in the club they don't even know each other, even if they want to. It's called incognito. Do you know this word?' I nodded and he continued. 'I'm telling you, man, this incognito business makes a lot of money. In Jo'burg there's already one, the Abdulla Club in Hillbrow, but all the English homos go there, there's nothing for the Afrikaners who don't like to mix.' He paused and seemed to be thinking, then took a deep breath. 'Hey, *Voetsek,* why don't you be a partner in the business? It will be like old times.'

I must say I was completely taken aback. Here I was thinking that I was the worldly one with all my Pirrou and La Pirouette training, but I simply had no idea. I was also deeply shocked that Pissy seemed to think that the term 'old times' somehow smoothed over what had happened at the big rock. 'A silent partner?'

'*Ja,* put in a bit of money, you'll get it all back pronto, man.'

'I have to go to England, to university, to take another law degree,' I replied.

'That's okay, man, it won't happen for another year, that's when my partner retires from his job and we still have to find a place and build the steam rooms.'

'I'll think about it,' I lied, 'but I must confess I have a problem.'

'What problem? I know the business, man, you can't lose.'

'No, Pissy, it's not that.' I hesitated, then said, 'How do I know you'll be honest? When you have a partner you have to trust him. You know how you said it would be like old times? Well, that's my problem, I haven't forgotten what happened that day at the big rock, and then to my friend Mattress.'

'Mattress? You mean the *kaffir* that was murdered?' Pissy looked down at the ground. 'Ag, man, that was such a long time ago when we were just kids, you hear? In that place, you know yourself, it was everyone for himself.' He glanced up at me and shrugged. 'I was only trying to survive, man. What must I say? I'm sorry?'

'No, don't get me wrong, I don't want an apology from you. You're right, it was a long time ago and what's done is done. What you and Fonnie du Preez did to me that day at the big rock is finish and *klaar*, we both know it happened to other kids as well, that stuff happens in institutions.'

Pissy looked relieved. 'So what is it you want?'

'Information. I want to know the full story. I'm going to tell you what I know, and then you tell me the rest. If you do, then I'll know I can trust you.'

'Okay, man, ask away.'

I told him about listening to him with Mevrou in the clinic while hiding in the hydrangea bushes outside the window, and how I knew he'd concocted the story of Mattress sexually abusing him. How Mevrou had believed him and her last words, or the last words I'd heard from her, were 'that *kaffir* is already dead, you hear'. 'Pissy, what happened when Mevrou took you to Meneer Prinsloo and they called Doctor Van Heerden to examine you?'

My memory is pretty good but Pissy Vermaak's was truly remarkable. In an earlier part I've already told you what he said transpired, right down to the funny bit when Doctor Van Heerden tried to take a snap of Pissy's bruised anus using Meneer Prinsloo's box brownie with Mevrou holding a torch. As Pissy recounted what happened I thought to myself what a brilliant student he would have been if he'd had a Miss Phillips in his life and been given the same opportunities I'd had.

'Okay, after the doctor had gone, what happened then?' I asked.

Pissy explained how Frikkie Botha was called in. This time I had the notes I'd made from Frikkie's painfully written evidence over more than five years, so I'd know if Pissy was lying. But again he recalled everything just the way Frikkie had written it down.

'One last question, when you and Fonnie were present was there any discussion, threat, implication or suggestion that Mattress might be dealt with, other than reporting him to Sergeant Van Niekerk?'

'How do you mean?' Pissy replied, not understanding my question. 'Meneer Prinsloo gave Frikkie permission to go three rounds with him in the boxing ring?'

'*Ja*, not that, some other threat. In the clinic Mevrou said "that *kaffir* is already dead, you hear". Was there anything else like that said in your presence, any further threat made to kill him?'

Pissy shook his head. 'No, man, just that Frikkie wanted to teach the *kaffir* a lesson before they handed him over to the police.' Recalling the incident, he laughed. 'Only he ended up himself with a broken jaw. That was one tough *kaffir*, hey?'

It seemed now almost certain that Mevrou had acted on her own. To an Afrikaner woman the sexual assault by an African of a child of her own kind would be the vilest crime she could possibly imagine. In her mind, death, violent and slow, was the only possible penalty and she'd have had little trouble persuading her six brothers to murder Mattress. She'd simply reacted the way her people had dealt with such problems for the last 300 years. I also had Frikkie's evidence that the Van Schalkwyk brothers had admitted murdering the *kaffir* when they'd been together in the *Stormjaers*, the seven-man Nazi-inspired sabotage cell when, during the war, they'd attempted unsuccessfully to blow up the railway culvert to derail a troop train. Frikkie, you will remember, sustained his terrible injuries and the six Van Schalkwyk brothers had run away and left him to die. By telling me they'd admitted to him that they'd murdered Mattress, Frikkie was hoping to exact revenge for what they'd done to him. With good behaviour the life sentences given to the six Van Schalkwyk brothers could be reduced to fifteen years, which meant they could be out in three years. If this happened I wanted to be ready for them. It was a promise I'd made to myself, at first as a small child half-consciously; it was also one I'd made to Frikkie Botha. It was also my major motivation to study law.

'There's something else I haven't told you, *Voetsek*,' Pissy said.

'What's that?'

'The bruises the doctor looked at and took the snap, they weren't only from Fonnie du Preez.''

'What do you mean? That's why he went to the reformatory in Pretoria. He also pissed on you and you performed fellatio on him.'

'*Ja*, the last two, but he wasn't the only one who fucked my arse or I sucked off.'

'Who else? It wasn't Mattress?'

He looked at me slyly. 'Can't you guess, hey?'

'Not Frikkie Botha?' I asked, looking surprised.

'No, man, I already told you he was straight.'

'Who then?' I said, relieved.

Pissy seemed to be enjoying himself. 'Meneer Prinsloo!'

'*What?* Meneer Prinsloo was sexually assaulting you? You were ten years old, for fuck's sake!'

'*Ja*, I know, it hurt a lot. It happened one Sunday when I'd had a fit the day before and I was in the sick room on my own because Mevrou was visiting her farm. Meneer Prinsloo came in to see me, and then it happened. After that it was every Sunday in the sick room after we came back from church and everyone had to work in the vegetable gardens and the orchards and there wasn't anybody around the hostel. Remember, I was always too sickly to go with you guys.'

The cruel, sanctimonious, sycophantic, Bible-bashing, hypocritical heap of excrement was also a paedophile. 'You poor little bastard, you never had a chance, did you?' I cried.

Pissy shrugged. 'Ag, *Voetsek*, it's easy to feel sorry for yourself in life.' He looked directly at me. 'You know what it's like, man. You were there. You an orphan. You haven't got any parents, a mother and a father, nobody loves you, you just a piece of shit. Then somebody powerful who can give you things and make life easier comes along.' He paused and looked down at his feet. 'If you a piece of shit anyway, what have you got to lose?' He looked up again. 'It was only on a Sunday.'

'Pissy, you were just a little kid, that fat bastard was committing a crime. Look, if Fonnie du Preez was buggering you, that's pretty bad, but it's two kids maybe experimenting, that kind of thing happens in institutions all the time. But Prinsloo *knew* he was sexually assaulting a minor, *knew* he was committing a crime. *Knew* he was destroying your life. Look, I'm a lawyer, you can still lay charges against him whenever you like, I'll help you mount the case.'

Pissy looked horrified. 'No way, man!'

'What do you mean? He's a fucking paedophile! He ought to go to prison!'

'Bullshit!' Pissy cried suddenly. 'Whoa! *Voetsek*, not so fast, man. He was kind to me, he said he loved me like his own son that he didn't have because "the Lord hadn't blessed him with issue". He brought me sweets, even sometimes a whole Nestlé chocolate. You yourself know what such a thing meant. It was Christmas every Sunday. Nobody was kind to me before.' He stopped suddenly and took a breath. 'Even then when I was only ten, I knew I was different. Later on I understood that I was a homosexual in my blood, from birth maybe. He said I could call him *Oom* Piet, and he'd be like a father to me.'

'A father doesn't fuck his ten-year-old son!' I shouted angrily. 'Thank God you got sent to Pietersburg and out of the bastard's clutches.'

Pissy threw back his head and laughed. 'No, man, even there he'd visit me. Twice a month. He'd take me in his big Plymouth to a hotel to eat something nice, then we'd do it after. Then later, after his wife died, he was transferred to be the superintendent at the Pietersburg orphanage. He's still there, he retires next year.'

'So how long did it go on?'

'The whole time, until I was sixteen and left the orphanage and came to Pretoria.'

'To work at the health club, which was more of the same?'

'*Ja*, but by then, like I jus' told you, I knew what I was. Look, man, you have to make the best out of life with what you've got. I worked hard at that place and learned everything there is to know about running a place like that: the steam room, laundry, front of house, kitchens, bar. I know all that stuff like the back of my hand.' He shrugged. 'You going to be the big-time lawyer and I'm telling you, man, I'm going to make a lot of money with a Turkish bath for Afrikaner homosexuals. Just another six months in the mines and I'll have my share of the money. Now why would I want you to make a big court case? It would fuck up my chances to start such a business. You think I'm mad or stupid or something?'

'Jesus, Pissy, what can I say? I'm just bloody sorry life happened to you like that.'

Pissy gave a short, sharp laugh, more like a bark. 'Life sucks, but then I'm an expert at sucking, man!' he said sardonically. 'Look, I know I was responsible for that *kaffir*, Mattress, being murdered and I'm sorry. When you become a big-time lawyer you'll re-open the murder enquiry, because I think that's why you asking me all these questions, isn't it? Okay, you got me out of the army, so I owe you big-time, man. But if you make me a witness in the case I won't cooperate and *Oom* Piet, Meneer Prinsloo, won't also, you hear? No way!' He paused and took a deep breath. 'Who do you think is going to be my partner in the club?'

'Oh, Jesus, no!'

'When he retires. It's not so stupid as it sounds, you hear? Meneer Prinsloo knows how to run a place. He's had lots of experience running an orphanage for boys, and these men he understands, you hear? He's also very respectable-looking, a fat old man with a gold watch chain, a *regte Boer*, who laughs a lot. He can give the Afrikaner customers a drink, talk to them, make them feel at home, run the kitchen and the dining room, he can tell them his funny chicken stories. The people who come to use the back part won't be nervous with him when they first come to the club. They'll know their secret is safe with *Oom* Piet. What happens out the back in the private steam room is my business.' He laughed and added gratuitously, 'He's a harmless old man. He can't even get it up anymore. For him the hanky-panky, it's finish and *klaar*!'

It was becoming obvious to me that there were two Pissy Vermaaks: the hapless, sobbing misfit that we'd seen in the barracks and a homosexual who knew his way around his own world and was a shrewd and cynical manipulator. Perhaps not even cynical, simply someone who lacked the normal moral standards most people accept as social behaviour. Knowing his background, this was hardly surprising and I wondered whether I might have assumed a similar philosophy if I hadn't received the breaks I'd been given in life. I confess, I hadn't realistically expected that he or Meneer Prinsloo would volunteer to be a witness. I'd have to subpoena them and hope for the best. But I was heartened by the fact that I now had something to hold over their heads. The case, if I could get it up, would almost certainly make the national papers. There had never been one quite like it before and the threat of revealing the details of a club for Afrikaner homosexuals might be sufficient to get them to cooperate in the witness stand.

I make no excuses for myself, in my own way I was being just as hard and cynical as Pissy. I knew I couldn't rest until I felt I'd done all I could to bring Mattress's murderers to justice. I also knew that my chances of doing so were not high, that to most South Africans the whole endeavour would seem a pointless exercise in jurisprudence. Some people in the law, even the judge, might think I was grandstanding, a young advocate looking for publicity. I knew that re-opening a murder enquiry that concerned an illiterate black man who looked after cows and pigs and six Afrikaner brothers and a sister, a family who many thought of as folk heroes and who'd already served twelve years in prison, was utterly pointless. Perhaps even cruel and vindictive, and it wasn't going to do my fledgling career in law any good, the legal Don Quixote tilting at windmills.

It must be explained, at the time, even the most liberal of South Africans, usually English-speaking, secretly thought of the African race as inferior to the white. A murder trial where there was nothing to gain but some sort of pyrrhic victory, which, in the process, reopened old racial wounds, was no honourable win for any system of justice. It might even have been possible that Mattress's wife and son, Mokiti Malokoane, also known as Joe Louis, didn't even know he'd been murdered. They might simply think he'd disappeared, as so many black men who left Zululand or their homelands to find a job to support their family had done in the past.

I hadn't tried to find Mattress's family. Perhaps, incorrectly, I reasoned that until I attempted to bring his murderers to justice there wasn't any point. (Who's the insensitive racist now?) I felt that by the time I was able to contact them, their grieving for his disappearance would be over. Then, if I were to win the case and see the Van Schalkwyk brothers convicted, at least they'd know that somebody cared.

It was almost time to leave Pissy Vermaak. I'd made arrangements to meet Mike Finger later in town for a drink, and to attend another heavily chaperoned dance at the YWCA. 'Pissy, I got to go. Thank you for being so frank with me.'

'That's okay, Voetsek, I owed you, but you got to promise you won't tell anyone at the barracks, you hear?'

I laughed. 'That's an easy promise. They're already so grateful you're gone, I'm a big hero anyway.'

Pissy laughed, then looked suddenly serious. 'Voetsek, maybe I can help you some more about the kaffir's murder.'

'Oh? How's that?'

Then he dropped his bombshell. 'Look, there's something else, something that didn't come out in the newspapers, in the Zoutpansberg Gazette. The kaffir's balls and prick wasn't there, they was cut out.'

I stared at Pissy, too shocked at first to comprehend. 'Jesus!' I exclaimed. Then I came to my senses. 'How do you know this, Pissy?'

'I've seen it.'

'Seen it? How? What?' I was sounding like an imbecile.

'Mevrou. She showed me. They were, you know, his testicles and cock, floating in this half-size canned-fruit jar, pickled in a half-jack of Tolley's five-star brandy.'

I felt, well, I didn't know at the time how I felt, numb I suppose. I know I wanted to throw up, then I felt incredibly sad and suddenly very angry. 'Pissy, you're a consummate liar, if you are making all this up I'll find out and I promise you I'll tell the mine about your epilepsy!'

'I swear it on my mother's grave!' he said, looking extremely hurt. 'I wouldn't lie to you about a thing like that, man!'

The fact that he didn't have a mother or even know if she was dead was by the way. I took a deep breath in an attempt to calm down. 'Tell me everything, Pissy,' I demanded. 'You've got a good memory, I want every fucking detail, right down to if she farted or sneezed or scratched her arse.'

He smiled, recalling. Mevrou would often scratch her bum, digging her stumpy fingers deeply into her elephantine crevices.

'It was the Sunday night after the Sunday when the murder happened and she'd come back from visiting her farm in the high mountains. After supper she said I must come to the clinic to take some medicine because, it was true, I had a bad cough and I must bring my pyjamas also, because otherwise I'd keep the dormitory awake all night. So I did. I had my medicine and went to bed in the sick room and I must have fallen asleep. I woke up, I don't know how late because how could I tell, the window of the sick room looked out on the long stoep and there was always a light on at night and the light was on in the sick room. Mevrou was sitting on the edge of the bed and she had one hand on my shoulder, shaking me.

'"Ja, now you awake, hey," she said. I'd seen her drunk on brandy before when, on other times, I was in the sick room. She'd sit in the front room till late and drink, and sometimes she'd wake me by giving me this big kiss on the mouth. Sis, man, with the brandy breath it tasted terrible. "You are my little skattebol, Kobus," she'd say in her drunk voice. Sometimes she'd fall over the bed, over my body, and I couldn't move until she got up. But now, this time she was different. Her hair was all over the place, some falling over her face, and her nightdress was pulled away from her one shoulder to her waist on one side with her arm out, so one big tit was also hanging out nearly to her waist. She had some sweat, like little bubbles under her nose, you know, where she had her woman's moustache, and her eyes were all blood-red. I can tell you, man, I was frightened she was crazy. "*Ja*, Mevrou, I am awake," I said, rubbing my eyes.

'"Some medicine for your cough, Kobus, sit up, *jong*," she said to me.

'I sat up but she wasn't holding the cough mixture and a spoon, jus' this small canned-fruit jar, half-full of brown stuff. I didn't know then it was brandy and I thought it must be some sort of medicine maybe she'd brought from their farm. You know, *boere medisyne*. "Look, Kobus," she cackled.

'"What is it, Mevrou?" I asked her.

'She held the jar up to the light. "Your revenge!" she said, and then she really began to laugh like crazy. She brought the jar down and held it in front of me, close, so I could see into the brown stuff. "What do you see? Tell me, Kobus!" She sounded angry.

'"I dunno, Mevrou, it looks like a black worm and two little eggs. Is it *muti*?"

'She thought this was very funny and laughed some more, like she was hysterical and couldn't stop, the tears were rolling down her fat face. Then at last she said, "*Ja*, Kobus, this is the *muti*, the medicine, you give a stinking *kaffir* when he puts his dirty black *piel* inside one of our children, inside an Afrikaner child!" She clasped the jar against her naked tit, holding it against her heart in both hands. "They going to send you to Pietersburg, to the orphanage there." She began to cry. "You like my own child, Kobus!" Then she put the jar down on the table near the bed. "Come to Mama, *skattebol*." She reached out and pulled me against her big breasts, the nightdress covered one and the other one sticking out. She started to rock me and she smelled of brandy and stale sweat from under her hairy arms, and she held me so tight with my face against her

I could hardly breathe and I started to cough. Then she let me go and she reached for the jar and handed it to me. "Here, hold it, Kobus, feel how it is to have revenge! That black cock is safe now, it can't hurt you anymore!"

'"*Nee*, Mevrou!" I pushed away from her. "I don't want to. It's not nice."

'"Kobus, lissen to me, I want you to hold it so you know an Afrikaner child is always safe from a dirty *kaffir*'s black *piel*. Here, take it, hold it," she put her hand on her naked breast, over her heart, "against your heart so you'll *never* forget! Then I'll keep it forever for you, you hear?" She smiled. "It's our little keepsake, *skattebol*."

'I took the jar and held it against my heart, I could feel it was thumping like anything. I can tell you, I was shaking all over my body. "Now, look inside, Kobus, you must be proud of your *Volk*, we God's own people, we don't wait for a so-called police enquiry, we have our own justice, God's justice, an eye for an eye. Suffer little children to come unto me, sayeth the Lord."'

Pissy looked directly at me. 'I guarantee, somewhere on the Van Schalkwyk farm is that canned-fruit jar.'

Half an hour later I met Mike Finger in a bar in town and we had a couple of quick beers. Apart from greeting him I didn't say much, my mind still reeling from the visit to Pissy Vermaak.

'You seem preoccupied, old chap,' Mike said halfway through the second glass of Lion lager.

'*Ja*, I apologise, I've just been to see Vermaak at the hospital.'

'That's decent of you, I would have thought you were glad to see the back of him.'

I smiled. 'My barracks owes you a big favour, Mike.'

'Not at all, you were right to come to me. He was, as you observed, genuinely sick, least I could do.'

'There were just one or two details I needed to clear up with him,' I said, explaining but not explaining my visit.

'Tom, I have news, I'm going back to Kenya,' he announced.

I was silent for a moment. 'I'm going to miss you, Mike. I hope we can keep in touch.' I extended my hand. 'I've come to value your friendship a lot.'

'That goes both ways,' he said, taking my hand. 'Drink up. Then one more beer before we go to that ghastly dance. I have something to suggest to you.'

I swallowed what was left of my beer and the barman poured two fresh ones.

'Tom, tomorrow the list comes out for the officer training interviews. I've spoken to Colonel Stone and suggested that if you agree, you come back with me to Kenya and do your officer's training with my regiment. The idea is that you get some first-hand experience of fighting the Mau Mau, and then we write a training manual for the Rhodesian Army.'

'Whoa! Take it easy. I'm due at Oxford for the Michaelmas term in October.'

'The training, because of the circumstances, is only three months, there's plenty of time.' He smiled. 'Besides, I have a sister, Sam, who goes by the unfortunate nickname among her friends of Midget Digit. She's only five feet and having a surname like Finger has decided drawbacks. Not just for her, at school the sportsmaster never tired of calling out, "Finger, pull your finger out!" I think you and Sam would get on very well.'

As I said before when he'd mentioned the possibility of officer training, it beat the hell out of working a grizzly. 'There could be a problem, if I train in Rhodesia the mine is obliged to pay my full copper bonus. I'm not sure this would be the case if I trained in Kenya.'

'Can't see the difference, you'd be seconded from the Rhodesian Army anyway, the way I am here from the Kenyan forces. Will you consider it?'

'When do I have to give you my answer?'

He smiled, and seemed a little embarrassed, then looked straight down into the foam-flecked top of his beer glass. 'Well, tomorrow actually.' He looked up. 'Tom, I'm sure you'll enjoy meeting my family.'

I grinned. 'What are you trying to say, Mike? That I'm not going to be given a choice?'

He took a deep slug of beer from his glass, almost emptying it, then placed it down with a smack of the lips. He grinned at me and said, 'Yes, something like that. You're in the army now, Rifleman Fitzsaxby.'

I was silent for a moment, nodding my head, trying not to look sheepish. 'By the way, you never did tell me why you were seconded to the Rhodesian Army?' I asked in an attempt to wrong-foot him, as he'd just done to me.

'Malaria and Major Chris Peterson of the Kenya Special Forces, the latter being the more serious and odious reason.' He glanced at his watch. 'Christ, we should get going if we hope to get a dance, I'll explain it all to you some other time, Tom.'

CHAPTER NINETEEN

A Mighty Smiting of Love and Hate

OVER THE SEVERAL DAYS before we left for Kenya, Mike Finger briefed me in depth on the state of emergency. Mike was anxious that I understood his point of view, which, I must say, often surprised me. The news coming out of Kenya was of a terrorist force that had reverted to barbarism, killing white settlers, with women and children being dismembered and their corpses burned. I couldn't recall a news bulletin or background commentary in a newspaper ever giving a reason why one particular tribe, the largest and the one thought to be the most 'civilised' of the six Kenyan tribes, would rise up to fight the British in such a fanatical way. 'Why isn't it a civil war involving all the tribes?' was one of my more obvious questions to Mike.

In all the discussions we'd had Mike seemed to be somewhat ambivalent about the state of emergency. He was Kenyan-born and his small dusty home town of Thika and the surrounding area of coffee and sisal plantations had been subject to attack by the Mau Mau, with one white family, close neighbours, murdered. Yet he didn't go on with the same rhetoric of hate coming from the Kenyan news sources, something I would constantly be subjected to from the farmers and settlers when I arrived there.

'Tom,' he'd often say, 'I willingly fight against the Mau Mau because as terrorists their methods are barbaric and cruel and cannot possibly be justified; they are killers, murderers of women and children, not just of whites but of their own people. We simply have to eliminate them.' Then he'd pause and say, 'But that doesn't mean that they don't have a good reason to fight us. They see themselves, no matter how fanatical and barbaric, as freedom fighters, and while you'll never hear it said among Kenyan whites or the British administration, we are largely to blame for this uprising.'

'Was this the reason you were sent to Rhodesia, I mean, for speaking out?'

'Certainly that was a great part of the reason. Malaria, as I told you, was another and a major quarrel with Chris Peterson when we were both in the Special Branch; he is now the commanding officer of the Kenya Regiment.'

'What happened there?' I asked him. 'You promised you'd tell me.'

'It was a bitter disagreement about the method of interrogation when we captured the Mau Mau. In order for you to understand you need to know more about the Kikuyu culture and you'll need to go to Kenya and see the situation for yourself. Perhaps we can leave this for later, Tom.'

As usual, Mike's briefing was thorough. He was someone who thought deeply and in detail, and his observations were seldom superficial. If anything, he was too serious and on occasion somewhat melancholy. With the prospect of his return to Kenya he'd taken to drinking whisky with beer chasers, and on several occasions when we'd been to Bulawayo I'd had to put him in the back seat of the military Ford sedan he'd drawn from the motor depot and drive him back to the camp to let him get out just before we got to the officers' quarters so that he wouldn't be seen with a training recruit bringing him home. He was what in those days would be described as a serious-minded young man with a tendency to worry too much. While he expressed an earnest desire to return to Kenya 'to finish the job', I sensed that it wasn't going to be easy for him. Anyway, in the matter of briefing me, he began with the topography of the country. I would, of course, learn it for myself so will put down a brief description here.

The Kenyan landscape has a taste of everything that is Africa. Savannah grassland, pancake flat, soft hills that fold into rolling green plains, harsh unrelenting rocky desert, fertile highland valleys and, most imposing of all, its mountains – the mighty Aberdares and the forbidding slopes of that second great African giant, Mount Kenya, a mountain that doesn't stand the least in awe of Kilimanjaro with its snow-capped peak squatting smugly on the invisible line of the Equator.

Mike's whole demeanour changed as he spoke of the mountains and the forests as if they were sacred places. 'Tom, Mount Kenya is the throbbing heart of Kenya and the Aberdares may be said to be its lungs, its breath, its very life.'

He described the impenetrable bamboo growing over razorbacked ridges where a mile away, as the crow flies from another ridge, may well be a day's march away. Within the deep green valleys, the sides of which fell almost vertically from the ridges, grew giant forest trees, each desperately competing to break through the dense canopy to reach the light – African mahogany, Cape chestnut, *Podocarpus*, meru oak and the enormous wild fig trees, also a feature of the slopes of Mount Kenya. Beneath the canopy was a world of vines and dense bamboo, where old man's beard hung ghost-like from the branches of the taller trees. Here it was always half-light, cold and misty with almost constant rain, a place to cause endless discomfort. Rising 13 120 feet above the forested ridges and dark valleys is the peak of *Ol Doinyo Lesatima*, where two waterfalls plunge for 900 feet to be swallowed into a deep gorge below. I recall Mike observing that 'The Aberdares is the most primal landscape on earth, beautiful in its terror and always unwelcoming.'

It was within the wooded valleys and razorback ridges of the Aberdares and the densely forested lower slopes of the extinct volcano, Mount Kenya, where the Mau Mau hid: two distinct groups of terrorists, one at each location who, although they fought for the same cause, seldom came in contact. From these two almost impenetrable hiding places they launched their uncoordinated attacks on white farms and on those Kikuyu tribesmen they considered traitors to the cause of freedom and the restoration of the land they believed they rightfully owned. In the main, these tribesmen enemies of the Mau Mau were known as the Home Guard. This armed and semi-armed, mainly African militia consisted of Kikuyu who had accepted Christianity or been promised land grants by the colonial authorities in return for their allegiance to the British and their willingness to fight against their own people.

I was curious to know why this Home Guard militia could be persuaded to fight their fellow tribesmen in return for agriculturally inferior lowlands granted to them by the British, who had robbed them of their rich and fertile ancestral highlands in the first instance.

Mike Finger explained it to me like this. 'The Kikuyu have a spiritual and emotional association with ownership of land that is the major factor in the Mau Mau uprising, which, by the way, the Mau Mau call the Land Freedom Army, or LFA.'

'Hardly a new idea,' I protested, 'the Zulu and Xhosa in South Africa and the Matabele in Rhodesia, as well as almost all other African tribes, have the same belief that land tribally owned is common wealth. A man's personal wealth is counted in the number of cattle and goats he possesses.'

'Of course, but it goes much further than this with the Kikuyu. Without actually possessing, that is *owning* and working land, he doesn't, in the beliefs of the tribe, qualify as human. There is an old Kikuyu proverb that states "One cannot eat what he has not sweated for".' Mike went on to explain. 'To fully understand this expression, it means much more than hard work in return for food, it means that without the means to create food from the soil a man may not be allowed to receive it.'

I looked at him curiously. 'You mean, don't you, they're considered to be lesser people? That's not so strange, landowners in any feudal society call the shots, you know, dominate the society. Peasants and landowners, the age-old struggle that eventually led to communism.'

He shook his head. 'No, I can see you don't understand, Tom. With the Kikuyu, land is everything, without it a man is completely emasculated, he is not allowed to take a tribal wife or to officially procreate. Landless Kikuyu are regarded as incomplete humans and therefore their offspring have no status within the tribe. Without land their lives and tribal association become meaningless.'

'So, by the colonial authorities granting the Home Guard land they grant them, in a real sense, the meaning of life?'

'You've got it in one. If they have to betray their own kind as a consequence, they argue that they are not fighting disaffected freedom fighters, they are fighting incomplete men, men of no substance, men of no spiritual value to the tribe.'

It was the lawyer coming out in me, for there seemed to be a contradiction to this rather neat analogy. 'But you've always maintained that a majority of the Kikuyu have taken the Mau Mau oath and are therefore seemingly in sympathy with them. If these freedom fighters are men of no consequence to the tribe, why would they take an oath of allegiance?'

Mike laughed. 'It's a mixture of things very African, but also practical, the oath is a critical and compelling component of the Mau Mau participation,' he explained.

'What exactly does taking the oath involve?' I naturally asked.

Mike thought for a moment. 'I was raised with the Kikuyu people, and at puberty was initiated into a Kikuyu age-set, the traditional manhood ceremony. I've mentioned in the past how they thought of me as an "inside-out man", a member of their tribe, white on the outside and black on the inside, and I'm pretty sure the oath of loyalty to the Mau Mau differed little from the normal oath of compliancy used in Kikuyu tribal ceremonies. You're going to hear all sorts of stories when you get to Kenya, most of them complete bullshit involving ritual cannibalism, necrophilia with goats, sexual orgies and the like. If I know anything about their rituals the oath will take place with some ceremony involving the eyes and intestines of a goat and the ingestion of animal blood, because almost any tribal ceremony involving an oath will have these components. What I do know is that they call on the old, *true* god, Ngai, to witness the oath. The people taking it swear to be united in their fight against the colonial enemy and agree to become involved in the struggle to take back the land stolen from them by the white man. As most of the tribe know, this is an honourable and just reason to fight, they can usually be persuaded to undertake the ceremony. Having taken the loyalty oath they discover it is totally binding, a deadly serious matter and one that can never be broken. The recipients, thought to be nearly 60 per cent of the Kikuyu tribe, are truly caught between a rock and a hard place. Fearing the power of the oath, the British administration has made taking it a capital offence and, conversely, the Land Freedom Army or Mau Mau work on the adage that you're either for me or against me. Neutrality doesn't exist, if you're against me you're my enemy and must die.' He looked up. 'Make no mistake, Tom. Loyalty is everything and ambivalence or resistance to the oath is potential death, so you see the ordinary Kikuyu people are in a no-win situation.'

Mike paused, then added, 'The second reason for taking the oath is a genuine recognition that under the traditional rules of land ownership these young men would not be robbed of their humanity. It is the fact that we white men and our colonial administration have expropriated the best of Kikuyu land without compensating or even granting them sufficient land elsewhere to meet their tribal requirements. This has left thousands of would-be traditional landowners with no means to acquire land so these emotionally castrated, young jobless men invade the towns looking for work and create the slums in Nairobi. In the fourteen years prior to the rebellion the city's population doubled. It was within these festering slums that, of course, the Mau Mau originated among the disaffected Kikuyu youth. The Kikuyu tribesmen – that is, other than some of their rich, self-serving, landowning British-appointed chiefs supported by the colonial administration – recognise this and support the Mau Mau cause. In a real sense the tribe is deeply affected; young men without the status and traditional means to marry and procreate means the Kikuyu people suffer in an ethnic sense, with nearly half of their young eligible bachelors unable to take their place in the tribal structure. Kikuyu women with no prospects of marriage to a man who owns land, or to avoid being sold off as wives to the hated Home Guards, have joined the freedom fighters in the forests. The Mau Mau have among them women who are said to have powers of prediction and they work directly with Mau Mau platoon commanders.

'Jomo Kenyatta, the political leader of the tribe, has tried to argue the Kikuyu's cause with the colonial authorities, pointing out the injustices and how, with some land redistribution, these might be remedied. In effect, he has tried to demonstrate how to bring the terrorism to a halt. But this would mean us white Kenyans giving back some of the land we've stolen. Of course, we're not willing to do this and, if you listen to my dad or any other Kenyan farmer, we will resist doing so, down to the last clod of earth. Instead we've put Kenyatta in prison, and consequently turned him into a martyr and a symbol of freedom, not only for the Kikuyu, but for all the tribes of Kenya.'

By the time Mike arrived back in Kenya, and I arrived for officer training in the Kenya Regiment, the emergency was thought to be almost over. In an operation named Anvil, the slums of Nairobi were being cleared and tens of thousands of Kikuyu suspected of being city Mau Mau supporters were summarily arrested; men, women and children were removed from their homes and incarcerated in detention camps or transferred to the already over-populated Kikuyu reserves.

Rural villages near Mount Kenya and the Aberdares suspected of supplying the Mau Mau with food and support had been razed to the ground. Huts were burned, crops destroyed, animals stolen to be eaten by the Home Guards and the villagers herded into barbed-wire-fenced, moated and fortified African gulags known as Home Guard posts that they shared with other rural suspects awaiting interrogation. The Kikuyu

Home Guards who ran the camps were, for the most part, illiterate and badly trained militiamen who were increasingly guilty of indiscriminate murder, rape and pillage. They practised these atrocities with the covert permission of their local white officers and the colonial authorities who, with a stroke of the governor's pen, would eventually officially absolve them of all crimes against humanity. The refugees herded into these gulags were helpless and without recourse to justice, the victims of a systematic purging that saw a great many innocent people die. The official colonial administration's reaction to the Mau Mau was to prove to be one of the most shameful human rights abuses in the history of British colonialism.

With their rural and city support system in tatters, hundreds of Mau Mau, starving and forced from the forest to look for food, were being captured in increasing numbers. A captured Mau Mau represented the black terrorist in every settler's nightmare and epitomised the official and settler view that they were subhuman creatures. A picture is said to be worth a thousand words and the photographs and newsreel pictures sent around the world of captured and dead Mau Mau were a major source of British propaganda.

Like all Kikuyu, the forest fighters didn't wash but would rub their bodies with animal fat. While a few still wore the tattered semblance of European clothes, most were clad in animal skins often shaped and stuck to the skin while freshly slaughtered, so that when they dried, they became an extension of the human skin underneath. This kept out the bitter cold of the forests and gave them the appearance of demonic wild men. Their eyes were deeply bloodshot, and their faces scarred and bearded. Their hair hung in dreadlocks to their shoulders, a hirsute fashion that would later become popular among Rastafarians but at the time was regarded as repulsive. They often had ulcers and ugly festering wounds and the stench they emitted would cause a capturing British soldier to turn away and throw up. Paradoxically, the corresponding smell of soap and toothpaste on a European often resulted in the captured Mau Mau following suit.

It soon became evident to anyone who cared to look at the situation that the Mau Mau or the Land Freedom Army never had a chance. They were loosely organised into two main groups, Mount Kenya and the Aberdares, and their raids and subsequent actions were opportunistic in nature. By the time we got to Kenya, properly organised resistance along military or even guerilla lines was impossible. The combination of British Forces, 55 000 troops, the Kenya Regiment and Special Forces together with the Home Guard completely controlled Kikuyu territory and the slums of Nairobi as well as the native reserves. The Mau Mau were effectively restricted to starvation within the forests.

It had taken a mighty army and air force to reduce the Mau Mau to the state they were now in. A lesson to be learned from this exercise, and something I picked up as part of the training I received, was that given the right terrain to hide in, along with strong motivation to fight for freedom and support from the indigenous population, a small guerilla force could stand against the might of a powerful and well-equipped military force. The Mau Mau had been all but defeated but it had taken a considerable effort to do so. Rhodesia would do well to sit up and take notice.

The cost in suffering was truly enormous. By the time the state of emergency was lifted, 100 000 Kikuyu had been imprisoned in detention camps. More than a million Kikuyu and Embu civilians had been shifted into 'secure' areas, such as the gulags and other camps. Up to 11 500 suspected Mau Mau had been killed already. If you counted deaths from disease and starvation in these 'protected villages', the total death toll was thought to be close to 150 000.

I was to discover that during the process of capture and interrogation Mau Mau prisoners and suspected terrorists were being beaten and tortured systematically by the British military, especially by the Kenya Regiment, headed by Mike Finger's nemesis, Colonel Chris Peterson. Peterson's regiment comprised, in the main, young locally born whites and British settlers who now owned the land the Mau Mau believed belonged to the Kikuyu people, and they had every reason to want to fight the terrorists. Under the direction of Peterson and a military intelligence officer, Major Dickson, a method of fighting known as pseudo gangs was initiated. These pseudo gangsters, as they referred to themselves, were made up of white Kenya Regiment officers and converted Mau Mau. They would enter the forests of the Aberdares and Mount Kenya to harass, search for and destroy the Mau Mau camps and, whenever possible, capture and kill the terrorists. The gangs, much praised within the white community for their bravery and commitment, were known to be notoriously cruel and unremitting in their harsh treatment of the prisoners they took alive.

It was in this area of the pseudo gangs that Mike Finger had come unstuck and the bitter disagreement between him and Chris Peterson had occurred. Peterson was a charismatic leader and a highly admired operator. He was said to have found an effective way of inducing Mau Mau terrorists to change sides and join one of his pseudo gangs to return to the forests to hunt down their former comrades. The news media at the time wrote extensively about Peterson's prowess and his deep knowledge of the psychology of the Kikuyu and the Mau Mau. This was reported in the London *Guardian* as 'completely mysterious to the Western mind, defying logic, fascinating and confusing and defying full comprehension'. Peterson was seen as some sort of white witchdoctor by the media and when asked would never reveal his technique for obvious reasons, implying that if he spoke about his methods this would alert the terrorists to them. When questioned he'd laugh disarmingly and say, 'That would be letting the cat out of the bag, old chap!'

Mike Finger was infuriated by this deception because all Peterson was doing was promising the interrogated terrorist freedom and a grant of land, in effect giving him the right to be a human being at last.

Mike explained, 'The poor, starving bastard has spent years in the misery and cold of the Aberdares or within the forests on the slopes of Mount Kenya. He is then persuaded by Chris Peterson that his cause is utterly lost, but by agreeing to take a cleansing oath he will be granted a pardon. Moreover, he becomes human by dint of being a landowner and the future father of many tribal sons. In return for this he is armed and returned to the forests to hunt down his former comrades.' Mike shrugged. 'It's not exactly a difficult decision to make when the alternative to taking a cleansing oath and a rightful place in the tribe is execution.'

Mike's problem was one of betrayal. Chris Peterson was making a promise he didn't intend to keep. The governor, Sir Evelyn Baring, had repeatedly insisted that the edict that no Mau Mau be given land under any circumstances was to be absolutely adhered to. The converted terrorist would never be granted a pardon or land of his own, and when the state of emergency was over he would be imprisoned. This subsequently proved to be true. What extra land was granted to the Kikuyu went to British-appointed Kikuyu loyalist chiefs and murderous Home Guards who, together with the Kenya Regiment and the Kenya Police Reserve, killed infinitely more innocent civilians than the terrorists did themselves. The Mau Mau who survived the gallows and imprisonment returned to being the non-people they'd been before the struggle. Mike felt strongly that Chris Peterson was using his deep knowledge of the Kikuyu people to betray their trust. 'I know the argument exists that the end justifies the means,' he protested to me, 'but I'm Kenyan-born and bred, so is Chris Peterson, and after this is all over we are going to have to live in this country with these people. While it may be my duty to kill the terrorists, I will not betray their tribe, their god or their ancient beliefs any more than I would my own.'

Mike had taken his complaints directly to Sir Evelyn Baring. He had pointed out that the Mau Mau were very much a spent force and could easily be defeated using conventional methods, that the idea of brainwashing and the cleansing oath was morally wrong and white Kenyans would live to regret the concept of the converted terrorist and the pseudo gangs. The result was that Mike was despatched to Rhodesia to recover from a particularly bad bout of malaria, where his high-minded principles could do no harm and the absence of the anopheles mosquito would cure the raging fever that was causing him to lose his judgement.

I recall saying at the time, 'Mike, don't you think you were being a little naïve when you went to the governor to complain about Peterson? He was never going to listen to you. Peterson is a big-time hero. He's been given the credit for the interrogation and confessions of the Mau Mau leader, General China, which provided the military with the inside knowledge of how the Mau Mau on the slopes of Mount Kenya were organised. Now he's captured General Kimathi who controls the Aberdares. The Mau Mau are being routed, and the pseudo gangs are proving to be an enormous success. They'll probably give Peterson some sort of medal before this is over. Governor Baring and the colonial administration don't give a shit about your sensibilities over betraying the Kikuyu people. Peterson and his secret methods are excellent propaganda and make bloody good newspaper copy, and besides, they're being made out to be a resounding success. They're not going to censure him over some sort of *Boy's Own Annual* idea of how to behave towards a bunch of restless natives who have the hide to ask for the land they traditionally owned to be returned to them.'

Mike sighed. 'Of course you're right, Tom. But there's enough Kikuyu in me to know that this is something I mustn't and cannot do. Call it superstition if you like, but Peterson will never be forgiven for this betrayal, not by me, and not by the Kikuyu people as a whole. This wasn't simply a promise of freedom and land, it involves a contra-oathing ceremony devised by Doctor Louis Leakey, the famous anthropologist, and is solidly based on Kikuyu sacred law. It's called a "cleansing oath" where the terrorist, now given human status at last, together with a promised pardon and a grant of land, swears upon *githathi*, the sacred stones, for a reversal of the Mau Mau oath. In Western terms this may seem justified mumbo jumbo, colonialism gone cleverly native, but to the Kikuyu, not to keep the promise made when the oath is taken is tantamount to destroying the whole tribe by insulting their god, Ngai. In Christian terms it is the equivalent of committing religious sacrilege of the worst possible kind. The Kikuyu are a deeply superstitious people but much of what we call ignorance and superstition is no different to our concept of religion.'

In the eyes of most white Kenyans, the once popular Mike Finger had become a laughing stock; people sniggered as he passed them in the street of the small town of Thika. He was openly called a *Kuke* apologist and a nigger lover. The inside-out man had brought his black inside out into the open. I was observing first-hand the Kenyan and English settler version of the Afrikaners who had called me a *kaffirboetie* when my friendship with Mattress had become known. The racism shown by the English-speaking whites in Kenya and the British colonial administration was every bit as bad as it was among the diehard *Boere* in South Africa. Only in this place they were free to put their hate into daily practice, not by murdering a Mattress in the dark of night and then hiding from the law, as I now knew for certain the Van Schalkwyk brothers had done, but by killing hundreds of black civilians without fear of official prosecution under the dual euphemisms of 'suspected Mau Mau' or 'attempting to escape'. It was open season on the blacks and it brought out the worst instincts in many whites. For a white man to possess a conscience in Kenya during the time of the Mau Mau was seen as a contradiction in terms. As a consequence Mike was often shunned in the officers' club, at a cocktail party or in the club in Thika. Many of his old schoolmates openly refused to talk to him.

We were driving down to the Fingers' coffee plantation on the first weekend leave pass I'd managed to wangle when Mike said, 'The hardest part is that I know both my father and my mother feel they have to apologise for me. Although she'd never say so, Sam, my sister, constantly jumps to my defence. She's naturally feisty and has practically come to blows several times defending me at the Gymkhana Club. I've begged her not to do so, but that's just not Sam, the Midget Digit, who hasn't a disloyal bone in her body.'

Mike spoke often of his sister and always in a fond and somewhat admiring voice so that I was now anxious to meet her. I confess when I first saw her, after the stunning Pirrou, I was momentarily disappointed when I was introduced. I guess when you're young every initial impression of a female is physical. (And I'm not so sure this only applies to when one is young.) Mike's sister certainly wasn't plain, far from it, but she wasn't glamorous either. She wore no make-up, not even lipstick, and had a light sprinkling of freckles across the bridge of her nose and dusting her cheeks. She had straight blonde hair cut in a no-nonsense style with a side parting, and falling just short of her shoulders, nice deep blue eyes, a generous well-shaped mouth, even teeth and a nose perhaps a little too straight, maybe even a fraction too sharp for her oval face. She wore baggy khaki shorts that reached down to her knees and somewhat scuffed plain leather sandals. What may well have been one of Mike's old school shirts, faded blue and too large for her small frame, was worn open to the third-top button and hung down to almost the bottom of her shorts. While she was small, five feet and one inch, she had an athletic body, nicely shaped calves and, because the shirt was too big for her, I couldn't see the bulges, if any, of her breasts. If she could be termed the girl-next-door type, she would also have to be described as a very nice-looking neighbour. Sam Finger, if not glamorous or beautiful, was nevertheless what you might call a very neat package, one that came fully equipped with a generous and infectious laugh and an open, direct and unpretentious manner. I would learn that she was an excellent horsewoman, a good shot – but only for the cooking pot – an all-round tomboy and a good sport. In terms of my previous experience of females, which only included Pirrou alias the temperamental La Pirouette, Sam was about as opposite in nature as could be, except that she too possessed a temper, though not one that ran to tantrums when she couldn't get her own way.

Mike's family must have heard the sound of the army Land Rover Mike had commandeered for the weekend, because as we came up the rather splendid driveway lined with flame trees, or as they are known in South Africa, Lucky Bean trees, Mike's mother and sister came out onto the terrace to meet us. Mike's father, it turned out, was attending a meeting and lunch for the local coffee planters at the Thika Sports Club.

The farmhouse, I observed, was like many I'd noticed in rural Kenya: three round thatched-roof *rondavels* or houses built together to form a single unit. The advantage, Mike had once explained to me, of a thatched roof is that it's always blissfully cool inside; the downside was that it needed to be replaced every five years or so, and, of course, during the state of emergency was very susceptible to fire. But it was far more practical than the ubiquitous corrugated iron favoured in most parts of rural South Africa. Thatch was plentiful and harvested on the estate and African labour was cheap. I must say a Kenyan farmhouse with its whitewashed walls always sat comfortably on the landscape. For once the European settler had adapted something appropriate to Africa instead of importing an architectural misfit entirely alien to place or climate.

Mrs Finger was a small, slim, good-looking woman in her late forties, with prematurely white hair cut into a soft bob that went well with her startlingly blue eyes, even more intensely blue than her daughter's. Her skin was deeply tanned (I would later learn from playing tennis) and was beginning to show the leathery effects of the African sun on what was once, no doubt, a perfect English-rose complexion. She wore bright-red lipstick, a plain blue cotton dress and a pair of leather sandals similar to Sam's, though hers were polished and neat. I noted that her toenails had been painted to match her lipstick, while, curiously, her fingernails were clipped short and remained unpainted; they were practical hands, or perhaps it was because she was a tennis player.

Mike called a greeting from the car and each woman, smiling, lifted a hand to acknowledge our arrival. An African appeared from the side of the house and came towards the Land Rover. 'Leave your gear, Tom, Githuku will take it to your room,' Mike instructed.

'*Jambo, Bwana* Mike,' Githuku said, smiling broadly as he approached us.

'*Ku salamu*, Githuku,' Mike replied, returning the greeting and the smile. '*Habari yako? Jamaa endelaya mzuri?* I hope you and your family are well?'

'*Ndio*,' the servant replied, smiling shyly.

Walking towards the two women, Mike called out, 'Not playing tennis I see, Mother?'

'Knocked out in the semifinals by Gladys the Man-eater,' Mrs Finger replied, laughing.

We climbed the terrace steps and Mike introduced me. 'May I introduce Tom Fitzsaxby,' he said in a surprisingly formal way. 'Tom, this is my mother and, of course, you'll have guessed, this is my little sister, Sam.' He suddenly lunged forward and grabbed Sam in a bear hug and kissed her while she squealed in delighted protest, then he turned and more formally did the same to his mother.

Hug completed, Mrs Finger smiled as I accepted her hand. 'You're to call me Bobby, Tom,' she said firmly. 'Welcome to Makindi.' She released my hand. 'Lunch is almost ready and the cook's baked an apple pie and there's fresh cream.'

'Sounds great,' I said, and then added for want of anything else to say, 'it's some time since I've had a home-baked apple pie.' Although, thinking about it, I don't suppose I ever had.

'Oh, don't expect too much, the apples are out of a tin from the south,' Bobby laughed, no doubt meaning tinned fruit from South Africa.

I turned to acknowledge Sam.

'You're supposed to be much bigger!' she exclaimed, looking me up and down. 'Six foot, at least.'

'You're supposed to be much smaller, Midget the Digit,' I replied, laughing.

'Watch out, Sam, Tom's a sharp-tongued lawyer,' Mike warned, grinning.

Sam flicked back an errant strand of blonde hair that was flopping over her right eye. 'The way Mike described you, with a Rhodes scholarship and all, I thought you'd be, well, tall and imposing, a bit frightening,' she said, laughing.

'I'm very unimposing, I'm afraid. There was a definite shortage of imposing, tall, frightening candidates when I applied for Oxford and I was very much the "next best" one,' I said, dusting off my Pirrou-taught manners. Then, bowing slightly, I smiled and extended my hand. 'By the way, how do you do, Miss Finger?'

Sam Finger ignored my outstretched hand and took a step forward and planted a soft kiss on my cheek. 'Lovely,' she said, 'at least I don't have to stand on a chair to kiss you, Tom Fitzsaxby.'

If I wasn't already in love with Mike's little sister, then I was well on the way to becoming so.

We turned to enter the house, led by Mike's mother. She stopped suddenly and turned back to face her son. 'I've spoken to your father and there's to be no discussing the war this weekend!' she said sharply. I was beginning to sense she wore the pants around the place. I would soon learn that she wasn't the only strong woman in the family.

Mike reached out and rested his hand on her shoulder, then bent down and kissed her lightly on the cheek. 'Sure, Mum, I promise.' Then he said, 'That's if Dad doesn't start up, you know how he is after a few Scotches.'

'Your father has promised to behave,' Bobby said firmly, brooking no further comment.

I saw the momentary expression on Sam's face as Mike made this remark about his father and told myself that Jock Finger might have a drinking problem.

'Oh, good!' Sam said quickly. 'That means we don't have to go into town to meet him for drinks, there's bound to be some nasty drunk at the club who wants to start a fight with Mike over the beastly war.'

'Does that also mean no dinner guests tonight?' Mike asked hopefully.

'Just the family, I've told your father no strays from the club, we want the two of you all to ourselves,' Bobby said without smiling. 'Drinks on the terrace as usual at sunset.'

'What? Doors not locked and bolted after dark?' Mike asked.

'We've decided we can't live like that,' Bobby said crisply. 'Besides, the dogs will warn us in plenty of time.'

'If they're not poisoned,' Mike said, almost to himself. 'Mother, please be careful, it's not the end yet by any means.'

'Perhaps if it's a nice day tomorrow, a picnic?' his mother suggested brightly, ignoring his remark. 'We'll see if the two of you feel up to it. Now come along, lunch is ready and you know how Wanjohi sulks when he thinks his soup is getting cold.'

'The cook,' Sam explained, taking my hand.

The rules for the weekend having been established, Bobby Finger entered the house.

After a lunch of vegetable soup, salad and cold roast beef, followed by a splendid apple pie and fresh cream, Sam showed me the garden, which was largely of her making. 'Mum plays a lot of tennis and so the garden has always been mine, though heaven knows who'll keep an eye on it when I go to horticultural college next year.'

My heart skipped a beat; Mike had told me about Sam going over to England to study horticulture. It was too early to process the thought of meeting her over there. 'I know a bit about vegetables and fruit, though not much about flowers,' I ventured instead.

She looked surprised. 'Were you a farmer once? Most men know nothing about the things they eat,' she observed.

I laughed. 'Well, a farmer in a manner of speaking, I suppose.' I pointed to the flame trees; sunbirds of every description, like bright jewels in the marvellous Kenyan sunlight, were flocking to the crimson blossoms for their nectar. Beyond the trees the peaks of Mount Kenya could be seen in the faraway distance. 'Sunbirds, how lovely they look,' I remarked.

'Tom Fitzsaxby, you haven't answered my question,' Sam said in a firm voice.

I turned to look at her. She stood, shapely legs slightly apart, her hands on her hips with a questioning look on her pretty face.

'What question?' I said, pretending not to remember.

'The farmer-in-a-manner-of-speaking question,' she replied.

'Oh, that, yes, well, when I was a little brat we worked in the vegetable gardens and orchards.'

We'd reached a wooden garden seat under an arbour covered with a vine of big hanging violet trusses that looked quite magnificent. 'Sit!' Sam commanded sternly, pointing to the seat. I did as I was told. Standing over me with her hands still on her hips, she sighed. 'Tom Fitzsaxby, if we are going to get to know each other properly then you have to answer my questions. I'm a naturally curious person and, besides, avoiding questions is being mysterious and means you'll be forcing me to jump to conclusions, which may not be fair to you!' She paused, looking serious. 'And that's not fair to me! You're hiding something, I just know it.'

I sniffed. 'Not much perfume, what's the name of the vine?' I pointed above my head.

'*Petrea*,' she said, then waited for my reply to her previous statement.

'Don't you think some things are best left unexplained?' I replied. 'I thought it was everyone's prerogative to hide the parts we don't like about our past.'

'No, you're not allowed to!' she said emphatically. 'That's why Kenya is in such a mess! I mean the whites. Everyone is hiding something. You know what they call Kenya?'

'They?'

'Outsiders, people from other places.'

'No, I don't believe I do. Is it something unpleasant?'

'A place in the sun for shady people!' Sam didn't laugh or even smile, as I expected she might.

I clucked my tongue. 'Sam, your brother is perhaps the least shady person I've ever met. Your mother doesn't exactly beat about the bush or appear to be remotely duplicitous. If talking about the war this weekend is forbidden, it would seem your father is a pretty forthright type as well. As for Miss Sam Finger . . . well, just observe her interrogating me, demanding the unvarnished truth or else misconstruction may ensue and future relationships may be adversely affected!' I was finding her directness both disarming and slightly alarming and was using my 'among clever people' Johannesburg-taught conversational language in an effort to keep Sam's forthright manner at arm's length.

'You're right, I'm being a stickybeak,' she apologised. 'It's just . . . well, Tom,' she seemed to think for a moment, as if she couldn't find the word she needed, then she shrugged and added ingenuously, 'talking over lunch and here, you seem different and I'm, well . . . curious.'

'I take it a stickybeak is someone who is overcurious to the point of being rude?' A hurt expression crossed her face and so I immediately added, 'Well, you're not being rude, Sam, but you're correct, I don't much like talking about my past.'

Sam looked relieved and moved suddenly to sit beside me. Quite unselfconsciously she reached out and took my hand in her own and brought it to her lips and kissed it. 'I'm sorry, Tom, I'm being a nosey parker. You were an orphan, weren't you? Mike told me.' She released my hand and I must say I wish she hadn't, there was something about her touch that felt wonderfully inclusive.

'*Ja*, a vegetable-growing orphan . . . also fruit, ask me anything you like about a cabbage, carrot, tomato, avocado pear, pawpaw, orange or granadilla!' I joked.

'Granadilla?'

'Passionfruit.'

She looked up at the arbour, thinking. 'Okay then, what's the Latin name for cabbage?' she challenged, giving me a cheeky grin.

I was well past the Cs in Meneer Van Niekerk's 'To thine own self be true' *Shorter Oxford English Dictionary*. '*Brassica oleracea*, but don't ask me about granadilla,' I laughed.

'Smart-arse!' she exclaimed, punching me playfully in the chest. Suddenly she looked serious, her blue eyes fixed directly on me, head tilted slightly to one side. 'Tom, the orphanage, it can't have been much fun, I know it's private, but will you —?'

'It wasn't too bad, I had a little dog, a fox terrier named Tinker, and a friend, a big Zulu named Mattress,' I heard myself interrupting her. Then, in the nick of time I caught myself. She was getting much too close for comfort. I rose from the garden seat, anticipating that Sam's next question to me would be about Tinker and Mattress. She was so gorgeous, open, ingenuous and spontaneous that I felt suddenly overwhelmed and emotionally cornered. I'd spent my life avoiding direct questions about myself. I was a world expert at parrying and deflecting intrusions into my past life. These days I relied upon hiding behind clever words and my seemingly laconic humour. 'Use words to defend yourself, Tom, clever, witty words, self-deprecating words, they are your new camouflage,' I said to myself. Sam simply ignored all the do-not-pass-beyond-this-point signs, oblivious of the minefields that might lie beyond. Now, suddenly no witty, parrying words would come, no clever jousting, only a clumsy and obvious scurrying for cover. 'You know, I've never seen coffee growing, Sam. Do you think we could go for a walk?' I asked.

Sam rose and glanced at her wristwatch. 'Sure, it's only three-thirty, I'll call the dogs and get a shotgun.' She saw my reaction. 'Sometimes if we're lucky there are guinea fowl,' she explained, then added, 'you have to hang them for four days until they're gamey, a bit whiffy. But then Wanjohi makes them into a wonderful casserole.'

But I knew that the prospect of finding guinea fowl scratching among the neat, weedless rows of coffee bushes wasn't why we were taking a shotgun along. I also knew that Sam Finger was someone I desperately wanted to get to know a whole heap better, even if I was finding her manner somewhat overpowering. Tom Fitzsaxby, the world-famous camouflage expert, was head over heels in love and taking a right belting from a slip of a girl who, seemingly, had never had anything in her life she wished to hide from the world.

'I haven't forgotten about Tinker and Mattress – was that *really* your friend's name?' Sam said, clearly warning me that I hadn't won, that she hadn't forgotten what I'd revealed to her in an unguarded moment. Then, like a schoolgirl, she skipped away across the lawn towards the house to fetch the twin-barrel twelve-bore from the locked cabinet in her father's study.

In the weeks that followed I would use every leave pass I could cajole, beg or connive to obtain in order to get down to see Sam at Makindi. Being with Sam Finger was like waking up to a sun-splashed morning after a wild stormy night, which, I know, is a pretty corny analogy, but there you go . . . everything was suddenly washed clean. Happiness, when you achieve it, is not a complicated emotion. But, then again, keeping one's life simple seems to be about the hardest task there is for humans to achieve, and happiness has simplicity as a major ingredient. Sam had definitely perfected the art of simplicity and loving, a process that required a lot of spontaneous laughter without the need for her to forgo her natural curiosity, strength and intelligence. I can tell you one thing was for sure, I was a goner – hook, line and sinker, finish and *klaar*.

Each time we met we would talk about the emergency but in a quite specific way. Sam had the knack of getting me to talk about my secondment to the Kenya Regiment and what had happened between visits to Makindi. She didn't believe in burying things, and she was aware that I was, almost on a daily basis, exposed to the interrogation of captured prisoners or suspected Mau Mau. I'd also undergone a training course in the methods of the pseudo gangs which, like Mike, I had found a pretty harrowing experience. In this case I had been prevented from talking to her as the pseudo gangster training was considered classified material. She'd wait until we were blissfully on our own, then smiling, big blue eyes fixed on me, head tilted slightly to one side, she'd demand, 'Out with it, Tom Fitzsaxby.'

'What?' I'd reply, knowing exactly what she required from me, and also aware that any obfuscation would not be tolerated.

'All the awful stuff that's going to fester if you leave it inside,' she'd say. I was never conscious that she did this for vicarious reasons. Sam was constantly exposed to the rhetoric of Mau Mau where the whites were never at fault. Like her brother, Mike, she was Kenyan-born and raised by a Kikuyu nanny, and they spent much of their childhood among tribal children, farm workers and house servants. Unlike her English settler parents, Jock Finger, small-time coffee farmer constantly preoccupied with coffee prices on the world market, and Bobby, a tennis-champion mother, who were away from home most afternoons when the children returned from school, Sam could understand both sides without being an apologist for either. While her parents' attitude to the blacks, like that of most whites in Kenya, was patronising, paternalistic and muted by a great sense of racial superiority, Sam didn't have a racist bone in her body. She actively craved a peaceful Kenya where everyone received the same opportunities and prospered equally according to their ability and efforts. In this desire she was probably an impossible dreamer. In Africa the downtrodden, cheated, beaten and enslaved are always the majority.

The week Sam and I finally consummated our love for each other began in much the same way, with Sam wanting me to talk about the past week so that we could then get on with the simple and lovely business of just being in love. We'd driven to a favourite spot known as *Ol Donyo Sabuk*, a small mountain overlooking rolling green plains. Sam had chosen a place for our picnic, below several small waterfalls. She'd spread a blanket some way away so that we could hear ourselves talk. Sam, if she had any faults, loved to talk. But then, it seems to me most women do. They seem able to talk about their feelings and anxieties with perfect strangers of their own sex and resolve them in concert, so to speak. I wasn't one of your great natural-born talkers, more a listener and lately a sometime witty replier (if that's a word), but definitely not given to spontaneous pronouncements or to exposing my emotions. Camouflage works two ways, with lots of words or very few. I guess, right from the beginning, not a lot of talking was expected from me. Until I went to boarding school in Johannesburg, the longest conversations I'd been involved in were directed to a constantly wagging tail and a pair of pricked-up ears and a Zulu with great big platform feet. Tinker and Mattress were both very good listeners. Then, of course, there was Gawie Grobler at the big rock, discussing shit-square news and the various viewpoints of his mythical uncle in Pretoria. Sergeant Van

Niekerk and Marie were also sometime conversation partners, they were the two grown-up people who didn't involve me listening to a diatribe that would result in fresh Chinese writing on my bum. Except for Tinker and Mattress, the others usually did most of the talking. Gawie in particular was a natural-born talker, so that it had come as no surprise to me that he'd studied law at Stellenbosch University. I felt sure that some day he'd become a famous lawyer.

I prepared myself to talk with Sam about the week I'd just experienced, although in my mind it wasn't all that different to the one preceding it. After a while you harden up, you can take more and force yourself to think about it less. Sam, by demanding my weekly verbal expurgation, was untying the knot that ties and binds so tightly around the neck of that invisible bag in which you deposit your conscience, when you become adjusted to what is basically unjustifiable and immoral.

'Sam, what can I say? The screening and interrogation is constant and the system so terribly unfair. Tens of thousands of young Kikuyu men from the slums of Nairobi are being arrested. They are herded into temporary barbed-wire enclosures like beasts, the military and police using rifle butts and *sjamboks*. There they face the *gikunia*.'

'*Gikunia*, that means a hooded man?' Sam said.

'*Ja*, that's it exactly. Each of the arrested men passes by a dozen or so hooded Africans standing at the entrance to this barbed-wire corral, that is, people with full-length cotton sacks over their heads and bodies with eye holes cut out of them. The hooded man or woman is purported to be a loyal Kikuyu who simply shakes or nods his or her head when an arrested man passes. A nod and he is handed a red card, a shake, white. Red means he's a Mau Mau and white, clean. Red means Langata Prison Camp for interrogation, ill-treatment and torture, white means he's sent to the Kikuyu reserve to basically starve. It's as arbitrary as that! How can that possibly be just? The *gikunia* are forced to come up with a decent quota of victims or else they are thought to be Mau Mau themselves.'

Sam nodded. 'Operation Anvil, everyone's saying how successful it is.' She sighed, then added softly, 'Cry, *the Beloved Country*,' quoting the title of Alan Paton's famous South African novel.

'It's the scale of the operation. Effectively Anvil has rounded up 50000 men, women and children living in the slums of Nairobi, 20000 of whom have been given red cards and despatched to Langata, the other 30000 sent to the hopelessly overcrowded reserves, their homes ransacked and their lives completely destroyed.'

'How can the authorities process 20000 suspects?' Sam asked, incredulous.

'Well, of course they can't!' I shouted indignantly. 'White officers simply go by appearance, if a man looks "suspicious", you know, the way he stands, the whites of his eyes, his demeanour, a sideways glance, anything, he is branded Mau Mau. Based on the assumption that more than half the Kikuyu have taken the Mau Mau oath they must, by definition, get some of it right. But it's not moral and it's not just! Arbitrary justice was last practised by the Nazi SS in Poland and Russia and the British fought a war to eliminate it!' I was getting very worked up. I forced myself to calm down and went on to explain to Sam that because my army brief said that I was a lawyer on secondment I was permitted to witness one of the last mass trials where the prisoners were all said to be confessed guerillas.

'There was no defence lawyer present other than a policeman and an army officer who read out the indictments,' I explained. 'No formal plea was entered on behalf of the prisoners. It seemed to me any pretence of a properly conducted trial had been abandoned. The hanging judge, unable to pronounce the difficult African names, allowed the black clerk to read them out. He didn't even gavel each name and make the hanging pronouncement. He waited until they'd all been called out, whereupon he simply slammed his gavel down and condemned them all forthwith to be hanged by the neck until dead . . . at the public gallows! Then he announced an adjournment for lunch.'

'Oh, Tom, how awful,' Sam said quietly, looking down at her hands resting in her lap.

But I hadn't finished. 'Sam, do you realise that in the last three years more than 1000 Kikuyu have been publicly hanged? In the entire history of the British Empire there have never been this number of civil executions performed in public!'

Sam suddenly burst into tears. 'Oh, Tom, what shall we all become?' she wept. 'I am so ashamed, so terribly, terribly ashamed!'

I took her in my arms. 'Sam! Darling, darling Sam, I really shouldn't talk to you about these matters. I apologise, I *really* do, it isn't fair.'

Sam pulled away from me. 'Oh, Tom, but you must! You can't keep all this awful stuff to yourself. It's turned my brother into a sad and ashamed person. He used to be such a happy one. I know he'll never be the same again!' Tears streamed from her wonderful blue eyes and down her freckled cheeks. 'Tom, I simply couldn't bear it if the sadness happened to you,' she sobbed.

I reached out for her. 'Come here, silly,' I said, trying hard to smile. 'How can I ever become unhappy with you in my life?' I kissed her on the forehead and then drew her head to my chest. How could I tell this lovely creature that the sadness had first come to me at the age of seven when my friend Mattress was murdered and it had never left me even for one day?

Seated on the picnic rug I held Sam, rocking her gently as if she were a distressed child. After a while she drew away from me and knuckled the tears from her eyes and rose and walked towards the highest of the waterfalls. I watched as she stood facing me, standing within the misted spray, her head raised into it, the sunlight, fractured by the falling water, forming a rainbow above her head. Her light summer dress was soon soaked, showing her lovely figure through the wet cotton. It was if she was cleansing herself, washing away the shame she felt for this lovely country. She lifted her arms and turning slightly she drew her wet hair away from her face and I saw the gorgeous curve of her breasts. Then she walked back and stood over me. 'Tom, please make love to me,' she said.

'Next to the waterfall,' I said softly. Taking her hand I led her back to the misty spray where the rainbow colours danced. We undressed and there, on the moss-covered bank of the pool where the white water crashed, Sam Finger and Tom Fitzsaxby made love.

I'm not much good at writing about such things. The words used to describe the loving of two people always seem so weary from overuse, so worn-out. I suppose I was an experienced lover and Sam, as she later confessed, a first-timer, but while making love may be a process that improves with practice, loving is not like that, it doesn't need a descriptive narrative punctuated with random adjectives. It becomes time suspended, a void into which you both plunge and where you hope you will remain blissfully together, forever. It is simply every meaning of the words loveliness and togetherness. Every gasp, every moan, every wonderful movement of Sam's gorgeous body . . . See what happens when you try to use words!

Pirrou taught me that most women don't experience orgasm during the process of making conventional love. And so I suppose I had been pretty well tutored to do what was required by a sexually demanding and sophisticated woman. Of course, I was an eager pupil and I guess I must have become a reasonably practised lover. Pirrou and, in particular, La Piroutte, always gave a commanding performance and expected nothing less from her partner. 'No came, no gain!' she'd sometimes laughingly quip.

However, nothing of the sort happened when Sam and I made love that first time. I know she climaxed twice, but it wasn't because I was the so-called 'practised lover performing my masculine magic on her tender young virgin body', nothing could have been further from the truth. I suppose we could have made love in the weeks before the waterfall. I certainly wanted to and constantly dreamed about doing so. I felt sure Sam would have agreed if I'd asked her, but here again the words of the ever clear-eyed Pirrou returned to me. 'Tom, the first time a virgin makes love to a man she is almost always disappointed. This is mostly because he has been pestering her for weeks, the bulge in his trousers dictating his every waking thought. In the end she usually relents, afraid that she may lose him if she doesn't. The first time for a woman should always be because she is truly in love and can think of nothing except wanting to release the bulge and possess and ravish her lover.'

Pirrou, as she usually was in matters amorous, proved correct. I don't believe I brought very much skill or experience with me into the act of loving Sam that first time. I just needed and wanted her so very much, and she me, that the loving took care of itself, a wholly overwhelming and wonderful thing, climaxing simultaneously. Afterwards we were entwined around each other, lying in the sun with our clothes spread out on a rock to dry. I couldn't take my eyes off her happy face. Every part of her neat body felt so very beautiful. 'Will you marry me, darling?' I asked.

She didn't answer at first. Slowly unclasping herself, then rolling a foot or so away, she raised herself onto her elbow, her head resting on her hand. 'Yes, but only after I've completed my horticulture degree. Then you'll have to buy a farm where I can grow *Brassica oleracea* and *Passiflora edulis* and we'll breed thoroughbred horses.'

'Cabbages and passionfruit, you and me, Fitzcabbage and Passionfinger,' I said. Then, trying to be too clever by half, I added, 'I guess you'll be the nag and I'll be the stud.'

'Passionfinger! Why, that's very rude, Tom!' she scolded, her eyes laughing. The warm afternoon sun and her gorgeous body stretched out in front of me did the rest. 'Hmm, I see!' she exclaimed, her blue eyes growing wide in a pretence of shock. 'Onto your back at once, Fitzsaxby,' she commanded.

I rolled onto my back and Sam mounted me. 'I assume you're a novice at all this?' I said happily.

Guiding me gently, Sam grinned. 'I'll have you know I've been riding since I was five.' She gave an ecstatic little shake of her pretty shoulders as all of me entered her. 'But you're my very first thoroughbred, darling,' she gasped, then lifting and lowering, she looked down at me. 'Beautiful saddle!' she said, settling into a perfect trotting rhythm.

So much for all my careful training! Though, I must say, I think both Pirrou and La Pirouette would have approved of Sam's riding technique and the commanding performance that followed.

Upon my return to Embu Barracks late on Sunday evening there was a message from Colonel Peterson for me to report to him at eleven hundred hours the following morning. We'd met on several occasions in the officers' mess, but always as commanding officer and junior subaltern, a nod of the head or a crisp greeting was the extent of the contact. I'd once shared his mess table, a common formality, though one where the junior officer was expected to answer when questioned, otherwise remaining silent. On that occasion, other than enquiring whether I was enjoying my secondment to the Kenya Regiment, no other direct conversation transpired between us and I ate my dinner in silence, grateful that I wasn't required to make any contribution to the conversation. Although I was good at conjuring up reasonably perspicacious questions and at fudging interest, with Mike's background brief, I might have found speaking to Peterson an awkward process. I should add that Peterson was a popular commanding officer and the other officers, mostly Kenyan-born or postwar settlers, seemed to enjoy and respect his company greatly.

At eleven hundred hours exactly Colonel Peterson's desk sergeant ushered me into his office. Upon entry I saluted and removed my cap.

'Sit, Fitzsaxby,' Peterson commanded, not looking up from the paperwork on his desk or returning my salute, indicating to me that our meeting was to be relatively informal.

I sat on one of the two bamboo wicker chairs in front of his desk and placed my cap on my lap and crossed my legs in an attempt to appear at ease. After signing the bottom of the typed page he'd been reading he put down his fountain pen and looked up at me. 'Good morning, Fitzsaxby, glad you could come,' he said, smiling briefly.

'Good morning, Sir.'

'I'm afraid that I haven't had time to review the progress of your secondment, but Captain Miles says you're making a good fist of it. I see you're a lawyer and have a Rhodes scholarship. Good for you, Rhodesian-born?' All of this was said in a peremptory manner. Peterson was obviously a man who cut to the thrust.

'No, Sir, South African.'

'Good. Then I'll get on with the reason why you're here. We want you to command a pseudo gang, a week's patrol on Mount Kenya; I believe you've already received instruction on harassment techniques. The Kikuyu in your gang are highly experienced and reliable, they're originally from the Aberdares, so they don't owe their loyalty to the Mount Kenya terrorists. They've been out on the mountain on two separate occasions so you'll be quite safe, though it's always a good idea to be on your guard.' He smiled. 'I don't suppose you'll enjoy the exercise much. That's all, do you have any questions?'

'Yes, Sir, when will this be?'

'Well, right away, you leave at fifteen hundred hours. I know it's short notice but Lieutenant Barnett has come down with glandular fever and his patrol is already scheduled for this afternoon. It will mess things up if you're not in your precise location by nightfall. You'll be briefed on your coordinates immediately when you leave my office. See Sergeant Pike as you leave.' I rose and replaced my cap, came to attention, saluted and turned towards the door. 'Oh, Fitzsaxby, by the way, this is a covert operation, no phone calls. I'm told you spend some time with Mike Finger's family at Makindi?'

'Yes, Sir, Mike Finger and I are friends. May I make a phone call to Makindi without mentioning the patrol?' I asked, then added, 'I customarily do so every night. It would be a concern for the party at the other end if I missed calling for a week.'

Chris Peterson smiled briefly. 'Certainly, you're a lucky man, Fitzsaxby, Sam Finger is an absolute cracker.'

I could feel myself blushing. 'Thank you, Sir, I consider myself most fortunate.'

I dialled Sam's number and Wanjohi the cook answered and explained that Miss Sam wasn't home and *Memsahib* Bobby was at tennis.

'Will you tell Miss Sam I will call in one week, Wanjohi?' I told him.

There was a moment's hesitation. 'You not call every night, *Bwana* Tom?' he asked, sounding confused.

I had forgotten that the Finger servants, in fact most Kenyan household servants, were proverbial stickybeaks and knew most of their white family's business, or so Sam assured me. My nightly calls would be a feature of gossip between their two African maids, Christine and Wanjika, and no doubt among the males as well. 'No, Wanjohi, *not* this week, I will call Miss Sam in *one* week, do you understand?'

'*Ndio, Bwana*, you will call one week. I myself will tell Miss Sam.' He hung up abruptly.

I knew that Sam would phone Mike and want to know what was going on and why I couldn't call for a week. Mike was in Nyeri on army business and I didn't know how to get hold of him, but I guessed he'd be able to work out what might have happened and put Sam's mind at rest. 'He has to attend a special course' is what he would in all likelihood say to reassure her.

The briefing was simple enough. I was given the coordinates for the week and my entry and exit point. We would need to cover five miles a day no matter what, a big ask. Five miles through the bamboo and undergrowth was no simple achievement. The point being that several gangs were operating within the mountainside forest, if we should fail to maintain our coordinates we might well find ourselves within the sweep of another pseudo gang. In the semi-dark of the undergrowth, the mist and rain, this might result in each of us mounting an attack on the other.

'You may come across rhino or even buffalo, and sometimes they'll charge, but do not under any circumstances give away your position by firing at them,' said the briefing officer, Captain Broon, looking directly at me. Of course I'd fire if my life was at risk, what was really being said was that if one of my pseudo gang was endangered he would have to take his chances with the rhino or enraged buffalo with only his *panga* to protect him. In other words, I was not to interfere.

I indicated the Patchett submachine gun I was expected to carry. 'May I leave my revolver behind?' I asked Broon. 'This and my pack are pretty heavy, I'd rather not carry the extra weight.'

'Sorry, old chap, tradition. A British army officer is never without his revolver while on active duty. When you come out of the forest you'll have a ten-mile walk to the rendezvous point where the truck will be waiting. You have permission, once you're clear of the forest, to smash your Patchett, but if you arrive back without your revolver, mark my words, you'll be in serious trouble. Righto, time to grease up,' Broon instructed, 'you're pulling out in an hour.'

What greasing up involved was taking a shower without soap so your skin and hair contained no residue of artificial perfume. In addition your mouth had to be thoroughly rinsed to remove any smell of toothpaste and you had to chew an aromatic twig that was readily found on the slopes of Mount Kenya. After this my arms, face and legs were blackened and my entire body was smeared with the same repulsive-smelling animal fat used by the pseudo gangs. Living in the forests the Mau Mau had developed an acute sense of smell and they could sniff the whereabouts of a European long before they sighted him. I wouldn't wash again until I returned to barracks in seven days and, meanwhile, I would brush my teeth by chewing the end of a green twig and using it as a toothbrush. After greasing and blacking up I was given a filthy shirt and a pair of shorts in disrepair and a repulsive dreadlocked wig to wear. After all this there was still no chance of my ever being mistaken for a terrorist; from my blackened face framed by the absurd wig peered a set of decidedly blue eyes.

The next seven days were not going to be easy, I spoke only a few basic words of Swahili and my so-called pseudo-terrorist gang spoke no English. My most efficient form of instruction was my submachine gun. Quite frankly, I was shitting myself. It was *Voetsek* back at The Boys Farm calculating the daily odds of staying alive and not liking my chances one little bit.

I'd long since learned that it was pointless to feel sorry for yourself, but I couldn't help wondering what I might have done to deserve this. I even speculated that it was Colonel Peterson's way of getting at Mike through me. There was certainly no love lost between the two of them. He knew, I reasoned, that I'd been visiting Makindi and why. In Bobby's tennis terms, it was game, set and match to the Colonel.

But there you go. This sort of speculation usually gets one nowhere. Commonsense and any sense of fairness told me that I'd replaced Barnett at the last minute, which hardly seemed like a premeditated action on the commanding officer's part. Besides, I'd trained as a pseudo gangster so why wouldn't I be chosen to lead a gang? Anyway, I would never know and there was nothing I could do about it. Hatching a conspiracy theory wasn't going to help.

What I did know was that I was a man deeply in love, with everything I had ever wanted about to happen for me – a beautiful, generous-minded and loving woman who, miracles will never cease, loved me as much as I adored her. Now, out of the blue I'd been handed a gang of brainwashed terrorists wielding razor-sharp *pangas* and ordered to spend the next seven days and nights smelling like a badly neglected latrine, cutting my way through forest undergrowth and bamboo thickets on the slopes of Mount Kenya. I told myself that I was going to have to rely on a bunch of known killers while we hunted Mau Mau whom only weeks before they'd regarded as their comrades in arms. All the instant pardons and promises of land grants Colonel Peterson had made to them, as well as his assurances that my gang was completely reliable, counted for nothing in my febrile imagination. Tom Fitzsaxby, sitting on the passenger side in the front seat of a Bedford army truck heading for Mount Kenya, was a very reluctant and frightened pseudo-gang leader.

Mike Finger had already explained the topography of the forest to me, but as we plunged into its mist-smudged darkness at first light, after camping on the outskirts the previous night, I wondered how I would possibly endure the conditions for the next seven days. The mist and the undergrowth restricted my vision to no more than 20 feet for most of the time. After an hour my ragged clothes were blackened with sweat and I was alternately hot and cold as freezing, intermittent rain soaked through to my skin.

I confess to my misery, while better men than me might have embraced the primal magnificence of the ancient forest, all I could think was that in the stygian environment the old man's beard hung from the branches of the taller trees like the tattered banners of doom. The very idea of being ambushed by Mau Mau or even charged by an angry rhino or errant buffalo filled me with the utmost dread. I knew I would be exhausted by the day's end. How was I to sleep knowing that sprawled around me was a gang of cutthroats ready to deliver me to their terrorist brothers, my bloody corpse disembowelled and offered as a sacrifice to their true god Ngai before being eaten as *muti* to make them prevail? It was complete nonsense, of course, it was simply a part of the British propaganda that the Mau Mau were accused of being cannibals, but my imagination was nevertheless running the full gamut of possible primitive savage behaviour. It was during the course of that first day that I discovered the bravado so redolent among the men in the officers' mess of the Kenya Regiment was entirely missing in my personality; I was, by nature, an abject coward.

That night I decided I would sleep sitting with my back against a tree with the safety catch of my submachine gun on my lap released. I had made the members of my gang clear the ground for 20 feet in front of me. I then had them build a wall of twigs and leaves 6 feet from me, completely surrounding the tree and too wide for a man to step over. This was so that any member of the gang attempting to approach me during the night would cause me to wake with the single snap of a broken twig and I'd let him have a burst of machine-gun fire in the guts. I opened a box of dry rations from my pack and started to eat. I must have fallen asleep halfway through my dinner because the next thing I felt was a hand gently shaking me. In the dawn light I opened my eyes to see a member of the gang standing over me and smiling. '*Jambo, Bwana,*' he said politely as he handed me back my submachine gun.

The six days that followed count among the more miserable of my life, although, apart from cutting through enough bamboo to build a Chinese village, we encountered no resistance or, for that matter, charging animals other than a troop of jabbering and indignant monkeys. Either the Mau Mau heard us coming and decided to move on or I was fortunate enough to enter a clean part of the forest. I was totally exhausted when we emerged just before four o'clock on the Tuesday, seven days after we'd entered.

It was then, for the first time, that I realised the stress my gang had been under. They too had been afraid and now whooped for joy, slapping each other on the back and hugging, every bit as happy as I was to be clear of the dark and dangerous forest. One of them, who I'd discovered spoke a smidgin of English, indicated that they wanted to go ahead to the waiting truck six miles off. I agreed, marvelling that they still had the energy to run as they moved down the lower slopes of the mountain shouting joyfully, determined to get as far away from the dreaded mountain forest as quickly as possible. Chris Peterson had been correct, they wanted no more of life as a Mau Mau terrorist. Their conversion, whatever had brought it about, was complete.

I destroyed my Patchett submachine gun, smashing it repeatedly against a large rock until it was beyond any thought of repair. If this seems like wanton destruction, let me add that I barely had the energy required to walk the two-and-a-bit hours to the rendezvous point; carrying it now I was free of the forest would have been quite beyond me.

Finally, I removed the itchy and repulsive dreadlocked wig and shoved it under an overhanging rock, then rested for a few minutes before setting off. I had to get to the waiting truck before dark, at around half past six, which was a steady enough march. As I set off the feeling of relief at leaving the forest was palpable. In the open, with the afternoon sunlight drying my clothes, I felt a lightness of spirit and even a sense of optimism. I'd persisted, survived and come out of the other side intact and the adorable Sam would be waiting for me at Makindi. I would be given three days' leave, and I smiled to myself as I imagined our reunion. I glanced back one last time at the monstrously magnificent mountain with its summit shrouded in roiling cumulus cloud. I have come back from the mountain, I said to myself. We have been through a mighty smiting of love and hate and this land cannot defeat us, our loving will prevail. I was sounding like the *Dominee*, but for once the biblical phrasing didn't sound pretentious to my ear.

I had been walking for half an hour or so and, as if as a reward, I came to a stream where a small rivulet from the great mountain flowed clean and pure. On either side of what appeared to be a crossing, bulrushes grew, the stream flowed free for thirty or so feet and then disappeared into them again. I couldn't see the customary pebbles and rocks redolent of any mountain stream, so I surmised the crossing to be quite deep. I didn't hesitate and waded in the gloriously cleansing water that quickly rose to my knees and then to my waist and continued to the start of my chest before I finally reached what seemed like the deepest part. I took a deep breath and sank down until the water covered my head, allowing the coolness to soak my clothes and cover my entire body, then rising slowly I brushed the sudden cleanness from my face and hair and began to wade out of the stream.

Then, to my complete shock, from the bulrushes emerged a Mau Mau terrorist screaming at me, a *panga* raised above his head. His knees kicked high as he splashed through the water. He kept coming towards me, and then I noticed her breasts, it was a woman terrorist coming to kill me. I had nowhere to retreat, the water was well above my waist with the deeper water behind me. I saw the great blade coming down towards my head, when her head simply exploded – blood, bone and brains splattering my face and shoulders as the force of the bullet from my revolver fired at point-blank range knocked her backwards into the stream, which had suddenly turned crimson around me. I looked in astonishment at the weapon I held in my hand. To my dying day I shall never know how it got there. I must have reached into the water, unclipped the holster flap and pulled my service revolver from it, then fired it inches from her face, no more than a couple of seconds before the *panga* would have removed my own head.

I stood alternatively howling and gasping for breath, unable to move, mesmerised by the blood in the water. Then, bug-eyed and semiparalysed, I watched as it dissipated, ribbons of scarlet curling among the green stems of the rushes, the water beginning, miraculously, to clear directly above where the woman lay. After a while, quite how long I can't say, perhaps five or six minutes, I began to move out of the stream, wading slightly upstream to avoid the headless body lying in some four feet of clear, clean water.

As I emerged from the shallows, my conscious mind seemed to return. I still held the revolver and I now returned it slowly to the wet leather holster. For a moment I contemplated pulling the Mau Mau woman's body from the stream, then realised if I did so the hyenas would devour her long before morning's light. Perhaps her comrades would find her and remove her body and bury it under one of the sacred wild fig trees that grew on the slopes of the great mountain, where the Kikuyu would sometimes go to pray to their true and great god, Ngai.

No, that's not entirely true, this somewhat poetic thought only just occurred to me. My immediate instinct was to get away from the crossing as quickly as my shaking knees could carry me in the event other Mau Mau were in the vicinity. The dead woman had obviously hidden in the rushes as my gang had passed through the stream and finally, thinking it safe, emerged just as I'd entered the stream. Seeing my blond hair and possibly my blue eyes she'd attacked, thinking I was helpless. Before leaving I returned briefly to the water, now clear and clean, and hurriedly splashed the gore from my face and hair, although the front of my shirt and even my shorts remained stained with blood.

I simply don't remember arriving at the rendezvous point or much about the trip home. Upon arriving back at the barracks, Sergeant Pike was waiting for me. He returned my salute. 'Jesus! What happened to you?' he exclaimed, looking at my bloodstained clothes.

'I'd better make a report,' I said, the full horror of what had happened suddenly returning to me.

'The commanding officer is waiting for you, Sir. I'll see you get a stiff brandy. Follow me, please.'

'I need to clean up first,' I said, looking down at my chest where the blood had dried and stiffened the material.

'I'm afraid that will have to wait, Sir. The colonel is most anxious to see you immediately.' I followed Pike to the CO's office. It was just after eight-thirty at night and I was almost too tired to stand. In my ragged, bloodstained clothes, no socks and battered boots, I must have made a strange sight as I came somewhat to attention and gave Peterson a weary salute. He didn't seem to notice either my salute or my bloodstained clothes. 'Ah, Tom!' he called, and jumping up from his desk walked towards me, taking me by the elbow. 'Sit, Tom,' he said in a surprisingly kind voice, steering me towards one of the wicker chairs.

'Thank you, Sir,' I replied, somewhat bemused, not understanding his sudden concern for my welfare. I reasoned that no message could possibly have been sent through to Embu base camp, as the truck in which we'd just returned hadn't carried a radio. Besides, a single Mau Mau kill was hardly worth a handshake from the CO. What then, I asked myself, was all the fuss about? All I could think about was making a phone call to Sam, though how I would manage to do this without breaking up hadn't yet occurred to me.

I sat waiting wearily as Peterson returned to his desk. There was a moment's hesitation and then he said, 'Tom, I have very sad news for you. Last night Mau Mau attacked Makindi and Sam and Bobby Finger have been murdered, together with all their Kikuyu servants and the dogs. Sam died clutching a shotgun. She'd killed five terrorists, three lay in the room beside her, one of them was their old cook who, it would appear, poisoned the dogs and let the Mau Mau into the homestead.' He glanced up at me. 'Christ! What happened to you?' he asked in alarm. Just then Sergeant Pike arrived with a tray upon which rested two brandy balloons.

CHAPTER TWENTY

Love is a Lonely Hunter

THE TWO YEARS AT Oxford passed somehow, mostly spent in the Bodleian
Law Library and the Bodleian Library of Commonwealth and African
Studies at Rhodes House where I buried my grief in law books. I felt sure
I would never recover from losing Sam. I spent the university vacations
alone, walking through various parts of Europe, and made very few
friends at Oxford where I was seen as a loner, always polite but seldom
engaged in any activity or discussion other than those involving my
studies. Towards the end of my second year I collapsed from malnutrition
and was taken to hospital where, on the third morning with a drip in
my arm, I finally came to my senses, although I was still so exhausted
the doctor insisted I spend two weeks in hospital. Tom Fitzsaxby was
beginning to recover from a devastating virus, a heartsickness named
grief, I had been powerless to control.

Up to the time of Sam's death, while life had held moments of
anxiety for me, I had never completely despaired. After Sam's murder,
a terrible darkness descended upon my soul, one that I was unable to
eclipse. This might have been because of some emotional weakness in
me, but it possessed me so completely that on more than one occasion,
just to stop the constant nightmares, I considered ending my life. Hardly
a week went by when I didn't wake up screaming from a recurring

dream. The Mau Mau woman was coming towards me, knees pumping, splashing through the stream. I stood, helpless in the chest-high water as the *panga* held above her head started to slice through the air, catching the late afternoon sun, about to split my skull open. Then, as I pulled the revolver trigger, the black woman's snarling face changed into Sam's and exploded, splattering me with her blood and brains.

There simply seemed to be no reason to continue except for a single word that always managed to wriggle through the darkness: 'Mattress'. I grew to hate its appearance and tried everything I knew to scrub it from my psyche. I told myself a thousand times that one murder on a dark night in Africa counted for nothing after what I'd witnessed in Kenya. I tried to convince myself that a single African's life was a mere drop in the ocean. So many had died and would continue to die on the Dark Continent that attempting to gain justice for a dead pig boy with platform feet was pointless.

At the wake held for Sam and Bobby Finger at the Thika Club, the worthlessness of an African's life had been demonstrated once again, not by wilful slaughter, but by sheer indifference. While the eulogies from friends continued into the late afternoon, I never once heard the three faithful servants, Githuka, the garden and odd-job man, and the two happy, always giggling maids, Christine and Wanjika, mentioned. They would have been well known to all those present, but now simply ceased to exist. By contrast, a friend of the Finger family, Jack Devine, a pompous and somewhat inebriated Englishman, a local sisal grower, after paying a sloppy and over-sentimental homage to the memory of Bobby and Sam, turned to Jock Finger to bemoan the loss of his three dogs. 'Such a terrible waste, hey, Jock? Excellent bitches, good ridgeback cross. You can replace a *Kuke*, but a good dog is hard to find. Wretched business all round, what.'

Jock Finger blamed himself for the death of his wife and daughter and had remained more or less drunk through the funeral service and the wake. Nothing Mike could do to comfort or sober him up helped. On the night of the murders Jock had been drinking at the club and towards midnight attempted to drive home. Three miles along the dirt road to Makindi he failed to navigate a sharpish bend and drove off the road and over a steep hump where the truck landed nose-first in a ditch on the other side. Too drunk to know if he was hurt, he fell asleep, waking in the early morning, bruised and battered, with a terrible hangover and a suspected broken arm. He managed to disentangle himself from the cabin of the truck and get back to the side of the road, where a lorry carrying road workers stopped and delivered him back into town, leaving him in the care of the cottage hospital. It was almost ten that morning when the first news of the murders reached him. Jock Finger had remained pretty well intoxicated ever since, so that an utterly distraught Mike, together with whatever help I could provide, tried to manage the tragedy and make the funeral arrangements. Devastated as I was at Sam's death, I attempted to comfort Mike, knowing that not only had he lost his mother and beloved sister, but the split between his father and himself was now beyond repair.

Three weeks later Jock Finger, still wearing a plaster cast, took his shotgun, the same one that Sam had used in the attempt to defend her mother and servants, entered his workshop and sawed fifteen inches off both barrels. He then loaded it with buckshot and walked some distance from the homestead, where he removed his dentures and put them into his shirt pocket. Bracing the gun butt firmly into the fork of a young Cape chestnut tree he placed the shortened barrels against his open mouth and pulled both triggers. Africa, the remorseless killer, had struck again.

Mike buried his father beside Bobby and Sam, and we attended yet another wake at the Thika Club. This time the wake turned into a disaster when Mike, somewhat pissed but still appearing to be in control, stood on the bandstand and delivered a speech. He told his father's assembled friends, among other gratuitous accusations, that it was they, the Kenyan whites and the iniquitous British administration headed up by 'that perverted bastard, Sir Evelyn bloody Baring', who were to blame for the Mau Mau uprising. The guests listened in astonishment for several minutes before Jack Devine, standing close to the bandstand, called out, 'I say, that's not cricket, old chap!' The guests began to murmur and Gladys the Man-eater shouted angrily, 'You're a bloody Mau Mau!' In a matter of moments the guests started chanting, 'Mau Mau! Mau Mau! Mau Mau!', pointing at Mike. With all pretension gone the rage and scorn they felt for him was apparent.

Gladys the Man-eater pushed her way through the crowd to reach the bandstand. She stepped up onto it, almost tripping in the process, although by some miracle not spilling the gin and tonic she held in her left hand. This she threw at Mike's face and followed it with a perfect tennis forehand. The flat of her right hand against his wet cheek sent Mike staggering backwards into the upright piano. The chanting stopped abruptly as everyone watched, delighted at the scene unfolding. Now Gladys the Man-eater moved close up to a surprised Mike. She was a tall, tanned, scrawny bottle-blonde with hair that fell untidily down to her shoulders, the centre parting showing dark at the roots. Swaying drunkenly, she jabbed her forefinger into Mike's chest. 'Even as a child you were a right little bastard, always playing with the filthy little nigger boys!' she shouted. Then she calmly placed the glass on top of the piano and turned to walk back to the cheering and clapping guests. Loving the sudden attention and with chin high, imperious over-powdered nose stuck in the air, she forgot the short step up to the bandstand. Stepping out into midair, arms flailing wildly, she plunged forward and crashed headfirst onto the corpulent Jack Devine, sending them both sprawling, spread-eagled on the dance floor.

In the confusion that followed I forced my way through the guests and up onto the bandstand where I took Mike by the arm. 'Ferchrissake, Mike! Come, let's get out of here,' I cried. 'These people are about to lynch you, man!'

With the guests crowding around the prostrated forms of Gladys the Man-eater and fat Jack Devine, we managed to reached the door safely. 'Quick, let's go!' I urged.

'No, wait!' Mike called. Turning to face the crowd, he yelled, 'Fuck you all!' Then he clenched his fist and raised his arm above his head and shouted, '*Uhuru!*'

Driving Mike back to Makindi, I started to laugh. 'Jesus! For a moment there I thought I was presiding over the demise of the last of the Fingers!'

Mike too began to laugh, the first time we'd laughed together in three weeks and four days. 'I guess my membership of the Thika Club is somewhat in jeopardy,' he grinned, sounding surprisingly sober. Then suddenly serious, he added, 'I grew up with those people, that sententious old fart Jake Devine is my godfather, ferchrissake. As for Gladys the Man-eater, she and Bobby were like sisters. Sam and I grew up thinking of her as some sort of surrogate aunt we were constantly forced to tolerate.' He gave a short laugh. 'She'd take off her tennis shoes in the lounge room and her feet always ponged to high heaven.'

'How did she get her carnivorous nickname?' I asked.

Mike laughed again. 'Blow jobs! She's famous in the district for them. Bobby gave it to her when some ten years ago she came across Gladys on her knees behind the tennis court pavilion pleasuring a standing Jock.'

'And she *forgave* her?' I asked, surprised.

Mike grinned. 'Of course! They were at school together in England. Gym frock always beats cock! But as I recall she gave Jock hell for months afterwards. Conjugal rights withdrawn until further notice, separate beds, that sort of malarky. She finally relented when Sam suggested to Jock that the next time they went to Nairobi, he book the Royal Suite at the Stanley, take Bobby to dinner and present her with a string of South Sea pearls. Sam, as usual, solved the problem.'

At the mention of Sam's name I started to choke up and drove on in silence for a while, trying to hold back my tears. Then, having regained my composure, I asked, 'Mike, have you thought about what you're going to do?'

Mike shook his head slowly. 'After that fiery little speech this afternoon I can safely carve the name Captain Michael Finger, in anticipation, on my tombstone. The army won't be giving me any further promotion and I'll be damned lucky not to be drummed out of the Kenya Regiment. Game, set and match to Chris Peterson.'

'I thought you were pissed; now I can see you're not. You gave that disastrous speech deliberately, didn't you, Mike?' I didn't wait for him to reply. 'I've bloody told you before, this is not a fight you can possibly win! It's obvious you were not brought up in an orphanage where you learn to bide your time, pick your target, strike fast, cover your arse and have a plausible alibi. You don't solve anything by making an appointment to see the bloody governor so you can give him a dressing-down. Or by accusing the white hierarchy in the district of being a bunch of lying, cheating, dishonest, exploiting, thieving, racist bastards. That, if I remember correctly, was only your opening sentence! Finishing off with "*Uhuru!*", the cry for freedom, now that was a *really* classy touch – that is, if you plan to be totally ostracised by the white community and, as you said yourself, drummed out of your regiment.'

Mike turned to look at me. 'Tom, I'm the last Finger. I don't have to shut up any longer simply because my views embarrass and compromise my mother and father or make things difficult for Sam, who, as you know, shared my views. What I said this afternoon is the truth and sooner or later the whites in Kenya *must* face the truth. These people are either in denial or stupid or both! My family lost their lives because of the cheating and lying, the duplicity and the racial arrogance of white Kenya. Gladys the Man-eater is correct, as a child I did play with the "little nigger boys". I regarded myself as one of them. I still do. I am not a *white* Kenyan, I am simply a *Kenyan*! I can't stand by and see my country torn limb from limb because white is always right. It isn't!' He brought his clenched fist down hard against his knee. 'It bloody *isn't*!' He was silent for a moment. 'Oh God,' he said softly, and then began to cry.

I stopped the car by the side of the road, shifted the gears into neutral and pulled on the handbrake. Then I grabbed Mike and pulled him towards me so that his head rested on my chest, my left arm holding him about the shoulders, my right hand cupping his head. And then I too began to weep. Mike wept for his family and his beloved country, and I because Africa had killed the woman I loved more than my own life and it had left me so cruelly to live.

After a while Mike moved away, and I pulled out the choke a fraction, pressed the starter button and we drove off. We were both silent for some time, recovering from our mutual blubbing session, when Mike said, 'I'll go into politics.'

'Sure, I can see all of white Kenya bumping and pushing each other aside to be the first to vote for you! Suggested slogan: "Let's give Kenya the Finger!"'

'Trade union official, black workers, that's where I'll start,' he said. 'In the meantime I'll grow coffee and marry a Kikuyu or an Indian woman.'

The sun was setting as we drove into the front gates of Makindi, the brilliant crimson flame tree blossoms blending into the scarlet and gold of the day's end. 'Well, I'm glad that's settled,' I replied dryly, then added somewhat sardonically, '*Of course*, you'll be having the wedding reception at the Thika Club with all the usual crowd present.'

Mike laughed. 'Mark my words, Tom Fitzsaxby, Kenya *will* change.'

'Yeah, but will Africa?' I asked.

I received a double first at Oxford, graduating in jurisprudence and African studies, and was encouraged to go further, with the university offering me a fellowship to Rhodes House. I thought about it, though not very seriously, as the wriggling word 'Mattress' simply refused to be scrubbed out of my psyche. I was going home to Africa where I had some unfinished business to attend to.

Curiously, the sea trip home from Southampton on the Union-Castle Line's *Bloemfontein Castle* proved to be the proverbial sea change I needed. The Suez Canal had reopened after the Suez crisis, but this one passenger vessel did the trip to Africa anticlockwise, my idea being to hitchhike from Cape Town back to Johannesburg and see my own country.

I fulfilled yet another ambition on my list of things to do one day. I'd always promised myself that I'd take dancing lessons at Arthur Murray Studios, and I was now able to do the next best thing. The ship had a dancing instructor, a vivacious older woman, who seemed to take a liking to me. She taught me the waltz and the foxtrot as well as the rumba and the tango, while several of the young women on board taught me how to jive and jitterbug, and were kind enough to invite me to limber up in their bunks. You'd have thought, wouldn't you, that I'd have learned to dance with Pirrou? But, as a professional dancer, she would never dance for recreation and so I'd missed out. With Sam my ineptness on the dance floor had never emerged; we'd both cherished the time we shared together and spent none of it at the Thika Club Saturday-night dance.

With the exercise on the dance floor and the good food on board, by the time I arrived in Cape Town I was fit, had gained weight and was returned somewhat to the old optimistic Tom Fitzsaxby. Imagine my surprise to find *Oom* Jannie, of the Steinway Baby Grand fame, and Hester, his wife, waiting to meet me at the docks.

I had written to him from England when the idea of hitchhiking from the Cape had occurred to me, mentioning the sailing date and day of arrival in Cape Town. I wrote to ask whether it would be convenient to call in on him. I'd received an airmail postcard with a picture of the BOAC Comet and one sentence in Afrikaans which when translated read: Come, please, Tom, you are always most welcome. Jan Odendaal.

Oom Jannie greeted me with a great bear hug. 'Ag, Tom, I said to Hester, no, man, this time he's not going to get away, we going to fetch him, hey!' Then holding me at arm's length, he declared, 'Now we not talking one night, you hear? We talking as long as you like and definitely more than one week!'

Before I could thank him, Hester chipped in. '*Ja*, Jannie is always talking about you, ever since he came back from the Transvaal with the pianos in the Rio.'

Oom Jannie released me and I turned towards her. '*Goeie môre*, Mevrou Odendaal,' I said, extending my hand.

She took my hand in both of hers. 'You must call me *Tante* Hester. It's really nice to meet you at long last, Tom.' *Oom* Jannie's wife was a big, handsome woman with steel-grey hair pulled back from her face, culminating in a bun at the back of her head. 'To have a piano in the house like that,' she paused and smiled at her husband, 'is to know somebody loves you a lot.'

'*Ag*, no, it was Tom's idea all the time,' *Oom* Jannie protested in an embarrassed voice.

I laughed, shaking my head in denial. '*Tante* Hester, let me give you *Oom* Jannie's exact words.' I pretended to think, although I had never forgotten them as they were quite the nicest expression of a man loving his wife I had ever been privileged to hear. '"You know, Tom, forty-three years is a lot of years and a lot of loving. Hester only asked me for one thing in all that time. When we got the first big wool cheque, only last year, the one when we became all-of-a-sudden rich, she said to me, 'Jannie, do you think now we can have an inside lavatory? I'm getting too old to go outside in the dark.' You can't pay enough for that kind of loving, Tom." Then he said he was going to buy you the Steinway,' I concluded.

Tante Hester stood there smiling, her eyes filled with sudden tears. 'Thank you for telling me, Tom,' she said quietly.

Oom Jannie was clearly embarrassed and, blustering somewhat, said quickly, 'You see, I told you, *ouvrou*, this boy is a whole dictionary, he never forgets words! When he told me why the shape of the pianos was so funny you should have heard him tell how the special sound it makes is made in Germany and it's called acoustics.'

'Look who never forgets now!' I laughed.

I had only one suitcase, mostly filled with books, and I followed my unexpected hosts to the parking lot. *Oom* Jannie, it seemed, had finally run the old Rio into the scrap heap and now drove a large Mack truck with multiple gears. They were both big people and so the front seat, the only seat, was pretty snug with the three of us.

'You know the floor polisher?' *Oom* Jannie said, as we got on our way.

'*Ja*, your *bonsella* from the pianos.'

'Let me tell you, Tom, Hester loves that machine, she doesn't let the *kaffir* women do the floor polishing, even old Martha, she won't let her, will you, *ouvrou*? Whoever heard of a *white* person polishing a floor, hey?'

'*Ag*, with a contraption like that a person doesn't have to even bend down, but you can't let modern machinery get into a servant's hands, they break everything right in front of your eyes,' *Tante* Hester declared.

'We lucky now we got electricity, it happened only last year,' *Oom* Jannie said.

'But you've had the floor polisher five years, even longer,' I said, not quite understanding. 'You mean you didn't have electricity until last year?'

'*Ag*, Tom, that time in that shop in Johannesburg, with the pianos, it was such a nice *pasella* I didn't have the heart to tell you.'

'And you just kept it, until now?'

'*Ja*, man, every week Hester polished the polisher,' he laughed.

Hester started to explain. 'Tom, in life a person mustn't get everything all at once, because then you can't appreciate it. First the lavatory inside the house. I can tell you, that is a very big blessing in a person's life. A person gets old and their inside doesn't always work at the right time. Then you must go outside to the *kleinhuisie* in the middle of the night, or maybe use a chamber-pot if it's only a number one. In the Karoo in winter it's icy-cold and dark and you nearly die to go outside if it's number two. So that's the first big blessing, now you got a lavatory right next to the kitchen and you just pull a chain and everything's gone, finish and *klaar*. It's a miracle from God, you hear? Then the piano, God gives you that for happiness and to praise His precious name and when the family comes to have a nice singsong, you can play all the old *boere musiek*. Now electricity all of a sudden comes right past the house, put in by the government for the abattoirs at Bakoondfontein. So now I have the floor polisher, and it's a big show-off, and in no time flat we got shining floors so you can see your face. Martha, who has been with us thirty years, she's getting old like me and now she doesn't have to do the polishing on her poor swollen knees.'

On the way to the Odendaal farm in the Karoo, a journey that took up most of the remainder of the day, the subject of *Skattebol*, *Oom* Jannie and *Tante* Hester's youngest daughter, who he'd once earmarked for me, came up. In fact, I brought it up myself, wanting to stack the decks early in case he still harboured the ambition of having me as his son-in-law. 'And what news of *Skattebol*?' I asked.

Oom Jannie turned to *Tante* Hester. 'You see, this one never forgets!' Then he glanced at me briefly before returning his eyes to the road. 'Ag, Tom, it's a sad story, but then again also a happy one, our *Skattebol* also did what Anna went and did. Remember?'

'Became pregnant out of wedlock?' I said, putting it as politely as I could.

'*Ja*, but this time, even worse, it happened with a *Rooinek*, a student from Cape Town University. He's a nice boy but he can't even speak Afrikaans. He's from London and is this architect out here studying Cape Dutch houses. Why does a man want to study old buildings, hey? They can't build them like in the olden days, it's just all this modern rubbish they going in for nowadays.' He seemed to be thinking, then said, 'The Odendaal family has been in this land a long time. *Skattebol* is the ninth generation and in the family Bible only one *Engelsman*.' *Oom* Jannie then quoted the words in the family tree in High Dutch, which, roughly translated, were, 'Samuel Thelonius Morris, Sea Captain, Cornwall, 1749, husband to Johanna Maria Odendaal, no issue'. 'That time we were lucky, the good Lord cut off that branch so we wouldn't suffer. We got an *Engelsman* who fired blanks! You'd think we should have learned our lesson the first time, hey? Now we gone and made the same mistake again.'

'What?' I asked, not understanding. 'I thought you said *Skattebol* was pregnant?'

'No, the baby is here already, a nice healthy child, thank the Lord,' *Tante* Hester said calmly.

'So what's the unhappy part?' I asked.

'This time the *Engelsman wasn't* firing blanks!'

We all laughed and then I asked, 'And the happy part?'

'Three happy parts. It's a boy child and they in love, two turtledoves *and* they married, so no disgrace. But the *Dominee* says, "No more shotgun weddings, Jannie. Two times is enough, God is not mocked, you hear!"' *Oom* Jannie chuckled. 'I told him, "That's orright, *Dominee*, all the bullets have been fired, I haven't got any more daughters."'

I spent two weeks with *Oom* Jannie and *Tante* Hester, and by the time I left these two dear and lovely people and met members of their family who came to visit, I felt thoroughly grounded. We'd spent the warm summer nights around the Steinway and I'd become re-acquainted with all the old *boere musiek* and songs. I was back home among a unique breed, Afrikaners, a people that were big-hearted, generous and loyal to a fault on the one hand, and narrow as a cut from a razorblade on the other.

Oom Jannie and *Tante* Hester exemplified all that is kind, loving and good in their people, yet it was readily apparent from the way they talked and behaved that they shared the Afrikaner racial antipathy towards the black people. This was despite the fact that they were paternalistic and caring to such old family retainers as Martha and several of the older men who worked on the sprawling Karoo sheep farm.

Three hundred years in Africa had turned them into the white tribe I had heard so often described from the pulpit by the *Dominee* in my childhood. Like all tribes, the *Volk* were more African in their ideas and attitudes than those they retained from distant European roots. The *laager* mentality and conquest that had won them their new tribal lands still existed. In their minds the ox wagons remained drawn in a tight circle against the black hordes and the God-given superiority and rights of the white man were to be defended at any cost. The concept of equal rights for all of the people of South Africa was anathema, as the doctrine of apartheid so stridently testified.

Of course, I knew all of this instinctively and it was just that I'd been away from it for a while, and it was different in its blatancy and openness to the rancorous and secret racism I'd experienced in Kenya. Britain's assumed right to expropriate the best land from the Kikuyu and give it to the whites, then to hold it at gunpoint and by murder, was disguised and explained by an elaborate exercise in obscurantism. They had devised a propaganda machine that pumped out high-quality mendacity to vindicate thousands of acts of institutional barbarism. The public hanging of over 1000 black men testified to this and was only one small example of it. They nevertheless continued to extol the virtues of decency, fair play, God, Queen and Empire, whereas the Afrikaner attitude, inexcusable as it was, was openly practised and vaingloriously defended.

Racism, wherever and however it occurs, is a repulsive, endemic and deeply atavistic human characteristic that appears to be present in most of humankind. Whether racism is openly practised or hidden, it is inexcusable. I felt that I had a better chance of obtaining justice for Mattress, a Zulu pig boy in South Africa than I would ever have for a Kikuyu goatherd in Kenya.

If, on the one hand, I found myself returning to my roots and the comfortable presence of *Oom* Jannie and *Tante* Hester, on the other my old ambivalence for the *Volk* returned. I had been with my host a week when late one afternoon, while enjoying a beer with him on the *stoep* of the homestead, the conversation inevitably turned to politics. What followed was not very different to all the other discussions I'd been involved in over the years. The blacks needed to be kept in their place, as they were growing much too cheeky for their own good. The African National Congress was a terrorist organisation and communist-inspired and should be hunted down and eliminated to the last member. The Nationalist Government policies were the right ones and the new *Bantustans* planned were a testament to this correct thinking and exemplified the principles of *baasskap*, leadership and the correctness of apartheid. The concept that the majority of the land rightly belonged to the white man as only he could keep it productive, and that sharing it equally with the *kaffirs* was as good as destroying it forever, was a notion I'd heard since the cradle. 'If you give baboons good land all you get back is soil erosion.' And so on, *ad infinitum*.

South African political views held by the majority of white people at that time, with a few notable and brave exceptions, were predictable and seldom polarised, even among the new Liberal Party that had opened its membership to all races and demanded equal rights for non-whites. But as usual there were qualifications and the old paternalism reared its ugly head. These so-called 'equal rights' would only be given to 'all civilised people', a neat cop-out that allowed the Liberals to have a bet each way. It was just that the Afrikaners were less subtle and more strident about expressing their racist views, while many so-called liberal whites sat wobbling on the political fence ready to fly off in whatever direction the wind blew.

Although, I don't suppose I could talk. I was back in my own country, which was on the verge of becoming a police state. I knew that I would soon be called on to make a stand. But I also knew that if I was to bring the Van Schalkwyk brothers and Mevrou to trial, a difficult enough task, I must steer well clear of the immediate taint of politics. I must be seen to be demanding *justice* for a humble farm worker and, at the same time, to be squeaky clean on the political front. In any other society my actions would not be questioned, but in South Africa, my ulterior and, in particular, political motive would be the cause of immediate speculation.

Listening to my host extolling the usual line of political cant, I decided that I couldn't continue to lend credence to *Oom* Jannie's blustering and bombastic jingoism, although I knew that I would achieve absolutely nothing by attempting to contradict the dogma *Oom* Jannie so vehemently proselytised. A *Boer* is by nature a stubborn creature but in politics he becomes intractable. I knew if I could bring the Mattress case to the High Court it would probably get national newspaper coverage, specifically in the Afrikaner press. So I decided to test the reaction to such a trial on my host. He was, after all, a salt-of-the-earth type, an Afrikaner to his bootstraps. *Oom* Jannie was, politically speaking, the Afrikaner equivalent of the English settler, of Jack Devine and Gladys the Man-eater of the Thika Club.

I waited for an appropriate time when the talk of politics seemed to have wound down. *Oom* Jannie sat quietly puffing on his *meerschaum*, looking out into the rapidly concluding sunset. 'Oom Jannie, I would like to ask your advice on a matter.'

The old man looked surprised. '*Jinne*, man, if it's about a woman don't bother, hey? No man understands what's going on in a woman's head. If it's about sheep, *that* I know. Also I know there's nothing going on in a sheep's head.'

I laughed. 'No, it's about being an Afrikaner, about the *Volk*. It's about bringing an attitude to peculiar subject matter.'

'Tom, I don't know about attitude to peculiar subject matter. You the educated one around here. I'm just a sheep farmer.'

'Oom Jannie, I want to tell you a long story. I'll try and make it as short as possible, but I'm warning you, it could go on for a while.'

'Then I better go get some more beer, hey?' He rose heavily, and with a sigh from his *riempie* chair, went into the house, returning with two large bottles of lager. 'Now we got electricity the beer is nice and cold for a change,' he said, smiling as he handed me one of the quart-sized bottles.

For the next hour I told him the story of The Boys Farm, of Mattress and Tinker, Pissy Vermaak, Fonnie du Preez, Mevrou, Frikkie Botha, Meneer Prinsloo, Sergeant Van Niekerk, and finally the murder of Mattress and how it had all occurred. I left out such details as the canned-fruit jar containing Mevrou's grisly brandy-pickled exhibit and Meneer Prinsloo's role as a paedophile. Then I told him about the sabotage attempt by Frikkie and the six Van Schalkwyk brothers in the *Stormjaers*, and the fact that they'd admitted to him that they'd murdered Mattress. I outlined how they'd planned to derail the train from Rhodesia and the subsequent explosion that had left Frikkie without a face and with a twisted and permanently broken body, and how the six brothers had left him to die under the railway culvert.

'I'm sorry to have been so longwinded,' I apologised, coming to the end of the story.

'No, man, you told it very good. You a born storyteller, Tom. What can I say? Such a terrible thing happening to you. I can hardly believe it.' He reached over and extended his hand and I shook it. 'Tom, from the first time I saw you I liked you. You a *ware Boer*.' Then suddenly growing misty-eyed, he added, 'I would be proud to have you as my son and Hester thinks the same.' He drained the last of his bottle of beer from his glass in an attempt to hide his emotion. '*Skattebol*, when she came the other day all the way from Cape Town to say hello to you, you could see she was sorry she didn't wait. *Ag*, I should have given her a blast of birdshot up the arse so then she couldn't lie on her back for that Cape Dutch *Rooinek*! But what can you do? These days children don't listen to their parents, they always know better.' His free hand flew up into the air. '*Boom*! Another shotgun wedding happens!'

'Thank you, *Oom* Jannie,' I laughed, handing him the bottle he'd given me, which was still two-thirds full. 'I would also be proud to *be* your son. But I must remind you, I'm *not* an Afrikaner . . . and that's where all the problems began.'

'If anyone tells you that you not a *ware Boer*, you tell them to come and see me, you hear?' He shook his head slowly and refilled his beer glass. 'How can somebody call a boy *Voetsek*?' *Oom* Jannie clucked his tongue. 'That's terrible, man!'

Oom Jannie was plainly feeling sorry for me but not quite knowing how to adequately express his feelings. Before he could sympathise any further and at the risk of sounding impolite, I said, 'Now, *Oom* Jannie, as an Afrikaner and a *boer*, I have to ask you an important question.'

'You the lawyer, Tom. Feel free, ask away,' he said, grateful to escape the prolonged task he may have felt sympathy for me demanded.

'That's just it, you see. I intend to bring the Van Schalkwyk brothers to trial for murder. Do you think this is the right and just thing to do?'

Oom Jannie looked momentarily puzzled. 'But they didn't kill him! He just lost his face in the explosion and they didn't make that explosion happen, he did that himself, an accident. No, man! No way, Tom! They *Stormjaers*, they *our* freedom fighters in the war, hit and run!' He drew a quick breath. 'Frikkie Botha took his chances, in war bad things happen.' He paused. 'But I admit they shouldn't have run away and left their comrade lying by the railway.'

'No, *Oom* Jannie, I meant Mattress, on The Boys Farm.'

'Who? Oh, the *kaffir* boy?' Then it dawned on *Oom* Jannie what I was suggesting. 'You want to do a murder trial for a black *kaffir*?' he asked, not quite believing his ears.

It had grown dark and the vast expanse of the Karoo sky was pinned with myriad stars, such a beautiful, beautiful firmament and such a totally fucked-up world below it.

I was fortunate enough to have been given the choice of joining several leading law firms. Pirrou, knowing I was returning to Johannesburg, had done her usual lobbying and when I arrived back at my Hillbrow flat I discovered half a dozen invitations from leading law firms suggesting that I come in to see them. Most of these were predictably Jewish with their practices heavily business-based or dealing predominantly with white-collar crime, whereas I wanted a firm that was mostly concerned with criminal law so, after attending every interview, I ended up refusing all the offers made to me.

Pirrou, probably prompted by her alter ego La Pirouette, was growing increasingly impatient and less than impressed that I seemed uninterested in the illustrious legal firms she'd worked so hard to influence. In a final effort to knock some sense into my head she convened a special dinner party, which included a judge of the Equity Court and a famous Johannesburg QC, Mervyn Rappaport. 'Tom, how you are perceived at the very beginning of your career will largely determine your future,' he advised me. 'People judge a young barrister as much by the name of the legal firm appearing on his letterhead as by his reputation. Besides, as a young advocate you won't *have* a reputation. Furthermore, you are unlikely to be briefed on any big cases from the confines of some unknown hole-in-the-wall legal firm.'

Rappaport's advice, of course, was absolutely correct, but I decided to ignore it and join the small, and by no means leading, Afrikaner law firm Kriegler, Cronje, Beyers, who specialised in criminal law. I was on a singular mission and wanted to establish a legal background for myself that couldn't lead to speculation that my case was politically motivated. By choosing an Afrikaner law firm I was also eliminating any accusation the Afrikaner press might take up by suggesting that the case wasn't truthfully about obtaining justice for the murder of a humble pig boy. Instead, they might assert that I was simply wreaking revenge on the Afrikaners, and Mevrou in particular, for the treatment I had received at their hands on The Boys Farm. I was also determined to conduct the trial in Afrikaans as this was the language spoken by most of my key witnesses and, of course, would be the language chosen by the defence.

Even though the Nationalist Party, predominantly representing the Afrikaner people, was in control of the country, they were totally paranoid that the world was against them and that liberal English-speaking South Africans were the internal enemy. A case such as the one I intended to bring against the Van Schalkwyks could easily be seen as a political attempt to show Afrikaners in a bad light and would definitely have a sinister political motive. The world was turning on South Africa, and in particular on the Afrikaners. The age-old racist division between the two groups of different-language-speaking white South Africans was being keenly exploited by the international media while, truthfully, the doctrine of apartheid had as many adherents who spoke English as it did among the *Volk*. Bellicose as the Nationalist Government appeared to be, they were nevertheless conscious of being made a pariah nation in the eyes of the world. The simple fact that I had been partly educated at Oxford would have been sufficient to send the Afrikaner press off on a witch-hunt, as it was a university that had often been referred to in the past as a hot-bed of communism.

The idea that six freedom fighters, for that is how the Van Schalkwyk brothers were seen by most Afrikaners, might be prosecuted for a murder of an unbelievably brutal and barbaric nature would have been anathema to the government in Pretoria. The Afrikaans press would immediately try to put a political spin on my motives, while the English-speaking newspapers couldn't be relied on to give unbiased reportage either. For instance, my attendance at Oxford would be given the obvious implication that my motives had nothing whatsoever to do with justice for an African peasant. Paradoxically, my stint against the Mau Mau would appear to be a contradiction to this almost certain accusation, and so was likely to be ignored.

In reading this, I sound somewhat paranoid. But as it turned out, all these precautions were well justified. I knew I would get only one shot at running the case and when the press, and possibly the Special Branch, came asking questions, to use an American baseball expression, I needed to have all my bases covered.

However, I am getting ahead of myself. My first task was to become a barrister or advocate, not an easy task for a neophyte lawyer. I also needed to earn an income and so was obliged to spend the next eighteen months as a lawyer learning my profession. But if I was to conduct the murder case myself, rather than act as a junior to a barrister, it was essential that I be appointed to the Bar. To achieve this I would need to be accepted by the Bar Council and while the quality of my degrees and the fact that I was of good character made this a possibility, my relative lack of experience in law suggested that achieving my aim might be very difficult indeed. The three senior partners in Kriegler, Cronje, Beyers were prepared to endorse me, but freely admitted that they had no contacts and influence or any capacity to lobby on my behalf among members of the Bar Council.

Cap in hand, I went back to Pirrou. Although we'd remained friends, she hadn't forgiven me for rejecting her efforts to get me into a decent law firm. She listened to me and then, somewhat purse-lipped, went into La Pirouette mode. In La Pirouette body language this was a flat refusal, she wasn't prepared to forgive me for allowing her to lose face among the *cognoscenti* of the Johannesburg Jewish law firms.

Thinking how I might overcome her antipathy, I decided to come clean. 'Pirrou, would you say I am someone who acts impetuously?' I asked.

'No, Tom, why do you think I threw you out of my bed?' She didn't wait for my answer but continued. 'You were technically the best lover I've ever had, but you were no Piccasso.' La Pirouette had lost none of her asinine expertise.

'You mean I'm not an original artist?' I said, parrying. 'I guess that's why I'm a lawyer – get all the essential details right and at the same time see the big picture, but don't get too emotionally involved with the client.'

'Not bad, you really *have* come along,' she said, an arched eyebrow almost touching her hairline.

'Pirrou, I want to confide in you, tell you a secret,' I began.

'Pirrou is not present, Tom. You'll have to tell it to La Pirouette,' she announced crisply, pulling back slightly and folding her arms over her small breasts.

'I can't, it's not a secret La Pirouette would be allowed to know.'

'You always were a clever little bastard!' she exclaimed. 'I taught you far too much about how a woman's mind works.'

I grinned. 'No, seriously, it's something I have never confided, never told anyone, except the farmer to whom I sold the three Steinways all those years ago, and then only recently on my return from Oxford and for a particular reason. It's something that up to this moment has driven my entire life, given purpose to everything I've ever done.' Throwing in the 'farmer and the three Steinways' caper I knew would be irresistible, even to La Pirouette.

La Pirouette, her curiosity suitably aroused, turned back into Pirrou. 'You'll have to take me to bed then. It's the only true confessional.'

'What about Marino the Supremo?' I said, surprised at the unexpected invitation, having on several occasions met her new, tall, tanned, good-looking and very attentive Italian handbag.

'Too much *nea* in the Neapolitan,' she exclaimed. 'I suspect he's a couple of generations South African with an Italian grandfather thrown in for good measure,' she said, grinning. 'Besides, it's not being unfaithful if it's done with an old faithful.' As always, Pirrou managed to condone her self-indulgence.

Afterwards in bed, where I must have performed adequately because there was no sign of La Pirouette's imminent return, I told Pirrou the story of Mattress's murder and of the railway explosion. This time I included the details I hadn't mentioned in the *Oom* Jannie version – Meneer Prinsloo's constant sexual assault on Pissy Vermaak and the contents of the canned-fruit jar.

'You poor darling, you've kept all this to yourself all these years. Oh, Tom, you are a strange one. Don't you realise that was quite a different world and that you don't live there anymore? You can't bring this Mattress back and nobody will have noticed his death, much less be affected by it.'

'Joe Louis and his mother would,' I replied.

'Joe Louis? Remind me, who was he again?'

'The son of Mattress, his Zulu name is Mokiti Malokoane,' I replied.

'Whom, by your own admission, you've never met?'

'Not yet, I have nothing to tell him or his mother.'

Pirrou leaned over and kissed me. 'Tom, my beautiful, beautiful, boy!' Then she drew back and sat up in bed looking down at me. 'Darling, you're a Rhodes scholar with a double first at Oxford. You can be anything you want. A brilliant barrister, chief justice if you want . . . you speak Afrikaans as fluently as the Prime Minister. You're going to throw it all away because of what happened to a black farm boy who looked after pigs when you were seven years old!' She shook her beautiful dark head, her lovely green eyes plainly confused. 'You must be stark, raving mad.' Pirrou had just given me the white liberal, English-speaking version of *Oom* Jannie's reaction.

There seemed no point in trying to explain. Besides, how do you explain stuff like that without sounding excessively self-righteous? 'Pirrou, will you help me?' I asked instead.

She seemed to be thinking. 'What did the *boer* who bought the Steinways say?'

'*Oom* Jannie?'

Pirrou nodded. '*Ja*, him.'

I imitated *Oom* Jannie's thick accent, trying to get the inflections in English that had been present in his Afrikaans. 'He asked incredulously, "You want to do a murder trial for a black *kaffir*?"'

Pirrou clapped her hands. 'Well, I never thought I'd agree with a *backveld* Karoo sheep farmer, but he's right, Tom.'

'Pirrou?' I left the implied question hanging.

'*Stoppit*, Tom! I'm *not* buying the poor little English boy from the orphanage shit! You're one of the most brilliant young men in South Africa and now this! You always had a stubborn streak; you should never have gone to those ridiculous mines or Kenya! Christ! What the fuck are you trying to do? Is this some sort of misconceived revenge? You've ignored the advances of some of the most prominent law firms in this country and spurned the advice of some of the most pre-eminent lawyers and joined, of all things, a second-rate, unknown Afrikaner law firm. Now, in one hit, you're going to destroy your entire future in order to bring to justice a family of *backveld japies* who murdered a Zulu pig boy!'

I remained silent. La Pirouette had reappeared, her green eyes hard as agate.

'I'm sorry, I have no choice, it's something I have to do.' I sat up, pulling the sheets away from my naked body, preparing to leave.

'All right! I'll try!' In the blink of an eye, La Pirouette was back to being Pirrou, her green eyes soft again. Then suddenly straddling me, she started to kiss me furiously, her tongue probing deep into my mouth. Then as quickly she stopped and sat up, arching her back and throwing her head back. 'Oh God! How I've missed you, Tom Fitzsaxby!' she cried.

'No more handbaggery, Pirrou,' I said firmly.

She looked down at me and her green eyes flashed momentarily, but then returned back to calmness. 'Just friends?' she asked, sticking out her hand. She simply had to have the last word.

Six months later, Israel Mausels, chairman of the Johannesburg Bar, signed a letter informing me that I had been admitted and could practise as a barrister. Advocate Tom Fitzsaxby was ready, at last, to take on Mevrou and the Van Schalkwyk brothers.

While I haven't mentioned this before, I have always been an inveterate letter-writer. Throughout the years I kept in regular touch with all those people who had influenced me on the way to adulthood and during my time in Rhodesia, East Africa and even throughout the two dark years at Oxford. I wrote to Miss Phillips in Australia, where her husband was the South African ambassador, on a monthly basis. And, while their own letters were few and far between, I wrote regularly to Sergeant Van Niekerk and Marie, as well as Doctor Van Heerden and Marie's mother, his wife, and finally to Meneer Van Niekerk of the *Shorter Oxford English Dictionary* 'To thine own self be true', school principal.

I had never raised the subject of the murder with the sergeant. *Oom* Jannie and Pirrou were the only ones to know of my intentions. Now the time had come to talk to Sergeant Van Niekerk. I called him at the police station in Duiwelskrans, and then took the train to Pietersburg where he met me in the police van and drove me back to the little *dorp* where it had all started for me. On the journey into town I didn't mention my reason for coming, instead we talked of old times and some of the better memories. The sergeant and Marie had moved into a more spacious but not overly large house with their four children. In calling him I'd used the excuse that I needed a break from work, and Marie had kicked two of the kids out of their bedroom and prepared it for me, despite the fact that I would have been just as welcome to stay at Doctor Van Heerden's, where there was no accommodation crisis.

When I'd suggested staying with her mother and the good doctor, Marie protested, feigning outrage. 'Tom, you must be mad to think we going to share you that easy, hey? Jannie and me, we've been looking forward to this day for years!' With child-bearing Marie had grown fairly stout and, while still pretty, had turned into a typical-looking Afrikaner country woman: square-shaped, competent in all things domestic, outspoken, a strict, no-nonsense mother who did a fair bit of yelling at her rowdy offspring. Saxby, the daughter whom I had been famously credited with delivering, was a lovely young seventeen-year-old with a shy smile and she blushed furiously when she was reminded that I'd been present at her birth. Sergeant Van Niekerk looked somewhat older around the eyes, his hair turned partially grey, but otherwise he hadn't changed a great deal. They appeared to still be very compatible and happily married.

The first evening we all gathered for dinner at the doctor's house where I was obliged to do most of the talking, trying to achieve a monster catch-up with everyone asking dozens of questions, mostly wanting more details on the things I'd mentioned in past letters. It was not until the following morning, when I visited the police station, that I was able to broach the subject of Mattress's murder with Sergeant Van Niekerk.

I should, in fairness, mention that he was no longer Sergeant Van Niekerk, but had been elevated to the rank of lieutenant. When I congratulated him he was quick to grin and modestly point out that this had come about from seniority and not from any special competence as a policeman. Although it was obvious a more able small-town police officer would be difficult to find anywhere. I had always known him as Sergeant Van Niekerk and even as an adult had never addressed him otherwise, despite several attempts he'd made to make me call him Jan.

I asked permission to continue to address him as I had always done and he laughingly agreed.

Settled in his office, and after the African day constable brought in coffee, the sergeant said, 'So now, tell me, Tom, what's the big secret, why have you come down?'

'Sergeant, I've come to ask you about a matter we were both involved in,' I began. 'Myself, when I was seven years old and at The Boys Farm and you, of course, as a policeman at the same time. I refer to the murder of the *Bantu* Mattress Malokoane who was killed by a person or persons unknown.'

'*Ja*, I remember it well,' Sergeant Van Niekerk said.

'Do you still have your investigation file?'

'Why do you ask? I didn't have the experience at that time; today, maybe it would turn out differently, hey?'

I ignored his premature attempt at justification. 'Is the case closed?'

'Man, I can't remember exactly, but I can take a look. It will be in an old file in the storeroom at the back.' He paused. 'But maybe not. The roof leaks, I can't guarantee it, you hear? Last year in the big rain we lost a lot of the old files to water damage.'

'Could you possibly find it, the file?'

'Tom, what are you trying to say? The native is long dead, over twenty years already.'

'Sergeant, I want to ask you to reopen the case. That is, of course, if you closed it.'

'*Here*, Tom, what are you talking about?'

'I think I have sufficient evidence to file an indictment in the High Court against Mevrou and the Van Schalkwyk brothers for the murder of Mattress Malokoane.'

Sergeant Van Niekerk's surprise was immediate and he jumped up from behind his desk. 'Whoa! *Stadig*! Slow down! What are you saying? You want to file a murder charge?' His hands flew above his head. '*Wragtig*! Against the Van Schalkwyks?'

I had rehearsed this moment too many times in my imagination to show any surprise. 'Ja, I'm asking you to be the police prosecutor, Sergeant,' I said in an even voice.

Sergeant Van Niekerk took several moments to recover and in the process resumed his seat. He shook his head like a boxer trying to shake off a punch, then looked directly at me. 'Are you mad, man? Only two years ago the six brothers came out of prison, the whole town turned out to greet them, they're big heroes in this *dorp*, you hear? It's impossible, man!'

I had prepared myself for this moment. 'Sergeant, you probably won't remember, but the morning after Mattress was murdered you said to Meneer Prinsloo outside Mattress's hut, "*Hy is 'n slimmetjie*". You called me clever and that was the first compliment I could ever remember receiving from a white person. Mattress was always saying nice things about me and perhaps that was one of the reasons I loved him. But when one of my own people said something nice that was a big moment in my life. Then later, after we'd met again in the headmaster's office, in your brother's office, afterwards you took me to the Impala Café and Mevrou Booysens served me the one-legged bowl of ice-cream with ten different toppings, that was when I decided that I could trust you. You were the first of my own kind I'd ever trusted. I knew then if you could you would find out who lynched Mattress and bring them to justice.' I paused. 'I still believe you can.'

'It's twenty-one years, Tom!'

'There is no statute of limitations on murder, Sergeant.'

Sergeant Van Niekerk, tapping a pencil against the desk, his chin resting on his chest, was silent for quite a while before he looked up. 'You don't know what you asking, Tom. It's easy for you. The people in this town they *verkramp*, they will never forgive me. I've got four kids and a wife and we have to live here, you don't. Let me tell you something, twenty-one years is nothing; it's still the same, the same place you left, you can ask Doctor Van Heerden or my brother. The people here, they diehards, only now it's *our* government in Pretoria so they feel even stronger. A dead native is nothing, man!'

I sighed. 'Sergeant, I do understand how cramped and narrow these mountain people are and that you and Marie and the kids have to live here. To be perfectly honest I expected you to refuse the offer to be the crown prosecutor, but I felt I had to ask anyway. I will act as both advocate and prosecutor.' I paused. 'Sergeant, you don't know how much I hate saying this, but I must warn you I may have to subpoena you as a principal witness.'

'*Ja*, I see,' he said.

'And I'm begging for your cooperation in the matter of police files and any evidence you may have gathered.' I hesitated. 'Sergeant, I don't want to hear that all of a sudden the files have been rain-damaged and lost.'

Sergeant Van Niekerk laughed. 'You're still a *slimmetjie*, Tom.'

'Last year was the worst drought in the Northern Transvaal in twenty years, Sergeant.'

'*Ja*, no problems, Tom. I will give you complete access to the files and cooperate in every way possible, including acting as a willing witness. I am still a policeman and will do my duty.'

I thanked him, then added, 'One more question. Sergeant, was the body of the murder victim mutilated in any way?'

Sergeant Van Niekerk appeared to be taken by surprise. 'You mean apart from being dragged behind a *bakkie*? Why do you ask?'

'Sergeant, I'm going to ask you the same question in court, but I'd like to know now if you're willing to answer.'

'How the hell did you know, Tom?' he asked, clearly bemused.

'Please, could you answer the question, Sergeant.'

'*Ja*, as a matter of fact, it was, but it was never officially announced, it was something people wouldn't believe white men would do.'

'And that something was . . . ?'

'Ag, the victim had his sexual organs removed.'

'And this appears in your case notes?'

'*Ja*, of course . . . everything.'

I must say, contrary to what you might expect, I was relieved that Sergeant Van Niekerk had refused to prosecute the case and understood that had he done so he would have been made a pariah in Duiwelskrans. All I had hoped for was his complete cooperation and now that I had achieved this outcome, I could spend the rest of the day and the next day or two examining the evidence in his files before returning to Johannesburg.

In fact, the files were brought to me and I got stuck into the evidence immediately, had a sandwich for lunch and decided to stay on at the police station after Sergeant Van Niekerk prepared to go home at six o'clock that evening. 'We'll keep your dinner warm in the oven,' he promised before leaving. 'If we're in bed just help yourself, Marie will leave coffee on the stove.' I was left with the night-shift staff, two African policemen who remained in the front of the station while I worked in the sergeant's office.

At around seven o'clock a black policeman entered the office holding a tray on which rested several small tin dishes with lids, a plate, fork and spoon as well as a starched napkin.

'The coolie, he is bringing this,' the constable announced, placing the tray down on the desk.

'Thank you, Joseph, is he still outside?'

'No, *Baas*, now he is going back,' he replied.

An envelope was propped against one of the dishes.

Dear Mr Fitzsaxby,

The sergeant is telling us you like very, very much curry. We are also sending chicken tandoori. Most welcome home again, we are remembering well the one-pound note.

Yours faithfully and so on and so forth,

J. Patel & Sons
Impala Café – Mixed Grills and Bombay Class Indian Curry

You can imagine my surprise when the following morning at breakfast and after the kids had left for school Marie brought a fresh pot of coffee and sat down with the sergeant and myself at the kitchen table. 'Tom, last night when you were working at the station, we had a family talk, you hear?' She smiled over at her husband. 'First it was only Jannie and me, then his *boetie* came over and then we called my ma and the doctor and they came too. We told them about what you want to do and how you asked Jan if he would be the police prosecutor.'

'*Ja*, Marie, I understand, I *really* do, his position in this town would become untenable,' I interrupted hastily.

'No, listen, Tom!' Marie said sharply.

'Sorry,' I said, suitably chastised.

'Well, we changed our mind, Jannie will do it.'

I raised both my arms. 'Whoa! It's not necessary for the sergeant to stick his neck out, I've already told him there's another way around the problem.'

'No, Tom, you wrong, it *is* necessary, a murder is a murder and in the eyes of God this is about a human being.'

'In my eyes too, Marie,' I said quietly.

'*Ja*, of course, we all humans. But Jannie is a policeman but also an Afrikaner; whatever the cost to us in this godforsaken *dorp*, in the end a person has to live with himself. A man has to do his duty. I want my children to be proud of their father.'

'Tom, it's not *just* the family's decision, I *want* to do it,' Sergeant Van Niekerk said firmly.

I was silent for a moment. 'Thank you, Marie, thank you, Sergeant. Now, may I say something?'

'Say away,' Sergeant Van Niekerk offered with a flip of his hand, obviously pleased that everything was out in the open.

'May I refuse?'

'What do you mean, Tom? You don't want him? You don't want Jannie to help you?' Marie asked, confused.

'No, Marie, of course I do. But there are two major parts to this trial, crown prosecutor and principal witness. I have spent almost fifteen years gathering evidence, and after reading the case file yesterday I realise I know more about the murder than the police do. What I don't know is what happened in the days following the murder. I was too young at the time to understand fully what was occurring. I can handle the dual role of prosecutor as well as advocate, but I *must* have a principal witness with impeccable credentials in the eyes of the judge. Such a witness is, of course, the sergeant. You see, I want to avoid a jury if possible. I'm going to ask the court to appoint two assessors instead, two lawyers, to act with the judge to reach a decision. It's taking a chance, I know, but in the present political climate and with the ongoing Treason Trial, I'm not at all sure I could get a jury in Pretoria that would reach a fair decision. If the police officer who investigated the murder is a witness, well, that's far more important in this context than if he acts as the crown prosecutor.'

Marie looked at me, still unsure. 'Tom, you're not just saying this, I mean, you know, to get us off the hook?'

'So, why did you ask me in the first place to be the crown prosecutor?' Sergeant Van Niekerk asked pointedly.

It was a good question. 'Well, in the first place, I hadn't read your investigation file.' I hesitated. 'I have to be honest, Sergeant, your reaction to the offer would have told me whether you would be a hostile witness under subpoena, or one willing to come forward voluntarily. I was always aware there was a lot at stake for you and your family.' I smiled. 'But there was a fair bit at stake for me as well, I stood to lose not only a dear friend but the first white man I trusted with my heart and soul. Your reaction yesterday and willingness to be a witness confirmed I had exactly the witness I wanted. It also told me that a child of seven can still be an excellent judge of character.'

'Ag, you right, Tom, I don't even know if I could do that job, you know, crown prosecutor. It's the High Court, I've never done anything like that, I'm a country policeman, mostly it's just Magistrate Du Plessis from Pietersburg.'

Marie rose from the table and put her ample arms around me, then kissed me on the side of the cheek. 'You're not only a good midwife and also a diplomat, but you've turned from a very nice little boy into a very nice man. I think you're going to be a pretty good trial lawyer, Tom Fitzsaxby. Thank you.'

'*Ja*, we both thank you,' Sergeant Van Niekerk said quietly. Then he said, 'You know, Tom, I'm glad. I'm still an Afrikaner, you understand? But I'm glad we going to do the right thing for a change, the death of that native boy, it's stayed on my mind a long time.'

'Marie, Sergeant, I appreciate how much guts it took to say what you've said this morning and it is me who needs to thank you and your family. You've all stood by me, defended me and cared for me from the very beginning. I love you all very much and have from the first green sucker, one-legged ice-cream, red book and "To thine own self be true" *Shorter Oxford English Dictionary*. As for nice people, just look who's talking!'

Before I filed an indictment with the High Court in Pretoria against the six Van Schalkwyk brothers and Mevrou, whose real name was Johanna Katrina van Schalkwyk, there was one more essential piece of evidence I would have to try to obtain. I didn't like my chances and when I returned to Duiwelskrans to inform Sergeant Van Niekerk of the possible existence of the canned-fruit jar and its brandy-pickled contents he couldn't believe his ears.

'The mutilation? Are you sure, Tom? That Vermaak kid was a born liar.'

'*Ja*, but how could he possibly know Mattress had been mutilated unless she told him or, as he said, showed him the jar? You said the evidence wasn't made public.'

I'd since learned that when Meneer Prinsloo had been transferred to Pretoria the new superintendent at The Boys Farm had dismissed Mevrou and she'd returned to the high-mountains Van Schalkwyk family farm.

'You're right, but would she keep it all these years?' Before I could answer, he did so himself. '*Ja*, she's a Van Schalkwyk, she would, *definitely*. They're all mad and bitter, that lot. It's a pity their life sentence got commuted to sixteen years. They're not true Afrikaner patriots, they're filth, vermin, but this *dorp* thinks they're living martyrs. Frans van Schalkwyk, the oldest brother, stood for the farmers' representative on the town council last year. Can you imagine? I'm telling you, man, he would have got in on a landslide, only I checked with Pretoria and you can't be a councillor with a criminal record. He can't even read!'

'So you think it's worth a try?'

'*Ja*, I'm game, but we'll have to go to Pietersburg to see Magistrate Du Plessis and ask him to issue a search warrant.'

'Will he cooperate?'

Sergeant Van Niekerk shrugged. 'Normally yes, I think so, but this isn't a normal case, Tom.'

We drove to Pietersburg and were well received by the veteran magistrate in his chambers, who, it was readily apparent, liked and respected the sergeant. When I was introduced the old man said, 'Ah, the true genius has returned.'

Sergeant Van Niekerk and I looked at each other, not understanding. 'I beg your pardon, Magistrate?' I said, somewhat confused.

'Tom Fitzsaxby! I never forget a name. Duiwelskrans railway station, 1945, when they were farewelling the Afrikaner genius, Gawie Grobler, from the back of a lorry. Now tell me, son, what has happened to you since then?'

You can get lucky in this world. Over a cup of coffee I filled in the intervening years and eventually got around to why we needed a search warrant. He puffed on his pipe for a while, then said, 'Tom Fitzsaxby, don't waste your great intellect on a rubbish case like this.' I was about to protest when he put up his hand to stop me and turned to the sergeant. 'Nevertheless Lieutenant Van Niekerk, you shall have your search warrant; sometimes a man has to go against his own better judgement.

This Van Schalkwyk woman, I remember her too.' He laughed. 'She once came to see me in the District Court, she wanted to report Doctor Van Heerden for leaving some kind of medical instrument in a dead native's stomach. "Was it an expensive piece of equipment?" I asked her. "No, Magistrate, it was a pair of tweezers," she replied. "Never mind, the Government can afford it," I told her.' Magistrate Du Plessis chuckled at the memory and we all laughed.

Sergeant Van Niekerk then asked, 'I will need three white constables from here to operate a dawn raid, Magistrate Du Plessis.'

'*Ja*, I will sign the authority with the search warrant; let me know if you find Exhibit A, Lieutenant.' We shook hands and I thanked him. 'Tom Fitzsaxby, take my advice, even the greatest genius will end up badly if he starts to defend dead *kaffirs* for a living. *Sterkte*, strength, *Advocaat*.'

I would have given a great deal to have been present at the dawn raid on the high-mountains Van Schalkwyk farm, but instead had to rely on Sergeant Van Niekerk for the details. A few prior enquiries had established which of the five houses on the property Mevrou lived in and the police had decided to go directly to her cottage on the far side of the family compound. They arrived at half past five, just as daylight began to appear, entering the compound and immediately setting off a dozen farm dogs. One of the dogs, a large Alsatian, attacked one of the police officers as he stepped out of his van and it was shot on the spot. The raid went badly from that moment on. Brothers carrying shotguns and rifles emerged from the various houses in their nightshirts with their wives following in voluminous nightdresses. Sons and daughters, the snotty-nosed wild kids that had once played outside the *Dominee*'s church on Sundays, now young men and women who were grown-up, were among them. Soon over thirty people surrounded the two police vans with the four policemen hopelessly outgunned.

Frans van Schalkwyk, the oldest brother, an enormous man in a dirty nightshirt and bare feet and brandishing a shotgun, stepped up to Sergeant Van Niekerk. 'Who *fokken* killed my dog?' he demanded.

'Meneer Van Schalkwyk, I have a search warrant to enter the home of Johanna Katrina van Schalkwyk,' Sergeant Van Niekerk said evenly, presenting the warrant to him, knowing he couldn't read.

Frans van Schalkwyk took the warrant, glanced at it briefly and handed it back. The six brothers had been incarcerated for too many years to have any respect for authority. 'Who says?' Frans demanded. 'Nobody is going to do a search, you hear? Now *fok* off before somebody gets hurt.' He kicked at the corpse of the dead dog. 'He's a pedigree, you'll hear more about this, Sergeant.'

'It's Lieutenant Van Niekerk, Meneer Van Schalkwyk, you've been away a long time. Now be sensible, man. I want to search only the home of Mevrou Johanna Katrina van Schalkwyk, that's all.' He turned, appealing to the gathered Van Schalkwyk clan. 'The rest of you we won't disturb, you can go back to sleep.'

'What you looking for, hey?' Frans van Schalkwyk asked. Through all this he was the only one to speak, the rest just stood slack-jawed and wary, not moving away.

'Canned-fruit jars,' Sergeant Van Niekerk replied.

There was a moment of stunned silence, then the whole Van Schalkwyk clan burst into laughter.

'Canned-fruit jars!' Frans cried. 'What the *fok* are you talking about?' Then he turned to the Van Schalkwyk women standing together. 'Does Johanna make canned fruit?' he asked.

Several of the women shook their heads, then one woman, an old crone much older than the rest, said, 'Not canned fruit, only pickled pork, she sells it at the church bazaar. They rubbish, pigs' feet, but some townpeople like it.'

This caused another bout of laughter. Pickled pork trotters were obviously something the clan didn't think much of. The laughter lifted the tension somewhat and Frans van Schalkwyk turned back to the sergeant. 'Only pickled pork,' he repeated.

'*Ja*, that's what I meant, we want to see this pickled pork.'

'She's sick,' Frans declared suddenly.

'That's okay, man, we won't disturb her,' Sergeant Van Niekerk said, gaining confidence. 'I don't suppose she keeps her pickled pork in the bedroom?' he added.

Sergeant Van Niekerk later confessed to me, 'Tom, I was shitting myself. I was gambling that after all this time and the fact that they didn't know why we were there, they'd clean forgotten about Exhibit A in the canned-fruit jar. That is, of course, if it was still in her possession.'

'But pickled pork? They could have twigged, guessed what you were searching for.'

'*Ja*, that, I admit, maybe. But the old woman said it first. I said canned-fruit jars. I just got lucky with the pickled pork part. The Van Schalkwyks, they make the best smoked honeyed hams in the Northern Transvaal, so when the woman said pickled pork, me saying we wanted to see the canned-fruit jars made some sort of sense. After that it was easy, man. I'm not married to a nurse for nothing.'

'Meneer Van Schalkwyk, we don't want to make trouble, but you see we got here a medical problem. Someone who bought Mevrou Van Schalkwyk's pickled pork, maybe at the church bazaar, got sick soon after eating one pig's foot. Doctor Van Heerden sent what was left in the jar to the pathology lab in Pietersburg. They still not absolutely certain, you understand? But now we must have the rest of the jars for testing. It may be this new pork poisoning that's going around.'

Sergeant Van Niekerk laughed as he told me. 'Tom, I don't know what is pork poisoning or even if a person can get it. "It's only a routine search," I told them.'

'*Ja*, and you bring three policemen and kill my dog for a *fokken* routine search?' Frans van Schalkwyk snarled.

'The dog attacked one of my men. Listen, this is nonsense, I don't want to have to arrest you, you hear?' At this the Van Schalkwyk males all started to laugh and Sergeant Van Niekerk heard the sound of several rifle bolts being pulled back and shotgun barrels snapping shut. 'They all stood there in their nightshirts and their dirty bare feet, the women too, you can see they also dirty and their hair is unwashed, they like wild people, man. It's filth standing there, holding guns and all the women have no teeth! I can tell the three young policemen with me, they shit scared.'

'I wouldn't blame them,' I said to the sergeant.

'Then a miracle happened, Tom,' Sergeant Van Niekerk recalled. 'The old crone stepped forward, she's munching her gums and her hairy chin is nearly touching her nose. "Give them the jars! That one is no good! Your *ousis* is a drunk and she's always made trouble. Now she's poisoning the pork with her dirty ways, she's not boiling the jars. For fifteen years it's only women and children here. Do you want to go back to Pretoria? I don't want you to be hanged for killing a policeman!" She pointed to the smallest of the houses. "Not for *that* one! Now listen to your *ouma*, Frans!" she squawked.'

'And that was it?'

'*Ja*, man, the old woman was the *baas*. After that they led us to Mevrou's house and surrounded it while we entered. "Go in, she won't wake up, she's too drunk," Frans van Schalkwyk said to me. "But you *only* take the pickled pork, you hear? Nothing else."'

Sergeant Van Niekerk shrugged. 'In the end, Tom, it was as easy as that. Behind three-dozen big canned-fruit jars of pickled pork we found this small half-jar that is Exhibit A. It was covered in dust and looked as if it hadn't been moved in years. I carried it out, inside my shirt, in case her fingerprints are on the glass under the dust. I also take two jars of pickled pork trotters with me, so they won't see what's inside my shirt. I hide Exhibit A inside the glove box in case someone takes a look in the police van. Then I go back into the house. We didn't even wake Mevrou up. You could hear her snoring in her bedroom. She's sawing down a whole forest. So I open the door and there she lies, like a great whale lying washed up on the strand. She's sprawled crossways on the big brass bed with her nightdress pulled up round her waist, her fat legs over the edge. Everything up her nightdress is showing. Then I think "fingerprints". I go back to the van and get the equipment – the ink pad and paper – and I go inside and she's still snoring, so I take her thumb-print and her forefinger, two good prints. I put the search warrant in her hand and close her fat fist tight around it, and she's still snoring like a sawmill and I wonder what she'll think when she wakes up and she's got two fingers turned black all of a sudden.' He laughed. 'Nobody can say later I didn't serve the warrant to her in person. Then when we leave and Frans van Schalkwyk shouts out, "Don't think you've heard the last of this, you killed my dog, you *fokken* bastards!"'

'Oh, that reminds me, Sergeant. Do you know where we might get a good Alsatian pup? It's just that, you know, after a while they may realise what we were looking for. For instance, Mevrou could alert them. If we deliver a puppy together with a note to say the pickled pork got the all-clear, it might just throw them off the track.'

Sergeant Van Niekerk thought for a moment, '*Ja*, I know someone, maybe their bitch is having pups.' He looked at me. 'You know, Tom, you weren't born yesterday, hey?'

The next stop on the witness trail was Pissy Vermaak who had recently opened for business in Fordsburg, an inner-city suburb with a high proportion of Cape Coloured and Indian people. It was the centre of an alternative city culture rapidly growing up in Johannesburg. I'd been with Bobby from the basement at Polliack's to Uncle Joe's Café, an establishment that featured African and coloured jazz groups and singers such as Dollar Brand and Kippie Moeketsi. I'd also been with Pirrou for the same reason and, as well, to eat at an Indian restaurant, The Bombay Bus, nearly as famous for its curry as the renowned Turkeys in the centre of the city.

The Lonely Hunter, Pissy's new bathhouse and members-only club, was only one street back from Uncle Joe's Café and sported its name on a small blue neon sign, at the time considered pretty posh signage. But my visit was at eleven in the morning when the club was shut; it only opened in the mid-afternoon. I'd called previously, asking Pissy if he'd visit me in my office. He'd insisted that he dearly wanted me to see his club and it seemed churlish to refuse. Pissy agreed to wait for me in the reception area. I'd braced myself at the prospect of meeting the odious Meneer Prinsloo, telling myself it was all in a day's work. But childhood fears never go away and as I entered the premises I could feel my heart pounding and my mouth going dry. Pissy, true to his word, was waiting – seated prim and cross-legged on a bright purple lounge in the reception area, all very modern in the latest Danish-style light-coloured pinewood.

'Howsit, Tom!' he called, rising to greet me as I entered. 'Welcome to the Lonely Hunter, let me show you around, man.'

'Kobus, we've got quite a bit to get through,' I replied hesitantly.

'Not Kobus, Tom. Now it's Pissy for keeps. Maybe I'll change it by deed poll, hey. In the club business Pissy is a good name.' He took me by the elbow. 'Ag, come, it won't take long, you must see where my copper bonus went, hey. To make a place like this, it swallows money,' he declared proudly.

Pissy's club was surprisingly well done, all in much the same taste as the reception area. It comprised a bar where patrons could be seated, an area extending from the bar with a dozen tables where drinkers could sit or order *à la carte* from the modern professional kitchen, a small gymnasium, men's locker room, toilets and a not very large steam room.

'The private one is much larger and is at the back, like that one in Pretoria, it's got a side entrance and you must announce yourself and your club number. All very hush-hush, you understand? We don't want rubbish.'

After the inspection tour he ushered me into a small private sitting room. Upon entering I received the shock of my life. To a small child grown-ups always look big. Meneer Prinsloo was a huge and vastly obese man whose looming, stomach-propelled presence had been the stuff of nightmares when I'd been a small boy. Seated on a small lounge sat what was certainly once a tall man, huddled, pencil-thin, clothed only in some sort of hastily fashioned nappy. Flaps of semitranslucent excess skin fell in scallops from his exposed body and limbs. His head was completely bald but for a few nascent tufts of downy hair and his face was beardless and the colour of putty, but had two great jowls hanging from his near-skeletal skull. His sharp fleshless nose assumed the appearance of a beak and his tiny agate eyes darted around the room, not able to focus for a moment on anything. They seemed to be the only objects in his pale, inert frame that possessed life. What was once his gargantuan, braces-busting stomach was now reduced to a large apron of skin resting on, and almost concealing, the dirty towelling nappy. The bones of his legs traced down to large, splayed feet with curved, yellowed untrimmed toenails extending beyond his toes. In fact, that was exactly it! Meneer Prinsloo had turned into a scrawny giant rooster, plucked and ready to be dropped into a steaming cauldron in hell, chicken soup for demons and devils.

'Cancer and then a stroke on the right side, then later two more,' Pissy said nonchalantly. 'Nice retirement present, hey?'

I turned to Pissy and spoke in a half-whisper. 'Can he hear us?'

'I dunno, man. Maybe yes, maybe no.'

'Does he understand what's going on?'

Pissy shrugged, indifferent. 'Who knows, man.'

'Pissy, shouldn't he be in hospital?'

Pissy thought for a moment. 'He'll be dead in a month, the doctor says so, it's cancer of everything, man.'

'And you *want* to take care of him?'

Pissy shrugged. 'He's dying, man, what can a person do?'

The room reeked of the pungent smell of urine and the pervasive smell of excrement. I sniffed. 'And you keep him here in this little room?'

'*Ag*, it's the cancer, it smells like that,' Pissy explained, then added, 'He lives in a shed in the backyard. I've got a *kaffir* girl. She changes his nappy and feeds him. Sometimes she washes him, but I think it hurts him when you touch his skin.' Pissy looked at me with a pained expression. 'I do the best by him that I can.'

'Pissy, why?'

'Why what?'

'Well, why have you shown him to me?'

Pissy looked momentarily confused. 'I thought you'd like to see what happened to him, Tom. Like it's your sweet revenge, man.'

I shook my head. 'Bullshit! Pissy, you're lying to me again.'

'No, Tom, I swear it! You not the first one.'

'Pissy, what the fuck are you trying to say?'

Pissy grinned. 'It's like, you know, my publicity campaign.' Then he added, 'It happened clean by mistake.'

'Your publicity campaign? Who is? Meneer Prinsloo?'

'Tom, you right, this room smells of shit. Come, we go sit at the bar, hey? Maybe a drink, a beer, Scotch, brandy, we got anything you want. I can make you an American cocktail, a Manhattan or a martini?'

Seated at the bar, Pissy poured me a beer and a Scotch for himself, then came from behind the bar and took the stool beside me. '*Geluk!* Luck!' he said as we touched glasses. He took a small sip from his Scotch and placed it down on the bar. 'Now let me tell you a story, Tom. About six months ago, one night sitting here at the bar is a lone stranger, that is what we call our private members from the big bathhouse at the back. They say it only to each other. It's not for public consumption, you understand? He's a bit drunk and he wants to talk, it's a Monday night so I'm not so busy at the bar. Then in the conversation he mentions Duiwelskrans where he grew up. I tell him me also, I once lived in that *dorp*. Then it comes out he was at The Boys Farm about five years before us. "I wonder what happened to that bastard, Prinsloo?" he says. I don't tell him I know. Then moments later, right in front of my eyes he starts to cry. I reach out and put my hand on his shoulder. "You okay?" I ask. "*Ja*," he sniffs, but then it's on again, he can't help himself. "I was only ten when he fucked me!" he said, then he cries and cries and it was just lucky the bar was empty. When, after a long time, he stopped, I say to him, "Me also, *ou maat*! Prinsloo did it to me also."' Pissy looked at me. 'Then we got *really* drunk, him and me. So I say to him, "Come, let me show you what happened to Meneer Prinsloo." It's late, the club is closed. I take a torch and I take him into the backyard and show him what's in the shed.'

'Jesus! So you decided to do the same with me. Meneer Prinsloo didn't rape me! I'm not a victim.' But, of course, that wasn't strictly true, I was simply a different kind of victim.

'No, listen a moment, Tom. I know that. But there's more. You haven't heard the end of the story.' He took a fairly hefty slug of Scotch. 'A week maybe goes past and the lone stranger comes back with a friend who he says wants to be a member. Then he tells me it's happened to him also at The Boys Farm and can he see Meneer Prinsloo. It's been six months, now there's ten already. It's on the grapevine and then there's others, not from The Boys Farm, but lone strangers who had the same thing happen to them, only at other institutions, and they also want to see what happens, what God does to a paedophile, they *also* want revenge.'

I was shocked. 'What? You've got him on exhibition?' I pointed in the direction of the private sitting room. 'In that miserable little room. He sits all day in that room on display?'

'No, normally we only bring him out at night. The *kaffir* girl brings him to the back door in a wheelbarrow, then her and me, we carry him in.' Pissy gave a bitter laugh. 'I told you in the hospital in Bulawayo, he's someone who knows how to run front of house, a very respectable old man and a good Afrikaner!'

'Pissy, that's unconscionable behaviour, it . . . it isn't decent!' I exclaimed, unable to think of a more reprehensible word.

'*Ja*, maybe, but who said I was decent? Now I got maybe fifty more members, lone strangers, all because Meneer Prinsloo is sitting in there dying for everyone to see. In the end his front of house paid off big-time, man!'

'You can't mean that?'

'No, you wrong, Tom, I do! If ten lone strangers have come from The Boys Farm, how many more, hey? How many more little kids like me has he buggered? Tell me, man, do you really think he deserves to die peacefully with clean sheets in a hospital? You know why I *really* brought him out for you this morning?'

'Yes, you told me, revenge.'

'*Ja*, that, but also something else.'

'What, Pissy?'

'Tom, I've got a life now. People know me. They like me, man. This is *my* club. To some people I'm an important man. Pissy Vermaak, club owner. It's only a few more days, then he's dead and gone, it's finish and *klaar*. I've been a lone stranger all my life, now when he's dead, who knows, maybe I can forget. But first can you do me a big favour? I dunno if he understands, but I think so. I hope so.' He pointed towards the room. 'The main reason why I have him in there is because the doctor said sometimes they have these strokes but they can still know what's going on around them. Inside their brain there's nothing wrong. I want the dirty bastard to see his victims and to suffer.'

'So, what's the favour?' I asked, curious despite my extreme disquiet at what he was telling me.

'Will you tell him you going to have a murder trial for the pig boy? It's all going to come out about him! The whole world is going to know what he did to helpless little boys. If you do this for me then I promise I won't put him on exhibition anymore and he can die in a hospital in peace.' Pissy gave me a wan smile. He sounded tired and looked a lot older than his thirty-one years on this earth.

I shook my head. 'I can't do that, he wasn't directly involved in the murder.'

'Oh, yes he was!' Pissy suddenly protested. 'It was *him* who also encouraged Mevrou and her brothers to do it. He was afraid people would find out about what he was doing to me! He told me himself, only two years ago, before he got sick and got the strokes. He said he loved me, he couldn't live without me, he couldn't take the risk people would find out!'

'And you will testify to this under oath in court?'

'*Ja*, of course.'

'But remember in Bulawayo you said you wouldn't cooperate.'

'Tom, I didn't know then what I know now. You know, I *really* thought that old man loved me. How can a man be so stupid, hey?'

'Pissy, in affairs of the heart there's no such thing as stupid, the need to be loved paralyses every sense except our emotional reactions. We will do almost anything and believe almost anything to be loved,' I said, trying to comfort him.

'Tom, you got your willing witness, I'll say anything you want.'

I laughed, partly to dispel the sombre atmosphere. 'No, Pissy, for once in your life just tell the truth. That's all we're going to need.' I glanced towards the door of the private sitting room. 'Now, do you want me to go and do what you asked?'

He shook his head. 'No, Tom, already I'm feeling a lot better.'

'And you'll take him to a hospice?'

'Hospice?'

'A place, a hospital, where he can die in peace.'

'*Ja*, I promise.'

CHAPTER TWENTY-ONE

Love Comes Full Circle

——————

WITH PISSY VERMAAK a willing and cooperative witness, Exhibit A in our possession, Frikkie's notes transcribed and carefully cross-referenced and annotated, together with the original scraps of notepaper all signed and, a month before his death, formulated into a sworn affidavit, I felt we had sufficient evidence to proceed. This information, together with the police files compiled at the time of the murder, was about as good as it was ever likely to be.

I appointed Janine De Saxe, a young lawyer who had a reputation for tenacity and determination, as my junior and assisting barrister. Before going into private practice she'd worked as the assistant to Judge Franz Rumpff, one of the three judges appointed to conduct the Treason Trials. She was English-speaking, but she spoke Afrikaans fluently and had worked in the High Court in Pretoria and knew her way around the capital city. While I was worried about any political overtones in the trial, Janine assured me that she knew most of the High Court judges, and in her own words insisted, 'These High Court judges don't generally play politics.'

I duly filed an indictment for murder against the seven accused in the High Court in Pretoria and received notice that two days had been set aside for the hearing on 4 and 5 June 1964, scheduled for courtroom

No. 13. I am not an overly superstitious person, but as a man of Africa and coming from the high mountains, no matter how pragmatic one pretends to be, there inevitably remained a tincture of superstition in a *backveld* boy that still dwelt deep within my psyche. The adjective 'darkest' is not conjoined with the name of the continent for no reason.

Then came a big shock: Judge Joe Ludorf was appointed to preside over the trial. Despite Janine's assurances that High Court judges don't play politics, I was worried. You may remember the name Robey Leibbrandt; the Nazi ex-boxer trained in Germany and sent to South Africa to organise sabotage. At his trial for treason he was famously defended by advocate and former National Party official and now judge of the High Court, Joe Ludorf. I was caught between a rock and a hard place. If I asked for a recusal and gave my reasons the case would immediately take on political overtones. To make matters worse, Ludorf, originally appointed as one of the three judges for the Treason Trial involving Nelson Mandela among others, had stepped down after pressure from the defence. I had an inauspicious courtroom number and a judge who, in his mind, might have translated the Van Schalkwyk brothers' sentences for treason into the two words 'freedom fighters' but, of course, I had no way of knowing. Janine, who knew him from her time in Pretoria, claimed that he was a pretty pragmatic character and pointed out that of the three judges the defence had objected to at the commencement of the Treason Trial, only Ludorf agreed to step down.

'You're overanxious and you've been working on this case in your head for too long, Tom. Ludorf is as good as we're going to get and that doesn't in any sense mean he's the best of a bad lot.'

We decided to remain silent and hope for the best and I was to be grateful, on more than one occasion in the ensuing weeks and during the trial, for Janine's calm and sensible advice. She also pointed out that the court had agreed to two assessors rather than a jury. 'If we'd gone into this trial with a Pretoria jury, *that's* when we would have needed to be worried,' she declared.

Both assessors were Afrikaners: Hansie Bekker and Tertius Viljoen.

They'd been around for a while and were thought to be highly competent lawyers, and said to be close to being appointed to the judiciary.

However, we were in for one further surprise.

The subpoenas were served on the seven members of the Van Schalkwyk family by a court official from Pietersburg. The idea was to keep Lieutenant Van Niekerk uninvolved, except as a witness for the prosecution, though, of course, the defence was almost certain to call him to the stand as well.

The murder indictment was front-page news in the *Zoutpansberg Nuus* where they'd dug up details of the original enquiry. In a highly inflammatory editorial the newspaper pointed out that nobody at the time had established a motive for the murder or named any suspects, and that ludicrously, the indictment was being brought eighteen years after the so-called lynching of Mattress Malakoani [sic], a pig boy at The Boys Farm, the orphanage on the outskirts of Duiwelskrans. The charge of murder was being brought by a thirty-year-old Johannesburg lawyer, Tom Fitzsaxby. They pointed out that the murder indictment against the six brothers, whom many people in the district regarded as Afrikaner *Volk* heroes, appeared to be politically motivated. As a clear indication of this they asserted that while the police enquiry at the time had found no evidence to suspect the Van Schalkwyk brothers, their subsequent imprisonment for treason made them ideal victims. Was this, the newspaper asked, the beginning of some sort of communist-inspired and ANC counterpoint to the Rivonia Treason Trial presently underway in Pretoria? Perhaps, they suggested, the forthcoming murder trial concerning a black pig boy was intended to discredit the Afrikaner people by making them out to be a barbaric and savage people. After all, Fitzsaxby was a graduate from Oxford, an English university well known for its communist leanings and ANC sympathies.

The writers then selected Mevrou for special attention. They pointed out that white English-speaking women were also detained in the Treason Trial. Then they asked, 'Is Johanna van Schalkwyk, now retired to the family farm, but at the time of the murder the much-loved and respected matron at The Boys Farm, to be the Afrikaner female sacrifice?'

Lieutenant Van Niekerk reported that the whole district was up in arms. That Saturday morning following the newspaper report the Van Schalkwyk brothers had come into town in a *bakkie*. The giant Frans van Schalkwyk sat behind the wheel and beside him was a hugely obese Mevrou, with the five brothers standing up at the back waving a large Transvaal republic *vierkleur* flag. A long length of rope tied to the rear bumper of the *bakkie* was a defiant token of their contempt. They'd driven repeatedly up and down the main street, tooting the horn, and were soon joined by at least thirty other vehicles, bringing the little mountain *dorp* to a standstill. In the following week, several hundred vehicles belonging to townspeople and farmers in the district sported a length of rope trailing from the rear bumper.

And then the bombshell! Of course, I should have seen it coming, but I didn't; Gawie Grobler accepted the brief to defend the Van Schalkwyk family. We read the news in the right-wing *Die Burger*, one of the two major national Afrikaans-language newspapers. They had been the first of the national newspapers to pick the story up from the *Nuus* and run with it, at first with only a couple of columns, but rapidly increasing as the furore spread from the sleepy little mountain town into the rest of the Northern Transvaal. In the weeks following the initial story, hundreds of motor vehicles in all parts of the province carried a makeshift length of rope attached to the rear bumper.

But it was when *Die Burger* picked up the story that the rope hit the big time. Inspired by the initial gesture of contempt by the Van Schalkwyk Seven, as they were now dubbed, Doctor Dyke, the erstwhile vet and Rhode Island Red blue-ribbon winner and notorious Boys Farm horse-pliers dentist, came up with a way to fund the defence of the accused. Now retired and the mayor of Duiwelskrans, he conceived the idea of the *Bloedtoufond*, the Blood Rope Fund. For a donation of fifty cents the donor received a short length of rope that clipped around and hung from the rear bumper of a motor vehicle, almost touching the road surface, with about four inches at the end of it dyed crimson. Soon enough, with the mounting publicity, blood ropes were selling like hot cakes. Within weeks, a cottage industry creating, packaging and posting the mordantly grisly items had been created by the ever-opportunistic Patel & Sons, who charged twenty-seven cents for manufacture, returning twenty-three cents to the fighting fund.

Gawie Grobler's acceptance of the brief to defend the Van Schalkwyk Seven added yet another unfortunate political dimension to the upcoming murder trial. The Afrikaner Genius, long the town's favourite son, was the logical choice as the defence barrister. *Die Burger* ran a feature story about him, going back to his days as an orphan at The Boys Farm. They described the hometown boy as a brilliant young advocate, educated at Stellenbosch University where he graduated with a double first in law. The article told of the early recognition of the boy's genius and the consequent encouragement he'd received from the recently deceased Boys Farm superintendent, Pietrus Prinsloo. It talked about the special relationship the boy enjoyed with its kindly matron, Johanna van Schalkwyk, now ironically and cruelly one of the accused. 'That boy was always thinking, even with lavatory paper,' she was quoted as saying. It described how the *Dominee*, also deceased, had seen a brilliant future for the orphan boy; how he had established an annual fete run by the church elders to help young Gawie with the necessities of life when he took up scholarships to Pretoria Afrikaans Boys High School and later Stellenbosch. The article recounted the amusing story told by the town mayor, Doctor Dyke, of a special fundraising idea at the first fete: 'Meet the Afrikaner Genius', where Gawie sat in an old armchair on a raised platform and answered questions from members of the audience at sixpence a question. 'I asked him to give me the theory of Pythagoras,' the mayor laughingly recalled. 'He told me right off, "The square of the hippopotamus of a right-angled triangle is equal to the sum of the squares on the other two sides", indicating to me that he was not only a highly intelligent boy, but also a very funny one. I recall I gave him two shillings.' Doctor Dyke was also quoted as saying, 'We, the good citizens of Duiwelskrans, want Advocate Gawie Grobler to lead the defence in this iniquitous and misconceived trial. Not only because we believe him to be a singularly brilliant advocate and the best man for the job, but also as a much-loved native son of this town. Duiwelskrans is very proud of our very own Gawie Grobler; we are a community where even an orphan is given every opportunity to grow and blossom. As a true Afrikaner he will surely defeat the dark forces of communism and the perfidious ANC ranged against us. Justice will be granted to the Van Schalkwyk family, who have already suffered so much as freedom fighters and martyrs in the struggle for independence by the true *Volk* of South Africa.'

The feature story in *Die Burger* was syndicated and appeared in dozens of smaller Afrikaans newspapers throughout the country, and sections from it were translated into the major English-speaking newspapers, among them the *Sunday Times*, the *Cape Argus* and the *Natal Mercury*. It was compelling reading and caught the imagination of Afrikaners throughout the land. Vehicles in the cities and small towns in every province began to sport the blood rope and soon there were sufficient funds to hire the best advocacy money could buy. But, of course, it was always going to be Gawie Grobler, *surrogaat*, Third Class Rooster and Afrikaner Genius, who would be leading the case; the town simply wouldn't entertain the thought of anyone else, no matter how big a high-up in the law he might happen to be.

It was back to the future, *Voetsek* the *Rooinek*, murderer of 26 000 women and children, versus the Afrikaner *Volk*. Let me tell you something for nothing, the shit squares were flying around so thick and fast in the hot wind that you couldn't catch one to wipe your arse, even if you wanted to.

Naturally, in all this errant publicity I was often featured, though usually in a trenchant and less than complimentary manner. There were also some humorous moments, one of them when Mevrou, in an interview with *Die Huisgenoot*, was quoted as saying, 'That English boy was nothing but trouble, you hear? A real little *kaffirboetie*! Cutting his finger all over the place and making trouble for everyone. Always answering back and never knowing his place. He had a little dog that caught some rats, that's the only thing good I can say about that one. When he left to go to that Pope's school my whole spirits lifted. I'm telling you, man, all of a sudden my head is going on a nice holiday!'

The story almost wrote itself and was tailor-made for the Sunday newspapers. The brilliant Stellenbosch double-first graduate versus the Rhodes scholar, the two 'genius' orphans with identical backgrounds are opposing young advocates in a murder trial. Afrikaner South African and English South African with the murder victim a black African.

The day of the court case arrived, 4 June 1964. Courtroom No. 13 was not one of the larger ones and the public and the press gallery was filled minutes after the High Court building opened. Many of the people seated in the public gallery wore a blood rope converted into a crude necklace. The small section of the public gallery reserved for non-Europeans was also filled to capacity. To my surprise I saw, among the darker faces present, Mr Naidoo of the Indian Curry Eatery where Frikkie Botha and I would eat on our way back to the park in the old days. Stompie from the kiosk outside Park Station, the purveyor of Pepsi-Cola, was also present. Pirrou was there, of course, as was Professor Mustafa, my old friend, the medical supervisor of Johannesburg General, and Professor Shaun Rack, my law professor at Wits. Meneer Van Niekerk of the *Shorter Oxford English Dictionary* 'To thine own self be true' sat with Marie and Mervou Van Heerden. Doctor Van Heerden and Lieutenant Van Niekerk had been called as witnesses and were waiting outside the court.

I was told later that a great cheer rose from the public gallery when Gawie and his junior, Herman Venter, entered and made their way to the bench for the defence. Though, I must add, the same happened, though perhaps not quite as strident an outburst, when Janine De Saxe and I entered and took our places for the prosecution. If the public gallery was not evenly divided, at least it was not completely one-sided. The court clerk entered and asked the court for silence and to be upstanding as Judge Ludorf and the two assessors, Bekker and Viljoen, entered.

Judge Ludorf, speaking in Afrikaans, opened the court proceedings by introducing the two assessors, one on either side of him. He then began his opening address, immediately creating controversy. 'I note with apprehension that some members of the public gallery are wearing what I believe is known as a blood rope. I now order the two police officers in the gallery to confiscate these items.' Gawie Grobler jumped to his feet. 'Yes, what is it, Meneer Grobler?' the judge asked, looking over the top of his spectacles.

'With the greatest respect, My Lord, I submit that the items in question are a part of a person's apparel, in essence no different to a necklace with a cross attached or a badge of affiliation, a statement of one's beliefs or membership of an association.'

I grinned inwardly, it was the same old Gawie of The Boys Farm, always wanting to have the first word. His objection, in my opinion, was ill-conceived and I wondered whether he secretly felt that his case for the defence wasn't as strong as he'd hoped, and wanted to appear confident and assertive from the first word. The judge was having none of it.

'Thank you, Meneer Grobler, I should remind you that this is my court,' Judge Ludorf said firmly. 'You may sit down.' He looked up at the public gallery. 'Would the police officers kindly confiscate the offending items.'

Gawie seemed about to return to his feet before thinking better of it and remaining seated.

It took several minutes for the blood ropes to be handed over, whereupon Judge Ludorf resumed his opening remarks. 'In the three months leading up to this trial there has been a great deal of regrettable publicity surrounding this case and I am therefore not surprised that the prosecution has asked for the court to appoint two assessors to work with me rather than a jury. I need not remind you that this is a court of law and only the evidence presented here will be assessed. The gallery will remain silent throughout and I would ask the members of the press to report the proceedings accurately and to refrain from the sort of hyperbole they have indulged in over the past weeks.' He cast a stern look at the packed press gallery. 'Although, alas, this last request is not enforceable and to rely on your good judgement and probity is, I fear, a contradiction in terms.' The judge had got his first laugh. He brought his gavel down several times demanding silence and then announced, 'I now ask the clerk of the court to announce the session.'

The clerk of the court was a small, thin, pop-eyed man with several long strands of dark hair derived from above the ear on the left side of his head and combed across to the right and stuck down on his bald pate. He commenced to read out the details of the murder charge against the Van Schalkwyk Seven.

Immediately after he had completed the indictment, Gawie Grobler jumped to his feet. 'My Lord, if it pleases the court, my clients have asked if Meneer Frans van Schalkwyk, the senior member of the family, may be allowed to answer the majority of the questions from the prosecution on behalf of the entire family.'

I stood up. 'Objection, My Lord.'

A grin appeared on the faces of the judge and his two assessors. 'Nice one, Advocate Grobler, objection sustained. I caution you that your request is improper, you well know that the defence is entitled to call whomsoever of the accused they require to the witness stand.'

'With the greatest respect, My Lord,' Gawie persisted, 'one of my clients, Mevrou Van Schalkwyk, is too ill to take the witness stand or even to climb the few steps into it. I ask for leave to submit to the court a medical certificate from a heart specialist to this effect.' He stepped forward and handed the certificate to the clerk of the court.

'Your client may take the oath from where she is seated and I am sure the prosecution will not object to cross-examining her from where she feels most comfortable,' the judge replied.

He glanced over to me, and I nodded and, half rising, said, 'Certainly,

My Lord.' I knew immediately where Gawie was heading: he intended to remove Mevrou as a witness if the case seemed to be going against him. He would claim her heart condition forbade her to continue. She was by nature a contrary and unpredictable woman and unlikely to stick to a strict line of enquiry and he didn't want a rogue female elephant on his hands. Mevrou had always been obese but now she was gargantuan, taking the place of three people on a courtroom bench. She seemed to be permanently breathless and Lieutenant Van Niekerk's description of her as a beached whale was entirely appropriate. I must say, if appearances counted for anything, then Gawie had a point. I wrote a note to Janine and passed it to her, requesting her to ask Professor Mustafa to be on stand-by to examine Mevrou if Gawie decided to pull this trick.

While all these goings-on seemed to have taken a long time, in fact they occupied less than half an hour. Judge Ludorf announced that I was presenting a private prosecution and that there would be no Crown prosecutor present. 'You may now outline the case for the prosecution,' he said, nodding at me.

'My Lord, Your Honours, at the heart of this case is the question of whether there is a clear motive for the murder of Mattress Malokoane. There has been a great deal of speculation that no such motive exists, that only one of the accused knew the victim, but not, in any sense, very well. Furthermore, in her work capacity she had no direct dealings with him. I intend to present evidence and show clearly that a motive for murder *did* exist in her mind and that she consequently involved six members of her family in a conspiracy to murder Mattress Malokoane. Thank you, My Lord, Your Honours.'

'Thank you, Meneer Fitzsaxby,' the judge said. 'I now call on the counsel for the defence.'

'My Lord, *Edelagbares*,' Gawie said, nodding at each assessor in turn. 'The defence intends to demonstrate that my clients are the victims of circumstance and conjecture. My learned friend has already pointed out that this case hinges on one person in particular, Mevrou Van Schalkwyk, who was, at the time of the murder, the matron of The Boys Farm. If, as I intend to prove, she did not instigate the murder of Mattress Malokoane she could not have coerced her six brothers into becoming involved. I intend to show that there exists no case against any of my clients. Thank you, My Lord, *Edelagbares*.'

It was all pretty predictable stuff: I say she's guilty, he says she's not, the opening to pretty well every criminal court case that ever was.

Judge Ludorf turned to me. 'You may proceed with the prosecution, Meneer Fitzsaxby.'

'I call Meneer Kobus Vermaak to the witness stand,' I announced.

Court cases are, out of necessity, tedious and drawn-out procedures and I have already written about much of the evidence I was able to gather, so I won't go into every small detail and procedure.

Over the next hour I led Pissy as he told the entire story of the incident involving the three of us at the big rock, leading to the intervention of Mattress where he lifted Fonnie du Preez and dashed him against the rock. I then turned to the judge and assessors. 'My Lord, you will have gathered that I was personally involved in the testimony you have just heard from Meneer Vermaak. I now ask permission to retain the witness while I take the oath myself and enter the witness stand and I respectfully ask that my assistant, Juffrou Janine De Saxe, act temporarily as counsel for the prosecution in order to question me.'

Gawie Grobler leapt to his feet just as I expected he might. 'Objection, My Lord!'

Judge Ludorf said, 'State your objection, Meneer Grobler.'

'My Lord, this testimony hinges on the recall of events given by a seven-year-old child. If it is taken from the original police interview, my learned friend knows that the testimony and evidence provided by a child of this age is not admissible in a court of law. I therefore ask that the prosecution be prevented from appearing as a witness in his own prosecuting procedure.'

Judge Ludorf turned to the two assessors and they spoke with each other for a few moments before he turned back to face the court. 'You may be technically correct, Meneer Grobler, but my learned colleagues and myself would like to hear the evidence whereupon we will decide whether to strike it from the record or not. Objection overruled.'

I took my place on the witness stand and was sworn in. 'Meneer Fitzsaxby, can you tell the court what happened immediately after Mattress Malokoane intervened at the big rock and the accident to Fonnie du Preez occurred.'

'Objection, My Lord, it was *not* an accident but the result of a deliberate action by Mattress Malokoane.'

'Objection sustained, Juffrou De Saxe will rephrase the question.'

'Meneer Fitzsaxby, can you tell the court what happened immediately after the incident when Fonnie du Preez was hurt?'

I then told the court how I'd gone to Frikkie Botha together with Mattress and told him what had happened, of how I had immediately been warned to say nothing or Tinker would be killed, whereupon Frikkie Botha had gone directly to the big rock and instructed us not to follow.

Judge Ludorf turned back to his two assessors and there was a fair bit of nodding going on as they talked quietly. He then turned back. 'The evidence we have just heard would appear to be pertinent to the case and is not subject to misinterpretation, even by a seven-year-old. It may be included in the record of proceedings.'

I returned Pissy to the witness stand and he told the court that, with Frikkie Botha's connivance, they'd invented the accident to Fonnie du Preez. He told how they'd evolved the story of how Fonnie stood on the rock urinating and had stepped back, slipping on a loose crust of rock that had caused him to fall and sustain a broken arm and nose and require stitches to the head. Then later, under intense interrogation from Mevrou in the sick room, Pissy had told the truth: that he had been regularly sexually assaulted by Fonnie du Preez, but then he'd lied again and told her that it had been the pig boy who had indecently assaulted him, that the real reason Fonnie had been injured was that he'd decided to 'teach the *kaffir* a lesson' and had come off second-best.

'Meneer Vermaak, did you have reason to believe that Mevrou Van

Schalkwyk believed you when you said the pig boy had sexually assaulted you?'

'*Ja*, definitely, I was crying a lot and she started to comfort me and I knew she believed me.'

'How did she comfort you, in what manner?'

'She pulled my head into her chest and held me.'

'Did she say any words to comfort you?'

'*Ja.*'

'Can you tell the court what she said? Can you remember her exact words?'

'She said, "Shhsh, *skattebol* . . . that *kaffir* is already dead, you hear."'

There was a sudden uproar in the gallery and Judge Ludorf banged his gavel and demanded silence. During this commotion I glanced at Mevrou who appeared to show no immediate reaction. Or perhaps her enormous size made it difficult for her to move, and her eyes were set so deep within the folds of her cheeks that they appeared as tiny pinpricks of light. When the silence returned, she suddenly pointed an arm the size of a large ham at Pissy. 'He lies, that one *always* lies!' she shouted.

'The accused will refrain from shouting out in court,' Judge Ludorf admonished, whereupon he adjourned the proceedings for lunch, announcing that the court would convene again at half past two. It is traditional for opposing barristers to meet before the court opens proceedings in the morning and to also take luncheon together. This is so each side can outline the line of enquiry they're going to take in the next session. I had arrived at the High Court early so as to engage Gawie in a mutual briefing session prior to convening in the judge's chambers for a pre-trial run-down. Gawie either deliberately, or because he was running late, arrived just in time to go into Judge Ludorf's chambers. As we adjourned for luncheon Gawie's junior, Herman Venter, approached to say Meneer Grobler apologised but would be unable to lunch with me. I explained that I thought it was important.

'I regret, but Advocate Grobler is simply not able to attend,' he insisted.

I should point out that this mutual and fraternal briefing is not mandatory, but I wished to inform him of the existence of the canned-fruit jar. I confess I was annoyed. Gawie had chosen, on several occasions during the lead-up to the trial, to demonstrate an uncooperative and unnecessarily arrogant stance towards me. I had put this down to his playing to the expectations of the people in Duiwelskrans and the Afrikaans press. Rather petulantly, I'm afraid, I turned to Venter. 'Would you please give a message to my learned friend: tell him he still needs to read the shit squares if he wants to know what's going on in the world.'

After lunch with Janine, I resumed questioning Pissy. He repeated how he confessed to Mevrou that he'd been sexually assaulted by the pig boy and she had then called the superintendent, Meneer Prinsloo, and consequently Doctor Van Heerden had been called in to examine him. Pissy then told of the subsequent meeting involving himself and Fonnie du Preez, Frikkie Botha, Meneer Prinsloo and Mevrou, where Frikkie had done a backflip and feigned surprise at the news of Mattress sexually assaulting Pissy, pretending to believe this new version of what had happened at the big rock, then how the boxing match had been arranged to teach Mattress Malokoane a lesson before handing him over to the police.

'Meneer Vermaak, was there any further occasion when you heard Mevrou Van Schalkwyk refer to the death of Mattress Malokoane?'

'Yes, once.'

'Can you explain the circumstances to the court?'

'It was the Sunday, a week after the murder, and I had a bad cold so Mevrou said I must stay in the sick room. I was asleep and she made me wake up and she switched on the light. I could see she was very drunk and you could smell the brandy on her breath. She held up this canned-fruit jar.'

Pissy then explained what had happened when the drunken Mevrou had shown him the jar containing the sexual organs. He finished with Mevrou's final words: '"Kobus, lissen to me, I want you to hold it so you know an Afrikaner child is always safe from a dirty *kaffir's* black *piel*.

Here, take it, hold it against your heart so you'll *never* forget! Then I'll keep it forever for you. It's our little keepsake."'

'My Lord, I have no more questions for this witness.'

Judge Ludorf turned to Gawie. 'Meneer Grobler, do you wish to cross-examine this witness?'

Gawie came to his feet. 'Yes, thank you, My Lord.' He turned to Pissy. 'Meneer Vermaak, we have heard in your testimony how you lied about the accident to Fonnie du Preez on the big rock, how "ostensibly" you told Mevrou Van Schalkwyk the truth that Fonnie du Preez *had* sexually assaulted you, then you withdrew this claim and told her that you had been sexually assaulted by Mattress Malokoane. Now you say Mevrou Van Schalkwyk believed your latest lie and threatened to kill, or cause to be killed, *Bantu* Malokoane.' Gawie paused, milking the moment. 'Tell me, Meneer Vermaak, which of your lies are truths and which of your truths are lies?'

Pissy, not intimidated by Gawie, replied, 'I already told you, man.'

'So do you expect us to believe the last lie you told?'

'You mean the one about the pig boy sexually assaulting me? No, man, that was a definite lie.' I have already remarked on Pissy Vermaak's mental acuity, he was not going to let my learned friend get the better of him.

'Meneer Vermaak, I now ask you, is not this ludicrous story of a mythical canned-fruit jar yet another fabrication, a figment of your overheated imagination?'

Pissy smiled. '*Ja*, I admit, with me it's hard sometimes to tell what is the truth. But with a thing like a canned-fruit jar with somebody's private parts floating around, that's not something even a person like me can just go and invent all of a sudden, out of the blue.'

'My Lord, I have no more questions for this witness,' Gawie said.

'Thank you, Meneer Vermaak, you may step down,' the judge ordered. 'I now call Doctor Van Heerden to the witness stand.'

Doctor Van Heerden told of examining Pissy and discovering severe bruising. I asked Janine De Saxe to hand me an envelope.

'Doctor, will you examine the contents of the envelope, please.'

Doctor Van Heerden removed four small yellowed and cracked photographs. 'Are these the photographs you took of the bruises sustained around the anus of Kobus Vermaak?'

Doctor Van Heerden looked at the photographs. 'Good Lord, these are meaningless, I simply have no idea.'

'Doctor, if you turn them around you will see that you signed and dated them four days before, or depending on the time the alleged murder took place, five days before the murder.'

Doctor Van Heerden turned each of the photographs over. 'Yes, that is my signature,' he confirmed.

'I tender these photographs to the court as evidence,' I said, handing the envelope to the clerk. 'Doctor, did you operate on the jaw of Meneer Frikkie Botha on the Saturday two days after you examined Kobus Vermaak?'

'Yes, he was brought into hospital with a broken jaw sustained in a boxing match at The Boys Farm. I wired his jaw and kept him in hospital that Sunday night and released him on the afternoon of the Monday.'

'That was on the Monday afternoon of the morning the body of the murdered man was discovered?'

'Yes.'

Gawie then cross-examined the doctor. 'Doctor Van Heerden, when you discovered Meneer Vermaak's bruising, did you ask how it happened?'

'I was well aware of how it might have come about, Meneer Grobler. I simply took the photographs and asked that the superintendent report the matter to the police.'

'And you were not curious as to who the perpetrator might have been?'

'I asked at the time, but the superintendent was non-committal. The Boys Farm tended to be a law unto itself. The photographs I signed later when Sergeant Van Niekerk brought them to me at my surgery.'

'And the superintendent didn't volunteer who he thought might be responsible?'

'No, he didn't.'

'And you didn't find that unusual?'

'No, as I mentioned before, Meneer Prinsloo, the superintendent, was a man who kept things close to his chest.'

'Thank you, I have no more questions for this witness, My Lord.'

The next witness I called was Fonnie du Preez. Fonnie du Preez worked as a bouncer at the Lonely Hunter and Pissy had persuaded him to be a witness for the prosecution. Quite how he had done this I can't say, but he'd told me Fonnie had taken one hiding too many in the ring and he was looking after him. 'Ag, what can you do, Tom, we go back a long way, man, even if it is the backside we go back to.'

'Meneer Du Preez, will you tell me why you were sent from The Boys Farm to the reformatory?'

'It was for misbehaviour, Sir.' Fonnie spoke slowly, his speech was slightly impaired.

'Misbehaviour. Was it sexual misbehaviour?'

'Ja.'

'Can you be more explicit?'

'Explis—? I don't know what means that word.'

'Can you tell me who you sexually misbehaved with?'

'Pissy . . . Kobus Vermaak.'

'Will you tell the court what form this misbehaviour took?'

'Lots of things.'

'Come now, Meneer Du Preez, I am led to believe that as an adult you are not inexperienced in homosexual matters. What precisely did you do to Kobus Vermaak?'

'I pissed on him and he sucked me off.'

'Is that all?'

'Ja, nee, also the other.'

'The other. Did you sexually penetrate him?'

'Ja, that.'

'How many times would you say this penetration took place?'

Fonnie frowned. 'I don't know, man. Lots of times. Pissy said he liked it.'

Fonnie then verified the true story of what had happened between us all at the big rock, graphically recounting the incident. He then verified the meeting where it was decided that Frikkie Botha would fight Mattress. While he was fairly slow-witted, he was a good witness, backing up what Pissy had maintained. Gawie declined to cross-examine.

The time had come to call Lieutenant Van Niekerk to the stand.

'Lieutenant Van Niekerk, were you the investigating officer involved with the murder of Mattress Malokoane?' I asked.

'Yes, Sir.'

'Did you do this investigation on your own?'

'Yes, Sir, the town only has one white police officer. I must do everything.'

'Would this be true if Meneer Malokoane had been a white man?'

'Excuse me, I don't understand the question,' Lieutenant Van Niekerk said, surprised.

'Are you qualified to do a murder investigation, Lieutenant?'

'For a non-European, yes, definitely. For a white man, no, I must call Pietersburg or Pretoria.'

'In the case of a dead man and in the absence of a coroner, would you not be required to call a doctor to establish the cause of death?'

'Not for a native boy. I would just ask the doctor to issue a death certificate.'

'Without seeing the body?'

'Ja, in this case the cause of death . . . a person doesn't have to be Einstein, you hear? You see, the body must be buried in three days. We do it quick, we don't have a place to put the body, only the shed at the police station. It was late summer and a body can stink very quickly.'

'Lieutenant, can you describe the state of the body of the man when you found him?'

'Ja, he had been dragged behind a vehicle, face down on a dirt road and his face was missing, and all the front of his body, the flesh and skin, was torn and ribs were showing, the bones themselves. Also the knees and the front of the legs and the insteps of the feet, they were worn down to the bones.'

'So, would you say there was no way of identifying him?'

'That is correct, but *ja*, I found a way.'

'Can you tell the court how you identified the murder victim?'

Lieutenant Van Niekerk pointed at me. '*You* identified his platform feet from a photograph, Meneer Fitzsaxby.'

'Ah, but as I was only seven at the time, my identification could not be accepted as evidence.'

'That is correct. But I believed you. You were a *slimmetjie*.'

'So, at the time, while you may have speculated, even *known* the identity of the murder victim, had *this* trial occurred at *that* time, you would not have been able to say with certainty that the murdered man was Mattress Malokoane?'

'*Ja*, I knew it was him, but you are right, I had no means of identifying him, except for his platform feet and the word of a child.'

'Would you say it could possibly have been someone else, another native with platform feet?'

'*Ja*, it's possible, such feet are not uncommon with the black people. But, *ag*, man, I was certain it was the servant from The Boys Farm.'

'Nevertheless you couldn't prove it?'

'*Ja*, that is true.'

'Tell me, Lieutenant, was there anything else unusual about the body?'

'Yes, it had been mutilated.'

'By the dragging of the body?'

'No, Sir, at first I thought this, but then I saw it was deliberate, the mutilation had been done using a sharp instrument.'

'Such as a knife?'

'Yes, it was well done, a clean cut.'

'What form did this mutilation take?'

'The penis and testicles, the sexual organs, had been removed.'

'I see, and was this discovery made known at the time?'

'No, Sir, at that time it was my decision not to reveal this particular mutilation.'

'Why was that, Lieutenant?'

'I didn't think it was nice. If the newspapers heard about it they would have made a big story. Only last year there was a ritual murder in the Tzaneen District. But that was a thing black people do, not white men. All the newspapers made a big gerfuffle. Not just the *Zoutpansberg Nuus*, the big boys, *Die Burger* and *Die Vaderland*, and also the English papers. I didn't think this was a ritual murder.'

'What did you think it was, Lieutenant?'

'Revenge for a sexual assault. Whoever did it wanted people to know why they did it.'

Gawie jumped to his feet. 'Objection, My Lord. This is pure conjecture on the part of this police officer.'

'Objection sustained. The witness's statement will not appear in the records. You may not proceed with this line of questioning, Meneer Fitzsaxby. The bench will accept that the police officer at the time did not divulge the fact that the body had been mutilated in the manner described.'

'Thank you, My Lord.' I turned back to Lieutenant Van Niekerk. 'So only you knew of the mutilation, Lieutenant?'

'Yes, but, of course, also the person or persons who did it.'

I turned to face the bench. 'My Lord and Your Honours, I have on two occasions attempted to brief my learned friend for the defence on the existence of the physical evidence I am about to produce. On both occasions my learned friend made himself unavailable. I crave your indulgences for this omission.'

Judge Ludorf turned to the assessors and a short conversation took place, whereupon he turned back to face the court. 'Most regrettable, Meneer Fitzsaxby. However, under the circumstances you may proceed with your evidence. Both you and Meneer Grobler will see me in my chambers at the conclusion of today's hearing.'

Janine De Saxe handed me a small canvas bag. 'My Lord, contained in this bag is the canned-fruit jar and contents alluded to by my witness, Meneer Kobus Vermaak, when the court reconvened after lunch.'

Suddenly the courtroom was in uproar.

'*Silence!*' Judge Ludorf thundered. 'I will have silence!' His gavel was working overtime and eventually the gallery was brought back to order. 'You may proceed, Meneer Fitzsaxby.'

'Thank you, My Lord. I will presently tender the exhibit in question to the court as evidence.'

'Objection, My Lord!' Gawie said, jumping to his feet. 'My learned friend has not proved that the contents of the canned-fruit jar are the legitimate and identifiable remains of the murder victim.'

I had caught Gawie completely by surprise. It was obvious that the Van Schalkwyks had not made a connection between the poisoned pork raid and Exhibit A. It may be possible that Mevrou had not even told Gawie about the raid. After all, I was certain that she was an alcoholic, in a state of *dwaal* most of the time. If I could prove, as I believed I could, that the contents of the jar had once belonged to Mattress, I was well on my way to proving her guilty. Although I had learned in life never to count my chickens before they have hatched.

'My Lord, I intend to prove that the contents of the jar are a part of the physical remains of the murder victim and that they are directly connected with the accused.'

Gawie was back on his feet. 'My Lord, the nature of this new evidence is such that I request time to consult with my clients.'

Judge Ludorf looked directly at Gawie. 'Firstly, your objection is overruled.' He turned back to me. 'Meneer Fitzsaxby, is the canned-fruit jar part of the evidence you wished to make known to Meneer Grobler, both this morning and at the lunch recess?'

'Yes, My Lord.'

'In that case, Meneer Fitzsaxby, you may proceed.'

With our Boys Farm backgrounds we had both learned in the cradle that self-conceit is dangerous and pride inevitably comes before a fall. The lessons learned early in life should never be carelessly thrown aside.

I returned to Lieutenant Van Niekerk in the witness stand. 'Lieutenant Van Niekerk, do you recognise the jar and contents I have given you? If so, would you please tell the court what you believe to be contained in the jar.'

'In the jar is a quantity of brandy and in it the penis and both testicles of a *Bantu* male.'

'Do you have reason to believe that, in all probability, they belonged to the victim, Mattress Malokoane?'

'Yes, I do.'

'Can you give this court your reason?'

'*Ja*, well, people don't keep the sexual organs of a native person for a keepsake unless they have a very good reason, even then —'

'Thank you,' I said quickly, wanting him to stick to the facts without confusing them with his personal opinion. 'Can you tell me where you found the jar and contents?'

'It was behind some large canned-fruit jars of pickled pork on the pantry shelf in Mevrou Van Schalkwyk's house on the family farm.' Lieutenant Van Niekerk then explained how I had told him of its possible existence, of me having originally heard about the jar and its contents from Pissy Vermaak; then how he had obtained a search warrant and what had occurred during the Van Schalkwyk raid. Gawie objected that Lieutenant Van Niekerk had employed deceit to obtain the evidence and asked that it be disallowed. Judge Ludorf overruled the objection, stating that the police officer need not have given a reason for conducting the search, that the search warrant from Magistrate Du Plessis was sufficient to enter the premises.

'Was there anything further about the jar that you wish to note, Lieutenant?'

'Yes, Sir. Under the dust we discovered Mevrou Van Schalkwyk's fingerprints.'

'Are you prepared to verify that you did not reveal the fact that the body of the victim had been mutilated and the sexual organs removed using a sharp instrument, in all likelihood, a knife?'

'*Ja*, I already said so,' Lieutenant Van Niekerk said, putting me in my place.

'Is it not possible that in the process of being dragged behind a motor vehicle the sexual organs might have been removed?' I persisted.

'No, man, you could see it clearly. When I was a young man on the farm we did all the slaughtering of animals: pigs, calves, sometimes if we could get one, even sheep. I'm telling you, there's no mistaking it, the native murder victim, his private parts, they was removed with a knife, I absolutely guarantee it.'

'Lieutenant, when you removed the jar that you now see in front of you from the premises of Mevrou Van Schalkwyk, did you also remove several jars of pickled pork?'

'Ja, I think, in all, it was thirty-six.'

'Did you get the impression that the pig meat was grown and slaughtered on the property?'

'Ja, the ouvrou more or less said so, but it is well known, you hear? The Van Schalkwyks, they keep pigs, and their honeyed ham is the best in the Northern Transvaal. They do everything themselves, they say this is their secret, only a Van Schalkwyk works on a Van Schalkwyk pig. Even the honey, it's from their own beehives, high mountain honey.'

'Therefore, it would not be unreasonable to conclude that at least one of the male members of the family would be an expert with a slaughtering knife?'

Lieutenant Van Niekerk shrugged. 'Ja, of course, it stands to reason.'

'Lieutenant, when investigating the murder, did you take a blood sample of the victim and submit it in order to ascertain the victim's blood group?'

'No, man, this was a dead kaff – a murdered native, we don't do that. I told you it was still hot weather and we had to bury him quickly, a body like that, with all that open flesh, you can't leave it lying around or you in big trouble.'

'I have no more questions of this witness, My Lord.'

Gawie then set about questioning Lieutenant Van Niekerk but yielded nothing until he arrived at the matter of the fingerprints, hitting the jackpot. 'In the matter of Mevrou Van Schalkwyk's fingerprints, there is no notation in your original police enquiry that you obtained the fingerprints of The Boys Farm matron. How did you come to obtain these in order to confirm a fingerprint match with those on the canned-fruit jar?'

Lieutenant Van Niekerk was then forced to explain how he'd taken a set of prints from the semiconscious and sleeping Mevrou.

'My Lord, I ask that the evidence pertaining to the fingerprints on the jar not be allowed. It is illegal to obtain the fingerprints of a citizen without permission if she has not committed a crime or has not been placed under arrest.'

Judge Ludorf sustained the objection. It was a moot point, but the damage had been done. The fingerprints on the jar were now evidence known to the judge and the two assessors.

'My Lord, I request permission of this court to allow the fingerprints of the accused, Mevrou Van Schalkwyk, to be taken in court and the findings presented at a later stage in these proceedings. I have a fingerprint expert standing by if permission is granted.'

The judge and assessors conferred for a minute or so before Ludorf turned to me. 'Gathering evidence while the court is in session is unusual, Meneer Fitzsaxby, but permission is granted. The court records will show that Lieutenant Van Niekerk acted willfully and abused the rights of the accused, Mevrou Van Schalkwyk.'

Lieutenant Van Niekerk retired from the witness stand and the fingerprint expert was called in and Mevrou's fingerprints were taken. I then presented Frikkie Botha's sworn affidavit together with his numerous notes. I selected only those notes that told how the Van Schalkwyk brothers, when with Frikkie in the unit of the *Stormjaers*, had admitted that they had murdered Mattress, describing to Frikkie how they had gone about it. I briefly outlined the bridge explosion and subsequent accident and the disappearance of the six brothers and presented the photographs of Frikkie after the accident. I did this only so that I could put his handwritten notes into context.

Just as I had anticipated, Gawie immediately objected, saying that the notes were clearly motivated by a sense of revenge. I deliberately did not argue this point. I then presented the notes in Frikkie's handwriting dated long before I had met up with Pissy again, by which time Frikkie had been dead some years. They told in detail of how Frans van Schalkwyk had told him how he'd performed the mutilation, finishing with the quote: 'Ag, it was easy, just like cutting up a pig, only the *kaffir*'s cock was bigger, man!'

'My Lord, if the information about the mutilation and removal of the murder victim's sexual organs was, as Lieutenant Van Niekerk told the court, unknown, I submit that in the case of Meneer Vermaak this information can only have come from Mevrou Van Schalkwyk in the manner previously described in his testimony. Furthermore, Meneer Frikkie Botha would have had no way of knowing this information other than if, in the intimacy of the *Stormjaer* fraternity, he had not been told about it. In other words, the information that the sexual organs of Mattress Malokoane had been removed could only have come from both the female and the male side of the Van Schalkwyk family. Apart from Lieutenant Van Niekerk, they were the only people in possession of this information.'

We had reached the end of the first day in court and I had concluded my evidence. As directed, Gawie and I met afterwards in Judge Ludorf's chambers, and the judge lost no time upbraiding us.

'Meneer Fitzsaxby, withholding important evidence from Meneer Grobler is bordering on the unconscionable. It is my firmly held belief that you could have persuaded him to spend time with you in order to share the details of your upcoming evidence.'

'Yes, My Lord,' I said, knowing he was right, but also knowing that there was no way I was going to be a servant to Gawie's arrogance.

'Meneer Grobler, your behaviour in this matter is reprehensible. Today you took a hiding in my court and much of it was of your own making. *Imperitia quo que culpa adnumeratur*, want of skill also counts as negligence. While the letter of the law does not require you to share information with your learned friend, a protocol, far older and more important than you or I, behoves that you do so. This is the essence of good courtroom conduct and the sooner you learn legal convention the better. Eventually you may both make good lawyers, but you won't do so by ignoring a tradition that has existed in jurisprudence for a thousand years. Law is about cogent and insightful argument, not about springing surprises on one's legal opponent in the courtroom. You will both meet in my chambers at nine o'clock tomorrow morning to discuss the procedures and the evidence that will be presented by Meneer Grobler in my court tomorrow.'

The following morning we met in Justice Ludorf's chambers and Gawie Grobler said that he had committed Mevrou Van Schalkwyk to the care of a leading psychiatrist overnight and intended to put the doctor on the witness stand, who would testify that his client was not of sound mind. Furthermore, he would be entering a plea of diminished responsibility in her case and in addition he would be asking for a verdict of manslaughter in the case of the six Van Schalkwyk brothers.

If things are going well there comes a time in a case where you believe you have your opponent on the ropes. This is when you have to be particularly careful not to be careless or give any indication that you know your opponent is in trouble. Gawie was doing all he could to save the situation. The last-minute plea that Mevrou was mentally disturbed was something he should have prepared for a lot earlier. With sufficient psychiatric examination, he might have just pulled it off. But you can never tell with a judge and I was glad that I hadn't put Mevrou on the witness stand where she might have demonstrated her mental instability. In my opinion, what Gawie was now doing was too little too late. Be careful, Tom, keep everything simple, I said to myself.

We returned to the courtroom and Gawie submitted his new pleas, the psychiatrist presented his diagnosis and I cross-examined him. 'Doctor, while your findings suggest that Mevrou Van Schalkwyk is suffering, at the present time, from diminished responsibility, can you say with any certainty that this situation existed twenty-three years ago when she was considering revenge?'

The psychiatrist thought for a moment before replying. 'You must understand that I only spent a short time with Mevrou Van Schalkwyk last night. Without prolonged and repeated psychiatric examination it would not be possible to make a definitive diagnosis. Therefore, it is not useful to speculate on the state of her mental health twenty-two years ago.'

The court refused to accept Gawie's change of plea. The fingerprint expert was called in again and he told the court that Mevrou's fingerprints matched those found on the canned-fruit jar.

Gawie's subsequent handling of the case was highly competent as he attempted to suggest that the contents of the canned-fruit jar might have been those of another *Bantu* male; that there wasn't any physical proof, such as a blood sample match, to connect it to the body of the victim. But, in the final analysis, this argument would, I think, have lacked conviction for the three men sitting on the bench. A verdict in a court of law is arrived at when the evidence put before a judge or jury is thought to be *beyond reasonable doubt*. With Pissy and Frikkie's evidence and the fact that the mutilation had been kept from public knowledge, taken together with the existence of Exhibit A, I was reasonably confident that I had done enough.

However, you can never tell. There was still the chance of a political decision. This was a South Africa living through the post-Sharpeville years: a government banning the ANC; the declaration of a state of emergency; the ninety-day detention laws without recourse for legal help; a country expelled from the British Commonwealth and one that had declared itself a republic in a 'whites only' referendum; and finally, the imprisonment of Nelson Mandela. Taken all together it meant that we were living in a police state.

Towards the end of the second day I summarised the case for the prosecution, and by mid-afternoon, after retiring to his chambers for less than an hour, Judge Ludorf and his two assessors, Viljoen and Bekker, returned to court. The six Van Schalkwyk brothers were found guilty of murder and each sentenced to twenty years and Mevrou to twenty-five years, pending a full psychiatric report. Janine De Saxe had been correct. Judge Ludorf had proved that the law still transcended politics.

I am aware that this seems like a fairly tame ending, that it would have been a better one if Gawie Grobler had demonstrated his obvious brilliance and we'd fought tooth and nail until the best man was left bloody but unbowed. The day after the court case was complete the English press anyhow referred to my conduct of the case by using a string of adjectives, 'brilliant' being the one most often employed.

In truth, it was nothing of the sort. I had spent the better part of my life finding evidence, thinking about it and working on how I would present it. I had taken years to compile my evidence and Gawie Grobler had been given a relatively short time to complete his. Therefore I had evidence and witnesses at my disposal that my learned friend did not know existed or, in the case of Pissy Vermaak and Fonnie du Preez, would have been unable to locate. He had only the police enquiry to work with and anything his clients may have told him. Both these sources proved to be fairly limited: Lieutenant Van Niekerk's enquiry had been restricted by the need to dispose of the body in a hurry, and the Van Schalkwyk family limited by their stubborn recalcitrance and stupidity. I had also enjoyed a great deal of luck. The discovery of the canned-fruit jar with its pickled contents was fortuitous to say the least. While he would have found the evidence of mutilation in Lieutenant Van Niekerk's murder enquiry records, he could never have expected the 'keepsake of hate', the physical evidence, to turn up. If I had finally triumphed, it had been a case of dogged persistence rather than a brilliant display of advocacy.

I had succeeded in obtaining justice for my friend Mattress and this gave me a great deal of satisfaction. It had been a long and sometimes weary road and, in a funny way, it meant that I could get on with the rest of my life. I also confess to having been proud of one aspect of the case. I had succeeded in obtaining a verdict without having to put Mevrou on the witness stand or bring Meneer Prinsloo into the proceedings. To have wreaked revenge for all the humiliation she had caused me as a child by demolishing her in court would have been to detract from the singular reason I was there in the first place. Pissy, who had inadvertently been the cause of the tragedy that brought about Mattress's death, was ironically the one who had enabled me to obtain justice for his murder. Life and death work in mysterious ways. He had kept his end of the bargain, and together with the tragic Frikkie Botha, their evidence had been the critical element in the case for the prosecution. In turn, I had avoided any adverse publicity or police attention he may have received concerning the Lonely Hunter club. Now you may think that I should have exposed Meneer Prinsloo for the vile creature he was, but I reasoned that this was not in Pissy Vermaak's immediate interest. It would be another court case for another time and one of Pissy's choosing, when I would make myself available *pro bono* if he wanted me to act for him and all the other victims, from The Boys Farm and elsewhere, who suffered and had their lives destroyed because of the monster Prinsloo.

At the conclusion of the case, I made my way over to Gawie, though in some trepidation. What I wanted to say to him was that he'd been unfortunate as the evidence at my disposal meant that I would have had to have been totally incompetent to lose the case. But, of course, I didn't want him to think I was patronising him. So I shook his hand and said, 'Perhaps we can get together soon, maybe talk about old times?'

He grinned. 'Lunch, so I can eat humble pie?'

I laughed. 'Gawie, this time it was me with the pound note concealed up my bum.'

Quick as a flash he replied, '*Ja*, and it bought you a green sucker!'

I laughed again and held out my hand. Gawie was still the Afrikaner Genius. 'No hard feelings, I really would like to get together.'

'I'd like that, *Voetsek*,' he said, taking my outstretched hand. 'We can catch up on the news on each other's shit squares.'

There was only one further matter I needed to attend to and this was to take place on the forecourt of the High Court building where all my friends waited for me to emerge: Pirrou; Professor Mustafa; Professor

Shaun Rack; Pissy; Mr Naidoo; Stompie the Pepsi-Cola vendor; Lew Fisher of Polliack's; Lofty van der Merwe, who was surprisingly still sober at this time of the day, though how he'd found his way to Pretoria was anyone's guess; Doctor Van Heerden and Mevrou Van Heerden, formerly Mevrou Booysens of the red-and-green-sucker-and-ten-toppings-on-a-one-legged-ice-cream-at-the-Impala-Café-fame; my loyal friend throughout, Lieutenant Jan van Niekerk and his 'To thine own self be true' brother, the school principal; and, finally, my beloved 'smelling of roses' Marie.

They cheered as I came out onto the forecourt and there commenced all-round congratulations and slaps on the back. People of every race in South Africa but one surrounded me, applauding the fact that justice had been served and the murder of a humble Zulu pig boy avenged. The only representative not present in this spontaneous cheering committee was a member of the African race.

After the unnecessary fuss had died down and I'd thanked my friends, I turned to face two people who stood waiting shyly several feet away. One of them was a woman who appeared to be in her late forties, who was barefoot and wore a faded cotton dress. Beside her stood a tall young African man, about my age, in a second-hand suit jacket and trousers that were too short and from which protruded a pair of magnificent platform feet.

'May I introduce you all to Mrs Malokoane and her son, Mokiti "Joe Louis" Malokoane, from Zululand,' I announced proudly. Love had come full circle.

Glossary

Afrikaans – language
Afrikaner – one person
Afrikaners – the people
Amabantu – Bantu people of South Africa
Amazulu – Zulu people
Askari – policeman or soldier
assegaai – spear

baasskap – leadership, domination
bakkies – utes, small trucks
bansela – variation of *bonsella*, a free gift
Bantustans – the homelands created by the Nationalist Government of
    South Africa
baraza – public meeting
barbel – mud-dwelling catfish
biltong – beef or game jerky, sun-cured beef
Blut und Boden – 'blood and soil'. A phrase used by Hitler to mean
    that people of German descent (blood) have the right to live on
    German soil. The same phrase was used to fuel patriotism and
    nationalism among *Ossewabrandwag* members in South Africa.

bobbejane – baboons
Boer/Boere – Afrikaners
boer/boere – farmers of Dutch and French descent
boeremense – country people
Boerevolk/Volk – Afrikaners
boerewors – farm sausage
boet – brother, younger or older
boetie – brother, usually younger
boma – an enclosure
bonsella – a free gift
boom – marijuana
braai – abbreviation of *braaivleis*
braaivleis – a barbecue
Broederbond – Brotherhood
buk – bend down

charras – South African slang for someone of Indian descent
chimboose (Swahili) – kitchen (slang)

dagga – marijuana
Dominee – preacher or the minister of a church
domkop – stupid person
donder – thunder, to beat someone up
dorp – village or small town
dwaal – confused

Edelagbares – Your Honours
eina! – ouch!
Engelsman – Englishman

fitina – intrigue, tribal rows
foksterriër – fox terrier

ganja – marijuana

gat – arse

githathi – sacred stones used in Kikuyu rituals

goeie môre – good morning

Habari yako? Jamaa endelaya mzuri? (Swahili) – I hope that you and your family are well

Here – God or Lord, used as in 'God, man!'

hou vas – hold tight

igwal (isiZulu) – a coward

ikhaya (isiZulu) – dwelling, house

in sy gat – in his arse

Induna (isiZulu) – big boss, headman

Injabulo, Baas (isiZulu) – a pleasure, boss

inyama (isiZulu) – meat

Itungati – Mau Mau forest fighters

izinyawo ezinkulu zika Mattress – Mattress's big feet

Jambo, Bwana – hello, Boss

jankers – punishment, detention (military slang)

japies – simpletons

Juffrou – Miss (an address, a sign of respect)

jy – you

kaffir – a derogatory term commonly used at this time to mean 'nigger'

kaffirboetie – a derogatory name for someone who befriends and is supportive of black people

kahle (Zulu) – it is good or well done

kaptein – captain

Karoo – a very dry, arid region covering a large part of central South Africa

kêrel – young man, chap, fellow, bloke

klaar – finished with

Kleinbaas – small boss. A semi-mark of respect used by Africans when referring to or talking to young white boys.

Kleinbasie – as above but used for smaller or younger boys

kleinhuisie – small house, outside lavatory

kloofs – ravines or gorges

knopkierie – club with a long shaft

koeksisters – a traditional Afrikaner sweet made of plaited dough, fried in oil then soaked with sugar syrup

kom gou – come quickly

kom hier – come here

krans – cliff, precipice, rock face, crag, high rock

ku salamu (Swahili) – a greeting

kuke – a derogatory name for black person and Mau Mau

laager – a camp defended by a circular formation of wagons

lekker – nice or good

maak – make

maak gou – hurry up

maats – mates, friends

magtig – powerful, potent, authorise

Magtig! – Oh Lord!, Good Heavens!

makhulu (Zulu) – big

Malokoane – a dance group leader playing traditional flute-type instrument

maroela – Afrikaans spelling of *marula*

marula – a much-loved tree found in the *veld*, one of Africa's botanical treasures

meerschaum – pipe

melktert – milktart, sweet tart akin to a custard tart

Meneer – Mister (Mr), used alone it means 'sir'

Mevrou – Missus (Mrs), a sign of respect

middag – afternoon
mielie – corn on the cob
mieliemeel – ground corn/maize
mieliepap – porridge made from ground corn
Miesies (Mies) – Missus or Madam, used by black or coloured people
    when addressing a white woman
mina (isiZulu) – I
musiek – music
muti/umuthi (isiZulu) – traditional medicine
my – me

Nagmaal – Holy Communion
ndio (Swahili) – yes
nee – no
Ngai – God
ngiyabonga (isiZulu) – thank you
nooi – sweetheart or young lady

om te braai – to barbecue
Ossewabrandwag – Ox-Wagon Fireguard. The *Ossewabrandwag* (OB)
    was a strong body originally founded by Afrikaners fuelled by
    strong nationalism for the purposes of maintaining their cultural
    practices and traditions. Driven by the intense desire to disassociate
    themselves from Britain and ultimately gain their independence,
    members of the OB actively opposed and attempted to prevent the
    participation of South African soldiers in World War II – these and
    other similar activities turning the OB into a militant, right-wing
    organisation.
ou – old
ouma – grandmother
ousis – older sister
ouvrou – affectionate name for wife

panga – a large and heavy-bladed knife (machete) used in farm work

pasella – a free gift, gratuity

piel – penis

platanna – literally 'Flat Anna': a spur-toed frog, dark green in colour
   with a yellow belly

regte – real, as in 'real man'

riempie chair – a chair with a seat made of interwoven narrow strips of
   leather

rondavel – a hut built in the round

Rooinek – red neck

sawubona (isiZulu) – literally 'I see you', a greeting

s'bona – shortened version of *sawubona*, a greeting

shamba – plots cultivated by each family

shaya (isiZulu) – hit, beat, smack

sjambok – a thick black rubbery cane, a rod that is four feet in length

skattebol – little treasure or treasure ball

skelm – rascal

slaap – sleep

slimmetjie – clever child, used sarcastically when referring to a child wise
   beyond his years

stadig – slow/slow down

sterkte – strength

stoep – veranda

stom – lips are sealed, dumb

Stormjaers – storm troopers

surrogaat – surrogate

tante – aunt

tickey – South African coin, threepence (pre-1961)

tiekiedraai – twirling-type of Afrikaner dance

toke – marijuana cigarette

totsiens – goodbye

uhuru – freedom
ukubonga (isiZulu) – thanks
umbulelo (isiXhosa) – thanks
umchamo (isiZulu) – urinate
umfana (isiZulu) – small African boy

veels geluk – congratulations
veld – field
verdom – damn, an exclamation
verdomde – damned, an exclamation
verkramp – ultra-conservative or unenlightened
verneuk – to cheat
vierkleur – literally means four colours: the glorious flag of the Republic
    of the Transvaal
Volk/Boerevolk – Afrikaners

wamana – of forty
ware Rooinek/ware Boer – real thing, a genuine *Rooinek* or *Boer*
Wragtig! – well, I'll be damned! (with an exclamation mark)
Wragtig – truly, indeed (with no exclamation mark)

Acknowledgements

My first debt of thanks must go to Celia Jarvis, who has done the research required for my past five books and to whom I dedicate this one. No request for information I made was ever too hard; no deadline, no matter how impossible, not met. Often she would work throughout the night so that I could have the information I needed on my desk in the morning. Simply, thank you – I know there have been times when it hasn't been easy.

I need to especially thank Marilyn Seaton McIntosh of Cape Town, South Africa, who acted as my researcher in that country. She too did more, more quickly than I could have hoped and always with great good humour and diligence. She was always conscientious in her guardianship of the rights, correct nomenclature and cultural portrayal of the different ethnic groups in her nation, and was quick to point out any aspects in my work she thought were inaccurate or unfair.

My researchers in Kenya were Tim Noad and Bumble Dawson-Darner, both of whom went to considerable trouble on my behalf and supplied me with detail and local colour I might not otherwise have known. I thank them both.

If a novel could be likened to a pie, then the crust is experience, the gravy the imagination, and the meat and potatoes the information other people so generously supply. I thank all of the following people for their help, information and advice, always generously given: Professor Richard Bauman, Professor of Law and Classical Studies, University of New South Wales; Sheila Bauman; Dr Jodie Braddock; Tony Crosby; Janine De Saxe; Adam Courtenay; Benita Courtenay; Clare Forster; Kerry Freeman; Christine Gee; Alex Hamill; Dr Ross Hayes; Rosali Hicks; Alan Jacobs; Christine Lenton; Dr Irwin Light; Sylvia Manning; Jon Mayled; Annette Stackman; and Graham Walker.

It is a rare book indeed that doesn't need the attention of a good editor and I certainly have never written one. Jody Lee, new to the role of editing one of my novels, gave me unstintingly of her talent, patience, opinion and plain commonsense. I am enormously grateful for the care and attention as well as the calmness, diligence and the many valuable insights she brought to the task.

Always in the background are the talented people who bring a book to fruition. To my publishers, Penguin, and those people within the organisation who labour on my behalf, my heartfelt thanks. Those to whom I especially owe my gratitude are Bob Sessions and Clare Forster, my personal publishers; Julie Gibbs; Susan McLeish; Saskia Adams; Anne Rogan; Ian Sibley; Lyn McGaurr; Sarah Dawson; Nicci Dodanwela; Kate Dunlop; Tammie Gay; Mary Balestriere; Deborah Brash; Cathy Larsen; Tony Palmer; Beverley Waldron; Carmen De La Rue; Gabrielle Coyne; Dan Ruffino; and Sally Bateman.

List of Sources

Anderson, David, *Histories of the Hanged: Britain's Dirty War in Kenya and the End of the Empire*, Weidenfeld & Nicholson, New York, 2005

Barnett, Donald L., *Mau Mau From Within: Autobiography and Analysis of Kenya's Peasant Revolt*, MacGibbon, London, 1924

Brookes, Edgar Harry, *The History of Native Policy in South Africa from 1830 to the Present Day*, N.P., Capetown, 1924

Bunting, Brian, *The Rise of the South African Reich* (revised edition), IDAF, London

Elkins, Caroline, *Imperial Reckoning: The Untold Story of Britain's Gulag in Kenya*, Henry Holt & Co., New York, 2005

Hewett, Peter, *Kenya Cowboy: A Police Officer's Account of the Mau Mau*

Mayled, Jon, *South Africa: For the children of Soweto* (manuscript), UK, 1990–2000

Libraries: Mitchell Library, NSW; National Library of South Africa, Cape Town; Mr Christopher Hunt – Imperial War Museum, Department of Printed Books, UK.

Newspapers: *The Cape Times* – South Africa; *The Argus* – South Africa; *The Star* – South Africa; *Die Vaderland* – South Africa; *Die Burger* – South Africa.

ALSO BY
BRYCE COURTENAY

THE POWER OF ONE

Born in a South Africa divided by racism and hatred, young Peekay will come to lead all the tribes of Africa. Through enduring friendships, he gains the strength he needs to win out. And in a final conflict with his childhood enemy, Peekay will fight to the death for justice . . .

Bryce Courtenay's classic bestseller is a story of triumph of the human spirit – a spellbinding tale for all ages.

TANDIA

Tandia is a child of all Africa: half Indian, half African, beautiful and intelligent, she is only sixteen when she is first brutalised by the police. Her fear of the white man leads her to join the black resistance movement, where she trains as a terrorist.

With her in the fight for justice is the one white man Tandia can trust, the welterweight champion of the world, Peekay. Now he must fight their common enemy in order to save both their lives.

April Fool's Day

In the end, love is more important than everything and it will conquer and overcome anything. Or that's how Damon saw it, anyway. Damon wanted a book that talked a lot about love.

Damon Courtenay died on the morning of April Fool's Day. In this tribute to his son, Bryce Courtenay lays bare the suffering behind this young man's life. Damon's story is one of lifelong struggle, his love for Celeste, the compassion of a family, and a fight to the end for integrity.

A testimony to the power of love, *April Fool's Day* is also about understanding: how when we confront our worst, we can become our best.

A powerful account of life and death from one of Australia's best authors.

The Australian Trilogy

The Potato Factory

Ikey Solomon and his partner in crime, Mary Abacus, make the harsh journey from thriving nineteenth-century London to the convict settlement of Van Diemen's Land. In the back-streets and dives of Hobart Town, Mary builds The Potato Factory, where she plans a new future. But her ambitions are threatened by Ikey's wife, Hannah, her old enemy. As each woman sets out to destroy the other, the families are brought to the edge of disaster.

Tommo & Hawk

Brutally kidnapped and separated in childhood, Tommo and Hawk are reunited in Hobart Town. Together they escape their troubled pasts and set off on a journey into manhood. From whale hunting in the Pacific to the Maori wars in New Zealand, from the Rocks in Sydney to the miners' riots at the goldfields, Tommo and Hawk must learn each other's strengths and weaknesses in order to survive.

Solomon's Song

When Mary Abacus dies, she leaves her business empire in the hands of the warring Solomon family. Hawk Solomon is determined to bring together both sides of the tribe – but it is the new generation who must fight to change the future. Solomons are pitted against Solomons as the families are locked in a bitter struggle that crosses battlefields and continents to reach a powerful conclusion.

JESSICA

Jessica is based on the inspiring true story of a young girl's fight for justice against tremendous odds. A tomboy, Jessica is the pride of her father, as they work together on the struggling family farm. One quiet day, the peace of the bush is devastated by a terrible murder. Only Jessica is able to save the killer from the lynch mob – but will justice prevail in the courts?

Nine months later, a baby is born . . . with Jessica determined to guard the secret of the father's identity. The rivalry of Jessica and her beautiful sister for the love of the same man will echo throughout their lives – until finally the truth must be told.

Set in a harsh Australian bush against the outbreak of World War I, this novel is heartbreaking in its innocence, and shattering in its brutality.